# A
# PLAY
## OF
# SHADOW

*Mellynne*

# JULIE E.
# CZERNEDA

# DAW BOOKS, INC.

**DONALD A. WOLLHEIM, FOUNDER**

375 Hudson Street, New York, NY 10014

**ELIZABETH R. WOLLHEIM**
**SHEILA E. GILBERT**
**PUBLISHERS**

www.dawbooks.com

Hallo, Poppa.

day's travel by oxcart

To the Barrens

Marrowdell

Upper Rhoth

Northward Road

Kotor River

Rhoth

Endshere

Weken

Kotor River

Lower Rhoth

Vorkoun

Essa

Lilem River

Channen

Avyo

Mila River

A
n
s
n
o
r

N

Mellynne

Thornloe

Sweet Sea

(Syrpic Ans or Mother's Elbow)

Eldad

Rhoth and Surrounding Domains

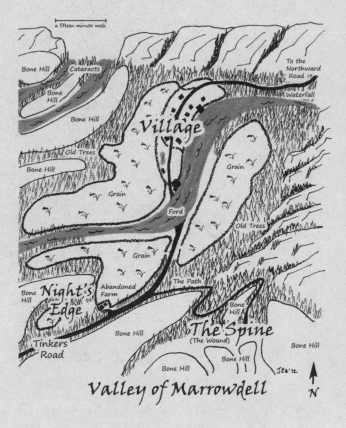

a fifteen minute walk

Bone Hill

Cataracts

Bone Hill

Bone Hill

To the Northward Road

Waterfall

Village

Old Trees

Bone Hill

Grain

Grain

Ford

Grain

Old Trees

Bone Hill

Night's Edge

Abandoned Farm

The Path

Bone Hill

Bone Hill

Tinkers Road

Bone Hill

The Spine
(The Wound)

Bone Hill

Bone Hill

Bone Hill

JC2'12

Valley of Marrowdell

N

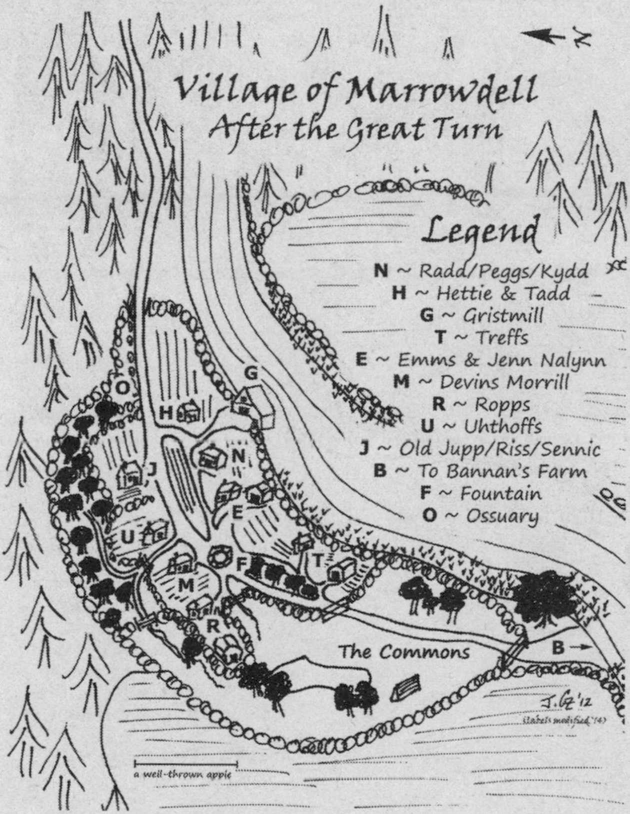

# Village of Marrowdell
## After the Great Turn

## Legend

**N** ~ Radd/Peggs/Kydd
**H** ~ Hettie & Tadd
**G** ~ Gristmill
**T** ~ Treffs
**E** ~ Emms & Jenn Nalynn
**M** ~ Devins Morrill
**R** ~ Ropps
**U** ~ Uhthoffs
**J** ~ Old Jupp/Riss/Sennic
**B** ~ To Bannan's Farm
**F** ~ Fountain
**O** ~ Ossuary

The Commons

a well-thrown apple

J.G '12
labels modified '14

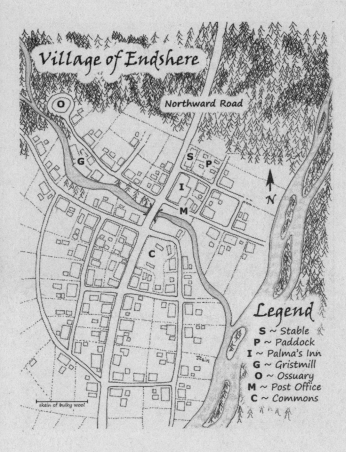

Village of Endshere

Northward Road

N

Legend

S ~ Stable
P ~ Paddock
I ~ Palma's Inn
G ~ Gristmill
O ~ Ossuary
M ~ Post Office
C ~ Commons

skein of bulky wool

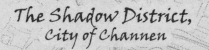

# The Shadow District,
## City of Channen

N

Sunset's Crescent
("The Straight")

Dawn's Blush
("The Crooked
Arm")

M

D

A

canal

S

H

# Legend

**S** ~ Sand's Crossing
**H** ~ Sect House
**A** ~ Artisans' Market
**D** ~ Distal Hold
**M** ~ Manor

Sarra River

2 minutes by rowboat

*TWENTY-THREE YEARS AGO, Within the World of
Roses and Rabbits ...*

Prince Ordo Arselical of Rhoth dipped his quill in the
golden inkpot reserved for matters of state. Tapping off any
excess ink, he pursed his plump lips in concentration and
scrawled his name below the rest. His secretary dripped a
precise glob of fragrant red wax and the prince pressed his
ring to it with a grunt of satisfaction, affixing the royal seal.

There. It was done.

He leaned back, arms crossed over his ample belly. From
their court portraits, his predecessors watched history being
made. The fools. Ordo smiled triumphantly at his great-
grandfather, who'd caved to Mellynne and given up so
much of Avyo, the great capital of Rhoth, without a whimper. At his grandfather, who'd squandered more wealth
building roads to places no one wanted to go. Last, but not
least, at his own father, whose extra chins rested on stiff lace
and who'd exacerbated matters with Ansnor until their domains had plunged into an undeclared, expensive war.

Fools, the lot.

Not he.

His secretary eased the next copy into place. The prince signed and sealed it, then waved off the man's attempt to collect the document. He rested his extra chins on a beringed finger to admire his accomplishment.

Let Mellynne complain. He'd signed and sealed the document to scour that domain's influence from Avyo's heart. The prince chuckled. Found use for that blighted road north, hadn't he?

Stiff with seals and fine print, approved by a thin majority of the House of Keys and a sufficiency of the House of Commons, today he, Prince Ordo Arselical of Rhoth, legally reclaimed wealth and property that should, after all, be in truly Rhothan hands. There might not be rejoicing in the streets, the populous at large more confounded than pleased, but behind closed doors?

Debt, that most useful of currencies.

Some repaid, so their owners believed, by yesterday's vote, for he'd chosen those Rhothan hands with great care. Others to wait, their obligation settled in place like unseen chains. With this pen and document, he'd begun the elevation of those who would—who must—support his ultimate goal.

The conquest of Ansnor.

Years it would take, perhaps the rest of his life, but was he not patient? And such a grand game, this, one to savor.

Ordo touched the now-hard wax and smiled.

Rhoth's future, and his legacy as its greatest prince, would be assured.

Time to commission his own portrait.

*Four Hundred and Seventy Years Ago, Within the World of Toads and Dragons . . .*

There was magic, enough. Beings who used it, or were it, or both. There was sky and earth and seasons, of a sort, though it didn't snow. How could it? Water stayed where it was summoned, in fountains and wells, and what rained from sky to earth in its seasons was mimrol. Silver and warm, mimrol carved rivers and filled lakes, spreading magic as it flowed.

Dragons hunted the air, kruar the ground, and toads, though cousins, stayed out of sight. Terst farmed and built, bringing peace where it could flourish, and avoided dragons and kruar too. All had their place, whatever they thought of it, or if they even did.

But there were those, the sei, who thought a great deal. Sei pondered what was beyond the ken of others, being as curious as they were powerful, and one fateful day the sei wondered . . . was there more?

And one day wondered . . . could they touch it?

And all would have remained as it was, with magic enough and peace, but on a day when the light of an unseen sun dimmed, on a day when anything seemed possible, one sei reached from the world of dragons and toads, into that of roses and rabbits . . .

Tearing both worlds open.

Making both worlds bleed.

Spilling magic.

The sei mended that tear, as best it could. Used itself like thread. Held on, accepting that penance.

While dragons and toads, as well as kruar and terst, explored what the sei had wrought.

*Today* . . .

There's a world of roses and rabbits.

There's a world of dragons and toads.

Writhing through both is the edge where they meet, for the sei holds, still.

Magic, wild and potent, lives there.

And so does Jenn Nalynn.

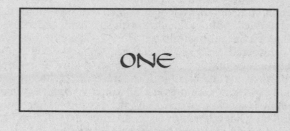

# ONE

WINTER STRETCHED ITS ICY FINGERS across Marrowdell in the hours before dawn, crisping leaves and sealing the commons' pond with a skin of ice. It breathed traces of snow over the crags and into crevices, snow that, like rain, avoided the Bone Hills altogether. It sighed at the rising sun and retreated, for now, leaving the air sparkling with frost.

Jenn Nalynn awoke to a rimed window and a nose much happier under the covers. Where it couldn't stay, of course, because this was Gallie Emms' writing room as much or more than her bedroom and lingering wouldn't be right. But in the loft she'd shared with Peggs, surely it had never been this cold.

Maybe it wasn't the Emms' fine loft. Maybe it was waking alone. Something, Bannan Larmensu would gladly remind her, that was her choice, not his.

Warmed by new and entirely unhelpful thoughts, Jenn tossed aside the quilts and stood, her bare feet glad of the braided rug. She dressed with haste, throwing on her second-warmest shawl. Her cold nose was a warning. The morning trip to the privy, however necessary, would be a chilly one.

She could, with a thought, with a wish, hold winter back. Reclaim the lingering warmth of late fall. Perhaps wake an aster or two.

Where was the harm in that?

Jenn lifted hands no longer tanned and well-callused, but glass and tears of pearl, aglow with soft light, and knew full well where the harm would be. "Here, I will not be turn-born," she whispered, willing herself flesh, willing herself back to what she was and intended to stay. Turn-born. A birthright both wondrous and terrible. If she were careless, Marrowdell would express her feelings as chill winds or warm, as storm or sunlight. If she were worse than careless and set her mind to a wishing, what other turn-born called an "expectation," Marrowdell would try to make it real, no matter the cost.

She could shatter the world.

Better to mind the baby, Jenn told herself firmly. Work, not worry, leads to accomplishment, Aunt Sybb would insist. She smiled, almost hearing Aunt Sybb's voice, then lost her smile, thinking of how long it would be until she could again. The ever-sensible Lady Mahavar spent the winter months in Avyo, where snow was a rare event and homes had indoor plumbing.

Hurrying winter simply to see their beloved aunt sooner was exactly the sort of thing she mustn't do. It wasn't fair to Uncle Hane, for one thing. For another—Jenn made her borrowed bed, nodding emphatically with each point—for another, life depended on reliable seasons, not those rushed by her whim.

Not that her whim would reach beyond Marrowdell. The valley sat where two worlds touched. Within that thin edge, Mistress Sand had warned her, was the limit of any turn-born's power.

And existence.

Jenn hugged her pillow, breathing in the rich summer scent of rose. Peggs' notion, to collect the fallen petals; Jenn's, to ask their permission first. Melusine's roses grew through the edge and were not to be trifled with, even by her daughters. They were partly of another world.

As was she.

Jenn closed her eyes. Beyond Marrowdell lay that world, the Verge, a place so utterly strange she hadn't been able to see it at first. She'd needed Bannan's true sight to reveal its sky full of dragons, not that she'd call something that wasn't blue or always overhead where sky belonged, sky at all. Yes, there were rocks, but the shapes were wrong and they could as easily hang in the air where sky should be as stay underfoot. As for what passed for lakes and rivers?

Her breath caught as she remembered mimrol's glistening silver.

Magic incarnate; that was the Verge. Its uncanny beauty ghosted her dreams when she wasn't careful. A promise. More. An invitation. Should she dare step beyond Marrowdell . . .

Jenn opened her eyes again. To step beyond Marrowdell used to mean taking the Northward Road, once her fondest desire. Still, the map hanging from the wall at the foot of her bed showed so much more of this world, she never tired of studying it.

At the same time, its exquisite detail and brilliant color, incongruous against the rough logs, were troubling reminders of its origins. That the treasure came from Bannan warmed her heart, but that the Baroness Lila Larmensu Westietas herself, beyond all reason, had had such an extraordinary and costly gift made for a miller's daughter? Worse, one with claim to her beloved brother's affections?

With all his big heart, Bannan believed Lila would welcome her into their family, once they met.

Would she welcome a turn-born? Jenn shivered from more than the chill air. As well for her peace of mind that even a baroness had to wait on the weather. The earliest their meeting could take place would be spring. Maybe by then, she'd have learned to keep her magic safe and hidden.

Maybe by then, she'd have come to understand what she was.

Work, not worry, Jenn reminded herself.

She climbed down the ladder to the kitchen, of habit mindful where she stepped. Though the kindest of hosts, Zehr Emms was apt to forget her presence and hang his saw on the middle rung, where it was beyond his little daughter's reaching fingers.

Warmer on the main floor, but only slightly. Jenn paused to stir the embers in the cookstove before adding a half-scoop of charcoal. She checked that the teakettle was full and set it to heat, then gave the porridge, left to cook over-night, a stir. Unlike the Nalynns' kitchen, separated from the rest of the main floor by a simple curtain hooked to the side when Aunt Sybb wasn't in residence, the Emms' boasted a solid dividing wall and door. The wall itself was a marvel. Zehr, a former furniture maker, had used his talents and the wood of the family wagon to fashion built-in shelves and cupboards, complete with clever fastenings and hooks; all of which Jenn quite admired. However, the heatstove was on the other side of the wall and, in the interest of pri-vacy and to keep little Loee, now able to crawl, where she belonged, the door between them remained closed at night.

She wasn't going to freeze, Jenn scolded herself. She scampered out the back door, running on her toes over the cold damp sod to the privy. Having taken care of the neces-sities, she went next to the larder, struggling a bit with the latch. What was the trick to it? There. Stepping down into the even colder room made her teeth chatter, so she worked quickly to load a basket with vegetables for tonight's sup-per. Just enough. Though the harvest had been good, winter in the north was too long for carelessness, even now, with shelves overflowing.

Not that she thought about winter. Nipping back up the steps, Jenn tucked the basket under an arm and wrestled the doors back together. Closing the latch was the easy part. Done, she stopped and gazed out over the valley toward Night's Edge, her meadow.

That by doing so she also looked toward Bannan Larmensu's farm was, she told herself firmly, entirely rea-sonable.

And blushed.

Hopefully by coincidence, the rising sun suddenly painted the sky with rose hues and brought a hint of pink to the Bone Hills.

She let her eyes follow the Spine, with its smooth mounds and long sweep, to where the Fingers stretched into the val-ley and spread to split the river, leading a tranquil flow by the village and fields, sending wild cataracts to the north.

By no accident or act of nature.

For the Bone Hills were neither bone nor hills, but what showed in this world of a being from another. The cliffs that girded the valley were gouged and scarred by its once-maddened reach; their worlds remained joined because it wouldn't—perhaps couldn't—let go again.

While along that strange connection, that edge, magic happened. On both sides.

Jenn tilted her head. The poor sei, trapped or trapped itself, couldn't leave Marrowdell. She could . . .

. . . just not, as she understood matters, as herself.

Still, wasn't it wonderful to know she could go beyond Marrowdell at her whim? To explore the Verge. To cross into other domains, for wherever the edge existed, as she understood matters, a turn-born could too. The terst turn-born couldn't deny her—she hoped they wouldn't want to—oh, how her heart pounded! The Verge was so very close . . . why she'd only to smell her mother's rose petals to feel herself almost there. Almost, but not quite.

Bannan thought of it too. He'd crossed with her, that once. Though he didn't say so, Jenn knew he was eager to go again. The man had no fear—or sense, according to Wisp.

Much as she loved them both, much as they loved her, deep inside, Jenn knew when she did cross next, she would do so alone. To see if she could. To understand matters.

To be sure.

"Ancestors Adream and Dazzled," she murmured. "As if I've time for traipsing about." Besides, being with Bannan was an exploration of a different kind, a wonderful kind, and the days passed in a busy, happy blur.

And in each day, its turn, when the light of Marrowdell faded and that of the Verge found her heart. Soon, she thought, oddly content. She would feel when to leave one for the other. She would know.

Others would, this very day. In fact, it would be the largest leave-taking of Marrowdell's short history. Hitherto only the smith, Davi Treff, and his family had journeyed to Endshere's fair, it being his mother Lorra and her friend Frann Nall who made items to trade and who, truth be told, enjoyed bartering more than breathing. This year Gallie and Zehr would join them, with little Loee, to meet the family of their new daughter-by-marriage, Palma, and nothing would do but their son Tadd and his wife Hettie come for the same reason.

At the last moment, Devins Morrill had announced, his voice barely cracking, his intention to accompany them; as this was in response to Palma's firm request that he meet her unwed cousins, his mother Covie had just as firmly insisted he wear his Midwinter Beholding coat, not the one for the barn.

Whatever coat, the weather would be chancy, Jenn fretted, not that she could change it for them. Worse, such a large group could draw the attention of bandits. Uncle Horst, sorely wounded this fall, might be back on his feet but was hardly fit to ride his horse, let alone lift a sword. People she cared about were going where she couldn't care for them; that was the crux of it.

If she worried too much, an axle might break, or a horse go lame, or some worse calamity stop them before the gate. That was how a turn-born's magic worked. This desire. That change.

And consequences. There were always those.

Jenn shook her head and pulled her shawl more tightly around her shoulders as she turned back to the Emms' house. Time to set the table. A light already shone from the side window. Despite last night's flurry of final preparations and excitement, including a predictably fussy Loee determined not to sleep and miss a thing, the family was awake. All through Marrowdell, tidy curls of smoke rose in the air as other cookstoves were roused to duty.

There. Lamplight in the Nalynns' kitchen window. Her sister, Peggs, up and stirring. They'd sit to breakfast, Peggs and their father, Radd Nalynn, with Kydd, Peggs' husband, taking the chair Jenn had sat in all her life.

Which was, she reminded herself happily, as it should be. She was welcome, always, at that table. At any table in Marrowdell.

Including the Emms', which she should be setting with bowls.

Still, Jenn couldn't resist one last look over her shoulder, toward her meadow. Toward Bannan's farm.

A light there as well now, to gladden her heart.

Her lips curved in a soft smile. On such a crisp morning, Bannan would surely walk to the village for a hot cuppa and a loaf of fresh bread. If they happened to meet, which of course they would, nothing would be more natural than for her to walk him home, for wasn't her meadow beside his farm?

And Wisp, Jenn thought happily. Her first, best friend, who always knew where she was and how, would be waiting.

Let the rest leave for Endshere. The Ancestors would watch over them and see them home again, while she enjoyed the company of those who stayed.

Nose and toes atingle from the frost, her heart brimming with warmth, Jenn Nalynn hurried indoors.

He was leaving.

Not for good or for long nor, for that matter, of his own volition, but Bannan Larmensu, once of Vorkoun and now of Marrowdell, greatly feared a certain lady wouldn't care about the details, only the fact. And what perturbed that lady?

He eyed the frost on his windowpanes, well aware Jenn Nalynn could have put it there.

Not willingly. She was as brave and good as she was powerful, and did her utmost to keep her magic under control. Magic.

Turn-born.

A person, he reminded himself, the same as any. Bannan swung his feet to the floor, pulling the quilt around his shoulders. A woman grown, full of possibilities and dreams he'd very much like to share. Along with a bed that'd be far warmer this winter with her in it; distracting thought. Bannan shook his head. He didn't doubt her love or his own. He couldn't doubt her good heart or intentions.

Jenn Nalynn was the one who needed to be sure. Ancestors Witness, wasn't her struggle to understand and accept herself the same one he'd fought, when he'd first learned he wasn't like other children? When he'd first looked into another's face and seen a lie? When he'd known he'd forever be different?

Truthseer.

Oh, how he'd hated that name, that gift, and the duty it had brought him, to be an interrogator for a heedless prince, to see nothing but darkness. It was only here, in Marrowdell, that he'd come to cherish his deeper sight. For here . . .

Getting up, Bannan tossed aside the quilt and dressed quickly. Here, he thought happily, were marvels, the greatest of all being Jenn Nalynn.

Surely she'd realize that for herself and soon. He glanced wistfully out the window toward the village. "I'd be Beholden if I didn't have to wait too long," he told his Ancestors, hopefully listening.

Not that he'd wait idle. There was work to do, he thought with still urgent joy. Work in his own home, by his own hands. The truthseer slid down the ladder to his kitchen, landing with a thump that stirred a grumpy blink from his house toad, warming itself by the stove.

"Fair morning," he greeted. The worthy creature understood most, if not all, of what it heard and deserved courtesy. Explaining that to Lila, Bannan chuckled to himself, would be an interesting conversation indeed. He stirred the coals before lighting a lantern. "Any sign of our dragon?"

While the toad couldn't speak so he could hear, it gave a huge and toothy yawn to reveal an eloquently empty mouth, then deliberately shifted closer to the warm metal.

The dragon, usually underfoot at mealtimes, had been scarce since the cooler weather. Were dragons like bears, to sleep the winter? The question, however intriguing, was unlikely to be answered before he had to leave.

Bannan opened the back door and leaned out, looking for his other frequent visitor. That he didn't see Scourge meant nothing. The old kruar, who looked enough like an ugly horse to pass for one, could hide his vast bulk behind a twig if he chose. And often did, ambush being a game he relished a little too much for a certain man's comfort.

To save time, and his toes, the truthseer stayed in the doorway and whispered, "Bacon. Baconbaconbacon." Should bring the idiot beast at a gallop.

Nothing. Good. The kruar and dragon must be hunting, or whatever they did together. An improbable truce kept them from each other's throats, as would otherwise be their nature and inclination. A shared past, common interests, and—to Bannan's mind—a mutual disdain for the younger of their own kinds, had them seek each other's company. Oh, and love of bickering. That too.

Under it all, the truth that neither belonged with their own kind, not anymore. They'd been forever changed: Wisp by his love for Jenn Nalynn, Scourge by his exile as a war-horse for generations of Larmensu riders.

Bannan had been the latest; he was determined to be the last. Beyond Marrowdell, the great beast had not only been mute; he'd forgotten who and what he was. Had he not found the Larmensus, with their ability to see the truth, Scourge would likely still be running loose, cheerfully hunting rabbits. Or men. The distinction seemed irrelevant when the blood lust was on him. The point being, the truthseer knew, that the kruar had come home, penance served and exile ended. And home was where he should stay.

Not that Scourge would agree. "Bacon," Bannan called again, louder. "Bacon and CHEESE!"

He counted to ten, then grinned with relief and closed the door. "Maybe they won't notice I've been gone."

The toad gave him a doubtful look.

"I know what you're thinking. If they do find out, the dragon will raid my larder—again. Which wouldn't be your fault, in any sense," he added hastily, house toads having a pricklish pride and, while peerless at keeping vermin out, having no such knack with dragons. Or at least Mar-rowdell's.

Humming to himself, Bannan made a quick breakfast of the last of the porridge from the pot, impulsively adding water to soften the crusty bits, then a full measure of fresh flakes to cook in case the dragon did move in—he hated being a poor host. Gulping down cold tea, he packed what little he'd need for travel.

Bedroll. Shaving kit—being beardless had begun as a simple disguise and was now his preference. He picked up his soldier's cup and folded the handle, tucking that into its usual spot in the saddlebag, then looked around for his sword and pistol.

Both of which he'd left behind in Vorkoun.

"Heart's Blood," Bannan swore, shaken. Were the old

habits still so close? "I'm a farmer," he declared, removing the offending metal cup and replacing it with the bulky, fragile, and far heavier one he'd used for his morning tea. Tir would mock him for it.

He didn't care. However ridiculous, the gesture made him feel better.

Bannan dug into a trunk for his riding leathers; home-spun didn't cut the chill. Ready, he came back to the kitchen and found the toad waiting.

The earnest regard of its oversized eyes made Bannan sit on a stool and shake his head. "You'll not leave me in peace till I admit it," he grumbled, hardly fair to the toad. "Heart's Blood. Here's the truth, then. The food doesn't matter. The dragon's welcome. It's Scourge I'm worried about. If he catches wind of this, the bloody beast will follow me. We both know it. And he mustn't. This is where he belongs."

Where those dreadful scars were the only thing left for Scourge to bear.

Closing its eyes, the house toad tucked its wide chin atop clawed feet, plainly considering the whole business beyond either of them.

The worst thing was, when it came to Scourge?

Bannan knew it was right.

For all their seeming silence, house toads had an abundance of opinion. Expressed, Jenn thought with some frustration, in the most awkward way possible. Like now.

"Will you please move?" she pleaded under her breath.

The Emms' house toad paled slightly, but didn't budge from the doorway, its huge eyes locked on hers with desperation in their limpid depths. ~ You mustn't try to leave, elder sister. You mustn't intervene. Marrowdell relies upon you. ~

Toads. "I know all that," she assured it, gripping the scraps of her patience. "I'm not going to—"

"Your pardon, Jenn?" Gallie looked up from her packing, absently shifting little Loee to a more comfortable spot on her hip.

Wen Treff talked to toads. Jenn wasn't ready to admit she did as well. "I'm not going—" she repeated quickly "—to have you wear yourself out before the trip begins. Please. Let me carry the rest to the wagon."

The older woman smiled. "Thank you, Dear Heart. Ancestors Beset and Bewildered, whatever would I do without you?"

Manage in her usual capable fashion, Jenn was sure, smiling back. "Glad to help." She lifted her armload and teased, "I take it there are no sausages in Endshere."

Gallie glanced ruefully at the table, covered with more coils of sausages as well as well-filled sacks and baskets. "I'm spoiling them, I know, but I can't visit Allin and Palma in their new home without Beholding gifts." Her eyes sparkled. "Won't they be surprised?"

Surprised would be an understatement, Jenn thought. Gallie and Zehr hadn't left Marrowdell since arriving with the rest over twenty years ago. "They'll be thrilled to see you," she said honestly. "It's a kind thing you're doing."

"It's no kindness to the horses, Gallie Emms, having you overload the wagon!" Lorra Treff made her entrance from the other room, Frann Nall close behind. Both were dressed for travel in their best heavy cloaks, scarves, and hats. Though their cheeks were equally flushed and foreheads beaded with sweat, neither would be first to admit they'd been a smidge premature in their bundling. "Leave all that."

"Now, Lorra," Frann protested. "We don't have as much ourselves this trip. You said it yourself."

Gallie brightened. Lorra frowned. Jenn tried to slip out the door over the toad but didn't make it in time. "We've enough. There's simply no room on the cart for—" Lorra eyed her burden and her frown became a scowl. "—sausages?! Ancestors Misguided and Mad, Gallie Emms, would you have us starve? Let Endshere feed its own."

At Gallie's crestfallen look, Jenn curled her arms around her bundle. "They've not tasted any as good as these."

Lorra drew herself up, the tallest feather on her hat collecting a cobweb from the rafter, to Loee's great delight. "And how would you know, Jenn Nalynn?"

It was true. And cruel.

The air in the room chilled. Frann stopped fanning her face with a 'kerchief and Gallie shivered. Which wasn't right and Jenn wished for warmth again too quickly, melting the butter in its flowered dish.

Loosening her scarf, Lorra dismissed the oddness with a brisk, "You should have my Davi look at your chimney, Gallie. Where was I?" To Frann.

"On your way to tell your son we'll be ready," Gallie informed her, with a frosty glint in her eye. "Not telling me how to pack for a visit with mine."

The matriarch of the Treffs drew a breath, ready and willing to argue.

A cough distracted her. Frann waved her 'kerchief apologetically. "The damp."

Jenn hid a smile. Though she'd not stayed abed a day anyone could recall, Frann had what Aunt Sybb called an expressive constitution, her nagging cough sure to arrive once confined indoors with Lorra for the winter.

"Lorra," Frann continued, "we must keep the house warmer."

"Psht. It's so hot my clay's drying." Lorra peered at her friend. "Ancestors Foolish and Fraught, how many times must I tell you to sleep with a heated brick?"

"And burn my—?" a second, deeper cough. Above the 'kerchief, Frann's brown eyes closed briefly, then opened with as determined a light as in either of the other women's. "We were discussing sausages. As Marrowdell's appointed trader," she stated, tucking the 'kerchief away, "the final decision on what goes or returns from Endshere's fair is mine to make. I see nothing wrong with providing samples," this with a slow smile, "of wares sure to be in demand next year."

"Samples?" Gallie echoed, eyes wide.

By her expression, Lorra might have bitten a sour berry, but she gave a reluctant nod. "Your sausages are the best I've tasted. Could be there's a market to be had."

"You're most kind, Lorra. Frann. But, Ancestors Witness, I'm not sure I could ever—"

Before Gallie could complete her highly reasonable protest at making sausages for more than Marrowdell's hungry and grateful population—not to forget one insistent and graceless kruar, who certainly wouldn't share—Jenn swooped in to grab a second basket. "I'll take those for you too."

And rather than argue further with the house toad, Jenn stepped over him, careful of her awkward and tasty burden.

Despite dawn's warning frost, the day was a splendid one for adventuring. Jenn quelled a touch of envy. As Aunt Sybb would say, to each the path before them and hers simply wasn't to be the Northward Road.

She'd also say envy was cousin to jealousy, neither being welcome guests. A caution suited to any turn-born, Jenn thought, comforted.

Besides, the sun shone brightly, with nary a cloud in the sky, turning the lingering leaves of the old trees warm russet and giving sparkle to river and windowpane alike. The hedges surrounding the village were bare, but their branches and twigs were more like the sides of a well-woven basket than walls. She'd a fine home, family, and friends. Jenn nodded to Zehr Emms, hurrying up the path to gather his family, and knew herself fortunate.

There'd be treats as well as necessities making the return trip from Endshere, including word from the Lady Mahavar, who wouldn't miss this final chance before the snows to send letters to her family. Everyone would be safely home again in a mere handful of days.

Meanwhile, for the first time in her life, she'd have an entire house to herself. Oh, and wasn't that an interesting notion? Hospitality was a homeowner's joyful duty, according to Aunt Sybb. Surely Bannan would accept an invitation for tea. She'd have to get one of Peggs' pies ...

If they bothered to eat at all.

Flushed by new and delightful possibilities, Jenn carried Gallie's sausages to where Davi's cart waited on the road. Battle and Brawl, yet to be hitched, stood dozing while Alyssa Ropp plaited their manes. The young girl stood tiptoe on a rickety stool, wobbling to keep her balance as she deftly worked ribbons into the stubby braids. "Fair morning!"

"Fair morning to you, Alyssa. Ancestors Sneaky and Sly," Jenn added with a laugh. One of the two packhorses tied loosely to the big cart had slipped her head under the tarp at the back to rummage about. Before she found something to her liking or, worse, broke one of Lorra's pots, Jenn put down the sausages and moved the horse out of mischief's way, giving her a pat of consolation. "Seems everyone's impatient."

"I wish I could go," Alyssa confessed. "Cheffy says Endshere's buildings are taller than the mill. And painted pink!"

Her only slightly older brother having relied on descriptions from their grown stepbrothers, Devins and Roche Morrill—the latter once notoriously untruthful and only recently, Jenn remembered with a small twinge, made just as notoriously honest—she doubted the last detail, but smiled anyway. "Next year, perhaps. You know Hettie's counting on you both to help in the dairy while she and Devins are away. I'm sure she'll bring you something special." Devins would be lucky to remember his own name, she thought, should some lass go so far as to smile at him, being painfully shy away from his beloved cows. Hettie would have to keep him from hiding in the stables.

"I'm sure Bannan will bring you something special, too," the kind-hearted child offered. "Here he comes now. You can ask him."

"But Bannan's not—" Feeling as though she moved through syrup, Jenn turned to look around.

To see the truthseer, dressed for the road, leading Uncle Horst's gelding from the commons.

It was all very reasonable. "Sennic asked me to go in his place," Bannan explained as he saddled Perrkin. "And I've purchases to make for winter."

"Endshere makes the best boots in the world," Alyssa piped in over Brawl's neck. "With bells and curled toes. Cheffy said so."

"I'll be sure to take a look," he replied solemnly, though boots he owned, sturdy new ones, with furred tops for warmth. He'd shown her.

His dark hair, usually loose to his shoulders, was tied back. He'd shaved but not with the fragrant soap she liked. In riding leathers and a handsome brown coat of doubtless modern cut, he no longer looked the farmer at all. Or was it the set of his shoulders?

He was leaving Marrowdell, for only a short time, and she would not, must not, dared not, let herself feel anything but helpful. "Have Frann check any deal you're offered," Jenn cautioned stiffly. "They know better than to cheat her." "They" being anyone not of Marrowdell, to hear Lorra tell it.

Bannan chuckled. "Wish I'd had her with me the first time." He tested the girth, then gave the gelding a piece of carrot. "Ancestors Witness, Tir was less than no help at all."

He was leaving Marrowdell and it was, Jenn told herself, reasonable and even right, for otherwise Uncle Horst would worry himself into trying to go with the others, none of them being soldiers. She mustn't feel dismayed or disappointed or worried or anything but—for an instant, she paused, abruptly confused what she was supposed to feel, if not all that.

Helpful. She took hold of a tie string from Bannan's pack and reached for the other.

Only to have him glance down at her with those too-perceptive eyes, a glow in their apple butter depths. His hand shifted to cover hers on the pack, warm and strong. "Thank you for understanding, Dearest Heart," Bannan said, his voice quiet and soft. "Is there anything I could bring back for you?"

Jenn's confusion faded. "Yourself," she whispered, and smiled from deep within, loving the way his expressive face mirrored both joy and a rather delicious frustration. Louder, for Alyssa, "A bag of sour candies, if you please, for my father. Any flavor will do. He's eaten all that Aunt Sybb brought, and they're good for his throat."

"Nothing more?"

"There's no room for more," she pointed out, turning practical. "You'll have mail—" which was Uncle Horst's job and meant something the truthseer should know and likely didn't. Jenn checked to be sure Lorra Treff wasn't in sight and Alyssa was safely behind Battle before whispering, "You mustn't let anyone look in the mailbag once you have it. Davi's burned Lorra's letter to the prince, and she'd be most upset if she found out. Give the bag and Kydd's honey-pots to Cammi—" the postmistress, having a sweet tooth and kind heart, took the 'pots instead of a fee the villagers couldn't afford, "—and she'll give you any mail for us."

Bannan chuckled. "A hazardous mission in truth, Dearest Heart, but one I'm willing to assume. Especially," with a wink, "since I expect mail of my own."

From his sister, he meant.

There could, Jenn swallowed, be one for her as well. She'd sent a letter to the Baroness Westietas with Aunt Sybb, a letter written in Jenn's best hand—the fourteenth such, as she'd found herself muddled at every try—thanking her for the map. She'd added a line about the weather. Another about the bountiful harvest—mentioning food should reassure a distant sister—and a final line praising her brother's courage. That had been the most difficult to compose. She mustn't imply a worrisome need for bravery in Bannan's new home, but Lila should know how much he was appreciated and valued.

She hadn't found a way to say she would protect him, always.

And now he was leaving. "You will be careful," Jenn told him, her voice thick. However capable he was, Bannan Larmensu was a man with a secret, a man who sought to leave behind his former self and occupation. Others would pay to find out, she was sure of it. "Promise me. There'll be strangers. You'll be staying—" with every intonation of ill repute and vile doings Aunt Sybb had ever managed to instill in a phrase, "—at the inn."

Even if *The Good Night's Sleep* was Palma's and by all accounts a fine and proper place.

He kissed the tip of her nose, making her eyes cross. "I promise, Dearest Heart. It's but a day's journey on horseback. We'll stay two nights at most, then be back. You'll hardly—"

"Ancestors Blessed, we've caught you!" Uncle Horst came up the road toward them, a pair of packages under his left arm, makeshift crutch under the right. "Uncle Horst" he remained to her and to Peggs, but to the rest of the village he was now Sennic Nahamm, in honor of his wife's Ancestors. He'd left his birth name behind long ago, and given his home to Hettie and Tadd, when he'd thought to leave Marrowdell.

Now he would stay, living with his wife, in her great-uncle's home.

Riss Nahamm walked with him, fingertips on his wrist. Curls of red hair kissed her cheeks and brushed the collar of her coat. Both of them were smiling. As they should, Jenn thought a little fiercely. As they should.

For the gallant old soldier had believed himself unworthy of happiness since the day of Jenn's birth, and Riss had loved him in secret all those long years. It had taken almost mortal wounds for him to accept her proposal.

And magic to save him, a turn-born's magic.

The sun felt a little warmer at the memory. Which was, Jenn realized, a turn-born's magic as well. She hurriedly thought about winter and snow and—oh, better still—washing day-old pots, that being a thought guaranteed to tame her impulses.

Bannan chuckled and nodded to the unharnessed team. "We're hardly rushing off, my friend."

"I'd prefer it if you did," Uncle Horst replied, his keen eyes lifting to the crags to the west. "Ancestors Wary and Wise, the weather can change in an hour this late in the season. I trust you to advise Davi as—" he paused, "—adamantly as I would."

Meaning that without firm support in any decision to leave early or turn back, the big smith would give in to his beloved mother's urging and Lorra, despite living in the north this many years and ample evidence to the contrary, continued to believe storms would wait on her convenience.

A strong mind didn't, Aunt Sybb would say, guarantee a wise one.

"Heart's Blood. As I should," gruffly. Uncle Horst put weight to his wounded leg. Riss bit her lower lip as the healed scars along his cheek and jaw whitened in pain.

"As I will," countered Bannan. He made a circle with his hands over his heart. "Hearts of my Ancestors, I swear to bring them home safely."

"Tadd knows what to watch for," Jenn offered. He and his twin had spent the past few summers with the livestock in the surrounding hills. They'd quickly learned when to take cover.

"That he does, Dear Heart," Uncle Horst conceded, then added with a nod. "As does our truthseer."

He didn't mean the weather.

"Then it's settled, with our thanks, Bannan," Riss said in her soft voice, her eyes suspiciously moist. "I've a favor to ask as well. My esteemed great-uncle would like this delivered to Palma. If you've room?" She took the first package from Uncle Horst and passed it to the truthseer. It was a leather portfolio, secured with thick drops of wax at every corner and loop. Old Jupp mustn't trust anyone not to read what he'd sent.

Or he valued it, Jenn reminded herself. She'd come to respect Marrowdell's eldest inhabitant; to like him, very much, truth be told, and to worry, a little. The former secretary of Avyo's House of Keys had brought trunks filled with documents to his exile, many containing secrets the current prince would not want revealed. Over the years, Old Jupp had compiled the juiciest in memoirs he gleefully planned to have published after his death.

Jenn hoped Riss would delay that publication until the prince joined her uncle as one of the Blessed. Marrowdell might be several days' travel from Avyo; it wasn't beyond reach.

"My pleasure," Bannan assured Riss. He tucked the portfolio deep inside a saddlebag, securing it before he came around to face Uncle Horst.

Who held out the second package. A slender one.

Something unhappy slid behind Bannan's eyes and he gave a sharp shake of his head.

"Heart's Blood! Don't argue." Leaning on his crutch, Uncle Horst used his free hand to strip the cloth wrap from what was, Jenn saw, his short straight sword. The one that had hung in its scabbard above the fireplace, by the bear claws, as long as she could remember.

The one for use on other men.

The gelding, Perrkin, lifted his graying muzzle and snorted with interest, being a soldier's horse and aware.

"I'm not arguing," Bannan said quietly. "I'm not taking it."

"Where's your warhorse? Without him, I don't see you have a weapon."

Scourge wasn't going? Jenn nodded to herself. She shouldn't be surprised. Beyond Marrowdell, outside the edge, the old kruar was voiceless and forgotten. He'd suffered that life till finding his way home. Why would he seek it again?

For love of this man, that was why, though the great creature would hotly deny any such attachment. Which meant . . . "You didn't tell him, did you?" she said.

Bannan half shrugged. "Even had I'd wished to, he and your dragon are off gallivanting." His way of saying they'd crossed into the Verge, which dragon and kruar could do at whim.

Well, that was inconvenient. Or convenient, Jenn thought with a little frown, unsure how she felt about the timing.

Uncle Horst had no such doubt. "Ancestors Unwary and Undone," he said roughly, thrusting the sword hilt-first at the younger man. "Every bandit worth the name knows Marrowdell travels to the fair, with goods worth stealing either way. The only reason they've never attacked is because they know me as well."

It wasn't a boast. Radd Nalynn, who well knew the measure of his friend, would make jokes about the wisdom of bandits, and the Lady Mahavar had relied on Uncle Horst to see her safely to and fro, until Tir Half-face and his axes took her service and his place.

Bannan—he'd been a soldier, too, a border guard and captain of others, including Tir. A life he'd left behind; skills he likely couldn't. Why shouldn't he arm himself? Wouldn't he be safer?

The truthseer's eyes found hers, as if she'd spoken aloud. "Swords end arguments," he said quietly. "I've never found them to win one."

Uncle Horst lowered the blade. "Trust me, Bannan Larmensu. The rabble who hunt the road will steer wide and clear if they see this. Or leave it here," he went on blandly. "If it turns out you were wrong, I'll see how it fits between your ribs."

The truth, if ever Bannan had seen it in a face. Silently, he held out his hand for the sword, belting the thing to hang at his hip. A soldier's weapon, as if there was doubt, free of gilt or tassel. The weight of it, the potential, changed his stance and darkened his mood. "I'll not draw it," he said, wondering who he promised.

"Ancestors Witness, now you look the part, truthseer, I doubt there'll be need. I'd not cross you." Spoken lightly, but there was something in the old soldier's eyes when Bannan met them that said otherwise.

This wasn't the leave-taking he'd planned, if he'd planned anything beyond being grateful if Jenn Nalynn didn't object to his leaving in the first place. He glanced her way. She'd lost her smile, but managed a resolute nod. "We'll be fine," she said, to his unasked question.

"Ready, Bannan?" Davi's deep voice brought up his team's heads, and Alyssa laughed as a ribbon pulled from her hand. He'd the reins of the other riding horses in one big hand. Marrowdell would be left with Wainn's old pony and a pair of weanlings.

Before the treaty calmed the border with Ansnor, the horses alone would have been a prize worth the risk of a sword. In Vorkoun, anyway. Perhaps Weken. Endshere and settlements farther north seemed oblivious to both the war and its end. Bannan supposed that was the way of the world.

"Ready when you are. We should get moving," he added without looking at Sennic.

Davi chuckled. "Mother's been saying that since breakfast." He handed the reins to Jenn and Alyssa. "We'll be off soon. C'mon, lads." This with a cluck of his tongue as he guided the big draft horses with a hand on each massive neck. "Mother's waiting."

Two pairs of ears flicked back, then the horses stepped promptly into their traces.

The Emms appeared, with Hettie and Tadd, and the area under the apple trees quickly became a bustle of activity as bundles and gear were sorted out. Bannan lost Jenn for a moment, then spotted her in earnest discussion with her sister and Hettie. Lorra and Frann arrived, faces flushed with obvious pleasure. More and more inhabitants of Marrowdell joined the fray, voices rising with excitement. The leave-taking was an event, after all.

A moth landed on his shoulder. Bannan squinted at it. "Are you coming?"

It waved an absent feathery plume, preoccupied with writing on its tiny curl of parchment. The moths were record keepers. News bringers, at times. And every so often, astonishingly—Bannan looked up at the sweeping pale stone of the Bone Hills—the moths were part of the immense being who held Marrowdell and the Verge together. Or spoke with its voice. A meaningless distinction, according to the dragon, who discouraged questions about the sei.

Or had no answers to give. Bannan grinned. "Keep track of things while I'm away," he requested, quite sure the moth would do so anyway.

To his surprise, it tucked away its parchment, moths having wee satchels for that purpose, and tiptoed along his shoulder to his neck. He held very still, despite the tickle, but couldn't help but start when it scratched busily on his skin. Done, it fluttered away, and he could have sworn it laughed.

"It wrote on you." Wainn Uhthoff had a gift for being unnoticed until he chose to be. He peered with interest at the truthseer's neck.

"What?" Bannan lifted his chin to make that inspection easier.

"I can't read," the youngest Uhthoff reminded him comfortably. "I remember the words."

Of all the books in Marrowdell, Bannan knew, even the ones Wainn's uncle, Kydd, had shredded into a lining for his beehives years ago. Books of magic, from Rhoth and beyond. "I should have shown you *Talnern's Last Quest*," he said ruefully, "before the dragon got his claws on it." His favorite novel had been thoroughly shredded as well; though returned, somehow neatly sewn back into the shape of a book, the words inside remained a scrambled mess.

Admittedly an entertaining mess. Neither he nor Jenn could read more than a line aloud to one another before bursting into giggles.

Wainn hadn't moved. "These words belong to Marrowdell." An uncharacteristic frown creased his forehead. "Wen said, if you leave, you won't."

If there was anyone closer to the Verge and its wild

magic than a turn-born, it was Wen Treff, who spoke to toads and heard the secrets within a heart. Bannan felt the weight of the sword again, but it wasn't that. Marrowdell objected to his leaving. Or warned him against it.

Why? A chill ran down his spine. To counter it, he clapped Wainn heartily on the shoulder. "Then I'd best come back, hadn't I?"

The younger man didn't smile. "Yes." He turned and left without another word.

"What was that about?" Jenn asked, giving Wainn's back a surprised look as she stepped close.

Bannan wrapped his arm around her, holding her slender warmth to the side without the sword, and pressed his face into her hair. "Hearts of my Ancestors," he prayed silently, then stopped, terrified to have come that close to doubt. "I belong here," he said instead, aloud. "I belong here and with you, Dearest Heart."

"You're doing the right thing." Her arms, strong and comforting, wrapped around his waist. "The others are glad you'll be with them. As am I." A squeeze, then she slipped away. "After all," her smile found his heart, "I'll be here to welcome you home."

Home, Bannan thought, almost dizzy with relief. That was the truth. Marrowdell was his home now and, moths and warnings withstanding, nothing would change that.

He wouldn't let it.

~

*A sliver of paper, touched by ink and fingertip . . . a drop of sleep, under the tongue . . .*
*And the dream unfolds . . .*
Mean, the room, full of dust and cobwebs, its walls of rough stone and wood black with rot. There's a shuttered window, curtained by a cloak.
A pair of lamps light a table spread with documents. A hand shifts them about, points to one.
Dim figures gather around. Heads shake. A fist comes down. Disagreement.
A finger pushes the document forward. Insistence.
*The dream falters . . . rebuilds . . .*

It rains silver.
And eyes glimmer from the dark.

She'd let him leave. There'd been a heartbeat, an instant, when simply asking would have kept him here, with her. But duty must, when duty calls, as Aunt Sybb would say, and she'd known he should and must go.

That didn't make it any easier.

So, having watched the precious caravan pass out of sight beyond the first bend of the road from Marrowdell, before the last echoes of hoofbeats and fare-thee-well's faded from the crags, Jenn Nalynn fled before she could change her mind.

And stop them all.

She ran through the village and climbed the gate into the commons, past Wainn's old pony, calling unhappily after his pasture mates, and the cows, half asleep as they chewed their cud in the sun. The far gate was open and the great sows, Satin and Filigree, didn't look up as she passed, too busy rooting through litter for the last of the acorns. They were as good as a gate, being unwilling to share their treasure with anything else four-footed; their boar, Himself, being the exception, but he dozed in the Treffs' warm barn with this year's weanlings.

The riverside oak rattled its brown withered leaves as Jenn moved through its shade, being an opinionated tree. She didn't pause. The water of the ford was shin-deep and bitterly cold, ice where it stilled among the brown reed stalks, but she didn't gasp or slow. Nor was she at all surprised when the path to Bannan's little farm came faster than it should, because Marrowdell knew where she wanted to be.

Night's Edge.

And with whom.

In the air, he was death and danger and all things perilous. A dragon, once lord. Almost, not quite, lord again.

Silly younglings.

Wisp settled to ground, leaving such pretensions in the chill air. He'd survived his penance. He'd no interest in earning another. Let a new fool rouse dragonblood and stir the cliff holds to battle.

His jaws gaped in a mirthless grin. Best way to trim the fat.

The ground was still frozen. He'd picked a sun-touched spot in the meadow, hoping for warmth, but was too early or too late. Late, was his gloomy thought. Marrowdell's sun waned already. There'd be snow soon. He shivered and snarled.

Warmth, sudden and welcome. Efflet, winged and clawed and foolishly fond of snow, had left their hedge to cuddle against his withered side. Lifting his head, Wisp hurriedly looked around for any sign of the old kruar. Finding none, he accepted the small beings' gift with a grateful sigh. Not that they'd be enough to keep him warm in winter.

Be warm he must. In the cold, dragonblood would first slow, then freeze solid like the revolting water in the river. Presumably also to thaw in spring, dragons being hard to kill, but none alive could claim to know for certain and Wisp wasn't about to take that chance.

Or leave the girl unprotected.

He'd find a way. Shelter he had, though of crystal and wood. Until now, he'd visited the girl but briefly in winter, crossing back to the Verge as soon as possible to bask in its heat.

No longer. A growl rumbled deep in his chest, disturbing the efflet. The outside world had found Marrowdell once. It could again. If he had to dig a hole under the truthseer's kitchen to stay close, live as he had among the turn-born, he would.

A moth shaped like a snowflake drifted near his face. ~I have news, elder brother. News!~

Wisp snapped before remembering the tiny creature could be more than it seemed. ~What news?~ he grumbled, annoyed to be relieved he'd missed. The moths, when not possessed, were prone to think anything worth recording.

~They are leaving, elder brother. Today!~

The dragon settled himself, rather smug. ~This is not

news to me.~ The fair at Endshere was the final exchange with the world beyond Marrowdell before winter. He would feel better once it was done, especially as the girl had reminded him there would be letters.

Wisp sincerely hoped none were for him.

The moth managed to look disappointed. ~My apologies, elder brother. I should have realized he wouldn't leave without your permission.~

~Who?~

~But you already know——~

The dragon parted his jaws meaningfully. ~WHO?!~

The moth landed at a safe distance, fussing with its plumes. ~The smith and the potter and the weaver and the milkmaid and the miller's apprentice and the woodworker and the writer and the tiny one and the truthseer.~

Bannan was leaving Marrowdell?

More importantly, his warm and food-filled home?

~Oh, that,~ Wisp replied airily. ~I knew that.~

Fine news, indeed.

Then, the best news of all. The moth startled up and away; the efflet deserted at the same time, leaving his side once more exposed to the cold. They sensed what he did and dared not stay.

A turn-born approached.

Not just any turn-born. Jenn Nalynn. Wisp sent a little breeze throughout the meadow to gather soft dry grasses, stealing some from the nest of a sleepy rabbit who thumped fearlessly at him, being one of hers.

As, he thought with undragonish pleasure, was he.

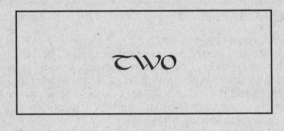

# TWO

*T*HE MEADOW KNOWN as Night's Edge nestled between Bannan's farm, two of the Bone Hills, and the Tinkers Road, isolated from all but a lovely view of Marrowdell by thick hedges and the old trees—who weren't trees, Jenn reminded herself, but the roots of neyet growing through from the Verge. That the valley was filled with such mysterious beings was still a delight.

That her meadow remained home to her favorite, her best friend, was something more than that. Had Wisp returned to his old life, hers would have been the poorer.

Though he could still be the most annoying, difficult, and stubborn . . . "I just want to talk to her."

A warm breeze tickled her ear. "Why?" It tossed her bangs. "You're talking to me, Dearest Heart. Am I not enough? Why am I not enough?"

Was that a hint of worry? "Nothing's wrong," Jenn assured him, rubbing her forehead. "I've some questions for Mistress Sand, that's all."

"Questions you can't ask me? You can ask me anything."

Oh, definitely worry—and a smidge of pique. If she didn't know better, she'd swear her friend was jealous. "Fine. I'll ask you." He'd made her a seat of dry grass, which was considerate, though the clumps of fur meant he hadn't been as thoughtful of the rabbit, but she was too restless to sit. "Mistress Sand said the Verge touches more than Marrowdell—" this being a marvelous revelation she and Bannan had discussed many times. "All I want to know is if it touches—well, if it goes to—"

"Endshere." Silver glinted in the air before her, and she felt a draft most likely from a wing. Wisp showed himself no more than ever, but Jenn had seen him both as a man, which had been her doing, and as he truly was. Claws like ancient bone, longer than her fingers, curved and serrated. A wiry beard below a long jaw of deadly fangs. Breath like steam; skin like finely woven silver chain. Eyes of deep, dark violet. One side, crippled, the other whole, but both wings entire and strong, a gift she'd oh-so-gladly given. "It does not, Dearest Heart," he informed her. "If it did, what would you do?"

She hadn't thought that far, to be honest. Jenn plopped herself down on the grassy seat with a sigh. "I don't know," she admitted. "Be sure they're safe. Watch over them."

"See the fair for yourself."

"I—" Swallowing her protest, Jenn lowered her gaze to her hands and searched her own heart. Was she still so shallow? No. "I'm uneasy," she said at last, sure of that much. "Whether it's because I can't help them, or because I shouldn't even if I could. Being turn-born's—" What was it? "—confusing," she finished, sure of that, too. "Wisp, I don't know my limits. I don't know how to find them without doing something I shouldn't." Oh, there was an understatement. "I need Mistress Sand." She patted the ground. "Here."

"The terst turn-born will not cross until Marrowdell warms again. Being sensible." Followed by a *snapsnapsnap* that sounded like chattering teeth.

House toads felt the cold. They moved indoors, taking up residence under heatstoves and in front of fireplaces.

Her poor dragon. Despite today's sunshine, the air had a nip to it that would soon be a freezing bite. Which she mustn't alter, Jenn reminded herself sternly. Instead, she undid her heavy cloak—the lined one being saved for real winter—and held it out awkwardly. "If you're cold—" she began, then shook her head and put the cloak aside. "Wisp. Come close. I'm warm enough for the two of us."

Grass bent and crackled. She let him decide if and how, reminded of how it was easier to catch a wayward piglet if one sat quietly and let it come. With a piece of apple, piglets not being foolish, but warmth was something she most certainly could see wanting just as much.

Something pressed against her arm, then around her back, cool and hard as stone. More laid along her thigh, then a long something that wasn't heavy but had odd sharp bits landed on her lap. Encased in dragon, Jenn spread her cloak over them both as best she could. "There. Isn't that better?" Though it was; she could feel for herself. What had been cool and hard warmed more quickly than stone could, and she would, in fact, shortly be too warm for the cloak herself and possibly break into a sweat.

Which was fine. After all these years, she finally knew who and what her little breeze was. He could be harmed—hadn't she done it? He could be lost—oh, how she'd feared it. Through it all, Wisp remained the bravest, truest friend there could be.

And deserved every kindness she could manage.

When the breeze found her ear again, it was decidedly formal, as if the dragon was slightly embarrassed to be, as Peggs would put it, snuggling. "If you truly wish to speak with the turn-born, Dearest Heart, I could convey your invitation. By word, not letter."

Wisp, as Wyll, had learned all about invitations. As for the letter? "I understand," Jenn said. Only turn-born could cross between worlds with more than themselves. What Wisp proposed was a meeting, but . . . "You said Mistress Sand wouldn't cross into—oh."

"The Verge is always warm," the breeze informed her, implying something wrong with a world unable to make the same claim. "It would be a show of strength to demand to meet at your crossing."

"My crossing?" Jenn echoed faintly. Did he mean the entrance to the Verge at the top of the Spine, where she'd crossed before? Where she'd faced—no, she thought firmly.

He couldn't mean that. It was much too close to the mad sei for even her comfort.

Not to mention some unfortunate rabbits.

The breeze found her other ear. "The terst turn-born would refuse, of course. They are not so brave as you, Dearest Heart."

She felt anything but brave.

The dragon might have been talking to himself. "A meeting at their crossing would put you too close to their home. No, it should be on neutral ground. Where I cross. That will do. You don't mind heights, do you?"

Worry about heights, when they were talking about crossing from one world to the next, where she would be away from all that kept her Jenn Nalynn and flesh?

Her heart filled with longing to do just that. And wasn't now, with Bannan away, the perfect time to try?

Which now wasn't. "Ancestors Forgetful and Foolish. Wisp, it's laundry day. I promised Peggs." A struggle once the air was so cold, and not something to avoid simply to go adventuring. "I can't abandon her." Not twice in a row.

What she'd unconsciously leaned against pulled away. As she caught her balance, the breeze chuckled in her ear. "Dearest Heart, do your duty while I do mine. There's no knowing when I'll find the turn-born to give your invitation. This day. The next. They travel the Verge, though never as quickly as I. I'll bring word."

Just like that, she was alone in the meadow. A disgruntled rabbit began stuffing grass in its mouth, the dried ends wagging up and down until it seemed to have grown a very odd and very large mustache. Jenn moved out of its way. "I've done it now," she told it, relieved, if she were honest. The die was cast. She was committed to crossing into the Verge, to meet with its powerful turn-born.

Where the warmth of her reception could depend on a dragon's manners. Or lack.

"Oh, dear."

The steady beat of unshod hooves on packed earth was their drum, the creak of leather and occasional snort their sole heralds. Bannan was reassured by the care taken by the villagers beyond Marrowdell's walls. They might have been ghosts moving down the mist-skirted Northward Road. Deer barely looked up as they passed; a young fox startled when they came around a bend.

Davi rode Battle, the extra burden nothing to the massive horse. His mother and Frann sat atop the cart load, a cozy nest having been made for them among the bundles and sacks; by midmorning, both were sound asleep.

Hettie and Tadd rode behind the wagon, holding hands when they thought no one was looking. They'd argued before setting out, she being large with child and he, to Bannan's mind, understandably anxious. But the women hadn't worried, most particularly her mother, who was the village healer, so how could the men?

Zehr walked more than he rode, admitting he hadn't spent much time ahorse the last few years, but cheerful despite his sore backside. He held the reins of his wife's mount as well, Gallie busy taking notes on the surrounding plant life, though it looked like all the rest to Bannan's eyes. Tiny Loee, preoccupied with her thumb, dozed in a sling at her mother's breast.

As for Bannan? After Scourge, Perrkin was a revelation: an honest, easy-paced horse who not only knew where they were going but wished nothing more than to please his rider along the way. He could get used to this, the truthseer decided, patting the aged gelding's sturdy neck.

Though truth was, after they stopped for lunch, he was in some danger of joining Frann, Lorra, and the baby, nodding off, then waking with a guilty start. Scourge wouldn't have put up with it, being expert at a jolting step or two if Bannan dared relax. Teeth through one's tongue was an unpleasant and highly effective alarm on patrol.

Which he was, so the truthseer fought his grogginess. Going ahead a bend or two and riding back helped, but it wasn't fair to Perrkin to ask him to travel the road more than the others. Instead, Bannan followed Zehr's example and dismounted to walk every so often, the challenge of keeping up with the team's long strides enough to keep his eyes open.

Not that eyes seemed much use. He hadn't realized how much he'd come to rely on Scourge's senses. Once the morning mist burned away, the sun dazzled. Now, afternoon's first shadows stretched like fingers from under the pines, clawing at the road's edge and hiding what they chose. His eyes played tricks, he thought, squinting.

Had he seen something?

Another fox, more likely than not.

The entire north, as much of it as he'd seen, consisted of steep-walled crags split at random by narrow, winding gorges. The road, like the tumbling water that sprang from cracks and seams, took the easiest path, winding anywhere the land could support it, ever-so-grudgingly sloping down to Lower Rhoth and civilization.

Toward Lila and home. He couldn't wait.

Bannan frowned.

The Westietas estate had never been home; he'd left the Larmensu holding a boy barely grown. Home lay behind him, in a land of—of—roses and sunsets that were—what were they?—where moths who took notes—which, his frown deepened, moths couldn't do.

Yes, he'd a farm of his own and soon, hopefully, piglets, but winter, he feared, would be long and lonely. If only he'd found someone in Marrowdell, as Lila had hoped.

Suddenly, his neck burned—or did it itch?

Bannan lifted his fingers to the spot and felt raised letters, hot as fire. As shockingly, at the touch, his memory cleared. "Jenn!" he cried, aloud and urgently, feeling the truth of it—of her—snap back into place.

He trembled, unable to credit he'd forgotten her, however briefly.

"'Jenn?'" Davi glanced down at him, bushy eyebrows raised. "Who's that?"

He meant it. The truth in the other man's face was like a knife in Bannan's heart. "Someone dear to me," he managed. Someone dear to all of them, before they'd left Marrowdell.

What was happening?

"Maybe you'll have a letter waiting," the villager said comfortingly.

"I hope so." The truthseer forced a smile, a smile he lost as he mounted Perrkin and sent him trotting ahead of their little group.

Ordinary sunlight crisscrossed the road, fallen leaves crunched rather than giggled, and what was wrong with him, that he'd any trouble at all remembering the love of his life? She'd kissed him this very morning. Held him tight then sent him on his way with one of her wondrous smiles.

He'd forgotten Marrowdell as well, at least everything strange and remarkable about the place.

Heart's Blood. Bannan swallowed. One and the same, weren't they, for wasn't Jenn Nalynn now turn-born and magic?

Wen had warned him. Leave and no longer belong.

Ancestors Dreadful and Dire, he hadn't thought it the truth.

Bannan twisted in the saddle. The others seemed unchanged and unworried. Because they couldn't see the Marrowdell he did? Or was it because they'd lived there most of their lives, taking so much for granted they didn't notice its absence?

Such questions died on his lips, unspoken, and he knew himself a coward, afraid to see the terrible truth in every face. That once beyond Marrowdell, even they forgot her magic.

He would not. Dared not. Ylings. They lived in the old trees—the neyet. The ylings had been left in the valley; the neyet grew through from the Verge for their own reasons and, once, had sacrificed themselves so the turn-born could build a village. A village to attract people, ordinary people, to harvest the kaliia, the grain that also grew from the Verge and was tended by the deadly efflet.

Jenn Nalynn had hair of gold.

The kaliia was the reason for the mill, too, for the turn-born—however dangerous and powerful—happened to like the beer they could make from that grain.

He did too, come to think of it. Tasty stuff. To turn-born it was more, Jenn had told him, the brew being their way of bringing some of this world with them into the Verge, for they wouldn't cross in winter.

Willingly would he drown in her eyes, their deep blue

purpled by magic. Her smile took hold of his heart and made it sing. When she laughed, the world brimmed with hope and anything was possible.

The road, the crisp air, even the patient horse beneath him faded as Bannan thought of Jenn Nalynn; he started when Tadd Emms rode up beside him and said his name.

"Is something wrong?" As if everything wasn't, the truthseer told himself grimly. Give him bandits. Anything but this betrayal.

"That's what I came to see." Though both twins showed their Naalish ancestry in a stocky build and tight black curls, with a sallowness to their skin despite its weathering, only Tadd had their mother's dimples. They weren't in evidence now, his features serious. "Hettie said you shouted a name she didn't know." After a quick, searching look at Bannan's face, he smiled broadly and leaned back in the saddle. "Jenn's. Jenn Nalynn. You remember."

"How—?" How didn't matter. Bannan's relief was akin to pain. "I do. Now. But Tadd, I—I forgot her." Said aloud, it sounded worse than impossible.

Tadd merely nodded, as if unsurprised. "What matters is you remember," with certainty. "We'd bet, Allin and me. If you would or not. I told him a truthseer might." His head tilted, like a curious bird's. "You have, haven't you? Remembered Marrowdell the way we do. Not only Jenn. All of it. The magic."

"Yes." With help. Bannan decided not to mention the moth. Though unoffended to be the subject of a wager—it was hardly the first time—he found himself abruptly indignant. "Why didn't anyone—" Ah, but he'd been warned, hadn't he? He took a steadying breath. "How is it you remember?"

Tadd found the ends of his reins of surpassing interest. Their horses, long-time companions, matched stride for stride in an easy walk. After a moment, he answered quietly, "We're different, Allin and me. We've known since we first left the valley."

Something they'd done each summer since being old enough to ride. Tadd's becoming the miller's apprentice and his twin living in Endshere, the question of who would graze the livestock beyond the valley next year remained to be settled. From what he was hearing, with what he'd felt himself, Bannan wasn't sure who else could. "Davi didn't remember Jenn."

"Not anymore." Tadd shrugged. "He used to, but she's changed, hasn't she? More—more Marrowdell than anyone else. That's what they can't remember, Bannan."

Jenn had told him turn-born couldn't live outside the edge. She'd done her best to accept that terrible truth. Now this? That outside, her very existence was forgotten? He'd have to tell her.

He couldn't imagine how.

"Does anyone else remember?" Bannan asked, dropping his voice below the clop of hooves on the road. "Sennic—Horst?" Surely the old soldier.

"He taught us to keep what makes Marrowdell special secret." A dimple showed. "'Course, once in a while we slip. I got in a fight at the inn last year, bragging about our grain, and Allin—well, fortunately no one believed him about the dancers in the trees. But Horst?" He shook his head and Bannan's heart fell. "Our first trip outside, we didn't know any better. Horst wouldn't talk about Marrowdell, so we didn't. Then Allin saw." Lower. "I did, too."

"Saw what?"

Tadd looked askance at him, then brought his horse closer. "You see when someone speaks the truth." He waited for Bannan to nod. "We see something—Allin calls it 'Marrowdell's light'—in a person's eyes. I can see it in yours.

"When we don't, when it's gone, the person has lost Marrowdell. We saw it leave Horst. Oh, he knew about home. About us. But when we talked about what makes Marrowdell special—what he'd warned us to keep secret before we left? He warned us not to make up wild stories. Said they'd attract attention. They weren't stories, Bannan." A resigned shrug. "Horst simply couldn't believe them, away from Marrowdell. He'd forgotten."

If not for the moth, Bannan thought desperately, he'd have done the same. "The others?"

"Hettie's lost it," with regret. "My parents. Loee hasn't, but she's a baby. The Treffs and Frann have. Devins. Naught's wrong with any of them." This was said hastily, as if worried what Bannan might think. "The light comes back, once they pass between the crags. Once home." His fingers circled his heart. "Ancestors Blessed and Bountiful. It's just—they won't remember having forgotten." He added, almost too quietly to hear, "Or believe us, if we tell them. Here or there."

"Tell me the Lady Mahavar remembers," Bannan pleaded. If Aunt Sybb forgot her youngest niece, if her letters from this time forward came without mention, Jenn Nalynn would be heartbroken. "She must."

"Aie. Her light's there, bright as yours." Tadd carefully examined his reins again. "Allin and I, we keep hoping to talk to her, when our paths cross each spring and summer, but every time there's no way to—the lady's not someone we—she's—" He looked up helplessly. "She doesn't care for magic."

For this was magic, no mistake.

Bannan reached out and gripped the villager's shoulder. "Hard enough to bear such a gift when you can't tell those you love. Harder still when you can see them change as you have. You've done well, Tadd. Both of you. Very well."

The other's eyes shone. "Allin said you'd understand if anyone could. We just had to wait until—"

"You saw," Bannan finished for him.

"Yes." Tadd beamed. "Which means I win for once!"

Their bet. He laughed. "Glad to be of service."

"We must talk again. With Allin." Tadd glanced over his shoulder and waved. "I'd best get back to Hettie."

"Thank you." And when they spoke, Bannan resolved to ask Allin about the Dema and the Eld, and their servants. Roche too. Much as he'd come to respect Qimirpik, it might be as well if Marrowdell kept its deeper secrets.

From Tir as well?

Ancestors Witness. Doubtless his friend would sleep better at night if he forgot Marrowdell's eccentricities. Why did it feel like betrayal? Because that's how Tir would consider it. He'd demand a way to remember.

Which there was. The moth.

As Tadd reined back to rejoin his family, who'd forgotten magic, Bannan found himself reconsidering it. Was this forgetting deliberate, with a cause and purpose? Or, like the dreams within the valley, simply a consequence of moving between a place saturated with magic and one—almost—without.

No wonder Scourge had wandered, lost.

Heart's Blood. He should turn around, now, before he was.

Should, but wouldn't. Dropping the reins, Bannan's fingers found that now-cool spot on his neck. The moth—be it the sei or Marrowdell itself—had marked him for a reason. Had saved him, that was the truth, and he was beyond grateful. He'd fulfill his duty, though the next few days would be an eternity.

It was then Bannan realized he'd let himself become dangerously distracted.

They weren't alone on the road.

"I'm pleased you're going at last, Dearest Heart." Peggs Nalynn Uhthoff brushed a lock of black hair from her brow, leaving a whimsy of soap bubbles above a shapely eyebrow. "Just tell me before you do."

"So you can worry?" Beckoning her sister close, Jenn moistened the corner of her apron and wiped the bubbles from otherwise flawless skin, then stood back and admired. Happiness sparkled in Peggs' eyes these days and, though always graceful, wasn't she now the most beautiful woman in Marrowdell, perhaps even in all of Rhoth? Now she moved as if hearing music. "Kydd agrees with you," Jenn declared with satisfaction.

Roses bloomed along those high cheekbones, but Peggs merely shook her head. "And you're changing the subject."

The subject being Jenn taking that first step beyond Marrowdell, though the process wasn't so much a step as a desire and intention to be somewhere and someone entirely not here and her?

Changing it was exactly what she wanted to do. "I'll hang these." Jenn grabbed an armload of steaming shirts and headed for the door. She paused to look over her shoulder. "I promise to tell you."

That won her the smile she'd hoped. "I suppose I should

be grateful you've decided to talk about this at all. If not with me, then with — " Peggs waved the big paddle, shedding bubbles "—someone."

By which she meant "someone" who knew everything. Oh, each and every resident of Marrowdell had their version of what had happened at the fall equinox, when the eclipse had passed over the valley on the Ancestors' Golden Day. Most believed Uncle Horst had succumbed to old guilt and tried to leave the valley, only to be mauled by a bear. How fortunate the tinkers had still been in the valley to help heal his wounds.

Most believed the mysterious and magical Wyll, once Jenn Nalynn's promised husband, had spurned her and also left, for good. Both events, it was tacitly agreed, had been for the best, Horst now happily married to Riss Nahamm and Wyll, never easy company, surely better off elsewhere.

Few knew the whole truth. Wainn and Wen, of course, who likely knew more. Bannan. Peggs and Kydd. Radd Nalynn, because his daughters had blurted it all out over supper and who, to his credit, had merely nodded and gone a bit pale. Aunt Sybb? It was difficult to say if the Lady Mahavar would bother with the truth, being unsettled by magic and toads at the best of times, and they'd promised their father not to disagree with their aunt's view of things, whatever that became.

Of the rest, Jenn suspected nothing in Marrowdell slipped the notice of Master Dusom, Kydd's elder brother, or Old Jupp, but none of them spoke of it. She hoped Uncle Horst had told Riss, which was their business and not hers, but surely Riss deserved to know he'd almost died defending Jenn Nalynn so she could reach the Verge to save the sei — and, not incidentally, Marrowdell itself — and that Wyll hadn't left at all, but had been returned to his true self.

A dragon named Wisp.

Jenn slipped through the doorway, her breath joining the steam from the damp clothing. It wasn't quite winter, but her fingers numbed as she hastily pegged shirts, shirtwaist, and — oh, yes — a pair of men's full undergarments that did not belong to their father. She managed not to drop them or blush.

Back inside, Jenn ducked under the line of clothing hung

across the kitchen and planted herself on the second last rung of the ladder that, before the equinox and weddings and all else, had led to her bedroom as well as Peggs'. "Nice underwear your husband has," she commented, reaching chilled hands toward the cookstove with its bubbling pot of laundry. Every window stood open despite the cold outside; it was that, or have the entire house smell of wet cloth and soap.

"I'm sure Bannan's are more modern," her sister retorted.

"Peggs!"

"When he wears any." With a wink.

Jenn launched a soggy sock. Laughing, Peggs caught it in midair and sent it flying back, but not before Jenn found another, then another. When they finally ran out of socks, the pair settled side-by-side on the stair, laughter subsiding. "Were you tempted?" Peggs asked quietly.

Jenn leaned into her sister's shoulder. "To stop him? For a moment. But the others need him. After all. There could be bandits."

"More likely a baby." Both chuckled then shook their heads. There'd been no arguing with Hettie, who'd pronounced, firmly, that babies were like calves and would be born whenever and wherever they chose. "It's because Bannan's away you're going now, Dearest Heart, isn't it?"

Was there anything Peggs missed? "I need to cross alone. I must."

She felt her sister tense, then relax. "Ancestors Witness. I hope you know what you're doing."

"Not in the least. That's why, you see."

Peggs fell silent. Jenn waited; her sister preferred to chew on a thought, especially when it involved change. Finally, "I've no idea what that world—the Verge—is like. How can I give you advice? Or help?" Her arm came around Jenn and hugged, hard. "Just know you'll be doing dishes the entire winter for two households if you aren't careful. Including the pots!"

Though the consequences of her not being careful in the Verge would be far worse, Jenn pretended to shudder. "Anything but pots. I promise, Peggs. I'll visit Mistress Sand and come straight back."

Perhaps having learned enough, she added wistfully and to herself, to welcome Bannan's interesting laundry into a pot with her own.

There. A glimpse of brown. Or was it black? Had he imagined it? No. Bannan trusted the wary flick of Perrkin's ear over his eyes. Something paced them through the shadowed woods.

If it was Scourge, the great beast had graciously allowed both man and gelding that fleeting look.

If something else . . . ?

Bannan spread the fingers of his left hand where it rested on his thigh before remembering there was no Tir Half-face to catch that guard's signal for caution. Then again, were they not a caravan of simple villagers? He turned easily in the saddle, hooking one leg over Perrkin's neck. The seemingly careless position would allow him to swiftly dismount with the horse between him and any attacker, a horse who might not have fangs, but who'd been trained to use hooves and teeth. "Ancestors Famished and Faint, Davi," he called to the smith. "When do we stop for lunch?" A meal they'd eaten already, at the same spot he'd camped with Tir on the journey north, giving the horses a breather and watering, and there was no plan to pause again.

The big man had been half asleep himself. To his credit, he understood at once, coming awake with a stretch and an outwardly cheerful, "Not long now. Past yon bend. There's a stream, as I recall." His own hand, twice the breadth of Bannan's and callused rock-hard by years working metal, wrapped around the hammer tied to Brawl's harness. He didn't pull it free. Not yet.

Tadd, riding by the cart, frowned. "Lunch? But—"

"Ooooh," Hettie groaned fervently, a hand on the swelling at her waist. "Oooh!"

Her husband looked horrified. Bannan, seeing the lie in her face, winked to acknowledge her quick wit. Though pale, she winked back.

The playacting roused Lorra, who fussily straightened her hat as she peered around. Frann, meanwhile, remained sound asleep. Devins, on the opposite side of the cart, glanced at his stepsister, made a face as if to declare his intention to stay out of any baby business, then pulled his hat down over his brows to doze again.

But didn't. Bannan saw the young man's hands gather the reins, ready to send his mount wherever necessary.

Lorra began to scowl. "What's the matter?" she snapped.

"A kick surprised me, Great Aunt, that's all." Hettie smiled, the little gap between her teeth giving her a mischievous look that was, Bannan knew, wholly appropriate. "She's a strong one."

"He," Lorra corrected—not for the first time. "Covie's guessing. And don't call me that. I'm not a hundred years old."

"My mother, Lorra Treff, doesn't guess." With a decided snap. Tadd, anxious now for a new reason, looked over at Devins; that worthy's shoulders were shaking suspiciously. "My mother's the best healer in Marrowdell!"

"Which doesn't say much, does it? I say it's a boy."

Bannan wondered if he should hope the bickering would distract any bandits.

Then Davi let go of his hammer to join the fray. "Now, Mother—a wee girl would be wonderful."

"Another girl, and we'll have to order in husbands by the handful!"

Frann woke up, blinked, and said happily, "You've had the baby?"

"You haven't, have you?" Tadd demanded. "I mean, you can't, like that. Can you?"

Devins leaned back and roared with laughter. Hettie's face turned pink.

Perrkin's ears went flat.

In one fluid motion, Bannan threw himself around in the saddle and dug in his heels to drive the willing horse toward the wall of trees. He put his hand to the hilt of his sword, but didn't draw it as they charged, hearing but ignoring the shouts from behind.

Almost in the shadows, he leaned back sharply in the saddle. The gelding almost sat in its urgency to obey, then half reared as now Bannan did pull free the blade. "Hold!" he shouted, thrusting the gleaming thing high as his blood pounded in his ears and all his better sense told him he was an idiot.

The martial display wouldn't impress Scourge in the least. Hopefully, it might deter a few faint-hearted bandits.

Unfortunately, it did nothing to slow the onrush of the huge and shaggy bear, mouth agape in a roar!

Perrkin, wiser than his rider, whirled and bolted.

While Lorra, never one to miss the essential point, shouted, "Save us! It's after the sausage!"

Later, Bannan couldn't be sure exactly what had happened, and was glad of it. He remembered turning the gelding back toward the caravan. The shouts and commotion as horses rightly contested being asked to stay anywhere close to the bear. The roars and snarls of what wasn't a huge bear after all, but a miserable and maddened creature, late to its den, bent on attacking anything edible.

Then the *smack!* as Scourge hit it from the side at full charge, likely breaking its back, but that hadn't been enough for the old kruar who'd . . .

The truthseer swallowed. According to Devins, who'd promptly lost his lunch at the side of the road, Scourge had ripped out the bear's entrails and tossed them high in the air.

Before diving back in to pluck out and eat its heart. While purring.

Drama done, the little caravan resumed its journey. The horses were understandably unhappy, an opinion they expressed by breaking into a jog toward Endshere and its stable as often as allowed. The villagers, who thankfully remembered Scourge as his warhorse, if nothing more, accepted with good humor that the beast had followed the caravan and heroically saved its master.

From what they emphasized had been a very small bear.

Bannan was almost offended, for Scourge's sake, if not his own; surely the beast had been large enough to bring down a horse or man, and enraged at that. Seeing the truth in their faces, he kept his peace. Perhaps the north harbored a different sort of bear.

As for the giant mass of flesh stalking alongside poor Perrkin? Bannan shook his head. "You could go home," he suggested quietly, again.

A roll of a still-red eye.

"Do you—can you remember? Home? What you are?"

Scourge might be unable to speak beyond the edge, but that curled lip eloquently dismissed any of his, Bannan's, concerns as trivial.

Fair enough. Scourge had brought him to Marrowdell in the first place. They'd make do. "Idiot beast." Bannan reached over to slap the dusty hide, avoiding a glob of bear blood. His voice thickened. "Hearts of my Ancestors, I swear I'll get you home again."

A shudder worked under the skin, whether at his touch or the alternative.

Well enough. They were safer for the kruar's company.

If not any mice in Endshere's stable.

The turn came, sliding night's deeper blue over the Bone Hills, leading shadows down the Tinkers Road to the village, spreading wide across the fallow fields. It roused efflet to whisper in their hedges, their eyes cold and pale as they watched for unwary nyphrit. They remembered, did efflet, how very many of them had died on the Spine, and took an accounting whenever they could.

Ylings, who'd also fought and died, danced and sang, catching the light of the turn in their hair, their number so great that the old trees, the neyet and their homes, seemed leafed in tiny stars. The turn passed and they hid again.

Giggling. Ylings preferred life to vengeance.

The turn reached the village and house toads tucked themselves under bed frames or stoves or burrowed beneath cushions, as house toads were wont to do, being loath to expose their true nature.

While Jenn Nalynn stood in the space between kitchen and main room, arms wide and head back, drinking in light.

She could be anywhere, and the turn would find her. Change her. Reveal her as she was. Earlier now, as winter approached. Unmistakable, always.

Jenn opened and closed her hands, marveling how they could feel the same, yet look so different. Fingers of glass, filled with opalescence. If she lifted them to her face, the glow made her squint. Which must be a memory of squinting, or its habit, since she had no eyes nor other features as turn-born. Another question for Mistress Sand, who hadn't said anything about the mask she and other turn-born wore in place of a face. A mask, moreover, that became a face, once the turn passed.

It was all quite remarkable. What mattered, Jenn supposed, was that she could see regardless. She smiled, just to feel her lips pulling and the crinkle of both cheeks.

Her smile grew wistful as glass became skin once more and her hands, merely hands. Like the toads, she avoided being seen during the turn; a task more easily accomplished now that the sun set before supper instead of during it when she should be helping. It was more than keeping her nature secret from those who didn't know—that some didn't being a feat to amaze in Marrowdell—it was that the change felt intensely private.

Although Bannan's magic let him see her as turn-born simply, as he put it, by looking deeper, he loved to watch her during the turn. She could watch herself in his eyes, see their astonished joy, hear the catch of his breath.

Her cheeks warmed. Two days. Three at most. According to Aunt Sybb, absence made a heart either fonder or forgetful. Bannan couldn't possibly forget her, though Jenn, now dancing around the empty room, couldn't imagine how it was possible to become more fond.

Should she, her heart, she assured that organ, pressing her hands to it, would no longer fit inside her chest.

A rumble from lower down reminded her it was, in fact, time to satisfy another hunger altogether.

The main room of the Nalynn home had changed since Jenn last lived in it. Some was the accommodation of an artist in the family, Kydd's clever slanted desk being under a front window and his latest watercolors pinned to the walls. The paintings were of Marrowdell's mill, with the colors of fall behind, though three were studies of Peggs' profile as he took full advantage of living with his favorite subject. Radd's bed remained where it had always been, with his favorite barrel chair brought in for the winter, but over the bed, where it would catch the morning's sunlight or evening's candleglow, he'd hung the sigil carved with his wife's name. Peggs had told Jenn he sometimes spoke to it, and admitted she did the same.

Radd smiled at his gathered family, resting his fond gaze on his youngest daughter. "Please say the Beholding for us, Dear Heart."

The eldest said the Beholding which, for much of the year, the best part, was Aunt Sybb. She'd never done it. Jenn glanced at Peggs, who merely smiled, then at Kydd, whose smile, if anything, was wider. It was a conspiracy, clearly. "I'd be honored, Poppa," she gave in, taking the guest's seat at the Nalynn table. She formed the circle over her heart with her forefingers and thumbs, silently hoping they were clean, and composed herself.

"Hearts of our Ancestors," Jenn began. "We are Beholden for the food on this table, for Peggs is the best cook in the world—" and blushing madly, though she shouldn't, considering the wonderful feast spread over the table, but Jenn had blushed herself at many a Beholding and considered this only fair. She continued, "It will give us the strength to improve ourselves in your eyes. We are Beholden for the opportunity to share this meal, for though we are two families now—" for some reason her voice stuck in her throat and Jenn coughed to free it "—we will always be one in your eyes and our hearts—"

Her father wiped his eyes and nodded vigorously.

"—and," she added, to be honest, "I'm nervous using Gallie's plates without her home." Those plates being family heirlooms and how they'd survived the twins no one knew.

Though, oddly, the plates presently on the table weren't the ones Peggs usually set, but white and porcelain with fine silver edges. A gift from Master Dusom. Jenn eyed them worriedly. She'd help with the dishes, of course, as would Kydd, but these?

First to finish before the food waiting for the lovely

plates cooled. "Hearts of our Ancestors—" she said firmly, only to be stopped as Peggs raised one hand, smiling very strangely.

A hand that reached for hers, the other taking Kydd's, who reached over to grasp Radd Nalynn's. From her father's face, he was as surprised as she.

Until Peggs said, very gently, "Hearts of our Ancestors, above all we are Beholden for the new life about to join ours. However far we are apart, Keep Us Close."

"'Keep Us Close,'" Jenn echoed numbly with the rest, then blurted, "You mean a baby?"

"We mean a baby," Kydd affirmed, smiling from ear-to-ear.

Oh, the ensuing excitement, because nothing would do but glasses be filled with summerberry wine, and once they'd had a sip their father couldn't stop laughing as he took them one at a time in his arms, Kydd as well and Peggs last of all, to whirl around the room, risking shins and toes and elbows, but no one was hurt because joy didn't hurt.

And Jenn caught herself with her heart in her throat about to wish it never would and stopped just in time.

Because babies weren't to be trifled with, nor was life.

Her big sister, bright-eyed and wise, pressed a basket of steaming bread into her hands and a kiss on her forehead. "Time to eat that supper you praised so highly, Dearest Heart."

When they sat, through no wish but happiness, the scent of roses filled the room and candleglow wrote "Melusine" on the wall.

Thanks to the girl, Wisp no longer limped down the path to his sanctuary, crystal cracking underfoot. Nonetheless, he chose that route, flying low along it, because crystal chose to die to warn him of intruders; a sacrifice he honored if didn't understand.

Dragonkind surely thought him mad.

Maybe he was. Wisp banked and twisted, both wingtips brushing stone. His current mission had nothing safe or

sane in it. Find the terst turn-born. No, find the one terst
turn-born of all their kind who cared for the girl. Surely her
kind thought Sand mad as well.

His jaw sank in a humorless grin.

Add the old fool to the list of those bereft of better
sense. According to the little cousins, Scourge had followed
his truthseer beyond the edge, returning of his own free will
to the land where he'd served his penance.

When he came back—if he came back—his kind would
doubtless laud him as a hero yet again. There'd be more
mating nonsense. Kruar couldn't help themselves.

Narrow heads, the dragon decided.

About now, they'd be setting their ambushes, while dragonkind grew wary or took to cliff dens. The Verge didn't have
night as the girl's world experienced it, with its darkness
and damp. Instead, here was the dimming, when the quality
of light went from gloriously fierce, dragon scale taking fire
and rock faces bleached to bone, to soft and subtle and sly.
The silver mimrol of river and lake reflected skies of ever-
changing color and hue. Throughout the·dimming, landscape became a play of shadow.

And hunters ruled.

During his penance, flightless and alone, as the light
faded Wisp had sought the shelter provided him by the sei.
Finished and freed, he'd thought himself well rid of it.

A curious visit another time—just to see if the sei had
removed the blue oval door in the rock—had discovered it
still there. A cautious poke of a snout through that door,
just to see if the sanctuary behind it remained, had led to a
step, then why not enter?

He'd turned and bolted out again. To be sure he could.
Before, the sei had locked him in during each dimming. For
his safety, or to keep him where they wished. He'd not
known why, nor cared.

The door proved to be his. Others assailed it, once in a
while, breaking claws and teeth in vain efforts to reach him.
He'd listen and yawn, then settle back to sleep. The incomprehensible sei, being mighty and negligent, might remove
his sanctuary without warning, or immure him in stone.

Or not. Pointless for a dragon to worry about such things.

Home again, Wisp yawned and curled tail over snout.

The blue walls having politely waited for him to still, closed in to almost, but not quite, touch. They'd become mannerly without the sei, or used to him.

Turn-born slept also, and Jenn Nalynn's quest wasn't so urgent that he need risk waking them.

As he dozed, Wisp snarled to himself.

When had he become mannerly too?

# THREE

$M$ARROWDELL SLEPT. PERHAPS the Verge did as
well. More to learn, Jenn decided, her rag-enclosed
hand closing the heatstove door. She resumed her spot on
the floor in front of it, well-wrapped in quilts and seated on
a cushion. Each quilt was a history, if you looked closely,
both in the scraps used—having come from everyone in the
valley—and the final pattern. None of it was random, Jenn
knew. Frann meticulously pieced this bit with that, laid
those in a spiral or inset block, her plan sure from the start
even if no one else could see it till the end, for she valued
records of every sort.

Jenn ran her fingers over the one on her lap. It was hers
and had been since she was born. As she'd grown, so had the
quilt, Frann adding scraps from clothing worn too long to
pass along. The fabrics were reminders and memories. And
warm, she thought, snuggling into it. The other quilts belonged to the Emms, and Gallie had been most definite that
she should use them, too, along with anything else she wished.

Which didn't mean being wasteful. A half-scoop of

charcoal in the heatstove would do for the night, and she'd lit only one candle. Aiming its mirror so the light fell over her lap made it look as though she sat in a tiny room of her own. Jenn arranged her desk atop the quilt. It was a short plank, well-sanded, with a hole carved into the upper right corner sized for an inkpot and a series of smaller ones for quills. Zehr had made it, having noticed their guest wrote letters whilst sprawled on the floor. Wouldn't do, he'd told her with a twinkle in his eye. Not in a writer's house.

She'd been inspired herself, by that writer. Oh, not to write books—she'd far rather read them—but to write lists. Aunt Sybb, Jenn thought with a smile, would approve. Or would, once over her astonishment her youngest niece considered organization of any value at all.

Organizing her thoughts, that was Jenn's goal tonight. Free of distraction and duty, tonight was the perfect opportunity to put in words the most pressing of her questions for Mistress Sand. Questions she was almost sure to forget or be afraid to ask, once distracted by the Verge itself. It seemed momentous to take a piece of the luxuriously smooth paper Bannan had given her and put it on the desk. She dipped her quill into the 'pot Gallie had left for her use, strained to see in the dim light, and wrote:

*Can turn-born have babies?*

Jenn stopped, aghast. She hadn't meant to—well, clearly she had, or the words wouldn't be staring back at her, the last one a little wobbly—but still, she'd been thinking about travel and masks and magic. She chewed her bottom lip. This was Peggs' doing. Between the news and the celebrating—not to mention Kydd's face and their father's—fine, and her own joy at becoming an aunt, which was suddenly a new distraction, because if she was an aunt, she'd need to be wise and wasn't.

Not yet.

"The baby's not even born," she told the Emms' house toad, who'd shifted closer and closer to the little stove as the coals took. "There's growing up, you know. By the time she's my age and ready to listen, I'll be—" Ancestors Ancient and Aged, she'd be old!

Inspiring another question, Mistress Sand having been a child once, according to Wisp, and now seeming as mature as Riss.

*Do turn-born grow old? Do they sicken and die?*

Darker, deeper questions than she'd originally thought. Her chin firmed. Good questions and important.

~Elder sister. The candle?~

A most excellent one, putting out more light than she'd expected, really. Puzzled by the toad's anxious tone, Jenn glanced at the candle, then winced.

The flame sat on the wick like a glowing balloon, wider and taller than any candle flame should or could, gleaming in the mirror like a little sun. The wax below wasn't so much melting as bubbling, and there were runnels pouring over the books she'd stacked to raise the candle exactly where it needed to be to light her desk.

Light presently filling the main room of the Emms' log home from rafter to toy-filled corners.

She'd made a wish.

Hurriedly, Jenn blew out the candle and found herself sitting in the dark with the toad, her important questions on her lap, and an open inkpot. "Oh, dear."

~You saved the home from burning, elder sister,~ the toad said, ever stout in its generosity.

Given this was her first night in charge, Jenn didn't find that a comfort. Not to mention the books, but the wax would come free of the covers; having read late more nights than naught, she'd plenty of practice at that. But saving the Emms' home? "You did, and thank you." Wishing not to wish didn't work at all; she'd tried. If the faint glow from the embers had been sufficient to put quill to paper in a legible manner, she'd have written another question.

How can I not be a danger to those I love?

A small foot found her ankle, a foot tipped with sharp little claws. ~We matter to Marrowdell.~ As if it had heard and dismissed her concern.

A cold foot. "We could not manage without you," Jenn said truthfully. She put the desk on the floor, careful of the inkpot. Aware of the great dignity of house toads, who weren't dragons but deserved every bit as much from her, she chose her next words with care. "Little cousin, I would find it a comfort if you sat with me a while. I mean no—" disrespect, she'd intended to add, but given the lapful of soft, heavy toad immediately making itself at home, she just smiled.

Marrowdell, every part and being, mattered to her.

Redolent of hay, horse, and warm mash, the inn's stable might have been any such near Vorkoun. Bannan held the lantern at eye level as he walked the well-worn floor between the long row of stalls, its light surrounding him. Battle and Brawl were outside, in the paddock shelter, the ceiling being too low for their heads, but the other Marrowdell horses were here, slack-hipped and already half-asleep. All had been groomed and pampered and now had a rest in store. There were more horses, for the fair drew from far and wide. Bannan took a good look at each. Most were the sturdy sort of use on a farm, thickset and hairy. Three nondescript bays caught his eye, stabled side-by-side. Good legs, wide chests, and recently shod. Fast, he judged. Their tack hung nearby, any metal darkened. By age or intent? He'd know more once he'd met their riders.

Eyes reflected cold disks in the light. Not a house toad, not here. The light found calico fur and a long tail. The barn cat, lying along a rafter, stared down as he past beneath.

Other than horses and cat—and any mice it may have missed—he was alone. The hayloft would be packed with sleeping guests later, but not this early, and he'd seen the stablehands at work repairing the far paddock fence. Such things happened, when strange horses were mixed together, though he'd have thought the plentiful feed would have kept them out of trouble.

Blowing out the lantern, the truthseer hung it on a hook and stepped into the second last stall, an arm over Perrkin's dappled shoulders. The aged gelding sighed and gave a little shake to rouse himself, a soldier's horse accustomed to the unfairness of life. "Not tonight, old friend," Bannan said gently, holding out the apple he'd brought from the kitchen.

Bristled lips worked soft over his fingertips, then collected the offering with a contented rumble. Scourge would have nipped the fingers, usually without drawing blood, but that depended on the treat. A mouse, preferably alive. He was out hunting his own treats at the moment, that being best for all concerned. Bannan gave Perrkin a final pat.

"—told you. Marrowdell's here."

About to call a polite greeting and reveal himself, Bannan checked the impulse. There was an odd smugness to the stranger's voice. Instead, the truthseer moved into the shadows near Perrkin's head.

"So you did." The second voice was deeper. Older. Light dipped and bobbed along the walls and ceiling as the pair went down the aisle, pausing as lanterns were raised at various stalls. "Ancestors Bountiful and Blessed. Well-loved, these beasts, and well-tended. They'll do nicely."

Heart's Blood. The damaged fence, taking the 'hands from the stable? Tir, ever-suspicious, would have spotted the ploy in a heartbeat. Bannan silently promised his friend to be less gullible in future. As for the sword he'd not wanted to bring and now would be most glad to have at hand? With his gear at the inn. Oh, he was every sort of fool this night.

He could die of it.

"Take them all, then?"

"That'd be greed to no point. There's only the five that'll fetch decent coin. We'll scatter the rest, stop anyone following too quick."

A bucket would have done. Something substantial he could send flying at a head. His hands searched, but Perrkin's stall offered nothing he could move. If the lantern on its hook had been empty of oil? No. Better to lose the horses than risk a stable fire. For all their sakes, he hoped the thieves felt the same. Bannan shook his head and patted Perrkin, then smeared straw and manure onto his clothes. With a grimace, he put some in his hair as well.

Then stepped half out of the stall and blinked sleepily at the men standing in the aisle. "Ancestors Witness." A feigned yawn. "When did it get dark? Have I missed supper?"

The two raised their lanterns. One was older and larger,

white-haired and neatly dressed. The other was in rougher garb, pimple-faced and wide-eyed.

The third—because if he was alone there'd be a third, wouldn't there?—just stood there, staring at Bannan through narrowed eyes. He had halters over both broad shoulders.

And a sword at one hip.

"Fair evening to you," replied the older man civilly enough. He appeared unarmed; under that loose fitting coat he could have a brace of pistols as well as knives. Or axes.

He could, Bannan decided, use Tir about now. Or Scourge for that matter.

Even Pimple-face had a short knife.

They weren't sure of him, yet, in the dim light. A caution about to end.

White-hair, the leader or buyer, smiled. "I'm sure supper's still to be had, young man. Take my advice, you'll wash before asking for it."

His best abashed grin on his face, Bannan made a show of brushing the filth from his clothes as he calculated the odds. The stable had thick timbered walls, and they'd closed the door. No chance a shout would carry to the stablehands outside. As for his foes? Even if they were fools enough to believe he hadn't heard them, the easiest way to be sure would be to let him by, then stab him in the back. Or knock him on the head, if they felt more kindly disposed.

The silent man, with the grim look? He'd prefer the stabbing.

Nothing to lose, then. "You fine gentlemen are making a mistake," he said cheerfully. "Between the railroad and the truce, there's no demand for horses. Sheep, now. They're your best bet."

Pimple-face laughed. "Haven't heard about the war? Where've you been?"

War? It was the truth he saw, but how could it be? When he'd left—why he'd left!—the Prince's truce had bound Rhoth and Eldad to Ansnor, the price of peace, ending generations of border raids and far worse, being access to mines and rail for the Eld's trains.

The stable's warmth, the light playing on their hard faces, the swish of a horse's tail, the smells, everything around him

snapped into sharp focus as Bannan's heart began to pound
with dread. By an effort he didn't dare show, he kept his tone
level. "We don't get much news up north. Who broke the truce?
Ansnor?" With what remained of Vorkoun—for the treaty
returned the portion of the city south of the Lilem to Ansnor,
stripping border patrols and garrisons from the rest—first
in her path.

And Lila.

White-hair raised a brow. "The truce holds, stranger. It's
Lower Rhoth shouting for reinforcements, including
mounts. Mounts we—" with a nod to his companions,
"—intend to acquire." Too casually, he hooked his lantern
on the nearest post. "Get in our way and die."

He'd die regardless, from the smirk on the silent man's
face. "Manners require I warn you very fine gentlemen that
Horst himself chose me as his replacement." White-hair
shrugged. Pimple-face swallowed.

The hitherto silent man spat. "That's what I say to the
old fool."

"I wouldn't," Bannan said and bowed, fingers to the stable floor. Straightening, he did two things at once.

Launched himself at White-hair.

And whistled.

The whistle was short and quiet. It was drowned out by the
anguished cry when Bannan drove an elbow into White-
hair's groin. As if he'd play fair, three to one. Following the
man as he crumpled to the dirt floor, Bannan searched under the coat for a weapon. A boot stomped near his head.
Before a second try, he was up and away, the hilt of a knife
in his hand. Flipping it so the blade lay against his wrist, he
used his empty hand to shove Pimple-face aside. The boy
stumbled into the back of a horse who grumbled but didn't
bother kicking him. Just as well. He held the remaining lantern in shaking hands.

The boot belonged to the third man. Dropping the halters, he pulled his sword with regrettable skill. His very long
sword.

Ancestors Unfair and Unworthy. Bannan flipped the knife again and threw it.

The sword batted it aside.

He'd never liked knife fights anyway. Win or lose, you were always cut by the end and the winner was whomever didn't slip in blood at the wrong moment.

"It doesn't have to end this way," Bannan assured the swordsman as he took a step back. "We could go into the inn and have a drink together." White-hair stopped moaning to spit out a curse. "Don't say I didn't offer," the truthseer continued blithely and whistled again. A little desperately, truth be told.

The sword point drew a little circle in the air as his opponent closed the distance between them. Get on with it, he hoped that meant. Otherwise, it appeared a plan to disembowel him.

Bannan raised his hands. Where was the idiot beast? "You don't want to do that."

"Ancestors Witness," the man said with a wide, unpleasant grin, "I most surely do." He tensed, the sword straightened to point at Bannan's stomach, then lunged!

The truthseer dodged into Perrkin's stall and scrambled up into the grain trough. Where next? The rafters were in reach; so would he be. He started to climb into the next stall—imagining Tir's face at this useless delaying tactic—when the gelding's ears went flat, every muscle bunched, and he let fly.

Both back hooves hit the swordsman squarely, sending him across the aisle to smack a post with a meaty thud. He slid to the ground.

"Take that!" Bannan crowed as he dropped back into the stall. Perrkin, blood still up, bobbed his head and pranced. "More apples," the truthseer promised.

The swordsman had been dead before hitting the post, a hoof having struck beneath his chin, breaking his neck. A soldier's horse, indeed. Bannan swept up the weapon and turned to the remaining two.

Lifting the blade, he smiled cheerfully.

Pimple-face set the lantern on the floor and bolted from the stable as fast as his legs could take him.

White-hair, on his knees, stared up. "Well?"

He'd met a few thieves. The ones who'd happily roll a drunk for his purse. Those who'd slit a dying soldier's throat for his boots. Mostly, their lives ended like this, caught and weeping, or defiant to the last. Bannan touched the sword's tip to the floor. "What's your name?"

"Ancestors Bloody and Bent." Teeth showed. "Join yours!"

Holding the sword hilt, the truthseer squatted to bring their eyes level. The worn clothes had been fine, once. Tailored and costly. Even now, the thief kept his beard neat, the ends gathered within a chased silver bead, and his boots showed polish as well as wear. "Not so long a thief," Bannan decided. "Merchant. Honest or not?"

"Honest, if you must know."

"I do know." The truthseer shook his head. "Merchant you might have been, but never an honest one. A smuggler's my guess."

The other's lips tightened, but not in denial.

Tir wouldn't approve. Tir, Bannan thought, needn't know. He wasn't a soldier anymore.

He stood, sword point down. "Go. On your own horse, if you can still ride."

White-hair rose to his feet with a wince and a scowl. "If this isn't some trick, let me take two. I'll not leave Bliss behind."

Defiance and a code of sorts. He'd made the right choice. "Agreed."

In the end, seeing the other man's discomfort—however deserved—it was Bannan who saddled the thieves' horses, then hefted Bliss' body over one and tied it securely. He pulled the dead man's coat over his head. Heart's Blood, he'd done that service too many times.

"Don't let me see you again," he told White-hair grimly, opening the stable door.

"I'm done with the north anyway." White-hair took both sets of reins in one hand and touched the dead man's coat with the other, giving Bannan a considering look. "Ancestors Witness. I hate to carry debt, hear me? For my own peace of mind, I should put a bounty on your head, villager, that's what I should do." The faintest of smiles. "But if I'd listened to 'should,' I'd not be here. Well, then." His tone grew formal. "By my Ancestors' Hearts, I or my kin will repay this debt. If you're ever in Avyo and need an honest smuggler, go to the inn under the Ten Bridge at dusk. Wear something red and ask the barkeep for Byng."

Avyo? He wouldn't be there. Shouldn't be there, even if he could, nor could Bannan imagine such a need.

Which didn't matter. The man before him spoke truthfully; he sought to do the honorable thing. "Ten Bridge, dusk, red, Byng," the truthseer repeated, as though committing what must be a closely guarded contact code to memory. "Now be off before I change my mind."

Despite Byng's fair words and intent, Bannan wasn't inclined to take any chances. He stepped from the stable to watch the smuggler mount, gingerly, then ride away from the inn and Endshere, toward Weken and points south. That duty done, he went back into the stable, there being blood to clean from Perrkin's hooves and the floor.

To find his way blocked by a large, sweaty mass.

"Now you show up?" he complained. "There were three of them, I'll have you know." Which Scourge would smell for himself. "Armed—" Bannan added indignantly, "—as I wasn't."

Voiceless, Scourge lifted a lip from a fang in answer. Scorn, that was, which he did deserve, having left his sword behind.

Scorn and an unflattering curiosity.

Bannan grinned and slapped the great beast cheerfully. "How'd I manage without you? Perrkin saved the day."

The old kruar glanced toward the gelding and purred deep in his chest. Perrkin wasn't the only horse in the stable to stir at the sound and whinny nervously. Scourge in a confined space with livestock guaranteed a sleepless night at best, panic at worst, but Bannan knew the cure for that.

He carefully didn't smile. "One of the thieves ran off. On foot."

Deep nostrils flared with interest.

"Kindly stand guard in case he comes back."

The massive head bent, the long forked tongue out to sample the smear of blood on the floor, then the head tilted to aim a gleaming red eye at him.

Heart's Blood, he looked wistful.

"No killing," Bannan said firmly. "Chase trouble off and leave those with honest business be."

Scourge stamped a great hoof to show his displeasure, but they'd played this game many times before; though he wasn't above having his fun with stablehands, especially any who thought to "catch" him. That, Bannan thought with some amusement, would be their problem. As Scourge wheeled to leave the stable, doubtless to skulk nearby, he added, "Don't be late, next time."

An ear bent. By no means an apology.

But it would do.

Endshere's inn, as suited the last public house on the Northward Road, was larger than warranted by the village alone. All travelers who came this far took their final chance for a warm bed, food and drink, and company by a fire. Many took advantage only to turn south the next day, daunted by the tales of that company, for what lay beyond Endshere wasn't for the faint of heart. At first, the land was riven by twisted valleys, few wide enough for more than the rivers carving them ever deeper. Steep ridges cloaked in desperate trees and loose stone shadowed the road; leaving the road was a surety of being lost.

Beyond that challenging terrain, the land smoothed and opened, but the Barrens were aptly named. Treeless and windswept, what lived there moved—or died—with the seasons. It was said the midwinter storms could freeze a horse between one step and the next.

Not that anyone could say they'd seen such a thing, but then you wouldn't, and live.

There were those who smiled at the stories and left the next day; those who listened, intent and fearful, but with no other choice. Endshere's inn would welcome them back, those who came back, when they fled south again.

And add their stories to the rest.

Having delivered a warning about the would-be thieves to the stablehands, who were properly chagrined to have been caught out, Bannan cleaned himself at the pump and

bucket provided for that purpose outside the kitchen annex
behind the inn, then went around front. The lower story was
stone, the upper of wood, both with abundant, deep-set
windows. Two chimneys sent pale smoke into the chill night
air, one from the kitchen and another, larger, from the end
of the main building.

The inn possessed a generous porch stretching from side
to side, overhung by a slate-shingled roof. A sign depended
from chains in the middle, proclaiming this *The Good
Night's Sleep*; locals called it *The G'night*. Lamps had been
lit in welcome to either side of the wide steps. Bannan took
those two at a time, eager to be inside, and pushed open the
carved double doors.

Would he ever stop pausing, ever so slightly, to gauge the
temper of those inside? Ever not check for exits? There
were, he supposed, worse habits. He made himself relax and
smiled, seeing heads raised in his direction.

And a hand. Davi, seated at a corner table, waved him
over. Just as well. The inn was filled to capacity, tin tankards
crowding platters and bowls on every table. Bannan
brushed shoulders and dodged elbows as he made his way
through.

The high ceiling was blackened by generations of soot.
Lamps hung from rafters and bracketed each half-curtained
window, their soft yellow light twinkling eyes and burnishing well-polished brass. A massive fireplace filled the right
wall, a cheery fire snapping in its shallow opening, though
the room was too warm already for a coat. The words
*Friends and Wine. The Older the Better.* had been inscribed,
neatly, into the mantel. Atop, a trio of large brass platters
leaned comfortably against the stone, and boughs of fresh
cut cedar added their pungent scent to the aroma of food,
drink, and those enjoying both.

A narrow stair on the left wall led to the rooms upstairs,
two steps to a small, but well-lit landing, the rest going up
behind oak panels. The table Davi had procured was against
one of those; as Bannan approached, the smith rose to his
feet with a broad grin. "Get what you want at the bar!" he
bellowed, to be heard over the din of voices. "Allin's buying."

The truthseer nodded and turned on a heel, narrowly

avoiding a huge tray stacked high with empty plates. The server behind the stack, a boy about Cheffy's age, leaned precariously to the side to see where he was going as laughing patrons piled more and more on top.

Before the inevitable, Bannan took the tray and lifted it over the boy's head to a chorus of cheers, the crowd as entertained by a bold rescue as disaster. "Where do these go?" he half-shouted.

Mopping his sweaty face with a sleeve, the lad gave him a shyly grateful look. "To the kitchen, good sir."

"Bannan—" But the boy was off, darting through the forest of legs. The truthseer chuckled and followed more cautiously.

The bar ran along the back wall, with the door to the kitchen to one side. Palma came out to meet him, wiping her hands on an apron. "We wondered when we'd see you. Fair festival, Bannan Larmensu!" she greeted with a warm smile. The serving boy peered around her waist and she pretended to pinch his cheek. "Thanks for doing my brother's work." The resemblance was plain, though Palma's mass of black curls was tied at the top of her head with a red ribbon and the boy's barely reached his neck. "Larah Anan, meet Marrowdell's newest settler. You'll not meet another who so loves his turnips," this with a wink.

He'd been found out. Bannan chuckled. "Well met, Larah." Unable to bow, he inclined his head. "Ancestors Blessed and Bountiful, that we are together again so soon." For Palma Anan had come to Marrowdell a bride and claimed all their hearts, before returning home. This was her inn, and her family's legacy.

Palma stepped aside when Bannan refused to relinquish the tray, his own grip on the stack less than trustworthy, and laughingly led him to what was more trough than sink. Hams and roasts and plucked poultry hung from hooks overhead, along with braids of fat onions and bunches of spice. On the wooden table that ran the length of the room, gold-crusted puddings fresh from the oven steamed in their crockery beside racks of cooling bread. A crisp-skinned lamb turned on a spit in the fireplace while a stewpot bigger than Bannan's arms could span simmered on the stovetop.

His lingering glances were noticed. "Hungry?" she teased.

"Famished."

"Out with you, then." With a flourish of her apron. "To the bar and tell Allin your fancy. On the house, mind," with a mock frown.

Freed of the tray, this time he gave a short bow. "My thanks." Bannan smiled. "And I've a package for you, from Master Jupp. I'll deliver it in the morning."

Eyes bright, Palma blew him a kiss from two fingers. "That, for not tempting with such a treasure while I've pots on the stove! Now off you go."

The bar sat on a raised portion of the flagstone floor, the rise convenient to prop a boot. Five barrels supported the wide top, joined one to the next by smooth planks. Nicely turned wooden pillars rose above each barrel to meet the ceiling, proof that Endshere's mill was used for more than grain. The top of the bar was a reddish wood, polished until it shone, and behind was a mirror the size of which Bannan hadn't seen since Vorkoun. Getting that unbroken up the Northward Road had been a feat.

The truthseer leaned his elbows on the bar top to hold his place. When sure those nearest him were looking elsewhere, he slipped a finger into his collar and pulled it aside to see what the moth had done.

From the sear of heat he'd felt on his skin, he'd half-expected an ugly burn. Or that nothing would show at all, the writing being Marrowdell's and magic.

But there it was. A set of tiny black marks, the whole of which he could cover with a fingertip and did, as the barkeep noticed him. Replacing his collar, Bannan pretended to admire his reflection. After all, the little mirror in his kit only showed the portion of skin being shaved and blade and there was, to his knowledge, no other mirror in Marrowdell. Not bad, he decided, jutting out his chin and tilting his head. He might never have worn a beard those many years. Or needed to hide his face from an implacable enemy.

Was that about to change?

The grim turn of his thoughts showed on his face, and

Bannan deliberately smiled at himself before giving his attention to the man coming toward him. "Keeping busy, I see," he observed.

Face flushed with pleasure, Allin Anan, for he'd taken his wife's name, stretched over the bar to slap Bannan on the shoulder. "Ancestors Fortunate and Favored! Glad to see you," he declared. "Glad to see all of you. I can't get over it. Mother coming?" He shook his head, his smile lighting the green eyes so like Gallie's. "Thank you for taking care of them, Bannan. Now, what can I get you? Anything."

Having seen the "anything" back in the kitchen, Bannan didn't attempt to decide. "A plate of your choosing, Allin, and something for a dry throat."

"Done." The barkeep smiled mysteriously. He waved Larah to his side and bent to whisper in his ear. As the boy ran to the kitchen, Allin produced a small brown cask and pulled a tankardful. "Try this."

Smelling the spice the moment he took the tankard, Bannan wrinkled his nose. "Heart's Blood, my nephews drink ginger beer! My young nephews. It's been a very long day, my friend," he coaxed, trying to return the offering.

Allin pushed it back, smile widening. "Then Palma's brew is what you need. Watch the—" as the truthseer gave in and raised the tankard in two hands.

A warning too late. Bubbles shot right up Bannan's nose. He sneezed, giving Allin a reproachful look. The barkeep merely nodded expectantly. Insult his hosts or drink the stuff? Holding his breath this time, Bannan raised the beer to his lips and took a mouthful.

Ginger it was. His eyebrows shot up as the smooth liquid landed in his stomach with a potent kick. "Tha—" he gasped in admiration. "Ancestors Witness, that's a fine brew."

"Isn't it?" Allin leaned across the bar. "Alas, there's only the one cask left. The weddings." Implying a delightful host of conflicting duties. "Would you let Frann know? Palma says she'd not forgive us if she doesn't get a taste."

Bannan drank reverently. "I may start to feel the same way," he warned. "This is almost as good—" As he hesitated—perhaps at his hesitation—his neck warmed where the moth had marked him. "—as good as the tinkers' beer," he finished, and took another deeper drink. "You remember it," this with a searching look at the other man.

Allin made a show of wiping the bar top. "I remember a great many things, Bannan Larmensu," he replied evenly, then looked toward the kitchen and raised his voice. "Larah! Take our guest's supper to the Treffs' table." His gaze came back at the truthseer, his expression wary but curious. "A discussion for tomorrow morning, when the room's not so full."

"And you're not so in demand." Bannan nodded and toasted Allin with his now-precious ginger beer, relinquishing his spot at the bar to a pair of new and thirsty arrivals.

He surveyed the room; being half a head taller than most here helped, but too many people were shifting around for him to spot a small woman who, moreover, would be seated. The inn was full of people who greeted one another and smiled and laughed. It was a welcoming place, the heart of a community, and he'd not seen it, that first time through. He'd been in a hurry to leave his old life behind, as if that could be accomplished simply by running from it. Suspicious of strangers. Wary of kindness.

Filled with rage. Hadn't Marrowdell shown him that unhappy truth?

Then healed him, or at least set him on a path to peace.

Tankard clasped to his chest, Bannan circled the room, turning sideways to fit between those at benches on either side of the long table down its midst, his attention more for the better seats near walls and windows. He found Lorra almost at once. She was deep in discussion with two women and a man he didn't know, hat feathers flicking back and forth as if she wore an aroused rooster on her head. Frann's hat — and its wearer — were nowhere to be seen. Finally, the truthseer shrugged and made his way back to the table, eager for his own supper.

The delay had been worthwhile, he decided, upon seeing what awaited him. Half a roast chicken, plums and apples tucked under its skin, lay amid generous slices of golden potato pudding on a platter; a bowl of broth swimming with button mushrooms and leeks sat on a nearby board along with a steaming loaf of bread; and a second board held an assortment of cheeses surrounding a jar of preserves. Daunted, Bannan sank in his chair.

Davi grinned. "Ancestors Witness, if you can't manage it all," he offered, "we're still hungry." Unlikely, given the mass of empty bowls and platters, topped with bones, in evidence, but Bannan'd seen the big smith eat before. His tablemates were larger still, their girth filling the remaining sides of the table. "Bannan Larmensu, Harty and Hagar Comber, Endshere's puny excuse for smiths."

They'd met before, when he and Tir had passed through Endshere. Bannan'd not bothered to learn their names, nor cared. This time, he inclined his head with all possible grace, murmuring, "Well met, good sirs."

Harty, the elder man, tipped his bald head in response. "Don't believe anything from this pot o'piss," he advised in a voice like the crunch of a boot on loose stone. "M'boy knows more 'an he e'er will, and he's a mere stripling!"

The "mere stripling," bigger than his father and with hands easily the span of a plate, smiled peacefully. "Well met, Bannan Larmensu." Hagar Comber had the dark curls of the Anan family—as did many in Endshere—on retreat from a broad forehead. Below bushy eyebrows, his brown eyes were bright and friendly. "Marrowdell's been good for you."

Bannan lifted his tankard in acknowledgment. "That it has," he agreed. How had he seemed to these villagers on his last passage through? Dour, dark, and bitter, he feared. Oh, and a fool too. A hasty one. He took a swallow and grimaced, but not at the ginger beer. "It's taught me how very much I don't know about farming."

That brought a laugh. "Tell us now," Harty said, big fore-arms crossed over his chest. "How long did Upsala's sorry old ox last? I'd have bet it'd drop dead the first day."

Why that one-eyed trader—but he'd been a fair mark, after all. What did he know of oxen? Being able to tell the truth, Bannan'd learned long ago, was a poor defense against being cheated by an expert. "Got my wagon to Mar-rowdell." As for the rest? That once in Marrowdell, the ox had strayed into fields protected by the invisible efflet and been summarily executed for that trespass?

Before he could think what else to say, Davi spoke up.

"And then the beast dropped dead!" After the roar of laughter subsided, he added, "Didn't go to waste," and licked his lips. "Speaking of which," with a cheerful wave at the spread before Bannan.

So what the others remembered made sense to them, beyond Marrowdell. It just wasn't the whole truth. "Help yourselves," the truthseer offered, uneasy again. It didn't help that though the chair had a cushion of sorts, it hardly made up for an unaccustomed day in the saddle.

He'd grown soft. Though there had been the fight.

Which, he reminded himself, Perrkin had won. A matter not to be ignored. About to speak of it, Bannan closed his mouth. Why ruin the joy with which the three smiths were adding to their own platters? Scourge was guarding the stable. Ill news could wait.

Besides, he should eat. So the truthseer circled his fingers over his heart and bowed his head, a private and personal Beholding being enough in a gathering like this, and moved his lips soundlessly. "Hearts of my Ancestors, I am Beholden for this food, for it will give me the strength to return home. I am Beholden for this good company and their fellowship. Above all else, I am Beholden for Marrowdell's Gift, so I not forget the who holds my heart. However far we are apart, Keep Us Close."

The chicken was Allin's reminder to him of Marrowdell, which had none, so despite his flagging appetite, Bannan made himself eat some of it. Then he had to taste the pudding, rich and sweet, and by that point, his tankard emptied and refilled with more ordinary but still excellent beer, he found himself enjoying the banter of the other three men, old and good friends.

Much of it concerned poor Devins, and Palma's eager cousins. "Do I have it right?" Bannan asked incredulously. "There are twelve of them?"

Harty nodded. "Ancestors Lustful and Lovelorn, e'er-one's hunt'n a husband and helpmate. 'M surprised you escaped. He won't, poor lad." He pointed a well-gnawed drumstick at the nearby table where Devins, in his best coat, sat bolt upright at one end as if on trial.

And wasn't he? The benches to either side of the same table were filled with keen-eyed young women, intent on learning everything possible about this latest prospect. At the end across from Devins sat an elderly woman wrapped, despite the warmth of the room, in layer upon layer of heavy wool. Every so often her thin hand would stretch from the bundling to tap a small, carved tankard and one of the cousins would hurry to refill it.

Bannan looked to his companions. "The lady?"

"Their great-grandmother." Hagar smiled. "And mine. Great Gran'll 'ave her say when the rest'r done." Said with an air of anticipation.

Poor Devins indeed, Bannan decided. He'd confessed to wanting a family; from the look of it, he'd have an entire town if he wasn't careful.

"Caryn Anan is close to a Blessed Ancestor herself," Lorra Treff said, none-too-quietly as she came up to their table. "That's no reason to hang on her every word." She waved her son back down when he rose to offer his seat. "I'm looking for the other old fool. Where's Frann Nall?" Her lips thinned. "She has to explain herself!"

The Combers glanced at one another. They knew what this was about, Bannan guessed. By his frown, Davi thought so too, but he spoke to his mother, his tone placating. "Frann went upstairs a while ago. She looked tired."

From Lorra's expression, he might have suggested the other woman had gone back to Marrowdell. "Ancestors Frustrating and Futile! Of course she's not tired. We slept most of the way here. And why? Because trading starts tonight, not tomorrow!" Her lips thinned. "She's hiding from me, that's what she's doing. And she'd better, after what she's done!"

Harty coughed and Hagar buried his face in his tankard. Big Davi's eyes went from one to the other, then back to his mother. "What did Frann do?"

Indignation stiffened Lorra into a black-hatted statue. "She—" almost spat, "—traded our barrels of ash for a flute and a cup of ginger beer!"

Bannan kept his face straight with an effort. Hagar choked and his father turned an interesting pink.

"Ancestors Witness, Frann does like ginger beer," Davi said, reasonably, if not wisely.

"And the rest of us like being clean!" Lorra glared at her

son, feathers tipping forward. "Our barrels always go to Endshere's ashman for an admitted pittance of lye—Heart's Blood, the woman will never admit she can't barter properly—but no, not this year. This year, she trades our hard work for a trinket and drink! It's that thief, Upsala. He played on her weak mind. A flute!" She paused to let them contemplate the enormity of this offense, then swept the table with a stern look. "I want you to get it back."

"The ash?" Harty raised his big hands as if holding back a tide. "Trade's done, Lady Treff. Can't be undone."

Bannan smiled to himself. *Lady Treff?* It had to be the hat.

Her son sighed. "Mother—"

"Now!"

To Bannan's surprise, Davi shook his head. "It can't be undone. Not if we want to trade here."

"The wagon was well-loaded," the truthseer observed, breaking the ominous silence that followed this nigh-on and, for all he knew, unprecedented rebellion within the Treff household. "Surely we've something else this ashman would take for the lye."

She might be furious, but Lorra Treff hadn't become who and what she was by ignoring opportunity. A brow lifted thoughtfully. "There may be. I must speak to Gallie at once!" Feathers dancing, the formidable head of the Treffs turned and was swallowed by the crowd.

"Ancestors Grateful and Glad, Bannan," her son said with relief. "You've saved the day and I thank you."

"We thank you too," Hagar chimed in, raising his tankard for a toast. The others did the same.

"A flute?" Bannan mused, eyeing Davi.

The smith refused to take the bait. Instead, he yawned. "I'm off to check my lads before getting some rest myself."

The truthseer held up one hand. "About the horses—" he began. As he recounted the attempted theft, the faces of all three men clouded with outraged anger, but the two from Endshere, he noticed, also showed guilt. "I left Scourge on watch," he finished, knowing Davi would be satisfied by that, then turned to Harty. "You've had other thefts. Why didn't you warn us?"

The smith hesitated.

"Yes," his son answered. When his father gave him a quelling look, he shook his head. "They'll hear the rumors soon enough, Da. We're not to talk gloom and doom at the fair," he continued. "It's bad for trade."

"So's thievery," Davi said grimly. "What rumors?"

Bannan lowered his voice. "Is Rhoth at war?"

Davi stared at him, shocked, but Harty spoke up. "Not so's you'd notice." He glanced over his shoulder, but no other patrons of the inn appeared interested. "Yammering t'now. Our arse o'a prince thought Mellynne wouldna notice his doin's, y'see. Well, t'have." With dour satisfaction.

Hagar leaned forward. "Mellynne demanded an envoy be sent to Channen to explain. Ordo had no choice but comply."

The elder Comber put a hand flat on the table, scowling darkly. "Aie. And no one's heard from t'envoy since, have they?"

"The border's been closed—" his son countered.

"More like he's dead," with gusto. "Or inna cellar, fed to rats!"

An envoy?

Heart's Blood.

"Who?" Bannan demanded, though he knew the answer, didn't he? Who else had the credentials for such a mission, familiar with Channen as well as the truce? Who else would Ordo risk without hesitation?

Being young and new to court, without influence or ties.

"Do the rumors give a name?" he insisted.

Harty began to shake his head, but Hagar caught Bannan's urgency and frowned in thought, then his face cleared. "A baron. It was a baron. West—something."

"Westietas." A flash of recognition in the other man's eyes. Ancestors Dire and Disastrous.

Emon Westietas. Lila's earnest, unsoldierly Emon.

"Tell me everything," Bannan urged, abrupt and harsh. "Quickly!"

"You've 'eard it." Harty stood, bumping the table so piles of dishware rattled and slid. "We want no trouble w'the prince," he said gruffly. "Come, lad."

"I'm sorry—" but they were gone. Bannan ran a hand

through his hair. He'd startled them, scared them, to be truthful. Where were his skills as an interrogator? But this wasn't any interrogation. This was about Lila—

"Bannan." He looked up to meet Davi's frown. "What is it?"

"I know this baron," Bannan admitted. "He's family."

The big smith was a guileless man. Concern warred with confusion on his face. "If you're noble, what are you doing in Marrowdell?"

"Trying to be a farmer." Bannan's lips twisted. "Westietas is my sister's husband." It didn't bear imagining, what Lila might do. "If only I knew more."

"There's the mail," Davi observed.

Of course! Lila would have written. He'd have news— Bannan half rose, then slumped back down. "I was told to pick up our bags in the morning."

"Cammi keeps them in the inn's storehouse. Here." Fingers slipped into a vest pocket and returned with a large black key. The smith looked sheepish but determined. "She lets me check for anything that might upset Mother. Come," the key went back into hiding with a little pat. "We'll visit the horses together then see what's in the mail. Help us both sleep better," he added keenly.

Bannan nodded, unable to say a word.

Friends indeed.

Sleeping in a bed alone, in a room alone—and a bed and room not her own—had taken some getting used to, but Jenn Nalynn had done it.

Sleeping in a house alone?

She sat up, hugging her pillow. That was harder.

She missed the little sounds. She hadn't realized how they'd filled the space around her heart. Zehr's boots on the floor below, Loee's cries for attention, Gallie's quiet murmurs. Without them, the house felt empty.

Because it was, Jenn reminded herself. Or almost.

A lump shifted near her feet, the Emms' house toad having taken her invitation to sit on her lap to being welcome on her bed and who knew where else? It was like sleeping with a cold rock, which would be fine in summer, but by then the toads were trying to cool themselves.

Moonlight shone through a gap in the curtains; the papers on the desk were pale and her color-filled map faded. Worst of all, the shadows stole any extra light and grew, if possible, darker.

She was not wasting a candle because of shadows. Use only what you must, Aunt Sybb had told her, and not a bit more. She'd meant her fine stationery, which had come in quite handy this past summer and been completely used up by the end, but it applied to candles and their improper use, Jenn was sure.

She could wish the moon a little brighter.

Not that she would. Jenn hugged the pillow tighter, suddenly curious. Could she? Was the moon part of Marrowdell and the edge, or part of the wider world beyond? She wanted to know so much she almost asked the toad.

But didn't. Such questions distressed them, whether they knew the answer or not.

Instead of wishing at the moon, Jenn carefully climbed out of bed, claiming one of the quilts for a wrap, then went to the window and drew aside the curtains. So invited, moonlight streamed inside. She looked out, holding her breath so she didn't fog the glass. Another crisp night.

The corner of the Emms' barn. Their slumbering garden. Beyond the hedge, the river and fallow fields. Beyond those, the forest and crags and the gleaming ivory of the Spine.

She didn't feel so alone, looking out like this. As if Marrowdell itself was company. Jenn touched the glass over the Spine with a finger, exhaled to leave a circle of breath. The sei had filled her with its tears. In this, she was something other than turn-born. But what?

A question not for her list, for Mistress Sand would not speak of the sei. Like the toads, such questions distressed her.

The moon, being high above, was likely as far beyond the reach of turn-born as it was of toad or woman. From so high, Jenn thought, surely it must shine down on Endshere as well.

Taking her finger away, she pressed her lips within the circle of breath, leaving a kiss.

Bannan feared no question or truth. When he came home, she would tell him everything she learned from Mistress Sand and they would puzzle at the rest together.

Smiling, Jenn climbed back into bed, careful of the toad, and fell fast asleep.

Bannan lay on the straw mattress he shared with Devins and Davi, staring at a ceiling he couldn't see.

No letter.

He'd emptied the mailbag and turned it inside out to be sure. Watched in silence as Davi took his turn going through the mass of letters, the smith pulling out three to fold and shove deep into a pocket, all with a fearsome scowl. Whomever kept attempting to write to Lorra Treff had a sure enemy in her son. A story lay there, understood the truthseer; not one about to be shared.

But nothing from Lila, not for him, or for Jenn.

Nor one from Tir, which he'd also expected.

There had been a beribboned package of letters from the Lady Mahavar, coated in formidable wax seals. Correspondence for Gallie and some for Frann. Lorra too, so Davi was selective. Master Dusom had the most waiting for him, being engaged in dialogues with fellow scholars, but there was a small elongated box wrapped in dark waxed paper and string for Master Jupp and an uncommon rolled parchment for Covie Ropp that might, Bannan hoped, be from her son, Roche.

There could be news of the situation in Channen in any or all of those. Or none, since why would such troubles matter to anyone in remote and magical Marrowdell?

Lila could take care of herself and the boys. She would take over Emon's political duties in capable fashion and run the estate, truth be told, with more attention, for Emon had little love for administration, preferring to closet himself with his sons to test some mechanism or other.

Which made sense and was reasonable except for one thing.

The lack of letters.

Bannan pressed the palms of his hands against his eyes, then made himself relax. A long day was behind him, a busy one tomorrow, and if he had to question everyone in Endshere about these rumors, so be it.

A soldier's skill, to sleep on the eve of battle.

As he lay, listening to the deep peaceful breathing of the other men, he knew it was a skill he'd lost.

~

*A snip of thread, touched by skin and warmth . . . a drop of sleep, under the tongue . . .*
*And the dream unfolds . . .*
Stone rushes by, then stops, too close. A figure runs past, sword gleaming. Then another. A third.
Silence. Darkness. *Dread.*
Light. A hand beckons. *Trust.*
All the while something rustles above. Something hunts below.
And everywhere is shadow.

A moth had brought Wisp's summons. If, Jenn thought with a touch of doubt, the white pebble in her hand was from her dragon and not some confusion by toads. She sat at the kitchen table to finish her tea and ponder the question.

Though they were generous creatures, she'd never seen nor heard of a toad relinquishing one of their precious stones. And wasn't giving her a white pebble exactly the sort of cleverness certain to amuse Wisp? Satisfied, she closed her fingers over the little thing. Today it was, then.

Last night, she'd found herself discomfited to be in an empty house; today, she relished it. Breakfast was a hunk of cheese and a loaf's end, washed down with hot sweet tea. Having dressed first thing in hopes of this journey, her list of questions and a token for Mistress Sand in her pocket, she'd only to decide on footwear.

Radd Nalynn, each winter, sewed his daughters new winter shoes. The waxed thread and well-oiled leather made them close to weatherproof, though the bottoms wore out, especially Jenn's. It wasn't as if she could help it, since it was take either the road or go over frozen fields on her way to Night's Edge and, yes, she usually ran, being in a hurry, which led, admittedly, to holes. But they could be stuffed with straw and Radd did his best.

She supposed, having stopped growing, that boots with thick soles might be in her future. Doubtless they'd be as awkward as the proper shoes Aunt Sybb insisted she and Peggs don at suppertime or when wearing their best or second-best dresses, and not let her feel the ground at all.

Barefoot would do.

Then there was the whole issue of the Verge, a place purportedly free of winter and cold. After some discussion on the matter with Peggs, Jenn planned to do as the turn-born did when crossing into Marrowdell as tinkers, namely leave the clothes she needed here on this side of the edge, at Bannan's farm. The turn-born used his barn and left trunks of crystal and stone for that purpose. Bannan surely wouldn't mind if she left her things in his house.

Where she could check to see what Wisp might have done.

Having banked the fire in the heatstove, because she couldn't know how long she'd be and the Emms' house toad would appreciate some warmth, Jenn left the white pebble where the little cousin would find it, then went out the kitchen door, closing it behind her. She tied a white dish towel around the handle, this being the signal she'd arranged with her sister.

Her fingers lingered on the loose knot. The Verge. Was she ready? Jenn firmed her chin and turned away from the house. If she wasn't now, she never would be.

Banners snapped in the crisp morning breeze as a band played and children ran laughing between the bright tents in Endshere's commons. Prized stock stood in rows, ribbons in tails, hooves agleam with lacquer, waiting the scrutiny of knowing eyes. Tables groaned beneath the industry of the local inhabitants, from foodstuffs to, as Alyssa had predicted, fine boots, while narrower trestles were arranged in a circle to offer baked goods and beverages to those wandering the fair.

A fair as proud as any Bannan had experienced, if the smallest. Much of what would change hands sat in barns delegated as warehouses: grain and other produce from those farms within a day's travel—any farther, he'd been assured, as well go to the larger village of Weken and get a better price—along with lumber, firewood, ash, and lime. Tools and ploughshares hung beside harness and saddlery, and sacks of feed lay atop barrels of flour and other staples. Everything would change hands, over the coming days, to ensure all would be ready for winter.

Ears attuned to any conversation not about Koevoet's well-hung bull or Moniq's exceptional pastry, Bannan took his time roaming the tents. He admired and praised, newly educated in the difficulty of making what he'd taken for granted, and left pleased smiles along with coin at several booths. Among his first purchases were the requested hard candy for Radd's throat, in every flavor, as well as large bags of a reddish sweet preferred by children, the truthseer having witnessed Larah Anan's wide-eyed longing, for Cheffy and Alyssa.

With one for Larah as well.

After that, well, how could he resist a soft little hat for Loee, with ears like a rabbit, and booties for Hettie's babe-to-come? Hatpins for the senior ladies of Marrowdell, each with tiny feathers at their tip, came next. Heavy mitts for Anten and Devins. Blue ribbons for Davi's draught horses. His coin went farther than he'd expected, buying tea and little woven bags of spices he'd have thought ordinary in Vorkoun and knew were prized here. Candles and oil. Quills and paper. Thread.

He spent far too long and too much at a table of books. None were new; all were precious. A dogged set regarding the essentials of farm life by Elag M. Brock made him smile, that being Gallie's pen name, but he left it on the table for someone else. After all, he could ask the dear lady's advice in person, over tea, any time at all.

Within an hour, Bannan was down to his last few coins. The saddlebags over his shoulder were filled to bulging, and he'd a selection of books tied together with a strap. Despite a notion of what he wanted for Jenn, and some quiet questions, he'd not found it. Nor had he heard more news about Channen.

The truthseer purchased a pumpkin tart crusted with roasted seeds and took it to an empty bench. The news could wait, he decided. Hadn't it already? Allin and Palma should be his best sources regardless, innkeepers having an ear for travelers. They were with their families, sharing a celebratory breakfast before the busyness to come later in the day and night. He'd take Palma the package from Master Jupp and find a moment to ask his questions. Which left—he went to lick his fingers—the question of the gift for his beloved.

His hand paused in midair. Before his eyes, a procession approached, others clearing the way with smiles and no few comments. Heads high, the twelve women walked up to the refreshments, Devins firmly in their midst.

By the light of day, Palma's cousins were similar only in that none were older than Hettie. Half had the dark curls of the Anans, but the others ranged from fair to fox-red, with one possessing remarkable freckles.

Riding garb, suited for livestock handling, was worn by four of the women; three wore pretty hats and had ruffled dresses showing beneath fair-day cloaks; a pair had the leather aprons of carpenters while another pair those of fine white cloth; and the last, the one of freckles, had a hunting bow over her shoulder.

The twelve formed a half circle in front of the baking table, and waited, eyes on Devins.

The hapless young man, his face crimson at being the center of attention, stepped forward to stand in mute agony before the amused baker. Presumably, he was there to buy a treat for himself and one of the twelve. But which one?

Chuckling, the truthseer finished licking his fingers and went to the rescue.

The river flowed through the valley, foreign geese and ducks bobbing along in its midst. They took their rest

before flying south to where it wouldn't be winter, Master
Dusom had taught, an incredible thought to a younger Jenn.
Now she felt an unexpected kinship, being about to make a
similar journey, and waved at a small group of ducks as they
floated past. They seemed to be enjoying the ride, though
she hoped they'd take off before the river plunged from
Marrowdell beyond the mill.

The Verge being full of its own hazards, Jenn planned to
be more cautious than the ducks, who paddled in soon-to-
freeze water and chanced waterfalls.

Holding her skirt above the water, she waded across the
ford with extra care. The cold numbed her feet but better
numb than a slip and full dunking. Once the river froze, she
could cross anywhere.

Behind her the village was awake and busy. Cows lowed,
impatient to be milked. She'd offered to help Covie and
Anten, but they were content to have Cheffy take a greater
responsibility. He was growing up, Jenn thought, remembering a sweet chubby baby fond of her hair.

She'd have Peggs' to hold come summer, and Hettie's
sooner still. The cycle of life, Aunt Sybb called it, how new
people to love arrived as others became Blessed Ancestors
to watch over them. New people and love were, in Jenn's
opinion, very good things. The rest, she chose not to think
about.

She stamped warmth back into her feet and legs as she
started up the road. The old trees—the neyet—no longer
leaned attentively when she passed beneath. They slept
through winter, even in the Verge, according to Wisp who
would know. Yling, who lived within their trunks, did not.
Though Jenn watched, none showed themselves.

Perhaps, like the toads, they didn't approve.

Jenn would be more than happy to know why, but the
house toads merely seemed anxious about any change and
she'd yet to understand a yling. Wisp couldn't either, but
she'd been surprised and a little chagrined to fail, having
made a wish to understand and be understood that had
worked for more than just Eldani and Ansnan. Wisp had
laughed at her and oh, the joy of it, that he still would.

Where the Tinkers Road bent sharply to the right, she
stopped at the opening to the path that climbed, switching

back and forth, to the Spine. Bannan had remarked that it looked like any other path in any other woods, now, but it wasn't, being the way to what Wisp had called "her crossing" which was her personal door into the Verge. To anyone else, the top was a meadow, not as nice as Night's Edge, broken by upthrusts of ivory that seemed stone to anyone else but were really bits of the sei holding onto this world.

A pair of wicked red eyes glared down at her from the shadow where branch met trunk. Jenn met the glare and raised an eyebrow. With a frantic scrabble of claws, the eyes—and their owner—disappeared. She wasn't at all sorry that nyphrit ran from her now. They were cruel and spiteful, even if small, and dangerous in number. Hadn't they almost killed Uncle Horst, surely the greatest fighter in the world?

Nyphrit did have one use. House toads ate them, with great pleasure.

The path and her crossing could wait. Jenn turned away, walking more briskly now that her feet were warm. She left the road at the entrance to Bannan's farm, passing between the old trees into sunshine.

Hard to imagine the little house, now tidy and well-loved, had sat empty and abandoned since before she'd been born. Fresh cedar shingles lay warm and golden over the roof, windowpanes glistened, and the door hung from sturdy new hinges. A bench waited on the porch and, most importantly, a small well sat before the house, water brimming in its stone heart. Water that, like the fountain at the heart of the village, was Marrowdell's bounty and would not freeze this winter.

Jenn admired the garden with its neatly trimmed summerberry stalks and tilled soil, ready to plant in spring. If Bannan had needed to do anything more to cement his kinship with those in the valley, which he hadn't, of course, it would have been the eagerness with which he'd sought advice and applied it. His larder, the door locked against ordinary intruders but likely not proof against a peckish dragon, was as full as any in Marrowdell. When he returned from Endshere, his barn would become home to two piglets, earned by his help mucking out stalls for Anten.

She stepped up on the porch. The door stood open the

right amount for a toad to come and go—a very large toad—and there, sure enough, was Bannan's, regarding her soberly.

Which toads couldn't help but do, having such huge and melancholy eyes.

"Fair morning," Jenn greeted it patiently. This close to Night's Edge, Wisp, and the Verge, she didn't feel particularly patient, but you couldn't hurry a toad. "May I come in?"

~Elder sister,~ it replied, ever-so-earnest. ~In this moon cycle, I made twenty-one eggs. I caught three squirrels and one cricket. No foul nyphrit lived to enter my family's home. I matter to Marrowdell.~

"You do indeed," Jenn agreed heartily, casting a longing look beyond the toad into Bannan's neat house. "May I come in?"

~You may not.~

She blinked. "Pardon?"

It sank into itself, clearly distressed, but didn't budge. ~You may not.~

"But—I mean no harm. I just want to leave some clothes here and—" she almost said "check on the dragon" but stopped before making matters worse "—and return for them," she finished lamely.

~If I may, elder sister, would it not be more convenient for you to leave your clothes in the house of our elder brother?~

"Well, yes, I suppose it would be as convenient, but—" Jenn craned her neck, trying to see if anything might be amiss inside that the house toad, for whatever reason, mightn't want her to see, then looked down at the creature. "Why can't I come in?"

~The truthseer is not here.~

About to argue she knew full well where Bannan wasn't, she hesitated. Either his house toad took its duties more seriously than those in the village, who simply stayed out from underfoot regardless of who came or went, or Bannan had left instructions she should respect. "Then I'll wait until he is," she said, having no wish to challenge the proud creature, then she smiled and added, with a small curtsy, "You're a most excellent guardian."

The house toad puffed into a smug ball, rocking on its

wide stomach. ~I will watch and hope for your return, elder sister.~

An odd thing for it to say, Jenn thought as she walked between the silent barn and slumbering summerberries. Almost troubling. She went through the gap in the hedge around the farm to the path her feet had made over the years alongside the field, now fallow. Why would the toad need to hope? She was turn-born and could cross from one world to the next at her pleasure, and had, moreover, no intention of being late for supper here, Peggs having invited her.

House toads fussed, that was the truth of it, being responsible sorts and prone to think the worst. They couldn't cross on their own, having been stranded here by mistake long ago, and probably, she nodded to herself, feeling better by the moment, found the entire notion of crossing a worry no matter who did it. She would visit Bannan's toad on her way home to reassure it.

Comforted by obligation, Jenn Nalynn entered Night's Edge.

~She's HERE!~ a wail from the sky.

~She's COME!~ a cry swooping up through the ground. Dragons fussed and complained throughout the meadow, not that they let themselves be seen.

Worse than little cousins, they were. ~SILENCE!~ Wisp roared, claws scoring the soil. He would much rather have scored a side or three, but they knew better than come so close.

Complain to him and fuss, oh, that they dared. Useless younglings.

He sniffed the air, felt for their presence.

Alone again. A welcome touch of wisdom, though he'd no doubt their fascination with Marrowdell's turn-born would lure them back once she was in the Verge.

A fascination mixed with dread. His jaw gaped with amusement. Wisdom indeed.

"Wisp?"

She was nervous and couldn't, even if she tried, hide it

from him. They'd been connected this way since the sei appointed him her guardian. The sei, oblivious to what mattered to lesser beings, hadn't bothered to sever the bond once the girl became turn-born and powerful and beyond the care of a mere dragon.

A dragon more than content to have her stay near his heart.

"Here!" he sang to Jenn Nalynn, sending a breeze to tickle the bangs from her forehead and another to hasten her steps.

"This way."

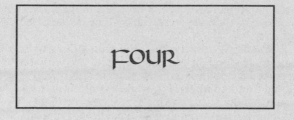

# FOUR

*T*O CROSS BETWEEN worlds sounded an immense and weighty undertaking, a task for scholars and those trained in magical arts.

Jenn stumbled and caught herself with a quick grab of Wisp's tail, having stepped from dried flowers and grass onto plates of crystal that cracked and sobbed blue tears. She tried to avoid cracking any more, but the things were everywhere.

As was sky, oddly beneath her feet as well as ground, a sky shot through with colors that tasted of carrots and spice as she breathed them in and felt the rush of wings and goodness, she was going to be sick . . .

Guessing what ailed her senses, Jenn let herself be no longer flesh, but turn-born and glass, calming her thoughts to wait, not want.

The Verge quieted around her, resolving into a down-sloped path, cobbled in weeping crystal, between spires of—rock, she decided to call it, though what kind of rock shimmered she surely didn't know.

The last time, she'd been on a mountain, or close to one, with a vista spreading in all directions. Granted, it had been a confusing vista, but most impressive. This? This, she began to frown, was sneaking down a cramped hallway of rock, with only glimpses of something other. To keep her from seeing more—or to keep more from seeing her?

~This way.~ Words she felt, rather than heard, Wisp say again. No longer a breeze in her ears, though she knew he could speak that way here, but a voice inside of her, deep and grim.

A dragonish voice. From— She spun around to find Wisp waiting. He stood on two good legs and two withered, using his spiked tail to prop himself straight. Silver scales caught the light and splintered it, while his glorious wings hung open, trembling at their tips as if eager for flight. His face was long and disturbingly well-fanged, with that wiry beard hanging from his chin. Idle steam curled up from paired nostrils. During her scrutiny, amethyst eyes gleamed with— yes, that was amusement.

And pride. That too.

All at once, his head flipped to one side with a SNAP! of those jaws. Something squeaked and died with a gush of cinnamon. Wisp tossed it aside, giving Jenn no more than a glimpse of spines and a long body.

~My apologies, turn-born,~ the dragon said, wiping his fangs along a scaled leg with toad-like satisfaction. ~I should have let you handle it.~

"No need," Jenn replied faintly, quite sure she didn't want to handle anything of the sort.

Wisp turned with sinuous grace and limped down the path. His clawed feet tore open crystal but weren't, Jenn noticed as she followed, the first to do so. Paired stains preceded the dragon, stains he assiduously avoided.

So she did the same, trickier after his feet left their share, but once broken, whatever the crystal leaked was slippery and she'd no intention of falling.

Then did, right on her rump.

Jenn took a breath, or hoped she did, for her body didn't feel as it should or did, and didn't breathing seem more like eating? Thinking about it, she felt she'd had her fill and could stop any time, but that made less sense than most of the Verge and she wouldn't start her time here by doing other than she would at home.

Which probably wasn't sensible either. She got to her feet, Wisp well ahead by now, and resumed walking. Ancestors Witness, she most certainly hoped Mistress Sand would help her understand all of this.

*Disagreement.*

Jenn stopped again. She knew that feeling, too well. Turn-born must agree, or their expectations, their wishes, would fail. One or more of them had just disagreed with hers.

But she hadn't made one . . . had she?

It seemed she must have. No hoping, then, even to herself. Anticipation was probably wrong too, though so would be doubt. Jenn brightened. With turn-born here and paying attention, at least she couldn't make more rabbits, that being her other thoughtless wish in the Verge.

Asking Mistress Sand's opinion of those rabbits was also on her list, if she got that far. It was, come to think of it, a very long list for a short visit.

~Here.~

Ancestors Dizzy and Distracted. She'd stopped to argue with herself and now Wisp was a flick of a tail going around a corner.

Jenn hurried forward, keeping a worried eye out for spiked things as well as puddles. This was her dragon's true home and she did her best to think kindly of it, but it wasn't making a very good impression.

She followed around the corner only to find herself alone at the end of the rock crevice, faced with a blue oval admittedly door-sized, but lacking handle or hinge.

~Step through.~

Into rock?

A shadow slipped over her, cold and ominous. Jenn looked up too late to see what cast it. Whatever it had been, she should take shelter, "Could a turn-born be eaten?" being near the top of her list.

Shelter where? Her eyes came back to the blue, which wasn't like the dark tears of crystal but rather the loveliest such color she could remember. Richer than a spring sky, this blue, and smelled of pie. Her color, something reminded her, though why that should be, Jenn couldn't imagine.

She reached out and touched it.

The blue oval split from its center outward along five seams, opening like a flower touched by the sun.

Shelter and a welcome. Jenn stepped inside without further hesitation.

"Ancestors Beset and Besieged." Bannan held up his hands in mock defense. "You looked in need of help."

Devins glared. "I was doing well enough till you interrupted!"

Not the truth, but the words rang with abused pride. In hindsight, he should have left well enough alone, and the younger man to his fate. The twelve cousins stood nearby, their heads bowed in murmured consultation.

No doubt about the young man he'd thought to rescue from their clutches. Seeing the stubbornness in his face, Bannan switched tactics. He took hold of a shoulder and pushed Devins ahead, gently but firmly. "Help me with the mail and you're free to go back to them. If that's what you want."

This time, the blush confined itself to a reddening along Devins' cheekbones. "How am I supposed to know?" he muttered, giving in to walk with the truthseer. "They're amazing women," this with emphasis. "Accomplished. Sure of themselves. A man would be lucky to spend his life with any of them. Ancestors Witness. I don't know what they see in me, Bannan. Roche was always the one girls wanted."

Bannan smiled to himself. That the gangling young man beside him, yet to gain his full growth, lacked the restless ambition of his brother and father? All to his good. Devins was free of bitterness and, like his mother, Covie, a healer in his own right, sure and gentle with the dairy herd he loved.

And something more.

When Devins forgot himself, and truly was himself, an air of peace and content surrounded him as soothing as a warm fire on a chill night. If Devins Morrell grew into the man he promised to be, he'd become the heart of Marrowdell.

The man he was now continued miserably, "They really should be after you anyway. You're unattached and not that old."

Bannan wasn't sure whether to laugh or grieve at the reminder of how Jenn was forgotten. He settled for a rueful shrug. "Maybe they've heard about my cooking."

Though it was, in fact, an interesting question. As Lila put it, he made a decent impression at court. Hadn't he — and Tir — fended off their share of propositions on the way north, albeit not from these women? Why not now?

Be grateful, he told himself.

The two left the fair, dodging wagons, horses, and chickens on the dusty road. The famed Northward was here tamed to a short main street bordered by buildings, except for the commons where the fair was being held. South of Endshere, the road passed through tidy farm fields; north, beyond the bridge they now crossed, it met the mill road. The inn sat at that junction, its stable the last building before the Northward shook itself free of civilization for good.

The mail wasn't the least of his duties and Bannan would be glad to have it done. Cammi'd let it be known she'd be at the storeroom to receive and dispense mail from midmorning till midafternoon; no sooner and, at the risk of unclaimed mail being offered to the highest bidder the next day, no later. Apparently this was no idle threat. It had become a tradition of the fair for young men and women to abandon small packages for the auction, the oft-desperate eagerness of the person bidding for those being a favorite entertainment for everyone else.

The highest bidder for truly unclaimed mail would be the local magistrate, this being Endshere's way of paying their postmistress a bonus for her year of service, with such mail simply moved to his loft until spring.

Hettie and Tadd, faces wreathed in smiles, waved at them on their way to the fair. Devins' eyes followed them wistfully.

Bannan didn't let him slow. A queue had formed in wait,

snaking around to the front of the inn, and he'd yet to retrieve Marrowdell's sack from his room. "Hold a place," he
ordered briskly. "I'll get our mail."

As if back on patrol and in charge.

Which he wasn't, nor wanted to be. The truthseer
stopped, facing Devins, and prepared to apologize, but the
other looked more puzzled than offended. "I thought you
were carrying it."

The bulging shoulder bags. Bannan hefted the string
with the books. "I did some—" shopping implied coin,
which those in Marrowdell rarely saw or could spare. Where
were his manners? "I did some trading of my own. Gifts for
those at home." He tilted his head at the inn. "If you'd be so
kind, Devins, as I meant to say, would you hold my place in
line while I drop these in my room and get the mail? There's
lunch in it for you."

That earned him a broad smile. "Done!"

Bannan leapt the steps to the inn and hurried through
the doors, almost colliding with big Davi Treff. The smith
had his arms full of well-wrapped bundles—Lorra's pottery
samples—and, sure enough, his mother stood behind him,
eyes narrowed against the burst of sunlight. "Fair morning!"
the truthseer greeted both.

Or was it? Davi's nod was gloom itself while Lorra's face
bore no expression at all. "Fair morning," she said. "Your
pardon, Bannan, but we've no time to waste." With a nod to
her son.

The truthseer held the door for them. Either Lorra's
aggravation with Frann's impulsive trade still rankled, or
something else hadn't gone well. Hopefully their day
would improve. Marrowdell counted on this fair to garner
vital supplies. He let the door close, shutting out the sun,
and felt the weight of the bags on his shoulder as an accusation. Ancestors Reckless and Rash. Had he misspent his
coin? While his purchases seemed good ones, the money
could have gone into the village pot to everyone's
benefit—

"Fair morning, Bannan!" Allin finished tying on his
apron and waved. "We'll be out in a moment. I'm helping
Palma start up." He disappeared into the kitchen.

Palma. Her package. Another gift, most eagerly

anticipated. He'd not second-guess his purchases, Bannan decided, happy again.

A familiar figure sat hunched on a stool at the bar, wrapped in layers of dark wool. As the truthseer walked past, he looked into the mirror and found his gaze caught by a pair of pale eyes, rimmed in white, set in a face so wrinkled he couldn't tell if the ancient smiled or frowned. He gave one of the villagers' short bows in polite acknowledgment. "Fair morning, Mistress Anan. My name is—"

"Bannan Larmensu." Soft, her voice, but with a crisp edge to it. A wizened finger crooked, indicating the stool by her side. "Call me Great Gran. Everyone does. Sit, boy!" when he didn't obey at once.

He'd owe Devins supper as well, the truthseer thought, but set his purchases down on the bar and took the stool. "I'm honored—"

"You're busy and I'm a daft old woman, but we've business, we two."

Ah, the unwed cousins. Bannan smiled and shook his head. "I'm not—" But the wizened finger tapped the bar top and he closed his mouth.

"Better." Another tap. "I've what you've been hunting."

"I don't seek a wife," he blurted.

"That's what I told my granddaughters." Her tiny booted feet were well off the floor. One swung forward to kick a crate he hadn't noticed till now, being in the shadows under the bar. "You seek a gift—the right gift—for your dearest love."

He stared at her, dumbfounded.

Great Gran's chin curled toward her nose as her whole body shook. Laughing, he realized belatedly, and at him, without doubt. After a moment, she stopped and dipped her head, peering up at him. "I see what binds a heart, Bannan Larmensu, as you see the truth. Your love is in Marrowdell. A daughter of Melusine's." Sharply, "Hush! I'm neither your enemy nor a fool."

For he'd started—how could he not?—about to protest she mustn't speak that name, no matter they were alone for the moment. Taking a breath, he asked, with care, for she was no one he'd dare offend, "May I ask, then, who you are to me?"

Her finger traced a line within the grain of the bar top's gleaming wood, then stopped. "One who has lived in Marrowdell—and witnessed its magic."

"But—"

"Surely they told you. Of the first to settle Marrowdell?"

They had, but the first to live in the homes built by the turn-born hadn't stayed long. "What made you leave?" he asked quietly, but he could guess. "The dreams?" For in Marrowdell, the Verge crept too close to sleeping minds, strange and, to most, disturbing.

Within her wool, she shivered and nodded. "We loved the valley. Named it. Tried to make it home. Oh, I was fine. Better than fine." A pause. "Things changed. My family and the others fled. They died," as calmly as if relating a history of strangers. "A storm caught us on the road, without shelter. I survived."

Bannan laid his hand near hers, palm up. A finger, cool and dry, touched it then curled away.

"Don't pity me, boy," she snapped, but kindly. "Ancestors Witness, I've had a good life here. Outlasted three husbands, I have, and raised fine children. Tho' for too many years, I thought I must have dreamed it all, for no one here believed me. The great toads. The magical light. Dancers in the trees. Then people moved into Marrowdell again, people like Melusine, who could thrive there, and I knew it was all real."

People who'd stopped here on their journey. Oh, and thinking that, wasn't something else more than likely? "Lady Mahavar."

"Sybbie?" Another laugh. "We're good friends. How else would I know you, Bannan Larmensu, once of Vorkoun? Sybbie and I share news over a bottle of Marrowdell's wonderful water every fall. Have done for years."

The Northward Road, Bannan realized to his chagrin, had its sentries after all, albeit older and better bundled than he'd expected. "Great Gran," he said with a little bow, "you must have thought me a rare fool when I came through before."

"Oh, and you're not one now?" But a tiny eye winked. "Don't be so hard on yourself, boy. I saw some potential. For Marrowdell, if not here."

Like Aunt Sybb and Mistress Sand, this woman would be his enemy if he threatened those she loved. Like them, she'd be a priceless ally if he held her trust. Bannan bowed deeper in acknowledgment, then looked up with his heart in his eyes. "I have seen Marrowdell's marvels," he confessed. "Among them is Jenn Nalynn, the love of my life."

"Sybbie's youngest niece. Ah." He began to sweat during the weighty pause that followed. Abruptly, Great Gran spoke again. "Here's a curious thing. Those who forget Marrowdell's magic have forgotten her too. I would ask you why . . ."

The truthseer pressed his lips together.

Another silent laugh. "Well enough. Listen, then, while I tell you of this—" a second light kick at the mysterious crate.

When Great Gran was a young woman, Endshere had been little more than a scrape alongside the Northward Road. Toil and time it took, in great measure, to wrest farmland from the grip of trees older than Rhoth itself. There were those who endured, understanding they built for the future, not themselves.

And those who fled the overwhelming forest, seeking easier work in Weken or the cities of Lower Rhoth.

A rumor started, no one later could say how, of a valley to the north already cleared and planted, with empty homes and a mill waiting. Surely a fantasy, the sort dreamed by those weary of ax and chain, of fire and stump. No one was willing to pack up and move deeper into the wilderness without proof.

Then, one day, a man arrived. He came in a wagon, but was no settler, being past his prime in years and frail. Tralee was his name, Crumlin Tralee, and he stood on a barrel in Endshere's poor excuse for a commons to speak at length and with passion. He'd come, Crumlin told them all, to gather families for a new settlement, one where the hardest work was already done.

Clods of mud and worse were thrown his way, for those

who believed in Endshere could ill afford to lose a single strong back. But there were those who listened, for Crumlin was an educated man and well-spoken and convincing.

Not that any guessed what else he was.

So when Crumlin and his wagon of belongings left Endshere for the promised northern settlement, others went with him.

He hadn't lied. Marrowdell was as welcoming and fertile as any could hope, and the families settled in, filled with joy and expectation. Crumlin himself took the house farthest from the rest, being, as it turned out, solitary and unhelpful and concerned with his own affairs.

No matter. They had the valley and new homes. All began as well as anything could.

Until the dreams.

Few at first, and dismissed. More, as time passed, and worse. The valley, it seemed, didn't care for them. Barely tolerated them.

Actively hated them.

What started as quiet concern became urgent flight. Though Crumlin argued against it, calling them cowards and nearsighted and fools, the would-be villagers began to pack everything of value and wouldn't listen.

Despite having no love for Crumlin, once wagons were loaded and ready to depart, the good people went to fetch him, unwilling to abandon anyone to the valley.

But he was gone.

Food had rotted on his table, meaning he'd left days before and in stealth, abandoning them. Outraged, the villagers scavenged his house, viewing it only just to take Crumlin's expensive things; he having led them to such a dreadful place and them returning to Endshere the poorer and in some disgrace.

Had the frightened folk needed aught else to push them on their way, it was the ominous build of clouds to the north, and the growing chill to the air.

"Bones and wagons lay on the road, left till spring," Great Gran finished.

"With you the only survivor." Bannan shook his head.

"Was I?" Her head tilted. "Only the bears know. The people of Endshere gleaned what they could; a debt fairly paid, to my mind. As for this?" another kick at the crate. "If it returns to Marrowdell, brings a smile, it'll pay for its keep in my attic these many years. It is—" with triumph "—what you asked for in the market."

Why wasn't he surprised? "Ancestors Blessed. I should have come first to you, dear lady," he conceded graciously.

Wrinkles creased with, he thought, satisfaction. "Now you know better."

Bannan smiled and reached for his purse. "What do I owe you?" Tir would protest, but he'd not haggle a price, not with this lady.

"Keep your coin." She shifted within her wool wraps like a bird settling into a nest. "I would have a story of Marrowdell, tonight by the fire."

It was more than the truth. Did he not feel the wistfulness of that, the aching need, as if it were his own? Speechless, the truthseer nodded.

Her finger crooked toward the stairs.

Dismissed, Bannan stood and bowed, then bent to retrieve the crate. Careful of Great Gran's booted toes, he managed not to grunt in surprise at the weight, sparing himself another laugh at his expense. The saddlebags and books would have to wait on the bar.

Anticipation, sweet and proud, made him grin as he carried his gift away.

Jenn would never expect this.

Whatever she'd expected in the Verge, it hadn't been the most comfortable chair imaginable.

Made of rock.

Which it wasn't. She needed more words, Jenn thought, stroking the silky blue whatever-it-was with delight. She'd stepped through the flower-petal door into a small, but pleasing space, bright—though there were no lights or windows and the door had closed—and warm. Being dressed for summer, the warmth was something she appreciated;

her cloak, scarf, and heavy tunic had remained behind, in Wisp's house.

Though wasn't here more his home than the clever little dome of crystal and wood he'd built in Marrowdell? "I hadn't thought dragons lived like this," she said aloud.

Wisp snorted. He'd stayed as she'd found him, curled into a ball, his bearded snout resting atop his good hip, tail covering his clawed feet. The twin puffs of steam rose to the ceiling then vanished. ~I live like this,~ he corrected. He lifted his long head to gaze around, staring longest at the now-folded petals of the door. ~You've changed it.~

She had? "How? What's different?"

~It's better,~ Wisp assured her, which, though uninformative, was certainly reassuring. Jenn settled back into the softness of her own seat, a seat that had formed itself from one wall and fit her to perfection. The dragon's jaw dropped open in one of his smiles. ~As for how, Dearest Heart? Only you could know. This was built by the sei. Only sei can change it.~

Not reassuring at all. Jenn jumped to her feet and started to pace, only to find the wall moving away from her so she could, presumably, pace forever in the same direction which wasn't pacing at all, but walking through a mountain. She stopped. So did the wall. "Oh dear." How very odd.

~Sand is outside.~ Wisp's eyes half-closed.

"Ancestors Blessed." At first relieved, Jenn began to frown uneasily. "Why doesn't she come in?"

~Thanks to you, she cannot.~

Rather than say "oh dear" again, Jenn stared commandingly at the petal door. When nothing happened, she ordered, "Open!"

It refused.

Well, this was a bother. She went to the door and touched it gingerly; her finger sank in and came out again, as if nothing was there, but something was. She could lean on it.

Though she'd matured beyond stamping her foot in frustration, to her aunt's relief, the temptation to do just that made her twitch. "What should I do, Wisp?"

His eyes were fully closed, his head back on his hip and not a care in the Verge, her dragon. If she believed the pose, which she didn't. "Wisp. Please," Jenn urged. "We're trapped in here!"

~We are not,~ he disagreed serenely. ~This is a sanctuary. It grants protection from the dangers outside. Beyond counting they are, in the Verge, and most quite deadly, but none dare challenge you, Dearest Heart.~

Oh, her dragon was enjoying himself. Enjoying her newly powerful self, was the truth of it, and as much as Jenn appreciated his extraordinary confidence, having none of her own, she didn't think it wise of Wisp to make assumptions. "Mistress Sand is outside," she pointed out.

~As a danger should be.~ A thoughtful pause. ~She grows annoyed. Turn-born, until now, have intruded here at their whim. I like this much better.~

"She's not a danger, she's our guest." As well as someone Jenn preferred not to annoy in any sense. "Could you talk to her through the door? Ask her to—" wait a moment, while they prepared tea? The humor of it struck her and she laughed.

The petals unfolded, letting in a blast of heat that dissipated almost at once.

Mistress Sand stood in the opening. About to rush forward happily with her arms open, as she'd always done, Jenn froze in place. This wasn't the Sand she knew.

This was a vessel of glass and light, shaped as a stocky woman. Instead of a face, she wore the mask of one. Wood it might have been, or weathered shell, but its features were fixed into a stern, almost judgmental expression. An incongruous shock of thick white hair topped her head and where eyes and mouth should open, light spilled forth, light of every color Jenn knew.

And some she couldn't name at all.

She looked down at herself, startled to find herself of ordinary flesh clothed in her very ordinary third best dress, with bare and—wasn't it typical?—blue-stained feet. Not the blue, which came from the broken crystal and made her stomach roil, but the stains. She couldn't seem to go anywhere without stains.

~Sweetling.~ Like Wisp's voice, not the one she'd come to know, but something new, yet the word and intonation were familiar. Jenn looked up again, light fractured to rainbows by the tears in her eyes. ~May I enter?~ Mistress Sand asked.

No endearing "-na?" at the end of the question, but there wouldn't be, in the Verge, where turn-born spoke to one another in their own tongue.

Which didn't need a tongue at all.

Overcome, Jenn sat on the floor to catch her—was she breathing? Ancestors Bewildered and Beset, she couldn't tell. It didn't matter. What did? Manners. The world would be a better place for everyone, Aunt Sybb often said, if everyone had better manners. Clinging to that, she managed to say, "Please come in, Mistress."

The creature of glass stepped through. Her mask faced the dragon's raised head, then dipped in a brief nod that seemed polite. Wisp, to her astonishment, did the same. Manners, Jenn thought, growing steadier. Who'd have thought?

She really should stand up.

Before she could, the floor lifted her, forming into a different comfortable chair. Another formed a short distance away and the turn-born sat in it as if well-used to such magical happenings. As of course she was.

Sitting up, face to semblance-of-face, Jenn felt much more herself. "Thank you for coming."

~Your dragon made it sound urgent. Is something wrong, Sweetling?~

Wisp curled a scaled lip.

"Not wrong, but—" She was doing everything backward. Jenn retrieved the homely little pot from her deepest pocket and held it out. "Peggs and I thought you'd enjoy some honey."

~Honey. ~ Sand took the pot. Not having pockets, or discernible clothing for that matter, she set it on a small shelf the wall provided at her gesture. ~While I welcome a taste of Marrowdell, and thank you and your sister, this can't be why you're here.~

"No. It's—I've questions." Jenn reached into another pocket to pull out her list, unfolding the paper. It couldn't have looked more out of place; she had the distinct feeling, despite the mask, Sand was amused. "There are rather a few," Jenn added, turning the paper over and back again.

~And neatly written.~ Definitely amused. ~Ask away.~ Sand sat back, glass fingers resting on her thighs. Her feet, Jenn couldn't help but notice, bore no stains at all, though she must have come this way.

"You were here first, waiting for us," she blurted, remembering the paired footprints. "But where? I didn't see you."

~She was in here. You shoved her out.~ Wisp amused at Sand's expense didn't feel like a good idea. Jenn shot him a warning look he completely ignored.

But the turn-born laughed, or rather Jenn felt her laugh. It was an itchy sort of feeling, but somehow still contagious. ~Dragons enjoy displays of power. The more meaningless and dramatic the better.~ The mask tilted. ~As you entered, the sanctuary sent me outside to wait. You, being sei, controlled it without need for my assent. It is a marvel.~ With admiration.

Eating apples hadn't made her into a tree. Swallowing tears didn't make her a—whatever a sei truly was, Jenn decided, intending to be firm on that point. What she truly was, well, that puzzled even her dragon.

As for her being "a marvel," well, that simply meant dragons weren't the only ones in the Verge to enjoy displays of power, a thought Jenn kept to herself as she consulted her list. She didn't have all day, being expected for supper, nor, she supposed, did Mistress Sand, though asking when turn-born ate in the Verge was right there on the back of the page, between could she visit and did they marry? She turned the paper over quickly. "I should start with the most important—"

Before she could choose, Mistress Sand asked, ~Why do you wear this seeming?~

Jenn studied her own hand. "I don't know." Nor could she remember changing from glass to flesh, for she'd walked down Wisp's path as a turn-born. "Shouldn't I?" Not on her list, but important to find out, she thought suddenly.

~It's a risk. Flesh can be harmed. Cut. Drowned. Eaten, not so likely, but you look a tasty morsel to those of the

Verge who cannot sense you as—~ Did she imagine hesitation? ~—turn-born.~

~And sei,~ Wisp added promptly.

A glass hand turned over, conceding the point.

"If you prefer, I'll be like you," Jenn offered and, with a shiver and wish, became glass and pearl. She felt no different, though tapping her fingers on her knee made a sound like tiny bells and if she cupped her hands palm to palm, she could pool their inner light into a glow bright enough to read in bed without a candle. Though turning pages was awkward.

Wisp snorted.

Mistress Sand laughed again. ~Best stay as you were, Sweetling.~ She'd shaded her eyes, or where eyes would be. ~Without a mask, you've no face I care to see.~

"No—" Jenn hurriedly reached to where her face should be, relieved to feel one, albeit one of glass. She frowned—or thought she did—at the turn-born. "I don't understand."

Mistress Sand's mask aimed at Wisp, then back to Jenn in question.

It hadn't occurred to her to exclude him from this conversation. She shouldn't and wouldn't, Jenn decided, no matter if the terst turn-born wanted it otherwise. "I'll only tell him anyway," she admitted, being honest.

Wisp, being prudent, offered no opinion. There was, however, a distinctly predatory gleam in his large, wild eyes she was sure meant they'd have to talk later.

~Very well, Sweetling. The light within us—~ Mistress Sand touched fingertip to breast ~—comes from both worlds. Our masks hold back one, so others may see us by the other.~ Raising her hands to the mask, she warned, ~Be ready.~

Jenn nodded, though how she could be ready for what she didn't—

Sand removed her mask.

A fine way to work up an appetite, Bannan decided, all this running about with packages and bags. Admittedly, his growing appetite likely had as much to do with the aromas wafting through the inn as Palma and her family worked their own magic in the kitchen. But he'd done his share of stair climbing, he had.

There'd been the run up to his shared room with Great Gran's interesting and heavy crate. With no time to investigate the contents, Bannan had covered it with his bedroll before running back down to retrieve his purchases from the bar.

Though he wouldn't have guessed her able to move so quickly, there was no sign of the elderly woman.

Up the stairs he'd gone again, with his saddlebags and books, putting those beside the covered box, then grabbed the outbound mailbags.

Those Bannan had run down the stairs and outside to where Devins waited in the queue. Not alone. Four of the cousins were keeping him company, a much less intimidating number, and by now they'd moved close to the front of the line.

Where Bannan might have stayed, but for forgetting the honey pots for Cammi in his room. Up and down once more. The inn started to fill with hungry customers.

Ancestors Famished and Faint, was that cabbage soup? He loved cabbage soup.

His return with the honey came just as Devins was trying to convince the dubious postmistress to take Marrowdell's mail. Swooping into his place, Bannan bowed politely—if breathlessly—at Cammi, offering the honey.

Oh, the smiles then.

The two, and larger, bags destined for Marrowdell safely in his keeping, Devins and entourage thanked profusely—and promised lunch—well, then it was up the stairs one final time to exchange those bags for Master Jupp's package and he'd be done.

Bannan put the mail with the rest, pushing the wide straw mattress aside to make room. They'd be cramped for space, but there was no question of loading the cart yet. Endshere swarmed with strangers; after his misadventure in the stable, he wasn't about to trust any of them. As warning, he placed Horst's sword on top.

The truthseer eyed his pile with pride, then had a twinge of conscience. Substantial, it was, and Perrkin shouldn't

have to carry heavy saddlebags in addition to a man's
weight. He'd walk most of the way, Bannan decided, cheer-
ing up.

Master Jupp's well-sealed leather packet under one arm,
he ran quick fingers through his hair to tame it, and went
out of the door, more than ready for his meal.

"Wait . . ."

"Who's there?" Bannan called, his tone friendly even as
he put his back to a wall. He glanced this way and that. The
hall and stairwell were empty. The hoarse whisper must
have come from one of the three other rooms, but those
doors, like his, were shut.

"Help me . . ." Faint. Pained. And from the door he faced.
Frann and Lorra's room!

One stride took him across the hall. He threw open the
door.

Sunlight streamed through lace curtains into the inn's
finest room, crossing the rumpled sheets of the canopied
bed to pool welcomingly in chairs arranged by the small
fireplace. The room was chill, the fire gone cold, and Frann
lay sprawled on the floor in her nightdress.

She raised her head slightly as he went to his knees beside her, her eyes dull and unfocused. "What's wrong?" he
asked gently, searching for injury, seeing nothing obvious.

"Don't tell—don't tell Lorra." Whispered with effort.
"I—I fell. An—cestors Stupid and—I fell."

"It's all right." Heart's Blood. From the rawness in her
voice, she must have called for help every time he'd so
cheerfully clomped up and down the stairs. Pushing aside
that guilt, he laid the back of his hand along her cheek to
find it icy cold. "Let's get you back to bed." Carefully, an
arm under her shoulders, the other supporting her legs,
Bannan stood. One of her hands fluttered, in protest or trying to help. "It's all right," he soothed again. "You're light as
a feather."

And was. The winter clothes—long sleeves, heavy skirts,
and shawls—had disguised her fragility. Bannan laid Frann
gently on the bed, wrapping her first in the sheet, then adding every blanket in the room. "Rest, dear lady. I'll bring—"
Who, if not Lorra? "—someone."

Frann might not have heard. Her eyes closed and she

shivered under the covers. Delaying only to rekindle the fire, Bannan went for help.

Help, in the capable form of Palma, her mother, Gallie Emms, and, in short order, Endshere's healer and his apprentice, shooed anyone else from Frann's room and closed the door.

"But—" Hettie pressed her lips together and sighed instead. Tadd put his arm around her, looking over her head at his father. Zehr shrugged, settling Loee into the crook of an arm while Devins stared helplessly at the door.

Word had spread quickly, as it would in a village. The wonder was that it had reached all of Marrowdell but the Treffs. "We might as well wait downstairs," Bannan suggested.

They nodded, following him down the stairs to the nearest table. The truthseer chose a seat where he could watch the door. When Allin spotted them, he hurried over, abandoning his customers.

Who nodded one to the other, knowingly.

"What ails Frann?" Allin demanded as he sat beside his twin. They were no more alike than any two brothers near in age would be, but identical concern filled their faces.

"We don't know yet," Hettie answered. Her hands rested over her unborn. "The healer wouldn't let me stay."

When Covie, Marrowdell's healer and Hettie's stepmother, would have, Bannan knew. Allin, well aware of this, nodded. "Frann'll be well cared for," he assured her. "Gallie will make certain of it."

"If only we knew what was wrong."

"Perhaps the journey—" Bannan offered.

"Nothing of the kind!" Lorra Treff arrived at their table like a whirlwind, her giant son drawn in her wake. He looked anxious. She looked furious.

Or terrified, Bannan thought with sympathy. He rose to his feet and offered his arm. "May I take you to your friend, dear lady?"

As he'd hoped, the courtesy made her pause, rather than rush past and up the stairs as she'd clearly intended to do.

"It was the mutton," Lorra declared, eyes snapping to Allin. He suddenly found the tabletop of great interest. Her eyes came back to Bannan, brows knit in a frown. "I told Frann to avoid it, but she's no sense of taste. She woke queasy this morning. Serves her right."

The truthseer kept his arm waiting. "Then you must tell the healer at once."

"Heart's Blood. That idiot's with her?!" Shoving past Bannan, Lorra dashed for the stairs. Such was her speed, her hat flew from her head, landing three tables over amidst tankards and plates of sausage.

Davi followed, sending an apologetic glance over a massive shoulder.

As Bannan sank down in his seat, Zehr spoke up. "Lorra and Master Shedden—the local healer—had a disagreement, last fair. Cynd told Gallie," he explained.

"'Disagreement?'" The truthseer raised an eyebrow.

"A loud one." Zehr handed Loee to Tadd, then shook his head. "Ancestors Brash and Bitter. Wasn't our place to ask what it was over. For all we know, it was Lorra."

Bannan kept his peace. A ready tongue—and temper— didn't mean Lorra had been in the wrong. Ancestors Witness, didn't Lila have both? He rubbed his chin, feeling its roughness. Hadn't shaved today. Hadn't eaten, other than the baking at the fair. Not that he'd appetite left.

Gallie Emms paused on the landing, looking for them. She didn't smile as she came to their table, her eyes touching briefly on her sons and husband. Taking Loee, she sat on the bench and pressed a kiss into the baby's curls, only then looking up. "Lorra and Davi intend to take Frann home. Now."

Hettie paled. "We'll be on the road in the dark."

"We won't. Davi claims his team knows the way and Lorra suggested—" her tone implying anything but a suggestion, "—those who prefer can follow tomorrow on horseback."

"I could ride to Weken," Tadd offered. "Bring their healer."

"There's none better than Covie," countered Hettie. "Lorra's right about that."

"If Lorra leaves now, who'll finish the rest of her trades?"

Allin looked from one to the other. "Ancestors Witness, I'm as worried as you about Frann, but Marrowdell depends on these goods. You'll run out of lamp oil and medicines. Lorra was bartering for barrels of salted fish as well as lye and who knows what else. The cart was to go home full."

"Now it goes home empty." Zehr half smiled. "Won't be the first winter we've managed without luxuries." He exchanged a glance with his wife and lost his smile. "Dear Heart?"

Gallie hugged Loee, her eyes troubled. "You want to go with them. Tonight."

"We can't let Davi and the others try this alone."

"There must be another way," she argued.

As one, they turned to Bannan.

Not only, the truthseer realized, because Horst had sent him to counter any of Lorra's follies that might endanger the rest. If anyone here knew the risks at night, he did. Years along the border, creeping through the dark. More often than not, they and their enemy would stumble into one another, flailing swords and firing pistols in a confusion that would have been laughable if it hadn't been for the dead.

The Northward was a road, not a battlefield. They could die on it as easily, and for no better reason.

"We go together." Bannan rose to his feet. "Be ready to leave at first light."

"But Lorra—" Hettie began. At his look, she stopped and nodded. "We'll be ready."

"I'll inform the Treffs," the truthseer told them.

He'd thank Horst for that duty once they were all safe in Marrowdell.

Before, light had poured out through the gaps in Mistress Sand's mask that marked where her eyes and mouth should be. Now, mask in her hand, all but her hair disappeared within coruscating beams, impossible to bring into focus.

With a cry, Jenn looked away. It was like trying to stare into an inferno, one that sent sparks flying hot into her eyes.

She wasn't at all surprised to find herself flesh again, nor to feel tears wet on her cheeks.

~Some things you must see for yourself, Sweetling.~ Calm and sure.

A cautious peek revealed the turn-born had donned her mask once more. Jenn shuddered, but gazed directly at Sand. "That's not what happens when I show my other self in Marrowdell." If it had, Bannan would have told her at once, being truthful and ever-curious. Peggs too, though her dear sister would have found a way to say it that made having a face of fire sound both reasonable and good. Which it wasn't at all.

~Curious, but unimportant.~ Mistress Sand shrugged. ~This is how terst see us. How turn-born see each other. Those of Marrowdell are neither.~

As if they didn't matter. Did Mistress Sand forget her fondness for the villagers here, in her own very different world? Another question, one Jenn wasn't sure she'd want answered. "Then—here—I should have a mask," she concluded.

~No need. Stay as you are. I enjoy seeing my Sweetling.~

A spiked tail beat against the rock. ~Jenn Nalynn will not stay here or with you. The Verge is hers as well and she intends to travel it. What of other turn-born? What of the terst?~

Wise Wisp, Jenn thought gratefully.

Mistress Sand appeared discomfited. ~I don't advise leaving this place or seeing others. You've much to learn, Sweetling. We don't even know how long you can stay in the Verge.~

There was a limit? "You were in Marrowdell for five days," Jenn ventured. She could be happy with that, five days surely long enough to explore and perhaps have a small adventure without missing too many chores at home or worrying Peggs.

~Days? Others of your kind die within moments of crossing,~ the turn-born said, the words leaving a chill inside Jenn's heart. ~They go mad and harm themselves or become prey. Ask your dragon.~

~I haven't eaten one of you,~ Wisp replied. ~Yet,~ he qualified, tongue wrapping thoughtfully around a fang.

"Wisp!" Though suspecting she was being teased, Jenn couldn't help herself. "You mustn't!" She was, however, careful not to make that any kind of wish.

From the pleased tilt of his head, he knew.

Jenn folded her list and returned it to her pocket. Those questions could wait. "How will I know when I need to go home? Will I—will I go mad?"

~If you do, I promise to eat you before anything else does,~ her dragon vowed. Amethyst eyes closed, then opened.

She chose not to believe him and was oddly comforted.

~I can't say how you will know.~ Mistress Sand told her. ~For us? When it's time to leave your world, we feel what is inside of us trying to stay, as if your world would reclaim what we've borrowed.~ She held out her arm of glass and sand. ~I know of no turn-born who has lingered past that warning. Why would we?~

It did seem a test unlikely to go well, Jenn conceded. She had a sudden, quite horrible, thought. ~The sei's tears. It couldn't claim those back, could it?~

Mistress Sand hesitated, then shrugged. ~Who knows what a sei could or can't, would or won't? Don't disturb them, Sweetling. Don't seek their attention.~ With grim finality.

*Disagreement.*

The turn-born's head rose sharply and the air grew stifling and thick. Jenn met the hot glow marking the other's eyes, refusing to back down though shaken by the speed of what must have been instinct, for she'd not consciously realized Mistress Sand had tried to force her compliance.

Which wasn't right and mustn't happen again. She found herself becoming angry. Angrier than she could remember being. So gloriously angry that the air in the room snapped and crackled as if a storm brewed and why shouldn't it—

~Temper, here? It will harm only your dragon.~ Calm, as if speaking to an irate child.

"Peace, Dearest Heart!" whispered a breeze. "Sand's caution is wise. No one in the Verge tempts the sei's notice." As her anger faded, the breeze warmed. "Always remember, there are turn-born who do not love you."

Jenn lowered her gaze to her hands. Glass fingers filled

with pearl and light, clenched into fists. She'd made Mistress Sand—who did love her and was her protector—stare into her unmasked face, which had been cruel.

She watched glass become flesh, nails biting into callused palms, and sighed, letting her anger go as she looked up again. The air calmed around them. Wisp closed his wings with a shake from head to tail, pointedly resuming his curl on the floor. She was sorry to have alarmed him.

"I came to learn, Mistress," Jenn protested, stung. "You should trust me."

~Trust you? I do. You've such a good heart.~ Then the turn-born shook her head. ~It's mistakes I fear. Ask questions of the sei, Sweetling? That's a mistake the Verge could pay for. Do you understand me?~

"There are rules." Ones the turn-born obeyed, to keep themselves and those around them safe. Rules, Jenn thought with a wild rush of hope, to make sense of the Verge. Or some sense, she added to herself, eyeing the wall that had moved ahead of her.

Wisp made a rude noise.

Mistress Sand ignored him. ~You could say that.~ Slow and consideringly. ~Certain actions have consequence here. We don't bring ourselves to the notice of the sei, for the consequence?~ A palm turned up. ~From nothing to the destruction of the Verge. Sei cannot be predicted or understood or trusted.~

She'd no intention of bothering the sei, and every hope they—or it—would ignore her too. A promise being foolish at best, Jenn nodded, very politely. "And the masks, Mistress?"

After a pause every bit as expressive as one of Aunt Sybb's, during which Jenn did her best to look attentive and not obstinate, the turn-born surprised her with a chuckle. ~Masks are good manners, Sweetling. Taking advice from those who know better?~ A finger pointed. ~That's good sense.~

The words left a shiver behind, a reminder she faced no one so safe as her aunt. "What advice would you give me, Mistress?"

~The most important you've heard. The next? What's to

be born, will. What's about to die, will. Turn-born can't oppose nature.~

Jenn started to object, "You healed Uncle Horst . . ."
then stopped.

~Healing's no more turn-born magic than your finding
the lost or Bannan's truth sight.~ Almost gently. ~It's a terst
gift, Sweetling, and one we were glad to use, but make no
mistake. Had he been worse, or slower to reach us, that
brave man would be bones in the ground.~ Mistress Sand
made a sound like a cough. ~Best advice of all, Sweetling?
Stay close to your family.~

Wisp uncoiled his neck, lifting his head to stare at the
turn-born. ~You have none.~

Mistress Sand didn't flinch. ~We do not. Being no longer
terst, nor welcomed by those who birthed us.~

Her dismay must have shown on her face, for the turn-
born reached across the distance between them to lay her
hand on Jenn's knee. ~We have each other, Sweetling. It's
not the same, but then, neither are we.~ Her hand withdrew.
~You asked for rules. I give you what is our one and our
only. Turn-born must agree.~

Was that a rule, a consequence, or simply a statement of
fact? All three, Jenn decided. In Marrowdell, there was no
one to disagree with her magic. That she hadn't done anything lastingly dreadful—there having been, of course,
Night's Edge—was more due to luck than wisdom. "I wish
there was another turn-born in Marrowdell."

~So do we all.~ But there was a hint of a smile behind
the stern mask. ~Don't doubt yourself, Sweetling. You've
come to me with your questions. Turn-born here should do
the same.~

Encouraged, Jenn pulled out her crumpled list. "If you've
time," she said shyly, "I've more."

In the stable, Davi tested the straps on the cart, throwing his
weight into the pull. The wood creaked in reponse.

The big smith hadn't protested leaving in the morning, or
packing Marrowdell's few acquisitions now, instead of then.

No longer smiling and all too quiet, he'd joined their preparations with a fierce will. "I'll be in the loft," Bannan said, coming around from the other side. Devins and Tadd had volunteered as well. He put his hand on the hilt of his sword. "I won't sleep."

The smith shook his head. "Get your rest. We'll need you tomorrow." He tossed a bedroll into the space in the cart left for Frann and Lorra. "Ancestors Witness, anyone tries to steal this takes me too."

Bannan gave a grim nod.

Worry clouded everything. Gallie, Loee, and Zehr were now in the room across from Frann's. To everyone's surprise, Lorra had merely nodded when told of the dawn departure.

To no one's, she'd banished the healer and his apprentice, and ordered meals brought to the room.

Perrkin and the other Marrowdell mounts nickered a welcome as Hettie entered the stable, laden with a tray of covered dishes. "I've brought supper," she announced briskly. "Where would you like it?"

Bannan patted the top of his crate. He'd had no chance to open it, but there'd been room after all, not that the reason was good. They'd tried their best these hours past, but trade was trade. Though sympathetic, no one in Endshere was ready to make a quick deal to Marrowdell's benefit, especially without Frann or Lorra involved. They'd leave their remaining goods for trade with Allin, who'd do what he could with them through the rest of the fair. As he'd warned, the cart would return home empty, but no one argued otherwise.

Anything, to get Frann into Covie's care.

"Any change?" Davi asked, taking his bowl.

Hettie nodded. "She's awake at last. Won't eat, but Gallie said Frann drank some sweet tea." She fretted at the ends of her shawl. "Ancestors Bothersome and Bound. Someone needs say it."

Bannan gave her his full attention. "What?"

"Something's not right. When she first woke up, Frann was furious with Lorra for changing her room without permission." The young woman's eyes were round and anxious. "How can she not know where she is?"

"Ancestors Blessed," Davi said, warm and hearty. "Frann's confused, that's all. She must have bumped her head. Like Tadd, that time on the ice. Right, Bannan?"

He'd looked for such an injury and hadn't found one, but what they needed to hear wasn't more reason to worry. "I've seen it before," the truthseer agreed, choosing not to elaborate. Blows to the head weren't always fatal, but few soldiers who survived them were the same afterward. "We're doing the right thing, taking Frann home."

He wasn't sorry, seeing the relief in their faces.

Hettie left soon after, needing rest herself. Once they'd finished their meal, Bannan went to return the tray to the inn. He owed Great Gran her story and tonight would be farewells, to Allin and the Anans.

Stepping from the stable, warmed by horses, into the night air, he found himself in winter. Stars twinkled like specks of ice in the black sky and the ground was hard, the grass crunching beneath his boots. Smoke wreathed rooftops; his breath fogged around his head.

The truthseer walked faster, trying not to shiver. If this was but winter's start in the north, best he study how the villagers dressed for this weather. Vorkoun and the marches rarely stayed below freezing for long and the only snow to last was on the peaks.

It'd be different here.

Marrowdell's folk made ready to leave before dawn the next morning. The cold reddened cheeks and noses, biting at fingers bared for work. The horses might have been on fire, the way steam rose from their backs and puffed with each snorted breath. Battle stamped, jingling his harness rings, impatient to be away. To head for home.

In complete agreement, Bannan warmed his hands under Perrkin's saddle blanket as long as he could, then gave the aged gelding a cheery pat. Home it was. When had he last felt such anticipation at the word? Then again, he'd never had someone, not just some place, waiting.

"There you are," Palma said, ducking under Perrkin's head. Apparently the morning wasn't cold enough, in her estimation, to require more than a lacy shawl around her shoulders. She smiled and pressed one of the small packages from the basket over her arm into Bannan's hands. "Something for the trip."

A hot and fragrant something. "My thanks," he said most sincerely.

"Please give my thanks to Master Jupp, would you?" Palma shook her head, black curls bouncing. "I'd hoped to send some of my manuscript back with you, but it's not ready."

"You've the winter to work on it, then."

Her smile was replaced by a small, worried frown. "Winter's harsh on our elders. Bannan, after what's happened to Frann Nall, I worry about Master Jupp, at his greater age, living in Marrowdell. We'd make him welcome here. Please tell him so." Then—innocent of what she said, because hadn't she forgotten too?—she added, "Marrowdell has nothing we can't offer here, and better."

Which wasn't true. It had magic. It had dragons, and house toads, and a silver road flowing between living hills that marked doorways to another world. It had Jenn Nalynn.

Heart's Blood, without the moth, he'd have forgotten too. He'd have urged Frann to stay here, would have headed south after Lila, would have lost . . .

Everything.

Warmth on his neck, ice in his heart, Bannan thanked his Ancestors once more. To Palma, he bowed. "I will tell him of your generous offer. However, I suspect," he smiled at her, "he'll be more interested in reading your manuscript."

She blushed but, given the newly determined glint in her eye, Bannan knew the book would be finished and in Master Jupp's hands the moment winter eased again. Ancestors Hale and Hearty, the elderly gentleman best stay in good health or Palma would have his head.

A commotion broke out, horses shifting with alarmed whinnies, voices shouting: "Get away!" "Move!" "Heart's Blood! Bannan!!"

Only one thing could possibly cause such a stir.

Scourge.

Hastily returning his package to Palma, Bannan bolted for continuing shouts. He should have told the warhorse that plans had changed. If the idiot beast thought the villagers were somehow stealing what he'd been ordered to protect, there was no telling what he'd do.

A shout louder than the rest. "I'll have you made into sausage!!"

Lorra? Worse and worse.

He dodged Hettie's mount and suddenly stopped, as stunned as the rest surrounding the cart.

Frann lay amid a wealth of blankets, Scourge's massive slobbery head in her lap, while Lorra, swearing like a soldier, flailed at the rest of him with her hat. Frann appeared unconscious, and the great beast?

Was humming.

The sound was deep, running along the nerves. The hair on Bannan's neck stood on end and, though he'd never heard it before, he knew it for what it was.

A warning.

Amazed Scourge had tolerated her this much, Bannan grabbed Lorra around the waist and carried her bodily out of range of the warhorse's back hooves, earning a few curses and swats of the hat in the process. Ignoring those, he handed Davi his mother and turned back to the cart.

In Marrowdell, he could ask the bloody beast to explain himself. Here, unsure how much Scourge even remembered of himself, he supposed he'd have to treat him as a horse.

A very large and disturbed horse, who'd somehow found it necessary to climb half into a loaded cart to be close to a sick woman.

It wasn't, Bannan thought, sorely puzzled, the sort of thing Scourge did. Eat someone or something helpless, yes.

He went to the front of the cart and climbed onto the driver's seat, hands open. To his relief, Frann seemed in no immediate danger, other than being afflicted by hair and drool. Scourge had placed his front hooves to either side of her; though it looked as if he'd rested his heavy head on her chest, it was held slightly above her. Muscles strained along the beast's shoulders and neck. Sweat steamed.

Dripping on poor Frann.

"Idiot Beast," Bannan said firmly. "Get off!"

Red-rimmed eyes glared. Scourge flattened his ears and his lips rippled over fangs.

Humming, as he had at Lorra.

Heart's Blood. Could it be? The truthseer sank to the wooden bench, holding up a hand to ask patience from those watching. After all their years together, something new.

For some reason—making sense only within that narrow skull—was Scourge protecting Frann from the rest of them?

Ancestors Compassionate and Caring. He'd have smiled, if it wasn't for the real danger posed by those great hooves and fangs. His tone free of any challenge, Bannan tried again. "No one's harmed Frann. We're taking her home, where she belongs, so Covie can look after her. Or we will," he corrected, "once you get off, you great lump."

An ear flickered, then nostrils flared, showing red. Unconvinced, that meant.

Growing desperate, Bannan circled his fingers over his heart. "Hearts of my Ancestors, I swear we mean her no harm. We need you to guard her on the road home. There could be," with all the sincere innocence he could muster, "another bear. Or bandits."

He hadn't realized how intimidating the hum had been till it stopped.

Lips closed. Rage left the eyes. Neck curved in a noble arch, Scourge, Protector of the Helpless, stepped off the cart.

Lorra Treff smacked him across the rump with the remains of her hat. She climbed in with Frann and glared at Bannan, still on the driver's seat. "Well?"

"Ready to go," he assured her, jumping down to let Davi take his place.

As Bannan mounted Perrkin and reclaimed his package from Palma, everyone bound for Marrowdell falling into their traveling order around the cart, Scourge pranced ahead, unaffected by hats or mutters about sausage stuffing. Soon enough, he'd melt into the forest alongside the road.

Bannan hoped.

The question of why the great beast had defended Frann would have to wait for Marrowdell, where he'd once more have a voice.

Scourge explain himself?

Bannan settled into the saddle, appreciating the gelding's easy gait, and chuckled.

He'd not bet on it.

If the lack of towel on the Emms' door handle wasn't clue enough, the marvelous smell of rich hot pudding Jenn inhaled when she stepped into the kitchen prepared her for Peggs being there and waiting, lanterns lit.

If not for her sister's pounce and the tight hug that followed. "Sorry I'm late—" Jenn squeaked with what breath she had left, her arms around her sister in an equally fervent embrace.

For hadn't she left the world and returned again?

And missed supper.

"I'm fine, Dear Heart," Jenn said with quick remorse, feeling Peggs tremble. "Wisp stayed with me and Mistress Sand did come. She answered so many of my questions—" though not all, and few to any comfort. "You know how I am once distracted," she finished disarmingly.

Another close-to-painful squeeze, then Peggs pushed her away, keeping a grip on her shoulders. She studied Jenn's face, her eyes huge and dark. "Ancestors Tried and Troubled. Distracted in your meadow's one thing. You were in the Verge!" A hard shake. "Late? I've been terrified. I'd have come after you if I'd known how!"

"You mustn't think that! Where I went, you can never follow." Jenn couldn't help the harshness of her voice. It was more than the truth. "I have to know you won't try. Ever. Promise me." She waited for her sister, now grim-faced, to nod before going on more calmly, "You mustn't fear for me there, Peggs. Not like this. The other world is strange and beautiful—I wish I had your skill with a brush, but we don't have the colors, not here. As I am strange, now, and no longer just your sister." She cupped Peggs' face in her hands, rising on tiptoe to press a quick kiss on her nose. "But I'll always be your sister."

"Will you always come home?"

Words like the tolling of a bell. "If you cook me supper,"

Jenn countered, making it light. She sniffed and pretended to follow her nose to the covered pudding. "Especially my favorites."

"Dearest Heart." Her sister shook her head, not quite smiling, then did. "What isn't your favorite?"

Jenn made a face. "Liver. Are you ready to hear what Mistress Sand had to say?" She set about making tea for them both, the familiar movements easing her heart when what she had to say, what she now knew, did anything but.

Peggs sat at the Emms' table, her eyes bright with curiosity and more than a little dread. "Not in the least. Don't let that stop you," she added, determined. "I want to know."

Oh, she'd guessed that. Jenn took a deep breath and managed to smile over her shoulder. "I'll start with the mask."

Explaining about the mask took them to a second cup of tea, as Jenn had to talk around mouthfuls of delicious and steamy pudding. Peggs poured for them both, her forehead creased in thought. "I've not seen such a light," she confirmed. "Could you make your own mask, here?"

"I've no idea how. They're magic of some kind." Jenn wrapped her hands around her cup. "Let's hope Mistress Sand is able to make me one, or I won't be visiting anyone else."

"Unless you stay your woman-self," Peggs pointed out, ever quick to the point. Then laughed. "Listen to me. Talking about magic and your Verge as if I know."

"It's new to me too." Jenn toyed with her next spoonful.

"Dearest Heart." Her sister sat again, and reached to touch her hand. "You learned something more troubling than turn-born masks and etiquette. What is it?"

They'd made a promise to one another, not to keep secret what was important, and this was. Jenn put down her spoon and fished the crumpled ball that was her list from her pocket, pressing it flat on the table. She rested her fingers on the paper. Fingers of skin and whatever strangeness lay beneath.

"Mistress Sand said there was no knowing about me, because all other turn-born are terst and—and different." Jenn's cheeks warmed. "She told me how it is for them." The rest stuck in her throat, as if the words couldn't decide the proper order.

"'It—?'" Peggs echoed. Enlightenment dawned on her lovely face and she blushed, a little, too. "Well?" She coughed and went on firmly. "How is 'it?'"

Like eating or breathing or dashing to the privy or anything else of flesh and blood, instead of glass and light.

"A memory, made real." Jenn turned her hand palm up. Life creased and callused the skin. Faint scars marked her latest misadventures with paring knife and turnip. A woman's hand, like any other's in this world, with its own history. What Mistress Sand had told her? Words could be scars, too, and these she doubted would ever fade. "'Memory, for a turn-born, is its own expectation.' Magic, Peggs." Saying it aloud, to her sister, eased something tight inside and she looked up, grateful. "I remember what I was, before. How I felt. What I felt. I expect to feel and do just as before." She picked up her tea and took a deliberate swallow. "So I still can."

"'Still can?'" Peggs went ghastly white. "What do you mean?" She snatched Jenn's hands, pulled her around so they faced one another, knees almost touching. "That you could—you might forget?"

"Only if I let myself," Jenn said simply, though it wasn't simple at all and terrifying to consider.

Mistress Sand had been clear on that point. The turn-born who let themselves forget they were once flesh inside as well as out soon forgot all else. She'd shrugged as if it was of no consequence, and perhaps it wasn't. Those who forgot made no more expectations. Ultimately, they vanished . . .

. . . as if forgotten themselves.

"I won't," she vowed, ever so glad of Peggs' warm grip, of the concern writ in those expressive eyes and mouth, of being with someone who couldn't forget to breathe. "This is what I am and intend to stay. Mistress Sand said so long as I think of myself as a woman—" Jenn squeezed her sister's fingers. "—I'll be one. Besides," she managed to lighten her tone, "I'm to be an aunt."

Peggs had that look, the one where she was thinking things all the way through. Jenn waited.

Finally, her sister let out a long breath. "Ancestors Blessed and Beloved, you'll be a wonderful aunt." She added serenely, "But not a mother."

The first question on her list. Mistress Sand had been startled; Wisp, of course, hadn't cared.

Hearing the answer—though hadn't she known as soon as she'd learned she was no longer flesh but its memory?—Jenn had been numb. Numb then. Numb now. She supposed she might be upset eventually, but what hit hardest and first was the reminder of what she was now. If she was honest, she'd had no desire for a baby of her own, being too busy learning to be an adult.

Until denied.

Aunt Sybb had written, in her latest and wonderful letter, that there was no one truly childless, who had family and friends, and no one ever loveless, who loved those around them. While she couldn't have known—or could she?—Jenn had taken comfort in those words. Because she did love those around her, with all her heart.

Jenn looked at Peggs. "'But not a mother.'"

"Well enough," her sister nodded. She let go of Jenn's hands to give her knees a quick little pat. "Ancestors Witness. I suppose you can't stop your moon potion, though it'd be nice, wouldn't it?"

Jenn felt her mouth fall open and closed it, before saying with great care, "Pardon?"

"If you must remember yourself as you are," her astonishing sister said, quite as if they discussed the cooking of turnips, "it stands to reason you'll bleed at your moontime if you don't. Take it, that is. Unless you could forget just that bit?" She sounded hopeful.

Peggs had started her on the potion this past fall, with a more complete explanation of its use than whispers or Hettie—whose dislike of its taste had provided ample demonstration of its effectiveness—had hitherto provided. Taken diligently, moon potion not only prevented unsought births but reduced or even eliminated a woman's moontimes—a boon particularly in winter, when the cold discouraged bathing.

"I wouldn't know how," Jenn responded. Even if she did, convenience hardly seemed worth the risk of forgetting. She grinned. "Besides, you'd be jealous."

Her sister laughed. "I would indeed." A keen look. "Feel better?"

"I do," Jenn said and did, much to her surprise. She picked up her list. "I didn't get to ask about the other turn-born—what their lives are like in the Verge."

"Maybe you'll see for yourself, once you have your mask," Peggs said, clearly having decided the Verge, despite its strangeness, could be approached as any other well planned social foray. Sure enough, "Did Mistress Sand enjoy the honey?" When Jenn nodded, her sister beamed. "I'll make you a basket next time. With pie."

She wasn't wrong. Peggs' pie could melt a heart, let alone improve a disposition, and she'd not send one unless confident her dish would return safely.

Magic of its own.

"Pie it is." Jenn tucked away her list, the better to hug what surely must be the best sister anyone could have.

And to leave the matter of certain other questions, and their answers, for the return of Bannan Larmensu.

After gaining a promise to be informed when her sister again left this world, and another promise to return in timely fashion, Peggs left, satisfied at last. The Emms' house toad hopped out from beneath the cookstove, warm from Jenn's supper, and settled on her feet.

"I do want to go back," she confessed. "I'll be very careful."

~And not late again.~

Good advice, from an honorable source. Jenn chuckled. "I agree." At least until she knew Peggs wouldn't worry. Or, she thought pragmatically, had the new baby to fuss over instead of her sister. "Being on time, though. It's not going to be easy." Sitting in the Emms' very nice, ordinary kitchen, filled with sights and smells—and chores—she'd known all her life, all Jenn could think of was how wonderful it had been to be somewhere new. Wisp's blue home, the weeping crystals, and even the narrow rock crevice were the most exciting things she'd seen since, well, since she'd last been in the Verge. "There's so much there!"

~Did you see any of us, elder sister?~

She bent over to meet its unblinking regard. "No. Should I have?"

The house toad deflated slightly. ~Perhaps not. Turn-born, if you forgive my saying—~ She had to nod before it would continue. ~—are best avoided. But we can tell that you, elder sister, are not the same.~ This last added in haste and with such sincerity Jenn could hardly take offense.

Though she was, now, curious. Curious was better than longing for another world, and ever so much nicer than worry over being more memory than real. Easing her toes from under the toad, she slipped from the chair to sit on the floor in front of him. Or her. With toads, "it" did seem the safer pronoun. "How so?" She'd not thought to ask the toads, who were full of caution and cared most about Marrowdell, any of her questions.

It blinked at this. ~You are different, elder sister.~

Jenn made sure she was comfortable. This could, she suspected, take a while. "Because I'm from Marrowdell or because of what—of what fills me."

It held up its chin, gaining an authoritative demeanor belied only by the long toe it stuck into its mouth. ~Yes. You are different.~

Never give a toad options. She sighed as quietly as she could. At least "different" seemed a good thing. To a toad. "The next time I cross, would you like me to find other house toads?"

Out popped the toe. The toad puffed into a quivering wart-covered ball, eyes closed and half-buried in flesh. It looked, Jenn decided after a moment, enraptured.

Or seriously ill.

No, this must be joy. How delightful! Now she could travel the Verge on a mission to please someone else, which was both virtuous and kind and felt better for many reasons than being simply curious. "Then I will," Jenn Nalynn promised with all her great heart.

Forgetting all about magic, just when she shouldn't.

~Did it go well?~ From a wall.

~Are we safe now?~ From above and below. ~Is she gone?~ Dragons pestered and dragons plagued and Wisp came close to swatting the nearest on his way home again.

A home the girl had improved, however unwittingly. At the thought, he grew unusually magnanimous. ~I was in charge, you fools. Of course all went well.~

The pause that followed was too dubious for his liking.

But it wasn't a pause. Wings no longer troubled the air. The younglings had scattered.

Heeding that warning, Wisp crouched and sprang.

Only to find himself pinned within claws, well above the rock crevasse and home.

A gaudy emerald face, bearded and fanged, dipped to aim a great eye at him. Shaped like a dragon, his captor, yet not.

Sei.

Wisp didn't struggle, though his wings were painfully crimped and, yes, his better leg was bent nigh to breaking. It would do no good, other than possibly annoy this most powerful of beings; while the notion had its charm, he'd only just fulfilled his penance from the last time he'd annoyed them.

He satisfied himself with a snarl of protest.

~You cannot stay here.~ A voice to shake bone. ~You must return to her world.~

He'd heard those very words the day Jenn Nalynn had wished him into a man, a transformation the sei had finished before sending him back to live as one. Wisp sincerely hoped the sei wasn't planning to do that again. Once was enough.

Or was this something else? A danger?

~What's wrong? Is there a threat?~ Now he did try to free himself, the effort as much use as a nyphrit's wriggling within a toad's stomach. ~If you want me to return to protect her—~ the sei would know who he meant, beyond doubt ~—let me go!~

Wings that had beat to hold them in the air stilled, as if the sei could no longer be bothered. Not falling from the sky made Wisp unsettled. Being unsettled made him angrier. ~Let me—!~

~You must return to her world.~ As oblivious to others as ever. Sei were supposed to keep busy contemplating things beyond the ken of dragons, vast and imponderable things of interest to nothing else. All were safer that way.

This one, he greatly feared, had developed a taste for interfering. ~Why?~ he dared demand.

~You cannot stay here. You must return to her world.~ The sei's head lifted away.

Wisp readied himself to bite whatever sei-flesh he could reach.

Just in time, for a bite might have been unwise, the being spoke again. ~A storm rides the road.~

As the dragon tried in vain to make sense of that, the claws holding him opened and he dropped.

It had happened before, the sei's lack of care leaving him broken on the rocks.

But he was no longer that Wisp.

With a snap and roar, he opened his abused wings. Their first powerful beat saved him from the rocks. Their second, even stronger, swept him around and away.

The third sent him soaring toward his crossing to Marrowdell.

And Jenn Nalynn.

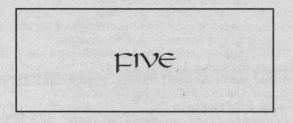

# FIVE

*T*HE ROAD INTO Marrowdell was shaped by the river leaving the valley. It twisted past the waterfall in the valley's narrow mouth and bent into the forest to keep secret the trout pool. Where the river calmed, between field and forest, the road too grew straight and level. Shortly before the river spread through reeds and passed the mill, the road passed through the gate into the village itself.

Tomorrow, near to supper, Jenn planned to be waiting on that gate. And the day after, if necessary, since they could be away longer. If she couldn't sit still—or if the wind turned bitter, as was happening more and more of late—she might wander up to where a little path led to the trout pool, and wait there. Wouldn't Bannan be pleased to see her where they'd first met?

Not, she told herself hastily, exactly where. Then, she'd been in the river, which she wouldn't be now, with it nigh to freezing. Then, she'd been trying to save Wisp—who she'd wished into a man named Wyll and was about to be drowned—and if Bannan hadn't arrived on his great horse, like a hero from a story?

Well, then, there wouldn't be a now, would there, with Wisp again a dragon, herself a turn-born, and Bannan holding her heart. When it came to it, Jenn thought soberly, then had been a moment so fraught with chance and change, the wonder was it hadn't slipped away, lost.

She put more effort into scrubbing. Weren't thens and nows like the Northward Road itself? It had brought the exiles here from Avyo. There was no going back.

Not that any of them would. Marrowdell was home; now, to her joy, to Bannan Larmensu as well. There were things to be said and understood between them; serious as those were, they couldn't diminish her happiness.

She wouldn't let them.

Jenn wrung Zehr's undershirt and put it in her basket, pushing steam-dampened hair from her forehead with the back of one hand. She'd insisted the Emms leave their laundry, having learned this summer the best way to wait was useful work, much to her aunt's relief. By this time tomorrow, the house would be tidy, dishes done and food waiting, with a pie or two if Peggs had them to spare.

And she'd be at the gate, watching for everyone, of course, but surely she was allowed to be especially pleased to see one tall and handsome farmer.

Ancestors Particular and Prepared. What to wear?

Jenn frowned thoughtfully as she stirred the bubbling pot of laundry. She hadn't cared before becoming adult and falling in love, except for shoes whenever Aunt Sybb would expect them and not to borrow Peggs' last clean pair of simples unless it was a dire emergency because her sister would find out and demand them back at the least opportune moment.

These days, she made sure to have her own clean clothes, and to mend any holes promptly. If ribbons found their way into her hair, said hair more often brushed than before, well, no one commented. Except her father, who would smile.

Bannan, she'd noticed, also dressed with extra care when he came to visit, something considerably easier for him to do, having brought from Vorkoun such fine and modern fashions as leather pants and high boots.

As for his undergarments? Dimples appeared in her cheeks. Oh, she wasn't about to share the clever details of those with Peggs.

What to wear to welcome Bannan home was, alas, up to the weather. Much colder, and she'd be such a round bundle of sensible wrappings, her love wouldn't be able to tell her from Anten Ropp. Who was, truth be told, a bit round himself.

Jenn's lips curved in a smile. Her truthseer would know her on sight. He always had. He always would.

If she wore a mask?

Her smile faded. Jenn moved the laundry pot to one side, putting the filled kettle in its place, and fished socks from the hot water. Bannan had seen the truth about Mistress Sand and the other tinkers long before she had. A mere mask couldn't fool him.

What it could do was ease her travels through the Verge. Mistress Sand hadn't promised. She'd been evasive—doubtful, in fact, her fellows would agree, being none too sure about Jenn wandering where she would—but had admitted there was a maskmaker among the terst who might be convinced.

If so, Wisp would be told and arrangements—whatever those might be—made.

Jenn took the final head-high basket of clothes into the front half of the house, pleased with her cleverness. Ropes crisscrossed the room, waiting and ready. There'd been plenty up in the loft and why go out in the cold, with this warm and empty space?

She hummed as she pinned, careful to put nothing where it could drip on the Emms' bed, with its wolfskin cover. Any movable furniture she'd pushed to the walls. The heatstove glowed a cheery red, having been given a little extra charcoal; Jenn hung Zehr's thick sweater above that.

Pinning the last of Loee's tiny clothes, she turned to find herself trapped. Shirts and dresses draped their arms in her way, while linens made castle walls.

Jenn ducked under and slid between, making a game of it. The laundry won each time it smacked her bare skin and had an advantage, since she wore naught but a shift, her other clothes being among those trying to catch her.

Back and forth, she wove through the room, getting more and more damp. Once at the heatstove, she dropped cross-legged to the rug to dry off. "Loee would love this," she assured the house toad. "What do you think?"

The house toad gave her a look that could only be described as disgusted, before hopping between dripping pants to the dry refuge of the kitchen.

Well, yes, it was messy, and she'd best mop a puddle or two—or three—but by morning, she thought with pride, all would be dry and ready. Practice with the iron would do her good, though she'd best start with her own things, in case of another accident.

That should keep her—

A burst of cold air. "Heart's Blood!"

Zehr? They were home! Jenn jumped to her feet, immediately tangled in a pair of leggings and then a pillowcase, and wouldn't it have to happen that an entire ropeful came down as she struggled?

She freed herself in time to pull the sweater from the stove before it was more than steaming—she hoped—then stood mute and guilty in the midst of what was not, in any way, a tidy homecoming.

Gallie came up beside her husband in the doorway to the kitchen, Loee in her arms. All three looked tired, cold, and shocked. "I'll put on the kettle," Jenn offered weakly. "Leave this to—"

Breezes flew and breezes chuckled, warm little breezes she knew, oh so well. Faster than an apology, the laundry was plucked from its pins, spun around and dried, then folded neatly, and pressed, on the bed. The furnishings she'd carelessly moved aside were nudged gently to their rightful places, with even the ropes and pegs whisked from sight.

As a finale, a little breeze tickled Loee's hair and she giggled, reaching out with both hands. Gallie smiled and even Zehr chuckled.

Which was all wonderful and remarkably good timing on her dragon's part, but timing was the question.

Uneasy, Jenn crossed her arms over her still-damp shift. "I didn't expect you until tomorrow."

Zehr looked as if he might explain, then sighed. "Care for them, Jenn, please. I must see to the horses." He kissed

Gallie on the cheek as he left, pulling up his hood before going out the door.

Gallie sagged with relief when Jenn took the baby. "Go and rest," she urged. "I'll take care of her."

"Dear Heart." About to protest, Gallie sighed. "Thank you." She made her way to the table and sat, slowly removing her scarf and mitts.

First things, first. Jenn laid the baby in her crib, stripping off her winter wrappings. A change came next, then a newly washed and dry blanket. Before she was finished, Loee's thumb had found its way into her mouth and her eyes drifted closed.

Grabbing a nightdress to pull over her shift, Jenn went to the kitchen. Without a word, she helped Gallie shed her heavy winter cloak, then put a blanket around the woman's shoulders. Tea, strong and sweet came next. Gallie's hands curled around the mug and she gave a grateful nod, too weary to take a drink.

What else would Peggs do?

Jenn pulled out the big frying pan and set it on the cookstove to heat. In went butter, then thick slices of potato and sausage. By the time the door opened again, letting in the cold and Zehr, she'd cut bread and cheese, and put plates on the table. He took the mug she passed him before bothering to lose his coat or boots, murmuring, "Ancestors Blessed."

What had happened? Where was Bannan? Jenn swallowed her questions. "Come and eat," she said, in her sister's easy tone, the one that promised all would be well if everyone was well fed. After a day of winter travel, coming late like this?

It certainly wouldn't hurt.

There wasn't a bone in his body that wouldn't ache tomorrow, after that ride, but Perrkin came first. They'd pushed the horses, as much as themselves, and not only to beat the dark. There'd been a chill to the wind chasing them along the road, sapping the strength of the healthy, let along the frail.

"Give the old boy a whiff of this." Anten Ropp passed

Bannan a bucket of steaming mash. Sure enough, though half asleep from the brushing and warmth of the barn, the gelding eagerly plunged his head into the offering. "The cows had their share." The village cattle, used to Perrkin and the Uhthoffs' riding horses as winter stablemates, hadn't budged from their doze. Wainn's old pony, however, had firm opinions about treats and who deserved them. He'd been appeased with his own portion.

Anten continued, "We'll rub his legs and keep an eye on them all." The dairy farmer's "we" included Cheffy and Alyssa, already busy beneath the contented horse.

"I'm Beholden—"

"Ancestors Worn and Wearied, Bannan. You look worse than the beasts. Go." More gently. "You've help, here. Take it, my friend. You're home, now."

Unable to argue, Bannan gave a grateful nod and left Perrkin to be properly spoiled. The horse's tack he left in Alyssa's capable hands, but he shouldered the saddlebags, heavy with his now-frivolous purchases.

Once outside the barn, he whistled.

Nothing. Where was the bloody beast?

They'd arrived after the turn and sunset, relying on Davi's team at the last to find the road within the shadows under the old trees. When they'd come through the gate, the other horses had been too spent to do more than nicker in anticipation. For home it was. The village had appeared before them like a dream, welcoming lights in windows, fragrant smoke rising from chimneys.

Including the Emms', where Jenn Nalynn would be helping Gallie and Zehr. Their early return might have taken the rest of the villagers by surprise, but they'd quickly come forth to welcome the travelers home.

He'd lost sight of Scourge on the Northward Road before the junction to Marrowdell, not that he'd seen much of him at all. He hadn't worried. After all, a march like today's would barely touch the reserves of the mighty beast.

Bannan whistled again. With a last longing look toward the Emms' home, he turned and headed for the Treffs'. Scourge should have bolted for the Verge, but somehow, the truthseer couldn't believe it.

Battle and Brawl had been taken to their well-deserved

stabling; the still-loaded cart sat outside the house. His crate might as well wait there; he'd need the cart and team to get it home, but it wasn't a good sign that the precious mail and what other goods had come from Endshere were being neglected.

Wainn was sitting on the porch step as Bannan approached, and stood in greeting. "You came back." With undisguised relief.

"I did." The truthseer resisted the urge to touch the moth's writing on his neck. "How's Frann?"

A hot, fetid breeze slipped across his cheek, forming words in his ear. "I should be with her. They have no right to deny me!"

Not in the Verge. Nor willing to show himself. Ancestors Blessed, at least the beast hadn't tried to break into the house.

Yet.

"Frann is in bed," Wainn replied calmly. So Scourge hadn't shared his protest. "Cynd is heating a brick for her feet. Covie is brewing something that smells awful. Davi is pacing."

Bannan glanced at the closed door. Curtains covered the windows. He couldn't, now that he paid attention, hear a thing. "Lorra?"

The other shrugged. "Davi wants her in bed, with a warm brick for her feet. Covie too. But she won't. She made him move her chair into Frann's room and she sits there. Wen will stay with her. She says it's the only way her mother can help her friend, but I don't see how." With honest puzzlement, "Could you rest if Lorra stared at you?"

"She's keeping Frann company," Bannan explained, though he suspected—had Lorra not been as exhausted as the rest—she'd have preferred to hover over Covie to argue about ingredients.

The breeze snapped, "I should be in there!"

Idiot beast. "Your pardon, Wainn," Bannan said, more curtly than he'd intended, but he was, admittedly, looking forward to bed himself and this business with Scourge had worn thin back in Endshere. He should have guessed it would worsen once the beast could again speak. "I've things to settle before my own rest."

"Rest well. It's good you found your way back, Bannan," Wainn said. "Very good. Wen feared you'd be lost."

The truthseer paused. "Tell her I almost was. And that Marrowdell saved me."

Why and how being the questions he couldn't answer.

Home was past the Treffs' barn, down the road through the commons and across the river, a journey now as safe as any to make at night. Bannan went the other way, around the house to the hedge that marked the river's bank, and there he waited.

It wasn't long before a patch of shadow shifted closer. "I should be in there."

From imperious demand to what sounded more like desperation. "You wouldn't fit through the doors," Bannan said finally, attempting reason despite a growing belief this was something else entirely. "What is this about, Scourge? Why do you want to be with Frann?" To the best of his knowledge, the woman had ignored the kruar, being familiar with those unfriendly beasts the tinkers brought into Marrowdell.

A heavy breath left plumes in the chill night air and a hoof almost the width of Brawl's, with a sharper edge, scored the frozen ground. "I stayed by my first truthseer. I took his final breath and carried it into battle. I killed and, as my enemy died, I gave that breath in my truthseer's honor. This," another line in the ground, "I would do for Frann, who has lived a brave life within the edge."

"Your—you mean my father's uncle. Kimm Larmensu." Bannan stared into the dark, imagining more than seeing twin red glows. "He died of old age, peacefully in his bed." After which the warhorse had refused all riders but the next Larmensu truthseer, Bannan's father.

When a mudslide had roared down, engulfing not only trees and fields, but stone walls and slate roofs and lives, wiping the Marerrym estate, his mother's legacy, from the earth? Thirty-one had been lost that day, including his mother and father, Ancestors Dear and Departed.

Scourge alone had survived. He'd made his own way home, cut and bruised and battered, to seek out his new rider, Bannan. To insist, truth be told, on that rider.

Ancestors Witness, he'd been so small. The struggle to ride the great beast had nigh killed him.

"Yes," the breeze almost gentle. "My truthseer died away from battle and would have lost all honor. It was my honor—" this with immense pride, "—to save his."

He'd never known Scourge to pause over those killed on patrols, other than to ensure what appeared dead, was. This? Kruar beliefs, Bannan supposed. Beliefs strong enough to continue to move the great beast beyond the edge. He dared asked what he hadn't, yet. "What else could you remember, away from Marrowdell?"

An uneasy silence. Then, more breath than breeze, an admission. "You. To stay with you. No one else in that world sees me as I am. Away from that truth, I forget."

Both of their futures had been saved by the moth. Bannan stepped close, lifting a hand to find that strong neck, and laid his forehead against Scourge's wide cheek. "Hearts of our Ancestors," he whispered, eyes shut and fervent. "We're Beholden above all else to be here, where we belong. However far we are apart, Keep Us Close."

Scourge bore the embrace for an unusually long moment, then sidled away. "We are here," the breeze told Bannan, "and I am myself. Leave me to my duty." The slightest of rumbles from that massive chest. "I will stay by Frann."

"Outside."

Loud, now the rumble, but Scourge didn't argue.

Ancestors Frazzled and Fraught, he was tired. Cold. That too. Probably hungry, if he thought about it. Enough of this. "I think you're wasting your time," Bannan said as cheerfully as he could. "We made it back and Frann's comfortable. Covie's an excellent healer. I'll bet she has Frann up and playing her new flute in no time."

He waited for a reply.

And heard only the winter wind.

They'd explained, Gallie and Zehr, though Gallie had spoken most, Zehr having begun to nod before a second cuppa. The rush home had been because Frann had taken ill, or tripped on a rug, or eaten bad meat, though Gallie had quite liked the mutton at the inn and certainly no one truly blamed Palma's cooking or kitchen. Except Lorra, but she did have a temper.

And was afraid for her friend. The same fear filled the eyes meeting Jenn's, despite the effort Gallie made to be cheerful and mention, several times, how glad they were to be home where Covie could care for Frann and Frann could recover in the comfort of home.

So when Jenn saw them to bed soon after, closing the door between main room and kitchen, she stood there a moment and tried not to be afraid herself. Which wouldn't help matters and could possibly—

"Dearest Heart—"

She moved, or he did, or the kitchen somehow shrunk to put them in each other's arms before the word finished leaving her beloved's lips, lips she found were chapped and cold and felt better than anything had ever felt against her own. And she would have been happy to stay in that kiss forever except that the kettle was hot and he shivered in her arms.

"Tea?" she asked brightly.

In answer, Bannan held tighter, burying his face in her neck. Jenn stayed where she was, though she was certain he'd feel better for a hot drink and doubtless a spot of supper, because something more was wrong.

And holding her helped.

It wasn't magic, she thought, but was, all the same.

Finally, he pulled back enough to look at her. "Tea," he agreed hoarsely.

For the second time, Jenn made tea and put the frying pan to work, but this time her every move was followed by loving eyes. Bannan's regard became such a distraction she came close to burning both sausages and eggs, and stuck out her tongue to dissuade him, but he seemed incapable of looking elsewhere, as though afraid she'd disappear.

Which she had, hadn't she? Jenn put the plate in front of him, planted a firm kiss on his lips, then sat on the other side of the table with her own mug. Unlike Gallie and Zehr, Bannan circled his fingers and said, "Hearts of our Ancestors, I am Beholden for this food for it was prepared with love—" There was, she saw with relief, a twinkle in his eye when he went on, "and the best I've ever eaten. I am

Beholden to be home again. Above all, I am Beholden to be with my beloved Jenn. However far we are apart, Keep Us Close."

"'Keep Us Close,'" Jenn echoed gently. "Eat," she ordered. "I know about poor Frann. You can tell me the rest afterward."

That earned her a look, but Bannan was clearly too hungry to resist. She sat and watched him with unexpected pride. She'd cared for Loee, then Gallie and Zehr. Now, she cared for Bannan. There was something to this feeding of people. Maybe she could cook for Peggs one day.

Jenn grinned. Her sister sit back and let someone else use her kitchen?

Bannan raised a questioning eyebrow.

"I was thinking about Peggs." Her grin widened. "Oh, I get to tell you the news! I'm to be an aunt. I'll be asking for your advice, being an uncle already."

"Congratulations." He smiled and looked pleased, but wasn't, she thought, not completely.

Which couldn't be about Peggs and Kydd, for she knew Bannan was very fond of both, but had to be about being an uncle.

Meaning Lila. "You've had a letter," she guessed. "Something's wrong in Vorkoun."

He put down his fork and sighed. "What's wrong is that there was no letter from Vorkoun, Dearest Heart. No letter or news; just an abundance of rumor. That Emon's missing in Channen. Detained by those who rule there, or come to foul play, or, Ancestors Lewd and Lost, maybe willingly, though I greatly doubt that. That there's trouble brewing between Mellynne and Rhoth over our treaty with Ansnor and the Eld." He laughed without humor. "To no surprise, the cost of the prince's train grows."

Places Jenn had once dreamed of seeing for herself, but as a child dreamed, she remembered with an inner twinge, glossy with adventure and wonders, heedless of different people or their needs. "Your sister must be worried. If you hadn't signed the bind, you could go to her," she said, wondering if he now had regrets.

"The bind?" A humorless smile. "A piece of paper older than you are. I don't deny there'd be risk, but they'd have to catch me first." The smile disappeared. "Trust I've the skills to reach Vorkoun undetected, Jenn, but to what end? There's nothing I could do there Lila couldn't do better — and she'd have my ears for taking the chance. No. I made my choice. This is where I belong." He reached across the table to take her hand in his. "With you."

Jenn lifted his hand to her lips, then let go. She searched his tired face, saw the worry drawn there, and realized what else troubled him. "What will your sister do?" she asked quietly.

"That depends on what's happened to Emon," Bannan Larmensu replied, the words slow and heavy. "Lila takes care of those she loves. She always has. Always will."

Somehow, Jenn was sure he didn't mean by making tea or feeding them.

Still, care was care and she found she approved, knowing this about Lila. "You'll stay the night," she told Bannan, who been through enough today without having to start a fire in a cold dark house and, most importantly, had come home, to her.

Bannan hadn't expected to be comfortable, the bed being far too short for his length and meant for one, not two. Nor had he expected to sleep, his mind awhirl and fretful and inclined to the worst.

Which was fine, since he wanted neither comfort nor sleep, not with the woman he loved tucked against him so her heart and his beat as one.

But the beat of Jenn's heart eased his from race to peace and, somewhere between desire's kiss and tender's touch, he fell fast asleep.

The cheery clatter of pots opened his eyes. Sunbeams trailed through the room, catching a corner of the map on the wall. Lila's gift it was, as much as his, since she'd commissioned a splendid new one when he'd asked her for any map at all.

The corner touched by light held Mellynne, Rhoth's neighbor to the west and south, and there it was — the strange weave of road, river, and canal that was Channen, the Naalish capital.

Lips, warm and soft, brushed his ear. "You've told me Emon's been there before," Jenn whispered, her arms going around him. "That he has friends. He's come back."

As he'd done. Filled with quiet joy, Bannan traced the line of her thigh where it crossed his. This wasn't the moment for worry. "Dearest Heart—"

"'Dearest Heart,'" she echoed, low and husky. "''Tis morning and we really—" a kiss at the edge of his jaw, "—must—" a nibble just under that sent a shiver down his spine and warmth rushing elsewhere, "—help Gallie."

"Must," Bannan agreed amicably, reaching a little farther. Jenn stifled her laugh against his neck and matters would have proceeded admirably . . .

Except that she sat straight up, staring at him, and the sunlight couldn't match the glow from within her glass skin, nor the fire that replaced her eyes.

"What's—" But he knew, didn't he? Bannan sat up too, despite the gooseflesh pimpling his skin, and touched the mark on his neck. "A moth gave me this, before I left Marrowdell."

"'Keep Us Close.'"

She was upset, he understood that. "Always. Jenn—"

"That's what it says." With a shimmer, barely seen, she became flesh once more, her dear face troubled. "Why would a moth write that in your skin, Bannan?"

To save me—the words stopped in his throat, for he had no idea why the moth, or Marrowdell, had acted, and to believe it was kindness was to mistake what ruled here. "To step beyond Marrowdell," he said instead, "—to go outside the edge—means to forget her magic. A few remember. Most do not. I wouldn't have, without this." He touched the mark again.

"'Forget her magic.'" Jenn stood and began to dress, seeming oblivious to the chill in the room. She shot him an unreadable look over her shoulder, her eyes purpled. "Me."

He'd worried how to tell her. He should, Bannan thought ruefully, have remembered who she was and her astonishing courage. "Yes. They—I—forgot your very existence.

Until I touched this," again to the mark, "and then I remembered. Everything. It was the worst moment of my life," he finished.

He could see only the side of her face, but did a smile round her cheek? "I must thank the moth, then."

"How did you read what it wrote? I didn't know you could."

Inside her shirtwaist, Jenn muttered, "I can't. It's not—" the words came clearer as her head came through, "—as if I can read what they write in their journals." She paused, her eyes meeting his. "But what's on your neck? That's clear to me."

He'd freeze if he sat like this a moment longer. Bannan got up and pulled on his clothes, cold as they were. "You've another heritage, besides Rhothan and turn-born," he suggested, shrugging on his shirt.

Jenn looked out the window. "Sei." Ice-cold, that word, and full of foreboding.

Bannan went to her, wrapping his arms around her waist to draw her against him. "It's not all you are."

"Is it not?" Jenn said, stiff in his embrace. "You were there. Is not sei what fills me now? Am I more than its tears?"

He tightened his grip and pressed his face into her golden hair. "Ancestors Blessed. I wish just once you could see yourself as I see you, Jenn Nalynn. As all of us see you. You wouldn't think such things."

She turned to face him. "What I think," Jenn told him, "is that we're late for—"

His lips found hers.

Late, they'd most certainly be.

She'd been the one worried about being late, and they were, by the sounds from below. A coo and giggle from Loee. Zehr, walking in his boots. Gallie's quiet question and his deeper answer.

Breakfast well underway, in all likelihood finished and tidied, while they lay abed. Bannan had drifted back to sleep in her arms, his face peaceful, and Jenn wouldn't move or disturb him.

Selfish, that was, as much or more than kind.

To feel his strong length against her, from toe to shoulder, was to find her toes and shoulder. The bristle of his regrowing beard, smooth one way, rough the other, discovered both fingertips and the soft inner surface of her wrist. The scent of him filled her nose and throat, giving her lungs, while his warmth drove the beats of her heart.

The magic of the edge was stranger than she could have imagined. Beyond its reach, others forgot her.

Within it, she could forget herself.

It didn't have to be so. The moth, or sei, had helped Bannan remember. Lying like this, with Bannan solid and real—yes, even his occasional snore and how her leg under his was numb and surely would be pins and needles soon—helped her be solid and real too.

For how long?

It didn't matter.

She'd asked Mistress Sand. "Do turn-born grow old?"

"We weather," that worthy had replied. "Like anything left outside for years. Slowly enough."

"How slowly?" she'd questioned, this being alarmingly vague. Jenn was aware there were sorts of wood that crumbled after a winter and others, for Zehr had taught her, that would stay unchanged for lifetimes after those who'd built with them were bones.

But the turn-born wouldn't say, or couldn't. Jenn wasn't terst, after all.

"We do grow weary," Mistress Sand had said next, to no question or perhaps all of them. "Weary of each other. Of the unending debates over this expectation or that or none. Weary of remembering what we were." She'd laughed then, and claimed Jenn should have no such difficulty, living as she did with family and others who were as real as could be and would keep her whole too.

Leading Jenn to wonder if this was why, more than Marrowdell's mill or beer, the turn-born came every harvest: to be with people who remembered them, so they would not forget.

Instead of that, which came needlessly near doubt of friendship and kindness, she'd asked, "Do turn-born die?"

Jenn rested her cheek on Bannan's chest, listening to the

ceaseless thud-thump of his heart and steady sigh of his breath. She tried to make her breaths and her heartbeats match, but they didn't, quite. She almost crossed her eyes watching how her breath moved like a playful breeze through the fine hairs near her nose and mouth, surely tickling.

They were late, after all.

There was a world with her, here in this small bed, a world as entrancing as any map could show or magic realm produce.

Turn-born, Mistress Sand had told her, did not die as other beings. Oh, they could take injury, while flesh, as readily as before. Heal from such harm, over time, or stay turn-born to avoid it. Until memory failed.

Die?

A turn-born was, she'd said bluntly, until a turn-born wasn't. Their passing left no bones to bury, though that wasn't terst custom, nor so much as a tidy pile of rock or sand or shattered glass to mark place and moment. Best, Mistress Sand had finished, to do as other turn-born and not dwell overmuch on the future.

So one day, Jenn thought as she lay with Bannan, a day she couldn't predict, she would be . . .

. . . then not.

What did matter was to prepare those who loved her for the eventuality, as best she could. Though she most certainly hoped it was an eventuality far removed from now . . .

"We could wait for lunch," Bannan murmured, eyes still closed, and rolled over to bring her close.

. . . for she quite liked now.

The breeze in Bannan's ear nipped like frost. "Tell me again why I agreed to . . . this."

The truthseer hid a grin as he adjusted the ox yoke around Scourge's neck. It hadn't been easy, coaxing the kruar from his vigil by the Treffs', but he'd a trick or two. "Cheese."

A red forked tongue slipped between lips that might have been those of a horse, but were not, collecting drool. The kruar hunted for himself; that didn't mean he spurned the occasional tasty bribe. Though "this," the man admitted, was pushing that limit.

But he'd no other way to hoist the heavy crate into the loft, not without spoiling his surprise for Jenn Nalynn. Marrowdell's inhabitants were as curious as they were helpful and nothing stayed secret.

Though today was different. Davi hadn't lingered after delivering Bannan's belongings. The rest of the village, including Jenn, was busy with an inventory of supplies. Sennic and Riss would ensure all knew what must be rationed at once.

And what they must do without, until the world thawed again.

At least his gifts had proved more useful than he'd thought. The candies could be crushed to add sweetness to winter baking, the spices and tea shared between every household. The lamp oil was added to the village store; with care, it could last till the days grew longer again. Wool from the gloves would mend socks and mittens.

Loee adored her hat with bunny ears and Hettie promised to pass her baby's booties on to Peggs', once outgrown.

The books brought murmurs of real pleasure. Wainn would "read" them, in case the paper was needed for tinder. Of that, they would have had sufficient for the winter, but the Treffs' fireplace roared, trying to warm Frann. No one argued with the need, though word was, unless Davi could move his forge stone into the house, other homes must make do with less.

Jenn's gift? Bannan smiled to himself. No need to share or worry about anything but surprising the love of his life. He'd do it here, in his bedroom, a room he hoped would become hers as well, forever. There'd be kisses, surely, and—

A hoof stamped impatiently and the truthseer took the hint, moving with dispatch to fasten the hook in the rope net around the crate. "Gently now!"

That caution earned him a baleful eyeroll, but Scourge stepped into the harness with all the care he could ask, lifting the load with ease. The pulley hoist Bannan had affixed to the roof beam creaked as it took the strain. "Hold there!" he commanded.

"More cheese."

"Ancestors Greedy and Gluttonous," Bannan muttered under his breath, knowing full well the sharp-eared beast would hear. Louder, "Not a crumb if you let it drop!"

Amazing, how smug that long face could look.

Wasting no more time on Scourge, Bannan dashed into his house. He jumped to pull himself through the opening into the loft, ignoring the ladder, unsurprised to find the house toad waiting. The creatures had a vested interest in anything that entered a building under their protection. "Off my pillow," he told it firmly. After a considering blink, it shifted to squat in the middle of his bed.

It'd have to do. Bannan hurried to the open window. The crate hung within reach, as planned. He took hold of the netting and pulled. The crate swung back and forth readily enough, but no matter how he strained and tugged, there was no tipping the awkward thing to fit it through the window.

Heart's Blood. Tir—or any villager—would have known better. Only one thing for it. Bannan leaned out the window. "Scourge! Hold it there!"

"More cheese," came the sly answer.

Easier to promise if the kruar would tolerate a cow on the farm, but no, Bannan had to trade with the Ropps. "All I have," he promised recklessly. "I'll be back."

He dropped to the main floor, found what he needed, and climbed back up. With a grimace of regret, he lifted the ax over his shoulder and took aim at the windowsill.

"What's this?" Wind rushed through the window, flapping Bannan's shirt and tossing his hair in his eyes. "Can it be?"

Flinging aside the ax, Bannan threw himself at the window. Ancestors Beset and Bewildered, why now? The dragon had the worst timing. So long as—

"It is! A cart cow!"

—too late.

With a squeal of outrage, Scourge lunged, tossing off the yoke and the crate plummeted toward the ground. Netting burned through Bannan's fingers as he made a futile grab. "Wisp!!" he cried.

The crate stopped, midair. An elegant nostril, traced by

steam, appeared nearby and gave a sniff, then vanished again. "Curious."

Scourge pawed the ground. "Come down!" the breeze snarled and snapped. "Come down so I can tear out your guts and feed them to nyphrit!!" He lifted his head and roared.

"Idiot Beast!!" Bannan shouted back. "Find your own cheese! As for you—" he stopped short, unable to glare at what he couldn't see. He looked deeper and thought he glimpsed the silver edge of a wing against the early morning sky. Good enough. "As for you," he said, glaring at the wing, "since you've cost me my help, you can take his place. I want that—carefully—put in here."

The crate jiggled.

"CAREFULLY!"

The crate spun slowly. "It's too big," Wisp informed him. "It won't fit."

Ancestors Tried and Put Upon. The truthseer collected himself. There was no ordering such a powerful being. "Then all is truly lost," he said and gave a theatrical sigh. Scourge, who knew him full well, snorted, but the crate paused. Bannan went on, "It was to be a surprise for Jenn Nalynn."

One he'd not seen himself, yet. Pinning his hopes on Palma's Great Gran—on an item brought here once before, which had seemed at the time a poignant coincidence, then stored in Endshere for a generation, he trusted somewhere dry, though who was to know?—might be the height of folly, but what choice had he? There'd been no more time to hunt a gift, nor coin for it, and it could be perfect.

Or not.

As for Lila? If there were answers in mail yet to be read, he'd no reason beyond his own impatience to hurry those who'd received them. There'd be no commerce outside Marrowdell once the snow began to fall and, as if to make his heart ache, a too-white cloud hung over the northern crag waiting to do just that. The world outside the valley would have to wait, as he would.

But this, Bannan thought with a longing look at the crate, might bring a bit of joy. Once he'd got his prize safely out of the dragon's clutches. "A shame to disappoint her," he finished, gesturing hopelessly at the window.

A little breeze tossed Bannan's hair, then dashed

hither-thither through the loft, as if looking for answers. The house toad's eyes sank into its head as bedding fluttered around it, but refused to budge. "Why would Jenn want a box?" Wisp asked reasonably.

"Stupid dragon." Scourge, now in better spirits, half-reared. "It's what's in the box."

"In the box? What's in the box!?"

Heart's Blood! Bannan stared helplessly as the crate split apart at every seam, wood splintering and flying in all directions, followed by clouds of sawdust and bits of string and ripped paper.

He covered his face with his hands and shook his head.

"What is it?"

Bannan peered between his fingers, then let his hands drop. "You didn't break it!"

"Of course I didn't," the breeze said testily. "What is it?"

Suspended in midair, the wide tapestried frame looked shabby and worn, its once-bright threads stained by damp. "Just needs cleaning—" the truthseer began, fighting disappointment. What had he expected from an attic in Endshere?

Then the precious silvered glass within the frame caught the rising sun and took fire. With a startled cry, Wisp almost dropped it.

But didn't.

Bannan realized he'd stopped breathing and gasped with relief.

"Old fool. It's naught but a mirror," Scourge announced, clearly bored. "Haven't you seen one?"

"I didn't live as a horse," Wisp countered, but the kruar was already trotting toward the village. Without his cheese.

Bannan stood aside as the mirror floated through the open window and came to rest against a wall.

Noting the house toad's attention fixed, still, on the window, the truthseer turned to face it. If he looked deeper, with greater care, something filled that opening. Something with claws that dented the wooden sill and eyes of wild purple. "Thank you," he said, bowing to the dragon.

"What is this, truthseer?" Wisp demanded.

The creature loved her too. "It's hope," Bannan answered honestly. "Just . . . hope." Hope that if Jenn Nalynn could see her glorious self with her own eyes, see herself as turn-born as well as woman, even as sei, she might be more content with all she was. "She hasn't seen what we see, Wisp. Now, she can." He glanced at the shabby thing and amended, "After I give it some care."

A considering pause. Then a breeze, heavy and unseasonably warm, found his ear. "A mirror, in Marrowdell. Hope may not be what you find in it, truthseer." A whisper, fading. "Fool."

Marrowdell. Where light came from more than one world. Ancestors Dim and Dull-witted, what had he been thinking? Heart sinking, the truthseer forced a lopsided grin. "I'm in love with a turn-born and talk to an invisible dragon. What else could I be?"

Silence answered. The dragon had left.

The house toad leapt from the bed to squat on the floor in front of the mirror. Its great brown eyes blinked slowly; so did its reflection's. "Ancestors Blessed and Bountiful," Bannan said with relief. It was just a mirror.

The toad went closer.

Wisp enjoyed teasing him; it wouldn't be the first dire pronouncement he'd made simply to be a nuisance. There'd been that time—

Suddenly, the mirror became black and within that darkness, eyes blinked again, deep within the glass. Great yellow eyes, without source in this world.

*Rustlerustle.*

The toad leapt to the opening in the floor and dropped through to the kitchen, rattling pots with its landing.

The truthseer grabbed a quilt and flung it over the mirror. He staggered back until his legs hit the edge of his bed, then sat with an annoyed grunt.

Was this what had driven poor Crumlin to flee the valley ahead of the rest?

"Not just a mirror," Bannan said with disgust.

A breeze found his ear and whispered, again, "Fool."

Covie Morrill had been a baroness in Avyo, wealthy enough to have had servants at her beck and call. A baroness who, before being exiled, wouldn't have washed her own face, let alone a chamberpot.

Jenn couldn't imagine it. The Covie she knew was as deft caring for the sick as she was helping in the dairy, a person so strong and kind and capable, you felt better the moment she took her first look at you. She'd not failed to cure anyone—villager or livestock or fallen bird—though it had been a near thing with one of the calves a couple of years ago, the silly beast having wedged itself between gate and barn wall only to panic, breaking its own leg.

Hadn't Covie helped Uncle Horst, after the worst of his injuries were healed by terst magic?

Surely, Jenn thought, she could help Frann, who'd returned from Endshere a shadow of herself.

"There." Covie passed Jenn the basin of warm water and now-damp towels, before easing Frann back against what had to be every pillow the Treffs owned. She put her ear to Frann's chest, then rose, nodding to herself, and pulled up the blankets. "Much better. Rest, now."

"I should be up," Frann protested feebly. "We're to leave for the fair." She put a hand to her head, as if feeling for a hat. "I need to dress."

"Later," Covie assured her. She took the strayed hand and tucked it back under the covers. "First, a short nap. Lorra's doing the same." She stroked the woman's brow, then ran a finger slowly down her nose, between her eyes. "Aren't you tired, Dear Heart?"

Frann blinked once, then again, more slowly. "I suppose I am, a little. Be sure to wake us both, soon. We mustn't be late." Her eyelids fluttered then closed.

Feeling oddly drowsy herself, Jenn followed Covie out of the bedroom.

Davi and Zehr had been hard at work, the past two days, rearranging the Treff household to accommodate illness. Frann was now in Lorra's bedroom, not that she seemed aware of the change. Lorra had insisted, her room being larger, brighter, and freer of draughts, according to her, and her bed superior in every way.

Jenn hadn't noticed any difference, in the rooms or their furnishings, so she thought Peggs must be right, that doing anything was better than feeling helpless, especially for someone like Lorra Treff.

Who'd done more than switch bedrooms. The fireplace in the main room proving insufficient to keep Frann comfortable in bed, Lorra sent Davi to bring in the stone that heated his forge. When that proved impossible—just as well, Radd had said to his daughters—she'd had her son wrestle the big cookstove from the kitchen at the back of the house, into the main room, rigging a clever arrangement of pipe to carry the smoke to the chimney. She'd banished her pottery wheel to the barn, to make room for table and chairs near that heat, but left Frann's loom and supplies where they were, ready and waiting.

As were Frann's flutes, the old and the new.

Covie led the way into the kitchen, where Cynd, Davi's wife, was at work. The bake oven warmed the room, melting the night's frost from the windows. Jenn put the washbasin on the counter and hung the towels to dry over the oven. "I've brought a book for Frann," she said, pulling it from a pocket. "It's new, from Bannan. I could read it to her, if you think she'd like that."

"Good Heart. She would, I'm sure." Jenn saw Cynd's hands clench on her apron as she turned to Covie, her sister-by-marriage. The two had grown close after Covie's husband died; closer still when Anten, Cynd's brother, had lost his first wife and later—gladly—accepted Covie's proposal. "Lorra said Frann would be joining us at the table for supper. I've made her favorite custard."

"That should help her appetite," the healer said approvingly, though Jenn noticed she avoided the matter of Frann rising from bed. "Though please keep making that broth I showed you. She should have as much as she can manage."

"I will. I have." Cynd's face paled beneath its freckles. "Covie—it's been two days. Shouldn't Frann be better by now?"

About to go back to the bedroom, Jenn paused to hear the answer. To her surprise, Covie hesitated.

"Frann will get better, won't she?" Jenn asked, very quietly.

"The broth," the healer said at last, which wasn't an answer. "And rest. Time will tell."

A sunny bright day, though the air had a bite to redden cheeks and nose; she wore her second heaviest shawl just in case. The few wizened leaves left on the oak swayed and spun. They'd stick till spring, the tree refusing to give in to winter.

Which was silly, Jenn thought, since everything must, yet brave of the tree, to cling staunchly to the memory of summer. She appreciated that effort, newly aware of its importance.

However certain, when it came to seasons, to fail. Winter wouldn't be denied, by oak or villager, being relentless and certain. The ice along the riverbanks still melted where the sun found it, but the water was gaspingly cold. Crossing the ford as quickly as she could, Jenn paused to dry her legs and feet. To do so, she set down her basket and sat on the rock everyone used for the same purpose; everyone who didn't have waterproof boots, that is. She should have put a request for such boots in her letter to Aunt Sybb, but who thought of wading in icewater at summer's sweet end?

Next year she would, Jenn nodded to herself, rubbing her toes back to life with the end of her shawl. This was Bannan's first winter in the north and they'd all promised to help him. She'd help him best by providing a good example.

A warmer bed for them both being out of the question, this winter.

"Ancestors Blessed." Her cheeks flared with warmth of their own and Jenn snatched up her basket before hurrying along the Tinkers Road, determined to think no more about that.

So of course she could think of nothing else when she stepped into Bannan's farmyard, and slowed her steps to regain her composure. This entire business of beds and warmth was getting out of hand. Yes, they'd shared hers, but they'd not shared his—

Yet.

They had, she recalled fondly, shared the rug before the

fireplace, and each of the chairs. The table. Not to mention the loft of the barn and, when the sun shone, the soft dry grass behind his house, and the—

"Not helping," Jenn muttered under her breath. She came to a flustered stop, staring up at the loft window, and gripped the handle of the basket until the wicker creaked a protest, lunch being the reason she was here.

Wasn't it?

Oh, and then didn't her breath catch and her heart pound? For she remembered, well and truly, having breath and blood, as well as desire and hope. The matter of Bannan's doubtless fine bed was what Aunt Sybb would call delicate, meaning neither of them spoke of it, as if there was no fine bed upstairs, while both of them thought of it, because there most certainly was.

Oh dear.

Yes, a bed was furniture and anyone could have one. But this bed was in this house, his house, with him in it. If their places were reversed, she'd be in it and this would be her house. So, if both of them were in it?

This would be their home.

She wasn't ready. She wasn't sure. Wasn't—

—a woman.

Still, Jenn thought, she knew more of and about herself now, thanks to Mistress Sand. Soon, she might come to know enough to seize the chance, being ever-so-in-love, and Bannan willing, which she was certain he was. A home together might have happened after all.

Except it was too late.

Winter was coming to the valley, with its long dark nights; Uncle Horst and Riss had finished their urgent inventory of Marrowdell's supplies. The village could make do, to everyone's relief, but only if everyone shared what they had. It meant fewer lamps to burn oil and fewer rooms lit by candle.

In other words, one less house being a home.

Tomorrow Bannan would seal his against the weather and move into Devins', an arrangement appreciated by all despite, Jenn gave a resigned sigh, what might have been.

She hefted her basket and began to smile.

It wasn't tomorrow yet.

The weather changed on the third night, an angry wind keening through the treetops and rushing through opened doors. Before subsiding, it rattled shutters and whined along walls as if frustrated Marrowdell's homes were well-caulked and snug. By morning, the river hid beneath a skin of dark ice and the sky was the color of lead.

By afternoon, Bannan's helpers arrived, cheeks rosy from the cold. "Ancestors Blustery and Bold, we're due for a storm," Kydd announced, shedding his cloak into the truthseer's waiting hands as he entered.

Dusom nodded. "Past due. It's good we're here beforehand. By the signs, it'll be a bad one."

Wainn, who kept his long, gray scarf wrapped around his neck, pushed past the others. "They worry it's Jenn Nalynn's," he informed Bannan, "but it's just a storm."

The elder Uhthoffs exchanged rueful looks. "Here we'd thought to ask you," admitted Kydd. He ruffled his nephew's hair. "Should have known."

"Yes, Uncle."

Bannan smiled as he hung cloaks on pegs, more content than he'd thought possible, considering he was about to lose both house and privacy for however long winter lasted in Marrowdell. Yesterday, with Jenn, had been more than a last gift of time together, more than lovemaking and laughter. She'd made it more, tidying cushions, running her fingers over mantel and windowsill, helping him decide what to take and what to leave. Like someone leaving a beloved home.

A beginning, he believed with every fiber of his being, hardly able to sleep for hope. This spring. This spring and its first flower and he would ask her again. By spring, this spring, Jenn might find peace with herself and all that she was. Be willing, by spring, to make this home hers too.

If not, well, he would wait, however long Jenn needed or wished.

The truthseer turned back to his guests. "Thank you for coming." He beckoned the three to seats by the fire. "Rest yourselves. I've mulled wine. And biscuits." For a wonder, since the dragon tended to steal them.

As for the dragon?

Though Bannan couldn't be sure, he'd his suspicions. His house toad, no longer willing to go into the loft despite the regrettable mirror being wrapped and hidden under the bed, had dragged a plump cushion close to the cookstove for its own bed.

Now, though without toad, that cushion was pressed flat.

A warm spot that would chill by nightfall, as these were the last biscuits from his new stove until spring. That said, Ancestors Needful and Necessary, Bannan had no doubt he'd keep baking since Devins wasn't a cook, preferring to take his meals in other households. Biscuits now and then was the least Bannan could do in return for Roche's old room.

As for his? The place had solid shutters and working doors now. Maybe it would be a short winter. Maybe he could visit, as the snow permitted.

Bannan had informed the dragon and his house toad. So far, neither had expressed an opinion, well enough, nor assured him they'd be fine, which was becoming a worry. Foolish of him, he supposed, both having survived winters long before he'd arrived, but he couldn't help it.

"You're a grand host, my friend. Yes to both." Dusom, the elder brother and Wainn's father, took the seat nearest the small fire, holding out his hands gratefully. "Brrr. I'm not as young as I used to be."

"No one is," his son said after a moment's careful thought. He choose to sit cross-legged on the rug. The house toad, having noticed, slowly edged closer. When Bannan glanced at it, it stopped at once, sitting tall and proud as if watching for mice.

He couldn't take it with him. Devins' house had a toad and there was only one per house or barn, not that anyone could say why. The dragon didn't know and Scourge didn't care.

Bannan loaded his tray with filled mugs and a basket of warm buttered biscuits, one of which he casually dropped near the cushion. By the time he served the Uhthoffs, the toad, clearly unconcerned, was leaning, eyes closed in bliss, against Wainn's leg.

Perhaps that problem was already solved.

"Welcome, all." His share of the warm and fragrant wine in hand, Bannan sat to enjoy the moment. A snug home. Friends such as these. What matter winter's first storm? Though he should, the truthseer reminded himself, seek advice from those familiar with such weather.

"So, Bannan," Kydd said, eyes alight with curiosity. "You've been mysterious since coming home. Something happened to you in Endshere, didn't it?"

A scholar, was Kydd, of magic as well as history. Dusom was an astronomer and teacher, a keen observer of what made Marrowdell special. As for Wainn?

Wainn was part of that.

"Wen worried Bannan wouldn't come home," that worthy offered through a mouth of biscuit. He licked a runnel of butter from his lips. "Marrowdell helped."

"Oh-ho!" Dusom settled back, mug in hand. "So there is a tale."

"More than that," Bannan said, abruptly serious, for his invitation to sit had another side to it. Despite Tadd's caution to the contrary, Jenn had agreed he should share the truth with these three. "Have any of you left the valley, since first arriving in Marrowdell?"

Kydd and Dusom shook their heads. Wainn reached for another biscuit.

He'd thought not. "Of those who have," he informed them, "all but a few forget what makes this place different from any other. Its magic. Its connection to the Verge. Its other inhabitants."

The toad snuggled closer to Wainn, as if disturbed. As well it should, Bannan thought.

"Heart's Blood!" Kydd went pale.

Dusom leaned forward again, his deceptively sleepy eyes alert. "'All but a few,' you say. Who is safe from this forgetting?"

"Tadd and Allin. They remember—and more. Once outside Marrowdell, they can tell who else, by looking into their eyes. According to them—" Bannan counted on his fingers with each name, "Lady Mahavar. Dema Qimirpik. Roche Morrill."

When Tadd had revealed what he'd learned from his twin, Tir had been a sorrow, Qimirpik an unexpected joy, and Roche? Bannan hadn't been surprised. Jenn Nalynn had wished Roche to speak only the truth; to himself, it appeared, as well. Though for all their sakes, he hoped the demas kept the self-centered Morrill close and content.

Kydd rubbed his forehead. "Ancestors Bemused and Bewildered. Davi and Lorra. Frann, these many trips. Every one forgot?"

"Sennic too." When he'd returned Horst's sword, difficult as it had been, Bannan had heeded Tadd's warning not to question the man. He'd seen for himself how the others arrived back, slipping on Marrowdell's magic like a pair of comfortable old slippers left by the fire. As for the former soldier's sharp look, well, he'd had his encounter with the horse thieves to relate.

To Perrkin's glory, if not his own.

"You failed to count yourself," observed Dusom.

"I remembered no more than the rest," Bannan said, proud his voice was steady, "till this burned into my skin to remind me." He pulled aside his collar.

Dusom and Kydd stood to take a closer look, then sat back down. Both appeared shaken. "If these markings are words," the latter said slowly, "it's no language I've seen before."

Words Jenn Nalynn had read with ease; words part of every day's Beholdings, said by any and every one in Rhoth. Words, she and Bannan had concluded, that must be the intention of the markings, not the means. "I believe it's a wishing, of a kind," he said, choosing his words with care. "It was written by a moth the morning we left."

"I saw. They're Marrowdell words." Wainn tilted his head. "I can write them for you, Uncle."

"Do not, please, for anyone," his father commanded gently. "I doubt these are words any of us should write, until we understand their source."

If they ever did or could, Bannan thought, but he wasn't the scholar. "You won't be able to question the others about this, Dusom," he cautioned. "They've no memory of having forgotten."

"Yet remember Endshere, do they not?" At Bannan's nod, the older man half smiled with relief. "Good. So, strange as it is, this 'forgetting' only matters outside of Marrowdell."

Kydd helped himself to more wine, offering the pitcher to the others. "Aunt Sybb," he said wonderingly. "Much about that dear lady becomes clear, especially her feelings about magic and our little friends here." With a bow to the toad.

Who yawned toothily.

"However troubling to contemplate," Dusom mused, "perhaps we should be grateful Marrowdell protects her magical secrets."

"All of them?" His brother gave Bannan a troubled look. "What of Jenn?"

"To those who leave Marrowdell and forget," the truth-seer replied grimly, "Jenn Nalynn might never have been born."

Wainn's eyes widened. The toad leapt away.

Seemingly of its own volition, the cushion slid an arm's length from where it had been, explaining the lack of biscuit on the floor.

Here, then, and listening, was Wisp.

Perhaps not the best outcome, to have the dragon learn all this from him, instead of Jenn, especially inside his fragile house. Ah, well. Bannan collected himself. He could hardly stop now. "There's worse." He touched his neck. "Without this, I wouldn't be here."

"What do you mean?"

"Before its magic took effect, I—" Heart's Blood, where was his voice? He coughed. Took a gulp of wine. "Ancestors Desperate and Despondent—I forgot her too. Our love— was gone. I was about to make my way back to Vorkoun, believing I'd found nothing in Marrowdell." His free hand became a fist. "And I'd have lost everything."

Wordless cold nipped his ear. Rebuke. Fair, he supposed. No one had forced him to take the road.

Other than duty and honor—and Sennic, who was both. All valued by the dragon. So maybe the nip had been something else.

Fear.

For him? Or of how Jenn might have reacted had he abandoned her? It could be both, Bannan conceded, and not wrong.

Free of the opinions of dragons, Wainn's forehead un-creased as he smiled, wide and happy. "Now you're home."

As if the outside world, and what happened there, could be ignored.

Kydd nodded, though the troubled look hadn't left his eyes. "What of Scourge? Devins said he came with you — fought a bear."

"He did." Bannan hesitated, then told the truth, "Like before, Scourge only knew himself through my gift. I fear — had we'd been separated, had I forgotten Marrowdell and left him behind — he'd have been lost."

A wicked hiss had the older Uhthoffs glancing around for a source, to settle, rather uncertainly, on the kettle. "Old fool," the breeze snapped.

"He was brave to follow me," Bannan countered, "and saved us on the road."

Kydd had fallen silent, doubtless thinking it through. Sure enough, "Magic like Marrowdell's has its place, then," he declared abruptly, "despite what small amounts may slip into the wider world. I admit I'd hoped it was so, that there were limits. Imagine this —" an encompassing gesture, "— in Avyo?"

"By reputable account, there's magic in Channen," Dusom reminded his brother. "If confined to a particular physical location, or remembered by few, it would explain why Mellynne itself does not rely upon it."

"Indeed!" Kydd's lean frame quivered with excitement. "But what of her exports — works of art that defy explanation —"

Bannan raised his hand to interrupt. "Your pardon, good friends." He gained the brothers' attention, Wainn being preoccupied wrapping his scarf around the toad. "There's more you should know. I heard disturbing news in Endshere. News of trouble between Mellynne and Rhoth."

"With our prince, when isn't there?"

"Kydd." Dusom frowned. "I've heard of a trade dispute. Do you have other news?"

Bannan kept his report brief and to the point. By the end, the brothers looked as worried as he felt.

"Envoys are inviolate," Kydd protested. "Ancestors Witness. Are you sure?"

"Rumor's never trustworthy," Bannan acknowledged. "But I had the same tale from a thief from Avyo as from locals at the inn—men who, moreover, gave me the envoy's name. One I know well. Baron Emon Westietas. My sister's husband."

"Ancestors Blighted and Beset." Dusom, who rarely swore, shook his head.

Kydd finished his wine in a quick gulp, setting down his mug. "You could tell they spoke the truth."

"As they knew it, yes." The truthseer shrugged. "It's not proof."

Dusom's face clouded. "It explains what's happened to a colleague of mine. Recall Jym's latest letter, Kydd? Jym Garnden is an astronomer at Sersise," he explained to Bannan. "As long as I've known him, he's spent the winter in an observatory in mountains north of Channen. This year, his invitation was revoked." Dusom sighed. "This trouble is unfortunate beyond words, my friend. We will ask the Ancestors Blessing at the Midwinter Beholding, and hope for better news in spring."

Because nothing moved north after the first snow.

Bannan rose and went to the fireplace, squatting to use the poker on the remaining embers and stare into the final, crackling flames. Warmth on his face, none in his heart. "Lila could have sent word," he said finally. "She knew the road would close. Why didn't she?"

"She thought to spare you the worry," suggested Kydd.

"Lila?" Bannan stood and turned, shaking his head. "Never."

"While the road's clear, there's always the chance of a messenger," Dusom offered.

His brother nodded. "That's it. A messenger. Still time for that, Bannan."

Not, he guessed, that there'd ever been such a courier come to Marrowdell. They lied to comfort him; he let them. "Something to watch for, then. Now. What say we finish the last of the wine, my good friends, then be off? I'm packed and ready—"

Wainn stood. "Too late."

"For what?" his father asked, raising an eyebrow.

In answer, the youngest Uhthoff walked to the door and threw it open.

Snow swirled in like a dancer, wrapping him in its arms.

He turned with a laugh, drops winking on lashes and hair. Beyond Wainn, outside, the farmyard already wore a coat of white, what little could be seen of it through wind-driven flakes.

"That's it, then," Bannan said, numbed by more than the cold wind. Ancestors Lost and Left.

The road south was closed.

It was too late.

~

*A fleck of paint, touched by a hand . . . a drop of sleep,*
*under the tongue . . .*
*And the dream unfolds . . .*
White. Everywhere white. Snow.
It softens, smothers. Tricks.
A face looms, strange and distorted. *Terror.*
Red sprays, dotting the snow like rose petals. More—
Russet fountains. Crimson waterfalls—
*The dream falters . . . rebuilds . . .*
White. Everywhere.
White.

Snow kissed her eyelids and patted her cheeks. Jenn stuck out her tongue to catch a flake, the first snow being the tastiest, only to have the wind snatch her breath and send icy fingers up her skirt. Which wasn't polite or comfortable, so she pulled up her hood and headed for home.

It wasn't a blizzard, yet, but wasn't weather to fool with, something she sincerely hoped Bannan understood. She'd told him how they'd tie ropes as guides to the barns, and how, if a rope snapped, it was better to sleep with the livestock than risk being lost. Not that he'd livestock yet, other than Scourge, but the warning was important. That no one in Marrowdell had strayed in a storm, to fall asleep forever, was due to such care.

Ankle-deep the snow, and light. Other than the cold, it was like walking through thistle fluff, fluff that filled the air as well. The apple trees to her left were dark blurs and, without the light in the windows, she couldn't have guessed which of the larger blurs ahead was the Emms' barn, and which the house. Jenn glanced across the road to the closer welcome of the Morrill home. Bannan, this very afternoon, had settled in with Devins. She wasn't entirely sorry. It was safer in the village.

And he was near. She'd invite him for supper tomorrow, if Gallie agreed. Or should such an invitation include Devins? Neglect half of a household, Aunt Sybb would say, and do harm to both. Not that Devins and Bannan were a married couple, and Devins usually took his meals with the Ropps, but his kindness at taking Bannan into his home should be rewarded.

Her toes reminded her they were walking through snow and Jenn stretched her legs, just as eager to be indoors.

Only to stop as a tall shape formed out of the blowing snow. "Greetings, Jenn Nalynn."

"Greetings, Wen." Jenn blinked in surprise.

Wen Treff wore no hood, likely because a toad usually rode her shoulder, safely tucked within her mass of wild hair, nor a cloak, which was more puzzling. Jenn blinked again and realized she'd been wrong.

Wen's cloak was the snow. It hung around her, now a sparkling cape, now scarves afloat, now a snug coat, or was it a cape again? Dizzy, Jenn focused on Wen's calm face. "I was just—" she'd started to shout to be heard, then realized whatever tamed the storm around the other woman now encompassed her as well, and lowered her voice. "I was with Frann. She's sleeping. So is your mother," she added, for surely Wen worried about them both.

Gray eyes regarded her. "Mother lies on her bed, lying to herself. She will not rest."

Jenn sighed and hugged herself. "I hope she doesn't make herself ill."

"Mother is stronger than that." Wen's head tilted like a bird's. "You were gone."

"I came back," Jenn countered quickly.

"This time."

What did that mean? She shivered and not from the cold. "This is my home," she assured the uncanny woman. "I'll always come back."

"Hearts would break, if you did not."

Had Wen been talking to Peggs? About to protest, Jenn subsided. It was nothing but the truth. "I will come back," she said then, unafraid to put all her will into the promise. If she couldn't bring herself home, what good was magic at all?

Nothing happened. Jenn felt a smidge of disappointment, though what had she expected, trumpets? Of course she'd return from wherever she went. That didn't take a wish.

Pale lips smiled, as if Wen had heard. "Jenn Nalynn. Tonight you must seek what is lost. That is your gift, as it was Melusine's."

To be honest, Jenn thought, it was her most useful magic, especially when it came to strayed piglets or eggs, and one the villagers had employed even before she'd been aware of it. To be lost in such a storm, be it cow or horse, or piglet, would be to die. "What's lost?" she asked urgently, ready to help.

A pair of dark, limpid eyes peered from Wen's hair, claws gripping a shoulder. ~She mustn't, elder sister,~ the house toad protested. ~Stay home. Stay safe!~

~Peace, little one. Our Jenn will do neither. She has a good heart.~

What she wouldn't do was disregard a toad's advice. Was it anxious because of the storm or something else? "Where," Jenn asked with sudden doubt, "am I to seek what's lost?" If the Verge, on some business of toads, whatever it was would have to wait. A storm meant everyone would be needed, if only to clear snow from the road and paths.

Could she? No more wishing, Jenn decided hastily, till she could be sure of the consequences.

Wen's arm lifted, her finger pointing. "Seek the lost, Jenn Nalynn." The snow-laden wind obliged, dying down to reveal the road through Marrowdell, then the gate, then beyond. When she let her arm fall to her side, swirls of white again hid the village. "Before it's too late."

"But—"

Wen Treff and her toad vanished into the snow, leaving Jenn standing in the midst of what was, now, a storm.

With, apparently, a mission. She blinked away the flakes

once more smacking her in the face—Marrowdell being much less courteous to her than to Wen—and started walking through the growing drifts.

She'd best stop for her winter shoes first, and a thicker scarf.

As for what she was to seek?

She supposed she'd know that once she found it. Or it found her.

Snow.

He didn't waste breath snarling at the horrid stuff, breath that would enter him cold and steal his heat. Breath he'd need.

~ 'A storm rides the road.' ~

A storm with snow. What other kind of storm could it be, here, at this dreadful time of year?

At least the water of the river was rock hard, a phenomenon he might have enjoyed had the air above it been decently warm.

Beyond a dragon to question how the sei knew the weather coming to Marrowdell, or on the road into it. Assuming weather was the storm. Sei, Wisp had learned, weren't above metaphor.

If it sent him, whatever the storm, it was something important to the girl.

Efflet purred and whispered on every side, catching flakes in their claws, collecting the white stuff into drifts and shapes. Wisp passed a growing mound that looked suspiciously like his own head; another that might have been an ox. A dead one. Come winter, efflet tended to humor. Maybe they felt free of their duty.

Duty was warmth. Duty was power. Without duty, the dragon knew, he'd be curled up at home.

Instead of this. To the excitement of efflet, who tried to keep up, and the curiosity of ylings, who fluttered in their russet cloaks to treetops to watch, Wisp flew across fields, forest, and waterfall to where Marrowdell's road bent out of the valley.

With each beat, he did his utmost to ignore what had

happened to the truthseer and his old enemy. A dragon, forget himself? He'd have roared a denial, challenged that fate, but it was too cold.

And he was too old to trust the unknown.

Finding the road, Wisp stayed low, angling to follow its twists and turns. The wind strengthened, howling between the crags like something alive and hungry. It drove the snow sideways, hammering rock and tree. An eagle couldn't fly in this. A man would be blind.

It was nothing to a dragon, born to own air.

Cold was the enemy. It gnawed and bit, making itself a thorough nuisance. Frost grew from his beard. As if that weren't insult enough, ice began to coat his scales, adding weight, changing his shape.

Crazed sei. How far did he have to go? How would he know when he was there?

A wall of stone!

His icy body refused to turn and avoid the obstacle. Roaring his fury, Wisp flew straight, taking the earth way.

Death was entirely possible. He hadn't tried this since being broken.

Ice shattered, left behind as, to his joy, his wings beat through rock as easily as air. Taking a breath, he inhaled the rich heady scent of the bones of the world.

Better still, there was heat within the mountain, heat to thaw him.

Not that he could linger. The road hadn't ended; it had met the one the villagers called the Northward that led to their former homes.

Turning, reluctantly, Wisp flew out and back into the storm.

And the cold. Loathsome, but no longer lethal. He'd a way to warm himself and would, again. First, to be done with this command of the sei.

The Northward Road had been built by pick and shovel, not magic, just as terst made their marks on the ground in his world. Like other dragons, Wisp had sneered at the toil of those who had to walk. After having to do the same, as a man, he highly approved of well-maintained paths.

Stairs, he would never like.

There!

He dropped from the air to the road near several mounds of white, drawn not by the shapes, but by the enticing scent of blood. His tongue licked out, tasting the air.

Horse.

He crouched, head whipping around, wary of ambush. Not that anything in the girl's world could challenge him—or see him, for that matter—but instinct wasn't to be dismissed.

And he hated surprises.

Once satisfied, Wisp spread his wings and hopped from mound to mound. It was graceless, but efficient. He sent a breeze to clear the snow.

Tried to send a breeze. What he managed sputtered mournfully, then died away. The wind wailed in triumph.

Beyond the edge, then, magic was untrustworthy. So be it. Growling to himself, the dragon scratched at the mounds until he could see what lay beneath the snow.

The first four were horses, their bodies cold and hard. One had been scavenged, but not the rest. Yet.

Next, he found two men, apart from each other. Neither wore a coat nor had a weapon. Neither were familiar. There was another mound, the same size, under the trees. Wisp ignored it. He wasn't here for the dead.

The wagon, with doors and curtained windows like Aunt Sybb's, lay overturned. Snow cupped it like hands.

A sanctuary? Or a tomb.

Wisp took hold of a window and ripped the side from the wagon, tossing it behind him.

An ax spun through the air. He caught it in his jaws and tossed it aside too, delighted by its familiar taste. The warrior! Wisp sent a breeze to shape words, to command the other to come out.

Nothing happened. Nor could he form any other speech. This—this must be what had happened to Scourge! They were silenced by this world. How was it possible?

What worse was to come?

Wings quivering, fighting the urge to lift into the air and flee, Wisp limped to the ruined wagon.

Inside was the man he'd tasted, Tir Half-face, bundled in more than one coat, ice on his mask and short beard. The eyes above the mask were closed, as if he'd spent his final strength to throw the ax. A row of other weapons lay in reach. Wisp angled his head. Tir had lain like this across Horst's threshold, on guard that first dreadful night when Wisp—Wyll, he'd been—couldn't guard himself.

What did Tir guard now?

As if in answer, the coats moved!

Wisp jumped back, then forward again, neck outstretched. He used a clawtip to pull aside the topmost layers.

Two boys huddled within, against the body of the warrior. One slept, or was unconscious.

The other?

That boy's eyes were open. Eyes of amber, flecked with black, like molten gold starting to cool.

Eyes at first puzzled, then round with wonder.

Take his magic. Steal his voice. What did it matter? Wisp spread his wings and roared his defiance. This world would not rob him of what he was.

For in those astonishing eyes, he saw a dragon.

And knew what the sei had sent him to find.

# SIX

*T*HE EMMS HADN'T wanted her to leave. Standing in the warm kitchen, Jenn most certainly hadn't wanted to go. But duty does, when duty must, as Aunt Sybb would say, or nothing would ever be accomplished.

And she'd a lost something to find. So Jenn smiled brightly, saying if she wasn't back soon, well, she'd have stayed for the night with Peggs or perhaps Hettie, and they mustn't worry. After all, it was just a bit of snow.

A bit of snow now up to mid-calf, with drifts sliding around every wall and tree and rising on the lee side of hedges. With a shrug, Jenn set off.

It would have helped to know what was lost, but she knew where it must belong, in Marrowdell and out of the storm, which was the main thing. The wind was being helpful as well, having shifted so that she could see her next few steps, though now the snow flew sideways, making her feel slightly tipped.

Unless that was being shaped as a turn-born, for she'd left her flesh and skin self as soon as she'd left the Emms, stripping off her mittens to reveal the light of her hands and wrists. The light was needful and no longer feeling the cold a wonder, though she was ever-so-careful to pay attention to breathing and walking, in case those slipped her mind.

Though they hadn't, not in the valley. Here she seemed herself, even when not quite, and hoped for the best.

She stayed otherwise dressed, because one never knew when that might matter even on a night like this . . .

Going where no one else should be.

The village gate hung open. Livestock wasn't loose to roam the village this time of year, nor was it sensible to leave the gate to freeze closed. It wasn't much of a gate, truth be told, being more to mark the end of the village than serve as a barrier.

Jenn trudged through the opening, refusing to take note of any more boundaries. Though there was another, ahead, she couldn't ignore.

Where the road left the valley lay the end of the edge and her existence.

Then whatever was lost best be found before that, or she couldn't help it, could she?

She could shorten any path she knew, Marrowdell being ever helpful in that regard, but she'd risk missing what she was after. The entire business, Jenn decided, dodging a lump of snow that came free from a branch, was more mysterious than it ought to be. Wen could have simply told her what to find.

Unless it was a house toad. They were pricklish about their dignity.

Jenn shook her head. Toads stayed close to warmth in winter. One wouldn't be out here. It wasn't pleasant to think Wen might not know what she was to find.

Leaves rustled to either side. Winter-brown leaves that somehow never fell from their trees. Ylings.

She looked up. "Do you know what I'm to find?"

Leaves tumbled and jumped and ran along branches, until most were on the side of their trees farthest from the village.

If not an answer, then a guide of sorts. "Thank you!" Jenn called, giving the best curtsy she could manage, being so bundled. It was more a dip and bounce, but the leaves fluttered crisply as if pleased.

Farther, then.

Like a sheet tossed over a set table, snow disguised everything beneath. Jenn held out her hands, reasonably sure stepping where it was flat would keep her on the road.

Though she seemed to have been walking longer than she should. Had she gone by the path to the trout pool, or not? She stopped to listen for the waterfall, but the wind laughed and gibbered too loudly to make out any other sound. It was most aggravating.

Was there a way to tame a storm like this, without harm? Given this was only the first of winter, Jenn decided to add the question to her next list for Mistress Sand.

Unsure where she was, she walked more and more slowly, until finally she stopped altogether. Snow pressed around her, sparkling in the glow she cast, until Jenn felt encased in diamonds. Which was very pretty, but how was she to help anything else, if she were lost too?

"Why are you here?" a whisper beneath the wind, hot as the air was cold.

Scourge! Jenn lifted her hands, straining to see through the snow. "I'm looking for the lost."

"Aren't you?" Grim amusement. "Come." A mass of snow-covered darkness loomed beside her, a hairy and most welcome mass.

Jenn reached for him and the kruar shied away. Of course. She changed into flesh at once, only to be plunged into darkness.

Oh, and didn't the air bite then? She gasped and shivered, but this time, when she stretched out her hands, she touched warm hide. Moving her hands, she found he'd knelt for her to mount, which was unexpectedly kind. Taking hold, carefully, of his mane, she fumbled her way onto his back.

With a powerful lurch, Scourge stood. "Will you continue the hunt?"

"I must," Jenn told him. "But only within Marrowdell. We mustn't go beyond the edge." A rumble she took for agreement, for he began to move.

Relieved of the need to watch where she was going, and heated by the great body beneath hers, Jenn closed her eyes and relaxed. According to the others in the village, Melusine's gift, and hers, was magic, but it wasn't like a

Rhothan wishing, involving tokens and words, nor at all like a turn-born's. Perhaps she should talk to Covie, whose ability to comfort and heal might just be a little magical itself.

Finding seemed more something she was, than did. If she set out to find something, it always found her first. Most often she knew what it was beforehand, as when she'd recovered her mother's ring, but occasionally, as now, she didn't. She'd been digging potatoes when her fingers found Gallie's pen, lost since spring, and, though her skill finding piglets was unmatched, she did tend to carry apples in her pockets so they loved her.

She'd helped the wounded sei find its way back from this world into the Verge, without apples or love involved.

Pens, piglets, and immense magical beings. Each had their proper place and sometimes needed a little help to find it. She was, Jenn decided, like a signpost.

Scourge came to a halt. Where he'd stopped was no different, as far as Jenn could tell, from where they'd been. No, that wasn't true. The wind had shifted, coming now from her left.

Where the road bent north, leaving Marrowdell.

And wasn't that a thought colder than the wind? To be within steps of where she wouldn't be at all?

Jenn gave Scourge a grateful pat. "I guess we'll have to wait," she told him, rather breathless.

He shook his thick neck, dislodging snow from his mane. "For what?"

"I—" About to say she didn't know, Jenn hesitated. Wrong to wait, in such a storm. She knew it. She slid from the kruar's back. "What's looking for me, what we've come to find, I fear it can't get here. Something's stopped it. Would you go—"

He was off before she could finish her plea, a triumphant neigh ringing off the looming cliff; she should have known a dangerous hunt was more to Scourge's taste than plodding along the road.

The air grew colder still, with night and being alone. When her teeth began to chatter, Jenn resumed her turn-born shape. By the light of her hands, she could tell the snow was easing, slightly. She found a place to sit and wait, hoping it wouldn't be for long.

It might have been moments, it could have been an hour, before she heard the crunch of heavy steps approaching. Jenn stood, peering anxiously into the darkness. Steps accompanied by a slithering sound, like the runners of a sled.

A breeze, sharp and urgent. "Help him, turn-born! Quickly!" With the command, the kruar came into view.

His neck was bent, head down and low. Because, Jenn saw in horror, his fangs were sunk into Wisp's throat! By that hold, Scourge was pulling the dragon through the snow toward her. "Hurry," the kruar urged. "He freezes!"

She could see it for herself. Wisp was encased in ice, wings tight to his body and limbs as if he'd wrapped himself to keep warm.

Warmth he would have, here and now! Jenn wished with all her might, and the snow melted from her feet outward. Tiny sprigs of green popped up, along with mushroom buttons and a row of little lily flowers. A mole startled from its hole and dove down again.

The wave of untimely spring met Scourge's hooves and he danced out of its way, disappearing into the dark with a snort.

Spring found Wisp and the ice began to drip. Jenn pulled hunks free as it cracked and splintered along his scaled sides. He wasn't moving. Why wasn't he moving?

A twitch! Breath steamed from his nostrils. Once, then again. "Oh, Wisp!" She ran her hands over his wings, using their light to search for any injury.

"Dearest Heart." Faint, that breeze, and colder than winter, but so very welcome. He shivered violently and his wings opened.

Out tumbled three bodies, those of a man and two children. They were unconscious and cold to the touch but, to her joy, alive! "Brave Wisp. Wonderful Wisp." Jenn tore off her cloak, wrapping the children as best she could, then changed into flesh to give them her own warmth. "Get Bannan," she told Scourge. "Bring help!"

Hooves beat into the distance. Spring faltered and faded around her, the storm taking hold again.

Instead of fighting winter, Jenn wished the road to the village short and clear, and held on.

Devins gathered clothes in his arms as he went through the main room. "I'm sorry about the kitchen, Bannan," he apologized, not for the first time. "I'll get to it right away."

"Ancestors Beholden and Blessed," the truthseer chuckled, tossing a shirt to his host, "you should have seen my room at home. And my first barracks. Took Tir to show me how to make a bed that didn't fly apart."

Devins relaxed enough to smile at this. "You'll have to show me."

"Done. And we'll do the dishes together. I'm no guest." Bannan clapped the other man on the shoulder. "Trust me to pull my weight."

A warmer smile. "That'll be more than Roche ever did," Devins admitted. "He wasn't one for daily chores. Unless hunting from dawn till dusk counts. Take a seat. I'll put on the kettle."

"Most welcome." Bannan sat, taking stock of his new home. It looked to have been neglected by both brothers. The rafters were festooned with years of cobwebbing and dust, and dark with soot above the fireplacc. Thc scarred floor appeared to be swept by pushing any dirt under the furniture. The furniture itself—the pair of high-backed chairs, a long table, and grand sideboard—must have come from Avyo with the baron, but the legs were lashed together with leather straps as if frequently broken, and marks on the once-fine table showed where knives had been repeatedly driven into it. Where not covered by worn squirrel and rabbit pelts, the original color of the threadbare upholstery on the chairs was long gone, as was—the truthseer shifted—any cushioning.

Fixable, all of it. An abundance of possibilities for the long winter ahead, should he find himself idle. At the thought, Bannan rose. Much as he'd appreciated the Uhthoffs' help— and horses—in the end he'd chosen to bring only what would add to Devins' kitchen, plus a minimum of clothing and effects for himself. His house toad had disappeared during the packing and wouldn't be found, leaving Bannan to wonder if the creature planned to stay on guard and keep mice—or whatever else—from nesting in his belongings.

So long as the creature didn't freeze.

Great Gran's strange mirror he'd left under his bed, well-wrapped. Let the eyes enjoy the view.

The stores in his larder would stay there until needed in the village, though Dusom had said they'd go in turn to clear the snow from its door, to prevent it being buried beyond reach by midwinter.

What had fallen outside by sunset, to the top of his boots, was already more snow than Bannan had seen in his life. He couldn't imagine the amount that must fill the valley by winter's end. No need. He grinned as he searched one of his packs. See for himself, wouldn't he?

There. The last of his brandy. It should go well with whatever hot—

A thunderous bang shook dust from the rafters. Putting down the bottle, Bannan rushed to open the door before a second kick could break it down, for there was no mistaking Scourge's version of a polite knock. "Idiot beast," he began, gasping in the blast of snow and cold. "I was going to tell you—"

Another blast, this in his ear and hot as fire. "COME!!"

Heart pounding, the truthseer snatched up his coat and scarf even as Devins came at a run from the kitchen, eyes wide. So Scourge had shared his alert. "Get the others," Bannan ordered, stamping feet into boots and making sure he had his gloves. "Follow us."

Then it was out into the storm, a quick mount, and a leap into the night.

Torches flared to life throughout the village as they rode through. Voices called one to the other; horses were being brought from their stable. No denying Scourge knew how to raise an alarm.

Why? Bannan pressed flat against that great neck. "What's this about?" he shouted.

"Your sister," the breeze told him.

Ancestors Wild and Willful. "She's come in this?" Of course she'd come in this. What was a storm to Lila Larmensu? He'd have dug in his heels, desperate for speed, but once Scourge stretched out, nothing could have run faster. Best of all, free of the pretense of a horse, the kruar stayed atop the snow, leaving no mark. The village gate passed in a

blur and they plunged into the darkness beyond. Bannan
shut his eyes, trusting the kruar to see.

But it wasn't the kruar's long legs that brought them
sooner than they should or could to the bend in the road.
Before Scourge had fully stopped, Bannan dropped to the
road, staggering forward, knowing who waited, if not why.
"Jenn!"

"Here." Hard to hear through the wind, but close.

"I can't see you!"

Then he could, light glowing from her hands and eyes
and mouth. She crouched beside Wisp, the dragon in plain
sight. He lay limp as a corpse, huge eyes closed, but a reassuring tendril of steam rose from his nostrils.

"Bannan!" Jenn moved, lifting her hands, and by their
light, he saw limp figures between her and the dragon. "We
have to get them to the village."

"Them?" He threw himself to his knees beside her,
hardly noticing the ground beneath was green instead of
white. "Tir?! And—" Words died in his throat. It wasn't possible.

But was.

Heart's Blood. Lila had sent him a message after all.

Her sons.

Horses and men arrived by torchlight, welcome help and oh
so needful. Bannan quickly lifted one nephew, then the
other into waiting arms. Davi dismounted to help ease Tir
in front of—yes, it was Sennic, somehow astride Perrkin.
The old soldier put his good arm around the unconscious
man. "Are there more?" he demanded.

Jenn, now flesh and blood, gazed into the blackness beyond the torches, then shook her head. "None I need to
find." At the conviction in her voice, Bannan felt a chill that
had nothing to do with the storm.

Lila wouldn't have sent Tir alone with the boys. Something was terribly wrong. Where was she? Had she come?

Was she lying under the snow?

He refused to believe it—to even think it. Tir would tell
him. He'd have the truth soon.

"Then let's get out of this," Sennic ordered, and turned his grateful horse to head for the village and warmth.

Dusom leaned down to give Bannan his torch. "You'll bring Jenn?"

"Yes." Once they saw to the dragon, who'd disappeared at the approach of the villagers.

The others safely gone, the truthseer turned to find Jenn running her hands over the ground where Wisp had lain. "He's gone," she said worriedly. "He was so cold, Bannan. Barely moving."

"Worry not." The breeze was temperate, though Scourge rumbled, stamping an impatient hoof. "The old fool will be warm enough. He flies the deep earth. It is how dragons elude us." With reluctant respect. "I'd not known he still could."

Putting the dragon beyond their help, while his nephews and Tir—and answers—were on their way to the village. Bannan beckoned Scourge close then tossed the torch into the snow, trusting the kruar's night sight. Mounting, he reached down to help Jenn climb up behind him.

Her arms circled his waist as the kruar began to move through the snow and he felt her shiver. "Ancestors Blessed," he said hoarsely. "How do I begin to thank you?"

Her arms tightened. "Hush, Dearest Heart. I wasn't alone. Wen warned me. It was Wisp who found them and saved them; Scourge who helped him find me." She fell silent.

It was a question.

"Werfol and Semyn," Bannan answered. "Lila's sons." Wind caught the words and spun them out into the snow. Snow that would have buried them and Tir, if it hadn't been for Marrowdell.

The next question unasked was one he couldn't answer, not yet.

Why?

The Nalynns' house toad scampered under the nearest chair as they carried in the storm's refugees. Not Wisp, to Jenn's continued concern. She'd some doubt when it came to Scourge's understanding of dragons; certainly hers appreciated warmth when he could find it. But what mattered now were Tir and the children.

Who were Bannan's nephews.

The boys, barely conscious, were tucked into Radd's bed, warmed stones placed around them. Covie had checked their fingers and toes, pronouncing them sure to be sore but without frostbite, and given them a draught to help them sleep till morning.

Tir sat on the settee, wrapped in quilts, eyes closed. He hadn't stopped shivering. The healer tsked unhappily at the condition of his hands and feet, insisting they soak in barely warmed water before she examined them again. Anten had lost three toes one winter and Jenn sincerely hoped that— or worse—wouldn't happen to Tir. Covie smoothed a poultice on the tips of his ears, also bitten by the cold, and, after gently removing his mask, over patches of white skin unprotected by his wiry brown-and-gray beard.

Jenn set the mask on a shelf. It wasn't the crudely hammered one she remembered. Though also of metal, this had been made with skill and care. Soft leather lined it and formed the straps to go around Tir's head. The old one he'd tilt with a thumb to free his mouth for drinking. This had a clever arrangement that would let him slide the lower portion over the upper. The finish seemed dull until she'd taken a close look, tipping it into the candlelight to find it wasn't dull at all, but covered in fine detail, like scales. A bit like a dragon, she thought, charmed by the notion. Aunt Sybb's doing, this was, as would be the sturdy, well-made boots Covie had cut from his feet.

Boots could be restitched. Could a family? Jenn looked at Bannan. He sat on the bed beside his nephews, his eyes never leaving their faces. Every so often he'd touch their hair or cheek, as if making sure they were real. Her heart ached for him.

Tir's lips moved and Covie beckoned to her.

Jenn leaned close. "Li-l-la," he whispered, teeth chattering. "Let—r. P-poc—"

"Bannan!"

He came at once, crouching to meet Tir's barely open eyes. He put a hand on his shoulder. "Easy, my friend."

"Tir's brought a letter," Jenn told him. "It's in his pocket. I think he said it's from Lila." Tir nodded at this and tried to smile; his badly chapped lips cracked, beading with blood.

"Ancestors Blessed—" Bannan bowed his head, eyes closed, and shuddered.

Tir understood before Jenn. Losing his smile, he managed, "Li-i-la d-didn't come!" with all the vehemence he could muster. "I'd n-never leave h-her. S-sir."

"I know." Bannan looked up, his eyes suspiciously bright. "Don't call me that."

"M-make m—me." Another smile. "S-sir."

The truthseer shook his head. "We'll discuss your poor attitude later. Rest." His voice grew husky and low. "You've earned it and more, this night."

Jenn went with Bannan to the dining table, where Kydd and their father were sorting what had arrived with their new guests. "A fight," Radd said quietly, pointing out dark stains and tears.

Kydd glanced at Tir. "He won, or the owners of these coats would still be wearing them."

Men had died, that meant. Jenn wanted to be sorry, but wasn't, Tir having saved the boys and himself from more than the cold. "There's a letter for Bannan in a pocket of Tir's coat, Poppa. From his sister."

Peggs, coming from the kitchen with a tray of hot drinks, overheard. "Ancestors Witless and Wanton. That letter best contain a good reason for risking these poor boys in a storm," she declared fiercely, "or I'll be writing their mother, baroness or not!"

"Peggs!" Jenn admonished, keeping her voice low.

"I hope it does too." Bannan laced his fingers through hers.

Radd, having the coat, was already searching the pockets. He straightened with a frown. "Nothing. I'm sorry."

"Let me try." The miller passed him the garment. Instead of going through its pockets again, Bannan flipped open the front of the coat, kneading the lining with his fingers until he felt whatever he sought. Taking out his knife, he made a small slit, then pulled free an envelope crusted with wax seals. "Lila makes Sennic seem a trusting sort," he commented wryly.

Cracking the seals to open the letter, he read it then and there. Peggs silently handed mugs to her husband and father, another to Jenn. She gave Covie hers and the one for Tir, since by the look of him, the man was sound asleep, then came back to stand near Bannan, leaving his close by on the tray.

The truthseer shook his head, thrusting the letter at Jenn. "Ancestors Perplexed and Puzzled. Does this make any sense to you?"

Jenn took the baroness' letter and read.

*Little Brother,*

*I send you greetings, salutations, and your nephews.*

*High time they saw a real winter, and life beyond the estate. Emon would agree with me, were he here, but he's been sent to Mellynne to talk their merchants out of suspending trade, improve the rhetoric between our governments from shouting and threats to mere shouting, and basically save us all from Ordo's latest folly. He took Cheek and Scatterwit. They'll keep him entertained between sessions.*

*As for the boys?*

*Hearts of my Ancestors. By this letter, I, Baroness Lila Larmensu Westietas, hereby place my sons, Semyn and Werfol, wholly in the care of my brother, Bannan Marerrym Larmensu, to live with him in Marrowdell until such time as I, or my husband, Baron Emon Westietas, come and retrieve them, or until adult by law.*

*This I declare my heart's will, by my seal in blood.*

*Do you good, brother, having them around. They're fine boys, if too biddable of late. I blame the new staff. Your nephews know how to be Westietas. Teach them what it means to be Larmensu.*

*Show them a dragon. I may have promised.*

*However far we are apart,*

*Keep Us Close.*

Midway down the page, beside the formal declaration, was a rusty brown thumbprint. Blood. Lila's blood.

Jenn thought the letter made perfect sense in one way: Lila had sent her sons to live with Bannan. In any other, it made none. She found herself agreeing with Peggs. Sending children into danger wasn't what anyone should do unless—and this must be what put such unfamiliar strain on Bannan's face—the risk would be greater, had the boys stayed at home.

She gave back the letter. "Who are Cheek and Scatterwit?"

"Emon's crows." Bannan ran a distracted hand through his hair. "Heart's Blood." He passed the letter to Radd, who read it in silence then passed it to Peggs, Kydd leaning over her shoulder. Covie took it last, after looking to the truthseer for his consent, given with a nod.

As the healer read, Peggs gazed at the bed and the sleeping boys, her expression going from distress to one Jenn knew very well. Determination. Sure enough. "Poppa," she commanded briskly, "Kydd will bring down your summer hammock and the heavy quilt. The boys should stay where they are tonight. And Tir." Who, having slumped over on the settee's cushions and begun to snore, would have been cruel to move, were it even possible. "I'll put on extra porridge and bread for the morning. Covie, let me know whatever you need."

"I will."

Radd and Kydd nodded in complete agreement, the latter heading off on his mission to collect bedding for his father-by-marriage. Jenn hid a smile.

Bannan bowed his head. "My thanks."

Peggs handed him his neglected but still-steaming mug. "Jenn will help me put out a supper." A frown as she assessed her sister's damp state. "After you change, Dearest Heart. As for you, Bannan, you'll stay the night, of course. Kydd can fetch you anything you might need from Devins'." With that, she spun on her heel and headed for the kitchen.

Where everything could be fixed. Jenn shook her head in admiration.

Radd chuckled. "I wouldn't argue, if I were you."

"I wouldn't dream of it," replied Bannan, who seemed overwhelmed. "Though I regret disrupting your home."

"Speak no more of that." The miller's eyes rested on the sleeping boys. "They were sent to you, but they'll be cared for by all of us. Now come. Sit with me. You too, Covie. Tell us about your nephews."

Her father saw how Bannan struggled to keep his worry in check. Not the least of those worries must be what the villagers would think of having new mouths to feed this of all winters. Radd would reassure him. They'd manage.

Another worry, Jenn took care of as she followed Peggs. Sweet dreams, she wished the boys, as she'd learned to do, as only a turn-born could.

So Marrowdell would let them stay.

Why, Lila?

Surely Tir would know. Must know. However desperate he was for that conversation, Bannan let his friend rest. In all their years together, he'd never seen Tir Half-face so spent. A lump filled the truthseer's throat each time he thought of how close he'd come to losing all three.

As for the dragon, Jenn, and Scourge? How had they known?

Ancestors Forlorn and Forsaken. What if they hadn't?

Busy staring into his cup, he started when the neck of a bottle appeared in his view. He glanced up as Kydd, smiling, tipped a generous dollop of amber liquid into his tea before doing the same for Radd and Covie. "Try this before the food comes," the beekeeper advised, pouring his own.

"My thanks. To families, wherever they are." The healer took a goodly swallow. Village rumor, namely Hettie, said the mail had brought encouraging news from the demas if not directly from Covie's now-distant son. Roche had apprenticed with a respected lens maker, in an Ansnan town on no map Bannan had ever seen. Dema Qimirpik had vowed to keep his eye on the young man.

"Ancestors Blessed and Beloved, watch over them all," the truthseer agreed earnestly, taking his own drink. A welcome burn down his throat nestled in his stomach; most welcome, after being out in the storm. "Thank you for your care, Covie."

She nodded graciously. "Thank me by keeping an eye on Tir. He'll need to stay off those feet for a few days, and keep applying the medicine I've brought. His toes are soft, still." This with a confidence that warmed Bannan even more than the drink. "They'll blister, badly, and forever feel the cold, but he shouldn't lose them."

"By the Hearts of my Ancestors," he vowed, "I'll sit on him if I must."

The others chuckled. "I'd help," Kydd said, "but I fear our doughty warrior would toss me over his shoulder."

"Your lads. Eight years and five, you say?" Radd raised an eyebrow. "They're alike in size. Who's eldest?"

"Semyn." Bannan leaned back in his chair, hands around his cup. "He's the one with red in his hair. Werfol's the family weed." "Weed" being Emon's pet name for the boy, the baron swearing Werfol grew out of shoes so quickly he could support a tannery. Seeing Radd smile, the truthseer went on, "Semyn's the image of his father; Werfol takes more to the Larmensu." Though appearances were deceiving, Semyn already a strategist like his mother and Werfol inclined to tinker—and break—whatever he laid hand upon. "They're both—wonderful." And well-loved. Emon spent every minute he could pry from his work with his sons and Lila, while her love for them all was as fierce and beautiful as her own heart.

See a real winter? Life beyond the estate? She hadn't even bothered to lie well. Lila scattered her family for a reason. Whatever it was, he'd see them together again, Bannan swore to himself. See them whole, again.

Or die trying.

They'd left him one of their precious candles, but Bannan snuffed it out and made do with the glow from the heatstove, wanting neither to waste the light, nor disturb the rest of those who deserved it. Radd snored gently. He'd slung his hammock from waiting hooks in the rafters, settling in with the ease of long practice, for this was how he slept on the porch spring and summer, giving his sister his bed.

Buried under quilts, Tir slept on the settee. Covie had bandaged his feet in loose wraps, finishing with soft scarves. Time, she'd said, would tell.

Bannan sat in a chair by the wide bed. The dim light caught on round young cheeks and noses, suggested shape beneath the covers, but couldn't give color to the hair on the pillows. No matter, he knew it well. Among his belongings was a tiny wooden box, containing a curl from each precious head, a keepsake from Lila. He could picture sunbeams finding red highlights or brown, touching skin freckled or tan.

No need to imagine what sagged the mattress near the foot of the bed. He looked deeper, glimpsed the violet of a wild and vigilant eye, and bowed his head in thanks.

The dragon had returned from wherever he'd gone to warm himself, to keep watch too.

"Hearts of my Ancestors," he prayed soundlessly, in the dark. "I'm Beholden for their safety, for losing them would have broken all our hearts. I'm Beholden for the kindness of these people, who shelter us despite their own need. I'm Beholden for the magic of Marrowdell, for without it Jenn Nalynn and Wisp and Scourge could not have saved them from the storm. Most of all, I would be Beholden if Lila could know her boys are with me and well. However far we are apart—" he choked at the last, but it didn't matter. Risk winter's wrath on the Northward Road? Despite having no Scourge of her own, Lila wouldn't hesitate.

Unless she chose to risk something worse.

Dark thoughts. Bannan shrugged beneath the quilt over his shoulders. Dark thoughts were the only ones he had.

"Sir."

A whisper. It flickered open a pair of young eyes, gleaming in the embers' light. Bannan leaned forward to kiss Werfol on the forehead. "You're with me, Dear Heart," he murmured gently, "and safe. Sleep now. I'll be right here."

He waited until the boy's eyes closed again before going to Tir. "What can I get for you?"

A whisper, hoarse but amused. "Dancing women in scanty clothes, sir, an'a bottle o'the finest, but I'll settle for making my report."

Bannan smiled, the stiffness of his jaw telling him how set it had been until now. "Good to hear." He felt for another chair and brought it near the settee, sitting down. "Mind you don't overdo, or Covie will have my head."

"How're the lads?"

"Better than you," Bannan assured him. "Asleep." Or

listening. He wouldn't put it past them and Radd's snores had taken on an artificial air. Fair enough. "Ancestors Crazed and Confounded, Tir. What's this about? Yes, I've Lila's letter, saying the boys are to stay with me. I don't need to see her face to know the lie."

"Aie, Sir. The letter's to prove you've right to the boys, should anyone else come after them." Tir's voice, though low and raspy, took on a familiar cadence. "I went to the baroness after the Lady Mahavar was settled at home, to pay my respects and because—begging your pardon, sir— your sister would have cut off more than my ears if I hadn`t told her your situation."

Bannan nodded. "Go on."

"When I was done, she asked me if you were in a safe place. I told her you were, though now I'm back, I'm wondering, sir, why." A meaningful pause, then, "She'd the boys ready within the hour. My guess is she'd been waiting for somewhere to send them."

The truth. "Why?"

Tir shifted as if uncomfortable, then sighed. "The baroness didn't say. No need. Whatever the baron's up to in Channen? There are those eager to change his mind on certain matters. The boys—they'd be leverage, sir, wouldn't they?"

Bannan felt cold. "There's nothing Emon wouldn't do for them," he agreed. Which didn't explain why they were here, with him. "Lila would have kept them safe. And her staff." Handpicked, the lot of them. Her standards were nothing if not exacting, and she wasn't above using his gift to check their loyalty. When he'd been there.

"Not all hers," Tir said darkly. "Not anymore. The prince suggested Vorkoun's noble houses accept Ansnans into their employ. Show support for the treaty. The baron had no choice. Your sister sent her two best with us—you'll know the names: Rowe Jonn and Seel Aucoin. Meant leav'n not a one at the estate I'd trust."

Worse and worse. "Where are Rowe and Seel?"

"Can't say, sir. We'd left in secret—didn't send word even to Lady Mahavar, who'll by now think the worst o'me—but we were betrayed. By Weken, we'd hunters on our trail. Passed Endshere by night, rather than risk a stop, but outrun riders, us with a loaded wagon?"

Bannan could see the moment, understand every choice, all too well. "They hung back."

"Aie. So me and the lads could make a dash for Marrowdell and help. The hunters caught up to us right as the storm hit. There'd be but one way past those brave men, Ancestors Dear and Departed. I'm sorry, sir."

A whimper, stifled and soft, from the bed. "Go on," Bannan said, hearing pain in his own voice.

"We're here, as your sister wanted."

"And the hunters?"

With grim satisfaction. "Won't be making reports, sir."

"Good." Bannan rose to his feet. "Rest, now."

"Sir. Bannan. The wagon—the baroness sent supplies for the five of us—we can't abandon it."

Of course she had, the truthseer told himself, feeling a pang of memory. How many rainy afternoons had they spent, sprawled on a carpet, adding cutlery and potato slices to their ranks of toy soldiers because Lila insisted armies moved on their stomachs? Ancestors Calm and Collected, sitting here in the dark, in this valley so remote few knew it existed, he could almost hear her calculating the burden of five extra mouths on Marrowdell. She'd sent what would compensate.

While he'd bought candy at the fair.

"We'll go for the wagon in the morning, Tir," Bannan promised. If the storm subsided by then. The wind still rattled the shutters every so often. Maybe there was a limit to how much snow could fall in a night.

Or a winter.

He settled himself back in his chair by the bed, wrapped in a quilt. Lila'd been beset and surrounded, a situation she'd not tolerate. She'd made her first move, to put her children out of reach. What next? Bannan pulled the quilt tighter, sinking his chin to his chest. Whatever she had in mind, his role was to be here, with Semyn and Werfol.

Whatever she had in mind, he'd hope no more blood would spill.

As well hope snow had limits.

Lila had none.

"More playmates for you, Dearest Heart," Gallie told Loee as the baby nursed.

Zehr smiled. "I'll see if Covie kept any of the twins' clothes. We passed them along for Cheffy," he explained to Jenn. "They'll be well-worn. You know the lad."

"That's what patches are for," his wife countered with a laugh. "We'll have Bannan's nephews snug as can be in no time at all."

The Emms hadn't been this happy since their return from Endshere. No one had. Despite the uncertainty and worry surrounding Semyn and Werfol's arrival, Jenn decided, they couldn't have come at a better time. Children, Aunt Sybb had said, were the surest remedy for grief. She'd also said children were the surest distraction—or was that interruption?—but all in all, her meaning was the same. Marrowdell's worry over Frann's illness had eased, however slightly.

"I'll let him know," Jenn promised, gathering the dishes.

"Leave those, Good Heart," Zehr told her. "You go help Bannan and your sister. I'm sure they'll be making plans where the boys will stay, and Tir."

"Perhaps you should be part of those plans, Jenn Nalynn," suggested Gallie, eyes atwinkle. "After all, a bed shared is a warmer one."

Oh, and didn't her cheeks flame at that? Jenn muttered something incoherent, which made Gallie laugh again, but kindly, and ran to bundle up for the trip to the Nalynns' very full house.

Once outside, her breath hanging in the air like a cloud, Jenn stopped to admire the storm's handiwork. For under a sky of brilliant blue, Marrowdell was now white.

Glistening snow pillowed rooftops and clung like frosting to windowsills and logs. It lay in sharp-edged drifts that curled between buildings and hedgerow, here waist-high, there up to her chin. The wind had scoured to the turf in places, but never in a useful path. They'd be shoveling for days.

The river had vanished beneath lapped scales of white, as if a giant snake lay along the valley floor. Beyond, the fields were full of odd shapes and lumps. Efflet sculpted the snow, Wisp had told her, not the wind. She couldn't wait to take a closer look.

First, to Bannan. Jenn began pushing through the snow. The snow pushed back. Or something under it.

She stopped and tilted her head, considering the matter. "Fair morning."

A long, slender mass of snow rose abruptly to hang in midair. Jenn narrowed her eyes. "Wisp?" More snow lifted in answer, this time in the shape of spread wings. "It is you! I've been so worried—"

"I've a way to warm myself, Dearest Heart." The little breeze sounded decidedly smug.

He'd recovered, that meant, and she wasn't to fuss, but finding her dragon encased in ice was, Jenn thought with an inward shudder, something she'd never forget. "I'm glad. You were very brave, Wisp, to save the boys and Tir. But how did you know?"

"I didn't." He shook, and snow flew in all directions. If not for the impression made by his body, she might be alone. "The sei sent me. Into the storm." A snarl. "Beyond the edge."

Brave indeed. "Come with me," she asked impulsively. "Bannan will want to know what you found." It wasn't as if Wisp hadn't been in the Nalynn home before.

Though then, he'd been a man, and Wyll.

"I'll come with you. I'll stay with you." The breeze lifted snow and spun it. "Here is the best place to be, Dearest Heart, and to stay."

As if they played in the meadow. As if nothing was wrong. Which made her suddenly certain something was and this wasn't play at all. "Wisp. What happened out there?"

Snow became one column, then two. "Horses died and men died," the breeze told her airily. The columns touched at their tops then collapsed. "I did not."

But he might have. She'd seen it. Had not Scourge dragged him back to the edge, and to her? He'd never have left the boys and Tir. He'd have frozen with them. "The sei shouldn't have sent you," Jenn said, trying her best not to be angry, but she was. "I don't understand why it didn't ask me—"

A clump of snow landed with a wet smack, right on her nose. She staggered back and almost fell. The breeze chuckled. "Because only a dragon could have saved them, Dearest Heart, and only I would have tried."

Well, yes, there was that. Jenn stealthily gathered up a handful of snow and formed it into a ball, then launched it where she thought he might be.

The ball swerved in midair. It made a glorious arc over the Nalynn roof and sleeping roses, disappearing beyond.

A surprised shout followed.

Jenn covered her mouth with a mitten hand, stifling a laugh.

Another ball of snow rose over the roof, coming this way! Though well thrown, it hadn't a chance against a playful dragon. The ball stopped midair, then flew back.

A second shout, this time more outraged than surprised.

Jenn hurried through the snow, taking shelter beneath the rosebushes. As she armed herself with more snowballs, the air above filled with them. Some blew apart into tiny blizzards. Some were sent flying back, faster than they'd come. A few disappeared as if swallowed. Which was hardly fair, no matter who was on the other side of the house. She began to throw her own. "Take that, Wisp!"

Though she hadn't made a wish, snowballs formed themselves all around her, soaring through the air with hers to converge on one spot, near the hedge. A shape fought free and, with a roar she felt in her bones, the dragon took to the air, shedding snow as he flew.

Jenn dusted off her mittens. "We won!" she told the snow around her, certain she wasn't alone. She got to her feet, freeing her scarf from a thorn, and turned.

To meet a snowball.

Jenn blinked snow to find Bannan, so caked himself in white he might have been one of the efflets' sculptures. Only his eyes showed, and they were full of mischief. He had, she realized belatedly, more snowballs.

With a ringing whoop of battle, Jenn launched herself before he could throw another, toppling him into the snow. Which might have worked, but he wrapped his long arms around her and rolled them both until they were more snow than person, and laughing so hard it was impossible to catch a full breath.

When finally they paused, wrapped in each other, Jenn

freed her hand to wipe snow from his dear face. "You do realize," she said cheerfully, nose-to-nose, "Wisp started it."

"Thought as much." Bannan's eyes sparkled. "He's in a good mood."

"He's glad to be home." Despite the layers of coats and cloaks and whatever else between them, Jenn decided she quite liked snuggling in the snow and would have been glad herself to stay like this, assuming no one walked by to see them.

"As am I, Dearest Heart," Bannan said, giving her a cold, wet, and thoroughly pleasant kiss. Then he jumped to his feet, offering his hand. "Sennic's sure the weather will hold for the morning, so we're off to fetch Lila's supplies."

Jenn took his hand to pull herself up. "It will hold here," she assured him.

A smile that warmed her heart. "Many thanks. And I ask another kindness, Jenn, much harder to accomplish."

She waited.

"Sit on Tir for me." Bannan shook his head. "I caught him trying to find boots. Ancestors Dutiful and Dazed, the man has more heart than sense. He hasn't said as much, but I know him. Now that I've the boys, he thinks to return to your lady aunt."

"He'll have to heal first," Jenn pointed out. "By then, even Tir will see why no one travels once winter takes hold."

They'd begun walking around the house. The truthseer paused to kick at a drift, and gave her a wondering look. "Worse than this?"

By the Midwinter Beholding, the village would shrink from wide fields and open roads, to narrow shoveled paths connecting the fountain to homes and outbuildings. Houses would be buried, marked by holes at doorways and windows, with steps cut into the snow packed on roofs in order to reach and clear the chimneys.

Which was handy for making slides, too. Winter had its joys; children knew where to find them. How many would be new to Semyn and Werfol?

Thoughts full of what was to come, Jenn settled for, "You'll see."

When they came around the house, Davi was there, busy

checking the runners on what had been the village cart and was now its sled. Battle and Brawl tossed their big heads, ringing the bells attached to their halters. Pretty, the bells, and Jenn loved them.

The only guide in the dark or storm, those bells, should horse or villager become separated.

Not today. Today was beautiful and clear; though Jenn didn't make a wish yet, she intended it stay that way till all were safely home.

Anten and Kydd were there, already mounted, with Tadd just arrived, leading his horse and Perrkin, who must be for Bannan, though she'd have expected Scourge. Tools and shovels had been loaded onto the sled, along with packs and firewood. Precaution before prevents regret later, Jenn remembered Aunt Sybb telling her and her sister, though she'd been referring to moon potion and womanly cycles, not being stranded overnight in the cold.

The packs would have contained moon potion, had Cynd been going. The older women had resumed its use, after Gallie's unexpected pregnancy. Jenn glanced toward the Treffs' house, knowing where Cynd would be and why.

The door opened and Radd stuck his head out, asking calmly. "Is the blizzard over?"

As the others laughed, Jenn noticed what she'd missed before. Ten paces from the Nalynn doorway the snow was marked only by footprints. Within that boundary, dozens of spent snowballs lay in tidy rows, for all the world like potatoes waiting to be planted.

Wisp.

An interesting winter lay ahead, if her dragon chose to play in it. It might be wise to establish a few rules.

She smiled to herself. Or not.

Marrowdell was in fine spirits this morning, with the storm passed and adventure in the offing. That the adventure would involve hard work—the snow doubtless having buried the boxes and the wagon, from Tir's unsettling description, having toppled on its side—didn't appear to matter to those who'd volunteered.

What did matter was the promise of supplies. Though none said it and none ever would, Bannan knew what had been careful rationing before would have been dangerously tight with Tir and the boys added. He'd sleep better.

Once they were back.

First things first. "I'll check on the boys," he told Jenn.

"Shall I come with you? We haven't been introduced." With an anxious frown.

"They'll love you," he assured her, kissing her nose. "As much as I do—"

"Ancestors Late and Laggard!" Davi cursed loudly. "Are we going today or not?" He climbed into the sled and took the reins, face creased in an unfamiliar scowl.

A man beset with troubles, giving his time. "Your pardon," Bannan said quickly. "Start on your way. I'll be right behind." He waved at Tadd to wait with Perrkin, then gave Jenn an apologetic smile.

"Go," she told him, smiling back. "I'll introduce myself after I change."

The village echoing the sound of bells and hooves crunching snow, Bannan hurried to the Nalynn home. Radd, about to leave, stopped him at the door, chuckling. "Your pockets?"

Puzzled, Bannan reached into one, finding it full of snow. As were the rest of his pockets and the tops of his boots. Taking off his coat to give it a shake, he discovered a great lump in the hood, sure to melt down his neck. "I've a great deal to learn about snow," he said ruefully as he stepped inside.

The miller laughed as he closed the door behind him. "You'll get plenty of practice here."

Tir had moved to a chair at the family table, his mask back in place. He grimaced at Bannan, nodding at the food before him. "Unfair tactics, sir," he complained.

A bowl of thick rich soup. Half a loaf, already buttered. Pie, steaming from the oven. Peggs' doing, this was. The truthseer managed to keep a straight face. "Impossible odds," he agreed. "Just as well you've orders to stay off your feet as much as possible."

Tir gestured with his eating knife. "Ancestors Fattened and Filled," he said with mock gloom. "Suppose it's doing m'duty, sir." Bright blue eyes looked sidelong at Bannan. "You're off, then?"

"Once I speak to the boys."

"Brave as any soldier, the pair o'them." As if embarrassed, Tir traded his knife for a spoon, then tapped his mask. "M'lady's doing." He slipped up the lower portion before pouring in soup. Another glance. "The lads won't want you to leave, sir, not so soon."

Bannan felt weight settle around his heart. "It's necessary. You know why."

"Aie." Tir paused, a frown furrowing the scars on his forehead. "Can't promise the wild things haven't already done their work. We heard howling, sir, most o'the way."

"Then I'd best not dawdle," the truthseer said lightly.

"Sir." Almost a protest. "They were strangers."

"Perhaps not to me." Bannan rested a hand on his friend's shoulder and bent to speak in his ear. "I'll waste no chance to learn who came after you." He straightened. "Mind you listen to the healer. Peggs isn't the only Nalynn keeping an eye on you."

He took Tir's resumed interest in his hearty meal for assent.

The boys were in the kitchen, standing shoulder to shoulder at the worktable. Semyn, his lower lip between his teeth, was cutting carrots while his younger brother lined the pieces back up as if they were a puzzle to solve. Over their heads, Peggs gave Bannan a dazzling smile. "Your uncle's back," she told the boys. "They've been excellent helpers," to Bannan. A second look and she pulled out a cloth to hand him, miming rubbing his head.

Bannan reached up to discover his hair was indeed soaking wet. "I was playing in the snow," he explained and almost mentioned the dragon.

Not yet. He dried his hair, using the moment to study the small and solemn faces aimed up at him, noting with dismay the pallor in once-rosy cheeks and purple bruises beneath their eyes. Tense, the pair, and ready to bolt. Despite being here with Peggs, in the most homely house imaginable, they were still afraid.

Heart's Blood. Shaken, the truthseer returned the towel

with a small bow and deliberately easy smile. "I won't be long," he promised. "I'll play with you this afternoon."

"We will look forward to it, esteemed Uncle," said Semyn, with a deeper bow of his own. Every bit the baron's son.

Well enough, Bannan thought, returning the courtesy. Manners could be comfort and shield.

Werfol wrinkled his nose at his brother. "Father took us up the mountain last summer to play in snow. You didn't like it."

"I daresay it wasn't snow like Marrowdell's," Peggs said smoothly. "Why don't you get dressed and see for yourselves? You can play outside till lunch. I'll ring a bell when it's ready."

Two pairs of dismayed eyes snapped to their uncle, an uncle who felt very much the same way. Bannan did his best to look delighted. "A splendid notion, Peggs."

"Do you think so, Uncle?" Werfol asked him, looking up through long eyelashes. "Truly?"

Of course he didn't. Let them roam a strange place on their own? Lila'd have more than his ears.

But Lila wasn't here, and he couldn't have her sons start their lives here being afraid to go out and play. "Of course I do," Bannan said heartily. "There are other children here. Cheffy and Alyssa. You can introduce yourselves." What else might entice them? "There are barns. You can visit the animals."

"Alone?" Semyn asked, abruptly sounding much younger.

"Marrowdell is full of kind people," Bannan replied, though his heart went out to the boy. Had they ever simply wandered without guard or nursemaid? "If you need anything, knock on any door."

Semyn considered this, his brow furrowed like his father's in thought, then nodded dutifully. "Is there a map, Uncle, we may borrow? We mustn't get lost."

"Or miss lunch," Werfol added.

Peggs laughed. "You'll hear the bell, Dear Hearts. Marrowdell's not big enough for a map. Stay within the hedges and gates. Open any door you like. We're friendly folk and everyone knows you're here." She tilted her lovely head. "Now wish fair journey to your uncle, so he and the others can be on their way."

Bannan stepped around the counter and squatted, his arms open. The boys came into his embrace, pressing their soft cheeks against his. They trembled, or he did, or both, and for an instant he wondered if he was wrong about all of it, about leaving them, about giving them freedom . . .

About Marrowdell.

Then a breeze found his ear. "Go, fool," the dragon ordered peevishly. "They are in my care!"

He laughed. He had to. And it was the right thing to do, for the boys stood back and looked at him with the beginnings of real smiles.

Marrowdell, Bannan thought gratefully. He should never doubt it.

Dragonlings needed little more than the occasional snap and snarl to remind them of their lowly place, which was safely distant from their elders. Especially from their elder's meat, tails—or jaws.

Not so children. They demanded such care that the villagers took turns and seemed exhausted most of the time. In Wisp's experience, as babes, they were at their best asleep. He'd tuck the girl in thistledown and clover, watching dreams play beneath her delicate eyelids. Awake? That had been more challenging. The ways her tiny toddling self could find to get into danger had appalled him. Even the newly hatched had more sense.

Fortunately these two were into the vastly more interesting stage that followed, being able to move on their own and talk. Wisp followed at a distance, fascinated.

After going outside to wave good-bye to their uncle, they'd evaded all other elders almost as easily as the girl had, at the same stage. It must be a skill children acquired when ready to explore their world, though the boys seemed less curious than desperate.

Wisp wasn't sure what they were after. They'd been fed and were well dressed, yet from the moment they'd

believed themselves unobserved, they'd made sure to stay
that way, going around the back of barns and crouching to
hide behind drifts.

The elder carried a kitchen knife. The younger—Wisp
tasted the air—the younger had taken food.

Where did his duty lie? He'd saved them once, which
should have been sufficient, but for some reason he couldn't
quite leave them. Perhaps, the dragon told himself, he hadn't
finished saving them yet.

Though what threat there could be in the village, he
couldn't imagine.

Still, it was a dragonish game, furtive movement as if all
were potential enemies, and one they'd clearly practiced.
He saw no harm in it. He even helped, here and there, surreptitiously clearing the deepest snow from their path.

The elder, Semyn, couldn't see him and didn't notice.

The younger, Werfol? Wisp wasn't sure. His golden eyes
flicked here and there. Twice he stopped to stare, seeing
what only he could; without a word, Semyn took his arm to
pull him along. Something else, the dragon judged, well
practiced.

At each barn, they'd stop to peer through gaps in the
wood, only to move on. Whatever they sought, they didn't
find it until the barn filled with cows.

This barn had a side door, light enough for two small
boys to slide open. They slipped inside.

As did Wisp, unsurprised to find Semyn and Werfol, who
were themselves most surprised to be confronted by the
barn's guardian.

~Elder brother?!~ The Ropps' house toad, having leapt
in the boys' path, now puffed in alarm. ~Who are these?
What do they intend!?~

~Let them pass, worthy little cousin,~ Wisp told it.
~These are the truthseers' kin. They mean no harm.~ They
certainly couldn't do any. The knife Semyn held outstretched and shaking might damage a vegetable, but his
arm hadn't the strength to puncture hide with it. ~They
were told to explore the village.~

The little cousin shrank, slightly, but didn't budge. ~I
guard,~ it said, inclined to be stubborn. ~I do not want them
here.~

Werfol stared at the toad. The toad stared back. "Semyn," the boy said uncertainly. "This isn't a toad."

"I don't care what it is. It's in our way." Semyn firmed his grip on the knife and gestured with it. "Shoo! Go!"

In their stalls, the cows turned their heads to watch. The pigs, half-buried in straw like great boulders, ignored the entire business. The old pony nickered, wanting attention.

The barn being warm, and inclined to curiosity, the dragon settled himself on a rafter.

~Elder brother.~ With as much reproach as a toad dared. ~They must leave!~

~Patience, little cousin. I would see what these newcomers do.~

Semyn raised his knife but didn't move.

Neither did the toad.

Werfol stepped between the two. "Let me try." Without waiting, he went to his knees in front of the toad. "You're a guard, aren't you? You protect this barn."

"You're wasting time."

"I am not." The younger boy reached slowly into a pocket, bringing forth a carrot. "We brought this for the pony," he said to the toad.

The old pony's nostrils flared with interest. The house toad blinked, slowly, then shrank to its normal size. ~It is proper for children to bring carrots, elder brother.~ Having pronounced judgment, it hopped into the shadows.

"Well done, Weed. Now hurry. He has a halter. There should be a saddle."

Ah. So that was their plan. Wisp laid his head along the wood, vastly amused. He'd watched the girl with this pony. It would take more than a carrot to convince such a wise and self-centered creature to leave its cozy stall.

But it soon became clear these boys were well accustomed to horses and ponies. Before the pony could finish its treat, it wore a blanket and saddle, the girth tightened by small, but knowing hands. When it balked at being led out, the elder boy jumped in the saddle, legs giving an authoritative squeeze. The surprised pony found itself walking forward, Werfol hurrying ahead to widen the door.

Why the little thieves, Wisp thought with some admiration.

The little cousin scrambled to stop them. ~ELDER-BROTHER!~

The dragon yawned, sending a breeze to slide the door closed. ~No harm done,~ he assured the outraged toad, now swollen into a fierce ball in front of Werfol.

The boy cautiously edged around the toad, then put both hands on the door handle. "Help me, Semyn!" he cried. "I can't open it by myself."

The delay gave Wainn's old pony time to remember it didn't have to obey a rider but should, always, the house toad. Moreover, it remembered wanting to have nothing to do with going out in the cold. Blowing out through loose lips, it turned and walked back into its stall, ignoring its rider's now tearful efforts. As a final insult, the pony lowered its head, closed its eyes, and to all appearances, fell asleep.

The toad gave itself a proud shake and returned to normal size. It did not, however, abandon its post by the door.

Semyn slid off the pony.

"What are we going to do?" Werfol demanded, taking hold of his arm. "We can't stay here. Mother said we'd be safe. She lied, Semyn! She LIED."

"I know." Semyn hugged his younger brother, the pair a picture of misery. "We'll find another way, that's all. We have to."

They were afraid?

An intolerable situation. In their meadow, the girl had spoken of leaving Marrowdell, but she'd been happy, imagining wonders beyond this world and eager to see them for herself. He'd been the one filled with fear, hiding dread.

A dragon lord's penance, just and deserved.

~Keep them here, little cousin,~ Wisp ordered. With a silent roar, he leapt into the air, then plunged into the ground.

It wasn't to be theirs.

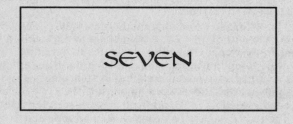

# SEVEN

"*D*O YOU THINK they'll like it?"

Hettie examined the little book with care. "I'm sure they will. The poor lads." Her eyes filled with sympathy. "They've been through so much." Passing the book back to Jenn, she heaved a great sigh and took up her tea, a determined smile on her face. "Ancestors Blessed, little ones recover before their parents do. You'll see."

She and Peggs had been deep in a discussion of children, babies, and their upcoming care when Jenn arrived. To be honest, it was more a case of Hettie holding forth and Peggs listening with both fascination and horror, Hettie having helped raise her younger brother and sister, and being present, as Peggs had not, to assist her mother-by-marriage with the birthing of innumerable calves and piglets, not to mention Gallie Emms' daughter.

Not being pregnant, Tir had excused himself and now snored, peacefully, if not-so-quietly, on Radd's bed. Not to be pregnant, Jenn supposed it was still worth learning. After all, she planned to help Peggs, when her time came.

However, she'd interrupted and now they discussed her book. Jenn held it in both hands. It was a very well-read book, with rounded corners, soft to the touch. When the spine had fallen apart, years ago, despite her always being careful, Frann had sewn the pages back together, her stitches so even and sure Jenn thought them much better than the original. Remembering, she ran her finger along the threads.

"It's a kind and generous gift, Dearest Heart." Peggs hesitated, then went on, "But can you bear to part with it? It's your favorite."

"That's why I want Semyn and Werfol to have it." Jenn put the little book on the table. "Aunt Sybb says actions are what matter. This—this is the most special thing I have from when I was their age." She stroked the faded cover, feeling the bumps of the title. Something you had to do, since the gilt had worn off before she'd learned to read. If she closed her eyes, she could see every page, with its whimsical illustrations—three in glorious color—and wonderful words. This was the book that had first taught her the world was wider and deeper and vaster than Marrowdell.

Peggs tugged her braid. "Then it's perfect. I'm sorry they aren't here. I sent them out to play, but they'll be back for lunch. Join us?"

Jenn shook her head. "I promised Gallie." She glanced around the room. Everything was in its place, as if there'd not been four extra guests staying the night. There remained the question of where they'd spend the coming ones. "Will they stay with Devins?"

"I'd not wish that for anyone," Hettie said, then pointed at Peggs. "Don't give me that look, Dear Heart. You've seen the inside of my stepbrother's house. If he hopes a certain cousin of Palma's comes to visit this spring, he's work ahead if she's not to turn right 'round and leave. As it is, I swear mice wouldn't step inside."

Hopefully an exaggeration. If true, Jenn thought to herself, then Bannan shouldn't be living there either. Yes, he'd cleaned up the long-abandoned farmhouse, but that didn't mean he should have to do it again for a winter's lodging. She should help and would.

"'A night with a willing host is better than a month in a

palace,'" Peggs countered, something Jenn didn't think Aunt Sybb had ever said. Then again, her sister was prone to creating her own sayings.

"I'd like to try the month first." Hettie laughed, hands on her swollen belly as if the baby laughed too. "Especially if the palace has a bathtub I can climb out of without calling for Tadd."

Peggs' eyes widened. Time to escape, Jenn decided, before more intimacies came to light. "My thanks for the tea and company," she told them as she stood. As for her book? "Please don't wait to give Semyn and Werfol my gift, Peggs." Surely a small entertainment would be welcome, while they waited for Bannan to return, and give her sister a little peace.

"As you wish." Peggs came with her to the kitchen door, passing her item after item of winter wear. "Though you should be here, to see their faces."

Jenn wrapped her scarf around head and neck. "I've all winter to do that."

"Oh really?" Her sister dangled a mitten out of reach. "So this has nothing to do with being afraid to meet Bannan's family on your own?" Something she saw in Jenn's face made her lower both arm and voice. "Dearest Heart," she whispered, suddenly serious. "I was only teasing. Semyn and Werfol are children who'll need all our love and care. It's not like—" Peggs stopped.

Jenn gave a rueful grin. "Not like meeting the terrifying Baroness Lila Larmensu Westietas?" She recovered her mitten. "You're right, as you always are, dear sister. I'll come back as soon as I'm finished my chores."

"Promise?"

She claimed her other mitten. "I do. Now go. Talk babies with Hettie."

Peggs blushed, as she'd hoped, and gave her a quick hug.

"Just wait till it's your turn, Jenn," Hettie called cheerfully.

Jenn met her sister's eyes, comforted by the understanding she found there. "Two of us is more than enough," Peggs replied archly, then gave her a quick kiss on the cheek. "The boys will love your gift," she added. "And you. Go help Gallie."

Outside, Jenn paused to take a deep cold breath. When she exhaled, a plume much like a dragon's hung for an instant in the air. In every way, she felt and seemed and was an ordinary woman, even to herself. Time would tell otherwise, she supposed.

Putting aside such thoughts, she started her morning's errands for Gallie. First to the Ropps for more cheese, Loee's newest teeth making such foods a matter of some urgency. On her way, Jenn waved a greeting to Master Jupp. He wore his tall hat and dark winter cloak, with a colorful scarf wrapped several times around his neck, its tasseled ends down to his knees. The scarf had come from Avyo with him and only Riss knew how many times it had been mended, but its reappearance marked winter had arrived as surely as the first storm.

For his constitution, Master Jupp walked to the village fountain and back, once a day, rain or shine. In snow, he used his second cane as well, though his path was cleared before those leading to the barns. Kindness, Jenn thought with some pride, abounded in Marrowdell.

And took different forms. In dangerous weather, when no one, especially the elderly, should be out of doors, the entire village could hear Master Jupp shouting for his canes. Riss, having tucked both in the loft, would ignore her great-uncle's outrage and put on tea.

Though Jenn was ever-so-curious as to how Uncle Horst was fitting into the Jupp household, she hadn't found a way to ask. He seemed—

A breeze flicked the ends of her scarf, then pushed from behind. A breeze, Jenn noticed, that didn't touch Old Jupp's scarf at all. Someone wanted to play. Again. "Wisp. I've no time to—"

"Come quick! Come now!" Urgent and harsh and not playful at all.

She turned to look east, her thoughts immediately with Bannan and the others. "What's wrong?"

The breeze, rather rudely, pushed her around again. "The barn. Hurry!"

The Ropps'?

Oh dear! Hurry she did, newly worried. Cheffy and Alyssa were doing more adult chores—especially today, with Anten off and Covie preoccupied with her patients—and while gentle, the dairy cows were substantial beasts. Accidents could happen and how kind, Jenn thought as she ran through the snow, of Wisp to watch over the entire village.

When she reached the side door, the breeze having insisted on it, it slid open to let her through, then closed behind her.

Going from sun and snow to the relative gloom inside the barn, Jenn stopped, wary of taking a step before she could see. "Cheffy?"

"Fair morning."

Not Cheffy or Alyssa. The greeting came from lower down than she was used to, in a shaky, fearful voice.

"Fair morning," she replied out of habit, then blinked, her eyes adjusting.

There, in the middle of the aisle between the stalls, was a house toad puffed in full fury. Beyond the toad, for some reason the subject of its ire, were the children she'd last seen asleep in bed.

~Elder sister! I have defended my home from thieves. They came to steal the pony, but I did not permit it!~

Thieves? Little boys, and unhappy ones at that, who stood shoulder to shoulder as if awaiting punishment. One slightly taller, Semyn, with reddish brown curls peeking from his hood, freckles on a snub nose, and eyes that odd shade between blue and green. Werfol would be the other, with the same delicate build. His eyes were downcast, but tears streaked both faces.

Jenn glanced at Wainn's old pony, asleep under, yes, that was Devins' saddle.

First things first. "Well done," she told the toad, then looked to the elder boy. "You owe this fine toad an apology."

Though confusion flickered across his face, Semyn obediently bent to meet the toad's glare. "We shouldn't have tried to—to take what wasn't ours and we're sorry."

~I accept.~ The toad blinked its great eyes, then let out an opinionated huff to return to normal size. ~Do not trust these newcomer children, elder sister. We will be watching them.~ Grimly.

"It accepts," Jenn told the boys, leaving out the rest. It could be the toad's prickly sense of honor, but watching the two seemed prudent in any case, given they'd chosen mischief for their first outing. She waited for Wisp to vouchsafe his opinion, certain he hadn't rushed her here to appease a house toad, but no breeze tickled her ear and she'd not ask. The boys had heard her talk to a toad. An unseen dragon?

That could wait.

As the toad hopped away to resume its usual post, she found herself at a loss. This wasn't at all how she'd imagined meeting Bannan's nephews.

Done now. She'd mend what she could. "My name is Jenn Nalynn. You've met my sister, Peggs, and my father."

"Lady Nalynn." The elder boy gave a deep, graceful, and achingly familiar bow, sweeping the barn floor with the tip of one mittened hand. Vorkoun manners. Bannan's. "My name is Semyn Westietas," he confirmed in what Aunt Sybb would call a too-proper voice. "This is my brother, Werfol. We meant no harm."

Perhaps not, though Wainn's old pony doubtless held a different opinion, but there was, Jenn decided uneasily, something seriously amiss. Werfol didn't bow. He'd yet to speak or even look at her, come to that, his eyes glued to the toes of his boots.

"Call me Jenn." She squatted to bring herself to their level and Werfol hunched, as if expecting a blow. Worse and worse. Jenn reached out her hand, as she might to soothe a nervous rabbit. "Is something wrong?" she asked softly.

Eyes shot up to hers, golden eyes flecked with black, eyes that widened in shock.

Eyes that *saw* her.

For a terrible instant, neither of them moved. Jenn couldn't breathe. Heart's Blood, why hadn't Bannan told her—

Werfol screamed!

Semyn grabbed his brother, freeing her from those eyes. The boys ran past her. Jenn heard the barn door open. Knew they were gone.

Didn't move.

Couldn't.

Why should she?

Winter's frozen air slid along the floor and around her. It was nothing to the chill in her heart.

Had Bannan not experienced yesterday's storm, he would, he decided, believe winter the most beautiful time of year. The trees wore elegant lace over their dark green robes and every stick, shrub, and fencepost was topped with a jaunty cap. Even the crags towering over the valley were bedecked in puffs and swirls, like some confection ready for a feast.

The road was a blanket of snow, but the path beaten the night before—by horse, then kruar and dragon—made an easy passage. Without the wind, the air was crisp rather than bone-numbing and Bannan took an appreciative sniff, smiling at the tang of woodsmoke. A magnificent day for the boys to explore their new surroundings and make friends. To start forgetting.

Which reminded him of a promise. Bannan brought Perrkin beside Tadd's mount. The miller's apprentice shook his head. "It's too soon," he said without prompting. "We're still in Marrowdell."

Bannan lowered his voice. "Kydd's growing anxious." More than anxious, truth be told. The beekeeper had begun to lag, looking over his shoulder as if memorizing what they left behind, or now loath to leave it.

"You shouldn't have told him." A shrug. "Ancestors Witness, Bannan. It's not as if there's something to be done about it. Either Kydd will remember, or Marrowdell's magic will slip in and out of mind without him knowing the difference."

What would happen to him? Bannan wanted to touch the marks on his neck; he kept his hands quiet and on Perrkin's neck instead, refusing to doubt. Either the moth's protection would last or, as Tadd so bluntly put it, he'd never know.

Nodding, he eased his weight back in the saddle. Perrkin flicked a curious ear, but slowed his pace. Kydd noticed and closed the gap. His lean, handsome face was beaded with sweat despite the chill. "Ancestors Beset and Besieged," he muttered once they were riding beside each other. "Part of me wants to turn back, Bannan. I'll not deny it."

"And not know?"

The beekeeper grimaced. "Being the point." He shook himself, patting his horse, and fixed his gaze ahead. "You're right, of course. I must, even if the result be my own ignorance." He laughed, albeit grimly. "Ah, Marrowdell. You continue to test me."

There was much to admire about this man. Bannan's lips quirked. "Can we be sure Marrowdell isn't playing games?"

"Test or game. Either one can be lost." Kydd urged his horse to longer strides. "Let's find out."

They fell silent as Davi's team turned with the road. The winter muted the waterfall as well, though Radd had assured Bannan that those rapids, as well as the northern cataracts, wouldn't freeze. Horses stepped, leaving craters in the snow, blowing clouds into the air. Leather and wood made their creaks and complaints, while bells rang with each bob of the team's great heads.

First Davi and Anten, then Tadd left Marrowdell. Kydd followed.

As Perrkin stepped off the edge and into the outside world, a thought came to Bannan. This was a crossing, like those into the Verge.

A crossing anyone could take except . . .

"Jenn Nalynn," he whispered, over and over, simply for the joy of her dear name in his mouth. "I remember you." Each time, he felt that reassuring warmth on his neck. "Jenn Nalynn."

Kydd turned in his saddle, lifting a brow. "And who might that be?"

For a sickening heartbeat, Bannan believed him, then looked closer. "Liar," he accused happily. "That wasn't funny."

Tadd stopped his horse to let them join him. He gave the beekeeper a quick searching look, then nodded, his relief plain to see. "Marrowdell eyes," he proclaimed quietly. "We'd hoped, Allin and me. I'm glad."

"Ancestors Blessed." Bannan clapped Kydd on his shoulder. "We'll celebrate tonight, I promise."

They started moving again. When the beekeeper began

to stare at Davi and Anten, Bannan had no trouble guessing what tempted him. "I wouldn't."

Kydd looked sheepish. "Was I that obvious? But it's fascinating—now that I'm not terrified—" he qualified. "To think these men, friends I've known most of my life, suddenly possess different memories . . ."

Bannan didn't smile. "What's not terrifying about that?"

Kydd's mouth opened then closed. He gave a suddenly grim nod.

Moments later, Davi raised his hand, then pointed right. They'd reached the turn onto the Northward Road.

Bannan freed Sennic's sword from his coat, borrowed again that morning, and sent Perrkin to the fore. The others gave him sober looks. "Be wary, my friends," he told them. "Tir might not have accounted for all on his trail."

If not, well enough.

Captain Ash would have some questions.

Children didn't always tell the truth. Children could be cruel and thoughtless and, as everyone knew who wasn't a child, children didn't understand all that adults understood.

None of it mattered. Jenn shed her clothes as she ran, for they hadn't hidden what she was. She didn't need them. They were a lie she wore, a pretense.

Children pretended.

She wasn't a child. Or a woman.

As turn-born, she crossed the river, heedless of ice or slush, and ran until she could no longer be seen from the village. Until she could no longer be seen by a child.

But it didn't help. Werfol's scream rang through her, in her. How? She didn't have ears or eyes, she had holes full of light, so maybe it rang in her heart, but she had none, not really, but oh— Ancestors Scattered and Stone, she felt it, she truly did, with all that she was.

She stopped, forced to her knees by its weight.

A breeze found her. "What's this?" Dismay. Fear. The breeze whirled, picking up snow as if it were flower petals. "Dearest Heart. What's wrong?"

With an effort, Jenn lifted her head. "I've seen myself,"

she told her dragon, the words like splinters. "At last, I have. Don't worry," for he did, she knew, and for very good reason, but for once Marrowdell ignored her.

For which she should have been glad and quite possibly curious. Jenn found herself too full of pain to care.

Wisp let his shape find the light and settled into the snow before her, tail curled in a question. Laying his head at her feet, he gazed up with eyes both purple and wild.

Waiting.

Something stirred inside her. Thought, slow and sluggish. Dragons didn't care for the cold. He'd almost frozen, to save—

She shuddered.

Those poor boys. What they'd been through, she couldn't imagine.

"Dearest Heart?"

Jenn looked down.

The dragon rolled his head until only one eye showed and gaped his slender, deadly jaws no more than the width of her hand. Fangs like shards of bone glinted with fresh moisture. "If it would please you," a coy whisper, "I could eat the youngest."

"WISP!" She pulled her feet from under his head, which rose on that long neck to meet her gaze as she stood. "You mustn't! You can't! Don't even—"

Jaws snapped with satisfaction. He had her.

Oh, her wise and wicked dragon. Jenn touched the tip of his scaled snout. "You wouldn't," she said, relieved beyond measure.

"Not today," Wisp replied archly, as if to remind her what he was. "Probably not at all. You know what he is."

"A truthseer." Jenn sighed. "I wish Bannan had warned me."

Her dragon rose on his two whole legs, using the opposing wing for support. "What does it matter, Dearest Heart? The child saw you for all that you are." With a hint of pride. "It is why the sei sent me to find him." Both wings spread wide as he slowly reared in place, every muscle taut, magnificent and sure, then winked out of sight.

But wasn't gone. She heard—felt—his other, soundless voice. ~Like you, I found myself in his eyes.~

"He wasn't afraid of you." Afraid of her, yes. Terrified out of his wits was more like it. Jenn shook her head. "It couldn't have been worse, Wisp. I can't go back."

A breeze, teasing and soft. "Because a child saw the truth and couldn't understand it. What would your lady aunt say, Dearest Heart?"

Which was unfair and . . . when had Wisp learned to invoke Aunt Sybb? She supposed it had to happen eventually, the dragon spending more time in the village.

So long as he didn't start writing to her aunt. Jenn couldn't imagine what the Lady Mahavar would think of such correspondence. Most likely it would restore her suspicion regarding toads.

What would she say? Oh, Jenn knew. Hadn't she heard it recited every time her younger self asked "why" once too often for her father's patience, or Peggs' or Gallie's, or anyone's. Aunt Sybb had said a child grows by questions. Fail to answer just one, and stunt that growth.

Believing that, Aunt Sybb was the only adult who'd never failed to listen and answer. She'd admit—readily—what she didn't know, oh but that wouldn't be the end of it. Regardless of time of day or weather, she'd hustle them over to Master Dusom to consult that worthy. If he failed, well, there were his books.

On occasion those books failed too. Aunt Sybb would make a note, then appear to forget, but her winter letter would contain a separate page just for Jenn, her question at the top, and the answer, found from someone in Avyo, beautifully written below.

Though she'd needed Master Dusom's help to understand the answer, as often as not; Aunt Sybb considered exotic new vocabulary to be a bonus.

Sparkles midair distracted her; tiny diamonds sewn on a bodice of sky blue.

Snow, disturbed from the branches of the old trees—by yling or squirrel or wind—that took its time landing.

Or something—someone—played with sunbeams, simply for beauty's sake.

In Marrowdell, any or all could be true.

Wise Wisp.

"Aunt Sybb would say," Jenn answered at last, "that Werfol's asked a question, and deserves an answer." She nodded to herself. "I must explain to him how he can see a normal woman, with this," a tap on glass, "beneath. I cannot fail." Being turn-born had its drawbacks; had she a face at the moment, she would have scrunched it to demonstrate the seriousness of the problem.

"He's going to scream again. I just know it. Wisp, I could use some advice."

None came. She looked along the Tinkers Road, this way and that, and even checked the old trees for shed snow or sagging branch, not that Wisp, when he chose to hide, would leave such telltale signs, but sometimes he did, for her.

He'd left. On business of his own or, more likely, because he'd helped all he would, being a dragon.

The rest was up to her.

Jenn wandered the field, among sculptures she hardly saw, delaying the inevitable. For each new plan she came up with, she found one flaw, then another, until her mind whirled with possibilities that chased themselves into dread.

Until she couldn't think at all. Was this how a soldier felt, before a battle?

Not that she knew, exactly, how that was. There'd been a book. Plagued by Roche and Allin, Master Dusom had produced a war account written by one of his ancestors. His students had hoped it would be exciting, with gory descriptions and a grand victory, but it proved packed with charts and formulas—from provisioning to how to predict travel time over varied terrains. There'd been a section on tactics, but dry and dealing with what hadn't worked—in the opinion of the author—because those in charge hadn't done the appropriate calculations beforehand. Master Dusom had been delighted to set them problems afterward.

Uncle Horst wouldn't speak of his life before Marrowdell, not even to Riss, according to Peggs, who'd become closer to the older woman since both had newly revealed loves to compare.

She could ask Tir, Jenn thought, then shook her head. He'd tell her all manner of stories, without doubt, but since he loved most to tease her, how many could she believe?

Leaving Bannan Larmensu, but not really. He wasn't so far from that life that she'd willingly remind him of it, having seen the pain on his face when others did.

She wasn't a soldier anyway, when it came to it, nor was gaining Werfol's trust in any sense a battle.

At least . . . she truly hoped not.

Jenn had started for home, to consult with Peggs, only to realize a significant problem. What had she been thinking? Her clothing lay strewn along the road. Yes, her simples were in the commons where she could dress unseen, but the rest were within the village. Leaving two equally unsavory choices: walk through the village almost naked . . .

Or as turn-born.

A sensation either way, with neither having a good outcome. Few of the villagers had seen her other self. Or her naked self.

It was all most embarrassing.

Fine time for her dragon to leave on his own business. Though Jenn had little doubt Wisp would find her predicament highly entertaining and not be helpful at all.

She wandered into the field of sculptured snow to delay having to make that choice and to ponder what to say to Werfol. Semyn seemed to take his lead from his brother. Hopefully, he would in this as well.

Once, Jenn thought practically, she had clothes. Definitely not a soldierly problem. Unless . . . she laughed, imagining the dignified author of Master Dusom's book arriving in camp in skin and naught else.

As if her laugh had been a signal, whispers broke out all around her.

Efflet.

"Is this your work?" Jenn spread her arms and turned. She hadn't been paying attention. Now she did.

The wind might have scoured that hollow in a snowdrift, then laid a sharp line atop its curve, but no wind she'd seen would add a pig's snout or curly tail. Beside the snow pig was the neck and head of a horse—a good likeness of Perrkin—while beyond that was something less familiar.

Something she could have sworn hadn't been there an instant before.

She stepped around the horse head to take a closer look.

Heavy forearms bent across a broad chest. Above, a head, flatter and wider than any she'd seen, held low. Round eyes, set within thickened lids, stared back at her, while two pairs of wings stretched down into the surrounding snow.

Whispers slipped by and away, returning in greater and greater number, as if her attention to this one of many had sent efflet swirling like a flock of little birds. Soon, she felt herself surrounded by an ever-moving cloud.

Yet not a snowflake tipped or toppled.

Jenn turned away from the sculpture and the whispers fell silent. She turned back, and they began again.

How curious.

So she went closer still. Like any child, she'd shaped snow and been proud of the results.

This was different.

From a distance, the efflets' snow sculptures had seemed almost crude, easily mistaken for the wind's accidental artistry. As she approached, Jenn was astonished. For each step she took shifted the light glinting from the flakes, adding exquisite new detail.

Revealing the mastery of the efflet.

The eyes had pupils, slit with a softly ragged edge. The eyelids had stubbled lashes and the head a mouth, lips pressed hard against rows of teeth, their tips flat and just shown. What she'd assumed skin seemed now more likely fabric, as if eyes and mouth peered from within a hood.

Or mask.

Muscle corded bare arms, reminding her of Davi Treff at his forge. Over the broad chest lay a chain, with others depending from it. Whatever hung at the end of the smaller chains was covered by the arms, as if being protected.

Or hoarded.

"It's very well done," Jenn offered, then frowned. Why this, in a field studded with snow pigs and horse heads and—she blinked—more than a few piles of nyphrit corpses?

At closer inspection she could see the wings belonged to a pair of other creatures, possessed of clawed hands.

Creatures she'd glimpsed, at the turn. Efflet. The sculpture was cleverly set into the surrounding snow, as if those with wings sought to pull free the one without.

Or attacked it, Jenn reminded herself; efflet being, in Tir's terms, bloodthirsty little scoundrels who tolerated no threat to their beloved grain.

Yet were brave and had fought for Marrowdell. So many things true at once could make a head spin, she decided, understanding Werfol a little better.

More whispering, as if impatient for her opinion. She walked to one side, to better see the snow efflet.

They weren't helping or harming the masked creature. Each was shown caught in a net, body twisted, wings sticking through. Beneath each were scattered other efflet, crumpled where they'd fallen.

She'd seen their bodies like this before, when efflet had died in terrible numbers so she could reach the trapped sei.

This sculpture, gruesome as it was, looked fresher than the others. Having noticed her presence, had the efflet made it for her? But why?

In Avyo, there were sculptures of stone or metal to commemorate important people or events, most commissioned by Prince Ordo. In Aunt Sybb's opinion, they were of use only to pigeons, but Jenn had thought, to herself, they sounded remarkable. She'd wanted to see for herself.

It seemed she had one of her own to puzzle over. "These are efflet," she said, pointing to the winged creatures.

The whispers intensified, then died away slightly.

Her gesture went next to the larger creature. "This is not."

More whispers, then less.

"Your enemy?" Jenn hazarded. "From the Verge." For surely nothing like this had ever walked in Marrowdell.

A solitary whisper here. Another there. Silence.

It wasn't disagreement. It seemed . . . confusion.

As the silence wore on, Jenn decided it was more than that. Frustration. She'd failed them, somehow. "I don't understand. I'm sorry, but I don't. Maybe Wisp—"

Snow flew as the sculpture was torn apart, flakes going hither and yon until she stood in the midst of a head-high blizzard and saw nothing but white.

"Wait! You don't have to—" She stopped, because they had.

The larger creature, shown trapped in the snow, remained untouched.

The efflet in the nets and the corpses around were gone.

And in their place, something else struggled within a net. Something larger, made not just of snow, but wearing clothing.

Familiar clothing. Hers.

Jenn took a step back, hands over her mouth. No monument, but a warning! Whatever this was, it hunted her too.

Or would, she thought grimly, if it could. Wisp and the turn-born had told her the Verge was filled with perils; here, it would appear, was one. "Brave efflet. I will be on my guard. Thank you," Jenn said with all her heart and whispers spread and grew until she might have stood midsummer amid delirious crickets.

Happy, incomprehensible whispers.

"Though it would be easier if I knew what this is or where I might find it."

She'd hoped for another sculpture. Instead, the whispers dropped to a concerned muttering.

She was going to have a long talk with Wisp.

On the bright side, Jenn thought, eyeing her clothed snow-self, the efflet had solved her predicament.

Frost clung to lashes and beard; what skin showed was the faint blue of a plucked fowl. Small things had begun to feast, as Tir predicted. The lips were gone, and the tongue. The remaining eye was useless, its color impossible to tell.

Bannan could see enough. Another stranger. He brushed snow from the front of the corpse. Tir had taken the coat and weapons, making it easier to reach inner pockets and belt pouches.

Davi, Anten, and Tadd were busy freeing boxes from the snow; Kydd had climbed onto the tipped wagon to locate more. They left him to this work.

As they should, Bannan thought. He was well used to searching the dead. They'd lay like cordwood, after a skirmish, or need to be fished from a stream. Sometimes they'd find bodies like these, frozen and abandoned; at others, they'd dig open fresh grave pits to count numbers and look for their own.

And for answers. Soldiers died from more causes than battle. It was worth knowing if your enemy sickened or starved. Especially before you could suffer the same fate.

Corpses meant information, not to mention newer boots and possibly coin, though the Ansnans who'd patrolled the marches were, as a rule, no better equipped than those of Rhoth. His fingers closed over a purse, half-full. Rather than waste effort to free it, Bannan took out his knife and sliced the leather, gathering the contents in his hand.

Coin it was. Two chocks with their middle hole, a couple of dozen sprats, and, lo, a large and still-shiny drogue. The sprats were next to worthless, but a chock would buy a round of drinks in one of Vorkoun's seedier inns.

Where the drogue would get your throat slit. The clumsy coin was worth three months' pay for a soldier and rarely the risk of carrying it. An advance payment. It had to be. The truthseer tucked the coins into his pocket, to be Marrowdell's gain.

There'd been something else. He sat back on his haunches, staring at the tangled clot of gray wool.

"What is it?" Kydd leaned over his shoulder.

"A soldier's luck." No surprise, Bannan thought. The treaty had put more than a few out of honest work. He teased apart the wool, expecting the usual trio of mother's hair, enemy bone, and cork.

Instead, tied along the strand was a tiny black vial, a rolled scrap of parchment, and a small reddish piece of metal. "These aren't the tokens my men would carry." He held out his hand to show the beekeeper. Tokens were used by the credulous—or knowledgeable, he thought suddenly—to perform Rhothan wishings.

When they worked, they were considered magic.

Had whomever sent this man, and paid him, given him these tokens as well?

Bannan got to his feet. "Can you tell what these were for?" Kydd being one of the knowledgeable sort.

"Perhaps." The former student of magic took the wool

and tokens gingerly. "But not here." He secured them inside his coat and nodded at the dead man. "If you're done, Davi's set to right the wagon."

"Tir killed three. There's another corpse."

Kydd shook his head. "Not anymore. The horses are gone, too." He pointed to the confusion of deep tracks and scraps of hide near the wagon. "We're lucky to find anything left. A winter bear." As Bannan looked a question. "That's our name for them. Bears like the one Scourge killed on the road are asleep in their dens by now. These stay awake. In winter, they come down to the valleys to hunt—Heart's Blood."

By the look on his face, he'd been struck by the same horrible thought as Bannan. What if the bear had found Tir and the boys?

"Sennic can tell you more, if you've a mind. Come," Kydd said, lightening his tone. "Let's see if Davi's as clever as we hope. That's a fine wagon."

"Fine" wasn't the word Bannan would have used to describe what Lila had provided for her sons' transport. Barely any paint remained on its thick wooden sides, sides that sloped to a narrow bottom. That slope kept goods from shifting or falling out, while the wheels, wide of tread and taller than he was, could handle the poorest road. A practical design, when your business was smuggling goods through the mountains to either side of the marches, for this was an Ansnan-built freight wagon.

With modifications. Some were to allow the use of horses, faster than the Ansnans' preferred stock, oxen, the rest to accommodate passengers. Four walls and a roof with cargo racks sheltered those inside. No seat for a driver. The reins went through an opening at the front. A strong ugly box.

They'd arrived to find it lying on one side. Logs had been placed to flip the wagon even as the four horses were dropped in their traces by arrows from ambush. Quick. Efficient. Brutal.

The attackers had not, however, been responsible for ripping free the door and half a side.

That had been the dragon.

The quarters inside had been tight, for Lila hadn't stinted. Cargo—wooden boxes and barrels—half-filled the wagon, formed into a floor and seats. Removed and added to the rest, they formed an impressive stack by the sled, more than it could handle. Righting the wagon so it could be taken to Marrowdell was, Bannan abruptly realized, more than the villagers' frugal nature.

Without it, they'd have to abandon the remaining supplies to Tadd's winter bears.

"Ancestors Witness. This is a sturdy wee cart," Davi declared, though the wagon was neither, being half again the length of the villagers', and if you asked anyone in Lower Rhoth, a proper farm cart having two wheels, not four plus a fifth at the tongue.

Likely no one in Marrowdell had known the difference, when they'd first arrived, being neither farmers nor carters. They certainly didn't care now. Davi called things what he wished to call them and so, Bannan felt upon time with the big smith, he should. The man had a gift for metal craft and engineering bordering on magic, and twice the strength of anyone else.

"The lads, Tadd, if you would." The draught horses had been taking their ease with the others, bags of feed over their heads. Tadd brought them, still chomping noisily, to where the chains lay waiting, hitched them up, then signaled they were ready.

The traces had been torn apart by whatever had taken the horses. Davi set them to collect every scrap, then shook his head in disgust at the result. "Ancestors Wanton and Wasteful," he cursed, whether at the bears or those who'd killed the horses Bannan wasn't sure.

They waited as the smith stood, his brow creased in thought.

Tadd swung his arms to keep warm. "We could bury the extra. Come back tomorrow."

Davi's frown disappeared and there was a gleam in his eyes. "I've a notion, my good friends. Remember the Eld?"

"Ancestors Willful and Witless!" Covie, who rarely lost her temper, was furious. She paced from one end of the kitchen table to the other, eyes locked on the woman sitting across from her. "I never took you for a fool."

Lorra glared back. "I took you for an excellent healer. That was my mistake! Stick to your cows, Covie Ropps."

"Would you care for a cuppa, Jenn?" Cynd asked politely, taking her basket.

She'd prefer a discreet and rapid exit, but having stepped into the Treffs' kitchen mid-argument, Jenn knew she was stuck in it now. "Yes, please."

Covie having fallen silent, Lorra turned her glower on the new arrival. "There's no need for tea, Cynd. Jenn's come for the boys."

So they were still here.

Putting aside, for the moment, the mysterious requests of toad and efflet, Jenn had followed Peggs' seemingly excellent advice on how to approach Werfol and Semyn to the letter. She'd changed into better clothes and left most of her hair loose down her back, though the difference attire made to children was, in her opinion, debatable. There was no doubting the value of cookies and sweets, and she'd added her little book to the basket.

She'd not been sure about the jar of pickles, but her sister had assured her with all seriousness that there was no telling what the Treffs had in their glass jars and Jenn should have some way to explain herself at hand.

As a jar of pickles?

They'd both smiled at that, which was Peggs' point.

She'd taken the last part of her sister's advice too. Don't wait for Bannan, Peggs had urged. Act now, so when he's home again all is well.

Which it wasn't, not at all. "If they've been a bother," Jenn began, prepared to apologize.

Cynd's "Of course not—" was drowned by Lorra's "Yes!" But Covie's blunt, "They're staying," seemed to end the matter.

Lorra huffed. "They are a nuisance and intrusion and unwelcome. I want them out of this house!"

They were children who'd sought shelter. Jenn bristled.

Covie flattened her hands on the table and leaned into Lorra's face. "Frann's smiling. Telling them stories.

Ancestors Blessed—she's some appetite at last! Taken broth and tea—hasn't she, Cynd?"

"And a buttered biscuit." Cynd carefully avoided the glare from her mother-by-marriage as she set a cup of tea before an empty chair and beckoned Jenn to sit. "Frann's enjoying the company."

"Uninvited company. Intruders!"

Covie leaned closer. Lorra tried to look away, but the healer wouldn't allow it. "Listen to me, Lorra," softer but no less firm. "You must let them stay. They've done more good for her than any of us—"

"Frann needs her rest."

"The boys napped with her this morning," Cynd observed, her attention all for the plate of fresh biscuits she put before Jenn, who began to see how this particular family worked out its many disagreements. "They were exhausted."

"She's doing them good too, then. Well, Lorra?"

"Cows," the Treff matriarch muttered rudely, then waved a dismissive hand. "Fine. I've no rights in my own house. Let the impertinent strangers stay." She rose to her feet, Covie straightening out of her way. Lorra turned to frown at Jenn. "Be sure to take them with you when you leave."

The odds being excellent Bannan's nephews would run screaming at the sight of her, again, she shouldn't promise anything of the sort. Catching Covie's eye, Jenn swallowed her doubt. "I will."

Once Lorra was gone, the healer dropped into a seat at the table, accepting a cup. Her face settled into weary lines. "I don't suppose there's brandy."

Cynd joined them. "It's in Lorra's room."

"Ah, well, she needs it more." Covie pinched the bridge of her nose, eyes closing for an instant. "Ancestors Difficult and Dense. For once in that woman's life, I wish she'd listen."

Cynd stared into her own cup. "I don't think she can. Not to this."

Covie nodded and both fell silent, busy with their own thoughts. Jenn sipped her tea and tried to be inconspicuous, but Cynd looked up with a small smile. "We've heard about Peggs. Congratulations."

The healer smiled too. "Ancestors Bountiful and Blessed. There'll be children everywhere, come summer."

Jenn didn't answer. Couldn't, was the truth, not right away. They changed the subject to let her remain ignorant of what troubled this house—whether out of kindness, or because she was younger, or for whatever reason. She gathered her courage. "Please. Tell me what's wrong."

Approval shone in Covie's eyes. Approval followed by such sorrow Jenn braced herself.

"Frann is dying."

She went numb, as if her blood had stopped flowing in her veins. Not that she had blood, but the feeling remained. Words roared through her. Words dreadful in their certainty.

. . . What's to be born, will be. What's about to die, will . . .

Ancestors Desperate and Despairing. In her worst nightmares, she hadn't dreamed to face either choice.

. . . Turn-born can't oppose nature . . .

What if Mistress Sand had lied? Been wrong?

What if she could—

Stay numb, Jenn told herself and tried her best, more afraid of her turn-born self in that instant than she'd ever been. Marrowdell mustn't express her feelings—any of them. Nor could she imagine anything safe to wish, not about Frann or anyone else. But how could she not?

Her heart began to race.

Suddenly, for no reason, she thought of blue.

Not the blue of eyes or summerberries, but the otherworldly blue of her dragon's door. As if the mere thought was a key or her touch, she felt herself inside that sanctuary, sitting on the stone that fit her better than any chair.

Safer than she'd ever been, and calm.

And as if being calm let her hear another, better voice, Jenn remembered once more Aunt Sybb speaking of the cycle of life, of babies born and those become Blessed, and she understood, at last. It didn't matter what she could or couldn't do.

What mattered was Frann.

With a blink, she was back in the kitchen, Covie and Cynd waiting patiently. "What can we do?" she asked, glad being numb made her sound even and adult and possibly sensible.

"Let her do what makes her happy. Keep her comfortable." Covie sighed. "Ancestors Witness, I deserve what Lorra thinks of me. I knew Frann wasn't strong—that she struggled last winter. I should have stopped her going to the fair . . ."

"How?" Cynd touched the healer's hand. "We all tried, even Lorra. Frann insisted. She felt well."

And hadn't been.

Jenn had to ask, though she knew the answer could take away the numbness and make everything sharp and real again. "How long?"

A look came over Covie then, as if she listened to what no one else could, then her eyes rested on her tea. "Soon, Dear Heart. That's what Lorra can't bear to hear. Very soon." The healer straightened and circled her fingers over her heart. "Hearts of our Ancestors," she prayed, "the time Frann has left is your Blessing, and we are Beholden to share it. However far we are apart, Keep Us Close."

Cynd put down her cup, bent her head, and started to cry, great racking sobs that made not a sound.

Tears prickled Jenn's eyes, but she took a deep breath instead. " 'Keep Us Close.' "

Why this, of all the buildings in Marrowdell? There wasn't pie.

Or peace. The old kruar prowled outside, grim as death and as conversational.

And hadn't coming here upset Jenn Nalynn even more than when she'd fled the village?

Yet the valley hadn't torn itself apart or whipped up a new storm. While he'd like to believe it was the girl's growing self-control, Wisp felt uneasy. This seemed more a sei's control than turn-born's.

Upset by the thought, he paced around the room. Doors on either wall stood ajar, their openings filled by curtains that stopped three-quarters to the floor leaving a gap convenient for a dragon, or boy.

At least the warmth was soothing. The Treffs' was the warmest place Wisp had been, this side of the Verge, other than the forge. He'd gone into the smith's stronghold once, out of curiosity, then fled. The stone at its core was hot enough to soften even his scales.

Turn-born meddling.

This warmth was welcome. The wheel was gone, the loom empty and against a wall. The only movement was the flutter along the curtains with each pulse of heat from the cookstove. Like breathing.

But not.

The house toad hopped from its hiding place. ~Elder brother, I did as you requested and allowed them to enter.~ It puffed indignantly. ~Was that wise?~

Daring little cousin, to challenge a dragon. Perhaps it was life with the Treffs. Wisp ignored the offense. ~We shall see. Where are they?~

~In the room that belongs to Mistress Lorra but is now home to Mistress Frann though the furniture is Mistress Lorra's and . . . ~ The toad, perhaps asking itself about wisdom, stopped.

Wisp waited.

The toad took a step, aiming its snout at the door beside the painting. ~There, elder brother.~

He'd overheard the conversation in the kitchen. ~The boys stay until our turn-born chooses to leave.~ Wisp informed it. ~They will be welcome to return anytime. If you think it wise . . . ~

The toad paled and shrank. ~Of course, elder brother.~

Satisfied, the dragon went to the curtain and slipped his head beneath.

Inside the room, sunlight played over a bed larger than Radd Nalynn's, covered in such a wealth of blankets, pillows, and furs Wisp had to restrain the urge to test their softness for himself.

The bed being occupied.

He stepped beside it, nostrils atwitch. Death filled the air, imminent and potent. A scent sure to gain attention, carrion being the easiest catch of all. One had only to wait.

This death's scent was distasteful, as would be that of a dying dragon. Wisp sneezed.

"Something's here, Semyn." The bed shook violently, then a head crowned with dark curly hair appeared hanging over the side. Eyes of black-flecked gold stared down. For a moment neither Wisp nor Werfol moved. Then, "It's the dragon."

Another shaking of the bed. "Let me see!" A second head, this crowned in reddish brown hair, appeared. Blue-green eyes peered this way and that. "Where?"

Werfol pointed, his finger almost at Wisp's snout. "There! Right there!"

Semyn squinted. "I wish I could see it."

"You have to—" The younger boy gave Wisp a beseeching look, his lower lip trembling. "Why can't Semyn see you?"

He was growing soft, that was the truth of it. Snarling to himself, Wisp caught a bit of sunlight, enough to glint on a scale or two, and reveal his eyes.

Semyn's widened until they looked about to pop from his head and Werfol smiled fiercely. "I told you!"

Wisp hid himself again.

"What is it, lads?" more whisper than voice.

Werfol sat up. "There's a dragon by your bed, Lady Frann. Semyn saw it too."

"I did!" said his brother.

"Might—I?"

Both boys threw themselves over the side of the bed again. "Please, dragon?" Semyn whispered.

"Please?" Werfol looked directly at Wisp.

Dangerous beings, children, the dragon grumbled to himself, wondering how he'd forgotten. Not seeing a way out that would please anyone but himself—and the Treffs' sure-to-be scandalized house toad—Wisp lifted his head above the bed.

Frann Nall lay nestled amid pillows like a bird in a nest. Around that nest were scattered trays, each cluttered with empty plates and cups. The remaining pillows, along with rolled blankets, had been piled into a formidable barrier at the end of the bed, presumably to defend against invading tray bearers.

"He's looking right at you, Lady Frann!" Werfol exclaimed. "Can you see him?"

What the dragon saw was weakness denied by pride. Her dark gray hair had been swept into a neat braid over one shoulder. A green scarf covered her neck, soft and glittering. Gemstones twinkled on her fingers and bone-thin wrists, with more crusted around a disk of red metal pinned to the dark jacket Frann wore over her nightdress.

Strokes of red marked sunken cheeks and skin already pale bore signs of powder, but her eyes were alight with curiosity. "Patience, Werfol. Marrowdell is shy," she told the children, in a voice more breath than sound. "Of all the times I played my flute under the old trees, only once did I glimpse its dancers."

That any ylings revealed themselves was a marvel.

Werfol looked pleadingly at Wisp. Semyn copied his brother.

He was going to regret this.

The dragon went to the foot of the bed, the only part of the room wide enough for his wings to open, and gave a single powerful beat to lift himself to a perch on the wall of pillows.

A few toppled. The rest were distractingly comfortable.

Hoping the little cousin was occupied elsewhere, Wisp wrapped himself in light.

"I told you," Werfol whispered.

With a gasp, Semyn took hold of his brother and tried to pull him back, clearly overwhelmed by an entire dragon. The younger boy shrugged free, insisting, "It's safe."

"It" certainly was not, Wisp thought, offended.

"Ancestors Grand and Glorious." Frann's eyes shone. "Look at you. Just look." Her fingers fumbled at her brooch. "See that, Baldrinn?"

"Who's Baldrinn, Lady Frann?"

"My lover." A secretive smile. "Lorra's, weren't you, Baldrinn, till you saw me? We didn't share so well, back then." Another fumble at the brooch. "I hear you, Baldrinn. They sing of dragons in Channen, but I've one on my bed, Dearest Heart. A dragon."

A dragon unaccustomed to scrutiny. But worse was about to come.

Werfol launched himself at Wisp, wrapping his small arms around the dragon's neck.

Wisp's entire body trembled with effort. The girl would be pleased he hadn't snapped off the child's head nor broken his fragile body.

It had been close.

The boy buried his face against scales able to withstand dragonsfire. "He's here to protect us, Semyn!" he declared. "I know it. The Bone Stealer can't take us now!"

Wisp shook himself free, as gently as he could. The boy tumbled unharmed on the bed, looking up with those golden, *seeing* eyes.

"Dearest—there's no such—" Frann paused to cough, her free hand bringing a cloth to her mouth.

Semyn tore his eyes from Wisp. "There is, Lady Frann. I swear it by our Ancestors. Werfol sees the truth and he saw the Bone Stealer in the barn."

Wisp lowered himself onto the pillows to consider the situation. He'd heard of this bone thief. In one of his summer night storytellings, Roche Morrill had told the younglings of a creature that built itself from the bones of badly-behaved children. Jenn had been especially well mannered for days afterward, until Kydd had found out and explained it was only a story. Roche had wound up sharing the sows' wallow.

A story to frighten children into obedience coupled with the glorious strangeness of a turn-born, arrived as they'd been awaiting some punishment for attempting to steal the pony. It made, the dragon supposed, a vague sort of sense.

It was a nuisance. The worlds held sufficient terrors. Why imagine more?

Frann lowered her cloth. "Do I speak the truth, Werfol?"

The little truthseer twisted to look at the woman. "Yes, Lady Frann. Always." He turned back to Wisp. "Even our uncle lied to us," too calm, too quiet.

The dragon was impressed. Rage brewed within that small body, a rage better suited to battle than hiding.

He must discuss this with the girl, before she faced the boys again.

The sound of the curtain being pulled and the sudden horror on the boys' faces told him it was already too late.

"Dragon, save us!" Semyn pleaded as he and Werfol cowered against Frann. "It's the Bone Stealer!"

Jenn Nalynn stood in the doorway, a tray in her hands. She met Wisp's eyes with something broken in her own. Without a word, she stepped back, letting the curtain fall.

A pillow hit the dragon's side, then a cup. He swung his neck around and brought it tip to nose with Werfol, who was on his knees, another makeshift weapon raised and ready. "You didn't save us!" the boy snarled, retreating not at all. "You're a liar too!"

Oh, he liked this one.

"Stop at once," Frann said with unexpected strength. "Look at me, both of you." She waited until the pair sat attentively, though Semyn kept glancing over his shoulder at Wisp. "That was Melusine's daughter, Jenn Nalynn. I've known her since she was born and her heart holds nothing but good. Werfol. Do I lie?"

"No, Lady Frann," with reluctance. The boy shuddered. "But—she's not like us. She's—" Words failed him.

"She's not." Frann patted the bed. "Let me tell you another story." She looked at Wisp, her eyes filling with memories. "It begins with a dragon."

The pillows being soft, Wisp curled himself at the dying woman's feet to listen.

# EIGHT

"*I*S EVERYTHING ALL right?" Cynd asked.

Jenn opened her mouth, then closed it, knowing she couldn't possibly answer.

There was a dragon on Frann's bed. Her dragon. Out in plain sight.

By the soft murmuring from the room behind her, Frann was telling the boys another story, as if a dragon on her bed was hardly unusual.

While she stood outside the curtain, having terrified Bannan's nephews again.

Something a dragon, apparently, didn't do.

Children—or at least Lila's—were more complicated than she'd imagined.

"Jenn?" With concern. "Is it Frann?"

"Not at all," Jenn denied hurriedly, and made herself smile as she stepped away from the door. "You were right, Cynd. Frann's enjoying the boys so much, I didn't want to interrupt."

What she wanted was a way to prove to Werfol, and so

Semyn, that she wasn't some dreadful monster sent to steal their bones. Bone Stealer. There was a tale told far too often, in her opinion, even if Aunt Sybb would say cautionary tales had their place. Surely there was a place for more about fluffy bunnies or songbirds?

"You're welcome to stay, Dear Heart," Cynd sounded almost shy. "Ancestors Witness, I'd be glad of company while I sew." She gestured to the table in the middle of the room, stacked shoulder-high with clothing, some to be taken apart for reuse, the rest in need of mending. New work waited on the shelves for Frann's nimble fingers to finish, but even without, there was sufficient work here, Jenn thought dazedly, to keep everyone in the village stitching. She'd not appreciated how much the Treffs sewed during the winter.

Cynd went around the table. "It's gone a little mad, hasn't it?" she observed, rearranging a towering pile of pants themselves in need of patches. "Frann keeps everything so organized and—" she took a sharp little breath. "Usually we work together. All of us."

Not today, with Lorra having taken to her room, leaving this—and Frann's care—to her son's wife, with Wen off on business of her own. "I'll stay and I'll help," Jenn said firmly. "Peggs would be happy to do the same, and Riss. Any of us. You need but ask."

"Ancestors Busy and Beset. You've chores of your own, Dear Heart. Frann—Lorra will be up again soon. You'll see." But the words faded into the corners of the room, filled with abandoned projects.

"Of course," Jenn said, for what else could she say? She went up to the table. "What's next?"

"There's Devins' work coat." Cynd stuck her arm up one of the sleeves, wiggling a finger through a hole in the elbow. "He's hard on clothes, that boy. I've this to patch it." "This" being part of someone's old pants.

Jenn decided not to ask whose. "I can do that."

Looking happier, Cynd positioned a second chair companionably close to hers in the sun streaming through the front window. They'd not waste oil during the day. Jenn left her basket—sweets, pickles, book, and all—on the floor. For reasons known only to itself, the Treffs' house toad had taken up a post in front of the basket, then promptly fallen asleep.

They started sewing. Unlike Peggs, Cynd didn't chatter as she sewed. Everyone knew she was a good listener, or had learned to be one among the more vocal Treffs, but Jenn couldn't think of anything to say. They stitched in sunshine and almost quiet. Almost, because without their voices, the fire in the cookstove snapped and snarled to itself, and she could hear the murmur from Frann's room.

Storytelling. The boys were luckier than they knew, Jenn thought with a pang, remembering her turn to listen.

Patch done, she started one for the other elbow; otherwise the coat would come back to Cynd sooner than later. She'd stitch and stay.

Wisp hadn't shown himself out of whim. Something was going on, in that curtained room, something important.

Perhaps, Jenn Nalynn thought as she stitched and listened, she need only wait.

And hope. That too.

"The Eld, sir." Tir raised both eyebrows, wrinkling the scars on his forehead.

Bannan grinned. They'd arrived bone-tired and famished, but triumph had a way of pushing such concerns aside. "Davi thought of it."

"It" being to copy the Eld wagons the demas and his sponsor had brought to Marrowdell this summer past. They'd lashed the tongue of Lila's wagon to the rear of the sled, leaving clearance for both to turn without collision, then hitched Tadd's and Kydd's riding horses to the sled, though Davi's magnificent team hardly needed the help.

Once in Marrowdell, they'd pulled the wagon and sled inside the mill for unloading, given care of the horses to waiting hands, then headed for home and supper.

"Ancestors Ingenious and Inspired," Bannan chuckled. "The rig worked like a charm." Saving another trip. They'd taken all they could free from the snow and left the corpses for the bear.

Dismissing that grim image, the truthseer looked around

the room, nodding in greeting. Peggs was there, and Radd, busy stitching a shoe. One of Wainn's, for that worthy sat nearby on the floor, the shoe's mate in his hands and the Nalynn house toad close by.

But no nephews.

"Where are the boys?" Bannan asked, disappointedly putting down the chest of their belongings.

"Covie sent word. They're at the Treffs'." Peggs, her arm around Kydd, spoke as though this were perfectly normal and to be expected.

The truth, but Peggs wasn't smiling. "When will they be back?"

"I don't know. They've been there all day."

"At the Treffs'?" Kydd sounded equally startled. "What of Frann?"

Bannan wondered the same. However well-mannered, Semyn and Werfol were normal, boisterous children, surely more than an ill woman could endure for long. Then he'd a happier thought. Hadn't Jenn planned to visit Frann as often as she could? She'd a gift for reading aloud; he'd lose all track of time when listening. "Are they with Jenn, then?"

Radd glanced up. "Jenn's at the Treffs'."

Which, while also true, wasn't what he'd asked. Bannan looked to Tir.

Who gave a not-my-fault shrug before bending to fiddle with the thick wrappings on his feet.

He'd been gone mere hours. What could have happened? "Something I should know?" he inquired, half-jokingly.

"Yes," Wainn said cheerfully. "The boys are hiding in Frann's bedroom and won't come out. Wen told me."

Bannan's hand fell where the hilt of a sword had been. With what he felt commendable calm under the circumstances, he asked the room in general, "Hiding from what?"

The house toad yawned, showing teeth.

Wainn didn't look up. "Jenn Nalynn."

Then it was a game. Likely involving the dragon, doubtless snow. Harmless mischief. His relief lasted until he saw the distress on Peggs' face.

If not a game, the boys were hiding out of fear and there was only one reason they'd hide from Jenn Nalynn.

But how? The day's turn had yet to come. The boys couldn't have seen her as turn-born, unless she'd willed it so.

Or they'd snuck up on her at the wrong moment . . . Ancestors Thwarted and Trapped, it was possible.

He couldn't imagine a worse way for them to meet. "Is Jenn all right?" the truthseer demanded, looking straight at Peggs.

Who knew what he meant. "Yes. She will be." She tried her best to smile. "Jenn's taken them her favorite book. And a jar of pickles."

" 'Pickles?' " Numb, Bannan waved away any explanation. "I'll be back." Once he'd done what he could to repair this.

Out he went, not feeling the cold, too busy feeling everything else as he half ran by the Emms' house. It wasn't until he neared their barn that he made himself slow to a walk. He'd gain nothing arriving upset.

And so very much to be lost, if he misstepped with the boys and they spent their winter terrified of the person he loved most.

Jenn should have been the one to decide if she would reveal her other self to Semyn and Werfol. She'd certainly have been the one to know how.

He walked past apple trees asleep and frozen, beside a garden hidden by snow, and hoped he was wrong. Maybe the boys had simply had their fill of strange faces, and gone to hide—

With Frann?

Bannan stopped at the path that led up to the Treffs' porch. The answers were through that door.

Or were they?

He gave a soundless whistle.

A dark nose came around the corner of the building, snorted steam, then withdrew. An invitation.

After checking to be sure he was unobserved—it being high on his list to avoid questions about Scourge and the Treffs—Bannan followed.

The kruar was waiting, neck and back coated in snow, the rest of him a shadow. For such a stealthy creature— unless he chose, Scourge left no mark in snow or mud—the well-trampled circle alongside the Treffs' doorless wall and hedges begged a question itself. One Bannan wasn't going to ask.

Nor did he bother to ask if the vigilant beast knew of the boys' arrival, Scourge being familiar with the boys' scent from Vorkoun. "Are they safe?"

The breeze snapped in his ear. "Am I not here?"

Ancestors Witness. First the dragon, now the kruar. He should have bet with Tir who'd take the greater interest in the boys. "I'd have thought you'd come with us," Bannan said, forcing his voice to be mild. "There's another bear. A bigger one."

Scourge tossed his head, flinging snow here and there. "Not hungry."

Bannan gave the trampled snow a closer look, then wished he hadn't. Blood streaked it here and there and, frankly, most of what wasn't streaked red was pink. He kicked a small hole. The disquieting stains continued beneath the new snow into the old. "What's all this?"

"Supper. Breakfast. Snacks." The breeze was coy, but lips curled away from fangs and the kruar's eyes gleamed red. Don't ask, that said, as plainly as if spoken.

"Idiot Beast," the truthseer responded, unimpressed. "Are your 'snacks' why Semyn and Werfol are hiding?"

A great hoof stamped, and there was nothing coy in the breeze that almost snarled, "You deserted them."

And didn't that hit home? "I'm back now—"

Scourge turned to show his hindquarters. Disdain.

Heart's Blood. Bannan spun on his boot heel to head for the porch, done with the kruar's foul mood.

A breeze followed, an unwelcome chill on his neck. "The dragon's a better uncle."

Furious, the truthseer checked in his tracks, about to turn and—what?

Tell Scourge he was wrong?

It would be a lie.

Wen came through from the kitchen. "Why is your dragon in our house, Jenn Nalynn?"

At the first word, Cynd gave a little start; no one in the

village was quite accustomed to hearing Wen speak. At the rest, she put down her mending with care and proclaimed brightly, "There's tea," bustling off to prepare yet another cup.

Leaving Jenn with Wen, in the heart of the latter's home. Wen gazed at her with interest, as did the toad in her hair. Not the Treff toad, Jenn realized for the first time, for that dozed by her basket, but another. A houseless toad. Or was Wen a house of different sort?

"Wisp is with Bannan's nephews. They're—" however odd, it was the truth, so she finished, "listening to Frann tell a story."

Wen nodded as if this made perfect sense. Her pale eyes went to the curtain across Lorra's door. "Mother?"

"Covie tried to tell her about Frann." Cynd arrived with her tray. She'd brought more for Jenn as well, and herself, as if tea of itself could mend the world. "Lorra refuses to listen."

"Why should she?" Wen took a cup but didn't sit. She rarely did, unless sewing; when she stood very still, like Wainn, those around her could forget she was even there. "Mother knows," she said calmly. "She knew first." A thoughtful sip of tea. "She's angry."

Which wasn't fair. "Covie's done all she could," Jenn protested, careful to keep her voice down.

"At Frann."

Jenn blinked at Wen. "But—but why?"

"Going first," Cynd explained unhappily, when Wen remained silent. "Lorra's older, Jenn. She expected Frann to lead the family, once she herself became a Blessed Ancestor."

Aunt Sybb was fond of saying the more you planned, the more could go wrong, which was something of a contradiction in a woman prone to lists and thinking ahead. Not making plans didn't work very well either, as a younger Jenn had discovered. As for being angry about a plan that didn't work? That made no sense at all. By that reasoning, her father should have been angry with her mother for going first and leaving him to raise two daughters alone, which hadn't been their plan at all, and she knew he wasn't.

Only sad.

Wen walked to the window and looked out. "Davi's back."

"Oh dear," Jenn said faintly. Bannan wouldn't be far behind. He'd look for his nephews, who were still hiding—from her—in Frann's bedroom. As plans went, today it seemed no one's were working.

"Frann's finished her story," Wen told her, without looking around.

In a world where she didn't terrify children, Jenn thought morosely, this would be when she'd go to the bedroom door, draw aside the curtain, and tell the boys to make ready for their uncle's return. A happy moment, in an otherwise sorrowful day.

She folded Devins' coat around the patched sleeve and rested her hands on it, with no idea what to do next.

All at once, a small hand appeared atop hers.

Jenn didn't so much as breathe as that hand's owner, Werfol Westietas, carefully stepped in front of her.

Standing at her knees, he gazed up at her, eyes gold and black and searching. Semyn joined his brother, waiting. He loved his brother and trusted his magic, Jenn thought, as she loved Bannan and trusted his.

At that thought, a smile rose up from her heart, a smile filled with her hopes, and found her lips.

Theirs trembled and tears filled their eyes, which hadn't been her intention at all. Before she could fix anything, Werfol and Semyn pushed under her arms and into them, Devins' coat landing on the floor. The little boys clung to her as tightly as they could, sobbing as though their hearts were breaking.

What had she done?

What she'd done, Bannan thought, standing in the doorway, was work her magic. He watched his nephews pour out days' worth of fear and grief with a lump in his own throat, grateful beyond words for Jenn Nalynn.

Who looked, truth be told, overcome herself, so he moved to where she could see him and smiled. "I see you've met."

She took a steadying breath and smiled very slightly back, then looked down. She tightened her arms around the boys and bent to press her lips to their heads, Werfol first, then Semyn. "Your uncle's here, Dear Hearts," she told them.

Two heads lifted, but the boys stayed where they were. Excellent taste, in Bannan's opinion, if a trifle unexpected.

A breeze found his ear, chill as outside. "You lied." It slid to the other ear. "He saw."

Four words that spread a chill inward as their meaning sank home and all became clear, from what had happened here to Scourge's fury at him.

Ancestors Perilous and Potent. The next Larmensu truthseer. How could he not have known?

Had Lila? His gift—he remembered its awakening the way he remembered his first broken bone; the break had been gentler. She'd found him, brought their father, stayed to make it bearable. Had it happened before they left, surely she'd have kept the boys close.

Bannan went to one knee, at a respectful distance. Which one—or both? It didn't matter. They were united in their anger with him. Heart's Blood. What had Lila sent him?

What only he could understand.

"I lied," said Bannan then, quiet and sure, "when I told you it was a good idea to explore the village alone. I lied because I was afraid and didn't want to give you my fear." The truthseer circled his fingers and put them over his heart. "By the Hearts of our Ancestors, I will never lie to you again."

Semyn glanced at his brother.

So.

Bannan waited. Werfol's eyes—he should have seen it—were no longer simply warm and brown. They'd gained the amber tone of his and his father's, presently burnished to a fiery gold.

By anger.

Anger that slowly faded. When it was gone, Bannan opened his arms.

To have them filled with his nephews.

For a moment, he closed his eyes to breathe in their scent, an intriguing mixture of horse manure and jam. A story there, no doubt.

One he'd get later. Bannan winked at Jenn. "We've work, lads," he announced, coughing the huskiness from his voice. "The goods your mother sent to Marrowdell need unpacking." He rose to his feet, leaving a hand on each small shoulder, and knew the decision had been made for him. "Then we're off to my home, yours while in Marrowdell."

Where he could grant Werfol peace and privacy, day and night, while he learned his gift. As he'd had. They'd manage. They were a family.

Two pairs of eyes looked up, suddenly brimming with curiosity. "What's your home like, Uncle?" Semyn asked. "Do you have extra horses?"

"Will we have our own rooms, Uncle?" Werfol demanded, not waiting for an answer. His brother elbowed him. Undaunted, the younger Westietas insisted, "I'm old enough."

Jenn chuckled. Oh, he had some fun ahead. "We'll see," Bannan told them, though he was determined to settle both in his room and take a mattress downstairs.

Between them and any danger.

"What we'll see are two less intruders in my house." Pushing aside the curtain over her door, Lorra Treff swept into the main room like an oncoming storm. "Well?" she finished, glaring down at Werfol and Semyn. The boys edged closer to Bannan.

"That's enough, Mother."

Bannan started. Where had Wen come from? Seeing his surprise, she smiled faintly, but her attention was on Lorra. "Frann's asking for you."

Werfol leaned around Bannan, studying Wen. The toad on her shoulder studied him in turn, then yawned, showing pointed teeth. The boy jumped, then giggled.

Whatever he'd seen, he'd accepted. A good start, Bannan thought, relaxing. "My thanks for letting the boys visit," he said, cheerfully ignoring Lorra's frown. "We'll leave you in peace, dear lady."

Without prompting, the boys stepped forward and bowed in perfect unison, fingertips to the floor. "Our thanks, Lady Lorra," they said together.

"And to the Lady Frann," Werfol added, Semyn echoing the words.

In the face of such noble courtesy, Lorra's lips twitched as if to smile, then formed a line again. But it wasn't so tight a line, and her frown seemed more one of weary habit than anger. "Knock next time," she said finally.

"We promise." "We will."

Appeased, the matriarch of the Treffs called, loudly, for tea then went into Frann's bedroom, Wen following behind.

The room felt smaller at once.

"Werfol. Semyn? Your winter clothes are on hooks by the kitchen door, with mine." Jenn informed the boys. As they hurried to dress, she retrieved a basket, nodding to the house toad who'd been guarding it. "My welcome gifts for your nephews," she explained, offering it to Bannan.

"With pickles," he said, winning a small smile. Though graceful, there was a hint of stiffness to her movements. Of care. Given the table loaded with mending, he might have thought Jenn had been sitting too long at that task, but he knew better. So after accepting the basket, Bannan put it down, then very gently took her face between his hands. She met his searching gaze without a flinch, her mouth curved in quiet joy.

Yet grief bruised her lovely eyes.

Scourge had known. "Frann."

She nodded, turning her face to kiss his palm. A tear followed, of such unexpected weight he looked to see if it were stone.

Just a tear.

Or the start of unimaginable magic.

With his nephews in Marrowdell. Heart's Blood. Bannan went very still, trying not to be afraid of the woman he loved, trying and failing.

Jenn Nalynn saw it. How could she not? Sorrow crossed her face, then resolve. Taking his hand, she pulled him to the window. "My heart came close to breaking today," she whispered. "Before I knew about Frann and since." Sunshine poured through the small panes and she held their hands, together, in that brightness. "This has been Marrowdell's answer. Dearest Heart, trust me. Never will I harm them. Never will I allow them to be harmed. I swear it by our love."

Was the sun warmer or was it simply the truth on her dear lips? Lips he found himself kissing, because how else could he answer? Lips that kissed him back and tasted of tears.

"Uncle?"

Well, they'd find out eventually. Bannan continued the kiss with great enthusiasm.

Feeling the lips against his curve into a real smile.

Along the northern wall of the mill, the wind had sifted snow like flour through gaps in the wood. Like the promise of spring, sunlight poured through from the west and south, laying bright bars over the floor and wide squares where it flooded through the many high windows, but it was light without warmth and a lie. Though the mill was frozen and still, there were signs of activity. The great millstones rested outside their case, their intricate patterns exposed, a pattern worn down during the last harvest and in need of renewal.

Turn-born had built the mill, but couldn't—or wouldn't—maintain it. No matter. The miller's tools were strewn on a canvas nearby. It would take till next harvest to chisel crisp edges back into the hard stone. Radd Nalynn had the skill, as did Jenn. Tadd would be learning it, as miller's apprentice.

Crusted with snow, Lila's empty wagon sat where, come summer, the Lady Mahavar's more elegant one would reside. Word having spread about the supplies, Bannan wasn't surprised to find most of Marrowdell, bundled for the cold, already in the mill. Even Tir had managed to hobble from the Nalynns', to take a seat where he could watch the proceedings.

However eager, they'd waited for him, a respect he acknowledged with a grateful nod when he entered, Werfol and Semyn at his side. The cargo—crates, barrels, and bags—had been swept clean of snow and arranged in neat rows.

Devins and the entire Ropp family were there, including Cheffy and Alyssa, who eyed his nephews with the hungry intensity of siblings who'd lacked other playmates. Riss and Sennic, though not Master Jupp. Given the cold within the mill, that was just as well.

But the Uhthoffs were there, and the Nalynns, of course.
Zehr with Gallie, holding the baby. Hettie and Tadd stood
nearby, holding mittened hands. Even big Davi had come,
to lend his strength yet again. If anything special Lila'd sent
would be a comfort to the Treffs, Bannan resolved in that
moment, it would be theirs.

Jenn left them, going to stand with her father and sister.

Bannan smiled at her, then went to the staircase in the
middle of the mill floor and climbed to the second step, indicating his nephews should flank him. "It is my honor to
introduce my sister's sons, Semyn and Werfol Westietas, to
my friends of Marrowdell."

The boys, ever aware of protocol, gave short bows. The
villagers smiled and murmured greetings. A shout rang out,
"I'm Cheffy!" as if the young Ropp couldn't risk his sister's
catching the attention of the newcomers first.

Semyn looked interested. Werfol had been pale since
seeing the crowd within the mill, but managed a smile.
"Semyn and Werfol have come to spend the winter with
us," Bannan said, not bothering with details. He touched
Semyn's shoulder.

"Good people of Marrowdell," the boy said, his high
voice clear and well-paced. "It is not our mother's intention
that we be a burden to you. We have brought these supplies.
Sufficient for—" Semyn hesitated and Bannan knew he
thought of the guards who hadn't made it this far, but the
boy recovered to finish gallantly, "There's plenty. Please accept our thanks and this gift."

The villagers bowed and Radd Nalynn stepped forward.
"Be welcome, Semyn and Werfol. You could not be a burden, for what we have is yours."

"Yes!" Werfol blurted. He nipped behind his uncle, startled by his own reaction or embarrassed. Likely both.

Bannan remembered. The truth struck nerves, those first
weeks. So did lies. He nodded gratefully at Radd.

The miller grinned back. "That being said, lads, who
doesn't like a gift, midwinter? Would you like to open the
first?"

With that, the fun began.

It didn't take long before the ooohs and ahhhs and

sincere appreciation of the villagers drew Werfol to join his brother in opening sacks and crates.

Bannan sat with Tir. "Did my sister expect a siege?"

The former guard shrugged, his eyes bright. "The baroness knows how to pack, sir."

Remarkably well, Bannan judged. There were barrels of oil and of fish pickled in brine, as well as crates of dried meat and sacks of beans. Lila'd even sent soap.

Knowing her boys.

Two crates contained dry goods, from seasonings to cane. All was of the highest quality. There were medicines Covie exclaimed over, and bandages.

Lila had, in fact, packed for a small garrison. That the goods she'd chosen suited Marrowdell's needs was, Bannan decided, coincidence. She'd been planning this for some time.

In which case . . . Bannan got to his feet. "It's a smuggler's wagon."

"Aie." Tir gave him a quizzical look. "But you can see it's empty, sir."

"It appears so," the truthseer said absently. Still. This was Lila, who'd sewn her letter inside a coat. "I think I'll take a look myself."

Not that he had secrets from the villagers, but Bannan was glad to see them preoccupied moving the foodstuffs from the mill to various larders. As he walked over to the wagon, Werfol caught up to him, then Semyn. Both were flushed and happy, and curious.

Both, Bannan thought abruptly, raised by his sister. He stopped at the wagon's torn side and turned to the boys. "I think your mother's left something for us to find."

"Momma does that a lot," Werfol said, giving a little bounce. "It's a game."

"Not always," from Semyn, who gave his uncle a sharp look.

"Not always," Bannan agreed. "She and I used to hide things for each other. We'd leave clues. Messages." There'd been that bottle of fine wine. A sword.

A severed head. Not a game at all, was it, Lila?

"Your mother picked this wagon for a reason," he went

on. "The wood of the sides and floor are strong and thick. So thick, people sometimes build secret compartments in them."

Werfol's eyes gleamed gold, then fell to the ground.

"What's wrong, Weed?"

"Uncle, must I go inside?"

Where they'd hidden from attack, then almost died, huddled with Tir. Bannan crouched in front of the boy, waiting until he looked up. "Not if you don't want to."

"He can hunt outside and under." With that, Semyn clambered into the wagon.

The younger brother cheered at once. "I can do that."

Though he itched to search himself, Bannan stayed back, watching the boys. Walking with his knees bent, Werfol fit neatly under the wagon. Tugging off a mitten, he ran those fingers over exposed wood, digging away the snow with his mittened hand as necessary, then moved to the next section. Semyn did the same inside.

Children with an exceptional teacher.

They kept going, methodical and sure. Where the snow was a thicker crust, the boys would kick it free. Bannan found a broom and helped move the growing piles out of their way. What the villagers thought of this "game" he couldn't guess.

Sennic knew it was more. He'd gone to sit with Tir and Bannan could almost feel the old soldier's eyes on him.

"Uncle!"

Urgent, that whisper. Bannan went to his hands and knees to join Werfol. "Show me."

The boy pointed to scratches in the paint, down the midsection of the wagon near the tongue. Bannan rolled on his back and pushed himself directly beneath the marks, reaching up to trace them.

His fingers recognized the shapes. A fox head. A flower. Crude and easily mistaken for damage from rock or chain, but there was no mistaking the Larmensu crest, once found.

"That's Momma's mark."

"It is indeed," Bannan replied, touched to think Lila used this with her sons, as she had with him.

Then a darker thought intruded. Lila wasn't sentimental.

Why, then, had she chosen her crest for this not-always-a-game and not the Westietas'?

Unless it was Emon's choice. When it came to scheming, Lila's husband, with his maps and mechanicals and boundless curiosity, was rarely far behind. Were there not an abundance of relatives, some of dubious quality, in Vorkoun and surrounds? Perhaps their smaller Larmensu heritage was the safer choice.

For a child, Werfol had been very patient. Now he squirmed close. "Can you open it?"

"I can try." Bannan drew his short knife and pressed the tip where the fox's nose would be, smiling to himself as the tip pushed through with little effort. He used the knife to dig out the clot of wood and glue, revealing a thumb-sized hole.

"The other sweet spot's here, Uncle."

"Thank you." The boy was right. The flower petal farthest from the nose was soft as well.

The moment he'd cleaned it out, Werfol tried to operate the catch, but his hand was too small for the span between. "This one's not for me, Uncle," he admitted, flopping back. "It's too big. You should try."

And why wasn't he surprised when his hand fit the cunning catch perfectly?

At once, a section of the underside of the wagon, as long as his arm and half that in width, sank down then stopped, its well-greased movement slick and silent. Bannan twisted and reached to feel what was atop the wood—

Only to have a small arm intercede. "Never use your hands, Uncle," Werfol said firmly, shaking his head at the dimness of adults. "You could lose a finger."

Ancestors Deadly and Dire. Lila set traps for her sons? Continuing to curse to himself, Bannan pressed the side of his face to the cold damp wood until one eye could see over the lowered panel.

A metal box was bolted to the top of it, connected by four now-taut wires to what he couldn't see and didn't doubt. There'd be needles, or blades. Poison was entirely possible.

Ah, Lila.

A trap, but perhaps one with a familiar key. Easing back down, Bannan felt along the crest until he found a third softness, which he removed. The rest might be Lila, but this trick was pure Emon. With fingers in all three, the truthseer turned the catch mechanism left then right again. He pushed up.

With a barely heard click, the bolt holding the box released. Working carefully, Bannan unhooked it from the now-loose springs and handed it to Werfol. Last, and to protect the curious, he reset the catch to seal the hidden compartment.

Semyn's face appeared, looking through the spokes of the wheel.

"We found something!" Werfol told his brother, and began to work his way out from under the wagon, box in his hands.

The older boy's eyes met Bannan's. "So did I."

Other than the mail or when Aunt Sybb arrived in spring with her thoughtful gifts, Marrowdell rarely saw surprises. Those it did, in winter, were not the sort anyone wanted, being thin ice or a larder door smashed open by a bear, its contents pillaged. The latter was, Jenn thought more cheerfully, less likely these days with both a dragon and kruar on the hunt, but thin ice remained a worry.

From comments she overheard, what Bannan's sister had sent were more than pleasant surprises; they'd make the difference between a good winter and a dangerous one. To her shame, she'd not been as aware as she should of what the village needed, relying on her elders to say how much could be spared or not and believing they'd been short, some years, but never desperate.

Which hadn't been true. Thinking back, there'd been winters filled with conversations muted when she and Peggs came into the room, and mysterious gatherings of adults at the Treffs'. Winters when their father would fill their bowls to the top, but not his own. Not to mention the winter when they'd run out of potatoes by the Midwinter Beholding, except for those saved for planting, and the year Anten'd slaughtered Satin's sister sow, Ribbon, who'd proved tough as shoe leather but they ate her anyway and were properly Beholden.

Jenn remembered thinking Frann and Lorra went to the fair every year for their own pleasure, while everyone else worked to bring in the last of the harvest, and felt even more ashamed. Marrowdell depended on Frann's careful inventory each fall of the village's supplies, and her and Lorra's trades in Endshere.

What they did there meant a good winter, or a bad one.

Aunt Sybb had known. She'd arrive each spring worn to exhaustion. She'd assure them it was merely the journey, yet wouldn't rest till she'd felt their cheeks and ribs, and seen them eat what she'd brought from the city.

Meaning her haggard appearance wasn't the journey at all, but a winter's worth of worry over what awaited her at its end.

As Bannan worried now.

"Here you go, Jenn!"

Next in line, she stepped up to take a barrel from Zehr, then went to Riss, who was overseeing where the new food-stuffs would be stored. The red-haired woman glanced up from her ledger, eyebrows rising when she read the symbol burned into the barrel's staves. "This one's come a distance."

Jenn tipped the heavy thing over to see for herself. "'Minaki Bay,'" she read. A name from her map, her new one. "That's a port on the Sweet Sea. In Eld!" The barrel bore stains and scrapes, perhaps from being in a ship's hold. A ship on a sea! Her heart began to pound. If the barrel itself was so remarkable ... "What's 'ompah'?"

"A long thin fish, like a snake, packed in brine." Riss laughed at Jenn's expression. "It's delicious. Ompah are brought by riverboat to Avyo. We'd have it, sliced, as the start of our Midwinter Feast." Her eyes softened at the memory, then she gave herself a brisk shake. "Please put it in your father's larder, Dear Heart," she ordered, smiling. "I'll make a note to save it for our celebration. Great-Uncle will be thrilled!"

Jenn headed for the Nalynn larder, her boots crunching on the packed snow. Other boots crunched in every

direction, the villagers determined to safely store this new
bounty before dark.

While pleased Master Jupp and, presumably, others
would be thrilled, she wasn't sure herself about a snake-like
fish. She did love the tough little barrel. Perhaps, if no one
else had a need for it, she might have it for a table. Once all
of the ompah had been eaten.

A breeze whistled passed her nose. "What's everyone
about? What's this? Why are you carrying it?"

"Bannan's sister sent us supplies. This," Jenn hugged the
barrel, "is full of fish caught in the Sweet Sea."

An incredulous silence.

"The fish aren't alive," she hastened to explain. "They're
put into brine so they don't spoil. Like pickles. Riss says
they're delicious." Something pulled at the barrel and Jenn
resisted, almost falling into the snow. "Wisp!"

The "something" let go.

"I've told you before," she scolded, glad the larder door
was in sight. "You can't just help yourself. We need these
supplies." Though she was to blame for his appetite for the
villagers' food, especially Peggs' pie. What he'd relished
while a man, he liked as a dragon and wasn't beyond theft,
to Bannan's occasional outrage. Still. "I promise to give you
some at the Midwinter Beholding. If you behave."

The larder door appeared to unlock itself and open,
ready for her to enter. A contrite gesture or a smug reminder the dragon could get at anything he chose with
ease?

She'd accept the gesture, and hope for the best. "Thank
you." Jenn climbed down and put the barrel on a low shelf,
as far back in the larder as she could reach. On her way out,
she paused on the top stair. "And for what you did at the
Treffs'."

"All are grateful for what you didn't do." The dragon being contrary.

And right, as usual. "As am I," Jenn whispered, coming
the rest of the way. He let her close the door herself, but the
latch moved before her fingers touched it, snapping shut.

A promise, perhaps, to leave the fish be.

"The sister sent something else," the breeze informed
her. "Hidden in the wagon. The truthseers found it."

"A surprise for the boys," Jenn guessed, though from what she'd learned thus far of Lila Westietas, it might be nothing so simple.

Or safe.

As for safe? The fields of snow were smooth from here, girded by hedge and tall dark forest, yet she'd no doubt the efflet were busy creating their art.

Leaving their warnings.

"What is it, Dearest Heart?" A gentle tug on her scarf. "Is it still Frann? Is it that?"

Jenn shook her head. "Wisp, what would hunt efflet?"

"Something unwise. Fierce are efflet and brave." Whispers broke out at this, gleeful and many, and snow swirled around Jenn's boots until she felt like dancing. The dragon added in his darker, grimmer voice, ~When they mind their place!~

Silence. The snow settled.

Amusement. "Nothing hunts efflet in Marrowdell. Why would you ask, Dearest Heart?"

She began walking back to the mill. "When I was with them, they built a sculpture, in the snow, of their kind caught in nets, being—being killed, by something with a hidden face."

"In winter, efflet have nothing better to do than spy on others and play in the snow." Still amused, her dragon. "Doubtless they heard how the boys confused you with the Bone Stealer and invented one for your approval."

It was possible, even probable, and Wisp knew the efflet far better than she, but somehow Jenn couldn't believe the creatures had been trying to entertain her. Should she tell him they'd shown her being caught?

"If they've troubled you, I can bite off a few toes," offered with the hint of a cheerful growl.

Maybe not. "Please don't. I'm sure they meant no harm," she said truthfully. "I was startled."

A petal-soft caress on her cheek. "Good Heart. And worried, were you not? Even over such deadly things as efflet. Be assured they are safe and we are." A whoosh of wind; perhaps a wingbeat? "Am I not here?"

Proud dragon. Rightly so, Jenn knew, but she felt less sure, now, that she shouldn't tell him about the depiction of her in the net. "If something were to hunt me?" she asked, almost lightly.

His answer, when it came, was in his other voice, deep and hot with rage. ~I would eat its heart!~

She could almost feel sorry for what might try.

Almost.

The sword hung with its partner on the wall, a string of what Bannan now realized were unusually large bear teeth looped over the hilt. A bow and quiver stood below, by a basket of fletching supplies, and an extra chair sat before the larger window, the sum of the soldier's material wealth brought into his wife's home. And her great-uncle's.

Master Wagler Jupp had been a person of great importance in Rhoth's capital city; he remained imposing within this small log cabin, seated at his wide and paper-strewn desk, surrounded by chests and tapestries. Moreover, he was a person of great age as well as accomplishment, with a scowl wrinkled into his face and a silver trumpet thrust into his ear, aimed at whomever he chose to hear.

He might, Bannan thought with an inner smile, have met his match.

Werfol and Semyn, well used to important, imposing— and, often as not, cranky—barons and their ilk, had, upon being presented, bowed and introduced themselves with such impeccable courtesy that Old Jupp had blinked once, then invited them for tea, pushing aside his still-wrapped package from Endshere's post.

By the second cup, he was listening with rapt attention to their stories of Vorkoun's court, interrupting only to ask probing questions Semyn would either politely deflect or answer in adult detail. Every so often, the old man would burst into a wheezing laugh that gave Werfol the giggles.

While Bannan and Tir sat by the window with the soldier, with what had been hidden in the wagon between them on a small trunk.

Sennic rested a blunt fingertip on the metal box. "Underneath. Clever."

He'd other words for it, the truthseer thought grimly.

Sitting in the frozen wagon, out of sight, they'd opened both finds, he and the boys. What they'd found? He'd alerted Tir with a look, collected Sennic with a word, and they'd come straight here.

Because at last he knew what Lila intended.

"Ancestors Chancy and Lost," Tir scowled. "More'n once I thought to leave that bloody slow wagon, sir, and take the horses. Far from me to criticize the baroness, but—" He shook his head, plainly wanting to do just that.

Sennic's half smile had no warmth to it. "What you didn't know, you couldn't tell."

"I'd not—!"

Bannan lifted a hand, waiting till Tir subsided. "Lila wanted you to care for her sons, not this." He picked up the leather pouch Semyn had found, undid its tie, then eased the contents onto the trunk, beside the box.

A lump of fine wax, dyed purple, and a simple metal seal, with a stout wooden handle; a golden ring, sized for a man's thumb; and last, wrapped in black velvet that Bannan eased open, a key.

Everything Baron Emon Westietas of Vorkoun would require to establish his credentials and perform his official duties in Avyo's House of Keys.

Or anywhere else in Rhoth, for that matter.

Tir sat back with a hiss, his eyes wide, while Sennic's face lost any expression. "These should not be here," he said starkly.

The sounds of the little tea party ceased.

Bannan met the old soldier's ice-cold gaze. "It's a little late for that."

"What is it?" Semyn handed Master Jupp his cane when that worthy held out his hand and the boys came with him to stand before the trunk. "Ancestors Blessed. I'd not thought to see such again," the old man said finally, eyes fixed on the key. "May I?"

"Semyn?"

The boy drew a breath, then took up the key in both hands. It was large yet finely made, its darkened silver shaped into teeth that were numbers, for this opened no lock, and a grip with fish swimming a waterfall ever striving for the star at its top. The numbers were Vorkoun's seat in the noble

House, the fish and star a symbol predating Rhothan rule but kept.

When Semyn's hands stopped trembling, he brought the key over his heart, his lips moving in silent prayer. Had he been the baron, and not the heir, he would have spoken aloud, proclaiming his right.

Had Semyn been the baron, and not a young child in hiding, Bannan wouldn't be as silently cursing his sister. Again. By sending these objects to Marrowdell, Lila strengthened Semyn's claim as heir should the worst happen, even as she prevented anyone else from assuming Emon's authority.

Including the Baroness Westietas. She'd cut herself loose, that's what she'd done.

There'd be no taking the boys home.

Invocation complete, Semyn offered the key to Master Jupp, who passed his cane to Werfol and tucked his trumpet under an arm in order to receive it in both hands. He pressed it to his heart for a moment before bringing it before his eyes to study. "Vorkoun," he confirmed, then handed the key back to Semyn with a graceful bow of his own, putting his trumpet in an ear to aim at the boy. "Is your father dead?"

"No, Master Jupp." Semyn wrapped the key and placed it with the other trappings of office. "Our mother protects his name."

Oh, and wasn't that wording precise?

Master Jupp smiled, exposing gaps in his teeth. "Just so."

"My dear sister's taken other measures." Bannan released the latches on the metal box and threw back its lid.

Inside were tightly folded documents, tied with black leather cords crusted with seals. There were two sets on each, one of green wax and another of brown, and the intricate crests pressed deep into the wax matched neither the Westietas' seal laying nearby nor the Larmensu crest.

The green seals were broken.

"Read and kept safe, till now," Sennic observed, giving his uncle-by-marriage a keen look. "Do you know the seals?"

Master Jupp had lost his smile. "Bring them to my desk."

Bannan brought the box and they gathered around the

former secretary of the House of Keys as he brought a lens to bear. "Under the light," he ordered gruffly, and the truth-seer obliged, moving the open box nearer to the large glass oil lamp that was the master's pride and joy.

"The green is Ordo's personal seal." Master Jupp straightened with a wheeze. "The brown ... Essa's baron, I'm certain." He used his trumpet to point, as if loath to touch the documents. "These were sealed long ago. See the cords? The fashion changed to silk ribbon while I was— before I left Avyo." His voice fell to an anxious mutter. "Ancestors Besotted and Betrayed ... is it possible? Was he such a fool?"

Then, so sudden and sharp Werfol jumped, "Close it! Close it now!"

As if what lay inside threatened them all.

Bannan closed the box and latched it. Face set, Sennic leaned on the desk to look Master Jupp in the eye. "What's this about?"

Semyn and Werfol stood nearby, their faces pale. The truthseer touched Sennic's shoulder, waiting until the other man looked at him, until he straightened and frowned with comprehension. "You know."

"I'm afraid so," Bannan admitted. He glanced at Tir, who gave a short, grim nod. The truthseer handed it to Werfol, meeting those golden, seeing eyes. "Whatever's in here, it's to be your mother's revenge should anything happen to your father."

Being Lila's son, Werfol hugged the box, a fierce look on his face.

Master Jupp said sharply, "What's in there could mean the end of Rhoth! Would the woman start a war?"

"For family?" Bannan tousled Werfol's hair. When Semyn came close, he pulled both to him and didn't bother to answer.

There was no need.

Wreathed in gold-brushed clouds, the sun rested just above the Bone Hills. As if she needed the reminder. The day's turn was coming, a turn Jenn had offered to spend with

Bannan and his nephews, to introduce Werfol to Marrowdell and let Semyn see what he could. Including her.

A grand idea, back in the village. Now? If she wasn't carrying everyone's supper, she'd head for home at a run.

As if sensing her doubts, or having his own, Bannan gave her a smile of encouragement. He carried his belongings on his back. Semyn and Werfol had stuffed what they needed this first night into flour sacks. They'd argued how best to hoist them over a shoulder, pretending to be sailors, then swung their sacks at one another all the way through the commons, laughing even when they missed and fell into the snow.

The pair had settled by the ford.

The once-untrustworthy ice was now firm and easily crossed, but yesterday's storm had filled the Tinkers Road with deep snow, save for the track broken by Kydd's and Wainn's horses. Bannan went first, to further pack the snow for the boys, but that track suddenly widened and cleared, snow flying upward and away.

Until there was room to walk side-by-side. Bannan laughed and bowed. "My thanks!"

Semyn froze in place. "W-what did that?"

"I saw little wings," his brother answered before Jenn could. "They moved too fast." With immense disappointment. "I couldn't really see them."

"They are called efflet," Jenn told him. "And maybe you will."

Bannan, delighted by Marrowdell's welcome, waved them onward with a sweep of his arm. "Home first."

Semyn and Werfol exchanged resigned looks before they followed their uncle, bracing themselves for the worst. Jenn hid a smile.

Sunlight glinted and glistened, warmer-toned as it sank to the horizon. The old trees overhung the road, snow along every branch, every so often dropping a soft clump.

Or something dropped it. Regardless, none landed on their heads.

"We're here," Bannan announced proudly and stopped at the opening to his farm to give the boys a good look.

Jenn was pleased to see the efflet had been at work here as well, enlarging paths begun by Kydd and Wainn. The fountain stood free on all sides, its sweet water unfrozen, that being one of Marrowdell's gifts. Snow remained on the roof of barn and house and filled the surrounding hedge, but the porch was swept clear and there was a path to the privy and larder.

A welcoming light shone in one window; a lazy curl of smoke from the chimney promised warmth.

"What do you think?" Bannan asked.

"It's very nice, Uncle," Semyn said, a little too politely.

Werfol nudged his brother. "It's very small, you mean. Smaller than our tack room at home. But nicer," he added quickly.

Bannan laughed. "It's big enough, I promise. Come." He led the way and the boys followed.

Jenn hesitated. From here, she could see the opening in the hedge that led to Night's Edge. As if noticing her attention, a little breeze flipped her bangs.

Wisp, reminding her what she could feel for herself.

The turn had begun.

Another flip. "I know," she mouthed.

Summoning her courage, she put down the basket and called out, "Wait." The three stopped and faced her. Jenn looked a question at Bannan.

In answer, he crouched between the boys, arms around their shoulders. "Semyn, Weed. Marrowdell's a special place. If you're quiet and patient, those who live here will show themselves as the sun sets."

"I've seen things already, Uncle."

Semyn squirmed to glare at his brother. "I saw the dragon too!"

"There's more." Bannan gave them a gentle squeeze then looked to Jenn with hope in his eyes.

So be it. Jenn unwound her scarf and shrugged off her coat.

Heartbeats later, the turn reached her.

She tipped her head back, feeling her form take its other shape. Lost in the sensation, it took her a moment to remember her audience.

Werfol looked pleased and a little smug. Semyn stood staring, his mouth open, then began to smile. "The dragon!" The . . . ?

Jenn looked down. Sure enough, Wisp lay coiled in the snow at her feet, steam trailing from his nostrils, by far the most interesting thing in sight.

Clever dragon. "This is Wisp—" she began.

Werfol pointed urgently at the nearest tree. "What are those?"

"I don't see anything, Weed." Semyn's face contorted with effort. "Where?"

"Now they're gone." Werfol frowned. "Why?"

"You scared them!" Semyn grabbed a mittenful of snow and threw it at his brother. "Uncle said to be quiet!"

"It's all right, Semyn. They're shy and don't know you yet." Bannan stood. "Thank you, Jenn."

The turn flowed past, on its way through the valley. As shadows lengthened around her, Jenn became her other self and Wisp faded from sight. She put on her coat and scarf, picking up the basket as if nothing untoward had happened. "We'd best get this inside and warming."

They waited for her. When she drew close, Semyn reached out as though to touch her, and Jenn held her breath.

Smack! A ball of snow hit her on the arm and Werfol ran past, laughing. Semyn, grabbing handfuls, took off after his brother.

"So much for the mysteries of Marrowdell," Bannan declared, looking rather smug.

Jenn wasn't at all surprised when a large mass of snow from the roof came WHOMP! down on his head.

"'Keep Us Close.'" The echoing words from around the table—from his nephews, from Jenn, and from Wainn, who'd stayed for supper—filled the room and Bannan's heart. He ducked his head to hide what surely was a stupidly happy grin, and cut generous wedges of Peggs' meat pie, slipping them onto waiting plates.

Despite poor Frann and whatever problems faced Lila and Emon, he couldn't help but be glad. The boys were safe and he was home. Ancestors Harried and Hasty, had it been only yesterday he'd left to move in with Devins for the winter? Tir had that bed until his feet healed. After that, Bannan planned to offer his friend room here, if he wished.

"We saw a real dragon," Semyn told Wainn, seated between the boys on a bench at the table. "He had smoke coming out of his nose!"

"He's our friend," Werfol put in. He'd been quiet to this point, staring so intently at Wainn he barely seemed to blink. The youngest Uhthoff didn't appear to mind.

Bannan understood. Werfol would learn how to suppress his gift; right now he couldn't help but see deeply and Wainn was—he was astonishing. To the deeper sight, he brimmed with joy and wonder, as if reflecting the best of the world out again. To look at Wainn Uhthoff with a truthseer's sight? Like warming cold fingers by a fire.

Jenn's fingers brushed Bannan's as she accepted her plate, leaving a tingle on his skin. He wanted to tell her how incredibly beautiful she'd looked at the turn, surrounded by the gold of the setting sun against the snow, her shape outlined in pearl and light. He wanted very many things, most of which, he realized ruefully, made newly difficult by the presence of small children.

A dimple appeared, as if she'd had the same thought.

The rest of the meal passed in a pleasant blur. Jenn and Wainn told the boys a little of Marrowdell. Semyn, already a scholar like his father, was delighted to hear Master Dusom would welcome them into his class, when those started again. Werfol, unimpressed by the thought of lessons, perked up at the mention of skates and shoes to walk on the snow, ready that instant to try both.

Bannan, who'd caught himself nodding over his tea, wondered if the boy ever tired.

In the midst of questions about, of all things, musical instruments—or was it eggs?—he must have nodded off again, for he startled awake at the touch of soft lips on his cheek. "We're leaving, Dearest Heart," Jenn said with a grin and a second, firmer kiss.

Which woke him completely, too late for more than a round of thank yous and good nights as Jenn and Wainn, already bundled for the outdoors and the ride home, cheerfully refused the leftover pie, and went out the door.

Leaving Bannan alone with his nephews.

Werfol and Semyn stood near the door, almost as if ready to follow Jenn and Wainn out of it.

He wasn't above bribery. "Is it too late for something sweet?"

"No, Uncle!"

"Momma always gives us a treat before bed," Werfol added to that.

Bannan raised an eyebrow, but let the lie go, for now. "Then we shall."

Semyn hesitated. "Uncle, Wainn said we were to introduce ourselves to the house toad."

"Of course." The toad he hadn't yet seen. He felt a twinge of remorse, for the toads were even more fond of courtesy than Master Jupp, and he shouldn't have brought strangers through the door without the consent of his.

He blamed the dragon, and the ridiculous amount of snow that had found its way down his back.

"May I introduce my nephews?" the truthseer said, and waited for a response, signaling his nephews to stay where they were.

A clawed foot appeared from under the cookstove. He'd not thought the creature could squeeze itself into so narrow a space, but there was another foot. The claws of both dug into the wooden floor then—with a pop!—out came the rest of the toad.

It waddled forth to squat before the boys in quiet dignity, somehow conveying a certain amount of scepticism.

"Uncle," Werfol whispered anxiously, "I don't think it likes us."

Semyn nudged his brother to bow. As they both rose, he addressed the toad. "Honored guardian, we are Semyn and Werfol Westietas, nephews of Bannan Larmensu. Our uncle has graciously invited us to live with him in this house. May we have your permission?"

"We promise to be good," Werfol added, his eyes bright with unshed tears.

They'd a history with toads, Bannan guessed. Just as well Wainn had given this advice.

The house toad waited long enough for the boys to worry, but not so long as to unsettle tired children. Giving a great, toothy yawn, it hopped out of their way, taking its usual station beside, not under, the 'stove.

Where a dented pile of cushions suggested another watcher had already made himself at home.

Ancestors Witness. What next? Scourge?

The truthseer yawned, more than ready for his own bed. He'd stuff a mattress with straw from his barn tomorrow. Tonight would be a bedroll on the floor, once the boys were comfortable upstairs. He'd be surprised if his eyes stayed open a moment.

His nephews came up to him. "The sweets, Uncle?" Werfol hinted.

Tomorrow, he'd ask Covie about the proper diet for young boys. "Just one." He found the little bag from Endshere and carefully put a piece of red candy on each offered palm.

Then a second. Lila had to know he'd be a terrible parent. "Sit with me a moment." Bannan took his favorite seat by the fireplace, waiting for the boys to climb into theirs. Their feet didn't touch the rug.

Heart's Blood. They were so young.

They were Lila's, he reminded himself, and Emon's. To think them ordinary children was to do them a disservice.

"Semyn, what else did you find in the wagon?"

They glanced at each other, then back to him. "Uncle?" Respectful and oh, so innocent.

"With the pouch."

Werfol shifted uneasily in the chair. Semyn shot him another look, a worried one, before turning back to Bannan. His lips pressed shut.

Good. He knew a lie would hurt his brother.

Bannan eased back, crossing one foot over the other. "Come now. My sister left something for you," he said. "Something she didn't want found until you were safe from pursuit. With me."

Blue-green eyes fixed on his, filled with an adult's resolve. Small hands gripped the chair's arms. His heart ached, that they'd learned such distrust, but wasn't it a survival skill, outside Marrowdell?

Hadn't he been the same?

"Whatever it is," the truthseer continued, "will have one meaning for you and your brother. It will have another, different meaning for me, her brother. Do you understand?"

"You can't have it," Werfol objected, his voice shrill. "Momma sent it for us."

Bannan laced his fingers together on his knee. "And yours it is. I ask only to see it. I'm afraid for her too."

Beneath a thunderous scowl, the little truthseer's eyes glittered gold. Bannan waited. Werfol didn't want to believe him.

But he must, for it was true.

The scowl faded. "Semyn."

"Weed—no!"

The younger boy slipped down from his chair and went to stand beside his brother's. "It's all right. Show Uncle Bannan."

Reluctance in every movement, Semyn pulled up his woolen vest, shirt, and undershirt. Beneath, around his small waist, was a belt of softly tanned leather, with compartments, like those worn by merchants and sailors to thwart cutpurses.

This had been made for a child.

A child who searched his face before opening a compartment to bring out its contents. What he held out on his palm, Bannan had last seen around his sister's neck.

Lila's pendant.

No ordinary frippery, this. Set in curls of silver, like a rock within rapids, the exotic teardrop-shaped stone changed color with movement, like water playing with sunlight. But its best trick?

The stone spoke.

Emon had bought it in Channen, where artisans worked in magic. Such objects were called endearments, being bespelled with a lover's soft whisper, a whisper heard only by those intended. Though Bannan had teased her when he'd found out, he knew Lila was never without the thing, going so far as to tuck it within her mail shirt when sparring.

Until now. Werfol touched it and smiled, his eyes closed for a moment. Semyn looked at Bannan. "It's Mother's voice." His own became husky. "She says she loves us. And 'However far we are apart, Keep Us Close.'"

Werfol opened his eyes. "'Keep Us Close.'"

He hadn't realized endearments could be respelled. Trust Emon, ever curious, to have found that out as well. Before he'd thought, he reached out his hand and, hesitating only slightly, Semyn gave him the pendant.

Cool the piece, and substantial. Feeling a fool, Bannan lifted it to his ear, the boys' eyes following the motion, but of course heard nothing at all. With a rueful smile, he returned the pendant to its rightful holders.

"You said it would mean something to you too, Uncle. What?" asked Semyn quietly.

That Lila had rid herself of a gift she'd suspected could betray her and there was only one place where magic would.

Channen. She'd gone to hunt for Emon herself.

"Uncle?"

Bannan let out the breath he hadn't realized he'd held. "Your mother has resources," he answered carefully, the word embracing a network of contacts and strong arms the extent of which even he didn't know. One thing was certain. Lila was uncannily aware of what went on beyond her walls; including, to his chagrin, details of his patrols. "This," he gestured to the pendant, "tells me she's not using them." Why, he refused to guess.

"Momma doesn't need anyone else. She'll find Poppa," Werfol said with touching confidence. "You'll see."

Semyn looked as though he might be sick, but didn't argue. Instead, he shook out its chain and hung the pendant around Werfol's neck. "Keep it safe," he admonished his brother, whose eyes shone.

"I will."

They fell silent after that, staring into the fire's fickle light. Tired, all of them, and heartsore. He'd take Wainn's advice, Bannan decided, and let the flames die out, relying on the charcoal in the cookstove to keep the house warm while they slept. At the thought, he yawned involuntarily, smiling when the boys yawned too.

"To bed, Dear Hearts." He'd shown them the loft where they'd sleep and, of no inclination himself to go outside, provided a chamberpot. "Take a lamp," he added, this being their first night in an unfamiliar place. "Leave it burning, if you wish." Lila having provided oil. "If you need anything, call me," he finished.

Werfol frowned. "You'll hear us? You're sure?"

If he didn't, the toad or the dragon surely would. Bannan smiled reassuringly. "I'll know if you need me," he promised, and Werfol relaxed. "Good night."

"Good night, Uncle," they said together and rose. They gave him a polite little bow when he'd have preferred a hug, but Bannan dipped his head, accepting the courtesy. He watched the pair climb the ladder, Semyn leading the way.

Then the truthseer closed his eyes, it being impossible to get up from his chair.

~

*A scrap of printed page, touched by skin . . . a drop of sleep, under the tongue . . .*
*And the dream unfolds . . .*
Light sings. Colors shriek. There's no end or beginning and all is falling . . . falling . . .
Unspeakable power writhes, searching for form, claims shape.
It must be seen. Must be. Cannot be borne—!
*The dream falters . . . lost . . .*

"Uncle?"

"What—" Ancestors Witness. Not again. He'd slept in a chair last night.

Groggily realizing what he'd heard, Bannan stirred himself. "I'm coming." He climbed the ladder into the loft, knocking a warning before his head passed the floor.

They'd dressed for bed in gowns and caps, but were sitting cross-legged on top of the blankets, their small faces somber.

Bannan sat on the end of the bed, guessing what was the matter. "This isn't home," he acknowledged. "But it's where your mother wants you to be. Where you're safe and with me."

Semyn plucked at a loose thread on his chest where the

Westietas' crest had been removed, as it had been from all their clothing. When he looked at Bannan, it wasn't the look of a child. "Why you, Uncle? Why not with our father's family?"

He'd thought to wait until morning for this. Maybe it was better said before they tried to sleep. "As Larmensu, we share a special heritage." Bannan touched a finger to Werfol's sock-clad toes. "You are a truthseer." He moved the finger to rest over his heart. "So am I."

"Weed?" A quick demand; though he hadn't known its name till now, Semyn trusted that gift.

Hadn't Lila?

The younger boy went on his knees, eyes wide and gold. "It's true," he breathed.

Semyn pulled his brother back. "What does it mean? Will it hurt him?"

"You've seen for yourself. It means you," Bannan looked at Werfol, "know if someone lies. It means in Marrowdell, where magic lies close to the surface, you can see what's different." He sighed. "It's already hurt, hasn't it."

Werfol nodded, then said, very quietly, "When people lie."

"Everyone did," Semyn burst out. "The new staff, our guards. Even—even Momma."

Werfol nodded again, his lips pressed together.

So Lila hadn't known. Werfol was younger than he'd been. A son, not a brother. Moreover, her house had been under siege, filled with untrustworthy faces. Little wonder her instinct had been to thrust the boys away from danger.

Still. "What did she say?"

"That we'd be safe. That we'd be together again. That Father would come home." Tears spilled over. "I could see they were lies. All of them!"

"Lies!" Semyn looked ready to cry himself.

Heart's Blood. "They felt like lies," Bannan said heavily, "because your mother was afraid."

They blinked like tired little owls. "Momma is never afraid," Semyn corrected carefully.

He'd thought so, once. "Your mother doesn't show her fear. There's a difference. Trust me when I tell you she's afraid for you and for your father, more afraid than she's ever been. What she told you, Werfol, wasn't a lie." Denial stormed across the boy's face and Bannan held up his hand. "It wasn't the truth, either. You'll learn the difference. What your mother told you," he went on gently, "is what she hopes with all her heart will happen. Do you understand?"

Werfol wanted to, desperately, but how could he? It was the hardest lesson of all, that the deeper sight must be interpreted, not blindly believed. "Enough for tonight," Bannan decided, overwhelmed himself. "Under the covers with you. We'll start your training tomorrow, Werfol, if you like, once we've moved all of your things here."

"And visit Tir?" Semyn asked.

Bannan smiled as he tucked the quilts around them. "And visit Tir."

"May we visit Lady Frann?" Werfol put in, snuggling close to his brother. "And Jenn? Will we see her too? And—"

Marrowdell being smaller than the Westietas' estate, Bannan chuckled, they'd be hard pressed to avoid anyone. "You'll see them all, I promise." He picked up the very well-loved little book from the nightstand and adjusted the lamp so its light wouldn't shine in sleepy eyes.

"Now, who'd like a story?" the truthseer asked.

And didn't see that a moth clung to a rafter, busily taking notes.

"Your sister wants the boy to keep up his training, sir."

"Not here," Bannan snapped. "Not that."

Tir gave him a look that said plainly as speech he wasn't about to take responsibility for defying Lila Westietas and anyone who did was a fool.

Fine. He'd no problem with either. Bannan put the practice swords and helms aside, leaving the boys' wooden pipes on the pile of goods to take home. "Semyn can keep up his music."

"A grand help that'll be, fighting for his life." His friend took a look at his face and added a placating, "Sir."

Bannan closed the pack, resting his hands on the top. The boys, brimming with excitement, hadn't stayed indoors long, determined to meet the other children. For the moment, he and Tir had the Morrill house to themselves, Devins being at the dairy, and he shouldn't waste it. He looked up at the man who knew him—and his sister—better than any now alive. "Lila's gone to Channen."

"And a week's pay says she left when we did." Tir's blue eyes regarded him. "What's to happen, Bannan, likely has by now."

His fingers tightened on the straps. "I know." He gave a helpless shrug. "I have to trust her."

"Oh, wouldn't go so far as that, sir. Wasn't it your sister who paid our trusty Ruthh to sew you inside your bedroll?"

And a challenging morning-after that had been. Bannan half smiled. "True. Any word from Kydd?"

"Aie. You were right—t'was no soldier's luck. Metal's Naalish starstone, worth ten times what's in the wagon. Parchment's blank—meant for a name, is his guess." After a grim pause. "Can't say as to the vial, or the proper words, but Kydd says—well, sir, he fears it's a wishing to force obedience. Not that he believes in wishings, sir, but it being Naalish—" Tir let his voice trail off meaningfully.

"It'd be real magic," Bannan finished for him.

"He thought so, yes. To use on the heir, would be my guess."

Implying someone who knew Semyn: a child, yes, but not one to be easily manipulated, not Lila's son. The rot in that house— "No wonder Werfol was so angry." At Tir's puzzled look, he added, "He has the gift."

Tir straightened from his slouch so quickly he spilled his tea, muttering an oath as the hot liquid found his hand. "Heart's Blood. Sir! I didn't know—I wouldn't have—"

Rare to see the former border guard tongue-tied. "Peace, Tir. Werfol's here now, and I'll teach him what he needs to know." Bannan reached over to put a hand on his friend's shoulder. "Thanks to you, whatever they'd planned—to force Emon's hand or use Semyn—has failed. That Naalish magic was involved is a clue we can give Lila and Emon when they come for the boys. I could pity those who plotted against them."

"No. Sir." Grim and final.

"'Could.'" Bannan picked up the pack, slinging over a

shoulder. "I'd best get these back. I've promised the boys a visit with Frann after lunch, and they'll want dry clothes." Along with Covie's advice on feeding the pair, he'd soon need advice on winter laundry. Ancestors Dazed and Domestic. He supposed baths would be next.

Tir nodded. "Good lads." He lifted a leg and flexed the ankle, waving his wrapped foot. "I'll be in boots any day, sir." A wink. "And there to help."

"Just be sure you're healed first," Bannan warned, then smiled. "Help will be most welcome."

"One more thing, sir, before you go."

The truthseer paused at the door. "Yes?"

Tir scratched at his beard, a habit when perplexed. "Yon idiot beast's acting stranger than usual. Are you sure the lads are safe 'round him?"

Nothing was certain about Scourge, but Bannan couldn't imagine—then he thought of the bloody snow, and could. "I'll have a talk with him."

"Best you do, sir. Before we have to explain to the baroness."

"I would not harm the boys." The breeze found him by the fountain, sly and cool along his jaw, proving there was no such thing as privacy when Marrowdell's other inhabitants took an interest.

As they had in Werfol and Semyn. Bannan couldn't see Scourge; he didn't doubt he was being seen. "Listening at the door, were you?" he said, continuing on his way. "Or did Devins' toad tell you? Rude, that is."

"Mine."

More than possessive. With one word, Scourge drew a line and claimed sole right to what lay beyond it. This was new.

Was it dangerous?

Despite now-serious misgivings, Bannan kept to his pace, doing his utmost to appear unconcerned. After all, he'd all the winter to work everything out, including the kruar, who'd not hesitate to challenge everyone or anything, including a dragon.

But not, Bannan thought with a lighter heart, Jenn Na-lynn. Let winter do what it would, he'd family and love.

As well as the surprise that had everyone talking. Om-pah for the Midwinter Beholding Feast.

Marrowdell seemed to hold its breath, the next handful of days, as if to allow everything—and everyone—to settle into place. Like the rest of those used to winter, Jenn found herself eyeing the sky, though there was no sign of another storm.

Like the rest, she found herself often at the Treffs', though not usually for long. Frann slept and Lorra brooded, a combination that saw Cynd and Davi taking tea with the Ropps more often than not, and made it difficult for anyone to linger.

The only ones unaffected by weather or illness were the children. By their second afternoon, Jenn smiled to see Werfol and Semyn playing with Cheffy and Alyssa, the lat-ter having finished their chores. By the next, the four were doing those chores together, much to the delight of Wainn's old pony who'd not been so fussed over in years. Mean-while, Tir had not only donned boots and easily walked to Bannan's and back, but shortly after moved his belongings into that now busy household.

Day followed day. The only guests Lorra Treff welcomed were Bannan's nephews. She'd sit with Frann to hear Semyn play his pipes, for he was a talented musician and well schooled, and listen, with unanticipated patience, as Werfol did his best to read from books beyond his age.

Hettie grew rounder and Loee another tooth. Master Dusom announced it would soon be time to recommence lessons, the weather unlikely to hold and young minds needing stimulation.

But it wasn't peace, Jenn thought as she took off her coat and hung it on its hook.

Marrowdell waited.

"Jenn. Thank you for coming." Cynd pushed back her bangs. "Here's the broth. You're sure you don't mind?"

"Not at all." Jenn smiled. "You've seen my stitches. Go.

Riss is there." "There" being the Nalynns' main room, today set for quilting. It would be a party as much as work, with a supper to follow. Those who weren't quilters but felt equally inspired to gather were already around the Ropps' massive kitchen table, testing their skill at nillystones and other games. At some point, the groups would merge and there'd be music and a bottle or few, with the night ending whenever inclined.

"We could take turns," Davi's wife offered as she began to put on her coat, then hesitated, one arm up a sleeve. "Maybe I should stay—"

Jenn wrapped Cynd's scarf around her neck. "I've books, and I'm sure you've left me some mending—?" A nod. "Then go. Enjoy yourself." She didn't make it a wish, but the other woman's eyes lightened.

"Fetch me if you need me."

"I promise." Having seen Cynd out the door, Jenn poured herself tea, then went to Frann's room.

Lorra sat in the big chair at the head of the bed, her eyes closed. Jenn quietly settled herself on the other side, there being a kitchen chair under the window, and rested her eyes on Frann.

She'd been frail. At some uncaught moment, she'd become paper and air, her skin prone to flutter, her only movement, breath.

Yet a spark gleamed in the eyes that met Jenn's and humor crooked pale lips. Frann glanced toward Lorra, then back, closing her own eyes, then opening them, and Jenn had to smile.

"Making fun of me again, is she?" Lorra grumbled, not opening her eyes.

"I believe so," Jenn replied, rewarded by the tiniest of smiles.

Lorra pulled up her blanket. "Good."

There being a still-steaming cup on the table beside the Treff matriarch, Jenn sipped from her own without guilt. She set it down and pulled out her book, finding the spot where she'd stopped last time. Before she could start to read aloud, Frann made a faint "shhh" sound, and glanced at Lorra again.

Who looked after whom?

Jenn nodded and sat back, flipping pages to where she herself had been. Frann smiled again, then closed her eyes.

The book was a new one, and entertaining. Jenn chuckled out loud, then looked up worriedly. She'd needn't have worried. Both women were sound asleep. Lorra snored and Frann ...

Did Frann ... ?

Frann took a deep breath and another. She'd been mistaken. Reassured, Jenn put the ribbon between the pages and put down her book. Mending would be quieter, so she went to the other room to fetch the basket Covie had left for her.

The afternoon passed. Jenn put buttons on a shirt and fixed what must have been a very drafty hole in a pair of pants. She was midway through an elbow patch when something caught her attention.

Ah. The turn. She'd planned for this—a trip to the privy would do nicely and, after so much tea, needful. Afterward, she'd heat some broth and see if Lorra would eat too.

Though Jenn rose to her feet as quietly as possible, Frann held out her hand.

She took it in hers. "Is there something you ... ?" No need to finish the question, Frann wasn't awake. The hand went limp and she gently put it down.

Lorra startled and sat. "What?"

Frann's other hand drifted toward her. Lorra stared at it before she edged closer and took it in her own. "You're not allowed," she said, so softly Jenn could hardly hear the words. "You're not. Not now."

But it was, Jenn realized, as Frann's breaths came slower ...

And sometimes didn't ...

Then did again.

Lorra looked up with such appalling grief in her eyes, Jenn could hardly bear it. "She asked to see the dancers again, the ones in the trees. I told her to wait for winter to pass. I promised, if she'd wait—" Her fists clenched over her mouth.

She'd no power to give breath or strength. She couldn't add so much as a minute to a life. She'd thought herself helpless.

But this, Jenn thought fiercely, she could do.

Even as the turn came and turned her to glass, she threw open the window and made her wish.

Marrowdell answered.

Instead of winter, spring burst through the opening, the air warm and rich with the scent of soil and growing things. Even as Lorra gasped, there came the sound of wings, then what seemed summer leaves and tiny stars filled the air above the bed, as if they'd but waited for the invitation—

And the ylings danced, their hands together, singing and laughing, dodging cobwebs and dust. Cloaks of aster petals and verdant green cedar swirled around them—

And a smile curved Frann's lips.

As one, the ylings dipped in salute, rose almost to the rafters, then vanished—

As Frann Nall let out a long, slow breath.

Through the window, then, came the kruar's mighty head as if summoned too. After a hum deep enough to rattle the windowpanes, Scourge opened his mouth and inhaled, giving Jenn a baleful look out of one red eye, then pulled back. She could hear him galloping away.

All at once, she could hear her own heart beat, for the turn had passed and she was no longer glass. She could hear Lorra's breaths, her sigh.

And nothing more.

"Well." Lorra put Frann's hand down on the bed and smoothed the hair lying over the pillow. "As always, you had to do things your way." She bent to kiss her friend's forehead. "And were brilliant."

She nodded at Jenn, then walked from the room, her head high.

Jenn closed the window, before winter, being back in its rightful place, could enter. When she was done, she turned to find the bed, and Frann, covered in rose petals.

Only then did she cry.

The wait was over.

And Marrowdell remained. A better end than might

have been; having survived, the dragon sincerely hoped there'd be no more tests of the girl's self-control. The little cousins had fretted themselves into hiccups and, till she'd sent him away, even he'd found it impossible not to keep asking how she was and would she be destroying the world anytime soon?

What would happen next? The villagers managed a feast for all other occasions. Surely this would warrant one as well. The larders held new and interesting food to try, food which, though tempted, he'd not steal.

There being biscuits, well-buttered biscuits, daily at the truthseer's.

Her grief would pass. Jenn Nalynn would come again to Night's Edge, though to be honest Wisp preferred winter at the truthseer's. He'd curl up on the bed with the children, once Bannan had said his good nights, and they'd whisper little stories to him as she had, when she'd been this small and not turn-born or grown.

Not, he thought with a quiet snarl, that she didn't still need him.

Not that there weren't still fools.

~What is the meaning of this?~

Efflet whispered and fluttered, but none dared approach.

The dragon stalked around the unfamiliar shape in the snow: the girl's "hunter of efflet." Not of Marrowdell, this grim creature, nor could he recall such within the Verge. The efflet could be fanciful, but their creations were most often real. Was this?

If so, he blamed the little cousins. Unlike the efflet and ylings, with their generations born here and died, the little cousins of Marrowdell had come from the Verge and re-membered it all too well. They told stories of that place to the others, the dragon knew. Hadn't he seen the toads' lost queen rise in snow every winter, glorious and regal and wise?

Foolish little cousins. They remembered with their hearts. Their queen sat her throne in the Verge, oblivious to her exiled subjects in Marrowdell, seething in her hatred of anything more powerful. No house toad, she. Nothing so amiable or small or trustworthy.

Dragons avoided her.

But this? This curious hunter of efflet. From whence had it come?

Wisp reached the other side and froze. A net hung by straps from the creature's shoulder. A net containing—

~NO!~ he roared, sending breezes to rip apart the offending snow, then drove himself through it, sending snowy arms and eyes and chains flying apart.

Satisfied, he turned around.

To see another sculpture of snow rise, another Jenn Nalynn shown trapped.

Wisp roared again. ~STOP!~ He sent wind, not breezes, to flatten everything in its path until the efflets' field became a featureless plain, white and even.

Snow flicked here and there, as if the efflet twitched nervously.

They should.

For an instant. Suddenly, everywhere, sculptures erupted. All the same. One pushed him aside.

How DARE they!

~What's this?~ from below.

~Why that?~ from above.

Dragons circled and dragons gossiped, curious and careless. They were drawn to his tempers, for what challenged a dragon lord was either entertainment or opportunity, and did some among them grow inclined to the latter, thinking him old?

Thinking him done?

Wisp launched himself upward, the beat of his wings driving a storm, the roar of his breath thunder! ~BE-GONE!~

Dragons fled and efflet cowered.

The intimation of something hunting Jenn Nalynn, that something would dare? Eat its heart? He'd rend flesh from its bones while it lived!

The old kruar snorted, neck arched as he stepped through the snow. ~Are you finished?~

Hovering above, for a vastly pleasant instant Wisp imagined plunging down, claws ready to slice to bone, jaws open to snap that neck.

Those had been the days.

Scourge stamped, the sound echoing through both worlds. ~I must have an enemy to conquer! You're in the mood. Come. Blood and triumph for Frann!~

There was something to be said for these days. ~A bear prowls above the village,~ the dragon observed. ~Perhaps two!~

A place to begin his search for the efflets' so-foolish hunter.

# NINE

*T*HE BODY OF Frann Nall was interred with those who
had joined the Blessed Ancestors before her, in Marrowdell's ossuary, on a morning without cloud or wind, in a
section of ground as soft and warm as midsummer.

For Jenn Nalynn had wished it so.

Lorra Treff had demanded that Frann be laid deeper
than usual, to leave room for her bones and those of every
other Treff, it being the Rhothan custom that, where possible, the bones of those close in life should mingle afterward.

Davi had done his best. They'd had to lower Frann on a
quilt, rather than carry her down, the hole being so deep,
which might have seemed a waste and indulgence, but Jenn
overheard Tadd telling Hettie there was a winter bear
nearby and the deeper the hole the better.

Lorra stood among her family, Davi and Cynd to her
right, Wen to her left, with the rest of Marrowdell around.
When the time came to fill the hole, Jenn reached for her
handful of still-warm soil and found herself facing Cynd.
The other woman stared at her in the oddest way, as if

angry, which couldn't be right, then stepped well back to let Jenn go first.

Not courtesy. Aversion.

Riss caught Jenn's eye, then gave a tiny shrug. She'd added anger at Melusine's death to that from her exile; she'd left both behind, long ago. Radd Nalynn, having seen, leaned close to his daughter. "Pay no attention, Dear Heart. Each grief takes its own shape."

Jenn nodded. Didn't hers feel hollow, as if she'd lost part of her heart?

Everyone helped fill the hole in the ground: Davi, Devins, and Anten with shovels, the rest by hand. Even little Loee was given a handful of soil to toss and was very quiet and solemn. Marrowdell stood together as Master Jupp led the Beholding. Winter slipped back before he finished, reddening cheeks and turning the ground as hard as rock.

Surely, Jenn hoped, a bear couldn't get through that.

Next, Lorra would lead the way back to her house, with all the village to follow. All the village waited, patient despite the growing nip in the wind. This first step away was the Far Step. To take it meant accepting Frann as a Blessed Ancestor, forever apart.

The feather atop Lorra's hat dipped once, then rose. She took the step, determined and alone, and Marrowdell followed behind, each within their own thoughts and sorrow. They filed along the path between hedges to the road.

When her turn came, Jenn felt a hand take hers and looked down to find Werfol, his face pale. Bannan stood with Semyn, Tir nearby, ready to follow them. She nodded at the child and they took their step together.

Hard, the Far Step, and momentous.

The next came easier.

And the next.

By the open road, voices were raised in conversation that grew louder and even happy. Now came the time for sharing of stories about the departed, the more the better, and there was no one here Frann hadn't touched.

With Werfol still holding her hand, quiet as could be, Jenn wasn't quite sure what to say or do. Was he upset or merely subdued?

Someone laughed, and he flinched.

Upset.

What would distract him? "I learned to dance to Frann's flute, Ancestors—Ancestors Dear and Departed." She'd not expected the exhortation, proper for the dead, to stick in her throat. "Frann was a wonderful musician. What would you say about her?"

Jenn waited a moment, but the boy was silent.

"What's wrong, Werfol?" she said quietly. "Frann did us both a great kindness, telling you about me. Surely you've something you want remembered."

"Frann didn't lie." An accusation.

Jenn looked around at the villagers, now moving briskly toward the Treffs' where food and drink and music waited. Everywhere was grief at Frann's loss. Everywhere, joy for her life. Those conflicting feelings washed through her too, coming in powerful waves, sometimes one, often both. Ancestors Troubled and Torn, how would this seem to a truthseer—especially one so young? "Werfol—"

He jerked his hand free. "I don't want to talk to you. I don't want to be here."

The other three joined them. "I'll take the lad home, sir," Tir offered at once. "I hardly knew the lady."

"We'll both go." Bannan swept Werfol up in his arms and the child buried his face in his uncle's neck. The truthseer's jaw muscles worked, his eyes full of sympathy. "Home it is, Dear Heart."

"Tir too." Muffled but determined.

"Aie," agreed the former guard. "Semyn?"

The older boy shook his head. "With your consent, Uncle, I would represent the family."

Bannan bowed his head gravely. "You have it with my thanks." He looked to her. "Jenn?" An apology.

Without need. "Go. I'll see Semyn home, afterward." She could see strain on his dear face, more than would be explained by worry over his smallest nephew. Was it Bannan's own gift or did he remember another moment like this? Jenn kissed him on the cheek. "There's no telling how long we'll be," she cautioned, Lorra as stubborn as she was exhausted.

"However long you need," Bannan said. "Frann welcomed me to Marrowdell, Ancestors Dear and Departed, and I'll always remember that." He hugged Werfol and added in a lighter tone. "Tir. I believe Weed's Special Eggs might be in order."

As they left, Semyn offered her his arm, his face solemn. Remembering how Aunt Sybb would accept the courtesy from their father, Jenn laid her gloved hand on the boy's arm and let him lead her to the others.

Most had gone by as they'd delayed for Werfol, but Hettie and Tadd waited for them, with Cheffy. Another child might have left her for his playmate; Semyn nodded a stiff greeting and stayed at her side.

Hettie's smile was tremulous. "I was telling Tadd how Frann helped us, after Mother drowned. Ancestors Dear and Departed. You were smaller than Werfol," to Cheffy.

"I almost drowned too," that worthy informed Semyn, who looked properly impressed. "Poppa says I swallowed most of the river!"

"Children," Hettie mouthed.

"And maybe a fish."

Jenn felt herself smile.

Tadd put his arm around his wife's shoulders. "I'll not forget the time Frann caught Allin and me nipping some clay from Lorra's pottery wheel. Roche told us it would make the best shot for our slings."

Roche having got the twins into trouble on many occasions, Jenn wasn't surprised. "What did Lorra say?"

"She never knew. Frann laughed and gave us each a bagful." His mouth drooped at the corners. "Ancestors Dear and Departed."

Despite the cold, the Treffs' door stood open in welcome, with one of Frann's bright weavings caught across the top. With so many warm bodies present, and all those wearing their best winter coats, there was no need for the cookstove which had been removed, presumably to the kitchen. When Jenn followed Semyn inside, the first thing she noticed through the crowd was that platters of food covered the table instead of mending.

The second thing were the threads. Bright yellow and blue, some white and others red, they'd been run from rafter to rafter until the ceiling might have been a loom itself. Where they couldn't stay, Jenn thought pragmatically, the threads being too useful. Someone would have to rewind each on its spool, a tedious task. She'd best volunteer to help, or it'd be Cynd for sure.

Until then, though, the effect was lovely, as if they all stood within Frann's weaving. In a sense they did, that loom having made much of the clothing worn by those present. Jenn could see the moment the realization struck as this person fingered a sleeve, or that person admired a shawl.

As for Lorra Treff? Her large and heavy chair filled the doorway to the bedroom that had been Frann's and there she sat, hat and all, Frann's brooch pinned to her chest. A statement's power, Aunt Sybb said, had nothing to do with its volume. She'd meant lowering one's voice indoors, no matter how exciting the news, but Jenn had no doubt, without a word said, what Lorra wanted known.

The room was out of bounds.

Like the threads, it would have to be temporary. Space in Marrowdell was tight as it was, and hadn't Wen spent most of her life in a tiny room in the loft with her brother and his wife squeezed into the rest? But there was no arguing with a Treff, especially Lorra, and today, no one would.

There were two other chairs. One had been claimed by Master Jupp and the other, Jenn noticed, had become a tower of gloves and scarves and hats. Everyone stood and chatted, conversations more animated once Davi came downstairs with priceless bottles of port, wiping the dust from them with the end of his shirt until his niece, Hettie, stopped him.

Jenn moved through the room, catching bits of this story and that, and it began to dawn on her how splendid and full a life Frann had had, despite being exiled or, perhaps, because of it. Astonishing any one person could have done all she heard; she supposed living so long a life provided an abundance of time for adventures.

Adventures remembered by those here, whether shared or by story. Memories that kept Frann alive in their hearts as truly as hers kept her whole and here. It was a startling connection and one Jenn wished to think about with great care.

Semyn came beside her. "I think Lady Lorra wants us."

Sure enough, her hand was up and beckoning. Jenn

swallowed a mouthful of pastry and made her way across the room, Semyn tagging behind.

Radd's eyes lit as they approached and she smiled fondly. Her father and Dusom stood near Lorra's chair, with Anten and Covie. Each had lost loved ones in Marrowdell; perhaps, Jenn hoped, they found comfort as much as offered it, being together.

"Come closer," with an impatient snap. "I've this for the boy."

"This" being a wooden case on Lorra's lap Jenn was certain she'd never seen before.

Semyn stepped up, and Lorra handed it to him. At her commanding nod, he undid the latches and lifted the lid. Inside was a flute, as different from the battered and much-loved instrument Jenn remembered Frann playing at dances as Aunt Sybb's elegant bay horses were from Wainn's old pony. In two pieces, silver inlay sparkled against the black of its pipe, and formed a complexity of keys and fragile-seeming mechanisms she couldn't begin to fathom.

"Well, boy? It cost enough. Can you play it or not?"

Radd put his hand on Lorra's shoulder. "Ancestors Kind and Patient. Give him a moment."

Semyn gave a short tidy bow. "I can, Lady Lorra." Jenn held the case while he took the two pieces and confidently fitted one to the other. As he brought the flute to his lips, an expectant hush filled the room and Lorra almost smiled.

"Aren't you going to ask her?" Sharp and angry, that demand, and from the looks all around, everyone was as shocked as Jenn felt. Cynd pulled away from Davi, who'd tried to put his arm around her, and came to stand before her mother-by-marriage. Her eyes had a feverish glitter. "Aren't you?"

Speechless, Lorra held up her hand in denial.

Cynd's stabbed at the bedroom beyond. "Do you know what's in there?" She whirled to face the assembled visitors. "Petals. Rose petals. Ancestors Dear and Departed," the words spat like a curse. She pointed at Jenn. "What's she done but that? Roses, when she should have saved Frann!"

Covie's face was like ash. "No one could have—"

"Jenn could—we all know it!" Cynd turned to face Jenn, who wanted to hide and couldn't. "You've powers. Real magic! Why didn't you save her?"

"Because she shouldn't." Wen Treff, who Jenn would have sworn hadn't been in the room an instant before, appeared at her mother's shoulder. Her head tilted like a curious bird's. "How do you think magic works, Cynd?" A long-fingered hand lifted, palm up. "Would you save this life?" Her other hand rose, then dropped. "And end this one?" Her face became shadowed, her tone implacable. "Would you trap Frann at death's edge, never to join her Ancestors?"

"No. NO! But—"

"Cynd." Lorra found her voice, and it was as gentle as thistledown. "Dear Heart, listen to me. Our Jenn, our wonderful Jenn, did do magic. She brought Frann her dancers, right there in her room. She made sure Frann heard music at the end. Ancestors Dear and Departed. Frann smiled, Cynd. I saw for myself. Her last wonderful smile."

Cynd's face crumbled and she went to her knees, head in Lorra's lap. Lorra put her arms around her.

There was a sob. Sighs. Someone coughed.

Then came the sound of a flute, achingly beautiful and slow. The notes soared, softened, pulled at every heart, and no eye was dry when Semyn Westietas lowered the instrument from his lips.

Cynd looked up. At Semyn. At Jenn. "Thank you. I didn't—I'm—"

Jenn went down beside her. "Don't be sorry. I'd not thought to explain—myself. This is new to me too," she admitted, and Peggs wasn't the only one to laugh.

Which was good and the best thing possible. Jenn stood, looking from face to dear face. "I can't change nature," she told them. "I wouldn't if I could. Even—even for someone I love."

"We're glad of that." Wainn slipped around his brothers and came next to Wen. The tip of a toad's nose showed through her mass of wild hair, the creature being cautious around Lorra, and Wen smiled.

This while Lorra looked from one to the other, a familiar frown taking shape. "What's this?"

"This is a gathering. We've an announcement." Wen took Wainn's hand. "I'm with child."

Wen? Jenn blinked, Davi roared something joyful, and

Cynd hugged her sister-by-marriage so tightly Wen's toad
let out a croak. Once past their surprise, everyone drew
closer to touch and smile—congratulations being ever so
much better to give than condolences—while Wainn, looking happily perplexed, found himself lifted off his feet.

"No!" Lorra surged to hers, hat feather touching threads
of red, green, and yellow, outrage in every line of her body.
"A child cannot replace her! Be mute again and forever,
Daughter, if that's what you'd say to me."

Master Dusom put his son back on the floor, leaving a
comforting hand on his shoulder. "Lorra!"

Wen kept her smile. "What I say to you, Mother, is that
the child and I will need this family's strength. Your
strength."

"Humph." There was a long, uncomfortable pause as the
two women locked gazes. "And room, I suppose," Lorra
snapped suddenly, slightly less angry, though Jenn was hard
pressed to tell. "Convenient!" She glowered at Wainn.

Who, being noticed, ducked behind Wen, who didn't
seem at all perturbed. "Wainn can't live here, Mother.
You're too loud."

"I'm—" Lorra sputtered.

Cynd coughed.

"What?"

"Davi and I were hoping—some day—to have the loft to
ourselves. To move our bed," Lorra's daughter-by-marriage
explained. "It's under the slope, you see, and a difficulty for
Davi."

The matriarch of the Treffs shifted her grim attention to
her son, who blushed but said bravely, "My head. I bump it.
Often." He warmed to his topic. "Almost knocked myself
out the other day when I was—" Seeing his mother's expression, the big smith retreated behind his glass.

"Just like that," Lorra grumbled at Wen. "You expect me
to stop grieving and start making a nursery. Knitting booties!"

"Grief doesn't end." Wen fixed her pale eyes on her
mother.

No, they weren't pale, Jenn realized, but aswirl with the
mad, nameless colors of the Verge. How had she missed
that—or was this new?

The villagers exchanged worried looks. Everyone could sense something more was coming, and it wasn't happy or good.

Wen continued, "My promise to stay ended with Frann, Ancestors Dear and Departed, who asked it of me for your sake. The day will come, Mother, when I cross the river and I make no promise to come back. You will grieve then, as will I."

"Leaving us with your get!?" Lorra lashed out. "Never!"

"Now Lorra. A niece or nephew," Cynd countered, once more the Treff peacemaker. She started to smile. "A granddaughter, Lorra, or grandson. Or both!"

Hettie—who likely lumped what Wen had just said with everything else peculiar about Marrowdell, namely best ignored unless you were about to step on it—clapped her hands. "Great-Aunt, just think. Another playmate for our little one!"

Lorra retreated to her chair, hands gripping the arms as she sat, a thunderous look on her face.

Of all the people in the room, it was the newcomer who dared speak. Having replaced the instrument in its case, Semyn chose that fraught moment to step forward and offer it back, giving a graceful bow. "It was my honor to play for you, Lady Lorra," he said solemnly. "Lady Frann, Dear and Departed, must have been a great musician, to have such a wonderful flute."

"She'd drive me to drink," Lorra muttered darkly, "playing at all hours." Her lips pressed together, then out came a grudging, "'Dear and Departed.'" Her eyes fell on the case, still in Semyn's hands. "Keep it."

The baron's son gave another deeper bow, eyes shining, and stepped back.

Lorra pointed at her son's glass in wordless demand. Pulling free hatpins, which Cynd collected, she took off her hat, also passed to her daughter-by-marriage. Filled glass in hand, only then did she look around at the faces regarding her with a mix of caution and hope. "Heart's Blood. What are you all waiting for? A story? The woman was impossible. Ancestors Dear and Departed. We fought. Constantly. That's the end of it."

She took a sip and glared at Wen, whose smile deepened. "A grandmother."

Covie raised her glass. "You won't be the only one." Gallie did the same and then Zehr chimed in demanding a toast for grandfathers-to-be, involving Radd and Dusom, and just like that, there was a different feel to the room as Marrowdell grew excited for its future.

Not all. Wainn's eyes didn't leave Wen. Had he known?

Wen wouldn't leave, would she? Besides, Jenn reassured herself, across the river was merely the other half of Marrowdell.

Unless Wen Treff meant to live in the Verge, but how could she, being flesh and blood? She was, wasn't she?

What would it be like, to call the Verge home? To fly with dragons—

Semyn touched her hand, and Jenn welcomed the interruption to what were, she admitted to herself, unsettling thoughts. "Jenn, might we leave? I'd like to know how Werfol is." He hugged the case. "And show him my flute."

"I'm sure we may," Jenn assured him. The rest were into another round, a smidge of pink on Lorra's cheeks. Ancestors Witness. Was that even a smile?

A good time to go.

Cynd, seeing them donning mittens, came over. "Jenn. Dear Heart." Her eyes filled. "I don't know what came over me."

"My mother would say you asked what everyone wondered," Semyn offered.

"She would?" Cynd looked startled, then shy.

The opinion of a baroness still having weight, Jenn thought, hiding a smile. "We'll start on the mending tomorrow, then?"

When Frann's clothing would be added to the load: what could be worn put aside for that purpose, what couldn't carefully picked apart at the seams to be pieced into quilts, braided into rugs, or used as patches and rags. Nothing would be wasted.

In answer, Cynd hugged her, winter coat and all.

Cooking over a fire most of one's adult life, while in fear of that life, favored meals both simple and quick, taste being

optional. There was, however, the occasional favorite to be
whipped up in a single pan, barring undue scorching.

With a wooden spoon, Tir divided what they'd affection-
ately called "That Bloody Slop" on the marches, and now
referred to as "Weed's Special Eggs," into quarters, the boy
having insisted some be left for his brother, and scooped each
portion into a waiting bowl. Bannan wasn't sure how much of
the boy's love for the messy mix of hot spice, beer, egg, stale
bread crusts, and sausage was its flavor, or Tir's fierce threat
to add, when he could find some, the eyes of blind fish and
salamander's fiery tails when no one was looking. Fearsome,
save that his eyes would twinkle above his mask.

Those eyes worried rather than twinkled as Werfol accepted his bowl only to poke listlessly at the contents once
the Beholding was said.

"I'll keep Semyn's share warm in the oven," Tir said. He
stepped over the toad, giving the pile of cushions a dour
look. "And I'm not dropping any, dragon, even if you try to
trip me again. I'm onto your tricks."

Not even this reminder of their invisible housemate
could spark interest in the boy. Bannan raised an eyebrow.
"What did I teach you, nephew?"

Surly best described the look this gained him. "That
what I see as a lie could be what someone wants to be true
but can't be sure about."

"And?" the truthseer prompted.

"And the people who loved Lady Frann want it to be
true that she's now a Blessed Ancestor and happy forever,
but the only thing true today, Uncle—" Werfol's voice rose,
"—is that her bones were buried in dirt! Everything else
was a lie! Everyone here is a bloody liar!"

"Mind!" Tir sat, a scowl drawing the scars on his head
white. He wagged his spoon under the boy's nose. "Being
what you are, lad, gives you no right to speak ill of others.
Especially good folk of faith."

Werfol scowled back, undeterred. "Liars aren't 'good
folk.' Liars are bad!"

Bannan put aside his bowl. "Enough." He waited for the
infuriated gold of those seeing eyes to cool before going on,
"What does your mother say to do, when you don't yet understand something and become angry?"

Long lashes brushed a round cheek, then lifted over a too-innocent amber gaze. "To count to fifty, Uncle, in Naa-lish. Backward, if I've been impertinent, but I haven't, have I?"

He resisted the urge to smile at the little scoundrel. "Forward will do." Seeing a flicker of triumph, he quickly added, "to one hundred. Sit by the fire, to give Tir and me peace for our lunch."

"May I not have my lunch, Uncle?"

Oh, now he was hungry? Before Bannan could reply, Tir, still scowling, snatched up the bowl. "I'll put it w'your brother's."

Werfol climbed down from his stool and gave a small bow before going to sit as he'd been told, the image of dejected dignity. Lila and Emon had their hands full with this one, Bannan thought with some admiration.

No, he did.

And wasn't that a thought to ponder? He and Tir ate in silence, it being difficult to talk over Werfol's clear and determined counting. The temper would pass; his mother's always did. Afterward, the boy would be able to listen.

If he knew what else to say. Bannan remembered all too well the turmoil of his parents' interment. He'd been dazed not only by grief, but by his own gift. Unlike Marrowdell— Werfol had no idea how pure and sweet their faith was— what seemed the lies around Bannan had been real, formed by malice and greed. If it hadn't been for Lila—

The house toad sat up, facing the door. "Company," Tir remarked. "I'm telling you, sir," he said as he shifted back from the table, "a dog'd do the same and keep your feet warm." The mysterious lack of dogs and cats in Marrowdell being a subject of which he never tired.

Bannan rose to his feet. "Ignore him," he advised the toad. He'd a hand on the door when the knock came, and opened it at once, smiling.

Finding himself eye to red flared nostril, he lost his smile. "What's wrong?"

A hoof scored the planks of his porch, but Scourge didn't push forward or raise an alarm. Instead, a breeze found his ear. "I have honored Frann. Her final breath joined that of my enemy," with dark satisfaction. "My duty is done."

Finally. "I'm sure she'd be impressed if she knew," Bannan said, as truthfully he could. When Scourge didn't budge, he narrowed his eyes in suspicion. "You're not coming in. I've furniture; you won't fit. We've discussed that."

"You're letting in a draft, bloody beast," Tir complained, coming beside Bannan.

A rumble. "I've come for the truthseer. It's time he learned to ride."

"Hate to say it—" The former guard slapped Bannan's shoulder. "—he's as good as he's gonna get by now."

Werfol's count slowed, but didn't stop, to Bannan's relief. He wasn't privy to Scourge's voice. Yet.

Tir chose to misunderstand. Bannan didn't. As far as Scourge was concerned, he'd trained generations of Larmensu truthseers to be his rider, replacing the old with the new. To the old kruar, Werfol was next in line.

And at five years old, in no sense ready to ride a full-sized horse, let alone a giant battle-proven kruar.

Heart's Blood. Away from Marrowdell, away from magic, the bond between truthseer and kruar had made sense, been a matter of survival. For both, Bannan freely admitted. Here, what was the point? Other than to make his current rider feel old.

He supposed it was habit. An inconvenient, untimely, and dangerous one.

Bannan stepped forward. "No." Scourge, head turned to fix him with a red eye, slowly took a step back. Bannan followed with another step. "Not." The kruar left the porch.

Another. "Now."

Head low, legs braced, Scourge curled his lips back from his fangs. "MINE," roared the breeze.

Bannan winced at a startled cry from inside the house.

That, the boy heard.

Ancestors Mad and Misbegotten. "Leave Weed out of this!" he shouted, as furious as the kruar and much colder, here in the snow. The idiot beast had grown a thick warm coat—he should know, he'd groomed it often enough—that feathered his legs and hung below his jaw. Add little balls of snow clumped here and there, and Scourge could be mistaken for an aged draught horse out to pasture.

Except for the drooling rage. That was kruar.

Bannan drew breath for another shout, not that shouting ever worked.

Scourge bent his neck to look around. With a nicker of happy-horse that would have put Wainn's deceitful old pony to shame, he gave a nose-to-tail shake, going from all-out threat to placid. As if the truthseer believed any of it.

The reason for this sudden change of tactic walked up the path, being Jenn Nalynn and Semyn, bright-eyed and rosy-cheeked.

Bannan waiting on his porch wasn't unusual. Waiting in his thick socks without a coat, fire still in his eye?

Oh dear, Jenn thought. What had Scourge done now?

Though it took him into the deeper snow, Semyn went by the kruar at a distance, familiar with the creature from his family's stable. Where he'd apparently not stayed in a stall, being of more use clearing any vermin, a topic Jenn had meant to mention to Bannan.

Well, here was her chance, and it might possibly improve tempers. She walked up to Scourge, standing in his shadow. He gave her a wary look. "Thank you," Jenn told him warmly. "I know how you protected the Treffs. It was very brave."

"'The Treffs?'" Bannan sounded surprised.

"Their toad told me only today." She stroked the kruar's broad shoulder, the only part she could reach, and felt his disquieting purr. "Nyphrit came in great numbers each night, drawn by—they sought to harm Frann." She shuddered at the thought. "You guarded the house so the little cousin could stay inside and warm. You were quite wonderful."

"I'd have done it," a dragonish breeze claimed with some indignation, "but it kept him out of trouble."

Scourge growled. Semyn scampered onto the porch to be with his uncle, who gently pushed him through the still-open door.

Where Tir leaned, amusement deepening the scars around his mouth.

"I see." Bannan's eyes hadn't left Scourge. "A moment

please, Jenn, while I settle something with our 'wonderful' idiot."

Well, she'd done what she could and, as Aunt Sybb would say, the only thing less welcome than unsought advice was the third to an argument. Giving the kruar a final, hopeful, pat, Jenn went into the house. She took Tir's arm and brought him with her, turning to close the door.

"I'd love a cuppa," she said briskly, stripping off her winter gear to hang on the pegs Bannan had put near the door. "Semyn?"

He didn't respond, having spotted his brother. Werfol sat in a chair by the fire, counting in a determined voice, a count that neither slowed nor stopped with their arrival. Which was odd of itself, and deserved explanation, but then Semyn joined his brother, sitting at his feet. Putting the flute case on the rug, he raised his hands and began to make small, rapid gestures.

Stranger still, Werfol stopped counting aloud to do the same. Their little fingers flew, every movement a mirror image, and both frowned in concentration. This wasn't play.

What was it? Tir appeared as nonplussed as she felt. "Tea there is. And lunch, if you like." He led the way to the table, having her take a seat while he poured a fresh mug, all the while staring at the boys, then added to his own. "Tell me, Jenn," he said, turning eyes full of mischief on her. "About the usual goings-on. I've been to more'n my share of Dear and Departed's." At her blank look he chuckled. "I'm guessing what with winter you'd no unwelcome mourners to show the door, but surely there was a scrap? The surprise? C'mon, girl. Share the news."

Jenn blushed.

"Both!" Tir leaned back, a satisfied gleam in his eye. "So was it—?"

Bannan's arrival was, she thought, a most timely interruption; Tir's glee for gossip being matched only by Covie and Cynd.

The truthseer rubbed snow from his socks, then gave up and removed them to hang on pegs to dry. He glanced at the boys but let them be, choosing to come to the table. Smiling at Jenn, he accepted the steaming mug Tir held out in silent question. "We've compromised." He took a swallow then grimaced, not at the tea. "We'll need the practice gear after all."

Had Tir eyebrows, they'd have shot skyward; he achieved the same effect by rumpling the scars on his forehead. "That'd be the gear you ordered not be used, sir. To be clear. Sir."

Bannan shot him a quelling look.

Tir chuckled. "I'll bring it from Devins' tomorrow, then."

Another mystery, on a day she welcomed distraction. Jenn couldn't help but grin. "So do I ask about them?" She indicated the boys, still trading gestures. "Him?" a nod at the door beyond which Scourge might or not be lurking. "Or the two of you?" She pantomimed the give and take between the men.

Bannan's lips twitched, then smiled back. "My apologies, Dearest Heart. Semyn?" The boy got to his feet and came promptly, Werfol turning in his chair to watch. "Please explain to our guest what you and your brother were doing just now."

"Counting, Uncle." Properly said, but with a dose, Jenn thought, of defiance. "You made Weed count."

"I did. For the same reason your mother would."

"I lost my temper," Werfol admitted. "Mamma lets Semyn count with me, Uncle."

" 'Counting?' " Tir wiggled his fingers. "This?"

"And more," Bannan said. The eyes of both boys widened as their uncle's fingers began to move as theirs had. No, thought Jenn. His were quicker and more assured.

"That's—" Semyn's mouth shut tight.

"A secret!" Werfol said, earning a stern look from his brother.

"A secret," Bannan's voice grew stern, "you were using in front of strangers."

"Jenn and Tir aren't strangers," Werfol stated.

Semyn nodded. "They're family, Uncle. That's what you told us."

Which was rather impertinent, but Jenn felt a warm glow and didn't mind a bit.

Nor, from his almost smile, did Bannan. "So long as you're more careful, outside these walls."

Tir coughed.

"Lila and I learned the signs as children. You've used a version," he told the former guard. "Our border signals have the same source." Bannan glanced at Jenn. "Naalish. I wondered if you could understand it."

She shook her head.

"It's Shadow Talk, Uncle. Poppa said so."

"Hush!"

Werfol glared at his brother. "He did. He knows all about it."

Semyn rolled his eyes. "And told us not to tell."

"He didn't mean Uncle!"

"You're terrible at secrets!"

"I'm better than you!!"

"Lunch," Bannan declared, ending the escalation. "Tir?"

"Aie, there's plenty."

"I'm not eating," Werfol muttered, putting his back to them.

Oh, he was in a mood. As Semyn sat to the table, his face flushed with temper, Jenn leaned to whisper in Bannan's ear, "Maybe I should go."

"Dear lady," he replied, his hand warm on hers. "Stay, please. I was sorry not to attend the gathering."

"Me too. There was a scrap, sir," Tir volunteered much too happily. "And a surprise."

"There wasn't really—there was, of a sort," Jenn corrected, because Werfol was present and already unhappy. "Wen announced she's with child." The rest didn't feel comfortable to mention.

Wen in the Verge? It didn't feel comfortable to think.

Tir served Semyn, and they paused for the Beholding, Bannan adding a heartfelt one for Wen and Wainn. "Keep Us Close," they finished together.

"Now, Jenn," Tir spoke up. "Tell us about the scrap."

When she didn't answer immediately, Semyn piped up. "Jenn won!"

"You did?" Bannan turned his head to face her.

While a breeze, sudden and demanding, shouted. "You fought? Who? Why wasn't I there? I should have been there. I have FAILED you!"

"Wisp!" she protested, covering her ears.

The dragon settled. The rest were staring at her and Jenn felt the blood drain from her cheeks, because she had, she told herself fiercely, blood and cheeks. "It wasn't a scrap, as you call it, and there was no winning or losing anything. Cynd—she wanted to know why I—why I hadn't—hadn't—" Jenn gathered herself. "Why I hadn't stopped Frann from dying."

"Heart's Blood." Bannan took her in his arms and held her so tightly she could feel the pound of his heart. "I should have been there," he said, echoing the dragon. "I'm so sorry."

She pushed, gently, and he released her. His apple butter eyes were filled with remorse, and she laid a hand along his cheek. "You were where you should be. Semyn was with me, so all was well." The boy straightened proudly in his seat. "He played for everyone. The loveliest music I've ever heard."

"Lady Lorra gave me the most wonderful flute, Uncle. I've never played one so fine before."

"We'll have a concert after lunch," Bannan declared. "Well done, Semyn."

And all would have been fine, but for what happened next.

"I can put it together." They all turned to see Werfol before the fireplace, a piece of the flute in each hand.

"Don't touch it!" Semyn jumped up, knocking over his stool. "Lady Frann wanted me to have it, Ancestors Dear and Departed. It's mine!"

Werfol's face contorted with rage. "LIAR!" He rammed the pieces together, and silver broke free, falling on the rug like bits of ice.

In the shocked silence, the boy's hands opened to let the remaining pieces drop. His lower lip began to tremble. "I didn't mean—"

Semyn shoved his brother aside and went to his knees by the flute. As he collected the broken bits of mechanism, he looked up at Werfol, tears of fury pouring down his face. "Who's the liar? You are!"

"Easy." Bannan moved between the two, putting a comforting hand on the younger boy's shoulder. "Mistakes happen." Jenn noticed he carefully didn't say "accident." "Instruments can be repaired. Werfol, do you have something to say to your brother?"

"I'm sorry I broke the flute."

Semyn looked to Bannan. "Is he?"

It was one thing, Jenn realized, to see beyond the ordinary to magic and wonder. Another, quite horrible, thing, to be the arbiter of truth within a family.

Before Bannan could answer, Werfol pulled away sobbing. He ran to the ladder, climbing to the top and out of sight.

Bannan winced at the loud thud from above. Werfol must have thrown himself on the bed. "That went about as badly as possible," he said, running a hand through his hair.

Jenn gave him a sympathetic look. She'd gone down on the rug to help Semyn and Tir find the fragments of what had been, from the look of the silver and ebony, an extremely fine flute.

Doubtless the very one for which Frann had traded Marrowdell's ash.

"Uncle. It can't be fixed. Not here." Semyn held out his hand, palm up, and on it were two halves of what had been a key. "We'd need an expert with this kind of flute. A master silversmith. Even Vorkoun doesn't have those skilled enough."

Something Emon's son would know. "Then we'll find those who are," Bannan promised. "Let's have everything in the case, Semyn, and leave it with me."

Tir gave him a warning look, but Ancestors Set and Determined, the shining trust in the boy's eyes was worth whatever he'd have to do. The Lady Mahavar would know who in Avyo to use.

Spring seemed farther away than ever.

"I believe that's all of them—oh. Thank you," Jenn said as silver glinted in midair, floating into her outstretched hand.

"Sir!" Tir scanned the room, then lifted a foot as if worried where to step. "Where is he?"

"Where you needn't worry." Bannan gave the dragon credit. It couldn't be easy to inhabit a room full of people. "My thanks, Wisp."

Semyn looked around too, then sat, shoulders slumped. He glanced upward. "I shouldn't have been angry. I've upset —"

A scream tore through the house, high-pitched and terrified. Werfol!

Bannan ran to the ladder, jumped to hook his fingers in the opening and heave himself through. "What is it? Are you hurt?"

The boy lay on the floor by the bed, on top of — on top of the mirror that should have been wrapped and safely out of sight under the bed! It wasn't wrapped now.

Nor did it reflect the ceiling or the boy.

A detail he hardly took in, frantic to determine why Werfol wasn't moving. No bump on his head —

Like Frann. Bannan's heart hammered in his chest. It wasn't the same. It couldn't be the same. "Werfol. Dear Heart!"

Werfol groaned, then spoke. What he said chilled Bannan to the bone. "Momma! Look out!!"

"'Momma?'" Fighting dread, Bannan looked at the mirror. Daylight in the room.

. . . Night in the mirror. Huge lamps, their shapes exotic and strange, splashed yellow over stone and rippled in dark water. A wall, nearby.

Nothing moved in the room.

. . . Everything moved in the mirror, as if he were moving. No, running, as lamps came close then fell behind. Turning corners. Water alongside. Always water. A bridge arched over. Staircase led up.

. . . There! The glint of steel and armor!

"They're coming! Momma! No!"

Somehow, Bannan pulled his eyes away. Taking hold of the unconscious boy, he pulled him away too.

Lila's pendant bounced against the mirror.

Which reflected a ceiling.

And daylight in a room.

"What's wrong with Weed?"

"I don't know, Semyn," Bannan said, wishing with all his

heart he did. He laid his hand on Werfol's forehead. Dark eyelashes swept colorless cheeks and the boy might have been asleep, but the skin beneath the truthseer's palm was fever hot. "Jenn's gone for Covie." She'd be there now, he knew, using her magic to shorten the road.

Magic.

He'd left the pendant around Werfol's neck. Put the boy on the bed before throwing a blanket over the cursed mirror. Though sorely tempted to smash it, he hadn't. Couldn't.

Because he was afraid he knew what magic had shown them. Channen.

Through Lila's eyes.

And her son's. Bannan lifted his hand. "Has he fainted like this before?"

"No, Uncle." Semyn sat on the bed beside his brother, almost as pale. "Weed gets angry. So angry he shakes sometimes. But that's mostly when people—" He swallowed and fingered the blanket over Werfol's legs, then went on very softly, "—when people lie to him. Nothing like this. I wish he'd wake up. I'm very sorry. I don't care about the flute. I don't!"

"This isn't your fault." Bannan ruffled Semyn's hair. "Trust me."

Tir didn't look around from the window. "Just say'n, sir. This place."

He wasn't wrong. Marrowdell changed everything. Bannan glanced up. To his deeper sight, silver glinted in the shadows above. The dragon perched there, presumably due to the lack of room on the bed. Wisp had been suspiciously silent.

Having included itself in the rush to the loft, the house toad sat where it had leapt, on the mirror, the blanket cover clenched in its claws as if holding something inside.

Something with eyes. And wasn't that another sort of nightmare?

Swords on a bridge. Ancestors Fearful and Fraught. What had Lila gotten herself into?

"They're here," Tir announced, leaving his watch. "I'll see them in."

Within minutes, Covie was up the ladder into the loft, Jenn right behind. "Stay," the healer said, when Bannan went to move out of her way. "You know the boys."

"I'll fill the kettle," Tir offered, backing down the ladder.

Jenn went to the side of the bed by Semyn. The boy reached for her hand and she took it in both of hers, sitting on the edge. Her eyes were blue again, like the morning sky, and the look she gave Bannan was both determined and worried.

While Covie leaned over Werfol, gently examining his head, then his neck. "He fell?"

"I don't think so." Bannan decided on the truth, such as he knew it. "I found him lying on the floor, atop that mirror. There." He pointed. She eyed the toad, which eyed her back. "There's some—some magic to the thing. I kept it under the bed, and wrapped. Not that I blame Werfol," he added hastily.

No, he blamed himself. And Lila. While he was at it, some blame belonged to the fat prince who'd started all this, and the train being built through Lower Rhoth to reach the mines of Ansnor, Ansnans likely deserving their share—

"Bannan." Jenn's voice found him, wherever he'd gone.

"My apologies, Covie. The mirror was where you see it. Werfol saw something in it that made him scream, then faint."

"'Something,'" the healer echoed.

"I—" saw it too, Bannan was about to say, then hesitated. What had he seen? Eyes, the once. This time? Had he truly seen Channen?

Covie held up her hand. "I don't need to know. He's had a shock, that's my thinking, and needs time to recover. Keep him warm, stay by him." She put a finger on Werfol's forehead, then gently drew it down to the tip of his nose. Had he seen a glow, where she'd touched? The boy let out a peaceful sigh, then rolled on his side.

"A bit of proper sleep," she said with reassuring firmness, "and he should be fine. Fetch me again if he isn't." She rose to her feet.

"Ancestors Blessed." Bannan bowed. "We're Beholden for your care and kindness."

Semyn slipped off the bed to bow. "That we are, Lady Covie."

The healer smiled at him. "I've not been that for a long

time." Her smile faded as she looked down at the wrapped mirror. "Whatever Werfol saw, Bannan, it wasn't fit for a child. I'd keep that away from him."

"I will."

"Then I'll be off. There's dishes to wash—and port—left at the Treffs'. Stay with them, Good Heart," to Jenn. "I don't mind a longer walk with the sun so bright."

Jenn blushed, warming Bannan's heart.

He glanced back at Werfol, and felt cold again.

～

*A sliver of paper, touched by ink and fingertip . . . a drop of sleep, under the tongue . . .*
*And the dream unfolds . . .*
The eyes watch and the eyes see and nothing's safe or hidden. A dream unfolds within a dream's unfolding, seeming real—
How can it be? Stones and dark water. Or is it quilts and black glass? *Distrust.*
Who sees whom?
*The dream falters . . . rebuilds . . .*
Through tears, light shatters.

There were possible things and there were unlikely things. This—this seemed impossible. Yet Bannan sat across from her, his eyes earnest, and Jenn had to believe. "You saw what Lila could see. Are you sure this wasn't your gift?" she asked with care.

"The image was in the mirror already. Lila," he corrected himself grimly, "was already there. I can't explain it. I just know what I saw." He sat back. "As for how? A truthseer too young for his gift. A pendant spelled with his mother's voice. Marrowdell!" with an encompassing gesture as much helpless as it was angry. "Let's not forget the fool who brought a mirror into the edge."

A mirror presently leaning on the wall beside the fireplace, bundled in thick oiled canvas itself bound by ropes.

Given Bannan's house toad remained, without blinking, on duty before it? The little cousin shared his opinion.

It was the mirror itself Jenn didn't understand. She'd helped Bannan unpack. Had spent more time, recently, in this house than the Emms', truth be told. "I didn't know you had a mirror," she ventured.

To her surprise, he looked embarrassed. "I'd hidden it. I—the mirror was to be my gift for you, from Endshere."

A breeze found her ear. "Fool."

So Wisp paid attention. From Bannan's shrug, he'd heard it too. "It wasn't foolish," Jenn countered. "It was thoughtful." Not that she'd imagined having a mirror or needing one. Come to think of it, wherever could she put one? "But—you didn't give it to me."

The toad puffed itself. ~The hard water looks, elder sister. Others see.~

"The mirror reflects from the Verge as well as here," her dragon clarified, the breeze unsettled and prone to snap. "The little cousin is wise. A mirror in Marrowdell is unsafe. It is dangerous. A fool's folly!"

"Heart's Blood. Will you give over? I know now." Bannan leaned forward, elbows on his knees. "Dearest Heart, I wanted a mirror for you because I hoped, with all my heart, that if you could see yourself—and your turn-born self—you'd come to accept both. To see the Jenn Nalynn I see and be happy."

"Then you were foolish," Jenn said, making the words light, though under other circumstances—which weren't the circumstances of now, with Tir and Semyn with Werfol, and Bannan having seen across the whole of Rhoth with a mirror—she'd have taken him in her arms and kissed away his worried frown. "Did you not know? I see myself in your eyes all the time. Where better?"

He came close to smiling, despite his worry. "Where better indeed." Then shook his head. "I should destroy it."

"Let me," offered the dragon.

"How can we?" Jenn heard herself say, then knew why. The mirror sat there like a silenced bell, waiting to be rung again. "It showed you Lila once. It could again."

"Ancestors Futile and Foolish. To what end?" Bannan

got to his feet and began to pace. "The mirror's shown us nothing we hadn't guessed. If we saw the truth, Lila's in Channen, doubtless hunting Emon. It's dangerous. She knew that before she left."

He argued with himself, not her.

Just then, Semyn's head appeared in the opening to the loft. To Jenn's relief, the boy was smiling. "Weed's awake!"

Bannan lunged for the ladder, but Werfol wasn't only awake but moving. His feet appeared in place of Semyn's head and he climbed down, moving away at the bottom to let his brother and Tir follow.

"Ancestors Witness. Awake and starving, sir, to hear it," the latter said happily once he joined them. "I'll find something."

An appetite had to be good, Jenn decided. She hung back, watching Bannan close his eyes tight as he hugged his nephew, content until a sly breeze found her ear. "Channen lies within the edge."

Did Wisp think she'd forgotten? Mistress Sand had shown her a bracelet of amber, like tiny eyes, from the Naalish capital and hadn't it been among her list of questions, when best to go, and what to trade?

Though admittedly well down her list, after birth, death, and peril. Yes, she could cross into Channen. Trade happened year-round there, though the turn-born hadn't seemed encouraging. Wisp knew that.

Jenn went to Tir, slicing ham being safer than anything her dragon suggested.

"You could take the truthseer. Find his sister."

"Hush!" Jenn whispered, now thoroughly flustered. Tir gave her a curious look that turned to amused comprehension at her muttered, "Dragons."

Bannan brought his nephews to the table, sitting across from them. "Help yourselves," he said, pushing forward a platter of biscuits. From the speed with which Werfol took one, he might not have done magic or fainted. Semyn followed suit.

Two biscuits floated into the air and vanished with a *Snapsnap.*

The truthseer tossed up a third. *Snap!* "The rest for us, please."

Tir scowled into the air as he put down a tray loaded with bowls, each filled to the brim and steaming. "Keep your—whatevers—out of my pudd'n!"

He'd set it cooking while Werfol slept, and it was a marvelous pudding indeed, the bread golden brown, speckled with dried summerberries, and topped with thick cream.

Semyn and Werfol's eyes widened. Jenn brought the tea, dolloping honey into the boys'. At Bannan's invitation, she sat, as did Tir.

The truthseer waited until everyone settled, then circled his fingers over his heart. Seeing this, the boys put down their spoons to do the same.

"Hearts of our Ancestors," the truthseer said, "we are Beholden for this food and hope Tir's pudding has improved over last time . . ."

This earned him a glare.

"We are Beholden for Covie's care of Werfol and for his recovery. We would be Beholden above all else if Lila and Emon return safely and soon from their—adventure. However far we are apart, Keep Us Close."

"'Keep Us Close.'"

Werfol picked up his spoon, then hesitated. He looked up, the gold of his eyes muted. "I saw, Uncle. I saw what Momma saw. She's in the Shadow District." He pulled the chain and pendant from under his shirt. "That's where this came from. Poppa said that's where all the artisans work."

"Because that's where the magic is," Semyn added matter-of-factly.

Bannan managed not to choke on his tea. Tir shook his head. While Jenn Nalynn? She'd gone very still, as if listening, and he didn't need to guess to whom.

Though he'd dearly love to know what the dragon had to say.

Later. To his sure knowledge, the boys hadn't been to Mellynne. "How did you recognize where your mother was, Werfol?" he inquired, keeping it to a curiosity over pudding.

His nephews, back to being two halves of a whole, gave

each other sidelong looks. Semyn shrugged and gave a tiny nod.

"Father brought home a map, but it wasn't a map, it was—" Werfol waved his hands as he groped for words.

"You might mistake it for an ordinary drawing, Uncle, but if you look at it like this—" Semyn crouched until his eyes were level with top of his bowl, "—you can see buildings and canals and bridges—"

"—and when you touch them, they say their names! Ancestors Witness, Uncle!"

Clearly the best part of the map. "Channen is a source of marvels," Bannan said agreeably.

Jenn frowned; not the reaction he'd expect in someone who dearly loved maps. "Shadow District. Why that name?"

"Because the sun doesn't shine there," Semyn answered eagerly. "But it only seems so. There are thick clouds overhead, always. Father said it's like walking through twilight. Every evening, there's fog as well."

"Sounds bloody awful." Tir put down his mug. "Why build a city there?"

Werfol gave him a surprised look. "For the magic."

"Father said the Shadow District was beautiful. He wanted to show us, but—" Semyn stared down at his pudding. "The situation became unstable."

Spoken like the son of a baron. Or Lila, Bannan reminded himself. The boys had been steeped in politics from birth; moreover, they were trained observers. He found himself asking, as he might of their parents. "Channen's Shadow District. Why is your mother there? What does it have to do with your father?"

"Sir." Mild, that protest. The look Tir gave him wasn't.

Bannan lifted a finger. Wait.

"Go on," Semyn told his brother. "Tell them what you told me, Weed. What you saw. Why you screamed."

"It was a shout," Werfol grumbled. "I was surprised, that's all. You'd have been too, you know, seeing that thing!"

"From the beginning, if you please," the truthseer asked, doing his best to sound calmer than he felt at this. "You aren't in trouble," guessing what would come next.

His youngest nephew gave him a relieved look. "I went to—go—under the bed, Uncle, but there was something there. I pulled it out of the way, and the blanket came off, and there were eyes, staring at me!" He spread out his arms to indicate size. "I didn't like those eyes. I didn't like them at all. When I tried to cover them up, Momma's pendant touched the glass." Werfol's eyes were shimmering gold. "I couldn't be scared then. I heard her voice and I knew I was seeing what she could see."

He frowned before continuing more slowly. "There were soldiers coming. I tried to warn her, but she didn't hear me. She started to run away, and she didn't hear me, and then—" a shrug, "—then maybe I was a little scared, because more were coming. I don't remember anything else, Uncle."

"You fainted," Semyn reminded him with brotherly satisfaction. "You ask about our parents, Uncle? Mother wouldn't be in the Shadow District unless she thought Father was there too. I've heard them talking about it. They said the true power in Mellynne lies along Channen's canals, not in its court. That . . . if Father couldn't bring those who fear an Eld influence in Rhoth to see reason, he'd have to seek out the shadow lords and—" a waver in that otherwise sure voice, "—if anything went wrong, he'd not so easily leave."

Heart's Blood. That they'd spoken like this in front of a child? No, Bannan reminded himself, not a child.

Emon's heir.

Who sat looking at him now with expectation written on his face. I've told you what you needed to know, that expression said, loud as words. Tell me what you're going to do about it.

Lila's son in truth. "What we can do," Bannan said heavily, "all we can do, is wait."

"Yes, Uncle." Semyn subsided. "If you say so." Werfol nodded; he didn't appear convinced.

Because of the mirror. He looked at Jenn, who'd suggested looking again. Did he dare? Could he control it? Or would the mirror show him what used it to spy on Marrowdell?

How could he not try? was the real answer.

Him, not Werfol. Never again. His resolve firmed on that point. Heart's Blood, he'd thought he'd lost the boy. Take that risk, for a look at what they could do nothing about?

Worse, to witness what they couldn't bear, for that was as likely as any other outcome. Lila wouldn't forgive him. He'd not forgive himself.

Bannan made sure the boy was looking at him. "Tell me what you think of the mirror."

"It isn't safe, Uncle." Werfol repressed a shudder. "There's something in it. Something that didn't want me to see it."

"If I keep the mirror in the house, what will you do?"

"Stay outside!"

Tir snorted.

Bannan's lips twitched. "Fair answer. Then the mirror goes out, into the barn." He studied the child's face, those eyes still aglimmer with gift, the round jaw as ready to set in determined courage as anger. "Werfol, I won't ask you to promise, nor will I order you. I trust your good sense to keep away from the mirror."

"I'd box his ears," Semyn offered, giving his brother an affectionate cuff.

Truthseers' eyes met, amber crossed with gold. "You can trust me, Uncle," Werfol said finally. "But we like to play in the barn. Isn't there somewhere else to put it?"

A breeze slid by Bannan's ear, cold and sure. "Not with me."

"I'll take the mirror," Jenn stated, her chin set in a line every bit as brave as Werfol's. "Wasn't it to be mine?" she asked as Bannan opened his mouth to object. "I'll keep it safe."

Said with the intensity of a turn-born's wish.

"Then it is yours," Bannan told the woman he loved and trusted, relieved beyond measure.

For the rest of their little feast, he thought how the day would end better than it had begun, with the easing of grief and pointless worry. Afterward, it seemed he was right, for Semyn played his pipes, and Werfol ate an extra helping of pudding, to Tir's delight, and Jenn sat close, holding his hand. Though he'd wondered how best to transport the bulky mirror, at some moment between pipe and pudding and hand-holding, it disappeared.

So he was a much happier man, when he kissed and was kissed on his little porch, and said good-bye to his love.

Until the dragon whispered in his ear what stole every bit of Bannan's peace.

"She can take you to your sister."

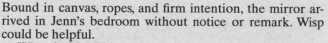

Bound in canvas, ropes, and firm intention, the mirror arrived in Jenn's bedroom without notice or remark. Wisp could be helpful.

When it suited him, that too. Meaning he'd approved.

Jenn eyed the mirror as she readied herself for bed. It leaned against the wall under the map and she'd meant to tell Gallie and Zehr, over supper, but they'd been eager to talk about the gathering for Frann, and Wen's news, and wasn't it wonderful for Wainn?

What they didn't say, being kind, was that no one in Marrowdell—except Wen, it seemed—had expected him able to start a family, Wainn having been simple of mind since his accident and in the care of the village.

Which wasn't the whole truth about Wainn Uhthoff, or even close, Jenn thought, but had kept her peace at the table, Peggs having told her Kydd was to have a talk with his nephew, it being unclear how much Wainn grasped of family matters.

Snuffing out her lamp, Jenn tucked herself into bed. Instead of lying back, she hugged her knees to her chest.

Staring at the shadow that held the mirror.

And so very many questions. She put her chin on a knee, considering.

A moth landed on her other knee. Jenn turned her head to gaze at it. "I wondered when you'd come."

The moth drew a slender jointed leg across one eye. When it spoke, its voice rolled through her with the crushing weight of the Bone Hills. ~I do not leave.~

Not moth, but sei. This was what had helped Bannan and sent Wisp to rescue Tir and the boys. "Why do you—" care wasn't the word. There was nothing of that feeling, nothing of compassion or empathy, in what faced her. Curiosity, perhaps. "What would you tell me?" Jenn asked, feeling her own stir.

"You are less. Be more." The moth fluttered into the air,

changing between wingbeats to a great looming stone, glistening of pearl . . .

. . . to the head of a dragon, green and strangely shaped, its body elsewhere,

. . . then to a sky, shot through with colors of such aching beauty Jenn stuffed a fist in her mouth to stifle her cry of longing.

"Come. Be more . . ."

As suddenly, she was alone in the dark.

Or was she surrounded by light, safe in a room of blue stone that knew her every need? She was filled with such belonging she might have found her true home at last, never knowing it was lost.

"NO!" Gasping, Jenn dropped her forehead to her knees, holding herself in a tight little ball. This was home. More home than Wisp's sanctuary in the Verge. More home than anything sei. Here, she was surrounded by memories. Here, she could remember herself. "This is where I belong. Here."

Words, against the will of beings so powerful they could reach beyond the edge and pull worlds asunder?

Beings, nonetheless, who spoke through a fragile white moth. The sei coaxed and confounded, Jenn thought, lifting her head. And confused, she mustn't forget that. But so far they'd merely offered her choices, that, and saved Bannan, the boys, and Tir. This particular sei, however mad, held the edge together with its own flesh. It made the Verge and Marrowdell possible.

She mustn't forget that either.

Ancestors Blessed and Beloved. For all she knew, the moth had been waiting in Bannan's loft to bring Werfol, pendant, and mirror together, simply to hurry her back to the Verge.

What had it said? "Come. Be more."

If Wisp knew the sei wanted her in the Verge, he'd not be so eager to see her take Bannan to Lila. If Mistress Sand knew, she—and all turn-born—could well blame her for the sei's strange interest.

And might not be wrong.

Jenn's thoughts were interrupted by a sound she couldn't place. *Rustlerustle.* It wasn't Loee, fussing before bed, or Zehr sanding wood. *Rustlerustle.*

From the mirror?

Werfol hadn't mentioned a sound. As to how a wrapped mirror could make one in the absence of mice, Jenn couldn't begin to guess, though this was Marrowdell and the mirror, by all accounts, wasn't behaving as mirrors did elsewhere.

How curious. Terrifying as well, but she wasn't a child.

Or woman. Jenn slipped out of bed, becoming glass and pearl. Seeing by her own light, she went to the mirror and undid the knots, careful of the string.

And let the canvas fall.

Each night, when Bannan put Semyn and Werfol to bed, he'd said his own prayer. That they not have nightmares. Thanks to Jenn's kind wish, or perhaps their own natures, they'd been free of Marrowdell's strange dreams.

It hadn't meant they slept well or easily. At first, Semyn would thrash as if running and Werfol would cry out. The dragon slept with them; perhaps their fear at night was why. He'd known from the start how Wisp had made himself at home. Known, and been grateful.

They'd been better of late, but tonight he'd no such hope. They'd asked for a familiar story, then another. He'd read until Werfol fell asleep and Semyn couldn't keep from yawning; turned down the lamp, but left it burning.

A hard day for them both. Bannan had waited till the bed creaked under more than two boys and whispered, "Call me, Wisp, if they wake, or have troubled dreams."

He'd gone downstairs. Played nillystones with Tir—been beaten soundly by Tir, in truth, game after game, but that was familiar. They raised the stakes from nuts to doing dishes and Bannan roused himself to the effort, winning once before losing and badly. "I'm done. Remind me again who thought this was a good idea?" he complained cheerfully.

"I'd be— Sir?"

He'd heard the faint cry too. "Wisp?"

When the dragon answered, the breeze had an uneasy feel. "The truthseer sleeps, yet speaks."

Bannan got up. "I'll check on them."

With a nod, Tir put away the 'stones. "Poor lads."

The loft was warm and peaceful when Bannan approached the bed, and he began to think it a moment's restlessness. A hint of silver caught his eye, then a ghost of steam. Wisp let him see where he lay curled at the boys' feet and Bannan didn't bother to look deeper.

Semyn snored, very quietly. Werfol's breathing was steady and slow. The truthseer touched the hair peeking from their caps and neither stirred. Nothing wrong, then, he thought with relief.

"Momma . . ." Werfol rolled on his back, the fingers of one hand clenched around the pendant. Eyes closed, still asleep, yet expression flickered across his face. Anxiety. He spoke in an urgent whisper, as if fearing to be overheard. "Where are we, Momma? Where is this?" Fear.

The bed creaked. "This is no dream," the dragon warned and Bannan's heart sank.

"Weed. Wake up," he called gently, putting a hand on Semyn's shoulder, to wake him as well.

The older boy's eyes opened. Werfol's did not. "Momma," he said, louder. "You shouldn't be here. No. No. No, Momma—!"

At the shout, Semyn pounced on his brother, giving him a hard shake. "Weed! Stop! Wake up!"

"What—?" Werfol blinked groggily, then shoved Semyn away with an angry, "You stop!"

"Easy, both of you." Bannan sat on the edge of the bed. "Werfol. You were—" not dreaming, according to the dragon, "—calling out to your mother. Do you remember why?"

The boy hunched into himself, gripping the pendant with both hands. "It was like before, Uncle. I saw—I saw what Momma could see."

Without the mirror?

Heart's Blood. The pendant! About to seize it and throw the cursed thing away in the snow, the truthseer froze. Would that make matters worse? He'd never heard of magic like this, he thought with rising fear, and put an arm around Werfol, as much for his comfort as the boy's. Had the mirror awakened some Naalish magic, or was this of Marrowdell?

Or both?

"Was she with Poppa?" Semyn went to his knees, his face pale. "Did you see him?"

"No." Tears weren't far away, from the tremble in the younger boy's voice. "I didn't see anyone else."

"What did you see, Dear Heart?" Bannan asked gently. "Take your time."

"A room. A nasty room. I didn't like it. Momma shouldn't be there."

What Werfol went on to describe, haltingly and without understanding, Bannan could picture all too well, being familiar with the requirements of keeping someone — especially a dangerous someone — prisoner.

Lila was locked in a cell.

"What should I do?" Bannan pulled a blanket over his shoulders rather than add more wood to the fire.

"You're asking me, sir?" Tir, well-bundled himself, scowled; without his mask, the effort contorted his ruined nose and chin. "Can't say I know about magic and such, but you owe those boys. The dragon's given you a way."

"Put Jenn in danger."

"Now, sir, that's just it. You say she's been to that place, the Verge, on her own. Ancestors Fine and Familiar. Maybe for her it's like you or me going to the pub." At Bannan's incredulous stare, Tir shrugged. "Just say'n, sir, we don't know what the dragon does. If he gave you the idea, where's the harm in asking?"

"You think I should go."

"All I know, sir, is Lila would for you. She always has." Tir settled deeper in the chair. "What I don't know, sir, is why we're still talking. You'd set your mind on it before coming down the ladder."

Set his mind to what? "Go to Channen," Bannan said heavily. "Rescue Lila from whatever jail she's in. For all we know, she's put herself there!"

"Aie," with admiration.

Though was this part of Lila's plan? Werfol had been frightened. He'd described staring through bars at dark water and wet stone. Lila'd paced, then he'd seen her fist hammer a closed door.

Seen a leather band around her wrist, and links of thick chain.

Semyn had gone quiet, after that. Had given Bannan a desperate pleading look.

Ancestors Foolish and Mad. "Fine. I'll walk through the Verge and hopefully not get eaten. After that, it's the Shadow District of Channen and hopefully I won't get thrown in jail with my sister. After that, oh, then we'll find Emon wherever he's been thrown and then—" Home? The truthseer shook his head, unable to think that far. "Nothing says Jenn will agree to any of this."

"Everything, your pardon, sir, about the lady says she will."

"There's the boys—"

"There's me." Tir grunted. "N'doubt the bloody beast and dragon too. 'Less they go with you." He sounded hopeful.

Into the Verge. That's what they were planning, in the calm sanity of a warm room. "You've no idea what it's like there," Bannan said, shaking his head. "What I saw was—" Astonishing. Remarkable. Altogether strange. "—it's an impossible place."

Tir, who did his utmost to avoid thinking of impossible things, looked uncomfortable, then shrugged offhandedly. "From what the dragon says, you'd not stay there. It'd be like crossing a road."

"Lila," the truthseer stated with certainty, "will box my ears."

"So long as she's around to do it. Sir."

"Ancestors Doubtful and Daft." Bannan rubbed a hand through his hair. "I can't believe I'm considering this. You're a poor influence, you are. You and that dragon."

Oh, and didn't a smug little breeze stir the fire at that?

The house toad moved closer to the flames. Marrowdell, it seemed, had an opinion.

"I'll decide in the morning," the truthseer decided, trying to reclaim at least some common sense.

But he knew, deep inside. If he had a chance to reach Lila, any way to help her?

He'd go. Be it through the Verge or over a cliff.
He'd go.

No more *rustlerustle*. Within its faded tapestried frame, the mirror gave nothing back but darkness, reflecting neither Jenn's inner light nor, when she changed, the faint glow of lamplight through gaps in the floor.

Making it not a mirror at all. She touched it, feeling the slipperiness of glass, like ice that had forgotten to be cold. If she was looking into the Verge, where was this or what? Not night. Wisp had told her that other world dimmed; it didn't go truly dark.

Dark? This was blacker than any shadow, an absence of light, drawn like a curtain.

Why had she thought that? Jenn ran her fingers over the glass, from one side to the other, to no effect.

There should be, she decided, something here. Was it lost?

If so, how might she find it?

Gallie kept a cup of charcoals and quills on her desk, along with a small knife for sharpening. Jenn brought the knife back to the mirror, then sat cross-legged on the rug in front. She went to tap the glass.

Only to have the Emms' house toad land in her lap, just missing the blade. Of all the times. "Careful," she admonished, shifting so its weight wouldn't numb her thigh. She went to tap the glass.

~No, elder sister!~

Jenn stared down at the toad. "Whyever not?"

~We know what's in the mirror.~ She felt it quiver. ~We do not want it to see you. Please.~

A warning not to be ignored. At once Jenn reached for the canvas to cover the mirror, but with the toad still in her lap it was beyond awkward and would have been hilarious if she hadn't been increasingly alarmed. "You'll have to m—"

In the mirror, darkness parted like eyelids, revealing a pair of great yellow eyes.

The toad leapt from her lap, bouncing off the glass. As it

went to attack again, Jenn grabbed it before it could hurt itself.

The eyes in the mirror were round, the pupils slit and black, with a softly ragged edge. They stared back at her as if equally astonished by what they saw.

Eyes she'd last seen made of snow.

The hunter.

Had she found it, or it her? Ancestors Dreadful and Dire. It was here, regardless. Or rather, not really here. "It's a reflection," she said aloud. "I don't think it can hurt us."

The toad squirmed until she let it go. To her relief it no longer tried to jump through the glass, but squatted between her and the mirror, puffed twice its normal size in threat. ~This is unwise, elder sister!~

She wasn't about to argue. The eyes neither blinked, nor moved. They might have been painted atop the black of the mirror, though Jenn doubted even Kydd could produce such intricate detail with a brush.

It was, however, an opportunity. "I've been warned about you," Jenn told the eyes grimly. "You've hurt efflet before. You would hunt me."

Nothing. Perhaps she should do something other than talk. "I'm not just Jenn Nalynn," she warned.

And let her other self show.

Pupils snapped to a thin line and the lids squinted almost closed.

Her light. She changed back at once, having at least one answer. The eyes were real and watching her.

More. They'd seen her as painfully bright, as a turn-born would if she were unmasked in the Verge. Which could be a clue, Jenn thought distractedly, had she anything but eyes and an intention in snow to consider.

"Do you understand me?"

Eyelids rose, though not as wide as at first, then lowered, then rose. *Rustlerustle.* As if stiff eyelashes brushed the glass from the other side.

Not speech, or none that she could understand. Might the almost-blink be "yes?" Remembering her mistake with the efflet, Jenn schooled herself not to jump to conclusions.

~Elder sister.~ A warning.

One she heeded. Jenn got to her knees and took the

canvas in her hands, ready to toss over the mirror. "I won't allow you to do any more harm."

And she didn't make that a wish, but wanted it just strongly enough to make her point. To her relief, the eyelids dipped and rose again. *Rustlerustle.*

"Good." She went to cover the mirror. One blink. Then another. A third. All with that soft, *rustlerustle.*

A protest?

A plea. There'd been a time she'd have been flattered something so strange begged for her attention.

Now Jenn felt a chill of foreboding down her spine. The eyes wanted something from her; she was no longer so naive as to believe it anything good.

"Better safe than sorry," she told the eyes coldly as she pulled the canvas back across. That she felt better and safer at once told her she'd been right.

~Wise, wise, wise, elder sister!~ The house toad settled in front of the mirror, clearly prepared to stay on guard all night. It blinked up at her. ~You mustn't let him think there's a way back.~

"'Him?' You know what this is?"

The toad shrank.

So there was something more to know about the eyes in the mirror, something the little cousin didn't want to tell her.

Something it might, if she found a way to ask. Jenn wrapped a quilt around her shoulders and sat on the bed. "I went to see Mistress Sand to protect Marrowdell and those I love. I don't want to make any mistakes. When I don't understand," she said gently, "that's what could happen. What should I know, my dear and brave friend, now?"

As she waited for an answer, she heard a *rustlerustle-rustlerustle.* Eyelashes against glass.

The toad heard as well and showed its teeth. ~When he was here, elder sister, he wanted to be there and caused great harm to do so. There, he can harm no one here. There~ with finality, ~is where he must stay. That is what you should know.~

Jenn blinked, working her way through "heres" and "theres." "Who is 'he?'"

The toad turned to face the mirror in answer. Nor would

it reply to how or why or when, returning only stubborn silence.

The mirror, on the other hand, never quieted. *Rustlerustlerustlerustle.* Long after she was in bed, the sound continued, as if the brush of stubby eyelashes could wear away the glass and let their owner out. *Rustlerustlerustlerustle.*

She'd slept through noisier. Jenn Nalynn put an arm over her ears, as if the sounds came from the hordes of enamored frogs along the river in spring.

And not from a magic mirror.

He'd known the mirror would be trouble.

Wisp rearranged himself, resting his jaw on the wood at the end of the bed. He liked it best when he could fit between the boys, gaining warmth on both sides, but they'd piled atop one another like frightened rabbits in a nest and he couldn't get comfortable.

He snarled without sound.

If people took his advice, as they should but hadn't, much would be better. The girl would be in the warm and beautiful Verge, away from winter and grief. They'd do a proper hunt, or as close to one as possible, the quest for the truthseer's sister noble enough to pique any dragon's interest. Return heroic and—

~Elder brother?~

Away from interfering little cousins, the dragon thought grumpily. That best of all. ~I'm asleep.~

There was a lengthy pause. Doubtless Bannan's house toad considered the ramifications of further intrusion, as another would imply he, a dragon, had lied. Wisp felt rather clever.

~It is truly a marvel, elder brother, that you can hear me in your slumber. Do I seem a dream?~

Proving little cousins could be clever too. Or too clever. ~You seem a nuisance.~

~For which I apologize, elder brother, but there is something we know that you do not and should. If you please.~

Wisp cracked open one eye. The house toad sat with a hind leg dangling through the opening to the loft; ready to leap to safety, yet bravely staying put. Little cousins did not lack courage.

Nor manners. He'd not had one risk waking him before. Vaguely curious, he opened his other eye, lifting his head to bring both to bear. ~Who are "we?"~

~All those left here, elder brother.~ It blinked and added with typical toad honesty, ~Except the nyphrit.~

Understandable. Nyphrit were wicked creatures, bent on eating anything that moved, not conversing with it; including other nyphrit, if slow. The little cousins conversed with everything else, and for everything else, ylings and efflet being without proper voice. If he'd cared, he'd have wondered what the ylings and efflet thought of the arrangement.

~If you please, elder brother, I would tell you so you may sleep without me.~

A very clever toad. Wisp was more than half-inclined to eat it. ~I'm listening, little cousin.~ He yawned, showing the extent—and sharpness—of his kind forbearance.

~What looks from the hard water, elder brother. We know who it is.~

~Do you.~ Stretching his neck, Wisp sent his head forward and down, until the beard of his chin brushed the rug on the floor. The little cousin grew a little rounder, but remained where it was. ~Who?~

~He lived in this house. The other villagers called him Crumlin Tralee.~

A dragon surprised was a dragon soon to die. Wisp went from speechless to furious. ~A villager? Impossible! I know them all. This is no name of Marrowdell!~

The toad cowered. ~Forgive my impertinence, elder brother, but it is and was. Crumlin came with the before-villagers. He brought the hard water—the mirror, elder brother—with him to Marrowdell. It stood here, in this room, and he spoke to it often. I know, elder brother, because I guarded this house then as I do now. When he was lost, the rest left and took the mirror with them. But now it's back and so is he.~ It stopped, giving him a troubled look.

About to snap a denial, the dragon hesitated. Caution thrilled along his bones. The mirror was "back?" Things of magic could have a will of their own, usually inconvenient, often dangerous.

Ask the toads' queen.

~Continue,~ Wisp ordered magnanimously.

Reassured, the toad pulled up its leg and settled into a proper squat. ~I was first to see the evil of the Lost One and warn the others. I matter to Marrowdell. I have produced more eggs for my home this winter than any other. I have——~

Wisp lifted his head, so; the toad, wisely, paused. ~What do you mean, 'Lost One'?~

~He who was Crumlin. He wasn't like the other villagers, elder brother. He knew of the Verge and wanted to go there. When the magic he brought didn't work, he did wicked things.~ With dismay.~He cut down neyet to reach ylings. He caught efflet in nets and nyphrit in traps. I would watch and warn as I could, elder brother, but my duty was to this house.~

Not dismay. Remorse. There'd been no elder brother or sister to tell the poor little cousin otherwise. Had the turn-born known?

They wouldn't have cared. Not before the girl.

~That was your duty, honorable little cousin.~ The thrill of caution became a painful tension shivering along Wisp's ruined limbs. ~What happened?~

What he heard was horrifying. Crumlin had been like the Ansnans, attracted by the magic within the edge. The Ansnans had tried to force their way into the Verge, in the process destroying their temple and most of Marrowdell, as well as exiling the little cousins.

From the toad's account, Crumlin had succeeded where they'd failed. He'd performed his magic using what he'd ripped from the helpless of the Verge and opened a crossing. Ylings had watched him disappear and, from what the little cousin said, all thought Marrowdell safe again. All but the other villagers.

They'd packed up and left, taking their belongings and the mirror.

~Why did you not tell me this before?~ Wisp demanded at the end. How could he not know? More than his pride was stung. This Crumlin was a potent threat.

The house toad blinked. ~We thought him dead, elder brother, until I saw him in his mirror.~

Dead he should have been. To survive, not minutes or

days, but years in the Verge? Without, the dragon thought grimly, coming to the notice of those who properly lived there. How had this Lost One managed that?

The figure shaped by the efflet looked nothing like a man. The eyes in the mirror—nothing like a man's. But he didn't doubt the toad.

The possibilities were, to say the least, unsettling.

Madness was likely.

Magic?

That he couldn't doubt.

~Why does he look through the mirror? What does he want here?~

Little cousins found questions about others alarming at best. This one shifted anxiously, as if about to jump, but made a gallant effort. ~It was his habit here, elder brother. He would stare at it while the others worked. They talked about him and were angry, but no one would interfere. What he wants now——~ It became a ball of distress.

~Excellent little cousin,~ the dragon praised, though he'd have preferred to snarl. ~Speak your thought.~

~The efflet, elder brother. They fear the Lost One wants to return to Marrowdell. That to cross again he needs more of what he took from them. That he would hunt—I dare not say more.~ The poor creature began to shake. ~You might eat me, elder brother.~

A pointless worry, the dragon being no longer concerned with toads.

Careful not to disturb the boys, Wisp launched himself up and away, moving through wood and snow as easily as he'd move through the earth. Free of the house, he wheeled in the air, heading for his crossing.

He'd seen for himself what the efflet feared.

Wisp tested the sharpness of a fang with his tongue. Jenn Nalynn, in a net?

Never.

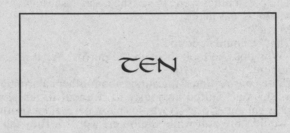

# TEN

*M*ARROWDELL, HAVING HELD its breath for Frann, let it out with an overnight storm. Snow, thick and quiet, filled in paths and laid a white blanket over the newest wound in the ossuary. There being no need to move around, and several more inclined to rest than usual—the gathering for Frann having dispensed with more than Davi's hoarded port—it seemed the day would be a quiet one and uneventful.

Appearances, Jenn thought wryly, were deceiving.

Porcelain that had survived passage from Avyo in a wagon, and a subsequent generation of use, smashed into pieces on the floor. "You're going where?"

It wasn't as if she hadn't been clear, though in hindsight she should have eased into the bit about the Naalish capital, rather than blurting it first.

"Peggs—" She bent to help tidy the mess.

Her sister stepped in her way. "Oh, no. You listen to me, Jenn Nalynn. This isn't a walk over for tea or whatever with a friend. This is—Ancestors Aghast and Agog!—you're talking about a trip to another domain! Do you hear your-self?"

Jenn looked to her father, who held up his hands. "I have to agree with your sister, Dear Heart. Such a journey would be dangerous."

"For anyone else," Kydd piped up, ignoring his wife's furious glare. "The Verge is Jenn's other home."

"And Channen?" Peggs retorted. "What's that? They don't speak Rhothan. They don't even eat ompah there! This is madness!"

The Nalynns' house toad yawned, showing rows of sharp little teeth. If an opinion, Jenn guessed it agreed with her sister, as did the Emms', still guarding the mirror.

Only one opinion mattered. "It's up to Bannan." There. She'd said it.

The crackle of flames in the 'stove, the sweep of a broom moving bits of a priceless dish; if the hush grew any deeper, Jenn thought with some frustration, they'd be deafened by their own hearts. "He's reason to go," she said quietly, but firmly. "A very good reason. Werfol and Semyn's parents are in Channen. Something happened, yesterday, to give us an idea where. Bannan hasn't asked me to take him," lest they jump to that conclusion and blame him. "I came to tell you I plan to make that offer." She met their troubled eyes, one after the other. "And to ask for your help. For everyone's."

"I see." Her father blew out his cheeks, his wont having made a decision. "I'll talk to Sennic," he offered, easing her heart. "Some things he's said—he's been to Mellynne, if not the capital."

"My brother," Kydd suggested. "He's corresponded with the Naalish for years. I'll see if Wainn can find me any text references to Channen."

"The Shadow District," Jenn specified.

His eyes gleamed with interest. "Indeed."

Peggs was still on the floor, sweeping pieces of plate. She glanced up, bright red on her cheeks. "You'll go and leave us with nothing. Ancestors Dear and Departed. At least we've Frann's bones!"

"Peggs!" "Dearest Heart!"

"Peggs' right," Jenn said quickly, stilling their objections.

"There's risk." Well beyond that posed by an unfamiliar wilderness, she could forget herself. Then there was Bannan.

She understood. Losing Frann made it harder, even for her, to imagine losing anyone else. Jenn drew her sister to her feet. "It's a risk worth taking, to save Semyn and Werfol's parents."

"There must be another way. Ask Mistress Sand! What of your dragon? Scourge? Why must it be you?"

"Peggs. Need you ask?" Jenn put as much confidence into her voice as she could. "I've our mother's gift. If they're lost, I can find them. Didn't I find the boys?"

Some of the anger left her sister's face. "What of Channen?"

"Its Shadow District is within the edge, like Marrowdell. A place where magic happens. A place where I—" Jenn let her other self show, "—happen. Who else should go, dear sister, but me?"

Peggs pulled her into her arms. "Ancestors Blessed," she prayed after a moment. "You'll need clothes. They don't wear what we do. That'll be for sure." She pushed Jenn back, keeping hold of her shoulders. "Not to mention your hair." Her eyes narrowed in thought, Peggs at her very best when planning. A nod. "Lorra might know."

"Before we do anything drastic," Jenn replied, "let me make sure this is what Bannan wants."

Though of that, she'd no doubt at all.

As snow clearers, efflet were, to be kind, unreliable. A ride on something strong, with long legs, would have done nicely, but Scourge, it appeared, would have no rider, if not Werfol.

"Idiot Beast!" Bannan pushed through thigh-deep snow, sweat stinging his eyes despite the cold. "You could—" he panted, "—make a path at least." A perfect use for the snowshoes Davi had promised to make for them, not that he'd remind the man during his grieving.

"Why?" Scourge walked alongside through the otherwise unbroken white coating the road ahead. Strolled, was more like it, flaunting his ease of travel, his hooves dancing over the snow. "She's coming."

No need to ask; there was only one "she" to kruar or dragon. The truthseer gratefully stopped, doubled over to catch his breath. "Where?" He'd made it as far as the path to the top of the Spine. It looked almost passable, if you didn't take note how the snow had drifted head high.

"Here," announced the breeze.

"Bannan!" Jenn trudged through the snow toward him, her cheeks flushed with effort. That her every step moved her twice the distance of his was simply part of what made her marvelous.

Her warm and slightly salty kiss another. They held each other for a moment, almost falling into the snow—

Which would have been fine with Bannan, but he'd been coming to see her for a reason—

They pulled apart, speaking at once so their words tangled together. "I'll take you to Lila," Jenn said as he said, "Would you take me—"

So of course they kissed again, toppling into the snow.

Not long afterward, though a sweet and warm while it was, Bannan found himself sitting at the Uhthoffs' long table with Jenn, surrounded by walls filled with books from floor to ceiling, to hear what Master Dusom and Kydd had to say about Channen's Shadow District.

It was, unsurprisingly, very little. "The Naalish don't speak about their magic." Master Dusom poured them cups of hot bitter cocoa, a package having been in his mail from Endshere, offering honey crisps at the side. A tall man and distinguished, with but a touch of gray in the thick black hair characteristic of the family, his hooded eyelids made him appear inattentive. Nothing could have been further from the truth. Marrowdell's teacher was renowned for his fierce intellect within and beyond the valley.

"I've an old friend who worked the barges one season. He said a strange thing." Dusom took his seat. "The greater canals that take shipping across Mellynne to the Mila River cup Channen like a mother's arms, but the lesser, within the city's heart? Those, he swore by his Ancestors, have neither source nor outlet, nor is any vessel permitted on their waters."

Kydd nodded eagerly. "Waters purported by some to be the source of Naalish magic, by others to be necessary for its use. Bannan, have you heard of 'Silver Tears' being sold in Vorkoun's market?"

The truthseer nodded. "For a pretty price." He raised an eyebrow. "I thought it a better swindle than most, for what seems ordinary water."

"Most likely," agreed the beekeeper, "given the real liquid is rumored to be among the most potent of tokens for a wishing." He slammed his hand down on the table. "Ancestors Dull and Dense! The vial!"

"The token Bannan found." By Jenn's unhappy tone, she thought of where. "You think it contains these 'tears?'"

Kydd's enthusiasm deflated. "Or goat's blood. I didn't dare open it, not in Marrowdell."

Bannan spared a moment to wish he'd been equally prudent with the crate.

"Still, if these tokens came from Channen," Dusom mused, "perhaps you could discover who made and sold them. From there, find who sent those men to pursue your nephews."

Locate one token dealer in an unknown city rife with magic? He supposed astronomers had a different sense of scale, being busy counting stars. Besides, Bannan told himself, he'd talked all this through with Tir, last night. The coins would be of more use, and far less risk, should they be searched.

Still, Dusom's idea had some merit. "We're looking for Lila, not Emon's enemies," Bannan reminded them, then gave a grudging nod. "But you've made a good point. We'll take the tokens. The hunt you suggest—she's the one to do it." He took Jenn's hand, knowing there was a limit to what he'd risk, even for his sister.

Her fingers squeezed his, then let go. "What can you tell us about the people, Master Dusom?" Jenn asked, tactfully changing the subject. "Peggs worries they'll be very different."

Did Jenn? Marrowdell and its village was the largest community she'd ever experienced. Forget dragons, the truthseer thought. A boisterous city crowd might be the greater worry.

Dusom chuckled, smiling at her. "People are people, Dear Heart. For all its seeming mystery, Channen's a trade city, with many tongues in use, and even more customs. You'll be fine."

"I speak Naalish," Bannan mentioned, in case she'd wondered. "Well enough."

Jenn, who by her magic could understand any language, even toad, smiled at that.

"And you may have local help." Dusom brought a small folded paper from a pocket, opening it and pressing it flat. From another, he produced a familiar brooch, laying that on top. "Lorra had a name for you. She's no idea if the man still lives, but if you can find him or his family, she was adamant showing this brooch will gain you aid without question." He shook his head. "I hesitate to guess what other debts that woman could call in, if she chose. Take it," he urged, sliding both toward Bannan.

The truthseer lifted his hands from the table. "Do you know what that is?"

The Uhthoffs exchanged frowns. "A piece of jewelry," Dusom replied. "Frann, Ancestors Dear and Departed, was never without it."

Kydd's frown deepened. "I take it you know more."

"This," Bannan pointed, "is Naalish magic. An endearment, bespelled with a message from a loved one. Semyn and Werfol recognized it and told me. They've one from their mother, hung as a pendant. They witnessed Frann listening to its voice."

Ever curious, the beekeeper picked up the brooch and held it to his ear. Disappointment crossed his face as he put it down. "Nothing."

"It would speak only to Frann, but the magic?" Bannan shook his head. "That's still within. I'm not sure we dare take such a thing into Channen."

"Dare we not?" Jenn replied. "We've asked our friends for help," she continued softly. "We should respect what they've offered. Lorra wouldn't part with this easily." She reached across the table to pick up the worrisome object, leaving him the paper.

He'd trust her instincts. Committing the name to memory, the truthseer passed the folded paper back to Dusom. "Please give Lorra our thanks."

"Something else was left for you." Kydd rose and went

to the pegs by the door. From under a coat, he brought something all too familiar. Horst's sword, with its sheath and belt. "Oddly enough, Sennic advised you not to take it."

"The dragons would laugh," Bannan agreed, then grew serious. "Sennic's right. I know enough of Channen to be sure a blade would be of more trouble than worth. Only city constables go armed." He grinned. "And those they do their best to catch."

"'Constables,'" Jenn echoed, as if tasting the word. "Canals. A city under clouds."

"'Dragons.'" Kydd came back to the table and sat, steepling his long, artist fingers. Over them, his face grew troubled. "Dragons and who knows what else. Don't mistake me, Jenn. I told Peggs the Verge is your other home, because that's the truth. You're part of it. But what of Bannan?"

She gave her brother-by-marriage such a surprised look Bannan almost laughed. "He'll be with me."

"And you won't leave him? Not even if you're tempted?"

Her surprise became something else. "What are you saying?"

"Kydd," Dusom said.

A caution and timely, the truthseer thought, seeing his breath cloud in the room's sudden chill.

His younger brother shook his head, either at the warning or Jenn's reaction. "The Verge is a magical realm. The real danger might not be the obvious. You can't know what might call to your turn-born self. What might try to lure or distract you, to leave Bannan unprotected. No insult intended," to the truthseer.

Who spread his arms. "None possible." He bowed his head to Jenn. "I put my life into your hands, Dearest Heart, without question or fear."

The air warmed again, but she didn't smile, as Bannan had hoped. Instead, she frowned and made to speak, then changed her mind, closing her lips.

Heart's Blood. It wasn't a lie.

But it wasn't the truth.

What hadn't she told him?

They would cross into the Verge at the turn, today, there being no need to wait and every reason to hurry. Bannan worried about Werfol as much or more than his sister, who they now knew languished in a cell.

About her too.

*Rustlerustle.*

Jenn ignored the eyes, still scratching at the mirror. Her bag, stuffed with simples and hair ties and her second-best dress, waited on her bed. The Emms' house toad squatted sentry on the floor.

They'd told the other villagers the truth, or most of it, so Werfol wouldn't be upset by what any villager said to him and, as importantly, so those they left behind would know where they'd gone and why. If not how. No other villager took the Tinkers Road to its end. All of them were comfortably convinced it led to where the tinkers lived, some place distant and foreign. Saying they were off to see Mistress Sand, to ask the tinkers about Lila, left most of Marrowdell content.

Those who knew about the Verge and Channen were left to worry. As Bannan, Jenn thought again, worried about her.

*Rustlerustle.* "Hush, you." She'd rewrapped the mirror, adding a leather strap. Before leaving to meet Bannan, she'd bury it in the snow behind the privy where it could "rustlerustle" to its heart's content. She wouldn't have Gallie or Zehr—or the baby—encountering great yellow eyes in their loft. Or let those eyes watch Marrowdell.

Eyes she'd explain at her first opportunity. Thanks to Kydd, Bannan knew full well she'd left something unsaid. Matters had happened rather quickly, that was all. She'd tell him all about the sei and the toads and the efflet and the—

*Rustlerustle—Crack!*

Jenn froze, hands on her bag.

*GrrissshSnapcrackle.*

She didn't need to turn to know what the sounds meant. The mirror—wrapped in canvas and rope and leather, leaning safely against the wall—had shattered.

Was whatever owned the eyes about to escape?

Taking a steadying breath, Jenn looked over her shoulder.

The toad, having leapt away, crept forward.

To her relief, the canvas around the mirror merely had a bulge at the bottom, where shattered bits of mirror would slide and gather. Nothing worse.

Just as well, then. Or not. Glittering specks of glass littered the floor, having slipped through folds in the canvas. Sharp broken glass couldn't be far behind.

~Be careful, elder sister.~

"I will." Once nothing else went *snap* or *tinkle*, she laid the mirror, in its wrap, flat on the floor. None of the glass must fall through a crack or get into the rug. Or anywhere else. Untying the ropes and strap, she eased open the canvas.

The frame remained intact. Behind where the glass had been was a piece of wood, stained as if once wet. She spread the canvas flat.

Glass piled at one end, all splinters and jagged shards like ice where it met stone, except ice wasn't this stygian black.

Eyes opened. Great yellow eyes. A pair in each and every piece, down to the tiniest speck.

The house toad launched itself under her bed.

To be honest Jenn found the regard of so many a little disturbing herself.

Eyelids rose and fell. Dozens. No, hundreds. Though faint, the *rustlerustle* of so many was like wind through a grain field.

Something white fluttered at the window, catching her attention. Not snow, but an unseasonable moth, trying to get in. The sei didn't appear to notice or require conveniences such as opened panes or doors, so Jenn opened the window for the small thing, moths being of Marrowdell. "You are welcome here," she told it, then turned to the glass. "You are not."

Every eye snapped closed, leaving black and featureless glass. The moth hovered at a cautious distance, pulling out a parchment upon which it inscribed a note with the tip of a leg. At some haste, Jenn thought. Then it rolled up the parchment, tucked it in the jeweled sachet moths carried, in Marrowdell, and flew back out the window as if she wasn't even there.

Well.

The eyes opened. "You weren't lost at all," Jenn accused. "You've been hiding."

No blinks. So it lied too.

She closed the window, pondering what to do. Gallie would be up to use her desk and where Gallie came, she'd bring the baby. Hopefully the eyes couldn't move on their own. To be safe, she bent to look under the bed. "I'll be right back," Jenn told the toad. "Please keep watch." It didn't look happy, but eased out and sat, staring.

And being stared at.

The Emms, having said their good-byes, had gone to visit Tadd and Hettie. They'd done so to keep Loee out from underfoot while Jenn packed and to distract Hettie, unhappy not to have a typical Marrowdell gathering to fare well the travelers, fresh snow and mysterious circumstances notwithstanding.

All for the best, as it turned out, Jenn relieved to avoid awkward questions. She took the largest stew pot from its shelf and hurried back upstairs armed with the pot, dustpan, and straw whisk.

She stood in the middle of the room, brandishing the heavy pot. "Fair warning," she told the pile of broken mirror. "Leave now, or suffer the same fate!"

Melodramatic it might have been, but the threat—or pot—had the desired effect. The black winked away, leaving sparkling glass. Jenn examined each with care, her reflection sliced into dozens of Jenns and Jenn pieces, but whatever—whomever—had spied from the Verge was gone.

Good. If eyes watched, she wasn't sure she could do what must be done.

Short work to sweep up the broken glass, dumping it by the dustpan load into the pot. Jenn used the whisk to knock free the few pieces still held by the frame, adding those to the rest, until all that remained were the specks that had escaped the canvas and frame. She mopped those with a rag dampened in her washbasin, putting the rag in the pot too.

After some thought, she shoved the canvas and ropes well under her bed, beyond the reach of little fingers.

Two trips down the ladder, one with the pot, the other with the frame. The pot, half full of glass, she set on the cookstove.

The frame? A pity, Jenn thought, running her fingers over the tapestry. Even though worn to bare threads at the corners, with the rest in desperate need of a good cleaning, this represented days, perhaps weeks, of painstaking work. The pattern, what showed of it, was hardly magical. Leaves and buds. Small flowers, some with bees. Apples of various sizes. How could there be harm in it?

She'd take no more chances. After knocking apart sides and back, watchful for more glass but finding none, Jenn used Zehr's saw to cut the frame, tapestry and all, into pieces that would fit into the pot.

Once every bit of the mirror was in the pot, Jenn used tongs to take a fat glowing coal from the cookstove, adding it on top.

She'd vaguely wanted more light from a candle, and it had answered. This time, her wish was deliberate and sure. She fixed her gaze on the ember. Heat!

In answer, its glow went from red-hot to white.

More, she insisted. Hotter.

Thread smoldered and fell apart. Wood snapped and caught fire, burning with the smell of apple.

Hotter still, Jenn Nalynn wished, and the pot itself began to redden, while within, thread vanished and wood turned to ash that crumbled and drifted up and away.

The pieces of mirror began to melt. They softened, flowing together until there were no pieces at all but a clear red puddle.

Before anything else could melt, including the perfectly good pot and the top of the Emms' 'stove—let alone the rest of the rather warm kitchen, Jenn changed her wish, or eased it, satisfied when the red of the puddle very slowly began to clear.

Leaving the pot, and glass, to finish cooling under the watchful gaze of the house toad—though she trusted the creature wouldn't get too close—Jenn went upstairs to finish her packing.

Sack filled, ready to go, she took a last long look around the loft. Oh, and didn't something catch her eye?

"Ancestors Crazed and Confounding," she muttered. There, in the shadows. A shard of mirror. "How did I miss you?"

She nudged it free with a toe. To her dismay it was black. Two great yellow eyes opened. Blinked. *Rustlerustle.* Again.

A plea perhaps, though a demand seemed more likely. With, she thought practically, no time left to deal with either. The shard being small enough to fit in an envelope, Jenn took the second last from her writing desk and tucked the glass inside, careful not to cut herself on an edge. She put the envelope, shard inside, into a sock from her bag. That sock she wrapped inside its mate, tying the top and stuffing the result to the bottom of her bag to be dealt with later.

She'd take the shard to Bannan and Wisp, and seek their advice.

Jenn paused at the top of the ladder. If she looked around again, it would make the moment seem more than it was, so she climbed down as if it were a normal day, watching for the step where Zehr sometimes left his saw. The kitchen was tidy, dishes for four dried and put away. The table would be set for three tonight, unless the Emms stayed for supper with Hettie and Tadd.

She wouldn't wish. She'd made one with Wen, to come back, and that would have to do. Though as Jenn left the Emms' house and her home, she wasn't entirely sure that had been a wish with turn-born magic.

Or simply one from her heart.

The Emms' house toad watched from its spot near the cookstove, offering no opinion as Jenn, using rags to protect her hands, carried the pot outside. She tipped it upside down behind the privy, pleased when the glass, now a clear lump with the faintest swirl of silver—more than silver, flickers of gold and hints of blue—at its heart, dropped free. The snow hissed to receive it, sending up steam; the glass crackled but didn't shatter and Jenn was satisfied. No more a mirror.

Though it would make an interesting find come spring.

"Uncle. We could go with you."

"We'd be very good. Wouldn't we, Tir?"

Under the blandishment of two pairs of so-earnest eyes, the former guard turned red. "Don't you look to me. We've duty here, and your lessons, and here's where you're to be when your uncle comes back."

"With Momma," Werfol said firmly. "And Poppa!"

Semyn nodded, trust shining in his face, and Bannan's heart thudded in his chest. So much for all his careful explanations. Where was Wisp when he needed distraction?

He put his pack on the floor. "Semyn. Werfol. Lads, I want you to listen to me." They nodded. "Ancestors Witness, it's not an easy road we'll take. There's no knowing what's at the other end." Another, slower nod. "Jenn and I—we'll do our very best. I can't—I won't—promise anything more. Werfol, you know I speak the truth."

The little truthseer nodded a third time, his eyes gold. "Momma said you were a hero, Uncle. No one else was allowed to know and we weren't to say, ever, but she told us. You'll find her. You'll bring them home."

And didn't that strike him in the heart? Tir coughed and Bannan took the boys in his arms. He kissed their heads and, though he didn't dare promise aloud, by every Ancestor he could claim, he vowed he wouldn't face these children again without their parents.

"Time to be off."

Bannan swallowed. Composing his face into a cheerful smile, he straightened and ruffled their hair as he always did. "Then I'm off. Mind yourselves and keep an eye on Tir for me."

"Couldn't we come with you a short way?" Werfol pleaded. "I like to watch the turn, Uncle."

His brother ruffled his hair. "Tonight let's watch from here, Weed."

They'd stick together. "Good," Bannan told them. "Tir?"

Tir snapped to attention. "Sir!"

Heart's Blood. Would the man never let it go? Bannan regarded his friend, then shook his head. "Still with that?"

A grin showed at the side of the mask. "Always, sir."

They clasped hands, then shoulders. Tir gave him a hard slap on one after letting go. "Watch your back."

"That I can promise." Bannan looked to the boys.

Semyn wore Lila's pendant. Werfol had found one of Bannan's scarves and had wrapped it around his neck. Seeing his attention, the pair bowed in unison, fingertips sweeping the floor with impeccable grace. "Uncle."

He wanted to tell them what to do if he didn't come back. To reassure Werfol his gift wouldn't stay all-consuming and tell Semyn that he'd make a fine baron.

Instead, he circled his fingers over his heart. "Hearts of our Ancestors, However far we are apart, Keep Us Close."

" 'Keep Us Close.' "

With their high voices in his ears, and Tir's low rumble, Bannan turned and left his house. He didn't look around or back.

He'd see it again when he brought Lila and Emon home.

"You should keep your hair like that, Dear Heart." Peggs tucked a stray lock back into Jenn's complex braid, her fingers lingering. Before they'd left the village, she'd checked everything Jenn wore, then produced a sachet filled with petals from Melusine's rose, the delicate bag newly sewn from a fine linen handkerchief embroidered with Jenn's name and hers, insisting that be tucked deep into a pocket.

She'd then made it clear there was no chance in either world of her family letting Jenn cross this time without them present. Kydd and Radd walked with them, and Peggs kept her arm linked with her sister's as if afraid to let go.

Truth be told, Jenn was glad of the arm and the company. The efflet had seen fit to clear the road. They'd not used the snow for more sculptures, either because they were satisfied or for some reason of their own. As for Wisp? She'd not heard or felt her dragon since he'd suggested she take Bannan into the Verge. Hopefully, that meant he'd be waiting for them at the crossing, smug they'd taken his advice and ready to be their guide.

If not? The turn was coming and she carried eyes in her bag. He'd be there, Jenn told herself.

"I'm sorry we weren't more help," Kydd said, not for the first time.

Radd marched alongside. "You were more than I was."

Jenn put her free arm through her father's and squeezed. "We'll have help, Poppa. Don't forget." When he glanced at Scourge, who walked alongside, she shook her head. "He's to stay with the boys." This earned her the glint of a red eye, then the kruar snorted and plunged ahead, his flagged tail the last thing they saw as he rounded the bend. "It's a sensitive topic," she said apologetically.

As they passed the path to the Spine, a figure stepped out to join them. "Wainn!" Kydd greeted, clapping his nephew on the shoulder. "Good of you to come."

Wainn smiled, but the look he gave Jenn was full of foreboding.

She tightened her grip on her family and didn't ask.

Be it Wainn's arrival or Scourge's leave-taking, they walked in silence to the opening to Bannan's farm. There, Jenn turned. "I know I said you could come all the way, but—"

"But this is far enough." Peggs smiled, though her eyes were suspiciously bright. "Go, Dearest Heart. We'll visit with Tir and the boys." She held up her basket. "I brought pie."

Then there were hugs and kisses and Jenn grew quite flustered and might have wept, but just in time Bannan appeared. There was nothing for it then but he be hugged and kissed and fussed over too.

Until Wainn looked to the Bone Hills and said quietly, "The turn's coming."

Jenn nodded. "However far—"

"No need for all that," Peggs stated in her do-not-argue-with-me voice. "You'll be home in no time. Come along, everyone. The pie's still hot." And because it was Peggs, and Peggs had thought to bring pie, she swept her family with her to the waiting house.

Not without casting a look back at Wainn, who hadn't budged, that threatened to lift him by his bootlaces. "I'm coming," he replied, then looked to Jenn. "Wen said to trust your heart."

Which didn't sound at all unreasonable and she would, of course. Jenn took Bannan's hand and smiled. "Thank—"

Her smile vanished as she met Wainn's eyes, for

Marrowdell looked back. "He doesn't belong here," the words slow and heavy. "You mustn't bring him back."

"'Him?' Emon?" Bannan asked sharply. "Why, what's wrong?"

"Nothing. It's not Emon," she replied. "Wainn—"

But the moment passed and Wainn smiled, himself again and without care in the world. "Peggs brought pie!"

"Jenn," Bannan pressed. "Emon?"

"Come," she told him. "I'll explain on the way."

What she could.

The turn was coming. They'd have been late, but the efflet had clawed a path through Night's Edge and into the old trees beyond.

The path he'd expected. Their slow pace along it was the surprise. After a moment, Bannan looked at Jenn. She gave him a determined little smile that didn't fool him for an instant. So, when they came at last to the forest edge, he stooped to give her a quick kiss on the cheek.

"What was that for?" she asked, her smile eased into something more natural.

"Everything. This." He waved an arm vaguely. "It's not snowing."

That won him a chuckle. "It doesn't always snow, Bannan."

"You could have fooled me," he assured her. He began walking backward, to watch her face as she followed. "We'll be free of it soon. No snow in Channen."

Her eyebrows lifted. "Ever?"

"Almost never."

The eyebrows drew together. "I'm not sure I believe you, Bannan Larmensu."

He clasped his hands over his heart. "You wound me, Jenn Nalynn."

"I—oh my!" She burst into laughter as he fell backward, landing on his rump in snow up to his elbows, which he hadn't planned. Still, the laugh was honest and contagious. He chuckled too, until he discovered to his chagrin he was stuck.

Smiling, Jenn offered her help. "Here. Wiggle yourself from the deepest part." As she pulled him free, she joked, "For your sake, we'd best hope there's no snow in Channen."

For both their sakes, he needed to know what troubled her. Bannan stopped her brushing him off. "This can wait, Dearest Heart. What is it? What did Wainn mean?"

Jenn met his gaze, her lovely eyes open and honest—and more purple than blue. A reminder of the coming turn. And her magic. "I looked in the mirror. There was—there is—something that looks back from the Verge."

The eyes. "It saw you."

She nodded. Ancestors Anxious and Uncertain. Was that good news or dire? "Could you tell what it was?" he asked, though he didn't know what to ask, was the truth. "What it—what it wants?"

"The efflet know. And the little cousins." Her voice became troubled. "All they'll tell me is that he—they call it 'he'—was once here and harmed efflet before crossing into the Verge. Like Wainn, they fear this thing, this hunter, wants to return to Marrowdell. That it would use me, somehow, to do so."

Dire didn't come close. "We mustn't go, then. We can't!"

"We must, Dearest Heart." Jenn's chin firmed. "And we will. The Verge is full of dangers we don't know," she added, being reasonable when Bannan couldn't imagine reason being part of this. "This one we do. He won't—" her voice sharpened, "—come back here."

There was no faulting her courage. "Where's the mirror?"

"Gone." With finality. "But the darkness—and the eyes—remain in a shard. I have it." The shoulder supporting her bag lifted and fell. "I couldn't leave it at the Emms'."

"No," he agreed numbly. "What should we do with it?"

"I don't know. If the hunter can use the shard to spy on Marrowdell, on us, shouldn't we take the shard into the Verge and leave it there?"

"And if that's what he wants?" It came out more harshly than Bannan intended and he gentled his tone. "Forgive me, Jenn, but this is—Werfol and Semyn slept over that thing. I brought it here."

"I'm not so sure you did," she said, touching his hand. "I mean, you did, but—what if there was a wishing involved? Some magic to bring the mirror to Marrowdell?"

Was it possible? Could an object persuade those around it—Great Gran, himself? Bannan shuddered. "Then we can't leave it here."

And hoped he wouldn't regret leaving the sword.

The turn touched the Bone Hills, sliding blue down their flanks. While Jenn, if she was like other turn-born, didn't need the turn to cross unless moving a wagon or other large object, crossing at other times would catch the attention of the turn-born of the Verge. Like a shout, Mistress Sand had warned her, where a soft voice would be more agreeable.

Good manners were never wrong, in Jenn's opinion.

What was? Wisp wasn't here.

Not knowing what else to do, she bent to look inside Wisp's home of crystal and wood. It was empty but for frozen moss. Straightening, she met Bannan's gaze. "I was sure he'd be waiting for us."

The truthseer shrugged. "We hadn't told him," he reminded her.

It shouldn't have mattered, Jenn wanted to say, but didn't. The bond between herself and Wisp was something she'd obviously taken too much for granted; she'd assumed he'd know and be here, ready to help. "I was counting on Wisp to guide us. I don't know the way," she admitted. "Not to the turn-born." Certainly not to the crossing into Channen.

They had a plan, as much as one could plan for the Verge. Wisp would take them to Mistress Sand, where they'd obtain the mask Jenn needed. Oh, and ask directions to the crossing. It seemed simple.

Not so, lacking the dragon.

"It's all right. We'll come back tomorrow." Bannan spoke lightly, but she could see it in his eyes. They'd said their farewells. Firmed their resolve and were ready, now.

Now it would be. "We'll cross to Wisp's sanctuary," Jenn decided. "We can wait for him there as easily as here."

"Or—" Bannan began to smile at something behind her. Jenn turned to see Scourge stepping from behind one of the old trees. "Ah! We've our guide!"

A lip curled. The breeze nipped Jenn's ears. "I'm to stay with the truthseer," the old kruar reminded them, sounding thoroughly offended and grumpy to boot. "I'm of no use in the Verge." He prowled forward, head low. "You prefer the dragon."

With a snap. Jenn winced but Bannan's smile only grew. "Testy testy. You know you want to show him up. Here's your chance. We need to reach the turn-born." He shrugged his pack into place. "If you're nervous, you can stay out of sight."

The massive head rose in outrage. "I hide from nothing!"

Which, according to Wisp, wasn't true; kruar hunted from ambush. In a sense, Jenn thought, it was more accurate to say they hid from everything. Until they attacked without warning.

Scourge with them might be a very good thing.

"Well, then. We'd best get going," Bannan said cheerfully. "Mustn't miss the turn."

A snort. Then another. Finally, Scourge lowered his head and spun away. Just as Jenn and Bannan exchanged disappointed looks, they heard, "MOVE! We won't cross here."

The truthseer laughed and took her hand, pulling her with him. "You heard the idiot beast!"

Scourge let himself sink, breaking a trail. They stumbled and ran behind him, Jenn gasping and laughing with Bannan. She couldn't remember the last time she'd laughed so easily. It should have made it impossible to move faster.

But once they went between the old trees and found themselves back on the Tinkers Road, she grasped where Scourge led them, and wished to be there.

And they were.

Where the road ended at the forest beneath the Bone Hills.

The turn-borns' crossing.

Where the dragon, indeed, waited.

Scourge stamped snow and glared. "Where have you been, old fool? I had to do your duty."

"Hunting." Something passed between the dragon and

the kruar then, something not shared with those on two feet. Jenn knew, because Scourge stilled, muscles tense along the curve of his neck.

Wisp must have been here awhile. Steam from his breath had melted snow, leaving an adorable but surely uncomfortable icicle on the tip of his snout. She resisted the temptation to run up and hug him. He was a dragon after all, and no less prickly about his dignity than a toad. But she could smile at him, with all her heart, and did.

Wild eyes regarded her. "You, they will fear," the breeze said with decided anticipation. The eyes turned to Bannan. "You, they might eat."

"No, they won't," Jenn countered. "I won't let them." She regretted the chill in the air, but on this she was utterly determined. "Bannan will be safe with me."

Wisp snapped his jaws, whether in agreement or dispute she couldn't tell and didn't care. The icicle broke off, dropping into the snow. "And what Bannan carries?"

"What I—?" The truthseer took off his pack, resting it on a bent knee. "It seemed heavy, but I thought Tir put in extra food." He undid the flap and lifted it.

A house toad blinked at the light, then squirmed with remarkable quickness deeper into the pack, long legs flailing.

The dragon pounced!

Bannan shouted as he was knocked aside, snow flying. The pack flew the other way, and the toad, neatly plucked, soared high in the air, then down again, to be caught in Wisp's jaws.

Jaws that didn't close, Jenn saw with relief, but held the toad firmly.

Bannan, snowier than ever, grimaced as he retrieved his pack. He made a show of looking inside. "Anyone else?"

"This little cousin was alone," the dragon told them. He tossed his head to the side and the toad into the snow. "And foolish."

Having spread its legs wide before landing, the house toad managed to stay on top of the drift. ~Take me with you, elder sister. I will be useful. I will guard your camp. I will make eggs—~

Jenn was given no chance to answer. Wisp interrupted, "What of your duty?"

The toad puffed itself into a joyous ball. ~I was of the homeless, elder brother. I have been gifted with duty to our elder sister. I matter to Jenn Nalynn!~

She'd her own toad? "I'm—I'm honored," she told it, though in truth her feelings on the subject were mixed. The little cousins were underfoot and opinionated at the best of times. To have one pay her special attention? Let alone one clever enough to hide in Bannan's pack? "You aren't riding in my hair," Jenn said hastily, to get that out of the way. There'd have to be more rules. Many.

Bannan had waited patiently through all this, privy to half of the conversation. "Jenn?"

"It seems I have my own guardian." Jenn did her best to look stern. "Who will be staying in Marrowdell."

Not happy now. ~Elder sister!~

"Stay!"

Scourge snorted. "It's time to cross."

And didn't that tingle in her very core agree? Wisp disappeared, Bannan, having shouldered his pack, began to walk with Scourge, who headed for the thick mass of tree trunk in front of them as if a door would open.

One would, Jenn knew.

~I . . . will . . . wait . . . ~

She looked back at the house toad. Having curled in its limbs, it sank in the snow. A thin line of white marked its lips and—were its dark eyes beginning to film over?

"Leave it," her dragon whispered in her ear.

But Wisp liked the cold no better.

The more she considered the situation, the more she realized there was really no choice at all.

"Jenn?"

"Coming!" She snatched up the toad, alarmed to find it felt more like a ball of ice than a living thing, and ran after the others.

She'd figure out what to do with her newfound "guardian" in the Verge.

Old trees filled the shadow of the Bone Hill, their thick trunks and intertwined branches forming a wall through which only a bird or squirrel could pass, a wall at which the Tinkers Road came to its abrupt end.

Bannan waited, hardly breathing, as the shadow lengthened around them, tinted blue over the snow. Small things stirred in the branches high above their heads, like dried winter leaves twisting on twigs. Ylings, curious perhaps, or wary. He hoped they'd show themselves to the boys while he was gone, the dance of the ylings, with their starry hair, being one of Marrowdell's best secrets.

Jenn stood beside him, her arms filled with toad. Scourge had given it a disdainful look, but Bannan felt better for the small creature's company. Homely things, toads, concerned with comfort and safety.

He watched the turn wash away her rosy cheeks and nose, and take the color from her lovely lips. Watched as her head lifted, hearing or feeling what he could neither hear nor feel.

She freed a hand as hard as ice within its mitten and he took it without hesitation. "For Lila," he said huskily.

The turn-born nodded, and they stepped forward as one.

Something landed on his head.

About to strike it away, Bannan felt the pat of tiny hands on his cheek and held still. The yling—for it could be nothing else—slipped inside his hood and settled somewhere in his hair.

He'd no more time to consider what that meant for the road became silver and soared up into the sky, or did the sky fold itself to meet them? What had been snow, between thuds of his heart, became warm and liquid. Not water, not this.

Mimrol.

He stood again within the Verge.

Silver flowed from his feet, for Bannan stood in the shallows of a lake that caught the colors of the sky and stroked them into long slow waves. To his right, forests of gold and purple rose taller than any trees he'd seen, their uppermost branches bending sharply as if to an endless wind.

Though the air was still and tasted sour, or was it sweet and did he—? The Verge played with the senses of those not born here. Bannan closed his eyes for an instant, then opened them again, looking deeper.

Three buildings stood on the shore to the left of the lake, their rooftops sparkling like gems. Around them was a wall of forbidding stone, but no gate barred the wide opening and a road led inside without sentry or watch.

Turn-born needed none.

"Warm, isn't it?" Jenn, already out on shore, was busy removing her winter clothes, rolling them into a tidy bundle. The toad sat nearby, its eyes barely open as if squinting. "Perhaps we can leave all this with Mistress Sand."

Bannan found her calm acceptance more startling than the strange world around them. He roused himself to move, stepping cautiously through the mimrol then out on what should have been sand.

Except that some of it blinked and slid away from his feet, so he moved with extra care. Jenn noticed and a dimple appeared in one cheek. "I do believe they brought me some of that," she commented. Ah, yes. The turn-born had provided boxes containing bits of the Verge, in hopes one would prove right for Jenn Nalynn.

Instead, she'd been filled by the sei's tears. "Do you know what it is?" he asked, curious.

She shook her head. A single lock slipped out of the tight coils of braids binding her golden hair; presumably Peggs' best guess at what would pass in Channen.

Bannan tenderly tucked it behind her ear. "We're here," he said with quiet awe.

"The first step," she cautioned, but looked pleased.

His pack safely free of toads, Bannan cheerfully stuffed his coat and other cold weather gear inside. Warm it was, like a summer evening.

And no brighter. "Is it almost night?" The sky itself had a glow, as if the sun of the Verge hid behind it. As for hiding, there was no sign of either kruar or dragon. Scourge was doubtless close by. Wisp? There was a busy splashing in the lake that could well be an invisible dragon taking a bath.

While the yling had made itself a nest in his hair.

~Marrowdell has night, truthseer, as does the outer world. The Verge dims but never darkens.~

The voice, more felt than heard, was unfamiliar. Smaller,

somehow, than either kruar or dragon, whom he had heard this way before. Bannan paused midway through shedding his vest. "Who's that?"

The house toad claiming to be Jenn Nalynn's opened its eyes. ~It has been long since I've been here, truthseer, but I haven't forgotten.~

"I can hear you!" Bannan grinned. "Greetings, friend toad."

It gave a delicate shudder. ~Little cousin, if you please.~ Within the Verge, the house toad showed its true nature, one he'd only glimpsed in Marrowdell. What had seemed warts were rich gems, wrinkled skin now the finest of mail. Only the eyes remained the same, limpid, dark brown, and huge.

No, they weren't the same. Now those eyes held an age-less wisdom, a quiet confidence he'd not noticed before. This was, Bannan decided, no ordinary toad.

If any were.

"We should go," Jenn said. She pointed at the small set-tlement. "Wisp?"

Something erupted from the lake, sending droplets of liquid silver glinting into the air. ~I will bring your mask.~

Her nose wrinkled. "Please ask nicely, Wisp." She glanced at Bannan. "Mistress Sand couldn't promise they'd make one for me. I hope so. If not, I'll simply stay like this."

~Tasty and fragile!~ Scathing that was. ~Would you be bait?~

"Scourge!"

"Don't pay attention," Jenn said and didn't appear overly concerned, finding a spot in the sand to sit that neither blinked nor moved. Bannan joined her. After a moment, her hand slipped into his. "It is beautiful here," she mur-mured.

"When things aren't trying to eat you."

"You," she pointed out. "If anything tries to bite me, I'll change. But I think we're both safe here."

True, they seemed in no immediate danger. Bannan did what he suspected Jenn was doing, and took a moment to simply realize where they were.

Not that the Verge made it easy. He could have sworn

the sky across the lake had been open. Now, a valley hung over them, a lake at its rocky heart. It was like being in the middle of dueling reflections.

Or inside a mirror.

"What is it?" Jenn asked, her fingers tightening.

"The hunter in the mirror. You haven't told me what he looks like."

"You've seen the eyes—" she began.

~He may not look the same here, elder sister.~ The toad yawned toothily. ~Or may. It's up to the Verge.~

How singularly unhelpful. Bannan frowned. "Then how do we watch for him?"

~I stand guard.~ The kruar, harsh and determined. ~I will know his stench. It will be of your world and not belong.~

He'd thought to coax Scourge to return to the boys. This seemed an excellent reason, Bannan realized, to change his mind. Though, "stench?" "Do we—do I—"

With dark humor. ~I'm used to it.~

Jenn leaned into his shoulder. Bannan looked down quizzically and she gave him a rueful smile. "Ancestors Blessed and Beloved. When I imagined coming here with you, it was more romantic."

He smiled back. "When I'm with you, everywhere is romantic, Dearest Heart." Then bent to kiss her.

~Move! NOW!~

Bannan scrambled to his feet, Jenn coming with him, and they bolted back to the sand.

Which blinked in offense and slid away, tipping them together.

Recovering his balance, holding Jenn, Bannan looked around, heart pounding. "What is it? What's wrong?"

The toad hadn't budged.

Scourge's ugly head appeared beside a purple tree trunk. ~Practice,~ the kruar announced slyly, then disappeared.

Heart's Blood. The truthseer glared where he thought the kruar likely was, not that glaring would bother the creature. After a moment, he shook his head. "We deserved that," he admitted. "This is no place to let down our guard, Dearest Heart."

Nor would Channen be any safer.

~They are not allowed!~

Wisp narrowed his eyes as grit blew around the turn-borns' courtyard and waited for the source of the little storm to subside. Riverstone stood with his arms crossed, Sand next to him, looking no less furious. Her little dog Kaj ran around barking while the turn-born known as Flint and Clay watched from a doorway.

There were three missing: Tooth, Fieldstone, and Chalk. The terst turn-born took their names from what filled their hollow bodies, materials taken from the girl's world. By that, she could be called "A Sei's Tears," a name sure to terrify.

Jenn was a better name. Safer. As was waiting out their tempers.

He'd lived here, as dragon, flightless and in pain. The sei's penance, it had been, before they'd sent him to the girl. When not serving the turn-born, he'd been under the kitchen, waiting to be remembered.

Waiting was wiser, with beings like these.

The grit settled all at once. Someone had finally disagreed. ~Why send you?~ Riverstone demanded.

Wisp and Sand had come to an understanding, over the girl. The rest barely tolerated his presence. Which might have had something to do with why he'd served a penance in the first place. Or simple dislike.

The dragon didn't care. ~She waits for a mask. As instructed.~

These wore masks, with features shaped to resemble man or woman, the terst being like the girl's kind. Riverstone's had a hooked nose and dark eyebrows. Shards of black stone filled his glass shell and white hair crowned his head. Light poured through holes where eyes and mouth should be. ~We have not agreed.~

Wisp looked at Sand. She held out a hand palm up, then tipped it over. Caution, that meant.

He was too old for this. The dragon snarled and advanced into the middle of the open space, wings high and open. ~Would you have her come here without?~

~Our Sweetling wouldn't, and you know it.~ Sand stepped forward; Riverstone hesitated, then moved back, conceding her precedence. ~Why has she come and why with these others, with Bannan and the little cousin?~

Much as he'd have preferred to snap, Wisp could almost hear Jenn's voice. Manners.

He loathed manners.

That said, they'd proven useful, on rare occasion. ~Jenn Nalynn asks your aid. She would cross into Channen with these others. It is a matter of some urgency.~

Riverstone leaned forward. ~She wishes to trade?~

Sand lifted her hand and he eased back again. ~Tell us this urgent matter, Dragon Lord, or is this something to hear from our Sweetling?~

As a man, he could smile and would, at this. Clever Sand. ~She would wish to tell you herself. It is personal and important.~

~Hence the mask.~ Sand turned to her fellows. ~I ask we reconsider.~

~And I ask Jenn come here, alone and not as turn-born, to explain.~

Wisp held in a snarl.

~We do not travel her world as we are in this one,~ countered Sand. ~Why should she? It is neither safe nor politic. What if she encounters other turn-born? Terst?~

~She should go back. Tell her so!~

The dragon let his wings beat, once, stirring the grit. A reminder, lest they forget. Jenn Nalynn had done this.

~We do not order one another,~ Sand told Riverstone. ~We do not interfere with sei. What our Sweetling will or won't isn't ours to say or forbid. Help for her or not, that's for us to decide. I ask we reconsider.~

They stared at one another, then Riverstone made a sharp gesture. ~It is not safe for them here, whatever help we give. I say give her none.~

Had the turn-born worn a throat of flesh at that instant, the dragon would have ripped it out with a joyful roar. However satisfying the thought, it wouldn't achieve what the girl needed. Instead, Wisp folded his wing, using the other to help him stand straight and proud. ~Let me take you to her,~ he offered as pleasantly as he could. ~If you explain the dangers, she might leave.~

The light where Sand would have eyes turned to him, but she said nothing.

Riverstone, less knowing, gave an appeased nod. ~Quickly, then.~

The dragon bowed his head. A man's habit.

Had he been able to smile like a man, he'd have done that too.

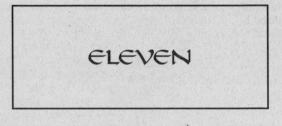

# ELEVEN

$L$IKE THREADS IN a loom, magic wove up and around and through the Verge. Jenn could feel it, almost hold it. Most, the strongest and deepest, was turn-born. How she knew she couldn't have said, but those threads came here, burrowing though the walls of the small settlement, knotted together by will, and she wouldn't touch them.

Though she could. That awareness brimmed in her like spring arriving in the valley, as full of possibilities and potential. Mistress Sand had told her the turn-born worked their expectations to heal and protect the Verge, that she mustn't interfere or more would be undone than she could imagine.

For the first time, Jenn could see it for herself. Was anything here untouched by an expectation? And not just one. Never just one. The more she looked, the more magic warped and twisted; here in what seemed a feather's tip, there through the core of a sleeping neyet, beyond, going wider and wider to encompass a mountain.

"Someone's coming. Dearest Heart? Wake up."

She drew back into herself, thinking of rabbits and meadows with more than a little remorse, and opened her eyes. "Wasn't asleep."

Bannan's eyes held their apple butter glow. "No?"

Jenn gave him a little push as she sat up. Truthseers!

They'd spread their coats on the sand, where it would let them, to go through their packs. After cautious sips from Bannan's flask, mimrol undrinkable according to Wisp, and a shared bit of cheese—though to be honest she'd felt neither hunger nor thirst—they'd tackled the rest.

The shard of mirror remained stubbornly black, with no sign of eyes, so Jenn carefully returned it to her socks. Frann's brooch and the tokens looked no different in the Verge, so Bannan put those away as well. The little bottle of moon potion Peggs had insisted she bring—in case they were stranded a month in a land without—was red instead of yellow, which was curious, but nothing in Bannan's pack appeared to change. The bag of rose petals, Jenn left next to her skin.

As for skin, Jenn had taken a close look at the markings on Bannan's neck. They'd not changed. She'd let out a small shriek when the yling popped its head out of Bannan's hair, four tiny hands gripping the top of his ear. It had disappeared even as the truthseer admitted knowing nothing of its purpose, nor did any of the rest of their small company offer an opinion, other than Wisp, who insisted ylings did as they chose and they should ignore it.

After that, they'd rested. She may have rested more thoroughly than she'd planned, but it was hardly her fault, Bannan's shoulder being very comfortable and comforting. Especially when Scourge had agreed not to give them any more "practice" for a while.

"Who's coming?" Jenn asked.

"Turn-born."

That had her on her feet at once, brushing sand from her clothes. Jenn tucked the strand of hair that refused to stay put behind her ear—again—and made a determined effort to stay as she was.

Mistress Sand and Master Riverstone. As they approached, Jenn stood and waited, seeing Bannan do the same. He had excellent posture, as did Werfol and Semyn when they thought about it, and she stood a little straighter herself, thinking it too.

Then she thought of yesterday and the day before and how the tinkers would miss Frann every bit as much as any in Marrowdell.

Thinking all this, Jenn ran to them, arms outstretched.

She surprised, perhaps shocked them. That didn't stop them from folding her into their embrace, though it felt like being hugged by statues. Jenn burst into tears. "Frann's died. I'm so sorry. She fell ill and passed away."

They stiffened. Then, ~And you did nothing,~ Master Riverstone said, the voice she felt more than heard filled with wonder and warmth. ~Dear Sweetling. Our Jenn. Sand knew, better than any of us.~

~Of course I did.~ Mistress Sand stroked her braids with a hand of glass. ~How is our Lorra?~

~She was there. I was—I was too.~ Jenn sniffed and fought for calm. She'd give them the better news, she thought. It was only fair. ~Wen's with child. So is Peggs.~

~More toys to make this winter,~ Mistress Sand declared and nothing could have eased Jenn's heart more.

These were friends.

They moved apart, at that, to gaze upon one another. ~I'll miss Frann's music.~ Master Riverstone shook his head. ~She had a gift.~

"Bannan's nephew plays beautifully," Jenn assured them.

As one, the turn-born looked at the truthseer. ~'Nephews?'~ Mistress Sand echoed. ~In Marrowdell. Are there aunts and uncles too, now?~

Bannan bowed. When he straightened, he met their regard with his own. ~My sister's boys have taken shelter in Marrowdell. Their parents are the reason we've come.~

After that, it was time to explain.

In the Verge, the turn-born were terrifyingly strange, the glow where eyes should be difficult to meet and impossible to read. Yet they grieved for Frann. By that, Bannan could see them as they'd been in Marrowdell, as friends and help-mates.

Yet dangerous. Ever that. Some things didn't change.

They weren't happy to risk Jenn, or to have Jenn as a risk. The distinction seemed unimportant. Bannan watched her more than them, her face expressive and honest. He feared how trusting she was.

He loved her the more for it. Didn't he face that choice, in the Verge? Fear or love? Everything here pulled at his deeper sense, used it, required it. He felt the strain of that demand, even as what he saw of this astonishing, impossible land tugged at his heart. Was there a limit to what he could stand?

A fear not to be dismissed. "We have to get to Channen."

They turned to look at him. Heart's Blood. He'd spoken aloud. Well, in for it, then. "The mask's important, Jenn, but so is speed."

"Lila," she said and nodded. "Of course." Though it hadn't been his sister in a cell he'd meant.

~The sooner you're out of the Verge, the better,~ Riverstone agreed, for any number of his own reasons.

~You'll be met in Channen. To get there? Speed you'll have,~ Sand promised.

Was that reassuring or terrifying? He'd prefer reassuring; it would most likely prove to be both. "Thank you."

~A mask, though?~ The turn-born faced each other for a moment. Sand looked away first. ~The terst will not. We would, but cannot. You must go without, Sweetling.~

Scourge snorted. ~Tasty.~

By the look on her face, Jenn did her best to ignore the kruar. Bannan, ever conscious of the turn-born, held back what he'd dearly loved to tell the idiot beast, "not helping" being the least of it.

~Elder brother? Elder sister?~

He'd forgotten the toad, in all the rest. The yling as well, though every so often came a tiny pat on his neck as if to remind him. The truthseer glanced down to find the toad had hopped into their midst, close to Jenn's now-bare feet.

The dragon wasn't impressed. ~Rash, little cousin, to interrupt.~

"Wait." Jenn crouched by the toad. "There's something wrong with it."

The toad did appear rounder than usual. Not as if it had

puffed itself up, but as if it had swallowed something too large for its body.

~It makes eggs, ridiculous creature,~ Riverstone stated. ~It has forgotten how to live here.~

~This is no egg-making.~ Wisp rose through the ground, forcing the turn-born to step back. ~Little cousin, what did you eat?~

Its voice was thin, like a thread about to snap. ~There was a moth, elder brother. I was hungry.~

"'A moth?'" Bannan met Jenn's worried look. "Maybe they aren't—" journal writers? parts of a sei? "—the same here," he finished anxiously.

The toad grew rounder still, until its eyes began to bulge more than Bannan would have thought possible. Its legs rose in the air as its belly expanded, clawed toes outstretched in a vain attempt to balance. Ever-so-slowly, the entire toad rocked one way, then the other.

"We have to help it!" Jenn cried.

~We must NOT,~ from Sand.

Jenn bit her lower lip, then gave a reluctant nod.

Wisp's tail curled to stop the toad from rolling away. He brought an eye half the size of the toad to almost touch the toad's bulging one. ~If you die of this making, I will take word to your kin.~

~I am honored, elder brother.~ So faint, Bannan could barely feel the words.

"But you mustn't die," Jenn said quickly. "I'll need you to guard me. I don't want to be eaten."

The toad tried to blink. ~I do my best, elder—~ Suddenly its mouth opened an impossible amount and the dragon leapt out of the way as something vomited out.

Something white and gleaming that spun on end like a tossed coin until, finally, settling to the ground.

The toad, shape and size restored, sighed with relief and closed its eyes.

While Bannan and the others stared down at what was, in fact, a mask. Or rather a face, for this was no crude shape, with holes for eyes and mouth.

This was a face, a face he knew and loved, captured in what might have been the finest shell. The colors of the

Verge played over it, highlighting cheekbones, blushing lips, shadowing eyelids still closed, as if asleep.

~So you are of use, little cousin.~ Scourge sounded amused.

Jenn moved first, picking it up.

~Sweetling, be careful!~ Sand warned. ~This is sei.~

"And mine," Jenn said firmly. Closing her eyes, she pressed it to her face and it was as if the mask winked out of sight. Her eyelids opened. "How does it look?" There was the smallest of tremors in her voice.

Having moved near, though what good he'd be against such magic was an open and worrying question, Bannan traced her jaw with a light finger, feeling soft, warm skin. "It's vanished. How does it feel?" he asked wonderingly.

She smiled, pressing her cheek into his palm. "Like your hand."

~A gift,~ Riverstone observed, his voice distant and cold. ~Why?~

~Why matters not. This is our Sweetling,~ Sand reminded him. ~That she has resources of her own shouldn't be a surprise. But does it work? That we must test.~

Jenn nodded and took a step to put herself away from Bannan. "Are you ready?"

In answer, Riverstone put his arm over his eyes and Sand covered hers with her hands.

Then Bannan found himself standing among beings of glass and light.

Alone in the Verge.

The instant Mistress Sand and Master Riverstone lowered their arms and hands, proof the mask worked, Jenn willed herself flesh again. She'd seen the stricken look on Bannan's face. Worse, she understood it. One of them, he thought her.

"I'll be this," she told him, stroking hands over skin, "unless necessary. I am this, Bannan." Jenn put her desperate hope into the words. She'd remember, she promised herself. She would. He must.

And he heard, she knew it, but believe? After years in

the marches, he could school his expression to show what he wanted and nothing more. Was the calm acceptance he showed her now a sham? Did he doubt her?

Bannan merely said, "Then we're ready to go to Channen."

~Keep wearing that,~ Master Riverstone advised.

Advice she couldn't help but heed. What they'd seen as a mask on the ground, what had shape and heft in her grip, was part of her. She'd felt it bond to what was within her, to the sei's tears.

Ending any question as to the sort of moth the poor toad had swallowed.

"Thank you for what you've done, little cousin," she told it, though it hardly had had a choice and now appeared asleep.

~I matter to Jenn Nalynn.~

She had to smile. "Yes, you do."

Wisp waited, silent, as did Scourge, for a wonder, both now at a distance and behind the turn-born. Jenn looked to Bannan.

By the light of the Verge, the amber of his eyes was darker, richer. Having dressed for the warmth, he wore a shirt, the neck loosely tied, leather pants, and tall boots. He stood with his arms slightly away from his body, his feet apart, as if his instincts told him to run, yet he smiled back at her.

He stayed. It was enough. Jenn turned to Mistress Sand. "What do we do now?" she asked simply.

A hand lifted. ~Go around the lake and up the slope. Wait by our spring for your guides. You can refill your flasks there.~

Bannan looked relieved. "Good to know. I'd planned to ask about water."

~We've put it where we need it and the terst, though most here drink mimrol.~

~Or blood.~ From the dragon and kruar.

"And food, Mistress?" he asked.

Master Riverstone shrugged. ~If you're in the Verge long enough to starve, it'll be too long and too late.~

Jenn didn't like the sound of that at all. "What do you mean?"

~There are things you can eat, Bannan,~ Mistress Sand said quickly. ~Ask your guides. Sweetling, you may feel you can live without food or drink and you can, longer than most, but not forever. Don't forget.~

They made beer from Marrowdell's grain. Enjoyed feasting. There was more to being a turn-born than a shell and magic, much of which familiar, and the reminder warmed a part of Jenn she hadn't noticed had gone cold.

"Then we should go." Jenn held out her hands, for Mistress Sand to clasp, and Master Riverstone. "Unless you've more advice?" She glanced at Bannan.

Whose rueful smile this time was real. "We'd take any and all."

Master Riverstone gave her fingers a last gentle squeeze, then let go. ~Move quickly through the Verge, is mine. Do nothing to attract notice. Ignore this mirror creature.~

Jenn tensed. She'd told them of the eyes and efflet; shown them the shard from the mirror, which had, perhaps now fearfully, remained black. ~What if he doesn't ignore us?~

A disturbingly happy snarl from the dragon.

Mistress Sand patted her hand. ~We've said we don't know this thing you've seen. If we do not, it's of no consequence, Sweetling. They die here, man or woman or child, too quickly to notice. Till now or yet, that is.~ The turn-born pointedly didn't look toward Bannan. ~If this mirror holds anything of this fool who crossed long ago, it's naught but a spiteful echo.~

Jenn nodded dutifully, hiding her doubt. Oh, how she wanted to believe what she'd seen was harmless, but hadn't Wisp warned her, often, that the turn-born of the Verge didn't always tell the truth? Even if they did, she suspected a certain arrogance. That what turn-born didn't know, couldn't be important?

Aunt Sybb had a great deal to say on the topic of willful ignorance, none of it flattering.

Mistress Sand clicked the tongue she didn't have. ~As for my advice? I repeat Riverstone's. The Verge is what it is. I add my own. We've arrangements in Channen. Follow the one who waits at the crossing, but be wary. Expectations go awry there. Too much of the Verge, might be. Too much

magic in those living there, might be as well. Most are
friendly folk and good traders, minding their own business.~ Darker. ~There's others, too interested for any one's
good. Know the difference, Sweetling and truthseer. Or you
won't cross back.~

Oh, dear. Yes, they'd spoken of magic in the Shadow District, but Jenn had imagined trinkets like the pendant or at
most wishings, like the ones Kydd teased Peggs about, to
produce larger babies or smooth wrinkles. Nothing of the
Verge.

Nothing to put either of them at risk.

When Jenn looked at Bannan, he dipped his head in a
grim nod. He'd known, or feared it.

He'd lived with his own magic, concealing it at risk of his
life. Though the thought was chilling, Jenn nodded back.
"Thank you for your kindness. We will take very great
care."

~Around the lake and up the slope, then,~ Mistress Sand
repeated. ~With luck, you won't meet any broods.~

With that, she and Master Riverstone turned and left.

Jenn and Bannan looked at one another.

"'Broods' of what?" he mouthed, eyes wide with mock
horror.

She couldn't help it.

Laughing, she took him in her arms.

They couldn't leave the sleepy house toad, so Bannan put it
into his pack, Jenn helping. Their fingers touched and min-
gled in the process, both chuckling at the awkwardness of
the limp creature. What had come between them—what
he'd put between them—was gone and he was beyond
grateful. They'd talk, he decided, losing himself in the wells
of beauty that were her eyes.

~Hurry. Hurry!~ the dragon snapped, though he seemed
in better temper. The mask had helped.

As had the departure of the turn-born.

Bannan kissed the tip of Jenn's nose before they both
stood. "Hurry it is." He looked over at Scourge.

Who deliberately pretended something moved in the—they weren't bushes, being more like fur, but had flowers, or were they eyes?

He made the effort to look deeper, rewarded by flowers again.

"Bannan?"

"Hurry it is," he agreed. If they weren't to ride, it'd be walking.

Walking it was. The sand curved away from the lake, as a beach couldn't, becoming a road of sorts, if you watched where you stepped. Jenn hinted such roadmaking was within a turn-born's power, and Bannan decided to be grateful.

There being shadows away from the lake he didn't care for at all.

Scourge padded alongside. Wisp, with his two ruined limbs, had taken flight. Bannan lost him in a stream of flowing silver, a river of mimrol now overhead.

"Do things change all the time?" he complained mildly.

Jenn grinned. "It seems so. But I feel," her grin faded as she thought, "it's more about what can be seen, at any time. I'm glad we've guides."

Guides they hadn't met and didn't know. "Are we sure we'll be able to see them?" he asked, only half joking. "Maybe Wisp and Scourge should stay with us."

~No.~ The dragon.

Taken aback, as he was, Jenn stared into the sky. "Wisp?"

~Once you are with those the turn-born have sent, I've another duty.~ From sharp and adamant, almost harsh, Wisp's tone gentled. ~If you need me, I will know. I will come. Never doubt that, Dearest Heart.~

Bannan stopped walking. "What about the boys? What of Werfol?" Surely the dragon had a soft spot.

~MINE!~

Ancestors Greedy and Gluttonous, if that wasn't predictable? "So you'll abandon us too." He was more relieved than otherwise; not something to tell the kruar.

Scourge rolled a red-rimmed eye. ~I will stay with my new truthseer. You may die here.~

Jenn's mouth formed a shocked "O." Bannan grinned. "I

can see you've thought it through. Just promise me you'll look after Semyn and Tir as well."

~They are mine.~ With affront he'd had to ask.

Jenn's lips closed into a firm line. No one was dying, that meant. He couldn't argue.

A short while later they came to what Bannan would have very much liked to argue with, and loudly. He and Jenn tipped their heads back as far as they could, trying to see to the top. "Slope, she called it? It's a bloody cliff!"

The rock reared from the sandy path, its surface veined in green, bronze, and black, sheer and glistening as if wet. The top, if there was a top, was lost in cloud.

Cloud that had a disturbing tendency to flock and whirl.

"We can walk up it." Jenn turned to him, eyes alight. "If Mistress Sand said to go this way, she'd expect it to be possible. They would have made it possible, Bannan. The turn-born."

With those words, she lifted her slender foot, toes spread, and put it against the rock. As if taking a normal step, her other foot rose to meet its mate and Jenn Nalynn stood out from the cliff, her skirt floating in midair. She laughed and waved to him. "It's wonderful, Bannan. Try it." She took more steps, quickly beyond where he could reach if he jumped.

Tiny hands patted him encouragingly. "Fine for you," the truthseer muttered. "You've wings."

"Bannan!" Heart's Blood, she was almost out of sight.

This was—Ancestors Mad and Delirious—this was the Verge. Tightening the straps on his pack, Bannan planted his boot against the rock.

It was like tipping on a plank. Suddenly, the foot on the rock was the foot on flat ground, while his other was stuck up behind him. Bannan staggered more than stepped forward, putting both feet on the cliff.

Which was now a road, easy and flat as could be.

Yet nót. When he tried moving faster than a steady walk, he lost his balance and almost fell backward.

Jenn, well ahead, or above, looked back—or was it down?—at him. He couldn't make out her expression, but her wave seemed cheery enough. "Almost there!" she called, and he smiled, waving back.

It was around that moment that Bannan realized the rock supporting his feet was occupied.

By things with teeth.

Ancestors Elated and Exhilarated. The more time she spent in the Verge, the more amazed Jenn found herself. The more at home. Not that this was her home, but she'd been more than a little anxious about this other world, being such a stranger to it.

But it welcomed her with open arms. Hadn't she the all-important mask, to make her acceptable to those who lived here, and now walked up a wall with ease? Being in the Verge, Jenn decided, was like being inside a story, one filled with unexpected wonders at every turn of the page. Pleased by the thought, she glanced back at Bannan and waved. He returned the gesture with a brave smile, being something of a wonder himself.

However the Verge appeared to her, she shouldn't assume it seemed the same to Bannan. They'd need to compare their observations, like the worthy explorers who'd mapped the roads through Upper Rhoth or sailed across the Sweet Sea to discover Eld. Were there seas here? Other domains than the turn-borns'? With each footstep, Jenn happily came up with more and more possibilities, though she—reluctantly—dismissed the notion of drawing a map. How could a road that went up as well as away fit on paper?

Not to mention a road that, just ahead, disappeared into a cloud that spun and whirled and—Jenn blinked.

Wasn't a cloud at all.

Running was out of the question. As, Bannan discovered, was walking on tiptoe. So, however reluctantly, he continued to plant each boot against what felt solid but, more and more, swam with things.

Things with teeth. He couldn't tell more about them, for their bodies, assuming they had bodies, blended into the colors streaking through the rock itself. The teeth, though, were regrettable—white and brilliant. Small, but sharp. They circled and gathered, like obscene little smiles.

Heart's Blood. Bannan wrenched his eyes from where he stepped, and what on, to stare determinedly ahead. Nothing for it but to reach Jenn Nalynn.

But where was she?

Something bumped his boot.

Another something.

He had to look down again. Ancestors Harried and Helpless! They were—they were eating his boots!

Regardless of the real threat of falling off the road—for falling might be an improvement—Bannan moved faster, wheeling his arms to keep his balance. Each time his foot touched, there'd be one or more bumps. The boots were—had been—his favorites and new, with thick soles. Ancestors Witness. Would they be thick enough?

One of the little smiles broke free of the rock, like a fish jumping into air, narrowly missing his hand!

Proving—oh, yes—there was a body belonging to that wicked set of teeth. A body he recognized, however much smaller and stubbier.

Dragon!

Brood, Sand had warned. He'd walked right into it, hadn't he?

Bannan shouted, half-warning, half-plea. "Jenn!"

More dragonlings erupted from the rock to snap at him, nipping holes in his shirt, pulling at his hair. The yling appeared on his shoulder, brandishing a spear, and accounted for one that fell tumbling through the sky, but there were more.

They were small and seemed able only to jump, then plunge back. Small mercy, Bannan discovered as he used his hands to protect his face. Their teeth resembled a rabbit's, rather than Wisp's long fangs, but were as sharp as they looked. The bag over his shoulders protected his back but confined the little cousin, whose desperate wriggles to join the battle threatened Bannan's balance.

All while the brood ripped and tore at his clothing, as if tearing away skin. It would take only the taste of blood, Bannan feared, to send them into a frenzy.

"Jenn—!" but she'd left him behind, surely thinking him safe.

A slash opened his cheek, spilling warm blood down his shirt. Bannan hunched, arms over his face, but his arms simply became the new target.

*Crunch.*

The attacks ceased. He lowered his arms only to flinch as most of a full-size dragon flew by his face and into the rock, the young scattering.

Flinched and might have fallen but for the mass behind him. Bannan grabbed for Scourge as the kruar snapped up a hapless dragonling. Once the truthseer felt steady, he voiced a heartfelt, "Couldn't have got here a moment sooner, could you? Before they were eating me?"

~Sooner and there wouldn't be enough.~ Another snap and capture. With purring.

"'Enough—?'" As if to answer his question, Wisp's head appeared from the rock, jaws crammed with little bodies, then slipped back again. "—oh," Bannan finished, now distinctly queasy. So dragons ate their young. Here he'd been pleased to have one sleep with his nephews.

Something he might not tell Lila.

Using a sleeve of his dragonling-shredded shirt, Bannan wiped the blood from his cheek, ignoring the rest. Shallow, the cuts. He rued the lost clothing more. "Where's Jenn? Is she all right?"

~Why wouldn't she be?~ as if he'd asked something ridiculous.

Maybe he had. Bannan sighed and started walking up—along—the rock again. By the feel of his feet, he'd need new boots as well as clothes. "Aren't you coming?" he asked, when Scourge didn't move with him.

~Tasty!~

Not for the first time, Bannan was grateful the old kruar didn't think the same about his rider.

Not that he'd mentioned, anyway.

Of course, Scourge was far from the only kruar in the Verge, as Wisp wasn't the only adult dragon.

Wasn't that a thought to put a shiver down the spine?

~

*A sliver of paper, touched by ink and finger's tip . . . a drop
of sleep, under the tongue . . .
And the dream unfolds . . .*
Up is down and behind is before and nothing is but
madness—
Nothing is but madness—
Nothing is—
*The dream breaks . . .*

Jenn was delighted to discover, upon closer inspection, that
what she'd thought a cloud was composed of dragons that
would fit in her hand. Like a flock of late-summer birds,
they flew in vast murmurations, tails and wings in constant
motion. Some flew higher than she could see, while others
plunged into the rock and disappeared.

On impulse, Jenn held out her hands as she might to
birds, but the baby dragons—was that the right word?—
were too shy to approach, though heads turned to watch
her as they passed and she thought a couple were tempted.

Bannan wasn't far behind, so he should see them too.
She hoped so; a flock of baby dragons surely a marvel even
in the Verge.

Ahead the rock split apart, a third bending up again—or
was it over—and the rest verging at a tangent to the right.
Between was something new.

Yet almost ordinary. It looked to be a grassy meadow,
surrounded by what she decided to call trees, in lieu of a
proper name for what had a woody trunk like a tree, but
instead of branches sprouted clumps of black feathers. The
feathers met at the tops, forming a canopy a little like a
night sky, complete with stars.

Stars that were ylings, who danced overhead, their hair
afire with light. Entranced, Jenn stepped from rock to
meadow.

With a startled gasp, the meadow being a far higher step
than she'd thought to take. It took her a moment to regain
her balance. She'd have to watch for Bannan and warn him
about that.

The short brown grass was pleasantly soft underfoot and

warm. The meadow itself, now that she stood within it, stretched like an open, welcoming hand, each finger and thumb a path whose end she couldn't see from where she stood.

While the palm was a depression, with a round fountain in its midst; a fountain so like those of Marrowdell Jenn didn't need the tangle of turn-born expectation to tell her who'd made it. She started walking toward it, then stopped to look back, abruptly uneasy.

"Bannan?"

He should be mere steps behind her. Mere steps—but what did that mean in the Verge? Where was he?

Jenn ran back to where the meadow ended and rock began, only to find herself confronted by tree trunks and darkening shadows. Their road was gone.

What had she done?

He was to be *here*. Now and *safe! WITH HER!*

Every wish she began slammed into *DENIAL* until she stopped, gasping, and fell to her knees. "I wasn't to leave him," Jenn whispered. "Ancestors Blessed and Beloved, how could I have left him?"

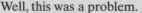

Well, this was a problem.

Bannan considered the wall of—stalks, he decided to call them—that had sprung into existence around him between one step and the next. They were topped by silky black feathers, like one of Lorra's hats, and seemed harmless.

He'd keep his distance.

As best he could. They grew, or sprouted, or stood, no more than two arm's lengths apart, though some touched and others merged. The ground was covered in what appeared brown fur—and might be—leaving him grateful for what remained of his boots.

Closing his eyes, he rubbed them with thumb and forefinger, seeking relief from the strain. Never before had his deeper sight cost him like this. Then again, Bannan thought ruefully, he'd not wandered a world where he'd needed to look deeper simply to see where to put his feet.

Pat. Pat.

Dropping his hand, he opened his eyes to find a yling—his yling—hovering just out of reach. It faced him, two hands gripping the barbed spear it had used to such good effect, another holding a shield made from polished acorn shell. Yling possessed two pairs of arms and one pair of legs, with hands at the ends of each. Its remaining three hands were held empty and open. He, for this was certainly male, wore a cape of purple aster petals. Wisp's doing, Bannan remembered.

Hair like threads of glass stood out from the yling's head; dark eyes regarded him.

Waiting. For what?

Bannan bowed, leaving his hand over his heart, fingers and thumb forming a circle. "By the Hearts of my Ancestors, accept my thanks for your courage, my friend."

The yling tipped his head, light splintering into rainbows around it.

How much did the creatures understand? "I must find Jenn Nalynn," Bannan said hopefully. "Can you help me?"

"Can I help you?"

The voice, querulous and high-pitched, seemed to come from everywhere at once. The yling dove into the truthseer's hair. As Bannan whirled around, searching in vain for the source, the house toad warned, ~Do not answer! Do NOT!~

"Can I?" the voice said again, abruptly high overhead. "Will I, is the better question."

~Let me out,~ demanded the toad. ~Our elder sister is near. Do not believe him!~

Good advice, Bannan decided grimly. The disembodied voice grated unpleasantly along every nerve; he needn't see who spoke to feel ill intent. He unslung the pack, tearing open the ties. The toad burst out between his hands to land on the furry ground, puffed and battle-ready.

Nostrils flared and red, Scourge plunged into the clearing, shattering wood to clear an opening. Plumes of black fluttered up and away, frightened from their hold. A furious wind followed on the kruar's heels, whirling splinters into a dizzying wall. The dragon's roar sent Bannan to his knees, hands over his ears, wondering why the ground hadn't shattered as well.

~SHOW YOURSELF!~

Jenn sat on one of the stones ringing the fountain, facing the direction Bannan should come. She'd tried to push her way to him through the trees and managed only to scrape the skin of her arms and tear the bodice of her dress. It was Peggs' second-best and, while she greatly regretted the tear, her sister did have a baby growing inside. Having witnessed the blossoming of Hettie's bosom, Jenn supposed Peggs was unlikely to fit into the dress again for at least a while.

Not that she truly cared about clothes at the moment. Ancestors Despondent and Despairing. She'd left Bannan behind. How could she have been so—so absentminded!?

The Verge. It sang through her. Songs of magic. Of wonders! Foolish, foolish to let the new and strange claim her attention, and now Bannan—

Jenn folded her hands just so, careful of the knuckle with the long scratch, prepared to sit on the stone as long as necessary. She'd done harm enough moving around. Those lost would stay lost, Uncle Horst had impressed upon all the children of Marrowdell, unless they stayed to be found.

She hoped she was the one lost and alone. If she couldn't sense where Bannan was, she supposed that made him a bit lost too, but surely he was with Wisp and Scourge. And the little cousin, not to be forgotten, as well as the yling.

Not that she could guess what use a yling, however brave, might be, nor why the tiny thing had climbed into Bannan's hair in the first place and crossed with them.

Though the man did have lovely hair. Thick, with waves Hettie envied. Soft to the touch—

This was no time to daydream about Bannan's hair, Jenn scolded herself, then sighed, a little. She'd been proud to think herself his protector. A splendid job she was doing of that. So much for being an all-powerful turn-born. Really, she wondered, how did they ever get anything done in the Verge, if they would disagree with something so simple as "please find my love" or "bring us back together?"

"Aren't you the lovely one?"

Jenn jumped, then looked around wildly. A voice! And not an inner one such as Mistress Sand's or a toad's, nor was it a breeze in her ear; this was, in fact, a real voice. A voice needed someone to speak it—

She was alone in the meadow.

Alone and uneasier by the moment, whether at the over-bold compliment or the voice itself, that being rather dry and dusty-seeming. Though perhaps the speaker didn't have the chance to speak very often. Didn't Master Jupp regularly need to clear his throat before any sound would come out?

"Can't you talk?" the voice said, its tone become one of pity.

"Of course I can." Problem was, what would be safe to say to such a strange voice? "Where are you?"

"Where are you, Lovely One?"

She cared even less for the flattery the second time. "My name's Jenn." Something told her to give it nothing more. "I'm here waiting for my friends." There. Now the voice knew she wasn't alone.

Though she was.

"'Friends.'" It said the word oddly, as if it had an unfamiliar taste. "Won't you, Lovely Jenn, be my friend?"

Friends, Jenn knew full well, were important. Aunt Sybb said true poverty was being friendless; though she'd add it wasn't easy to tell a true friend from false, then frequently go on to comment darkly on friendship being a poor gauge of trust. Their Poppa would remind his daughters, quietly and in private, that their aunt had lost friends during the exile and some of those, she'd loved dearly.

Thinking of Aunt Sybb and her family stiffened Jenn's spine. "Who are you?" she demanded.

*Rustlerustle.*

Heart's Blood!

She would not be afraid. She would not. Now she had "who."

Where was he?

Jenn pushed aside her dread, determined to find this sneak. This was her magic and the turn-born could not deny her.

There!

Too close for comfort. Much too close. Moving very

slowly, she looked over her shoulder into the water of the fountain.

And into great yellow eyes.

"Got you!" exulted the voice.

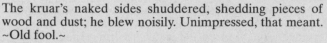

The kruar's naked sides shuddered, shedding pieces of wood and dust; he blew noisily. Unimpressed, that meant. ~Old fool.~

The dragon, having made himself visible, stalked back and forth, violence in his eyes. ~I'm the fool?~ His claws shredded the ground. ~You were to wait in ambush!~

~For you to scare him off?~

Letting the powerful beings bicker, not that he could stop them, Bannan settled his pack and tucked the house toad under one arm, where it seemed content. Done, he stood in the middle of the clearing and raised his forefinger.

Scourge's head lowered and turned to fix him with an abashed-looking eye. Wisp halted, claws deep in brown fuzz that, on too-close inspection, appeared to bleed.

"Where's Jenn?" Spoken, Bannan thought proudly, like a man both calm and collected. A man with priorities. Someone sensible.

~Where you were told to go.~ As if all this—all of it!—was his fault?

The truthseer abandoned calm. "Bloody idiots, the pair of you! Where's that?" He shook a fist under the dragon's long and deadly snout. "Is she there? Do you know? Is she safe?" He turned to Scourge. "And what were you after? That foul voice? Ancestors Misbegotten and Malicious, what was that?!" He was shouting. Who wouldn't be shouting! "You used me as bait AGAIN!"

~You haven't been eaten yet,~ Wisp pointed out smugly.

Scourge lifted his head, a noble curve to his neck. ~Tasty!~

Ancestors Witness, he'd give anything to tie their tails together. Was that within a turn-born's magic? He'd be delighted to request the favor, when next he had the chance.

Hoping for that chance, Bannan emphasized each word. "Take me to Jenn. Now."

~ 'Now?'~ Scourge.

~We're hunting!~ Wisp.

Though one pair was red and somewhat beady, the other whorls of wild purple, their eyes gave him the same astonished look.

Maybe he could find a way to ram them down each other's throats! As Bannan drew breath for another, likely useless, shout, the toad shifted under his arm. ~Elder brother, General, forgive my intrusion, but I too must go. The man you hunt seeks Jenn Nalynn. I am her protector!~

"'Man?'" Bannan heard himself as if from a distance. As Captain Ash, he'd felt the same exceptional clarity when his patrol entered the darkness close to their enemy, or when an interrogation drove past lies to some horrible truth. It washed away every emotion, leaving only focus and deadly will, and he was grateful—oh, yes—for that now. "Another man. Here," he stated grimly. "What is he? Another truthseer?"

The house toad, after a courteous hesitation for others to answer, launched itself into its own without breath or pause. ~Do you not know of the Lost One, truthseer? Who lived in your house and brought the mirror and was named Crumlin Tralee before he crossed at the cataract using magic he stole, and thought dead then though now, according to the efflet, isn't dead and never was and seeks our turn-born for her magic? How they know I cannot say, but I will protect—~

~Peace, little cousin.~ The dragon padded forward until the heat from his breath stirred Bannan's hair. ~What we hunt was once a man. What he is now?~ Somehow Wisp put the feel of a careless shrug into the words. ~A threat. One whose strength we don't know and the turn-born deny. Whatever he is, I will end.~

"I know the name." Bannan heard himself say. Crumlin. The man who'd led Great Gran and her family, those other families, to Marrowdell. Who'd been left behind.

Lost.

Heart's Blood. The mirror. Great Gran had meant it as a kindness; he'd seen the truth in her wrinkled face. "Why didn't you tell us?" Beyond betrayal, this. Or was it? Ancestors Witness, he was nose-to-snout with a dragon. But not any dragon. "You claim to value honor and duty," Bannan said harshly. "You've betrayed both!"

Wisp's long head turned so Bannan gazed into one wild eye and he spoke next as a breeze, hot and fetid and intimate. "Tell Jenn Nalynn a villager from Marrowdell has been lost in the Verge—trapped here—most of his life. Tell her I intend to eat his heart before he can so much as think to do her harm. What would she do, Bannan Larmensu? What will you?" The dragon moved back, jaws agape. "Now that you've a name and know our prey was once of your flesh, what does your honor and duty demand? Does it differ from mine?"

Bannan held to his dark focus, made himself hear what Wisp told him, forced himself to think. No innocent settler, this Crumlin Tralee, nor charlatan selling tokens in the market. The mirror—the rest of it—was proof they faced what was exceedingly rare in Rhoth, a true wielder of magic. More than that, a wielder who'd come to Marrowdell for his own purpose, like those who'd almost destroyed the valley.

As for the mirror? Bespelled to return or by unfortunate chance, it had given Crumlin a window into Marrowdell, to see the magic that was Jenn Nalynn. Yes, she'd destroyed it, but would she have, knowing the truth about its owner?

Would he?

Let alone how best to deal with Crumlin in the Verge, other than by the dragon's clear preference. "What is he now?" Bannan asked grimly. "Could he return to our world?"

~To survive in this one, who knows what he's become?~ Wisp balanced on his good legs and spread his wings. ~Well?~

"We're not your bait," Bannan snapped, then curled his arm more securely under the toad. "We find Jenn. We cross into Channen. And hope Crumlin Tralee has the wisdom to leave us alone, having seen who hunts him."

Those hunters regarded him, waiting for the rest.

"If he doesn't," the truthseer said at last, sure and cold, "we'll revisit the question of who eats his heart."

Scourge began to purr.

"You haven't 'got me,'" Jenn informed the eyes, being quite firm about it. "I found you."

A blink. *Rustlerustle*. The voice, still disembodied and seemingly from everywhere at once, chuckled as if she'd surprised it, but it was an uncomfortable sound, as though laughter was more foreign to the voice than speech. "Say we've found one another, Lovely Jenn. I'd prefer we not argue. About this. About anything."

She'd argue about not arguing, but that seemed pointless. Jenn stared into the water, but the eyes sat within the sky's many-colored reflection, as if they rode those heights.

She glanced skyward, to be sure she wasn't looking at a reflection, but there were only the myriad colors of the Verge, a rock or two floating high, and the black plumes of the trees surrounding her.

Plumes filled with watching ylings. They clung to the tips by one hand or two and weren't at all like the ylings she was used to in Marrowdell. These wore black feathers instead of petals or leaves and more than a few held shields that looked disturbingly like the fine silver scales along Wisp's back. There were tiny swords that might have been teeth and those without swords carried spears twice the length of their bodies.

"I—"

A hard cold grasp jerked her back toward the fountain! She looked down, horrified to find a metal band clamped around her arm from wrist to elbow. From it depended a chain, a chain that ended at the surface of the water.

While within the water, the eyes, once slit, had dilated and become round, like black pits. "Got you!" Another jerk on the chain.

Her free hand scrabbled over stone, unable to find a crack or crevice to grip, and her upper body was already at the fountain's edge. Another pull and she'd be over. Jenn pressed her knees against the outer wall, trying to use her own weight for leverage.

*Freeze!* she wished the water, but the expectation that

had built it wouldn't be denied. *BEGONE!* she wished the eyes, but they weren't really here and didn't obey.

"Help!" she shouted. "Help me!"

"I am helping," crooned the voice. "And soon you'll help me, Lovely Jenn. Come closer. Come."

"Bannan! Wisp!"

Jenn felt herself slipping. Felt the lines of an unseen net fall around her, taking her breath, taking her. She made herself turn-born and it made no difference.

The hunter laughed.

Bannan fell more than stepped into the open, losing both his balance and grip on the toad. The toad landed without difficulty, being used to flying through the air. The truthseer caught himself. "You couldn't — " he sputtered.

"Bannan! Wisp!"

"Jenn!"

Heart's Blood. She lay facedown over the edge of a stone-rimmed fountain, struggling! Bannan broke into a run . . .

Even as the toad hopped as quickly as it could and the yling flew from his hair and up, spear raised . . .

As Scourge plunged by him, joined by two other kruar out of nowhere, their crests intact and glittering like swords. The three roared and snarled as one . . .

Hair like flame, ylings dropped from above, converging on the fountain . . .

All to be tossed aside by the dragon.

Who got there first.

~MINE THE DEATH!~ Wisp roared as he hurled himself at what dared attack the girl, permitting nothing to get in his way.

Were those CHAINS?

He crashed sidelong into the fountain, jaws snapping at the metal. It gave, as did most of the bones in one leg and wing, the turn-borns' cursed creation being nothing like honest stone. Heedless, he pushed Jenn back and away, only then to feel the bindings of a net.

For something weaker. For something younger and foolish. For something that wasn't a lord among dragons!

Wisp sent breezes to rip the netting to shreds, snarling in fury. With his good wing, he spiraled up a bodylength, then two.

Then turned midair to plummet down at the eyes.

Instinct tried to stop him, warn him, make him flinch. The fountain was floored by the turn-borns' making and impenetrable. He couldn't pass through it.

Her enemy was there!

~DEATH!~ Wisp roared, oblivious to fear.

# TWELVE

$D$EAFENED BY THE dragon's roar, Jenn scrambled back to the fountain. Wisp was overhead now; somehow he turned, and she knew, to the core of her being, he was going after the eyes.

She couldn't stop him, not in time.

She gripped the stone, laced with turn-born magic, and wished. *LET HIM PASS!*

*Denial . . . denial . . .* the fountain was old, reworked, the voice of its magic distant, almost bored. Yet strong. Too strong.

A moth landed near her hand, or did she only think of a moth? Did she only imagine blue around her and the peace of that room?

Did she feel as large as a mountain? Or was she a speck . . .

Whatever Jenn imagined, just as Wisp, claws outstretched and jaws agape, hit the water of the fountain, with all her heart she *wanted* him safe.

Her hands sank through dust as the stone crumbled away.

The wind of the dragon's passing knocked her backward, but she saw Wisp go into the ground as if it were sky.

She'd done it.

Bannan caught Jenn in his arms as she staggered back, as the fountain collapsed, and the dragon, maddened and magnificent, drove himself into the earth with a roar like thunder. For moments afterward, he held her steady, or she, him. It didn't matter which, so long as they were together and holding, nor did it matter where.

What had she done? The fountain was the turn-borns', twin to the one in his farmyard, yet Jenn had destroyed it with a touch.

How—? That he'd seen for himself. Felt as well. The moth's writing had *writhed* on his neck, coming alive as Jenn Nalynn, for the briefest of moments, somehow became larger than the meadow.

Perhaps the world.

Ancestors Simple and Sane. He could fear such power. Likely should. Except that it filled the woman he loved and trusted with all his heart, so Bannan gave her a squeeze and chuckled. "You couldn't wait till I refilled the flasks?"

Jenn lifted her face to him. Though her eyes were huge and purpled with magic, she'd the beginnings of an adorable frown. "You're worried about—?"

Bannan interrupted with a kiss he'd meant to be light, but became hungry and nigh on fierce. She responded in kind, for they'd come too close to losing one another and this was but the beginning of their journey, and he felt as though he drowned in glory—

~There is water, truthseer, elder sister.~

They broke apart, gasping and giddy, to stare at the little cousin at their feet. Jenn's toad, Bannan thought, his heart pounding, best learn when not to comment or he'd stuff him in his pack again.

"Bannan, look!"

He followed her pointing finger in time to watch the fountain unfold like a flower where it had been, as it had been.

Water sparkled, reflecting the sky.

~Old fool.~ Scourge dipped his muzzle in the fountain, blowing bubbles. Not done, he stepped into it. Water lapped to his knees, no higher.

"I can't find him," Jenn said hopelessly.

"Wisp won't give up this chase," Bannan replied, thinking he knew what she meant.

"Him." She held up her slender left arm, encased in a dark metal band. Three links of chain hung from it and she caught those in her free hand to silence their rattle.

Ancestors Defiled and Disgraced! Such rage flooded him at the sight of the thing, Bannan knew himself as capable as the dragon of tearing out Crumlin's heart.

If not of eating it.

"Let me see," he said, or tried to say. Jenn nodded, standing still while he examined every part of it once, then again, searching in vain for a release mechanism or weakness. In his own world, he'd have guessed it iron, cold forged. Crude work or careless. The surface bore the marks as if shaped by a hammer, but fit her arm like a second skin.

Bannan stroked the back of her hand. "I see no way to remove it." Other than by whatever magic had bound her. Heart's Blood. If the dragon killed Crumlin, would the cursed band be fixed in place or disappear? He could come to loath all things magic.

Except that the greatest he knew regarded him tenderly, and gave a brave little shrug. "It doesn't hurt. But what of this?" Her fingers took firm hold of his chin, turning it to see the full extent of the bloody gash that ran from above his ear to near his lips.

He'd almost forgotten. "I learned where dragons come from," he quipped. "I'm fine, Dearest Heart. Scratches, that's all."

"Ancestors Witness. These are not 'scratches!'"

Nothing would do after that but a thorough examination, which he might have enjoyed under other circumstances. Once she discovered the bites on his arms, Jenn pushed him to sit by the fountain and eased the pack from his shoulders before helping to remove his shirt.

What was left of his shirt, and that a bloody mess. "It looks worse than it is," the truthseer insisted. "They were very small dragons." He decided not to tell her of their fate.

"With sharp teeth." Jenn bent to tear a clean strip from her dress, itself rent in a few places. One of those provided a distracting view of round soft flesh and, catching his look, she gave the bodice an irritated tug. "It can be mended. I hope."

"We'll look a pretty pair in Channen," Bannan said lightly, but it was a problem. He'd one more shirt, but Jenn's sack looked too small for a second dress. Not that fashions from Marrowdell would match the latest Naalish trends, but walking any city street in a torn garment would attract the wrong sort of attention.

Jenn dipped the strip in the water, though not without a shudder, and began cleaning his wounds, starting with one on his upper back he'd not noticed. "I've a shawl," she mused. "What about your boots?"

He stuck a toe through a hole, then pulled off what were, in truth, more the memory of good boots than usable footwear, tossing them aside. "At least we've found our guides."

The pair of kruar stood at a distance from Scourge, crests erect in continued alarm. Or respect. From what Bannan had seen of their kind, these were smaller than most, similar in size to Perrkin. There the resemblance to anything so safe as a horse ended.

Save for the saddles on their backs. Mistress Sand's "guides" in truth though, from the looks on their long faces, they didn't think much of that duty.

The truthseer couldn't blame them. Scourge's unhindered presence likely didn't help. He wore naught by a harness of scars, given to him by his own kind when they'd ripped the armor from his body, the leader's penance for having lost the war. That he'd survived that torture, to battle in another world and return, had only elevated Scourge among kruar.

Whose attention presently flitted between the old kruar and—more often now—him.

Oh, and didn't he know why? His wounds were minor but many and, no doubt thanks to the dragonlings, continued to ooze red. "Can you stop the bleeding?" Bannan asked very quietly, even as nostrils flared to catch more scent and Scourge rumbled a warning deep in his chest.

Jenn's eyes widened in understanding, then narrowed. "I can stop them."

"While a comfort, Dearest Heart, believe me, them we need."

~Worry not, truthseer, elder sister,~ the toad assured them pleasantly. ~All will be mended.~

"*All?*" Something stung Bannan in the back, then pulled. "Ouch!" He craned his head around to see, but Jenn was there first.

She smiled and settled back on the stone. "Hold still."

Another sting. Another! "*Hold still?*"

A yling appeared too near his face, needles in its—her—hands. She patted his gashed cheek, then began to stitch.

Gentler stitches than Tir's, if it came to it. Bannan held still as the creatures worked, quickly discovering that as each wound was sewn shut its pain vanished too. Could have used that skill after a patrol, when they sat to trade stitching favors.

On those who could be stitched.

Ancestors Doubtful and Dumbfounded, how many more escapes before the Verge claimed them?

And where was the dragon?

At first, watching the ylings sewing Bannan's flesh back together had made Jenn queasy, though she'd seen Covie do the same for her father after an accident with his chisel. That wound had healed, leaving a long scar.

She felt better when she noticed where the ylings passed needle and thread, Bannan's skin might have never been cut, save for the few smears of blood. The seamstresses worked with blinding speed, pausing only to pat him every so often.

Comfort, Jenn guessed. Though perhaps to be sure he stayed still.

To do her part, she gathered up the remains of his bloody shirt, thinking to bury them. Ylings swooped down to take the mess from her hands, then flew high into the plumes and disappeared.

Well. That solved a problem. "Thank you," Jenn said,

trying not to notice how the kruars' noses, including Scourge's, lifted to follow the blood scent.

"Your turn to hold still." Bannan smiled and dropped his gaze to her bodice.

That again? Jenn looked down to find two ylings hard at work. Their needles flickered like darts of light and their hair, this close, sparkled from tip to base. In hardly more time than she'd have taken to thread a needle, they were done and flew away.

There was no seam. The fabric, like Bannan's skin, appeared never to have been torn. "I thought Frann had tidy stitching," she commented, adding the 'Dear and Departed to herself.

Bannan flexed his arm. "I've no complaints. How do we thank them?"

Jenn dipped a finger in the fountain, bringing it to her lips as she would at home, and considered the matter. "Little cousin?"

The house toad sat against the fountain, its skin matched in hue to the stone. ~Yes, elder sister?~

"The ylings. Could you thank them for us?"

The toad blinked slowly. ~I could, if you ask it, elder sister, but they would not understand your gratitude. I fear they might take it as insult.~

"I heard that," Bannan said, reminding her of that helpful difference within the Verge. He went to run his fingers through his hair, then stopped with a wry grin. "Is there anything we could do for them?"

The toad crouched, as if wary of their response. ~Kill the Lost One.~

The eyes, that meant. Certainly it had been her dragon's intention. Jenn looked worriedly at Bannan. "Shouldn't Wisp be back by now?"

The truthseer shook his head. "There's no telling the sort of chase that thing could lead him on. He won't give up."

No, she thought, he wouldn't. For all his posturing, her dragon cared deeply about the small denizens of Marrowdell; the more, perhaps, because he hadn't always. The Lost One would regret making Wisp his enemy.

The metal around her arm felt suddenly heavier. Jenn

laid it on her thigh. "The eyes—he said he wanted to be my friend," she said bitterly. "I shouldn't have listened."

"Did you see him? More than those cursed eyes."

Something in Bannan's voice had Jenn searching his face. "Have you?"

"We'd an encounter," he admitted, his tone grim. "Only the voice."

That horrible voice. "I saw nothing more." But she had, hadn't she? In the snow. In Marrowdell. Jenn stood and went to her sack, digging out the bundle of socks. She brought it back with her, facing man and toad. "Whoever he is, whatever, doesn't belong in the Verge." Cautious of its sharpness, she pulled the shard from its hiding place. The black was gone.

That didn't make it safe. She stared at her own reflection. "He's been watching Marrowdell. That's where he's from, isn't he? From—from our world."

Bannan crossed his arms over his chest, eyes hooded. Considering what to say, she wondered abruptly.

Or what to leave out.

"Tell me all of it," Jenn insisted. "Everything you know. The Lost One has trapped and killed efflet in Marrowdell. They feared I'd be next. I almost was, Bannan."

A muscle clenched along his jaw. "He's killed ylings as well." The truthseer regarded her soberly. "I've been told the Lost One is—was—a man named Crumlin Tralee. The toads remember him. I've heard of him. Crumlin arrived in Marrowdell with the first settlers." He paused as though to give her time to absorb this, but Jenn nodded, certain there was more and worse. "Crumlin was no farmer," Bannan continued, his voice harsh. "Whatever lies he told the others, he came for the Verge and magic. He found a way to cross, long ago." A wave at the meadow. "And been here, it seems, ever since."

A man? She'd seen nothing man-like in the snow sculpture; Crumlin's eyes were stranger still. His voice, though?

Jenn shivered, putting the shard down on the stone. Like the fountain, it reflected only the Verge's sky, presently crimson with a set of floating mountains shaped like pie wedges. "Crumlin's gone now," she said, to reassure all of her protectors.

And herself.

Bannan came to her, put his hands on her shoulders. "We'll wait for the dragon. He'll tell us."

~We cannot.~ A new voice, like Scourge's but somehow thinner. Younger, Jenn guessed, though every bit as full of itself. ~The dimming comes. We must away now.~

~Or what? The dark is when we hunt!~ Scourge lifted a foot and set it down. The ground beneath Jenn's feet trembled, and the new kruar tossed their heads, eyes wide. ~Obey your riders.~ Though his crest had been cut away, leaving a stubble along the rise of his neck like broken knives, when he curved his massive neck, there was no mistaking who was larger—and more dangerous. ~Do you know my name?~

And that was either invitation or threat.

~We know.~ Despite their mass and armor, they appeared to move on tiptoe, ready to bolt. Once close enough to Scourge, they stretched out their necks, nostrils flared. Their crests chattered like restless swords. ~We know, Lord General. You are Scourge, the Malevolent.~

~While you are nameless!~ Scourge swung his head, smacking one in the shoulder. That kruar swung around to snap, teeth scoring red along tough hide, while the other pranced at a distance, snarling.

Faced with such ferocious display, Jenn wasn't sure if they should intervene or hide behind the fountain. To her surprise, Bannan chuckled. "We're in a hurry, Idiot Beast. She'll have to wait."

Scourge gave him such a look Jenn blushed.

Amused agreement. ~He's right. Mate later.~

"Wisp!"

Bannan ran with Jenn to where the dragon heaved himself up through the ground.

Despite the amused tone to his voice, Wisp was hurt and badly. One wing hung crooked and useless. A leg had been opened to the bone, skin flapping loose. There were what could only be burns along his jaws, though from what Bannan knew of dragons, they couldn't burn.

Unless— "You caught him."

Had the look in those eyes been meant for him, Bannan would have run for his life. ~Not yet. The coward fled rather than fight, covering his trail with what would have killed anything else.~

Scourge having arrived.

Not only the kruar. The air suddenly filled with dragons, full-sized and of every color, wheeling around them in a vast angry flock. Their wingbeats drove hot, dry air into Bannan and Jenn's faces.

Kruar roared a challenge! More than one. Dragons answered. They were, Bannan decided numbly, at the center of what could well be a resumption of the great beings' war. Or at least a bloody skirmish, for old times' sake.

But neither kruar nor dragon were the most powerful here. Jenn Nalynn became turn-born, her inner glow burnishing scales and hide. "Enough," she said quietly, and raised her hand.

The meadow became deathly still, then the dragons scattered, tail and wingtips the last to disappear. The kruar bent their heads, but didn't bolt, though the young ones trembled.

Wisp's lower jaw sank in one of his laughs. ~Dearest Heart.~

He claimed her and Bannan was happy to let him, quite sure the dragon was on their side.

"You're hurt," Jenn cried, flesh again and worried.

~This?~ The dragon flexed his broken limb. ~I will heal. And hunt again.~

Scourge growled approval.

Given how he'd seen the dragon heal before, it was no idle boast. Reassured, Bannan caught Jenn's wrist and lifted it so Wisp could see the band, careful to support the metal's weight. "You bit through the chain. Can you remove the rest?"

"Please, Wisp?" with the faintest tremor in her voice.

He could hate Crumlin more, the truthseer discovered.

~Be turn-born again, Dearest Heart,~ Wisp said. ~Come close.~

Jenn did as he bade her, becoming glass and pearl. Her inner light faded alarmingly where the band wrapped her arm. Trustingly, she held her arm near the dragon's jaws. Wisp took hold, finger-length fangs ticking against the metal like daggers of bone.

The dragonlings' sharp little teeth had sliced his flesh with no effort. This? A bad idea. A terrible one! The truthseer started forward. He was panicking and knew it, but those jaws around her slender arm were a nightmare.

But the jaws didn't close and crush. Instead fire boiled within the dragon's open mouth, writhing and white-hot.

Bannan shielded his eyes. "Jenn!"

"I don't feel it," she said quickly. "Clever Wisp."

Iron began to melt and drip, sliding over silver scales to drop to the ground with a sizzle and spit. Before they could cool, the house toad pounced, snapping each up with its tongue and what seemed boundless delight.

Ancestors only knew what it would make of them. Bannan refused to guess.

~There.~

Flesh once more, Jenn straightened, holding out her arm. "Bannan, look!"

He did more, running paired thumbs gently over her skin, turning her arm over to check the other side. Was it paler, where the band had been, as if she'd worn it for years? With a hand that wanted to shake, the truthseer rubbed his eyes and looked again.

"Bannan?"

Jenn's arm was fine, exactly as it had been. "Perfect," he affirmed. "How does it feel?"

"Normal. Is something wrong?" She came close, looking into his eyes.

"Other than our good dragon here looking like battle dregs?" he said, to distract her. The dimming—the Verge's night—was coming. He hoped so.

It was that, or his beyond weary eyes were losing the struggle to make sense of what he saw.

One of the kruar shifted its feet. ~Turn-born.~ Oh, the new-found respect in that voice. ~If we are to cross into Channen when we should, we must away.~

To Channen. The words were a weight he felt in his heart. What was he thinking, to risk Jenn there? They could turn back, now. Be home in whatever passed for hours here.

Face Semyn and Werfol.

"I'd best find a shirt," Bannan announced, doing his best to sound lively and ready for more adventure.

Hearts of his Ancestors, he'd be Beholden for less.

He'd rubbed his eyes, again. As before, Jenn pretended not to notice. Bannan's gift let him stay here, but not for long or forever, that was plain.

Unlike Crumlin.

She made herself use the name in her thoughts, for it was a truer name than "lost." She most sincerely hoped he was "one." Her dragon lay hurt—and how many others had Crumlin harmed? For what?

For what she touched, in the Verge. For what she was. Crumlin was a great fool, to think magic was something you took in your hand and used. As well put time in your hand or guilt or courage.

Or kindness. "Bannan?" Jenn pointed to the cluster of ylings. They held a shirt, his shirt, whole and clean, between them, somehow flying in a straight line despite their burden.

The truthseer grinned.

Dressed once more, they refilled their flasks, then turned to Wisp. ~Go,~ he ordered, almost peevishly. Perhaps, Jenn thought, the healing magic of a dragon prickled as it worked. She could, to her relief, see him heal. Bones shifted under his scaled skin and the deep wound on his leg had begun to knit.

It was not a process to rush. Jenn crouched in front of him, seeing herself in his wild beautiful eyes. "I'd not stop you hunting Crumlin," she said gently. "I don't want him to harm anyone else. But please, while I'm away and can't, dear Wisp, take care of Marrowdell."

Steam rose from his nostrils and claws dug into the ground. She waited, trusting her dragon, and sure enough, after that mute protest, he bowed his deadly head as might a man. ~I will.~

Jenn smiled from the bottom of her heart. "We'll be home as soon as we can."

~Listen to the little cousin, Dearest Heart,~ Wisp

advised. ~They have their wisdom. If they don't always employ it.~ That to the toad, presently half-inside Bannan's
backpack.

Then it was time to gather up her sack and say good-bye
to Scourge, but he'd left at some point when she'd been distracted by dragon. "The idiot beast's for Marrowdell too,"
Bannan told her, guessing why she was looking around.
"He's bent and determined Werfol learn to ride."

Oh dear. She was reassured by the twinkle in Bannan's
eye. They'd worked something out, he and the kruar, and
she wouldn't worry.

Their steeds stood waiting. Their guides. They'd not had
the best of introductions; she should remedy that.

Jenn took Bannan's hand and drew him to stand with her
before the pair of kruar. Whose eyes rolled and lips curled,
but who stood waiting nonetheless. "My name is Jenn Nalynn. Thank you for your help," she told them.

Bannan, more familiar with the creatures, bowed deeply.
As he rose, he said, "I am Scourge's rider," in a no-nonsense
tone. "We've gone into battle times without count. I trust
you will attempt to honor him." Spoken as if he had grave
doubts.

Both tossed their heads, crests rattling. ~We aspire to his
greatness.~

"We'll see." Turning away, he winked at Jenn. "Time to
go."

She gladly accepted Bannan's clasped hands, the saddle
being very high from the ground in her estimation. He
tossed her up and she put her leg across, glad to discover
that, unlike the saddle she'd used for Wainn's Old Pony, the
one on the kruar's armored back was kind to her skin and
a comfortable fit.

Bannan mounted as his kruar started to move, leaping
astride with easy grace. A yling flew down and into his hair
at the same time. Marrowdell's troop would stay together,
it seemed.

Leaving Jenn wondering where to put her hands, her
kruar's crest being every bit as sharp up close as it had appeared from a safer distance.

Suddenly the great body beneath surged into motion

and Jenn grabbed frantically for the raised front of her saddle before she was left behind.

She could swear the kruar purred.

Bannan hoped Jenn hadn't expected their first ride together to be peaceful and romantic, with them side-by-side and surely a stolen kiss or twenty. Not that he wouldn't prefer it that way himself, but they weren't on horses.

Nor did kruar enjoy riders. In his experience, they enjoyed being given direction by those riders even less. Bannan had never fooled himself Scourge obeyed without question. The great beast gauged every situation by his own standards and either agreed with his rider.

Or didn't.

These kruar were eager to complete their duty and be done with riders altogether. The Verge passed by in a blur of unexpected shapes and unnamed colors as they wove their way around obstacles that loomed in front.

Or under. Or over. He couldn't tell if the idiot beasts were deliberately choosing the most complicated path or if they couldn't abandon their instinct to go unseen. They moved in uncanny silence as well. Not that he'd argue.

What a kruar chose to avoid, Bannan did not want to meet.

Within a few mad swerves, he lost sight of Jenn and her kruar. After another, he couldn't be sure if they traveled uphill or down. The kruar hit a stretch where it could lengthen its stride; Bannan had to bend over the saddle to catch a breath. "Hang on, Jenn," he muttered.

~Our elder sister wants me to tell you that she is hanging on and hopes you are too.~

The toad. Bannan yelled into his sleeve, "You can hear her?"

~There's no need to shout, truthseer.~ With some offense. ~Of course I can hear our elder sister. I can hear you, can I not?~

Save him from toads. "Apologies, little cousin." Hopefully, this meant Jenn wasn't far ahead. "Does she see the crossing yet?"

A darker voice, amused. ~We are there.~

Bannan's kruar jolted to a stop and he barely saved himself from lurching forward onto its perilous crest.

Then the truthseer hung onto the saddle as perspective screamed and common sense failed. Look *deeper*, he told himself desperately, and tried, but not even his gift could grasp where they stood.

Unless it was possible, in the Verge, to be within a single drop of rain.

"Thank you," Jenn told her mount, knowing full well it hadn't been her skill—or tight grip—keeping her in the saddle through the violent ride.

It turned its head to regard her with one red-rimmed eye. ~I do my duty.~ But not as gruffly as it might. ~This is the crossing.~

She could feel it. Goose bumps rose on her skin, a reassuring reminder of what she was at the moment. In the Verge, it was too easy to forget. There was, however, one small problem.

They were, quite plainly, inside a drop of mimrol. While Jenn was relieved not to be drowning—which was another, not-so-small a problem to consider—she couldn't see how, or why, they were where they apparently were.

"We're in a drop."

The head swung back, the kruar unimpressed. ~Will you cross, turn-born?~

Not without Bannan. As if the denial had been a summons, the truthseer, still astride his kruar, appeared in the drop with her.

He let out a cry and pressed the heels of both hands into his eyes.

"Bannan!" She kicked her kruar as she would Wainn's Old Pony and, for a wonder, it stepped close enough to the truthseer's that she could lean over and put her hand on his arm.

An arm so tense it shook beneath her fingers.

It was being here that upset him.

So Jenn Nalynn wished them . . . there.

They were in a drop.

That fell,

fell,

fell . . .

Bannan put his hand over Jenn's on his arm, and prayed, "Hearts of my Ancestors, I'd be Behold—"

Not to die, not to smash into the ground, not to stay small enough to fit inside a silver drop, not to drown—

When none of those things happened, when what he felt next was rain on his own face, he opened his eyes one at a time.

He still rode, but what had been kruar appeared now as a chestnut horse with a shock of black mane. Jenn, on a bay with black points, was beside him. Their "horses" stood knee-deep in a small round lake banked with stone, more stone forming a walkway bounded by stone walls whose tops disappeared into masses of shadowed leaves.

The only opening in the walls was ahead, where the outflow from the lake, edged by narrowing walkways, slipped beneath an arched stone bridge. Huge lamps, like golden sentries, hung from the walls at intervals and their light caught in puddles and dark water.

For it rained.

Bannan held out his cupped hand, shocked when it filled with molten silver. Mimrol. Here?

"Is this Channen?" Jenn asked, sounding as unsure as he felt.

"It must be." If for no other reason than he no longer used his deeper sight, an almost painful easing of effort. Bannan gave himself an inner shake. They had to move.

Though where they stood deserved a second and third look.

The lake was more a fountain, filled with submerged wide irregular platforms stacked one upon the other. The kruar were on a middle one. To Bannan's left another two rose higher, but not out of the—was it water, or pure mimrol? A blend, he guessed, seeing how the pure silver drops that fell as rain slipped below the surface to gather, ever-so-slowly, on the platforms. Had the Naalish built them for this purpose?

Or did the mimrol settle out thus, over time?

He tipped his hand, watching the mimrol pour into the lake. Ripples spread from that point, but the silver stayed together, dulling slightly as it sank.

"Bannan. Someone's here."

Tir'd box his ears, Bannan knew, for letting himself be distracted by drops. Sure enough, a figure stood on the bank, hooded and cloaked, one hand holding a lantern on a staff. He—or she—appeared unsurprised to have horses and riders appear in the lake.

The turn-borns' arrangement.

"Greetings," Bannan said in Naalish, touching two fingers of his right hand to his left shoulder. The last he'd heard, it was still the salutation between persons intent on amicable business.

The figure did the same. "All is ready for you, Keepers." A man, and not a young one, by the voice. The Naalish turned and began to walk away.

Jenn's kruar lifted his head. "Do we follow, turn-born?" A breeze in Bannan's ear, with a hint of puzzlement.

"If this is the trusted person," now his, the mare interested in Scourge, with a decided snap. "We were to follow only the trusted person. Is it?"

That the kruar, on this side of the edge, were willing to speak in breezes—their other speech something he couldn't detect outside the Verge—was a relief.

That they were just as new to Channen?

Wasn't.

Jenn drew another deep breath. The Verge had an array of smells, none of which her nose would have predicted and several she'd seemed to "smell" with her eyes.

Here? She might have stepped barefoot into the river, midsummer; somewhere in the reeds, where rot bubbled beneath her toes and everything was rich and dark, like a well-made pudding. There were kitchen smells, too, though faint, enough to make her stomach rumble in interest. She'd not eaten much, in the Verge. Hadn't wanted to, there, but here?

Here she was hungry.

And rode a horse, or the seeming of one, which made her feel a great deal more comfortable than riding a fierce and armored kruar—which she still did, of course, but the camouflage was perfect down to the feel of warm hide.

Ears flattened and Jenn stopped the inadvertent petting she'd begun. Not a horse.

"We can't stay here," Bannan said quietly, but didn't move, as if waiting for her to decide.

The man in the cloak seemed harmless enough. After all, he'd expected them.

No, she thought abruptly. He expected turn-born.

This wasn't like Marrowdell, where the turn-born could cross unseen, then pretend to come by an ordinary road and be ordinary. This was the heart of a city. Here, Mistress Sand and the rest arrived as what they were, relying upon this man and his kind to keep their secret.

Insisting on it.

This wasn't the turn-born coming in friendship, and working together at the harvest, nor dancing till dawn to celebrate. What they did here was something very different and Jenn found herself more than uneasy and unsure.

She found herself afraid. How could she act that way? What should she do?

"We've been met, as promised," Bannan reminded her, his voice calm and composed, his face a mask, and he couldn't say what might be on his mind, she understood, for someone listened to them.

A stranger.

Worse and worse. Goodness. What would Aunt Sybb say?

That standing still was for statues, not people with work to do.

Jenn took a deep breath and steadied herself. She'd be herself, for weren't the turn-born individuals? As for Bannan, who could be anyone he chose, why, anyone waiting here would surely assume he was turn-born. Who else could appear out of thin air and rain?

Which was good and safe and important. Those who

knew of the turn-born must believe Bannan one as well. If they didn't—if they discovered a man could cross into the Verge and survive—

With a wish, with a thought, she could make everyone believe. This was the edge, her domain, with no one here to deny her.

Except herself. She'd vowed not to wish at people again. It wasn't right and it wasn't fair. Besides, they'd only just arrived.

And she was hungry.

Oh, and didn't she have a host of new questions for Mistress Sand, concerning the edge in other domains and how turn-born behaved in each and how people treated them?

Bannan waited. At Jenn's nod, he set his not-horse in motion with a louder, "We're coming." Hers followed.

They were on some sort of platform submerged in the little lake, for their mounts climbed down with care. One step, then two. At that level, water as warm as a bath lapped at Jenn's toes and she stretched out a foot to enjoy more.

"Do not." From her not-horse. From the way Bannan promptly brought up his feet, he'd received the same warning.

Why? Jenn looked down. The water was almost black, either because it was a bit boggy or because the sky above them was obscured by low hanging cloud. Or both.

The surface dimpled, as if something had floated near the top, watching them, then dove out of sight. A fish? Wen spoke to the fish in Marrowdell's river, but Jenn hadn't found them interested in talking to her. Just as well. She was very fond of pan-fried trout.

Her curiosity about the water faded as they approached the bank, replaced by a real concern how they were to get out of the lake, the stonework rising over her head. As if to remind her what they rode, Bannan's kruar bunched its hindquarters and sprang over that barrier like an ungainly rabbit, to land on the path beyond.

Jenn held tight as hers did the same.

Seeing Bannan dismount, she slipped her leg over and jumped down. "Thank you," she told her not-horse, with a determined and respectful pat on his shoulder.

The shoulder shuddered as if her touch was a biting fly,

but the beast came with her like a mannerly horse as she joined Bannan.

Lamplight caught on ripples in the water, reflections dancing overhead as they passed under the bridge. Something followed them, submerged in that mix of silver and tarnish. Several somethings. But they were small and in the water and Bannan Larmensu worried more about the dense foliage that overhung the wall where an ambush could wait.

Lamplight and stone, water and cloud. He'd looked deeper the once and wouldn't, he thought with a shudder, do so again if he could help it. Unlike Marrowdell, here the world of dragons overlapped this one as though in a mirror. What was ground and river there twisted above, topsy-turvy, within what was cloud and sky here.

No wonder mimrol rained down.

No wonder they'd had to fall to cross.

The truthseer refused to consider the return journey.

The bridge marked the end of the lake and the start of a canal that flowed away between stone banks, walkways, and walls as far as Bannan could see. Another bridge arched across in the distance. Here and there, planters—of the same ubiquitous gray stone—brimmed with greenery but if any were flowers, this seemed not their season. Looking up, he caught glimpses of lights in windows. Buildings loomed beyond the foliage that tumbled over the walls, indistinct and distant.

Their guide kept a few paces ahead, the hem of his cloak sweeping the stone with each step. The hood was separate, Bannan noticed, and the fabric of both, though so dark a brown as to seem black, flowed like silk. The air being summer-warm, the lighter material made sense. Or the man's raiment was designed to fold, quickly, into the smallest of bundles. A good disguise.

How quick, suspicion. How unavoidable, old habits.

How very welcome, both. What he'd learned as a farmer was of no use here. Jenn Nalynn walked beside him. She'd been shaken at first, and he couldn't blame her, but rallied with courage. Now she looked around with the beginnings of wonder. Her first canal. First bridge. First city.

In no way did he blame her, but Ancestors Dazzled and Distracted, a city had its share of nonmagical pitfalls and threats. They'd need to stay together.

Then Bannan found himself distracted as the path widened, the wall replaced, here, by the formal entryway of a building, complete with tall paired doors and wide, shuttered windows. A sign hung over the doors, proclaiming this a private residence, and chains crisscrossed the doors, proclaiming it closed. Four columns stood waiting, the sort that would support an awning for shade. The awning was missing—not that Bannan could imagine a need for shade here.

For privacy from above, perhaps.

"This way." The Naalish led them past the chained door to the opening to a narrow alley, hidden from view behind one column. Bannan had to turn sideways to fit and a horse couldn't have passed through.

The kruar followed without difficulty.

Bannan reached his hand back for Jenn's, more to be sure she was there than anything else. Her fingers squeezed his. Reassurance, that was.

Older stone formed the alley walls, damp and eroded, as though all effort to maintain the buildings to either side went to what faced the canal. Moss grew in cracks, interspersed with the waxy yellow of butter fungus. There were lamps, head-high, their glow dimmed by matted cobwebs. That they held oil was unlikely. Magic, Bannan decided uncomfortably, but whose?

"This feels like a trap," observed a kruar.

The other replied, "Who here would dare trap a turn-born!"

Bannan felt Jenn's hand tremble; she didn't speak.

The house toad squirmed in his pack, and was that a pat-pat on his ear? Ancestors Witness. Did they plan to ride him the entire time?

Another squeeze on his fingers.

The alley ended in stairs, steep and laden with filth that must wash down in heavier rains. Bannan let go of Jenn's hand to use his own along the walls. Better the dirt than to slip himself and fall on her.

They'd climbed one story, by his estimate, then part of another, when the hem of the cloak whisked away around a corner above. Bannan risked taking the four final steps two at a time, to spring a trap if one waited.

But what waited at the top wasn't a trap.

It was another city.

The people of Channen were wealthy beyond her imagining, Jenn concluded, if they could afford to let their city fall into such decay.

Or were careless of its repair. After all, Devins and Roche were no great housekeepers themselves. If someone like them owned this magnificent stone staircase, a work of art in itself—

No, even the Morrills would keep the steps clear of mud and dead leaves, though they might neglect to brush webs from the lamps. Jenn slowed to take a closer look. Each was a different sort of fish, the light coming from a globe of glass where a belly would be, with fins and tail and head of a greenish metal. They were ever-so-clever—

"Jenn."

At the top, Bannan was beckoning her to hurry. "Sorry," Jenn whispered to the kruar behind her, rather embarrassed to be caught gawking, but this was the most amazing and glorious place—under the dirt—she'd ever seen.

Until she went up the remaining steps and realized she'd seen nothing at all.

At the top was a small walled landing, cluttered with debris that crunched or slid underfoot, and roofed in drooping leaves larger than any Jenn had seen before. To the left of the landing was an arched gate taller than Bannan, made of black metal bars with a charming inset of flowers, also of metal.

The gate was open, the truthseer holding it so, but Jenn barely noticed. She stepped from the gloom and filth of the landing onto what she recognized as glazed tile—the Ropps having two pieces they brought from Avyo and now used in their dairy—formed into a—a porch, she supposed, for they'd come out onto another level.

Rather, another world.

At first she struggled to make sense of where she was, given where they'd been. There was no water in sight. Instead, a broad cobbled road ran like a river between towering buildings. They leaned and tilted, as if in conversation. Or did the clouds that wreathed their roofs press down? In places, buildings met overhead, with the road going right through them, and in all were windows with bright curtains billowing through their openings, for there was a breeze here, the air cooler and drier. There were doors, too, most open to offer bewildering glimpses of what lay within, but no yards or gardens between.

If sight bewildered, sound was worse, for they'd come up in the midst of what had to be everyone in Channen.

Ancestors Crushed and Crowded. People were everywhere. Leaning out of windows, going through doors. Meeting on sidewalks. The cobbled road could hardly be seen for the wheels of elegant carriages and carts, and the smartly moving legs of horses. Everyone in a hurry, and everyone talking or shouting, and everywhere clatters and loud thumps and was that music or was it her heart beating so quickly she felt ill—

"This way, Dearest Heart." Bannan took her hand, drawing her to his side. "Quickly."

Though she'd never been exposed to so many eyes at once, no one seemed to notice as they walked over tiles to where an open door promised shelter. Seeing that, Jenn was proud not to break into a run.

Safe inside, she found herself in a room larger than any in Marrowdell, other than a barn or the mill. More lamps curled out from the walls, these polished and gleaming. At the far end of the room were three doors, the rightmost being only half a door, like a stall.

As was the floor, of wood that more rightly, in Jenn's experience, should have been made into fine furniture and not a walkway for people.

And horses, for the kruar crowded in behind. They looked, if anything, more bewildered than she by their surroundings and Jenn felt a rush of sympathy. She supposed the expected arrival of horses explained the lack of furnishings, for there was nothing other than a set of familiar-looking trunks against a wall.

Arrangements, indeed.

The cloaked man closed the outer door, shutting out the din and them inside. Using two hands, he pulled off his hood.

Jenn found herself disappointed by her first up-close look at a full-blooded Naalish, though really, what had she expected? Most of Rhoth and all of Marrowdell had Naal-ish blood and this man might have been Anten's older cousin, with a similarly blunt nose and high cheekbones. His skin was paler, but in a place called the Shadow District her tanned skin might be thought odd. His gray hair was longer than Bannan's, swept neatly in a braid.

As for his expression? It was what Aunt Sybb would call a polite face, which showed nothing at all but pleasant attentiveness.

Bannan let go of her hand and touched his shoulder once more. "Our thanks."

The Naalish echoed the gesture. "I must apologize," he said, not sounding particularly sorry. "We'd not readied attire of the correct size or coloring. There will be a brief delay." Jenn thought she saw a flicker of curiosity in the other man's eyes, but he must have been well-schooled in the privacy of turn-born. "You will, I'm sure, wish to bathe." His hand lifted to point to the middle door, then shifted to indicate the half door. "As usual, your mounts are welcome to hunt the rooftops. We ask only that they leave any banded birds alone."

So he knew what they rode or had instructions, which was all well and good, and they needed a bath and wouldn't new clothes be a delight? However, hospitality, as far as Jenn was concerned, ought to include something more basic. "Forgive me, good sir, but is there something to eat?"

Bannan half smiled. "My thought as well," he agreed. "We've had a long journey."

Oh, then curiosity flared, but the Naalish restrained himself. "Refreshments await by the bath." As if they should have known.

Then he waited, as if they should know what to do next

too, so Jenn lifted her head and walked straight to the door
to the bath.

Hoping the tub wouldn't be outside and in view of
strangers.

The Naalish had taken their arrival in stride, a bland acceptance Bannan didn't trust. Though he'd seen no lie in the
man's face, a delay to obtain clothing could be a delay for
something else as well, including a message to bring constables or whomever else might care about strange turn-born
in their city.

They were tossing the 'stones, they were. High and wide
and wild. But the real truth was they couldn't move about
as they were. The turn-born who came here regularly to
trade had put measures in place, as they had in Marrowdell,
measures they'd use to their advantage.

Before Jenn could go through that door without him,
Bannan reminded her, "The horses."

She turned with a quick smile. "Of course."

The Naalish not volunteering to assist with that duty,
Bannan led the way through the half door, the kruar coming behind Jenn.

Behind the door was another empty room, with saddle
racks on one wall. It was more landing than room, for one
set of stairs led to a doorless opening that showed sky, while
another led down into dark water. The kruar prowled
around, nostrils flared. "Not a trap," the young male concluded with an "I-told-you-so" air.

The mare's lip curled. "There's always a trap."

"That's the attitude," Bannan said cheerfully, setting
down his pack—and the toad. "Let's get those saddles off."

That brought their heads around. " 'Off?' "

"You can't want to keep wearing them." Jenn went to
her mount, then turned to Bannan. "I don't see a girth."

He'd gone to the mare only to discover the same problem. The saddle appeared one of leather, simple yet well
fitted, but there was no strap to undo.

The truthseer looked deeper.

Armor and crest of shimmering blades. What had

seemed a leather saddle? A callus grown from the kruar's back, like proud flesh on a leg wound. Exactly like, he realized, for the armor beneath had been cut away to expose the flesh. Bannan shuddered as he regained his normal sight. "I don't understand," he said numbly. "The kruar who came to Marrowdell wore normal harnesses. Why this?"

A red eye considered him. "We are nameless. The turnborn do not expect us to be faithful."

"Or to return." With a familiar dark humor. "We will prove them wrong. We aspire to the greatness of Scourge the Malevolent!"

"You did this to yourselves," Jenn breathed, her hand going to the soft spot under the chin of her kruar. "You volunteered. How brave you are."

He could think of several other words for it. How many "brave" and naive youngsters had joined the border guard?

To join their Blessed Ancestors soon after.

"There are rules, in this world," Bannan said, harshly enough that Jenn lost her smile. "Rules you must learn and obey without question."

Heads lifted in offense, threatening the ceiling.

"Rules Scourge learned and obeyed." He frowned. "Would you do less?"

The mare's head lowered first. "Tell us these rules."

The bath wasn't outside.

And wasn't a tub.

It was pure luxury and they'd no time for any of it. After a quick supper from the refreshments, those being a tray of unfamiliar yet delicious fruits and cheeses, Jenn knelt on the lip of the tiled pool, and dipped a corner of a large soft towel into the warm perfumed scented bubbles, using that to give herself a quick, dutiful scrub. Though she held the towel over her face just a little longer than necessary, her eyes closed, to savor the scent.

Bannan stood looking out one of the high windows. The sun had set, but not so long ago. Thinking of worlds and suns, of her map—where it was, where they were now—made her a little dizzy, truth be told.

Jenn focused on here, which was remarkable enough.

The truthseer'd changed into the clothes brought by their cloaked Naalish, garments they were informed suited a moderately successful merchant. A blue, almost purple, jacket wrapped from neck to right waist across his chest, the front and cuffs trimmed in coin-sized gold buttons. The bottom of the jacket had a fringe of brighter blue threads, tied into clusters to allow the gold of his belt to show. The belt had compartments, disguised as decoration; to take the place of pockets, she supposed.

His wide pants, of muted lilac, were gathered snug above tall boots of excellent brown leather. In sum, Bannan Larmensu looked every bit the part, prosperous and handsome.

They were, however, indisputably no longer in Rhoth.

Wrapped around Bannan's neck was a collar of gold and blue that served as the upper part of his jacket. His shoulders from collar to the start of his arms were bare, as was his neck below the collar. The dark blue shirt under his jacket was similarly constructed.

His back was covered. That, at least.

"Are you ready?"

She wasn't, if the as-yet-unnamed Naalish meant allowing him, a stranger, to help her to dress, but one look at the clothing waiting for her was enough for Jenn to realize she'd no hope of puzzling it out on her own. "A moment, please." After waiting for them both to look away, she changed her plain simples for two satiny pieces clearly meant to serve the same purpose, then tucked her little pouch of Melusine's rose petals in the topmost for safekeeping. What she now wore was rose-red and petal-soft against her skin, not to mention distracting.

Perhaps she'd be allowed to keep them.

"Now, I'm ready."

There were, to Jenn's astonishment, pants of the same style as Bannan's, though hers were dark gray. They gave delightful mobility and she thought them most practical for adventuring.

She also thought it best Aunt Sybb not see her in them, the dear lady scandalized by an excess of calf.

The boots Jenn regarded with doubt, given her history with shoes of any sort, but when—with a little help—she managed to get them over her feet and up to her knees, they felt wonderful. Like Bannan's, they had two handsome buckles, at ankle and top, to give a secure fit.

Then came the top layers, the Naalish handing her one at a time, with instructions. First, a white blouse, its long full sleeves ending in tight brown cuffs. It went across the bodice and around her back, exposing not only her shoulders but a good portion of her chest and back. "Is there something to go over this?" Jenn asked, feeling the air move over her skin.

"Here." The Naalish handed her a white collar, showing the hooks at the back. Lace at the top and bottom, with a line of smooth ribbon in the middle, it was the width of her palm and stiffer than she'd expected.

But hardly what she'd hoped.

"Let me." Bannan took it from her and Jenn lifted her braid out of the way, much happier to have his fingers on her neck.

Silently, the Naalish gave the truthseer what looked like a necklace of golden beads but bore several hooks. He indicated where it fastened to the blouse, above the cleft between Jenn's breasts, and to the collar.

By the end of that, she could feel herself blushing and Bannan dared wink.

They still weren't done. She was to be dressed as the merchant's apprentice, so over the blouse and pants went a tunic of the same deep purple blue as Bannan's jacket. Around the top was a narrow froth of white lace, with more lace between her breasts. By this point, Jenn wasn't surprised that the tunic covered no more than the blouse. At least there was a hook with which to fasten the tunic to golden necklace and so her collar, ensuring no further exposure.

Instead of a skirt, the tunic split over her hips, with panels front and back ending at her knees. The panels were embossed with a fine pattern, and their edges were trimmed with black leather, studded with small gold beads.

"We're done?" she asked hopefully.

"Just this." The Naalish held out a corset of supple black leather, worked with a pattern of delicate leaves. When he went to put it around her waist, Jenn took it with a determined smile.

"I can manage, thank you." The corset fastened at the front, with good-sized metal clasps, and was more comfortable than it looked. Clothing complete, she felt as if she'd stepped out of a story, and no longer Jenn Nalynn but someone braver, someone more worldly.

So long as no one asked her a question. "Thank you for all of this," she told the Naalish, touching her fingers to shoulder. They were beyond fortunate to have such help. However disconcerting to have her shoulders exposed and the rest fully clad, this was the fashion here. Much as she'd appreciated the loan of Peggs' second-best dress, it wouldn't have served at all.

Jenn turned to Bannan. "How do I look?"

"Not yet ready. Please sit." The Naalish produced a brush and comb from somewhere in his cloak. "The pair of you."

Bannan grinned, she grimaced, and they sat, side-by-side, on a cushioned bench. Before the man started, Jenn discreetly plucked the leaf from Bannan's hair, letting it drift to the floor. When she checked a moment later, the leaf was gone. How the yling could hide in this room of water and tile, she'd no idea, but the creatures were adept.

For now, the house toad was content in Bannan's pack.

The truthseer's hair took little time, being gathered at the nape of his back into a braid that secured with a clip.

The Naalish paused to consider Jenn's.

Daunted by the pins, she guessed, Peggs having used dozens. "It stayed put," Jenn said defensively. Hadn't only one lock of her hair come loose, despite their adventuring? Repeatedly, but still. "You could leave it."

Though were she to think about it, her scalp did itch and prickle, which could become maddening if she kept thinking about it.

"I could not." A suggestion of a smile on the man's face, the first. "With your permission?"

Jenn nodded, unable to hold back a sigh of relief as the tight binding over her ear came loose, hair tumbling over her shoulder. Whatever else he did in life, there was no mistaking the competence with which the Naalish disassembled Peggs' efforts.

While pins rained down, Bannan moved to another seat

and leaned back, lacing his fingers around a knee. "You're here to facilitate our business, are you not?"

"In every way possible."

Why, he could direct them to where Lila was being held! Jenn almost held her breath, waiting for Bannan to ask. She'd not thought to find such help, so promptly.

Bannan gave her a look she couldn't interpret. "As usual, we've come to trade," he said, the slightest emphasis on the last word. "We've an interest in tokens, this trip."

He didn't trust the Naalish, she guessed, somewhat deflated; not enough to reveal their true purpose. Clearly, she'd more to learn about adventuring.

"I'm sure I can direct you," came the prompt reply. "Magic is, after all, the stock in trade of the Artisans' Market. Do you have a specific requirement?"

"The sort not on open display." Bannan's eyes had taken on their apple butter hue, and Jenn knew he watched for lies.

The fingers in Jenn's hair briefly stilled, then went back to work. "Birr, then. His stall is set against the Seahorse Bridge. May I offer advice?"

Bannan waved an open hand. "We welcome it."

"The Shadow Sect watches for such merchandise changing hands. They'd not interfere with you, of course, but Birr will be wary in their presence. I'll send word to clear your approach, but I advise you allow them time to leave."

The truthseer's expression didn't alter; lacking his skill, Jenn was just as glad to have the Naalish behind her so she could look as shocked as she felt. Semyn had told them those in the shadows here, along the canals, were the ones Emon sought. Could they be this "Shadow Sect?" If so, they were in the right place to start their search.

But that there was an entire organization here that knew about turn-born? That granted them the right to break laws?

Pots. Messy baby pants. Snowstorms and shovels. Jenn ran through her list to calm herself.

Bannan actually winked at her, which eased her mind even more. "You, then, are a member?" he asked the man.

"I did not — ? Forgive me!" The Naalish rushed around the bench to fall to his hands and knees between the two of them, dropping his forehead to the floor with an audible thud. "Only the Shadow Sect tends the Keepers of the Source," he chanted in a frantic monotone. "Only the Shadow Sect protects the Purity of the Source. Only the Shadow Sect dispenses What the Source Provides. By the Blessings of our Ancestors, we give ourselves to this service, as I give mine to you."

She'd never seen the like of it. Jenn stared wide-eyed at Bannan, who gave her a satisfied nod before turning his attention to the Naalish. "A service we appreciate."

The man didn't budge. "I erred in not proving myself to you, Keepers. When you make your report, it is of Appin you must complain. Appin Arkona."

"We will have nothing but praise for your work, Appin, if you finish it."

The Naalish lifted his head and Jenn, realizing he was ever so much like a house toad, smiled reassuringly. "My hair, please?"

That brought him back to his feet, two fingers to his shoulder. "At once."

As Appin—she did prefer having a name—took a brush to her hair, Bannan watched him keenly. "You were offering advice. Please continue."

"As you wish." Appin appeared to regain his confidence. "While I understand the affairs of our world are not yours, Keeper, I suggest the lady speak for you both as much as possible. Her Naalish is without flaw, while yours has a distinct Rhothan flavor. Trust me, it will draw unwelcome attention."

Jenn bit her lower lip rather than smile at Bannan's expression. After all, he'd worked to learn the language while she'd used magic, wishing to be understood and understand, with the result that others simply heard what they expected.

"Also, the lady must have her ears pierced at the first opportunity."

"Pardon?" Whatever was on her face at that, it was the truthseer's turn to keep his straight.

~What is wrong, elder sister?~ her toad demanded, instantly alarmed.

As was she, but Jenn swallowed and nodded as best she could with the man's hands in her hair. "If it's necessary."

"Absolutely so. No lady would be seen with naked ears, especially one of such beauty. I wish there was time for the gentleman to be tattooed. Such excellent shoulders."

The helpful Naalish had warmed to them, it seemed.

Bannan frowned and rose to his feet. "Our thanks for your assistance and advice, but we wish to conclude our business in Channen as quickly as possible."

"Of course." The man's fingers fairly flew through her hair. "I'll be but a moment."

Jenn met her love's eyes, trusting he saw the understanding in hers. Earrings and tattoos?

Lila and Emon. They were why she and Bannan had risked the Verge. It was time they went on the hunt.

Hunt. Jenn frowned, remembering Wisp and Crumlin and the shard.

Hopefully, by now, her dragon was in Marrowdell, Crumlin hiding in some hole, and the shard?

Oh dear. She very much hoped it would be safe where she'd forgotten it, on the turn-borns' fountain.

The dimming came and shadows played. Hunting; being hunted. A gibbering shriek ended in a crunch. Success for one, if not the other.

Wisp snarled a warning, not yet able to move. He hurt, but pain was an old friend. Harder to bear was the loss of his prey and he'd be ever so willing to kill something else. Making it hard to understand why the fool ylings kept hovering nearby. ~Go away.~

One dared come close to his eye, like the spark from a fire, and the dragon prepared to snap, then hesitated. The hands of this yling were filled with needles. One of those hands gestured toward his torn wing.

They'd sewn up the truthseer.

These weren't of Marrowdell. They weren't—his. ~Why?~ he questioned, suspicion always safer.

Others flew, the sparks in their hair the only light below the sky, to gather over the turn-borns' fountain. They danced up and down, stabbing with spears even a dragon respected, being tipped with poison.

Making themselves understood.

So. The Lost One hunted here, too. The turn-born should have dealt with this man the instant he crossed. As well as expect a sei to wipe the bottom of an infant terst. The powerful cared nothing for the small ones.

Had he, before Marrowdell and Jenn Nalynn?

Wisp extended his wing.

Dragons strengthened with age and little could penetrate the hide of an adult. The claws and fangs of other, older, dragons. The secret venom-filled fangs of kruar.

The darts and spear points used by ylings could do damage as well; by the sudden bites along his wing, so could their needles. Wisp brought his head around to watch, bemused how the small one pushed each needle through with seeming ease, then bent it back on itself to secure the seam. By the time it had moved to the next needle, the first had disappeared, the section of wing intact again.

Yling magic. Quiet. Productive. As powerful in its way, the dragon thought warily, as any in the Verge. What else did they sew?

They worked quickly, oblivious to his curiosity, turning to his leg once finished the wing. Others, warriors, hovered on guard or clung by a hand; at some point Wisp had become a roost for several and couldn't very well shake them off. They protected those preoccupied.

If they thought to protect him too, he'd not bother to argue, though he was heartily glad the kruar were gone.

Especially Scourge.

The old fool returned to Marrowdell for his own reasons; the girl would have him return for hers. Wisp snarled, startling the ylings on his snout into the air. ~Your pardon.~ They settled.

Only to startle again, spears at the ready, while the rest wrapped themselves in cloaks, dousing their lights to hide as leaves on the ground!

Ground with wretched fur to muffle any footfall. He could be safe in his sanctuary, asleep and uninjured. He could be in Marrowdell, snuggling with the boys. Wisp growled. He was too old for this; that was the problem. Did not dragons barely older take to the high cliffs?

Where admittedly most stopped moving altogether, too

busy hoarding their magic and plotting dire deeds to care about themselves, let alone the world below.

He. Was. Not. That. Old.

~WHAT DARES HUNT ME?~ Wisp roared, claws ready, daring whatever lurked in the shadows to strike.

*Rustlerustle.*

~YOU!~ Shedding ylings, the dragon lurched to stand on his one good leg, bearing with the pain of the others. ~SHOW YOURSELF!~ He didn't risk more movement, wouldn't again underestimate an enemy able to bend the earth itself into a trap.

*Rustlerustle.*

A flurry of wings, cloaks, and sparks converged on the dragon. Five ylings carried something between them, something they dropped before him.

The shard of mirror Jenn Nalynn had brought to the Verge!

The small ones stayed around the shard, the sparks within their hair enough to light it.

Or rather, to light the ground around the shard, for the surface was black and reflected nothing.

Easing back down, Wisp placed a clawtip in the center of the shard and set a breeze to whispering. "Crumlin. She is gone and you are lost. I offer a quick death."

Not that he'd any intention of mercy, but the man needn't know.

*Rustle.* Eyes opened, then crossed to stare at the clawtip neatly between them. "What are you?"

Mortified, Wisp opened his jaws to roar, then thought better of it. If this Crumlin kept to the shadows, coming out only to hunt the small ones, little wonder he was ignorant of the Verge's other inhabitants.

It was likely how he'd survived.

No longer. "I am your death," the dragon replied comfortably. "Face me now or wait in fear."

The eyes narrowed. "You won't catch me again. I'm too clever. Too quick. I'll catch you first!"

Tiresome creature. Wisp yawned. "Wait, then. I've other places to be."

He snapped up the shard and filled his mouth with dragonfire, until nothing remained of the mirror or eyes but the last echo of Crumlin's, "Noooo—!"

The ylings crowded close, patting the dragon with their tiny hands. He forced himself to endure for a moment, as they'd been brave and helpful, then snarled an end to such liberties.

Wisp opened his wings, finding the one healed by the ylings no less strong. With a single beat, he was in the air above the meadow, sparks glittering below.

With the next, he'd turned and begun the journey to his crossing, and Marrowdell.

Destroying the shard had been to rid himself of the bother of conversation.

When next he crossed into the Verge?

He'd rid them all of Crumlin.

"We don't wish to go to lessons," the elder boy exclaimed. "We wish to stay here, and wait for Uncle Bannan."

Wisp resisted the urge to open an eye. He'd promised the girl to return and had, but healing was best done asleep. Something far easier in his sanctuary than here. It didn't help that everyone seemed bent on making as much noise as possible.

~Elder brother.~

Let alone the little cousins.

~I'm asleep.~

Unfortunately, this was the truthseer's too-clever toad. ~No need to wake, elder brother. I know you can hear me in your dreams. Is everything all right? Did our elder sister cross into Channen? Have they succeeded?~

~Have you the ability to be silent!?~

Silence as, presumably, the toad considered the question.

"Master Dusom's expecting you on the morrow. You promised your uncle you'd go." Tir, the redoubtable warrior, was losing ground.

"Weed can do sums here and I'm to practice with my sword anyway. We'll work ever so hard, Tir. We promise."

Werfol joined the pleading. "We promise, Tir."

The man was seriously outmatched. Wisp bestirred himself and sent a breeze to Werfol's ear alone. "Behave or we'll eat you."

"Wisp's back!!" A joyful shout.

The dragon felt his control of the situation slipping. Had the girl been so difficult?

"Back? Ancestors Useless and Unreliable!" Tir bellowed. He grabbed a broom and started poking into corners. "Show yourself, dragon!" He passed a window and stopped to peer outside, wiping away frost with his sleeve. All of a sudden, he pounded his fist on the glass. "An' there's the other bloody fool!" He brandished the broomstick. "Open the door, Semyn, so I can smack one o'them at least."

"You mustn't!" Werfol cried, even as Semyn obeyed, letting in a cold draft and Scourge's head.

The broom lifted, which was promising, but to the dragon's disappointment, the old kruar meekly lowered his head. "I've come for the boys' lesson."

Tir gave his erstwhile weapon a frustrated shake then tossed it aside. "There'll be no lesson till I get a report! What happened? Where's Bannan and Jenn?"

Before Scourge could reply, Wisp wrapped himself in light and raised his head. "We saw them safely to the crossing into Channen where they were met by an escort arranged by the turn-born. I have returned to Marrowdell as its protector."

A derisive snort. "You returned to lick your wounds."

The dragon found himself surrounded by boys. "You're hurt?" Semyn asked worriedly. "Where?"

"Can we see?" Werfol, the more bloodthirsty. "Were you in a battle?"

"Lessons!" Scourge urged, but his cause was lost.

Tir Half-face pointed a stubby finger at the dragon, then brought it to bear on the kruar. "I'll have the whole of it. Now!"

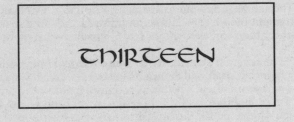

# THIRTEEN

*I*N THE SHADOW District, night was brighter than day.
Certainly it was livelier. The huge wall lamps were joined
by others on poles and hung from wires overhead, not to
mention the bright welcome from open doors and windows
as shops opened along the canals. Damp stone glistened by
that light, as did skin, bared shoulders rubbing in the crush,
for Channen's inhabitants had streamed belowground with
sunset, to walk and shop and feast.

Night didn't matter. Hadn't she found lost boys and a
half-frozen dragon in the middle of a storm?

Finding one woman among thousands, however, was
proving a different sort of challenge. Her gift worked here.
In short order, Jenn found a lost coin, a lost earring, and a
box of ribbons. More satisfyingly, she'd reunited a crying
child with his parents; less so, they'd been followed by a trio
of dogs—according to Bannan not so much lost as hoping
to be found and fed—until she'd stopped trying to find Lila
for a while.

Though under other circumstances, Jenn would have

been happy to spend more time with dogs, having not met one before.

In a city, she thought, something—someone—must be lost all the time. Perhaps if she could stay in one place, but they were moving steadily through the crowd, Bannan proving adept at slipping around and between without so much as a bump.

Though he heard her as speaking Rhothan, any Naalish who might overhear would think it their language. Convenient for their disguise, so long as Bannan answered in Naalish and kept his voice to an indistinct murmur. He'd done quite well so far, better than she could have, Jenn was sure, especially the time when a heavily burdened servant had trod on the truthseer's foot and he'd stifled a shout.

She plucked his sleeve. "I could try again."

His fingers covered hers, warm and comforting, but his gaze continued to sweep the faces of passersby and he didn't slow. "Thank you, Dearest Heart," he said gently. "But save your gift, for now. I fear it may not be the city. What if Lila isn't lost?"

His sister was lost, because Jenn wanted to find her and hadn't. Yet.

This firm conviction being difficult to put into words without sounding childish, Jenn nodded. "So we're going to the token dealer?"

"Not exactly." Instead of explaining, Bannan led the way under another arched bridge. They were everywhere, some merely for foot traffic, others so wide going beneath was like entering a tunnel. On either side of each bridge was a stair leading up to what would seem the surface of the city, if you didn't know how much of it was below. "We do need to find the Artisans' Market. It should be close."

He'd had directions from Appin, but Jenn wasn't so sure. The Shadow District was a maze of streets above and walkways below, made worse by how the canals flowed with what seemed no direction or sense that she could see. Just ahead, this one widened almost into another lake, with its strange sunken disks, then narrowed under a longer bridge than most, only to widen again, with more disks, beyond. If she looked the other way, well, it was more of the same. Cities seemed to try to be confusing.

"Up and over we go." He nodded to the stair by the bridge. They climbed single file to make room for the family with three laughing children on the way down. The adults courteously touched fingers to shoulder.

Jenn did the same. Bannan, now carrying the gilded staff Appin had assured them was required for a merchant about legal business, gracefully tapped the round top of that to his shoulder, as they'd seen others do.

Her sack remained with the Naalish, as did Bannan's pack and anything with pockets. Merchants, however, carried purses and he'd a small gold one, studded with square golden mirrors, hanging from a chain that went from shoulder to hip. He'd tucked the tokens and coins from Marrowdell, along with Frann's brooch, into the compartments along his belt. The purse, that fit in the palm of his hand?

Oh, that held the house toad.

With Appin out of the room a moment, they'd watched the stout creature squeeze himself in, doing their best to neither laugh nor gasp. Somehow it managed. The chain went through the lid, so Bannan had gently pushed that down.

Toad on his hip, staff in hand—with, no doubt, the yling clinging to him somewhere, perhaps part of the fringe on his jacket—they'd headed into the night.

Having climbed to street level, Jenn was charmed to discover the bridge was bordered by boxes of greenery interspersed with more benches, these in shadow rather than light. At the top of the arch, she knelt on a bench to look down, her arms crossed on the stone railing, her chin atop her arms.

Below, the canal was dark violet and impenetrable. Only where the disks lay just beneath the surface could she even tell for sure something was there. Light played over the water, or the water played with the light; nothing reflected as it would in a puddle at home. Instead, the shapes of buildings, of pedestrians, of bridges sprawled and bent, while ripples came and went, like suggestions of life.

Yet the air was moist and warm, as if summer had taken shelter here for the winter, and small creatures scurried along branches. Something trembled the leaves nearby.

Jenn took a second look, wondering if she'd glimpsed red little eyes.

Rabbits, she thought then, quite firmly, for nyphrit surely didn't belong in a place full of young children and not-found dogs.

"Jenn. We mustn't linger." The first impatience he'd shown, though it must, she thought, wear on Bannan to stroll the city instead of run through it.

"But we must, at least once." She looked around meaningfully. "Doesn't everyone?"

Bannan shook his head and almost smiled. "You're absolutely right." Leaning his staff against the bench, he sat with her, his back to the rail, arms along it. "As pretty a little bridge, Ancestors Witness, as ever there was."

"Little?"

"Vorkoun's span the Lilem," he explained. "The river's easily a hundred times wider."

Jenn turned to sit as well. Her love's fingers explored the shape of her shoulder, tracing the bones with a touch not so light as to tickle, sending gooseflesh down her arms and an interesting heat elsewhere. While that was certainly enjoyable, her curiosity was even more aroused and she'd have liked to ask how such massive bridges were made and how long they lasted, not to mention what ice did to their structures, if there was ice in Vorkoun at all, but . . .

This wasn't the time. "Melusine's gift—my gift—"

"It's all right." Bannan gave her a reassuring squeeze. "We'll find my sister without it, Dearest Heart. If Emon came to meet these shadow lords, Lila will have come here. My guess is she's being held nearby, somewhere. Unless she's escaped or been freed—which," abrupt dismay, "could be a problem."

"She hasn't, or she'd be here."

He gave her a doubtful look.

Jenn bent to look under the bench, unsurprised to find a child's shoe. She put it beside her where the owner could spot it. "I don't believe my gift has failed, Bannan. Perhaps it's not that I find what's lost," she mused aloud. "When I'm searching—" not that she did, so much as pay attention, "—things that are out of place, adrift, and yes, lost, find me.

I've been searching since we arrived. If Lila hasn't found me," she hazarded, "maybe it's because she's still a prisoner and can't."

"Or I was wrong about Channen, in which case I apolog—" Without warning, Bannan went white and Jenn knew what he'd thought, another reason for no Lila at all—

His sister injured.

Or worse.

"Don't think it." Jenn grabbed his hands. "You've told me about Lila. How careful she is—how strong and quick and wise. Dearest Heart. Bannan! What's more likely?"

He shuddered, then rested his forehead to hers. "Ancestors Awed and Amazed," unsteady. When Bannan straightened, his eyes gleamed with renewed hope. "A cell able to hold my sister? Who'd have thought!"

"A cell that could be anywhere," Jenn had to point out, for in that her gift had failed. "How do we find it?"

"Continue as we've begun. What I saw in Werfol's vision was no mysterious dungeon, but a jail like those of any city. My plan's to roam the market and commit a petty crime."

"Bannan!" Whatever would Peggs say? Let alone her father. "We can't!"

His grin was pure mischief. "Agreed. We'd do Lila no good in jail ourselves." Before Jenn could do more than scowl at him, the truthseer grew serious. "My first thought was to find a constable, spin a tale of needing to question a jailed thief about some missing goods. See the truth."

Which sounded reasonable, but . . . "Why tell Appin we were going to the token dealer?"

A shrug. "So he wouldn't know where we really went, while gaining a name for Lila."

Jenn stared at the remarkable man she'd only thought she knew. "That was—" devious and altogether not what she'd have done, but how better to throw the alarming Shadow Sect off their trail? "—very clever," she finished admiringly.

"Maybe." Bannan went to run his fingers through his hair, then stopped, likely thinking of the yling. "Maybe not," he said abruptly. "If my Naalish will expose me as Rhothan, I can't risk a conversation with a constable or anyone else. This Birr may be our only choice."

The difficulty with clever people, Jenn decided, was keeping up. "Why?"

"The most lucrative wishings—and their tokens—are illegal, even here. I'd bet the winter's dishes Birr's spent his share of nights in the city jail. He should know what we need." A decisive nod. "If necessary, we'll trade him our tokens for the information."

"You wanted them for Lila," she protested.

"I want Lila."

Flat and uncompromising. She'd feel the same, were it Peggs, Jenn thought.

Bannan searched her face. "Much as I hate this, Dearest Heart—" he began.

"I'm the one to speak to Birr," she finished.

"Are you sure?"

~Is this wise, elder sister?~ the toad asked at the same time.

"Of course," Jenn answered them both. "Just tell me what to say. After all, this city is your world, beloved."

Then, because they were alone for this moment and shadowed, because Bannan feared for her and mustn't, and because, most of all, she'd lost him once—

And would not again.

Between one heartbeat and the next, Jenn Nalynn let her other self show.

"As the edge is mine."

Like a glimpse of the Verge, seeing her shift between glorious turn-born and the woman who was equally so. His ally. His partner. The love of his life. Whatever Jenn saw in his face brought forth one of her magical smiles and Bannan might have happily drowned in it, then and there . . .

Save she jumped to her feet and held out a hand with a brisk, "Shall we?"

"Away, then," he agreed.

Down the other side of the bridge, then down again, taking the next staircase to the canal level. To his deeper sight, the ever-present dampness on the stone walls had a silver tint and what filled the channel between banks was nothing he'd swim in or touch to his lips.

Mimrol. No doubt as to the "Source" the Naalish, Appin, had spoken of with such reverence.

Magic rained here.

To be collected with care. Dusom's friend had been mystified to discover the lesser canals of the Shadow District didn't join those surrounding the city, but Bannan understood all too well. Let magic wash away? Be diluted?

Surely a waste, when it could be bottled for use beyond the edge. "Jenn." He lowered his voice, for they'd rejoined the crowds. "The 'Silver Tears' Kydd spoke of, sold by Channen for Rhothan wishings? It has to be mimrol. Mellynne's magic comes from the Verge. As rain!"

"The 'Source.'" She looked up, as if hoping for a glimpse, then sideways at him. "Is mimrol as lovely here as the Verge?"

Wistful. How often she'd ask him to describe Marrowdell's wonders, being, like any villager, unable to see them for herself until the turn. "No," he admitted. "It sinks and tarnishes in the canal. Those," he pointed to one of the submerged platters, "must be where something of it becomes solid."

"And no longer magic," she guessed. "Or the Naalish would dig them out."

Implying it would be worth collecting the rain as soon as it fell. Bannan took a closer look at the walls and walkways, their abundance of eaves, catchments, and gutters taking on a new significance.

As did the presence of so many, living within the edge. Marrowdell's dreams tested those who entered, chased those unable to bear them away. Clearly it was different here, but why? Was it that magic fell from the sky, instead of grew through the ground?

Or was it simpler than that? Had the dreams begun when Marrowdell's trust was betrayed?

"Bannan. We're here."

Sure enough, the stone walkways widened ahead, permitting a row of stalls to be set against the banks. The crowd slowed as people meandered from one offering to the next. There, any resemblance to the market at Endshere's fair ended. These stalls were rich tents, open front and back, their contents spilling out on tables or hung from easels. Colors blazed under plentiful lamps and music filled the air. Performers on stilts strutted through the mass of people, juggling balls of light.

"What do we do?" Jenn asked, eyes wide.

"Play our roles." Staffs like his, with its tip carved like a fat snake curled back on itself, were common. Others bore wings and some were more properly spears, though he'd seen no weapons. In sight.

Three women passed, gems sprinkled on their bared shoulders. Collars and skin were in evidence everywhere, and Bannan was relieved to see their clothing—which he'd thought conspicuous—was among the more conservative here. Tattoos were common; that some of those moved over the skin?

Magic.

"Walk ahead of me, slightly. My apprentice would identify merchandise worth my while. Admire each artisan's work, take their name, but don't step inside." This when her eyes lit. "And watch for a jewelry maker. We'll stop at the first."

Jenn fingered her ear, which showed to advantage, her hair rolled into a loose coil down her back. The Naalish had warned them; every grown woman, and quite a few men, sported earrings, some dangling below their shoulders. As one of those passed, the earring a chain of red-and-blue bells that quacked like ducks, she wrinkled her nose. "Not that."

"Your choice," he promised.

The first artisan worked with fire, his magic to instill images within the flames of candles as well as a portable hearth. The candles held portraits he was willing to do on the spot, while within the hearth's fiery heart curled a dragon.

Jenn stared at that a long moment, as if she couldn't believe her eyes, which she likely didn't, her own dragon nothing like the artisan's tame rendering. She left without taking the name. Bannan followed her to the next stall, hiding a grin.

Needlework dragonflies, larger than life and with

jeweled eyes, clung to the roof's edge over the second stall, their wings rarely still. Easels displayed more fine work, framed Beholdings for handfastings and weddings, their traditional words bespelled, so the labels claimed, with potent wishings for fecundability, faithfulness, and good health. The artisan responsible was named Dawnn Blysse; Jenn complimented her work from a cautious distance.

The yling leaned from his hair as they left, as though loath to leave.

The next stall couldn't be reached, hidden by a press of people ten-deep waiting their turn. Those successful were walking away with wooden mugs and blissful expressions, froth clinging to their upper lips. As Jenn looked over her shoulder, Bannan chuckled. "Emon told me of those. The wood's bespelled so the plainest beer tastes better than any you've had before. Lasts a day."

She smiled. "Just as well. Oh, look!" The exclamation hung in the air as Jenn slipped boldly around a pair of elderly men and dove into the next stall.

They scowled as he hurried after; the truthseer, not daring to speak, pressed his fingers to shoulder in apology.

Jenn was standing amid crates of baby rabbits, their bright eyes fixed on her. She exchanged a few words with the artisan, who held a larger version in her arms, only to back out so suddenly she collided with Bannan.

"You don't want to know," she gasped, moving onward.

~

*A snip of thread, touched by skin and warmth . . .*
*a drop of sleep,*
*under the tongue . . .*
*And the dream unfolds . . .*
Moonlight. Lamplight. Curls on a pillow.
Shape beneath a quilt.
Above the quilt, a dragon sleeps.
*The dream falters . . . rebuilds . . .*
Above the quilt, a dragon sleeps.
*The dream falters . . . dismissed.*
*A sliver of paper, touched by ink and fingertip . . . a drop of*
*silver, under the tongue . . .*

*And the dream unfolds ...*
Bright eyes, wise eyes, gaze back. A head tilts. *Inquisitive.*
A hand strokes the head, the thumbnail purpled and
broken.
Skyward.
Silver rains down.
While something rustles above. Some things hunt below.

Marvel. Wonder. Horror. Delight. Mere steps apart, within
a cacophony of music and voices such as Jenn hadn't imagined could exist in one place. Yet everyone else, including
Bannan, took the Artisans' Market in stride, oohing at this,
dismissing that, pausing to sip and chatter like Cynd and
Covie out in their gardens.

The Verge, being uniformly strange, felt ever so much
calmer. Here she went from magical beer mugs to—she
swallowed bile—self-skinning rabbits? What were these
people thinking?

As for her role? She'd but to walk up, Bannan and his
fancy staff in the wings, for the artisans to abandon their
clients or friends, mistaking her for someone who could order their work by the bargeload, to be shipped beyond Mellynne. Perhaps make them famous, surely that. Famous
beyond the Shadow District, as only the best at each art
form—as she'd heard more than once—was permitted a
stall here.

The best skinner of rabbits? Jenn shuddered, hoping for
better at the next.

She envied Bannan his ease working through the crowds,
though his height gave him an advantage. From where she
stood, the walkway was a moving maze of people, most carrying packages, and all cheerfully oblivious. At any moment,
someone would dash across her path without warning. Ancestors Trodden and Trampled. How she'd avoided colli-
sions so far was a—

And there was one, just ahead. Two young women
walked right into a dark-haired man. Bags went flying and
the crowd split around the trio as everyone apologized
while belongings were sorted.

As easily her as anyone, Jenn thought, becoming even more mindful of those around her.

So she noticed, when the dark-haired man walked past her, and saw how he felt his pockets, and heard—though he cursed in a low mutter— him say, "Heart's Blood. Now I've gone and lost it."

And wasn't surprised at all when, a few steps later, she felt the toe of her boot touch something on the ground.

Stooping quickly to pick it up, Jenn found herself with a clockwork within a golden case, the sort of thing that would fit nicely in a pocket and surely was what the man had lost.

Her gift at work.

"Another find?" Bannan shook his head. "Dearest Heart, you can't return everything lost."

Turning, she saw the man hadn't gone far, forced to wait by a round of spectators around an impromptu juggler. "This I can," she assured the truthseer. "I'll be right back."

Before Bannan could try to change her mind, she slipped between shoulders and boxes and a cart.

There. Jenn hurried up to the owner of the clockwork. "Excuse me, sir."

He seemed not to hear. Jenn touched his sleeve. "I believe you dropped this."

His head came around and he glared at her. "Go away! I don't understand a word you're saying!"

Which wasn't, Jenn thought distractedly, possible, but before she could utter another, the strange man spotted the clockwork. Without so much as a thank you, he snatched it from her hand, shoved it in his pocket, and pushed his way through the people beside him as if he couldn't leave her soon enough.

Though surrounded by people, she felt suddenly alone. This wasn't Marrowdell, where helping one another was like breathing. Aunt Sybb had said a whistling woman and a crowing hen never come to a good end, meaning there were times to behave as expected by others. Of course the dear lady would add, a twinkle in her eye, that there were times to do nothing of the sort, but they were playing roles, she and Bannan, and hers was to blend with those around her.

Who apparently did not chase after one other to return dropped clockworks.

She made her way back to Bannan. Though she'd been gone no more than a few steps, out of sight no more than an instant, his relief was plain and she felt worse. "I'll not bother again," she told him.

Reading her face, the truthseer carefully didn't smile. "It would speed our progress," he agreed, then leaned close to whisper, "Never regret a kind act, Dearest Heart, even to those who aren't grateful."

And she wouldn't, Jenn decided, stealing a kiss.

"I show the world what I choose," Rhonnda Taff explained as she worked. "If fashion follows me, that's because people are unoriginal sheep." The man who sat in her chair nodded agreeably, as did the twenty more waiting in line.

As a merchant's representative, Jenn had been invited to stand and observe. She watched the artisan deftly apply paint to a muscular shoulder, adding shading to the semblance of bare branches that began at the man's collar. Whenever Rhonnda's brush left the skin, the illusion became so convincing Jenn wouldn't have been surprised if a bird tried to perch on one of the twigs. "How long does it last?"

"However long I wish. This—" a light slap on the man's as yet unpainted shoulder "—is my canvas. The essence of my art is uncertainty." She smiled at the man.

Who looked, to Jenn's eyes, suddenly less certain about walking around with shoulders that looked like bits of a tree.

"If you wonder why my shoulders are bare," Rhonnda went on, "it's because there's no one else good enough to decorate them. A curse, I know." The artisan stared pointedly at Jenn and shook her head, the bells hanging from her lobes jingling. "Bare ears, though? Can't imagine going out in public like that."

"Thank you for your time," Jenn said hastily, and left.

She liked Bannan's shoulders as they were, she decided as she rejoined him, though she'd not mind them glistening with bubbles from the bath they'd missed sharing, or glistening with sweat, for that matter. At his quizzical look, she blushed. "On to the next," she told him.

It was wider than those previous, which was interesting. At Jenn's approach, a chubby brown bird stepped out to fix her with a beady-eyed gaze. It didn't appear magical but was certainly remarkable, being what Jenn had seen in books. A chicken! She bent to look more closely and it fluffed its feathers at her. Done, it walked away, deeper into the stall, making a clucking sound as arguing with itself.

Fascinated, Jenn followed, weaving through painted statues of people—life-sized, clothed, and mostly old—as well as of dogs and other animals, depicted about to play or asleep. The chicken, at home, moved its short legs faster.

So did she, loath to lose sight of it, to find herself moving through a curtain and into what must be a private part of the stall.

Statues here as well, but these were younger and naked. The chicken having disappeared under a cot, Jenn went to the nearest, a man perhaps Wainn's age, astonished how life-like it was, down to black eyelashes and shy dimples. Even efflet would be impressed.

Stone or clay beneath the paint? She couldn't help but touch—

The eyes opened, the mouth smiled, and a hand shot up to cup her breast while the other slipped between—

"Heart's Blood!" Jenn leapt back and would have struck the presumptuous creation, but its eyes closed as did its mouth, and the hands fell harmlessly to its sides.

"May I help you?" The artisan had come through the curtain. He flicked a finger at his shoulder then waited, sucking on a stick of red candy.

Jenn touched her shoulder hastily, then bowed to be safe. "My apologies. I followed your chicken." She frowned. "Why do you have a chicken?"

Out came the candy, to be aimed at the cot. "Hard enough to sleep here. The clucking helps. I'm Stevynn the sculptor. May I help you?"

Her role. "My name is Jenn. I represent a master merchant, interested in putting together a shipment of new works," she explained. "He's asked me to visit yours."

The candy stick pointed to the naked man who'd groped her, then waved to encompass the rest. "These are commissioned. Bought and paid for. Private. Since you're the one trespassing, I expect discretion." As he spoke, Stevynn tried to scowl, which might have succeeded except that he looked just like their father whenever he tried to scold her and Peggs.

Both men having faces more suited to laughter.

"I won't tell anyone." Not that she grasped what was so secret about these statues; many of the other artisans exhibited nude forms, though none that were so—active. "Have you anything smaller?" she asked, hoping he'd lead her elsewhere. "We've cargo constraints." The vague term Bannan had given her having proved its worth already.

Stevynn drew the curtain aside, nodding for her to go out. "I've samples of my public offerings. But my work doesn't travel well. This would be the merchant?"

Jenn looked to find Bannan stood just inside the stall, doubtless alarmed when she'd disappeared. He touched staff to shoulder in greeting, but didn't speak.

The artisan's brows rose toward his hairless scalp, but he turned his attention back to Jenn. "Trusts your judgment, I see."

"Yes." Flustered, Jenn went to the nearest of the clothed statues, a woman with a fiercely intelligent face. She'd been carved with shoulders bared, breasts rising like waves beneath a web of gold beadwork, and the more Jenn looked, the more realistic the woman appeared. "Your work is astonishing."

"Care for a sample?" the woman asked dryly, looking down.

While Jenn gaped, Stevynn pulled the candy from his mouth, wrapped it, and tucked it in a pocket. "My wife, Lianna. Always better at business. Please. Try for yourself."

After what happened in the back of the stall? Jenn began to shake her head. "I really mustn't—"

But Stevynn's wife had already gone behind the curtain, returning with a flat square of unfired clay on a tray, and Stevynn stood waiting, something of Radd Nalynn in the shape of his face, and something of hope in his eyes.

Where was the harm? Besides, she was playing the role

of someone who might buy this talented man's work. "What do I do?"

"Touch to see," the artisan sang, rather than spoke, "what yours would be."

As her hand reached, Bannan stepped forward, crying "Jenn!" and she tried to stop. Too late. She felt the cool of clay on her fingertip.

Stevynn took the square and held it toward Jenn, singing again. "The Far Step need not be your last. Behold my gift, your living past."

A figure pulled itself from the clay, as though rising from the ground. Colors ran this way and that. Cloth appeared and fluttered into place and with a final lift of her head, Frann Nall stood in Stevynn's hands.

She was no taller than a cup, no more alive than before, and heartbreakingly real. When she smiled and raised her hand, Jenn bolted from the stall.

Hearing Stevynn call after her. "Order soon. The full version takes five days in the oven."

"Ancestors Witness. I knew a man once," Bannan commented. "Had his dead horse stuffed and put into his hall. He really loved that horse."

Jenn gave him a sidelong look. She'd passed two more stalls without slowing and they'd begun to stand out from the milling crowd, but he didn't protest. "What they did there. It wasn't right."

"They harm no one."

"We don't keep our dead!" A passerby glanced at them and a flush appeared on the cheek he could see. Jenn lowered her voice. "You know what I mean. The departed leave their shape, to be Blessed Ancestors. It makes no sense to buy those—those copies! Besides," with familiar practicality. "What does one do with such a thing? Show it to friends? Stand it by the table for meals? Cover it to keep off dust?"

Not the truth. Not what drove her forward, as if in flight.

Bannan understood. Who better? Leaving for the border hadn't eased the pain of losing father and mother, only added the recurring one of fallen comrades. He'd learned. Only the dead could be left behind.

"Jenn. Jenn—!" when she didn't look around. He touched her elbow. "We didn't bury our grief with Frann's bones, Ancestors Dear and Departed. Or leave it in Marrowdell." He lowered his head near hers. "We carry it. Sometimes put aside, but never gone. Nor should it be."

"'Dear and Departed." A tear slid down her now-pale cheek. "She looked—real. She smiled at me."

The loss in her voice cut his heart. He lifted his head, making his own tone matter-of-fact. "Emon spoke of such statues. The movement's drawn from the bereaved memory of the person, as is the appearance. That's all they are, Jenn. The smile you saw was one you remembered. You don't need a statue for that."

She considered this in silence as they passed a stall with paintings that sang like the birds they depicted.

Then, "There were others, in the back." Was that another blush rising? "They moved—differently."

Love mimics? Emon, ever fascinated, had described those with great gusto. For a price, you could have the object of your unrequited lust, conveniently cooperative, if unreal. Being illegal, the originals more than willing to prosecute if their mimics were discovered, only added to the things' allure.

It was Bannan's turn to feel heat in his face. Jenn was learning more than he'd anticipated of city life.

"I've seen my first chicken," she announced all at once, her voice happier. "I think I prefer my eggs from toads."

Relieved, Bannan gently patted his purse. "Not that we need one now, little cousin." Though what the toad might "make" next was a question he'd like answered. Eggs from pebbles; gauds from the hearts of fallen enemies; a mask from a moth.

What might come from dragon-melted iron?

That disturbing train of thought ended as Jenn exclaimed. "Look at those!"

She carried her grief. Thinking that, realizing the truth of it, Jenn felt lighter. Had she thought to honor Frann's loss by burying that pain, by trying to forget? If so, she'd done them both a disservice.

Better this, the splash of ready tears as she gazed wonderingly at what Frann would have loved. Flutes, somehow suspended in the air, played themselves in exquisite harmony. There were small ones and ones longer than her arm. Some turned slowly, their intricate keys twinkling as unseen fingers rose and fell. Others were still and silent until she came close, then burst into trills that lay over the other notes like frost on a window.

"Are you all right?" Bannan asked quietly.

He'd known what to say because he carried more grief than she could imagine, yet lived life with such joy it spread to everyone around him. Despite that grief. Despite the scars he bore.

Or . . . could it be because of them?

Surrounded by music, Jenn touched her fingers to her shoulder as she met the truthseer's apple butter eyes, being unable, in this public place, to take him in her arms.

"I will be," she said, and saw his eyes glow with the truth of that.

They walked past the next artisan, a chandler. Jenn glanced inside, seeing rows of bronze candles on shelves set against the tent walls. Those ranks were unlit and oddly plain, in a market where everything moved or sang. They weren't alone in passing it by. Few so much as noticed it.

Then Jenn saw one candle was lit, on a pedestal in the middle of the floor.

A simple candle, with nothing remarkable about it, yet she slowed. When had she seen a candle burn with such golden light?

"What is it?" Bannan asked.

"I'm not sure." Jenn went into the stall, the truthseer at her side.

The closer she came to the candle, the gladder she felt. It was as though its flame shed happiness as much as light.

"Ancestors Blessed." The truthseer smiled, going to the other side of the candle. They looked at one another across it and, for no reason, both laughed.

Jenn looked happy, he felt—as if every weight had been lifted—that's how he felt and if a candle was responsible, Bannan couldn't imagine why this stall wasn't filled with customers.

Pat. Pat. The purse at his hip bumped and shook.

Unless the happiness was due to some drug and this a trap. Losing his smile, Bannan's hand dropped to the lid. "Jenn, ask it what's wrong."

Keeping her smile, she said gently, "Nothing's wrong, Dearest Heart. The little cousin's happy too." Her eyes gained the faraway look they had when she listened to what he couldn't, then Jenn chuckled. "We're expected."

They couldn't be. Bannan had time to worry before a man stepped through the curtain separating the private portion of the stall from the public and clapped, as if overjoyed to see them. A lion paced the skin of his shoulders and they'd never met, he was certain.

But there was something familiar about his round gentle face—The truthseer looked deeper.

To find pure joy.

He moved involuntarily to seize the man's hands, meeting a strong, sure clasp. "You see me," the man exclaimed with pleasure.

"I do," Bannan said huskily, unafraid to speak. There was nothing but good in this man.

Here was another like Wainn and Wen.

Touched by the Verge, and magic.

Leott was his name and Jenn knew, even without the toad's happy ~We're here! We've come!~ and Bannan's beaming face, that this was someone to trust. Without hesitation, they let the artisan lead them into the back portion of the stall. It wasn't a workshop at all.

But a perfect little home, with an elegant table and chairs, a comfortable bed—presently occupied by a bewildering array of dogs and cats—and a tidy kitchen. Nothing would do but they sit and have a drink with their host.

Who gave her a perceptive look as their hands touched. "You are turn-born yet of this world." Leott glanced at Bannan. "And a seer of truth." He sat, fingers steepled together, his face intensely curious.

The yling chose that moment to perch on the tips of Leott's fingers. Man and yling tilted their heads exactly the same way. "You're a brave one, to travel so far."

~I matter to our elder sister,~ the toad said at once.

Leott bowed to the purse sitting on the table, the toad having refused to budge from it. "You do, indeed, my courageous friend."

"You can talk to toads too," Jenn said with delight.

A modest touch of fingers to lion's nose. "I listen."

To more, she guessed, than toads.

Bannan leaned forward. "Are you a member of the Shadow Sect?"

A dog snarled and a cat hissed. Leott smiled at them and they subsided. "The sect sees a candlemaker," he said simply. "They don't see me. Few can."

Explaining, Jenn realized, why others had walked by without noticing the marvel within. "Your candles. I've never seen such light."

The yling flew to Bannan as Leott clapped his hands again. "Oh, but you have, Dear Hearts! You've traveled here from its true home." A wink. "I heard."

The Verge. The candle burned with its light. Jenn exchanged worried looks with Bannan, who said quickly, "Please be careful. There are those who seek what you've found."

"Fear not for me." The lion on his shoulders lay like a scarf, its huge eyes peaceful. "What I've found is my way to bring a little happiness to those who need it." Leott lifted his cup. "All those who do, if they possess an open heart, will always find me and be welcome."

A promise, Jenn realized in that moment, he'd made long ago and would keep, so long as he lived.

There was a bit of Marrowdell here, after all.

"I'm glad we've met," she told him, and smiled from the bottom of her heart.

Their visit with Leott had been like a moment home, safe and at peace. Once they left, the mist-stroked stone and dark, secretive water of the Shadow District served to remind Bannan how far home was. They were on their own here.

Except for unspent coins and illegal tokens. A name and a now-silent brooch. Oh, and a staff, purseful of house toad, and a yling, though he'd no idea where the tiny thing presently hid and worried he'd sit on it.

All assets of unknown worth in Channen. Not so Jenn Nalynn. Stall after stall, artisans warmed to the sincerity of her interest and more than one had rushed after her with work they'd kept back for a special customer or hadn't finished, but wasn't it remarkable and would she place an order?

If he'd been a merchant in truth, he could have loaded a barge three times over. Being nothing of the sort, Bannan made sure to confer with his "apprentice" after every visit, shaking his head like a man sorely tempted but short on funds to forestall further importunities.

He'd been sincerely tempted to ask Leott for help, but hadn't. Like Wainn, the gentle artisan was part of two worlds, yet not wholly in either. That Leott had avoided the notice of the Shadow Sect was a marvel; Bannan could only hope their visit, as Keepers, hadn't exposed him. In no way would he risk embroiling the man further.

Besides, they'd a plan, once they found the token dealer. Bannan had Jenn ask a passerby about the bridge they sought, learning they were almost there. Now, more than ever, they had to act their parts, though he was heartily sick of being mute.

Lila was going to hear about this.

"Earrings!" Jenn stopped before the jeweler's stall. "At last."

The jump from dark plots and danger made Bannan blink. "Pardon?"

"I need earrings," she pointed out.

"No one's noticed," Bannan managed. "You don't have to—"

"I do," with the faintly pitying look he remembered receiving from his sister at such times.

Without another word, Bannan gave her the lesser coins from his belt. He went to wait by the bakery across from the earring maker, there being chairs in front, and had almost lost the battle to resist the aromas wafting within when Jenn reappeared.

A fresh hot pastry might ease the sting of pierced ears. Bannan waved her to join him.

As she did, someone else moved aside. Subtle, that move, to stay at the edge of his sight without being obvious.

Familiar.

Bannan smiled warmly as Jenn approached, admired the dainty gold hoops in her ears, and marked the man well.

Friend, was the question.

Or foe?

The pastry brimmed with chewy nuts and crunchy sugar bits, as well as spices and a creamy cheese. They'd ordered tea as well, this being a bakery where one paid for food and it was brought. Jenn was torn which she enjoyed most: the treat or the new experience.

"Don't look around," Bannan said in a low, too-cheerful voice. "We're being watched."

Had he said it the other way around, she'd have looked at once. Jenn managed to finish her bite, keeping her eyes on the truthseer, then swallowed before asking, with what she felt admirable calm, "One of the Shadow Sect?"

"I doubt it. Appin said he'd send word to keep them away from us, to smooth our way with the token dealer." As Bannan sipped his tea, his eyes flicked over her shoulder, then back to her. "Whoever's watching, best we don't let him know we're aware."

"How do we do that?" Jenn asked dubiously.

The corners of his mouth creased; amused, if not ready to smile. "We go about our business as if nothing's wrong.

He'll keep his distance. I've naught but glimpses," he went on. "A man, middle aged. Dark hair, shorter than most. Quietly dressed. Middling height and weight."

Oh dear. "Did he pull out a gold clockwork?" Jenn asked, feeling her stomach roil.

Sharp. "Pardon?"

She grimaced and told of her encounter, finishing with, "I meant no harm."

"And did none," Bannan assured her. "If—if, being the word—this is the same man, we'll both keep an eye out. It's the watchers we haven't spotted that worry me," the truthseer admitted, finishing the ruin of her appetite.

Jenn ate the rest of her pastry anyway, washing it down with tea. A prudent adventurer—or villager, for that matter—never wasted food. It was an admirable saying. She wished she'd one from Aunt Sybb to take away the sensation between her shoulders of unseen eyes staring at her.

The whisper of cool metal against her neck was a distraction, happening each time she shook her head. Something she did surreptitiously, so as not to appear unfamiliar with earrings. Nor had there been need to poke a hole through her tender earlobe, as Appin had implied, though she'd girded herself for that unpleasantness. In a place where magic was poured into art, at least one artisan had created earrings that stayed where they were put without hurting at all.

The watcher, however?

Bannan put one of the square coins she'd brought back in change by their used plates, standing. "The next bridge is the 'Seahorse.' Birr's stall should be on the other side. Here." Blocking the sight of anyone else, he licked his thumb and used it to rub sugar dust from her nose.

The gesture was so like Peggs' Jenn felt all the distance between them. Before she could be sad, she remembered Aunt Sybb, who always said home stayed in the heart, however far away, and smiled.

All too easy, this slip back into Captain Ash of the guard. If he hadn't, Jenn . . . ? Bannan refused to follow the thought. He'd skills of no use to a farmer.

They were of use now.

As for the watcher he'd spotted, he'd know him again at a glance. Nondescript features, best for such work, but posture was hard to disguise. The one who watched them had either stood to patient attention at a guard post for hours or stood waiting on notice at court just as long.

Or both.

He'd observed the man slide a finger under his collar, though his modest clothing was well-fitted. Having fought the same impulse, the unusual garment at times feeling it was like to throttle him? Their watcher was Rhothan. He'd bet on it.

Jenn had done an admirable job of looking without being obvious, but they'd either lost their watcher or he'd fallen back to avoid notice. Was he the same she'd met?

And could this Rhothan be Emon's, staking out this part of the market in hopes of—of what? Finding Lila?

Bannan made a frustrated sound in his throat and Jenn looked up. "What is it?"

"I'm half inclined to accost our new friend and ask his business. It may be the same as ours."

A tiny frown. "And the other half?"

He laughed without humor. "Knows better than act in the dark." Lila and Emon could be playing a deeper game than he guessed. They'd not thank him for interfering.

And be at greater risk, should he fumble.

He'd his own game, such as it was, Bannan reminded himself. With a most able partner.

They stopped under the bridge, not the only couple to linger away from the brighter lights. "Here are the tokens," he said quietly, digging them from his belt. He snapped the strand of wool holding the three together. "Offer them all only if you must. The vial first. If you can, keep the starstone."

She tucked the foul things into her bodice, between white lace and soft creamy skin, and he fought back a protest, saying instead, "Did you want to go over what to say again?"

A small smile. "I'm all right. We can do this," Jenn told him, as if aware of his doubt.

"This" being Jenn to speak to the artisan, while he

watched for lies. They'd have to both enter the stall. Bannan rubbed the back of his neck, above the collar. "Unless, seeing what we've to offer, Birr calls for the constables or the Shadow Sect. An honest man would."

Dimples appeared in her cheeks. "Then let's hope he's not."

Heart's Blood, he loved this woman. "Let's."

The token dealer's stall leaned against the stone wall of the stairs leading up to the bridge. For support, perhaps. More likely, Bannan thought, for the discreet movement of customers, wishings most often highly personal. Foliage hung almost to the roof, shadowing the stall from any lamplight above; though lit inside, rather than be open for the display of wares, the stall had a flap across the front, partially closed as if to discourage entrance.

Jenn didn't hesitate, going right inside. Bannan followed after a carefully casual look up the stairs. They were empty, and no one on the walkway seemed to pay undue attention. Their watcher? Nowhere to be seen. Good. He ducked to enter.

Inside, a banner hung from the ceiling, its neat black letters declaring: "Birr's Custom and Imported Tokens—If I Don't Have It, Who Will?" A round-faced man, presumably "Birr," sat beneath on a tall stool behind a counter. Seeing them, he frowned. "You took your time."

"You weren't our first stop," Jenn Nalynn replied without hesitation or apology. She made a show of examining the multitude of items displayed on the counter. No two were the same, though there were groupings. Polished stones and gems; small stoppered bottles; folded paper squares; an array of animal parts, scales, pickled hearts, dried fins, more of that sort.

The largest group took pride of place at the center: bones, lovingly arrayed upon a swath of black velvet. They'd have had history, Bannan thought, such bones. Names and stories. Loved ones. Enemies. Now, all that remained was what value they'd bring from those who'd grind them to powder.

In hope of magic.

"We're here now," she said and touched fingers to shoulder. "I am Jenn. May I have your name, esteemed artisan?"

Bannan winced inwardly. Jenn wasn't to reveal they knew of this Birr, but he'd not anticipated a sign, especially placed where it couldn't be missed.

A sign she couldn't read.

But the artisan merely nodded. "I'm Plevna. Birr's gone for the day." He touched his own shoulders, their skin so covered with ink it gave the illusion of clothing. He glanced at Bannan, waiting for an introduction.

The truthseer tapped his own shoulder with his staff and didn't approach, a merchant making it clear his apprentice would speak. The artisan turned back to Jenn.

"Business, is it?" His eyes traveled from her head to her boots and back. "Well, then. What's your lie?" he challenged.

Plevna had expected someone. Was this a code, to identify the right buyer? If so, they'd walked into a dealing with nothing safe about it. The truthseer's fingers closed on the staff. He'd checked its heft and balance. As good as a club, should the need arise.

Jenn, being less suspicious, took the question for an honest one. "I'm here to offer you a token for information, which isn't a lie." She tilted her head. "Why would you want one?"

"I collect them."

The truth, however odd. Bannan relaxed his grip on the staff.

Plevna stretched his arms over his head, spine cracking, then brought them down, laying his palms flat on the velvet between the bones. "Everyone has a lie. Yours could be interesting. New, perhaps. Or not. It's our favored coin, we makers of magic." He smiled, exposing teeth with letters written in red upon each. "Come. Tell me yours."

The mass of shoulder tattoos, Bannan realized, were letters—words. He'd met token sellers whose pockets bristled with scraps of paper, each covered with wishings. He supposed this was more permanent.

"My lie," Jenn Nalynn said, the truth shining in her face to Bannan's deeper sight, "is that I speak Naalish."

After an incredulous stare, Plevna broke into a wheezing laugh. "Ancestors Clever and Convincing," he said at last. "I am impressed, woman. A spell is it? And a bloody good one. How much do you want for it? Come!"

"Your lie," she said calmly.

Bannan carefully didn't smile.

"Mine," the artisan said finally, wetting his lips, "is not for the telling. Not till I'm done with life and safe." A finger tumbled a bone, then stabbed at Jenn. "Birr told me to close and go home, business being so slow, but I stayed, feeling lucky. Here you are. If you're that luck, best be worth my time. A token for information, is it? What do you want to know? More importantly, what are you offering?"

They'd practiced what to say and how, so the truthseer waited for Jenn to ask about the jail.

She drew a sharp, triumphant breath. "You stayed open to be found."

Bannan's heart skipped a beat. It couldn't be—

Jenn set the tiny black vial, the roll of parchment waiting a name, and the red starstone on the counter. "You prepared this."

—but was. He could have hugged her as recognition flared in Prevna's eyes. Recognition and fear. The artisan leaned back, waving his hands as though to shoo the tokens from his sight. "Illegal. Forbidden. Not mine."

Fragments of truth. The man was an experienced liar. Trusting Jenn's gift, Bannan went to the door flap and let it drop, then spun on his heel to bring his staff whistling down.

To stop just above a skull.

"We don't care about you. We'll settle," the truthseer said grimly, "for a name. Who bought these tokens?"

"My customers expect privacy—"

"Do they?" He knew this dance. Instead of pursuing the name, Bannan took a tangent. "What does this wishing do?"

He hadn't expected Plevna to flinch. "Didn't say what or why," the man blurted. "I don't ask."

"But you know, don't you?" Purple, in Jenn's eyes. She wasn't happy with this man, not happy at all, and for once Bannan welcomed the chill in the air.

And the ominous snap as canvas walls swelled and billowed with the approaching storm.

~Surely sufficient, elder sister,~ the toad fussed.

It wasn't wrong, Jenn realized, coming to herself. Dirty pots, she thought determinedly. Days old. Greasy pots.

When the storm didn't abate, pots and cleaning being homely things, she made herself think of strangers brushing her hair.

The storm subsided, such as it was.

The token dealer, in her opinion a person unworthy of trust or the care of a Blessed Ancestor's bones—or those of more than one, spotting a second skull on a shelf—turned a peculiar color, then reached a shaking hand for the tokens. "Yes. Not that I myself would make such a thing—but I've heard rumors—"

Bannan's staff inscribed a small circle in the air.

"It's a wishing to bind a seer of truth. Gift and will."

Bones became dust; stones and gem shattered; bottles and stoppers and papers and bits of poor creatures burst into flames that quickly spread to velvet and countertop. Plevna scampered from his stool to cower in a corner. "I made them! I'll tell you! Stop!"

Flames being dangerous to others, Jenn wished, with more restraint, for them to cease.

And they did.

Bannan put his boot to the charred counter and pushed. It fell asunder, cold cinders and ash covering the carpet that was the floor. He held out his open hand. There, on the palm, were the tokens. She'd not seen him retrieve them.

"Start with who," he said then, harsh and unforgiving.

And Jenn didn't know if Bannan meant who'd intended to bind a truthseer . . .

Or the truthseer intended to be bound . . .

"Her name's Nellie and she makes flowers that blossom as glass. Her asters are too yellow." Having made her report, Jenn put her hand flat on Bannan's chest. "He told you where to find the city jail," she said quietly, mindful of the crowd. "Why are still we doing this?"

Because what had chased two little boys from their home wanted nothing so sane as ransom, and if it wasn't Werfol—for the token dealer hadn't known the target—then they'd been after him, scattering his entire family in their pursuit.

Covering her hand with his, Bannan nodded to the next stall in the market. "Not seeing our watcher doesn't mean we're unseen. A few more, Jenn, so they don't think the token dealer our true destination. Then we'll go." They'd been fortunate. Between the performers on the walkway and the music all around, the disturbance within Plevna's had escaped notice.

He'd escaped with blisters on thumb and forefinger to show for saving what they had to have. A name alone wasn't enough. A name, together with the tokens now back in his belt pouch? Proof.

The source of the flame firmed her round little chin and nodded back.

The truthseer watched Jenn, in her tunic and pants, hair of gold and shoulders of silken skin, as she went to yet another artisan. Framed images as tall as he lined the opening to the stall, each a card from the Whither Omen Decks employed by fortune-tellers across Mellynne and Rhoth. Bannan wondered idly if they'd ever told a fortune for a turn-born.

Then Jenn's hand lifted, beckoning him to follow, and idle wonder became alarm. Ancestors Beguiled and Gullible! Bannan laid his hand over his purse—and the toad inside it. "Tell your elder sister it's time to go."

From her frown, the little cousin had done just that, but Jenn simply waved more vehemently. Before she could shout, Bannan sighed and went to join her in the stall.

"This is Thomm."

Thomm was a slender young man. A thin scar ran from forehead to cheek, giving him a rakish look; knife cut, Bannan guessed, just missing the right eye. Though quietly dressed, in a simple black tunic and pants, the artisan's right shoulder and what showed of his arm were tattooed in the seeming of a chain whose links penetrated the flesh. Above his heart, exposed by his shirt, was a second tattoo: a pair of small black ovals, their tips overlapped so one flowed into the other.

He'd seen the like before. The ovals represented a fortune-teller's link to the limitless future. The chains? A vow to be bound by the truth. In Bannan's experience, the only binding involved the fortune-teller's fingers and the purses of fools. But that was in Vorkoun.

Thomm brushed fingertips over the nearest standing card. Its depiction of Prosperity—a figure wreathed in exotic flowers and fruits—bowed, even as the chain tattoo took on a golden glow.

Magic, indeed. Well, there'd be no fortunes told today. If this Thomm was like every other fortune-teller, he'd want to know his clients' present before peering into their future; they'd trouble enough hiding what they were. "Jenn." Silently cursing whatever Rhothan accent he supposedly had, Bannan bent his head emphatically toward the walkway.

"Thomm's been waiting for us," Jenn countered. "He's—"

The truthseer turned on the artisan, unable to restrain himself. "Let me guess. You've seen a future with us in it. One of profit."

Fingertips to chain. "It is not my place to view a Keeper's future," Thomm replied softly. "The only profit comes from What the Source Provides. By the Blessings of our Ancestors, I give myself to this service. And to yours."

Shadow Sect.

Waiting for them. Why? A thrill of suspicion ran along Bannan's bones. "Have you been following us?" he demanded, watching for a lie.

"We have not, and would not. But someone dared," Thomm said. "Shall we continue in private?"

It was the truth.

Heart's Blood. Bad enough the Shadow Sect knew of turn-born, of Jenn and himself. That, he'd hoped they could manage.

If they learned the rest—that they'd come to rescue his sister and her husband—how long before they discovered he wasn't turn-born, but something far more useful?

A man, able to live within the Verge.

With the tokens to bind a truthseer in his belt.

He should have let Jenn destroy them, but it was too late for that sensible notion now.

Thomm led them to the back, where a cloth-covered table waited. He gathered up the palm-sized cards strewn across the cloth, tapping them together into a pile. More of the life-sized cards surrounded the table, their figures looming as if trying to read over her shoulder. They weren't, in Jenn's opinion, at all pleasant, being shown in distorted postures. None had faces.

Faces were important. She'd a face—most of the time. Though Jenn doubted the blank ovals were meant to represent turn-born, she couldn't look directly at any of them, not even the one with the armful of small dogs.

Perhaps cards supposed to tell a person's future had to be blank, otherwise how could you use the same cards for someone else? Though why the figures had to move was beyond her.

Thomm waved them to sit, there being three chairs at the table. Bannan shook his head, so Jenn stayed on her feet. He'd gone quiet since the token dealer, with something in his face that made passersby move out of his way. Now?

Whatever he was now, wasn't a farmer.

Thomm wasted no time. "I apologize, Keepers. One of us noticed you were being watched. An attempt was made to detain this person. He eluded capture, but we have this."

He put a knife, half of its blade black with dried blood, on the cloth.

Jenn covered her mouth to keep in a gasp.

Bannan picked up the dreadful weapon by its ornate hilt, a humorless smile playing over his lips. "I hope no one died."

"Death in the service of the Keepers of the Source is our hope," Thomm said rather stuffily.

So someone had, Jenn thought.

Then Bannan did the strangest thing. He twisted the ball at the top of the hilt, then flipped it up with his thumb.

Revealing an empty space within.

"You know the owner," Thomm commented.

"I know the knife," the truthseer corrected. "May I keep this?"

The sect member touched fingers to shoulder. "As you wish, Keeper."

When the artisan went to obtain a cloth in which to wrap the blade, Bannan leaned his head close to hers, his whisper warm on her ear.

"It's Emon's."

Tir Half-face had listened, his face like stone. Having listened, he'd proceeded to swear imaginatively and well, until the boys' eyes were round as saucers and Scourge gave an admiring snort.

When he'd run out of breath, it being improbable he'd run out of curses or the passion provoking them, Tir had donned coat and boots because, as he put it, someone in the bloody village had better know more than dragons and toads about this Crumlin.

And would dragon and toad mind the lads?

As for Scourge? The mighty kruar had agreed to carry the man over the snow. It was that, Tir made clear, or he'd see to it the villagers no longer provided treats.

The old fool was nothing more than a stomach on legs. Useful legs, granted.

Once the door closed, restoring some semblance of peace, Wisp curled on his cushion by the cookstove, leaving the boys to mind themselves.

If he'd thought to sleep, that hope was quickly dashed. Bannan's house toad, having been assigned a task, attempted to complete it with pathetic eagerness.

To fail. Wisp could have told it boys weren't something to be herded; nor, having lived with the toad, could they be intimidated by a dignified puffball. He could have, but didn't waste the effort.

Besides, the result was entertaining.

Semyn and Werfol took eluding the toad to be the best

of games, not that the poor thing could protest, only to discover the joy of pursuing it with a pot.

The dragon was certain they planned to catch it, not cook it. He doubted the toad shared his confidence. Cushions flew and a stool toppled. The pot slammed down on wood, then carpet, once on hearthstone, and came close to his tail.

Eased aside, just in time.

SLAM!

Finally, silence, if he ignored the boys' gleeful giggles.

~Elder brother?~

Wisp yawned.

~ELDERBROTHER!~

~My thanks, esteemed little cousin,~ the dragon said with the utmost sincerity and no little amusement. ~The boys should fall asleep with no trouble at all now.~

A considering pause. Then, ~Must I remain in the pot, elder brother?~

Tempting, but the little cousin couldn't very well stand guard unless freed. Still. ~If you escape too soon,~ cautioned the dragon slyly, ~they may want to do it again.~

A longer, almost anguished pause. ~How soon is too soon, elder brother?~

Wisp heard Werfol yawn, but then came the WHOMPF! of a cushion accurately thrown.

~I'd wait a while longer.~

It wasn't much longer. A nose was bumped, to teary fanfare, followed by an angry push and a scraped elbow—and more sniffling. The dragon roused, sending breezes to right the toppled and tidy the messes. The boys, entranced by furniture picking itself up, forgot their tears and began to applaud.

Wisp left them the pot, showing himself beside it to be sure they understood.

It took them both to lift it, with care, off the house toad, leading the dragon to wonder how they'd manage to use the pot as a trap in the first place. "What do you have to say?" Wisp sent, adding a tiny sting to the breeze.

Werfol crouched, knees by his ears. "Thank you for playing with us."

Semyn, being wiser as well as older, bowed graciously. "Thank you, esteemed guardian, for letting us catch you."

And didn't the little cousin puff proudly at that?

"To bed now," the dragon commanded, sending a breeze to lift the boys into the air and up to the loft to forestall any argument. That it was a warm breeze and tender was no business but his own.

He followed, their bed being the most comfortable, and made himself at home at the end of it as they changed into their nightgowns.

Werfol slipped under the covers first. "Semyn," he whispered, as if a dragon couldn't hear, "let me listen."

"No, Weed." The elder brother climbed into bed. "Go to sleep."

"I can't sleep if I don't listen." The bed bounced annoyingly as Werfol flung himself from side to side. "Please, Semyn. Momma sent it for us to share."

Wisp held back a snarl. He suffered for the girl, that's what he did, being bounced when he could be undisturbed.

"You know what Uncle Bannan said."

Another bounce. "Uncle didn't say I couldn't listen. He just said not to fall asleep with it." Bounce. BOUNCE. As if the child would prove how not-sleepy he was. "Please, Semyn!"

SNARL.

A hushed silence. No one moved.

Satisfied, the dragon curled his tail over his snout and prepared to sleep at last.

"Wisp, tell Semyn to let me listen." Werfol wiggled from under the blankets to sit staring down. "Please? Please?" He tried a new tactic. "It's—it's important. I know it is. I should listen. Tonight."

Annoyance became wary curiosity. This was no simple child, bent on his own way. Or not just that child. This was a truthseer. A truedreamer. "Why tonight?"

Semyn sat up. "Weed, stop."

"I don't know why," a sudden fearful whisper. "I just know I should."

Wisp lifted his head, now thoroughly unsettled. "You would dream of your mother."

"He mustn't!" Semyn grabbed Werfol, wrapping his arms around the smaller boy despite his squirming. "Weed, Uncle Bannan—"

"Left you in the warrior's care, who left you—" the dragon pronounced smoothly "—in mine. Trust I know more of magic." And was far less squeamish when it came to offspring.

Not that he'd eat these two. They'd found their way into his heart.

Werfol had stopped struggling, holding onto Semyn as though to solid ground. "I'm afraid."

"Well then." Wisp tucked his snout back under his tail. He didn't bother listening to their whispered consultation.

He waited, as sure of them as he was of the girl.

The bed creaked. "Will you stay, Wisp? Awake? Will you stay awake if I do this?"

"Weed—" Semyn sighed. "We both will. Come here. Let me tuck you in again." A moment of restrained bouncing, then, "Put it around your neck. I'll help."

The boys huddled under the covers, twitching until they'd warmed, settling slowly. The dragon kept his head up to watch, having that duty. Their heads were side by side. Round cheeks and long lashes. Curls and caps. The embodiment of peace.

Yet not. A gem glinted in the subdued lamplight, the endearment on the pillow near Werfol's head, the chain around his neck gripped in chubby little fingers. His mother whispered to him in a voice no one else could hear.

Such strange magic. A dragon had no need of it. Would scorn it as weakness.

Other dragons were fools.

To have the girl's voice with him—especially now, when the glow of her presence was so faint? A pain worse than knitting bone or flesh, that distance, but he endured it. For her.

Still . . . to hear her say his name?

Bah. He was sentimental. Children did that. Babies were worse, with their cooing. Give him dragonlings any day.

He licked the drool from his fangs.

After a while, the little cousin leapt soundlessly into the loft, patrol complete. It took its station at the opening.

When a moth fluttered up and through, the toad prepared to pounce. ~Do not,~ the dragon advised, having witnessed the results. The moth perched on a bedpost, cleaning its eyes with a slender limb.

Marrowdell gathered.

And Wisp grew uneasy, suspecting the sei of taking too personal an interest, though it was beyond him to banish it.

"Momma?"

Semyn opened his eyes, remaining still. Extending his neck, the dragon brought an eye to bear on the boy still fast asleep.

"Momma." Werfol's face worked, a small frown creasing his forehead as if he thought very hard, or was puzzled. "I don't—"

"No!" He shot upright and awake so abruptly, Wisp barely moved in time.

"We're here, Weed. It's all right." Semyn climbed from the bed to turn up the lamplight, then came to sit beside the dragon. "You dreamed. What did you see?"

Werfol panted as if he'd been running for his life. Sweat beaded his face and his eyes were molten gold. "Momma. I saw—I saw what she saw. Like the last time. Semyn, she's still in that place!"

His brother laid a comforting hand on his leg. "Take your time, Weed. You said it was important to do this tonight. Why? Did you see anything else? Anything different?"

Impressed, Wisp left the questioning to the older boy, clearly accustomed to the vagaries of helping those with a gift.

Breathing steadier, Werfol met his brother's gaze and nodded. "Scatterwit was there. On the windowsill."

"Our father's crow," Semyn explained, never taking his eyes from Werfol. "Did you see Poppa? Was he there?"

"No."

Oh, the world of woe in that. Tears spilled over Werfol's cheeks and even a dragon could appreciate the depth of the child's disappointment.

"Scatterwit was. That's good, Weed. You know it is. She's the smartest."

A tiny nod. "And prettiest."

Crow. They'd fly over Marrowdell at times, and the girl would remark on them, but crows—and their larger kin—avoided the valley, being too wily to land in fields protected by efflet or trees infested with nyphrit. Wisp shifted his weight, gaining the boys' attention. "Does the crow matter?"

"Poppa's taught them tricks. They're very clever." Semyn glanced at Wisp. "More than tricks." Soberly. "Westietas' crows are messengers. Spies. They can understand words and repeat them—"

"I remember!" Werfol sat straighter. "Momma was signing! In the dream, I watched her fingers move." He sagged again. "Too fast for me."

Semyn leaned forward. "You know that game, Weed," he coaxed. "We play it all the time. Where Momma signs and we do our best. Try."

"I can't. They weren't normal words."

"Make the signs for me. Maybe I know them."

Werfol frowned but brought his hands above the covers. Hesitantly, he moved his fingers.

"That's 'tomorrow.' Good, Weed. Try another."

Fingers wiggled and bent, with growing confidence. Semyn stared at his brother's hands, his mouth working as if piecing together sounds.

Werfol stopped, clenching his hands together. "I did my best."

"You did." Semyn took a deep breath and let it out.

"Well?" the dragon prompted.

"Momma has to get out. Something bad is to happen or someone bad will arrive—I couldn't tell which." His face darkened. "Soon."

"Here?" Werfol's voice broke in the middle.

"No, not here, Weed. In Channen. Where Momma is. Where Uncle Bannan and Jenn plan to go." Semyn looked to Wisp. "They're in danger."

The young truthseer drew the covers to his chin, golden eyes wide and afraid, and his brother moved to put an arm around him.

"Worry more about those who would threaten them," Wisp assured the children, thinking of Jenn Nalynn with a rush of dragonish pride. All of Channen would be at risk, should his turn-born chose to act. He wished he was there to see it.

"Give me the necklace, Weed." Semyn took it, putting it around his unmagical neck. "Back to sleep now."

The dragon yawned. At long last.

"Might we have a drink first?"

"I am a little hungry."

As Wisp sighed, the moth left the bedpost, fluttering past the house toad, sinking through the opening and away.

Had it written a word?

Or simply listened.

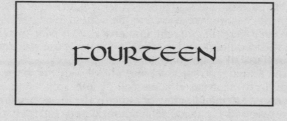

# FOURTEEN

*A*S IF TO remind them of the passage of time, when Jenn and Bannan came out, the crowd had noticeably altered, family groups replaced by those more interested in wine and dancing. To every side, stalls were closing, artisans packing away their work. Opposite them, the doors of inns and halls were flung wide, music pouring from each. Night in the Shadow District was full of life.

Life they now hurried past. Jenn looked wistfully at a group of dancers. Bannan noticed. "We could come again, Dearest Heart. Under better circumstances."

She tucked her hand into his elbow, there being other couples doing the same. "You mean when we aren't about a rescue?"

A glow in his apple butter eyes. "Exactly."

"I'd like that." But she wouldn't, Jenn told herself, put Bannan at risk from both Verge and Shadow Sect simply to dance, when they could do it in Marrowdell.

Though the music here flowed with a lively complicated beat and she found her feet, despite the boots, keeping time.

According to Plevna, the only jail in the Shadow District with cells of the stone Bannan'd described was the Distal Hold. The token dealer had used a shaky finger in the ash on the floor to sketch where they were to go: a distance from the Artisans' Market and across one of the larger canals. The 'Hold was within the main constabulary building, which to Jenn sounded both immense and daunting. Bannan, well used to tall buildings, had pressed their guide further, discovering the cells were restricted to the bottom five floors.

Which she still thought immense, given Marrowdell's mill had two floors and climbing between those was a task if carrying a filled bag of flour.

The floors at street level and above were for petty offenses or those accused possessed of sufficient wealth and influence to demand better treatment. The lower two floors were reserved for those felons considered a greater risk. Foreigners, be they drunken sailors or smugglers. Local Naalish, be they murderers, extortionists, or those who'd misused magic.

The view from Lila's window meant a lower floor. Bannan'd said either the local authorities had been tipped as to how dangerous she was, or someone was missing a head.

Jenn wasn't quite sure he was teasing.

They'd know soon. She looked up at him. "You're sure the knife was Emon's?"

Bannan had tucked the wrapped blade through his belt, beneath the back of his jacket. She supposed that was where its owner kept it on his person, knives of that sort forbidden in public placcs. "The hilt's Emon's design," the truthseer replied. "I don't know how many he had made. He gave them to his most trusted companions—which means I should have accosted our watcher," this with a rueful shrug. "Here's hoping he escaped the Shadow Sect unharmed."

Had it been her magic, Jenn wondered, drawing close someone connected to those she sought? If so, it hadn't been at all helpful, not if the man was hurt. She noticed Bannan's frown. "What is it?"

"The hilt's empty. There'd be gems for a bribe inside, or a written message, or both." His face lightened. "Emon's delivery was made, successfully."

Or someone had stolen the knife, Jenn thought, and managed to open it, taking what they'd found. They'd no evidence Emon was alive or even free, and knew nothing of his companions beyond the knife. Doubts she kept to herself, for Bannan, who had his own, chose to be hopeful.

So would she. "I'd like to come back," she told her love, twirling as they passed yet another outburst of lovely music. "To dance with you."

And was pleased to see him smile.

The Artisans' Market ended as abruptly as it started, the ever-present stone walkway continuing along the canal. Though there were still lamps set high on the walls, they were dimmer than those behind. Bannan found himself tensing whenever they approached an opening. Those were fewer and more narrow, the stairs within steeper and more utilitarian than those to welcome customers.

Jenn pointed at the canal. "Did you see?"

"See what?"

Here the stone walkway had no rail or raised edge, so Bannan bit back a protest when Jenn walked closer to dark water. "There was ... it's gone again. I must have frightened it."

Or "it" hid from sight. Bannan's skin crawled.

He gave himself a shake. The water, whatever its makeup, was no deeper than a horse's belly. Hardly the place for a monster.

Why had he thought monster? Ancestors Rattled and Ridiculous, when had his nerves got the better of him ...

... oft as not, when the danger was real. "Stay close," Bannan said quietly. He gripped his staff, wishing for Horst's sword. "Let's pick up the pace. Not too fast. We're hard-working folk, eager for home."

Jenn nodded.

The canal bent—buildings and stone walls between them and the music of the market—leading them into a hushed sweep of closed doors and shuttered windows. Either this section of the city slept.

Or was abandoned.

Not liking either option, Bannan walked briskly, Jenn beside him, glad their boots were soft-soled.

While alongside, in the canal, v-shaped ripples began to keep pace. First one, then many. Whatever made them stayed below the water.

Jenn grinned and pointed. "Do you think people here feed the fish as they do in Avyo? Aunt Sybb says schools gather when anyone is on shore."

"A bonus for those with nets," Bannan commented, keeping a wary eye on the ripples. He couldn't tell what made them.

Except it wasn't fish.

*Plunk. Plunkity. Plunk. Plunk.*

At the first raindrops, Bannan took Jenn's hand and to-gether they ran to the shelter of the next arched bridge. Just in time, for with no other warning, the clouds seemed to burst open, mimrol falling in great sheets. To his deeper sight, the canal was transformed by silver splashes and rings crisscrossed and spread, overlapping the ripples.

Ripples disturbed anew as the magic rain was greedily snapped up by pale yellow beaks that rose from the water then sank again. Dozens. More.

While an appetite for mimrol was unexpected, the beaks were as familiar as home. Bannan laughed with relief. "Turtles!"

~Mine!~Catch!~Catchyourown!!~Don'tpush~Catch!~ Catch!~Minemineminc!~Catch!~ Cold little voices, speak-ing all at once as if they never listened to one another. She'd not heard the like before. They sounded a bit like raindrops themselves.

"'Turtles?'" Dogs and a chicken were exotic enough. Turtles? They didn't live so far north as Marrowdell, or even Weken, according to Uncle Horst, though she'd seen them depicted in books. Along with tortoises, who lived on the land, and terrapins, found in brackish water, oh, and sea turtles rumored large enough to use as ships, but Bannan sounded certain in his naming.

Here were turtles. Since she could hear them as she did

the toads, Jenn suspected they were something else as well. She couldn't see more than blunt little faces, with jaws of yellow and scaled skin, for they seemed loath to be above the water. As for the rain, it looked like any rain she'd seen, though smelled older, which might have more to do with the canal not being a free-flowing river than the Verge.

She'd kept Bannan's hand. About to let go, Jenn hesitated, her eye caught by something white, near the top of the arch overhead. "Is that—what do you see?"

He looked up. "Nothing. What did you?"

"It can't be—" she started to say, then stopped, for it could. Hadn't one of Marrowdell's moths shown up in the Verge—to meet an unfortunate, if useful, end—so what was to prevent them being here? "It could be," Jenn announced worriedly, "a moth."

"Mellynne has moths. And bats, you know. As well as turtles." And didn't her love sound perfectly serious? Jenn suspected he found her amazement at what he took for granted highly entertaining. "Come. We'd best hurry."

She stuck a hand beyond their shelter. She'd been in harder rains, but not many. "Shouldn't we wait for it to end?" Was it ever the way she'd ruin new clothes? Not to mention her fine boots.

"On the contrary," he informed her gleefully. "Rain like this will empty the walkways and disguise us. Here's hoping it lasts till we're done and away."

With Lila rescued. Her heart pounding, Jenn nodded. Bannan bent to give her a quick kiss. She took hold of his jacket and made it a better one.

~Elder sister, the yling asks you let him finish his work.~

Jenn told Bannan, who raised a brow. "What work is that?"

She shrugged, even as the yling swept around their heads, his many hands filled with what appeared a thick mass of cobwebs. Easy to come by from any lamp, but why?

Even as she thought the question, she saw the answer. With a complex flip, what had been cobweb opened into two cloaks, one that drifted down to settle over her head and shoulders, the other over Bannan's. The moment they touched, what had been dust-coated silk transformed into a garment of soft shimmering gray to her knees. Warm, on her shoulders.

She'd missed warm shoulders. "Ancestors Clever and Kind. Please thank our friend, little cousin."

~The yling apologizes, but they will not last, elder sister, for he is but one.~

"Then we'll move quickly," Bannan said when he'd heard this, and led the way.

Jenn followed, admiring their yling cloaks. Like dew on a spiderweb, glistening beads caught along the hems, but nowhere else did the rain seem to touch.

This was what it must be like, she decided, to hurry down a romantic castle hallway late at night. Though in those stories, something with teeth or spears or dark magic waited at the end of the hall, but before that dire turning point came wonderful descriptions of how gowns brushed over rich carpets woven in the deserts of Eldad, and how silent, empty armor lined the walls, and torches.

There were always torches, though lamps were superior and cleaner. Come to think of it, why did castles have torches . . . ?

Jenn stepped in a puddle, jolting herself out of a train of nervous thought that had as much to do with not thinking as anything else. Every step took them closer to Bannan's sister, as they'd planned. It wasn't important that she'd not had time to prepare for that meeting or thought of what to say or—

"Lila will love you too."

"How did you—I wasn't—" She tried to frown at him. "So now you read thoughts as well as faces?"

A flash of white teeth in the gloom. "An accusation Tir makes, from time to time. Wholly unfounded, might I add. In this case, Dearest Heart?" His head tipped in a bow. "I guessed.

"Not—" Bannan went on with a grin as she pushed him, "—without some understanding of the ladies involved."

He'd made her laugh. Bannan locked that triumph next to his heart, the rest of him cold and grim. The rain had ended steps too soon, with the Distal Hold in sight, an edifice of the same weathered stone as the rest. Its windows, though lit, were tall and thin. Perhaps wide enough for a slender person to pass through; from here, he could see the dark web of bars, in case one tried.

On the other side of the canal, but no matter. They'd come to another widening, this time to allow the flow of gardens from the street to spill along the walkways. A bridge arched from here to there, a fountain against its base to mark where a good-sized stair climbed up. Above were the dazzling lights of more magnificent structures—perhaps the famed legislature of Mellynne, model for Rhoth's own—lights that haloed through remnants of mist and brightened the low cloud overhead, as if night wasn't allowed to approach.

Fortunately for those who preferred it, the branches from trees at street level drooped gracefully toward the canal, shadowing all below.

Bannan brushed cobwebs from his arms, the yling's cloaks having reverted to their source. Just as well. Cloaks might impede them. "We'll make for the stairs."

Jenn nodded, then whispered, "He knows what he's doing."

The toad, he presumed. Wise creature to doubt him. He doubted himself. But not Jenn.

And not Lila.

They'd been alone till now, due to the rain or their route or both, but as they approached the stairs a commotion rang out overhead and an outcry.

Coming for the bridge!

"There's another way across," Jenn said urgently. "Bannan, look."

"Ancestors Blessed." They ran under the arch to what she'd spotted, a crossing of ornate cobblestones, raised only slightly above the water. There were steps to it from the bank on both sides, with a second graceful fountain, mate to the first, across the canal.

By day, this would be a gathering place for officials and their guests, restful and beautiful. By night, with the ruckus above drawing ever closer and shadows lapping stone, Bannan felt a chill down his spine. "Maybe we should—"

Too late. Jenn, used to running across a river, hadn't hesitated. He watched, heart in his throat, as she stepped

nimbly from cobble to cobble and up on the other side,
turning to wait for him.

After that, he could hardly delay, could he? Though
Bannan made sure to plant his foot firmly in the middle of
each stone before stepping to the next.

And next.

And...the next rocked a bit, so he staggered and
stepped more quickly than he'd like. The canal wasn't where
he'd choose a dunking.

"Bannan!"

He tore his eyes from his footing to look for Jenn, only
then realizing the shout had been a man's. A man he—the
truthseer twisted around, stared up.

Emon Westietas looked down from the bridge. Their
eyes locked for a heartbeat, then two figures grappled with
the baron, pulling him back despite his struggles. "Run!"

"Run!" Jenn shouted, as the stones beneath Bannan's
feet shifted.

He looked down in horror to meet red eyes filled with
hunger. Necks stretched from their hiding places and fist-
sized beaks snapped eagerly at his feet.

Turtles! He was standing on giant turtles!

~EAT!~Catch!!!~MINEMINE~EATEAT!~ Deeper these
voices but just as cold and eager. ~Eat!~MEAT!~ Jenn
heard their cries with horror in her heart. Bannan jumped
from shell to shell as the remaining turtles, their clever trap
sprung, moved in to share the feast. Not that they appeared
to want to share. ~I was FIRST!~MoveOver!~EATEAT!~

They most certainly were not to eat Bannan or even nibble him. Jenn Nalynn stretched her hand to Bannan as she
*wished*.

And Channen answered.

Spears of ice shot through the water in every direction.
The quicker turtles dove; those preoccupied with Bannan
found themselves immured and nicely solid.

The truthseer didn't test the arrangement, but ran to her
across it, taking her hand to gain speed on the final step. He
whirled to face the bridge. "Emon!"

The three who'd been there were gone.

*Warm*, Jenn told the canal, not wishing harm or notice. As the ice weakened, turtles cracked themselves free, muttering ~Turnborn~ and ~Starvesus!~ and ~Notfair~. One paused to give her a malignant glare. ~Wewereherefirst.~

Rabbits, she thought, but left it at that.

Instead, she took a firmer hold of Bannan, in case he thought to climb to the bridge where there were lights and people—people who'd taken the baron away—and said the only word sure to stop him.

"Lila."

He nodded, though his eyes were wild. "This way."

That they'd been so close—and failed. Bannan pushed the thought aside. Jenn was right. No matter who'd taken Emon, they were gone now and Lila was close. He abandoned stealth for speed. He'd looked out the window through his sister's eyes and began checking over his shoulder once they reached the wall set with broken glass, meant to discourage too close an approach. Not this view. He stepped to his right, then again.

This. He spun around, eyes fixed on the rectangle of light that should—if their Blessed Ancestors would please pay attention for once—be his sister. "If anyone comes, warn me." He laid his jacket over the spikes and lifted his foot.

"I'm coming with you," Jenn said firmly. "We'll have warning."

Before he could argue, tiny hands patted him, then the yling took flight, hovering in the air with spear at the ready. At the same time, the purse banged and rocked against his hip until he pulled up the lid.

Out plopped the toad.

They weren't alone. He wasn't. And they were about to rescue Lila.

Ancestors Witness. Giant turtles. What a night! Tir won't believe this, Bannan thought, grinning as he jumped atop the wall and reached a hand to his lady.

How could they fail?

By being too late. Bannan hung for a moment by his hands, then let himself drop to the ground, knees bent to soften his landing. "She's not here."

"You're—"

"Certain? Yes." He found Jenn's arm in the dark and urged her forward. "We'd best not be here either."

"I don't understand."

Lila. Heart's Blood. No wonder Emon had shouted at him. She'd made her escape when she was good and ready, leaving her younger brother to look the fool.

Bannan laughed. He couldn't help it.

Jenn gave him a strange look. "Before you were happy she was in jail," she whispered, putting her foot in his hands for a boost.

"And now—" he heaved her up "—I'm happy she's not." Once she jumped down the other side, he took a few steps back, then ran to—

Ran to—

Ran—

He wasn't moving.

Why wasn't he moving?

He should know, Bannan Larmensu thought, fuzzily . . .

. . . before he stopped thinking at all.

She'd jumped and should have landed.

Why was she still falling?

Jenn considered the question, or the question considered her. She couldn't tell the difference.

Not that the difference mattered.

Especially while something pulled her hair and something else tugged her boot. The hair pulling hurt.

The boot tugging moved her sideways, which was highly disconcerting, for she fell at the same time.

Really, it was enough to make her laugh.

So she did, but it sounded wrong, so she closed her lips

quite tightly. Having lips. It was important, she thought fuzzily, to have lips.

For kissing. There were many good reasons for lips—her other boot was being tugged now—from smiling to talking to eating to . . . but kissing was—

Time floated by, or she did. In fact, when she did think about it, she seemed to be floating on her back, with something heavy and cold on her stomach.

How odd.

Voices, strange and cold. ~Carrycarry.~ and ~Don'tsink.~ and a plaintive ~Bite?~ followed by ~Mustn't!~

Then a tentative tug on her ear, accompanied by ~Shiny?!~ and immediately thereafter strong tugs on both ears. ~SHINY!!MINE!~

Squashed by a different and stern ~BEHAVE!~

The cold voices settled into a muttered ~carrycarrycarrycarry~ as if their effort was difficult and virtuous.

~We've come!!~

She cringed. Loud, this new voice. Harsh and unhappy. Worse was the question it asked next.

~Where is the truthseer?~

For she did not know.

~Elder sister?~

"Jenn?"

The first voice was familiar, though it felt like an anxious itch between her ears. The second, less so, and Jenn Nalynn kept her eyes shut as she tried to place it.

"Ah. I believe she stirs, friend toad."

Leott! The artisan who brought the light of the Verge into Channen. Jenn opened her eyes.

Tried to open her eyes. Ancestors Faded and Futile, why was it so hard? She struggled to raise herself to an elbow instead, but her arm had no strength.

"Easy, Jenn." A damp coolness soothed her eyelids. "You're safe now."

A breeze, hot and dry, found her ear. "Where is the truthseer?"

Bannan—!

She couldn't breathe. Was she drowning? Where was he? Hearts of her Ancestors, it couldn't be—she hadn't—

"Jenn. Relax. You must." Louder and sharp. "Patience, the lot of you, or you'll wait outside!" Gentle, once more. "Don't fight the spell, Jenn. I fear it may strengthen again. I'm looking for a remedy—"

What came after "spell" blurred into a sameness. Someone had used magic against her.

Was she not magic?

Jenn let go, willing to become her other self.

Nothing changed.

She thought frantically of the blue room and the sei's power, which was so much more than she dared hold, but for Bannan, she'd take it all, be whatever it demanded . . .

Nothing changed.

Heart's Blood. She was nothing. Could do nothing.

Was this death?

"Don't fight, Dear Heart." The cloth, for it had been that, lifted from her eyes and passed its coolness over her cheeks, then across her forehead. She clung to the sensation; it was the only thing real.

If she wasn't to fight, she mustn't think of—of anything but home. Home was safe and predictable. Piglets strayed and the mill wheel turned. Home was where roses bloomed—

Melusine's roses.

Mother, Jenn thought then, finding herself surrounded by tiny buds on thickened stems. Spring, surely, for the buds uncurled and expanded into serrated leaves, dark and glossy, while the tips of brown twigs shot forth bright green stalks heavy with the buds of what would be flowers.

And couldn't she smell them, as if they'd already opened and had summer and now cast their petals into her hands—

Jenn Nalynn opened her eyes, unsurprised to find her hands clenched over her heart. She didn't try to sit up, but pulled the little bag of Melusine's petals from her bodice, pressing it over her nose and mouth.

She took an endless breath, through cloth, through roses, feeling strength course through her like fire.

~Elder sister!~

Pouch and petals crumbled to dust in her hands. Jenn

looked up to meet the *knowing* eyes of the artisan who, like Wainn, like Wen, was part of more than this world. He clapped. "You're back!"

She sat, then rose to her feet, discovering she now wore a plain brown tunic and pants; by the loose fit, the artisan's spare clothing. The house toad gazed up at her. The kruar — hers — glowcred. He'd ripped an opening in the fabric of the stall and stood with his head shoved through, like an ill-tempered version of Wainn's Old Pony.

Leott squatted by the toad, and patted it on the head. "You can thank your friends," he exclaimed, bouncing back up. "They brought you to me."

~And the nyim,~ the toad added, ever generous. Giving her a name for the turtles of the edge, though she couldn't imagine them as friends and had a good notion where her earrings had gone.

"But not Bannan." Jenn regarded the kruar, who lifted his head uneasily. "Why?"

~He didn't jump the wall with you, elder sister,~ the toad explained. ~People were coming. I am your guardian. I but did my duty.~ With new trepidation, for a hot, bright glow reflected within its eyes.

Because she was turn-born. Jenn hastily returned to flesh, though relieved to be no longer trapped.

Not that trapped was how she felt, as herself. Never that. Her mind must still be hazed by the spell. "What was done to me?"

"An ill wishing," Leott replied. "The result you felt. I found the remnants on your boot."

Heart's Blood. She'd stepped into Bannan's hands after he'd gripped the sill of Lila's cell, pulling himself up to look inside.

"It was a trap."

As hangovers went, this must be the worst he'd ever had. Something he'd likely declared more than once, Bannan re-minded himself, hangovers thankfully being forgettable. Served him right, though, drinking when he was — when he was here with —

Who was he with—?

Something *burned* against his neck.

Jenn!

Ancestors Despairing and Lost, he'd been taken beyond the edge. But where? His eyes wouldn't open, so Bannan tried to say her name, to cry out. His lips cracked and bled and refused to obey him. His arms and legs might have been tied down to some hard surface.

Were they?

The truthseer froze at that, keeping his breathing even and slow. He'd been captured, once, by his own carelessness. Spent a night tied to a tree and innumerable days thereafter enduring snide comments on young idiots and their fool luck. Seen his captors fall before his eyes, his "fool luck" having been an earnest and deadly response by his patrol.

To this day, Tir refused to let him forget, not that the man would be more sympathetic this time.

A trap. Something on the wall they'd climbed or embedded in the stones of the windowsill he'd recklessly touched with bare skin. A trap to stop escaping prisoners, perhaps one in particular. Or to prevent a rescue such as they'd planned.

Which hardly mattered now. Heart's Blood, he was every sort of idiot to have brought Jenn with him into this, to have gone blindly forward as if the Ancestors always smiled on those who leapt without so much as a look ahead.

She'd gone over the wall. She might have escaped.

Or been taken beyond the edge with him and—

Bile rose in his throat and his head spun. No. NO! He wouldn't think it, let alone believe it. Jenn Nalynn was safe, somewhere. He had to get out of here. Find her. He tried to move his fingers, at least that.

"Sir." From behind his head. "He's awake." Something poked him in the ribs—a stiffened thumb by the feel. He'd have grunted, but whatever held him in thrall wouldn't allow it.

"Ancestors Tedious and Tardy. At last." Another speaker, his Naalish cultured and fluent, yet with the slightest of accents. Not from here, the truthseer thought, grasping for any clue. "Douse him."

A thick moist mass was pressed to Bannan's face, smothering his nose and mouth. He gasped and fought to breathe, a struggle worsened by a smell so vile gorge rose in his throat and for an instant it was an even bet if he'd choke to death in his own vomit or suffocate in whatever they were using against him. His head began to spin, his lungs burn—

The mass lifted away. He spat out a slimy remnant, realizing at once if he could spit, he could move! Tensing every muscle, Bannan leapt for freedom—

—and went nowhere.

He opened his eyes, turning his head from side to side. His first unpleasant surmise had been correct. Ropes wrapped his arms and legs, two more across his chest, securing him to what was, he could now see, a long wooden table.

Yellowed sheets, their bottoms stained, covered chairs set in a row before a wall. The lower halves of the wall's panels were swollen, what had once been rich dark wood coated in powdery rot. At a guess, the room had been flooded more than once by water that hadn't, yet, reached the portraits above the chairs. Thick frames, more dust and cobweb than gilt, surrounded women and men in uniforms crusted with medals, who stared at the truthseer as if he interrupted a discussion, then resumed their grim outward gaze.

From the vaulted ceiling hung a chandelier twice Bannan's height, a scant handful of its flames still burning. Shadows crowded close, hiding the rest of the room's size and shape, keeping secret any windows or doors.

All this he gleaned from the quickest possible glance, being more urgently interested in his captor.

And the truth.

"Fair evening." The cultured voice. The man sat in a chair, its cover tossed to the mud-streaked floor, set midway between Bannan and the wall of portraits. His back was straight, feet together in tall polished boots, and his hands, long fingers well-manicured, rested on his knees. He was dressed for a social function, his white shirt and collar trimmed with black lace, a jacket, also black, but textured with embroidery. He wore black billowing trousers clasped at the knee by golden straps, and looked every bit the Naalish but for the addition of a short wool cloak about his shoulders.

Beneath sparse fair hair, his face was even-featured, comely, aside from a nose that looked to have been broken more than once and eyes like blue ice.

Not a face he'd seen before, Bannan decided. Not one he'd forget.

Older by ten or so years, taller, more slender. Bookish, like Kydd, which made him more, rather than less, a threat.

"What, no courtesy?" the man inquired, lifting a brow.

"Untie me," Bannan suggested.

"Of course." A smile quirked his lips up and to the side, then the man snapped finger and thumb.

The ropes snapped too, their ends slithering to the floor.

"Sir!" A protest like any of Tir's, but the guard stepping forward was of different stuff.

The man wore a constable's livery, wanting only the plumed helmet and nightstick. It wasn't his, by the strained seams, and Bannan hoped the original wearer had lost only his clothing and dignity.

By the flat stare of those eyes, the dour set of the jaw, it was a faint hope, lessened further by brass at the knuckles. The truthseer kept his hands in plain sight as he sat, slowly, discovering in the process he was filthy. Dragged through a significant amount of mud and debris, that meant, and no need to guess by whom.

He swung his legs over the side of the table, fighting a wave of dizziness. To disguise the effort, he scrubbed the last of the vile substance from his face with the cleanest part of a sleeve.

Outrage, Bannan decided, lowering his arm, and set his face in an offended scowl. "Who are you? How dare you—"

"You don't know me. And I dare many things," the cultured man said smoothly. "A pleasure I've long anticipated, meeting you at last."

"I don't know who you think I am." Had the trap not been for Lila? Bannan did his utmost to look flustered, which wasn't difficult. "I'm a simple merchant—"

"Ancestors Witness, you're anything but that."

The truth.

Well enough. In Channen, did he not wear more than one disguise? This could work to his advantage. Sitting straighter, Bannan went for scorn. "Then you know I'm a Keeper of the Source. The Shadow Sect—"

"Greedy fools who'd wet themselves if they knew what they tended." The man's smile held a disconcerting appetite, as if he watched a feast being spread before him. "Not that they don't have their use. We do one another small favors, from time to time, making convenient— but enough of business. Hearts of my Ancestors, I am truly Beholden. Bannan Marerrym Larmensu, here." Sharply. "Don't waste my time and deny who you are."

Ancestors Desperate and Dire. The truthseer bowed his head, gathering his wits. What was a name? All manner of people knew his. People in Vorkoun and other, farther places. "Who are you?"

"Glammis Lurgan," too easily said. "You won't have heard of me. I'm a private man. A collector, of sorts. I've patrons with like interests, you see, and am known for my—quality."

True, and oddly disturbing. Bannan fought for calm, fought to remember he was the truthseer and should be able to deal with this Glammis, but he wasn't calm, not at all. Tempting to think it the aftermath of the spell, tempting but wrong. There was something about the other man that shook him to his core, and he was afraid he knew why.

"What is it you collect?"

"Today? You." Glammis waved a generous hand. "And your sister, of course. I'd thought to catch her here, so conveniently alone and unknown, while you were brought down from the north." An exaggerated shrug. "Alas, Lila's proved elusive. No matter. You'll make fine bait. Welcome to Channen, truthseer and key!" He leaned his head back and laughed. The chandelier's dusty pendants sang like discordant bells in echo.

As the enormity of his folly sank in, Bannan was left with one clear thought.

Lila'd have his ears for this, if Jenn didn't take them first.

It was then he felt tiny hands seize his hair in a desperate grip, as if afraid of falling.

The yling!

Jenn rode a hunting kruar across the mist-cloaked rooftops of the Shadow District, a toad clenched under her arm, and wondered rather desperately how she'd explain this to her sister.

Assuming they made it home for her to explain.

~Elder sister?~

"I'm a little busy." And she was, busy holding on. Though in the semblance of a horse, the kruar moved across sloped tile or flat stone with equal ease, but tended to pounce without warning, there being pigeons at roost for the night. She'd grown almost used to the crunching, it being the kruar's nature after all, but the leaping? That usually involved a drop to a lower level, leaving her stomach behind. Still, they were almost to the Distal Hold. She could see the palace lights.

~While I am honored by your care, elder sister, please, you need not carry me. I can manage.~

Oh dear. She must be squeezing the breath from the poor creature. When the kruar next paused, nostrils working at the air, Jenn put the toad on his shoulders, in front of her. "Are you sure?"

By way of answer, its claws dug into their mount's hide and its body flattened, eyes aimed forward. ~I will not fail you, elder sister. Onward, nameless one!~

~Fool little cousin!~ The kruar snarled and bucked, but the toad stayed in place better than Jenn, who yelped and had to change her hold.

A shape formed out of the shadow of a chimney. Jenn's heart leapt at the sight of Bannan's kruar, who'd gone back for the truthseer while she lay in the artisan's care.

Until she saw the empty saddle. "You didn't find him," she said, discouraged.

Defensive. ~The scent changed.~

Her kruar rumbled and pranced. ~Scent does not change!~

His snarled back.

"Stop!" Jenn softened her tone. "Please." This was more than a difficulty, she thought despairingly; she'd counted on the hunters. "If you can't smell him, how will we find Bannan?"

~We cannot,~ admitted one.

~You are turn-born,~ said the other, seeming perturbed. ~Do you not know?~

She slipped down, pressing her forehead to the side of the kruar for a moment, then took a step away. "Let me think."

Jenn went to the roof edge, no longer as wary of heights as she'd been, and sat beside a stone . . . whatever. This one had bulbous eyes, broad etched feathers, and the usual open mouth through which water would pour after a rain. She put an arm around it and gazed out at the Shadow District.

She might be looking over the world, with mountains and rivers and unreachable depths. Lamplight floated along canals and marched over bridges. Few lights showed now from the buildings above street level. More gleamed in the distance, below. Where there was dancing.

Where was Bannan?

"Keep Us Close," Jenn whispered, the part of the prayer she wanted, with all her heart, to be true. For no reason but hope, she held out her hand, palm up, and waited.

A heartbeat went by.

A breath came and went.

Then a moth white as snow landed on her palm, its toes prickly, and fussed with its wings.

Be grateful for small mistakes, Bannan told himself as his captors hustled him from room to room. He could almost hear Tir add, beware your own, they'll cost more.

The false constable had searched him, carelessly and in haste. He'd torn free the purse, displeased to find it empty; though had it remained full of toad, he'd have had a rude surprise. Tossing that aside, he'd felt Bannan's clothing for weapons, swearing under his breath, and stopped with a satisfied grunt upon finding the knife.

Saving his back from further bruising, Bannan thought almost cheerfully, should they throw him on another table.

His sodden braid, home to the suffering yling, the fool left untouched, as well as the belt, with its seemingly ornamental pouches. For now. He couldn't expect too much stupidity, more's the pity.

From Glammis, he expected none.

The wretched dining hall had been on a lower, long-abandoned floor of whatever building this was, its entrance through a panel that barely opened to let them pass, then closed behind as if never touched. Beyond lay a whole series of equally decrepit rooms and halls. He'd seen the like in Vorkoun, along the riverbank, where old buildings had sunk under their own weight; levels damaged by flood or at risk were simply sealed and forgotten, with new floors built above.

Yet there was magic here, still. At their approach, sconces along the walls flickered to life. By their feeble light, Bannan counted the footprints in the accumulated silt and grime. Too few to suggest anyone else had been here in years.

His hands were bound behind his back. He'd naught but what he wore, the guard having tossed Bannan's staff into the shadows with his purse, deeming the knife alone worth taking.

Glammis had a staff of his own, gleaming black, with a top carved into the head of weasel. What trade or guild it signified, the truthseer couldn't guess, but red jeweled eyes gazed wherever its master looked, giving the thing an eerie semblance of life. No doubt the staff concealed a blade or other, more subtle, weapon. This wasn't a man who went unarmed.

As for mistakes? Oh, he'd made his own, potentially costly. The tokens to bind a truthseer. Bringing them, in hindsight, had been foolish enough. Now they sat at his waist, waiting to be found and used against him.

Really, Bannan told himself, he'd had better days.

Of course, should Glammis have a supply of the dreadful things and if such a wishing could enslave him?

What he carried wouldn't matter. Nothing would.

They came to stairs leading up to a closed door, a door in better shape than any they'd passed so far. Glammis stopped, raising his staff.

"Sir?" the guard questioned with a frown. "We daren't take'm that way."

"I've wasted time enough." Discarding his cloak on the floor, Glammis reached inside his jacket, pulling out a twist of wool. "Hold him still."

That brought a thick arm around the truthseer's neck and a knife to his spine above his tied wrists.

Leaning his staff against the wall, Glammis put a booted foot on a stair, stooping to use the step above as a worktable.

The wool had secured tokens, as Bannan feared, tokens his captor now laid out in a row, ready for use.

The truthseer tensed.

"Here now!" the guard growled in his ear, tightening his grip.

Glammis didn't look up. "This won't harm you, Bannan Larmensu," he said pleasantly. "I know you must believe me, if I tell the truth."

Heart's Blood. Bannan refused to panic. The other might be sure of his name; he couldn't be sure of the rest. "I don't believe you. Why should I?"

"Because of what you are," with chilling confidence. Glammis finished whatever he was doing on the stair and stood, his hands cupped. "You must wonder how I learned of your rare and special gift . . ." — a smile — " . . . truthseer."

"I wonder," Bannan said politely, "if you're mad." The knife tip pressed; he ignored it. " 'Truthseer?' Next you'll tell me you believe in the Bone Stealer."

"And you don't?" Glammis chuckled. "The world isn't as it appears to those like Dokis here. I know it." A nod. "You see it. And you, truthseer, will find what I seek."

"Mad," Bannan repeated just as surely, hiding his consternation. This man wasn't after his gift to detect lies in others, or not that alone. He wanted something more.

Something perilous. What if Glammis meant to use him to learn about the edge and its magic, maybe even the Verge and how to reach it? To trespass against turn-born and sei?

Mountains had crumbled, the last time someone dared that utter folly.

Jenn would find him first. The edge was her domain, as was the Verge. All he had to do was return to it. To her. Bannan clung to that hope.

Glammis raised his cupped hands to his mouth, murmured something Bannan couldn't hear over the guard's ragged breathing in his ear, then threw open his hands.

Doing what? Nothing, so far as the truthseer could tell. He began to relax.

"A simple trick," Glammis said dismissively, implying all manner of magic at his disposal that was neither. He dusted his boots with a cloth, then went up the stairs.

"Get moving," the guard commanded, shoving Bannan to follow, but his voice?

It was a woman's! The truthseer turned and gasped. The false constable was now a scullery maid, albeit a substantial one, the illusion—for surely it was only that—complete to a spoon in the hand that, an instant before, had held a knife. In place of the helmet he'd donned, the man—maid—wore a lacy cap.

In horrible surmise, Bannan looked down at himself.

He was still a man, but that was the only thing familiar. He was now bone-thin, wearing a stained apron that draped him from neck to knee, with a beard, or its seeming, braided and long enough to reach his waist. There were sandals on feet, the right foot missing toes.

Toes, Bannan checked by flexing his inside his boots, he was relieved to still have. "How long—" he tried to say.

He'd no voice. The "maid" wagged her/his eyebrows, then nodded to the stair.

Mute and no longer recognizable, though the "spoon" in his back still felt like a knife, Bannan obeyed.

The reason for their disguises became clear when they passed through the door Glammis unlocked. A foyer lay beyond, sparkly clean and ornate, complete with lavish marble stairs that swept up on two sides and voices—along with soft music and the civilized chink of glassware—flowing back down.

Glammis stepped out like someone who belonged here, engaging the sole person in view, a passing servant, with a question. The young woman nodded compliantly and went up the stairs. As soon as she was out of sight, he beckoned.

A push encouraged Bannan to move. He and his guard kept close to the wall under the staircase, walking in no great hurry to a small door on the far side. A servants' discreet entrance, he judged it.

Glammis slipped through first. Once the door closed behind them, the guard became himself again, giving a groan of relief.

Bannan didn't bother checking his own state. His mind reeled with unsettling thoughts, from Jenn's fate to his sister to— "Where are we going?"

"To where I can work in comfort, without disturbance or discovery." Glammis walked away.

The guard gave him no choice but to follow.

They came to an outer door, secured by a key his captor produced from a pocket. The air outside was redolent of rain-damp stone and greenery. Another canal.

No, this air was fresher and what had seemed a canal stretched away in the dark, its water lapping against the bank. Lights bobbed in the distance. There were more lights and higher on the far side.

Heart's Blood. This must be one of the greater canals that split and tamed the Sarra River as it passed through Channen. On maps, the one to the west was named Sunset's Crescent, the one to the east, Dawn's Blush. Those on the barges called them the Crooked Arm and the Straight, since the westernmost meandered and bent and was prone to shoals.

By the look of it, this was the Straight. Stars twinkled overhead in a clear sky and there, there was the moon, delicately curved as always. But no mist. No silver mimrol. Had Bannan needed proof, here it was. He'd left the edge. Entered his world.

Leaving Jenn's behind.

From here barges traveled throughout Mellynne. They'd go to Rhoth. To the Sweet Sea and points east.

Barges like the one waiting, lamps unlit, tarped against the rain. Ancestors Adrift and Abandoned. Was that Glammis' intention? To take him from Channen?

"Your pardon, Bannan Larmensu," the name savored. "It's time I returned to the gathering upstairs or be missed. We'll wait, of course, but Ordo's so-secretive envoy won't be joining us as planned."

Emon? Bannan felt unsteady. What was going on? Who was this Glammis?

Someone who smiled, as if aware of the effect of his words; worse, as if relishing it. "I believe you're aware his wife was released from jail this evening? A misunderstanding. The constables have apologized profusely. Such things happen, when foreigners wander the Shadow District." Glammis raised his staff, contemplating the weasel's red eyes. "Unfortunately, the lovely Lila has since disappeared. The envoy will hunt for her, but these are dangerous times, as you know. I'm certain he won't be heard from again."

Bannan's blood went cold. "You can't—"

"I've nothing further to do with the matter. Dokis, secure him below."

"Sir!"

His captor gave a short, very Rhothan bow. "I trust you won't leave without me, truthseer."

Hearts of my Ancestors, Bannan prayed silently, I'd be Beholden for the chance to do just that.

Aloud, "I'm not what you think I am." Then, because it was true and might plant some doubt. "People will be looking for me."

"I do hope so." Glammis' lips quirked to the side. "I missed Lila earlier. Let's see how much she cares for her brother. Dokis, set the traps. I must collect her gift as well."

A satisfied, "Sir."

As he was pushed toward the barge, Bannan stumbled, his thoughts splintering.

Lila's gift?

"Below" proved to be squatting between the ribs of the barge, boots just out of the bilge sloshing along the shallow keel. There was a deck, of sorts, above. It was made of planks that could be taken in or out depending on cargo, or even set lower, to adapt the barge for livestock. Bannan, his neck already bent to avoiding cracking his head, supposed he should be grateful they weren't shipping cattle.

Dokis had brought down a barrel and lantern, its opening a slit that did little more than confirm how dark it was below. He sat, long knife across his lap, eyes fixed on the truthseer.

Who considered and abandoned notion after notion. The coins and brooch in his belt? Pointless. Dokis would simply search him for more and find the tokens.

A bribe from another source was now out of the question.

Emon had seen him. Tried to warn him. Heart's Blood. Was himself in the gravest danger!

If he'd the power of a turn-born right now, he'd wish Lila the great good sense to rescue her husband and leave Channen with him.

Probably take more than that, Bannan thought ruefully. His sister leave him? Whatever this "gift" she had—and hidden so successfully from him—it wasn't prudence.

Pat. Pat. For whatever reason, the yling stayed with him. Much as he appreciated the company, a messenger would have been of greater use.

Nothing for it, then. He'd have to overpower the brute and escape before Lila arrived. First, untie his wrists and ankles, the latter also secured by a ring screwed into the wood—implying a regular trade in those who needn't bother shouting for help.

While Dokis watched like a toad by an open door.

"Your master's mad," Bannan began conversationally, trying not to appear as if he strained against the ropes. Ancestors Untimely and Unwanted, whatever Dokis lacked as a searcher he made up for in his knots.

Was that a glint in midair?

Energized, the truthseer went on, "Mad and I'd not trust him. That sort? As like to tidy up loose ends when he's done, as remember a man's service."

"Shut up."

"I'm just giving my advice."

"I said—" Without warning, the man's eyes rolled up and he toppled gracelessly from the stool to lie facedown in the bilge water.

While above him, the yling raised a bloodstained spear in triumph.

Though he was woefully bedraggled. The light of his hair had dimmed and strain was evident on his small features. "Hurry!" Bannan urged, pulling at his bindings, but the yling was already in flight. Whatever his rescuer did behind his back, the ropes unwound themselves. Shaking the last free, the truthseer splashed through the bilge to pull up the man's head.

Only to set it down again. "Poison, I take it?" Heart's Blood, that spear had been in his hair and who knew where else?

Patpat. Then a painfully tight grip.

"Get out of here," Bannan translated. "No arguments, my deadly friend." He retrieved Emon's knife, leaving the lantern, then crept toward the ladder, as eager as the yling to return to the edge.

To freeze as a plank above him creaked, then something heavy fell.

The moth danced on her hand, as if unable to settle or unsure of its welcome. Jenn lifted it level with her eyes, careful not to wish or want or, as best she could, feel. "Help me find Bannan. Please?"

The moth froze in place. ~This you can do.~ Deep that voice, and vast. The Bone Hills spoke thus, being sei.

Lighter than a feather in her hand, the moth who was as well. Larger than the world, that too. Jenn swallowed. ~I don't understand.~

~This you can do.~

Oh dear. The words sounded promising but— "What is it you think I can do? I've tried my mother's gift. I've tried wishing as a turn-born and—and—as the other." She couldn't very well presume to say "sei" with one sitting on her hand. "Nothing's worked. Bannan's vanished in this great city, and we'd come to help his sister and her husband. Now everyone's lost and not where I want them—" Jenn closed her lips, but it was too late.

Had she gone too far?

The moth bent a plumed antenna with a leg, bringing it across a fathomless eye as though curious about itself. ~You are one. This you can do.~

Of course she was "one," Jenn thought. That was the problem. She sat here, alone on a roof, when she'd been supposed to stay with Bannan and find his family and go home.

Not that the little cousin and kruar weren't company, but—

Alone wasn't what the sei had meant.

She was "one."

The word filled her, finding empty spots and heartsores and worries she hadn't known. It answered and promised— and warned. Most of all, at last, Jenn understood.

She'd kept herself divided: woman, turn-born, sei.

It was time to put aside fear and be whole.

~I can do this.~ And her voice was vast yet familiar and how could it not be hers?

Jenn Nalynn cupped her free hand over the moth, then pressed her palms together. "Keep Us Close," she whispered, even as she became glass and glow, and tears of pearl.

She opened her hands and moved them as if tossing something into the air.

Moths bubbled from her palms, streaming into the sky. Smaller, yes, but just as white. They fluttered and danced into the mist. Dozens. Hundreds.

Thousands.

For this was her magic.

Enough, she decided, when it was, and lowered her hands, watching the last disappear into the night. In a sense, she'd sent an invitation. All that remained was for it to be accepted. If it was, those who were lost would find her.

Acceptance was beyond her control; a limit she'd set herself without qualm. As Aunt Sybb would say, grace lay in offering help, not imposing it. She'd also say a lady did not go barefoot in a city.

Wiggling her toes, for the artisan hadn't shoes to fit her, Jenn leaned against the stone statue. Desperate times. Bannan had been taken. Lila and Emon were missing. To be honest, she'd no idea where she was at the moment, other than here. Yet she felt at ease, more content than she could remember and whole as never before. What could be mended, would.

What she dared not touch, she wouldn't. She wasn't the sort of heroine to leap into battle, sword in hand, much as that was admirable and exciting. She was, Jenn realized peacefully, roses and tears and wishes.

After a moment, something cool and warty pressed against her side.

Air stirred over her head as the kruar came close and took in her scent.

"Now we wait," she told them. She'd done what she could, though what she could do still astonished an increasingly small part of her.

The rest? Began to fret—as usual—about meeting Bannan's sister and whatever should she say to a baroness?

The ladder led to the deck through a hatchway inconveniently left closed by the late Dokis. Bannan gave it a cautious push. The hinges were well oiled, to no surprise, but to raise it sufficiently to jump out, free and clear? Or even to take a peek? He'd be seen.

The yling could slip through a crack, but it was beyond Bannan to communicate the notion. He wasn't sure how well it was or strong, another worry, away from the edge. Besides, if there were friends above, he'd rather the tiny warrior not simply guess who to stab.

He eased back down, having a better idea.

The constable's helmet Dokis had stolen was too small for Bannan's head, but he didn't plan to wear it. Instead, he stabbed the tip of the dead man's long knife into the padding within, holding the arrangement up by the hilt.

More thuds from above. He was out of time.

Bannan braced himself near the top of the short ladder, Emon's knife free in one hand, the hilt and helmet ready in the other. He'd lift the hatch and show the helmet. If anyone waited above, Ancestors Favored and Fortunate, they'd strike at the wrong target, giving him time to strike the right one.

Which was a fine plan, except that when Bannan thrust up both hatch and helmet, a sword swept by both to rest lightly at his throat.

Lila Larmensu chuckled. "Really, brother?"

The sword slipped back in its scabbard and a strong, slender hand came down. Bannan took it, climbing out on the deck. Bodies lay strewn about. Three men and a woman, in nondescript clothes. Hired thugs, at a guess. No, two men, one woman. He'd mistaken the lonely head for a third.

Bannan shook his. "Messy."

The Baroness Lila Larmensu Westietas shrugged. "They were in my way."

Oh, he knew that tone. She was annoyed, as she'd put it. Furious was more like it.

Though it didn't show. She looked—Ancestors Witness, she looked wonderful, delicate face wreathed in a tumble of fine brown curls, large luminous eyes that seemed soft and gray, but would flash green without warning. As tall as he, Lila, but slim of build, almost frail.

A misjudgment how many had paid for with their lives? Whipcord and steel lay beneath that elegant femininity.

And a temper.

Bannan felt entirely within his rights to some temper as well. "I came to save you, you know."

A shapely eyebrow rose. "Did I ask?"

"The boys did."

Her eyes closed for the briefest instant, as if she summoned patience, then flew open. "And you left them," with an icy snap.

Heart's Blood. Not a thank you or an— Bannan chuckled. "I've missed you too," he said lightly, as sure of his sister's heart as his own. "Could we argue somewhere else? Your husband's in danger."

She raised a brow. "Why do you think I'm here?"

He nodded, conceding the point. He'd hooked his thumb in his belt. Now he spread those fingers in the sign for *enemy closing in.*

Her finger tapped the hilt of her sword in acknowledgment, the scabbard belted over a corseted tunic and pants similar to Jenn's, but in muted red. In plain sight, that sword, despite being illegal on Channen's streets.

Any comment being unwise, Bannan tiptoed around the pools of blood—though admittedly his boots and clothes were crusted in filth—heading for the bow and the ramp off the barge.

Lila touched his shoulder. "Not that way. Follow me."

She'd sliced an opening in the tarp, on the river side, and now quickly widened it for his bulk. Bannan felt every bit the foolish younger brother. How often had she told him, never use the obvious door? Those lying in wait hadn't been the only trap. "The ramp's bespelled," he guessed as he slipped through to join her.

Lila gave him a sharp look.

"Long story. Where now?"

She pointed along the narrow gunnels. "I'm going that way. You?"

Bannan found himself in the river, sputtering. Lila looked down, unsmiling. "See how much of that grime and stink you can scrub off. I'll be back."

There'd best not be turtles, the truthseer grumbled to himself, though to his deeper sight he was in nothing but ordinary water. Above-his-head water, but he'd grown up swimming in a river like this. Trusting the yling to have abandoned him, unless the creature longed for a bath as well, he dove under, but was still careful when rubbing his hair.

When he surfaced, Lila had clothing under one arm and a pair of boots in her hand. "Leave yours under the barge." She nodded toward shore, then walked away along the thin rail, as easily as if on a street.

A short while later, and smelling more like the river than whatever Glammis had him doused with—an improvement— Bannan checked the belt around his waist. The compartments remained sealed. "So, sister. Still giving me baths?"

After leading him on a dash through darkened streets, then down to the lesser canals, Lila'd stopped them in one of the alleys that held stairs to the upper city. Mist hung low, trapping light and smothering sound. Bannan looked deeper to be sure, reassured by the silver tint. He was back, inside the edge. Where Jenn Nalynn existed.

Where she must still exist.

Lila sat on a step midway between the cobwebbed lamps, a shadow herself. "Ancestors Baffled and Bewildered. What did you do? Crawl through a midden?"

Bannan twisted river water from his braid, then looked her in the eyes. "I was trapped by magic. The stench was what remained of the remedy, though I'd wager my captor knew to hide my scent."

"You brought Scourge!" As if it was the first thing he'd done right.

He'd be jealous tomorrow. "Something like," he evaded. "I've a story to tell." He stepped up to hold Emon's knife in the faint light where she could see it, feeling, more than seeing, her tense. "So do you. Who should go first, Lila?"

The knife clattered to the step as Bannan found himself slammed against stone, her arm like steel across his throat. "You," she suggested, cold and harsh. "Tell me who bled on the snow. Tell me why my sons sleep protected by a dragon." Lila leaned in, eyes feral green. "Tell me who is the woman made of power and why you traveled through madness. I love you like life, brother. I gave you my sons. But you?" Her voice lowered in threat. "You've given me nightmares."

Heart's Blood, it was true, every word of it. Unresisting, Bannan stared down at his beloved sister, feeling pity war with the beginnings of indignation.

Indignation won. "You've been dreaming me!? For how long?" Had he ever had privacy?

She shoved herself back. "For always. Don't look at me like that. What was I supposed to do? Tell my baby brother whenever I fell asleep, I'd see out his eyes? It took years for me to control it. To be able to sleep without dreaming. Would you have helped?"

Lila, with her knack for knowing when he'd had a rough patrol. Lila, with her uncanny insights into everyone and everything around her. "Ancestors Great and Glorious," he breathed. "I've never heard of such a thing."

"Then you didn't pay attention. Our nurse spoke of true-dreamers. Larmensu lore claimed our great-great—some bother of greats—grandfather to be the last with this gift."

The gift Glammis coveted. "Until you. A truedreamer." Bannan shivered inwardly, thinking of Marrowdell and a small boy. Ancestors Cruel and Calamitous.

"Sometimes." Lila grimaced and sank to the stair again. "What of you? I ordered a patrol up the Northward after 'dreaming blood through Weed's eyes, but the road was storm-closed. What of the boys? Tir—? My men: Rowe and Seel?"

Bannan sat with her. "Your men didn't make it," he said quietly. "Tir took care of those who hunted them, and the boys. The dragon?" He smiled. "His name is Wisp and he brought them in from the storm. I do believe he's adopted them. So's Scourge." He took a breath. "They sense what Werfol is. A truthseer."

"Heart's Blood." Rare to see Lila blanch. "It can't be—Bannan, no. He's so young. Too young for a gift."

"I know." He cupped her head in his hand and kissed her forehead. "Weed will be all right. He's a tough lad and I've started his training. Besides, Dear Heart, he has Semyn, as I had you."

"Semyn." Lila sighed like someone letting go. "I blink and he's grown, that one. Hearts of our Ancestors, I'm Beholden you were there for them both." With a snap, "Why aren't you still?"

He closed his eyes, then opened them. "Because Werfol has your gift as well as mine."

"Are you certain?" she asked, but her face was bleak and without hope.

"I see no other explanation. You asked why I'm here. Weed brought forth an image in a mirror. We saw this place," he gestured, "through your eyes. Then he dreamed on his own, seeing your cell—the chains. The boys insisted I come to Channen and I can't say I argued." The light flickered and Bannan glanced up. A moth circled it, which moths did. He looked back to his sister, crossing his arms on a knee. "Though it seems you didn't need rescuing."

Lila's grin lit her face. "Ever the hero. I appreciate the thought."

He found himself chuckling. "Trust me, I'll try to do better. What were you doing?"

"I 'dream Emon, if I've reason. He knows," Lila added, without apology to the brother who hadn't. She stared outward. "After he left for Channen, I discovered a malcontent among our original staff. I'd no idea how far the rot had spread, Bannan, but we'd already a house divided. I 'dreamed Emon at once, to find him in hiding, reliant on those I could no longer trust. I sent the boys to safety—or so I thought—with you, then came after him."

" 'Ever the hero,' " Bannan chided gently.

"My family."

No arguing with that tone. "The city jail?"

"It has windows," she said, as if amused, then went on more seriously. "I came in secret. Without knowing who to trust—or the city—I needed Emon to find me. Where easier? Besides, it was a safe place to truedream. There's risk, to what I do." She left it at that, though Bannan ached to know more.

Or did he?

"How did you do it?"

She shrugged. "Found an empty cell and made myself at home."

He raised an eyebrow. "And no one noticed?"

"M'name's Lornn Heatt," she announced with a wicked leer. "Killed m'layabout partner, I did, and would'a donnit twice if he'da let me." Her face and voice returned to normal. "Guards don't expect someone to put themselves in jail and I didn't need long. I put crumbs on my windowsill. Emon's clever birds spotted me by the second day. We conveyed messages." She grinned. "Emon wasn't happy."

No surprise there.

"I assured him no one knew who I was, my cell was doubtless more comfortable than wherever he was hiding, and that when he could do so without risk, he was to bribe a guard to get me out."

The truth, which was, Bannan decided, a surprise. Though if anyone knew how to mislead him, it was his sister.

Now was not the time for it, but before he could probe for more, Lila faced him, her eyes cool and gray. "Your turn, little brother. Was that your Jenn I saw, through Semyn's eyes? Is—that—what she really is?"

At the turn. Ancestors Blessed. Jenn worried about how to greet a baroness. He'd been waiting for this, the moment Lila would decide if she considered Jenn friend or— it had to be friend.

"Jenn is a woman, my love, and, yes, magic, too," Bannan said, treading with care. "You hadn't seen her before?" Oh, and didn't he blush, now appreciating what that meant?

Lila snorted. "I 'dream you only when I've no choice, Bannan Larmensu. Especially once you discovered what hung between your legs."

Yes, he could blush hotter.

She took pity on him. "I learned to silence my gift. It was that, or never sleep." Oh, so casually said. But he remembered a young Lila, always awake to soothe him from a nightmare. Remembered, now that he understood, her napping in the saddle. A soldierly skill, she'd called it.

Heart's Blood.

"These days, to truedream someone," his astonishing sister continued, "I taste something they've touched and use a sleeping draught to stay long enough to make sense of what I see." All the while helpless; risk indeed.

"So no," she finished, "I hadn't seen your new love as other than a blue-eyed woman who runs around barefoot. Until," her voice hardened, "Semyn saw her otherwise. Magic, you tell me. What sort? Dire or perilous."

"Good-hearted," Bannan countered, making her blink. "Brave. Jenn brought me here through a realm of magic— of the perilous sort—so we could arrive in time and save you. That realm—" as comprehension flared in Lila's eyes, "—would be the madness you saw."

"Bannan!"

The truthseer hunted for the right words, then held out his hands. "Our world," the right. "The dragons'," the left. He laid the palms over one another. "Where they overlap is something else again. On the dragons' side, it's called the Verge and teems with magic. That's where we traveled. My gift lets me see the truth of it; the beauty as well as peril. On our side?" He nodded to the mist overhead. "The edge. The Shadow District lies within it, as does Marrowdell. Magic slips through from the Verge. I see it here too."

"Magic," Lila echoed, looking around as though expecting Wisp to appear from a shadow. "So that's it." A tinge of color appeared on her cheeks. "I see what you see, little brother; I've never seen with your gift. But . . . sometimes I've 'dreamed what can't be real, yet I know is. Silver rain and blood-red eyes. Your dragons," with the tiniest of smiles.

"Because in the edge, sunset—the turn—reveals such things," Bannan explained, his heart lighter. "That's when Semyn saw Jenn as magic. Admittedly, he was more interested in Wisp."

He surprised a laugh. "I think I'd be too." She gave his ear a snap.

"What was that for?" he complained, rubbing the sting.

"To remind you, magic or no, I know best." Something grim settled around her. "And what I know is time's passing, little brother. Our friend Glammis went back inside. I'll not lose him."

Bannan stared at her. "You know who trapped me."

"I followed him here." Smug, that was. "To your good fortune."

"I was making my escape," he protested stiffly, choosing not to mention being used for bait.

Lila chose not to mention the three on the deck. "The manor is served by someone Emon trusts, who's set up a meeting—for tonight—with those who matter here. Glammis poses as a magic-user from Essa, having business of his own with the shadow lords—"

"It's no pose," Bannan interrupted. "He has a wishing to bind a truthseer, gift and will."

"Does he."

"Whatever else his business here, Glammis hunts those with the Larmensu gift. He would take our magic, Lila, for himself. Take us."

Her silence as she absorbed this stole warmth from the air. Then, an eyebrow lifted. "Indeed."

He heard the end of the man in that word.

"Whatever else," Lila echoed calmly, "I know Glammis serves those who wish to dissuade my dear husband from making his case." She jumped to her feet. "Let's fetch him."

"What of Emon?" The truthseer stood as well. "Shouldn't he be warned?"

Lila gave him a pitying look. "Once we deal with Glammis, he won't need a warning. Besides." She grinned. "When my clever Emon hides, even I can't find him."

"But I thought—" Bannan closed his mouth. Lila hadn't waited for Emon to free her from jail. Hadn't needed his help.

Hadn't wanted it.

"Don't think so hard, little brother," she suggested archly. "Your head will hurt."

"You—" All at once, the light dimmed. Both looked up.

The lamps to either side were smothered in moths, small and desperate. More climbed the stone walls, wings aflutter.

Then the mist above turned white, as moths filled the air like snowflakes that refused to fall. They settled in the alley, leaving one way open.

Up the stairs.

"Bannan . . . what's all this?" Was that uncertainty in her voice?

All was well—very well—if all was as he believed. "I believe, dear sister, we must leave Glammis for a while yet," the truthseer announced, heart grown light and trying hard not to laugh. "It seems Jenn Nalynn would like to meet you."

"I'd like to meet her too," Lila Larmensu stated, sounding not the least amused.

It wasn't until they were at the street level, moths to either side, that Bannan thought of something else.

"When you kept after me to write home—"

"It was so I could 'dream you," Lila told him. "If I didn't like what I read," she added, as if that were a comfort and not confirming his worst fears. "Your Jenn wrote to me. Did you know? Quite a nice letter."

Worse there was. Bannan couldn't find words.

Lila pushed him ahead of her. "Don't fuss, little brother. I'm no fool, to truedream magic."

They would say later that never had there been so many white moths in Channen, nor any so filled with magic. To follow one was to find your heart. So many did, that special night, nine months later midwives were the busiest they could remember, though every babe was healthy.

And not a one cried.

Strays, be they four-footed or on two, found homes that night as well, while constables stood by in amazement as their cells filled with thieves who'd followed the moths and wished, most ardently, to put what they'd stolen back where it belonged.

Well before sunrise, the moths had vanished. In the days after, the Shadow Sect quietly spread word of how the moths had been a gift of the Source to Channen, and all should be Beholden.

What went unremarked?

That most of the moths returned to a single rooftop, followed by those particularly invited . . .

To find Jenn Nalynn.

~Elder brother. Are you asleep?~

Giving up any pretense, Wisp cracked open an eye. ~What now?~

~Though it is the middle of the night, the warrior returns, elder brother. He moves with urgency.~

Not good news. The dragon eased himself from the bed, pleased his bones felt whole again. Though there was—he stretched his wounded leg—lingering weakness.

~Something must be wrong, elder brother.~

The man might want his own bed, Wisp thought, but there was no convincing the toad. Little cousins noticed the unusual, being meticulous beings and vigilant. ~Peace. I will see to it.~ Little he could do for Tir's comfort, but as Wisp flew to the lower level, he sent a breeze to liven the fire in the cookstove and move the kettle above that warmth.

Then, knowing the man, he brought a bottle from its hiding place and a mug.

The door opened, brusquely but with a care. Tir stepped in with a swirl of snow and cold, shutting out the night before beginning to strip. "Dragon."

Wisp shaped himself in light. "I am here."

Tir glanced at the loft.

"The boys sleep." He'd wait to learn the man's temper before going into more than that. "You've alarmed the little cousin."

The house toad, puffed by the fire, received a glance. "I saw no reason not to sleep in my own bed," the man said gruffly.

The toad glared, still unsettled.

Wisp sent a breeze to stretch out the hammock and its bedding.

"Not yet." Tir could move silently when he chose; he didn't bother to mute his steps as he went for the bottle. Taking off his mask, he freed the cork with his teeth, spitting it on the table. After pouring a quantity into his mouth, he swallowed, then wiped the ruin of his lips on his sleeve. "My thanks."

"I'll thank you," Wisp said, giving the breeze a nip, "not to wake them."

A wink. "Had a rough go, did you? Don't worry. T'lads expect noise down here. Too quiet will only wake them sooner."

He'd not thought of that.

Grabbing the bottle, Tir went to sit by the fireplace, stretching out his legs. The dragon took the hint and added tinder and a log, fanning the embers with a careful breeze. Dragonsbreath, though quicker, would have melted the brick.

"Books." The man paused for another pour and swallow. "Who'd have thought it?"

Wisp curled himself before the fire to wait for something of meaning.

"Don't be smug." The bottle lifted, a finger around its neck pointing at the dragon. "Kydd'll find you in one. You'll see."

Much as he respected the skills of the beekeeper—and abhorred his curiosity regarding things of magic—the dragon doubted that. "Are you saying you've learned from a book about this man from before?"

"First things to start with. I've a name for young Weed." A nod upstairs. "Truedreamer. And why I'm glad o'the wine, friend dragon," pour, swallow, and sigh, "is thinking who else must be." He settled a moment, fierce creases along his brow, then threw out his arm, almost losing the bottle. "That bloody woman! It's how she always knew— always!—when I was at fault. Or sir. She'd call us out before we'd stepped two feet through the door. Bannan'd blamed me for it, but it was her—dreaming us!"

The dragon refused to puzzle this out. "What did the beekeeper know of Crumlin?"

"Humph," Tir grunted. After a sullen moment, he cheered. "Can't see why you've had such trouble with that one. Must be over a hundred by now."

"I'm 'trouble.'" Wisp lifted a flawless wing and pretended to examine it. "And older still."

"For a man, that's gum-the-bread age. Anyway, this Crumlin—Crumlin Tralee—had family in Avyo, including a young brother of the same mind. This brother wrote a book on magic doings and don'ts Kydd said was rightly banned, though why he has it—" Tir stopped, by his blank stare working his way through the "having" of a book whose pages sheltered bees and whose words were lodged in Wainn's head. He gave up the struggle. "In this book, he brags of how his elder brother 'traveled north to conduct his greatest work.' That'd be our Crumlin," he clarified unnecessarily. "Not to be heard from again."

The dragon curled up to wait again.

"I didn't get the half of what Kydd said. But I know what's what." Tir lifted the bottle, only to put it aside. "What's in one world belongs to it. Nothing good's to come of this Crumlin's meddlin'," he stated. "Nothing good at all."

Wisp snarled to himself, in complete agreement.

"How can I know? What if she's 'dreaming me now?'" Tir muttered, squeezing his eyes shut. "Think it's funny, do you?" he said abruptly, glaring down at Wisp. "Wait'll Lila 'dreams you, dragon. Sees out your eyes!"

The dragon rested his long jaw on his hip, admiring how the firelight caught on his scaled hide. "A far more interesting view," he suggested slyly, "than through yours."

# FIFTEEN

"IT MIGHT NOT work," Jenn admitted to the toad curled in her lap. The little cousin was heavier than it looked and chill, but she didn't mind. What she minded, a little, was that every so often there'd be a disturbing "squeak!" and crunch from the dark, the kruar insisting they hunt around her.

After a louder CRUNCH than most, she winced. "How many mice can there be?"

A kruar purred. ~Not mice.~

Oh.

~I would eat the foul nyphrit too, elder sister,~ the house toad informed her poignantly, ~but none dare come close to you.~

"Because you are here to guard me, esteemed little cousin," she consoled it, smiling as it puffed with pride.

~Someone comes!~

The toad leapt from her lap to let her stand. "It's a friend—or family," Jenn warned, her protectors having demonstrated themselves the sort to eat first and look later.

The kruar faded into the shadows, leaving doubt.

Jenn hoped they'd be family. She also hoped, most earnestly, that whomever came didn't mind having to climb the rickety ladder from the back alley which was the route to this particular rooftop, that not having been something she'd thought about before invoking magic to draw them here.

Consequences, Jenn sighed to herself. Difficult to think of them all.

A moth danced in and out of a dark alcove near the back of the rooftop, then two. Suddenly a veritable storm of moths, all white and aflutter, appeared in the same spot.

Jenn held out her hands and they flew to her, sinking through the calluses of her palms in a flurry of softness before she could change and be glass. She squinted at her now-empty, quite ordinary skin, then rubbed her hands together, wondering. Was being one and whole, to be all at once? Surely not—

"Fair evening." A man stepped through a door she'd not noticed before, but should have guessed would be there.

He wasn't alone, for two other men came behind him, then a woman.

And she might have worried, to be faced with so many strangers, but the man who'd greeted her came forward and bowed, brushing fingertips to the rooftop and when he raised his head, she saw Werfol's smile.

By his dress, the man could have been any of those she'd observed sweeping the stones or carrying packages. He'd curly reddish-brown hair, gentle brown eyes, and a round, almost boyish face, but there was no mistake.

Jenn dropped in a hasty curtsy. "Fair evening to you, your—" Her wits scattered. What did one say? "Baron Westietas. I'm Jenn Nalynn." Which should have meant nothing to a baron.

His smile softened. "Of whom my wife's brother has written such glowing praise." A second, shorter bow. "Please. Emon. These are my companions, Bish," the woman, "Dutton, and Herer." The men.

All three wore swords strapped to their hips. They bowed as they were introduced, looking none too happy to be here. Bish had tight gray curls cut close to her head and keen brown eyes; black feathers had been painted on her shoulders and throat. Hair and beard grizzled, Dutton was heavier set, his shoulders scarred, face wrinkled beside his eyes as though he'd spent his youth staring at the sun. Emon's final companion?

"I've had the pleasure," Herer said, after his bow, being the man who'd lost his clockwork and knife. His arm was in a sling.

"You were watching us," Jenn blurted out.

"My apologies. When you spoke to me in Rhothan, I feared you were one of my lord's enemies, trying to expose me. I followed to see for myself." He touched the sling. "Someone objected."

Jenn winced. "I can explain—"

"Later, please, along with why you're here at all." Emon had lost his smile. "Where's Bannan? I tried to warn him."

"A fool risk," snapped the woman, Bish.

"As is my right!"

Bish bowed her head. "My lord." Her eyes glittered. "You're most welcome to be a fool, so long as we can save you from it."

They'd been the figures on the bridge, who'd pulled Emon back. Ancestors Plagued and Pained. They'd been close to finding Emon twice, Jenn thought, chagrined, only to fail. "I've asked Bannan to find me," she said, which was true however strange-sounding. "That's why you're here. I expect him soon."

"The moths." Emon shook his head, face filled with childlike wonder. "You've rare magic, Jenn Nalynn."

"When it works," she muttered.

Dutton and Herer exchanged looks; Bish almost smiled.

~Danger!~ Kruar erupted from their hiding place as two large black birds dove toward Emon!

Swords flashed even as the—crows!—veered at the last moment to avoid the leading kruar's fangs, cawing their alarm.

"They're mine," Emon said calmly. He lifted his arm and the crows spiraled down to land on it, fluffing their feathers as if thoroughly offended. "Cheek and Scatterwit." The latter put its head close to the baron's ear, taking a curl of his hair in its beak to give it an affectionate tug.

Jenn looked sternly at the kruar who, having sprung their ambush to no good purpose, did their best to appear ordinary horses, ears up and peaceful, though one had a very large toad clinging to the saddle and both stood on a roof where horses couldn't be.

"These are mine," she admitted, not attempting to explain.

"Remarkable!" He seemed ready to take a closer look.

"M'lord." Herer had pulled out his clockwork. "They've convened. We mustn't tarry."

The baron sighed. "For what good it will do." He gave Jenn a wistful look. "Unless you've some magic to change minds who stubbornly insist on proof."

"With respect, my lord baron," she replied stiffly, "that's not a proper use of magic at all."

He had a contagious laugh, open and joyous. "Emon, please. You're right, of course. We're left with my powers of persuasion, such as they are. As Herer says, we're out of time."

"M'lord. I beg you reconsider." Dutton's voice was the deepest Jenn had ever heard, like one of Scourge's rumbles. "You've done all you can without exposing yourself. There's naught to be gained from these shadow lords. We could be back in Rhoth—"

Emon shook his head. "I'd ill serve Rhoth if I didn't see it through. I'll meet with anyone who might bring some sense back to all this."

Shadow lords? "You're meeting with the Shadow Sect," Jenn said anxiously. "That's what he means, isn't it?" She looked to Herer. "That's who tried to stop you in the market."

"They're against us?" that worthy exclaimed, growing pale. "M'lord!"

"How do you know of them?" Dutton demanded sharply, hand dropping to the hilt of his sword. "Speak quickly!"

"Peace." The baron held out a hand, waiting until his companions relaxed their stance, if not the now-suspicious glares they bestowed on Jenn. "The sect has authority within the Shadow District for good reason, my friends. Magic walks here." He smiled at Jenn. "Have we not seen it tonight?" He gave her a curious look, his crows angling their black heads as though curious too. "Leading me to ask, Jenn Nalynn. Are you of this sect? Is that why you've summoned me?"

"No." How much to say? Jenn met his eyes, kind and wise, as well as curious, and thought that if Semyn and Werfol's father was someone to trust, his companions were another matter, being rightly concerned with protecting their lord. "The sect has been courteous and helpful to me as a—as a visitor here." Which wasn't a lie, if hardly the full truth. "I invited you to find me because Bannan and I thought you needed help." She made a rueful face. "I'm sorry to have disturbed you. You aren't in trouble, are you."

"Not for want of trying," Bish said dryly. "Our lord's put himself at considerable risk to move freely, away from Channen's official court."

"As was necessary." Emon shrugged, his crows bobbing to keep their balance. He noticed her puzzlement. "Jenn, those who'd blame Rhoth for their woes have been swayed by promises no one outside Channen could match or comprehend. The rest hold no grudge against us, but have been convinced by lies I couldn't refute as an envoy, trapped in meetings. If I was to find any leverage at all—any hope at all—it was here, in the Shadow District."

It sounded more desperate than hopeful. "What will you do?"

"The shadow lords wield great influence within Channen's House of Keys. Pray they'll listen. First and foremost, though. Please. I must know Bannan's safe," Emon declared, warming her heart.

"You will," Jenn told him, for she trusted what she'd done. Then, because Bannan would, she dared ask, "And the baroness? Is she safe?"

Emon ran a finger down the throat of the larger crow, Scatterwit. His thumb was badly bruised, the nail split, as if caught in a door; now that she looked with more concern, she noticed the purpling under his eyes and how he favored one leg. Still, he smiled at her question. "My Lila? Rarely."

Which wasn't an answer.

"M'lord, if you would do this, we must away."

"A moment longer," Jenn urged, answering to impulse. "Please."

"I—"

A sheet of white crested the side of the roof, moths spilling over in a blinding cloud. As Jenn held out her hands to retrieve them, she looked to see what—who—followed, her heart pounding.

And there he was. Bannan Larmensu reached the top of the rickety ladder and stepped onto the roof.

Followed by the woman who could only be his sister.

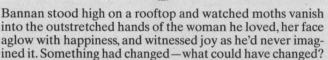

Bannan stood high on a rooftop and watched moths vanish into the outstretched hands of the woman he loved, her face aglow with happiness, and witnessed joy as he'd never imagined it. Something had changed—what could have changed?

Whatever it was filled his heart until it might have burst. Save that Lila stood watching with him, her utter stillness a warning not to ignore.

"Lila, this is Jenn."

Along with Emon, Ancestors Blessed, with his bloody crows, flanked by Dutton Omemee and Bish, whom he'd not seen since his last Midwinter Beholding with the family, two years ago. And their watcher, reasonably unscathed, likely missing a knife.

Not to forget the kruar, with toad.

PatPat. As if the yling knew he'd been counting.

Did Lila even breathe?

Jenn's smile disappeared as her hands dropped to her sides, her eyes locked with his sister's.

"Let me—"

Lila's head moved almost imperceptibly. No, that was, and Bannan closed his mouth. Heart's Blood. She'd judged Jenn a threat and why wouldn't she? Magic in abundance. A summons in the night? One that swept up her husband too? It couldn't be worse, and Bannan was lost for what to say or do—but he, Ancestors save him, he put his hand to the hilt of that wretched knife and despaired.

Jenn took a step forward, dropping an old-fashioned curtsy. "Baroness."

Lila gave a hard little gasp. "I've 'dreamed you."

Jenn froze, which was a mistake because now she was stuck at the low point of her curtsy, never graceful despite practice, and she would, she thought numbly, tip over in a moment which would be a disaster. "I dreamed you too," she admitted, though to be honest hers had been more nightmares of doing exactly what she was. Cheeks starting to flame, she looked up at the beautiful woman.

Seeing Semyn's eyes and Werfol's brow and, oh yes, Bannan's mouth. It was like magic, seeing them writ together in this one face and she began to smile, she couldn't help it, from her overfull heart. "I'm Jenn."

Then, of course, she did tip, and flailed her arms to save herself landing on the roof. Just in time, someone caught her wrist.

Lila.

She held very still, for the grip wasn't like Peggs' or even Bannan's. Fingers dug in, as though seeking bone. Punishing . . .

No, Jenn decided, meeting those vivid green eyes, asking a question. "I do bruise," she answered evenly, the matter of bones being complicated. "In case you wondered."

The hand loosened at that, but held enough to help her to her feet.

"Can you be killed?" Pleasantly, as if they discussed a late supper for those listening.

Fair enough. Jenn replied in kind. "I'd rather not find out."

Was that the hint of a smile? "So say we all." Lila searched her face, then frowned. "Are you dream or nightmare?"

"Lila," Bannan warned, low and unhappy.

A tip of her head. "My brother wants me to trust you." Now, at last, the baroness smiled, but it wasn't kind. "His taste in women hasn't been wise. You force me here with moths and magic, Jenn Nalynn. To meet you?" A deliberate look up and down. "Nothing inclines me to believe his taste's improved."

Earning Lila's trust would never be easy, not when it came to her family. The realization put Jenn oddly at ease, no longer afraid the baroness would reject her simply for being turn-born. They were the same, in their passion to protect.

Willing to die for those they loved.

Deeds, then, not words. "Then I look forward to your better opinion," Jenn said simply. "You aren't here for me." She stepped to the side, gesturing to Emon and his companions.

"Bannan!" Emon strode forward, crows lifting into the air. When the truthseer went to bow, the baron took his hand and drew him close with a fervent, "Ancestors Blessed and Beloved."

After the embrace, he frowned up at his brother-by-marriage. "Ancestors Witness, drawn you into this, has she?" Before Bannan could say a word, Emon turned to his wife, his frown deepening. "Where are our sons?"

Bannan tried to recall when he'd last seen Lila rendered speechless, then realized he hadn't. "The boys are safe," he interjected. "We came—" He ran his fingers through his hair. "We came to your rescue," he said lamely.

Emon's worldly and worthy companions were too polite to smile at this. They didn't have to—he felt fool enough. "I should have known better."

"As should I," the baron said bluntly. "Imagine my surprise to find no hapless wife languishing in her cell, and her brother playing in the canal."

About to object, Bannan found he couldn't.

"'Hapless,' am I?" The back of a limp hand rested across a brow. "'Languishing?' And misplaced the children?"

Pretense. Misdirection. Why? Seeing Emon grow still, Bannan eased closer to Jenn, wishing, among other things, to take his doubtless bewildered love aside and explain.

Explain his sister? Ancestors Witness, easier to describe walking the Verge to Tir. At least, Bannan consoled himself, Jenn hadn't let Lila intimidate her.

"We paid the constables, m'lady, but you were gone." Dutton frowned. "What happened?"

Gleeful, that smile. "Bribed twice? They'll miss me."

The rest looked confused. Emon scowled like a gathering storm. "You promised me no one knew who you were! That you were safe!"

"As you're 'safe' here. Really, Emon," she chided gently.

"Heart's Blood, woman! Don't tell me you used yourself as bait! That was never the plan."

"Wasn't it?" She locked eyes with her husband.

For it had been Lila's, Bannan realized, since the moment she'd sent the boys to him. Ancestors Battered and Bled. She'd aimed herself like an arrow at her husband's heart, using his love for her, his love for his dearest friends, to set her trap. She'd known Emon would tell his companions she'd come to Channen, that he'd order them to rescue her, if he couldn't.

She'd known they'd be betrayed.

The truthseer watched the same realization drain the righteous fury from Emon's face, leaving it bleak. "I see."

Something in those words altered her face as well. It might have been pity; it was nothing so kind as regret.

Gone the next instant. "Shall I continue?" Lila said briskly. She didn't wait, but looked around at them all. "Someone paid the constables to patrol another hall than mine, leaving the key to my cell."

"Did you get a name, m'lady?" Dutton asked grimly.

Lila smiled at him. "I did, indeed. My, the constables grew fat today. The man who'd bribed them first was Glammis Lurgan."

From their faces, the name was unfamiliar. Faces, Bannan knew, could lie.

"A bold plan, m'lady, to trap them into trying to take you, but I'm glad you weren't tempted to play along." Herer shook his head. "Begging your pardon, but even a confession from the man would change nothing. The shadow lords employ such tricks themselves. Why would they care? And if they'd been behind it—" He shrugged, leaving it at that.

"I'm flattered by your confidence, Herer, but that wasn't my intention. Besides—" Lila looked at her husband. "—I'd heard the name before. Glammis is a collector with an unsavory reputation. Not that any of his 'guests' have come forth to press a complaint."

Emon moved involuntarily, his face gone white, but it was Bish who spoke up. "How can we be certain, m'lady, Glammis wasn't simply after the next beauty he could spirit away? You're not exactly hideous," she added with a grin.

"A burden I must bear," Lila agreed. "But you're right, I couldn't be sure. So I followed Glammis—who is, by the way, not only Rhothan but has a revealing tang of Essa in his speech—to a large building on the Straight. Imagine my surprise, dear husband, when I realized it was the very same address Scatterwit here," a nod to the crow, "had given me in our last exchange. Where you plan to meet this night with the shadow court."

"A trap!" Dutton scowled. "I knew it, m'lord. We've enemies among them too."

The baron raised his hand for silence. "Go on."

They worked together now, his sister and her husband, letting the others chase this distraction. Bannan could see it, as plainly as if he watched Scourge toy with a mouse.

Just as merciless.

"Oh, I shall. A coincidence? Unlikely, as you rightly say, Dutton, but still. A servant proved more than happy to gossip. Said this Glammis is an annoying upstart of a Rhothan who claims—the servant was most unflattering—to be a magic-user. He comes regularly to the Shadow Sect, does some minor business for them in return for permission to ply his craft in Channen, import tokens and so forth, though she was surprised he'd returned so soon. All quite legal, if unusual.

"Yet I'm there but a short while when what do I see? This law-abiding Rhothan marching my brother, arms tied, out a side door."

Bannan saw Jenn tremble and reached for her hand. She squeezed his as though he needed reassuring. Given how close it had been—had Lila not been there? Had Lila been fooled by Glammis' traps? He squeezed back.

"Then Dutton's right, m'lord," Herer stated, his face

troubled. "The shadow lords are against us! They want to stop our mission so badly that when m'lady escaped their trap, their henchman took you, Bannan."

"Except that tonight isn't their trap," Lila said gently, "but mine." Her fingers moved. *Your turn.*

Ancestors Sly and Conniving. Bannan took a step forward. "Whatever his involvement in the threat against you, Emon, Glammis admitted he'd had no interest in your mission here." The truthseer hesitated. Bish and Dutton had served Emon's father; this Herer, he didn't know. "What I would say concerns the Larmensu, and your sons."

"After my wife," Emon said, bowing slightly toward Lila, "these are my most trusted advisers. There is nothing you may not say in their hearing."

Because he understood what his bloody-minded wife had done and why, and that he'd pay the price, should she be right.

The pair of them watched him, waited for him to finish it. Heart's Blood. He could hate them. Should. Jenn stood watching, perplexed but knowing to be silent. How dare they ask this of him, in front of her?

Unsuspecting, Emon's companions bowed to the baron and baroness, murmuring, "M'lord. M'lady."

*All of it, brother,* Lila signed then, and shot Bannan an unreadable look.

In the border guard he'd taken the name Captain Ash from his predecessor, earning a reputation as an infallible interrogator, his well-bearded face known only to his patrol and the lord commander of the border guard, who reported directly to Prince Ordo.

That Captain Ash was Bannan Larmensu? Tir had known from the beginning, having helped him assume that identity and protect it. Being young and a fool, Bannan had shared his accomplishment with Loiss and Renee, a pair of equally young fools who'd joined for glory and become his friends. Having watched both die on patrol, helpless to protect them, he'd let no one else come so close, made no more friends among the guard.

And kept secret his name.

Of course Lila had known; if she'd told Emon, he neither knew nor cared, trusting his sister.

But the deepest secret of all, that Bannan had inherited the Larmensu gift and was a truthseer? Outside of Marrowdell, that knowledge should belong only to their aged nurse, Lila, and Tir. That Emon knew? In no sense a worry.

That Glammis did? Was beyond terrifying.

Yet Lila wanted him to bare his secrets to these three. Wanted to show them the trap even as she sprang it. Would use him, as readily as her sword.

Bannan braced himself.

The mist wreathing the rooftop thickened and chilled; someone else expressing an opinion. He managed to smile at Jenn Nalynn; she didn't smile back.

In for it, then. "Glammis knows us as Larmensu. He knows some of that heritage possess gifts, though it's a secret we've protected all our lives. Gifts of magic. He knows I'm a truthseer. That Lila—" he waited, lifting a brow.

His sister lifted hers. No, that was.

Fair enough. "—is aware of it." Emon nodded impassively.

His companions, after shock flickered over their faces, grew grim and even more attentive. Not that Bannan had hoped to surprise a reaction. Not from such as these.

He didn't need one.

"Though Glammis went to the jail for Lila, he said he'd been hunting for me at the same time. These—" Bannan reached into his belt and took out the tokens, "—are for a wishing to bind a truthseer's gift and will. They were purchased here, in the Artisans' Market, by someone I now believe must be one of the 'like-minded' patrons he boasted of having. The Baroness Abeek Harrow."

Emon's companions shared meaningful looks. "We know the lady," Bish commented.

"My chief adversary and a dangerous one," the baron said grimly. "In no way am I shocked to hear this." He heaved a sigh of relief, his face clearing. "Ancestors Blessed, this is what I've needed, Bannan. Proof! Magic misused by one of the court? There's no greater crime here. Once I bring this to the shadow lords, name names, they'll collapse her influence in court."

"There's more." The next, Lila didn't know, not yet, and would be hard to hear. Bannan looked a warning at her.

"What?"

His fingers closed over the tokens. "These followed Semyn and Werfol to Marrowdell. To me." Surely that would be enough.

He sighed inwardly. Surely not.

With his free hand, he signed, *What now?*

Green flashed in her eyes and her fingers moved in answer, quick and sure.

*Captain Ash.*

Eyes with ominous gold in their depths. A jaw gone hard, muscles working along it. Stance become threat, any warmth of expression wiped clean. Jenn watched Bannan change, and it was a transformation as profound to someone who knew him—who loved him—as the cobwebs to cloak of the yling.

This man was a stranger.

It hadn't been shaving the beard that had disguised Captain Ash, nor keeping secret his gift. It had been that Bannan Larmensu, young and ready to hope, had cast him out.

To bring him back, now. Jenn looked to Lila and if she'd seen triumph or even satisfaction, she would no longer care for Bannan's famous sister.

Instead, she caught a glimpse of grief so profound, her own heart bled too.

Before resolve carved those delicate features in stone.

After an unreadable glance at Bannan, Herer took out his clockwork. "M'lord—our allies will do what they can to delay, but if we're to present this, we must go."

Ancestors Distant and Disregarded. She'd brought them together but wasn't part of this, Jenn reminded herself, being a miller's daughter from what she now recognized was a tiny village beyond the rest of the world.

Yet . . . wasn't she? Bound by love to Bannan, by Bannan to his sister, by his sister and Werfol and Semyn to Emon who'd come to Channen for the noblest of reasons, to bring peace.

To have this family threatened.

Bannan gave himself away to help. What could she do? Jenn let herself feel the expectations of the turn-born for this part of the edge, drawing them in as if they were her own. Peace. Privacy.

Through people as well. Preserve magic's source. Protect the Verge. Keep secrets. Whether intended or not, the turn-borns' desire had led to the Artisans' Market. To paintings that sang and magical beer mugs and so much more.

As well as the Shadow Sect and its court.

Woven through leaves and water and turtles and stone, their expectations, as in the Verge. No one thread to pull. No thread safe to cut. Everything was intertwined and dependent, and part of her admired their magic, seeing it as neat stitches and needful.

While another part twitched, as though uncomfortable. As if bound. Annoyed.

Which she wasn't, Jenn decided firmly. She was respectful and careful. Mistress Sand would be proud, to see her use such good sense. "I dare not help," she said out loud.

Herer and his fellow companions frowned as if she'd interrupted her elders, but Emon smiled. "You've done so already, Jenn, bringing us together. For that, you have my deepest thanks."

Captain Ash, who knew full well what she meant, merely nodded. Lila, who claimed to have seen her in a dream and whose "gift" Jenn was beginning to suspect, frowned as well, giving her a considering look, but asked no questions.

"I'll check the way," Bish said briskly and Dutton turned with her.

With one smooth step, Lila Larmensu had her knife to Herer's throat. "I'd like you to meet my little brother first."

"When you're ready, Dear Heart."

Those who didn't know Lila exceedingly well would think that an even tone. Might even think her calm.

They'd be wrong. Captain Ash met Emon's gaze, saw the same awareness there. Death hovered a hairbreadth above that blade, more than eager.

Good.

Herer, unaware, tried to protest. "My la—" He shut his mouth as the knife penetrated skin, blood beading, then starting to flow.

"You cannot deceive me," Captain Ash told the man. He glanced at the other two. "Or flee." He looked beyond them.

Bish turned her head very slowly. Eager for violence, the kruar had closed in, eyes rimmed with red, lips curled back from what belonged to no horse. Dutton, seeing her attention, looked as well.

The house toad, not to be outdone, bared its needle teeth.

"We've—" Dutton stopped.

Few kept talking, once they knew who listened. What listened. It mattered not.

"Someone here has betrayed their lord," Captain Ash began. No need to raise his voice; once they saw his face, they never looked away. "Has conspired with those who would betray Rhoth. Has aimed harm at innocents. Someone here would see Baron Westietas dead before allowing his mission to succeed."

He paused to allow protest, that ever-revealing lie, but there were none.

Ah, well.

The truthseer's attention returned to Herer. He took a moment to study the face, looked deeper. "Know this. I will see your lies. I will know the truth. Have you betrayed your lord?"

The knife eased its pressure to allow an answer. Eyes hot, cheeks livid, Herer shouted in fury, "I have not! Would not. I owe m'lord my life and more. I would die for Baron Westietas, whether you 'see' that truth or not!"

So it was one of Emon's oldest friends, or both. Unlikely to be neither. Deception. Mistrust. He sensed them, was drawn like a hound to a blood scent. "I see the truth," Captain Ash said and nodded.

Lila took her knife from Herer's throat and spun to Bish, as Emon himself, followed a heartbeat later by Herer, drew their weapons on Dutton.

"Ancestors Bloody and Bent!" Dutton swore. "It's none of us, m'lord!" He took a step.

Emon lifted his sword to forbid a second.

At that, the other man seemed to crumple. "I'd give my life for you, m'lord, you know that. I didn't betray you. I never would. Tell them, Bish," he pleaded. "Hurry and say it so they know."

Pleading signified nothing, nor did shouts nor sobs nor outrage. The truth counted for all and it shone in his face. How convenient, Captain Ash thought, nodding once more.

Everyone looked then to Bish, whose lips remained pressed in a thin line.

Ah, silence. How predictable.

How futile, against the fullness of his gift. "You'd help, at the estate, ready to take the baron's sons," Captain Ash said conversationally. *Truth, there, in her face.* "When that failed, you sent a pursuit—" *No.* "Or did you merely inform of the chance to gather in not only the sons and heir, but to locate the baron's brother-by-marriage?"

A hint of panic. "How—?" Her lips clamped shut.

*Truth.* Captain Ash gestured, as if being generous. "Only the baron and you three knew the baroness was in the Distal Hold. Only you could have betrayed her." He didn't bother to look deeper.

The baron's face was terrible to see. Lila's?

Bore the smallest of smiles, as if sharing a secret between close friends. For they'd been close, she and Bish, since Lila came to the Westietas'. Fought together. Betrayed? It was too small a word.

And mattered not to Captain Ash. He savored the hunt, lived to catch the lies. The best was to come, he could tell. "Having failed in all your attempts, what's left? Ah. Assassination. Secret, perhaps. A knife in the back." *No.* He smiled. "Public, then. Much better. The Rhothan baron linked to the treaty brought down in the heart of Mellynne. Ordo's not fond of Westietas, but the Eld would take it as a threat. They'd demand a show of strength and resolve. You'd win."

"Lies! All lies, m'lord! None of it's true, I swear!"

Everything was. He had her. "I condemn you, Bish Fingal, for betraying Rhoth, your lord, and all those who've called you friend."

Done. Always, victory was a disappointment, leaving him spent and grim, tarnished by the lies.

Fingers wrapped around his, warm and sure. Unexpected. Captain Ash started and looked down. Letters burned along his neck and . . .

He drowned in eyes like a deep endless pool, blue—no, they were purple—eyes that held the truth . . .

And his name.

Bannan.

He gasped as though coming up for air, Captain Ash stripping away from him even as he reached for Jenn Nalynn and buried his face in her rose-scented hair.

For an instant, an eternity, but it wasn't over, Bannan thought, heartsick, and looked up.

Emon stood closer to Bish. "Say you were bound by foul magic," he told her, his voice breaking with anguish. "Coerced!"

"Coward, I say!" Bish looked at him with such hate, Lila forced herself between. "You let my city be split apart. Gave away everything we'd fought for—everything we'd bled for and for what?" She spat.

"Peace." He turned away, shoulders slumped; his crows circled his head in silence and no one else moved.

Bannan watched Lila. She stared after her husband, then said gently, "Emon."

After a long moment, he lifted his hand, then flicked the first two fingers.

Lila turned back to Bish and bared her teeth. "Who is with you? Where were you to strike? When?"

"NOW!" With that shout, the other woman contorted her arm and silver flew through the air toward Emon!

Lila was quicker, knocking the weapon aside.

While Dutton's sword buried itself to the hilt.

The world became the rooftop. Jenn couldn't move, couldn't take her eyes from the man who clasped the woman to him, holding her as she collapsed, easing her down as life left her. He pressed his lips to her head with a shudder.

She'd thought it impossible to bear, watching Bannan become Captain Ash, but he'd come back to her. This—this couldn't be changed. Couldn't be fixed.

Hearts were broken.

When Emon approached, Dutton looked up, tears in his eyes. "I didn't see it. If anyone should have, it was me. I've failed you, m'lord."

The baron laid a hand on his shoulder. "We failed her. Ancestors Dear and Departed."

"Bish made her choice," Lila reminded them bluntly, putting away her sword. "Haven't you somewhere to be, husband?"

"Lila." Jenn heard the pain in Emon's voice. "I was a fool."

"Never that." She had a lovely smile, when she chose.

"If this had failed?" His gesture included Jenn and Bannan.

Lila raised an eyebrow. "Need you ask?"

Implying plans upon plans, Jenn thought, like layers of a cake, though what else Lila might have done, had Bannan not been there to see the truth, she couldn't imagine.

But Emon nodded, as if he'd expected no other answer, and for some reason, Dutton looked worried and Herer went pale. "Then we'll be off. May I leave this to you, Dearest Heart?"

A faint smile. "Always."

Leave what? wondered Jenn.

~We could help,~ offered a kruar eagerly.

Oh.

Bannan gave the baron the tokens, queasily glad to see them leave his hands.

"Pity we don't know the poor truthseer who was the victim of this plot," Emon said, looking to Herer.

The man bowed his head. "Unnecessary information, m'lord. We've more than enough for the court."

"I concur. Dutton?"

"Aie, m'lord." The older man stood. After pulling free his sword and cleaning the blade, he shed his bloody tunic, laying that over Bish's face. "We'd best change our route," he advised heavily.

As they gathered themselves, Bannan looked for Jenn.

She'd gone to stand by one of the roof's gargoyles, her hand resting on its head. When he neared, she whispered, soft and puzzled, "They were friends."

"More." Dutton and Bish had been lovers, off and on, but Jenn didn't need that grief too. Bannan said only, "Bish was one of Emon's guards when he was a boy." He put his arm around her waist and leaned his head against hers. "Ancestors Dear and Departed."

"What happens now?"

He lifted his head and stared into the night.

"Emon stops a war," Bannan said at last, "while Lila and I deal with Glammis."

Jenn turned, her hand flat over his heart, her face shadowed. "Not alone," she said.

And he heard thunder.

He didn't doubt her resolve or power, but this she couldn't do. The truthseer covered her hand with his. "It's beyond the edge, Dearest Heart. Where you—" where she didn't exist. Throat tight, he finished, "You could wait. There's the house the sect had for us."

The air fell still, mist unmoving.

"Jenn?"

"I'll wait," she agreed, when she might have protested, and he took an easier breath. "But—" this in a tone so like Peggs' he almost smiled, "—I'll come with you as far as I can, first, to see you safely there."

He kissed her. "Thank you."

His ease vanished in the next instant. Their faces still close, Jenn whispered, "Just be prepared, Dearest Heart. When you leave the edge, Lila may forget me."

"She dreamed of you—of the dragon. The Verge. Her gift—" He stopped. His hadn't saved him. They'd been within the edge when Lila'd spoken of Jenn.

He'd had no letter from his sister since Jenn had become turn-born, becoming part of the magic others forgot. Leaving no way to know except one. Leaving the edge.

Heart sinking, Bannan touched noses with his wise and gentle love. "Then I'll remember for both of us," he vowed.

~We could help,~ the kruar insisted with brutal enthusiasm. ~Tasty!~

"Tasty" referring to a person who'd followed her moths and come to her—who'd been lost, and stayed so—Jenn had to swallow twice before uttering a meek, "No, thank you."

She felt queasy as it was, watching Lila and her brother handle the matter with capable and—horrible as the thought—practiced ease. Having stripped any valuables to make the death seem a robbery, they heaved the body over the side of the roof and out, to land with a splash in the canal.

Where the nyims, the little cousin unnecessarily assured her, would do the rest.

Jenn eyed the toad, who eyed her back. It had gobbled Dutton's blood-soaked tunic while Lila and Bannan had been busy, using its front feet to shove the last section of fabric into its mouth. It didn't appear to be making anything from the garment.

Yet.

A tidy creature, the toad, and helpful. That being said, she would not, under any circumstances, ask what it found "tasty."

When the Larmensus came to where she stood, both looked for the tunic and Jenn nodded at the toad. Bannan grinned. "Don't ask, sister mine," he suggested, unwittingly agreeing with her. "Some things must be seen."

Lila nodded. As they prepared to leave, Jenn caught her giving the toad quick looks as if to surprise it in action. The toad, meanwhile, let Jenn lift it to its favored spot before the saddle where it flattened, claws in the kruar's hide, eyes intent. The kruar swung its head around, glaring, but didn't try to shed the little cousin this time.

The great beasts approved of Lila; Jenn's would carry both women. She went to mount first.

"Wait," Lila said quietly, stopping her. "Soldiers know. Their bones rarely go home."

Something Aunt Sybb might say, meant to comfort, but Bannan's sister wasn't like Aunt Sybb, not in this, so Jenn waited for the rest.

"You aren't a soldier," Lila said then. "What's happened

here—you need take part in no more of it. Please, Jenn, don't come with us."

Bannan, already mounted, gazed down. "Waste of breath, Dear Heart."

Lila hadn't taken her eyes away. At this moment, she couldn't be sure of their color, Jenn realized, nor was the other woman's face easy to read. "You doubt me," she decided suddenly. "You think I put the two of you in danger."

An eyebrow curved. "Am I wrong?"

Bannan's chuckle had a grim sound. "If we're ever in danger because of Jenn Nalynn," he assured Lila, "so is Channen."

"I wouldn't," Jenn said quickly, not wanting Lila afraid of her.

But Lila's lips formed a silent "Oh," at this, and her eyes held a new and alarming consideration.

Jenn turned and swung herself atop the kruar, determined to avoid whatever that "Oh" might mean. She offered Lila a hand to mount behind her. Accepted the other woman's hold around her waist.

Accepting what had just happened—how Lila could so easily lie to her family, force her brother to do what he hated, a friend kill another, toss a body aside—?

What sort of person could do all that?

A callous person. Unfeeling. Bloodthirsty as a kruar. She mustn't—couldn't—judge, Jenn told herself. All she knew of Lila came from Bannan's stories.

Until tonight.

The kruar sped away. They'd go by rooftop until the next canal. Jenn watched numbly as chimneys and spires flashed by, held on as the great beasts leapt down and down again.

The house toad rode along, seeming to relish the speed.

All at once, despite having no neck worth mentioning, somehow it turned to gaze back at her with one limpid eye.

~Elder sister.~ Filled with foreboding. ~Was the truth-seer's sister wounded?~

Why would it think so? Jenn dared let go of the saddle to feel Lila's hands. Like ice, they were, and trembling.

And it wasn't the rooftop ride.

It was all that a soldier saw and a soldier did and understood, being a soldier, they might do again and see.

It was a mother, desperate for her sons. A sister, leading a brother back into terrible danger. A woman, having left her lover to do the same.

Callous? Say brave and not even then plumb the depths of courage that rode behind her.

Jenn gripped Lila's hands in hers, held tight.

If, for the briefest moment, a head rested on her shoulder?

It'd be their secret.

The dead of night, they called it on patrol, when eyelids grew heavy and bodies ached with the effort to stay upright, let alone alert.

Riding a kruar across a slanted roof—of damp and moss-slimed tile, no less, so even those sure feet slipped, especially when lunging for ill-fated pigeons—was the best remedy Bannan could recall offhand. He refused to give any credit to the "nap" Glammis had imposed.

Though he'd very much like to know what had happened to Jenn, during that time. She'd different clothing and had lost her boots, but the change he sensed was far deeper and profound. He'd have tried his gift, if he wasn't hanging on for dear life. Of all the times for them to be caught up in one of Lila's schemes . . .

Not that there was, in his experience, a good time for that. Unless beer was involved. Jenn had seen for herself. Lila was a force of—imagination failed him. A force, she was. As for her being a truedreamer?

Ancestors Skinned and Gutted. He'd be doing more with his eyes closed, that's what he'd be doing. Or in the dark. Especially that. The dark would be fine.

Recognizing where they were, Bannan bent over the kruar's neck. "We must cross this canal, my friend. Down to the next bridge."

~We need no bridge.~ With some scorn.

Heart's Blood. The truthseer tightened his grip, hoping Jenn and Lila—and the toad—did the same as the body beneath him ran for the roof's edge, pulled in like a spring, then soared—

—over walkways and canal and, yes, several trees, to land like a feather on a roof on the other side.

~Across.~ Pride, that was.

And deserved. After a glance to be sure the second kruar, and riders, had joined them, Bannan gave his mount a firm pat. "Well done!"

A snarl answered, but he was used to that.

The truthseer looked down, then ahead. "The end of this row, if you please."

Hopefully with no more doomed pigeons.

Once on the walkway, shadows shifted and flowed around them, drawn by coils of thickening mist. The night cooled, Bannan told himself, and refused to look deeper in case he was wrong and something was curious. Bad enough small disks of light dotted the darkness of the canal. Turtles—nyim, Jenn called them—watched, no doubt hopeful he could be fooled twice.

The meeting place of the shadow lords might be a grand manor, but it sat amid rows of warehouses sure to be noisy and bustling by day. An odd choice for a group who traded in magic and valued secrecy, unless it wasn't from people they chose to hide.

Disquieting notion, that the Shadow Sect who claimed to serve the turn-born conducted their affairs beyond the edge, where none could reach them.

Not their business. "Do we have a plan?" Bannan asked his sister as he dismounted.

Lila grinned. "Go in; get him." She slipped from the kruar's back, landing lightly.

The truthseer rolled his eyes. "That is not a plan." It was, however, what he'd expected. "See what I had to put up with as a child?" he complained to Jenn as he helped her down.

"If you wish, the little cousin will ask the yling to scout ahead," the miller's daughter proposed calmly.

"What is a—" Lila stopped, eyes almost crossed as she stared at the tiny creature now hovering in front of her nose, light sparkling in his hair and glinting from the tip of the spear.

"Poisoned, that," Bannan said proudly. "Did in my guard."

"Explaining how you managed before I arrived," Lila countered. She stretched out her hand.

With an offended trill, the yling dove back into Bannan's hair.

Jenn took a few steps, then stopped, looking around. Mist wrapped her shoulders and stroked her arms. "How much farther?"

They joined her. "Past the next building, there's a servants' staircase," Lila pointed. "Once at street level, we cross the canal and it's but a few blocks to the river."

"The river." Jenn looked into the distance. "Is it the Mila?"

He understood the longing in her voice. Another name from her map, so close. "No. The Sarra," Bannan informed her. "Here it's split in two, but joins again beyond the city to flow into the Clairr at Essa. That goes south, along the border, to meet the Mila."

She glanced back, her face alight with wonder. "Then to Avyo where all rivers blend with the Kotor and go to the Sweet Sea!"

"I suggest the manor first," Lila commented dryly and Jenn nodded, growing serious again.

He hadn't told his sister about the edge. And wouldn't, Bannan decided, until he knew Lila could remember beyond it.

They took the route Lila'd discovered while following Glammis, to improve their chance of an encounter. When it was time to leave the walkway, the kruar agreed to wait near the canal, there being, apparently, good hunting in the bushes lining the wall above it.

And being still within the edge.

The little cousin, as the only one of them who could understand the yling, came with them, tucked under Jenn's arm. The truthseer, catching Lila giving it another close look, couldn't help himself. "They make eggs. Best you've ever eaten."

The toad, noticed, stretched out a leg, clawed foot flexing.

His sister made a face.

"Would I lie?"

"Whenever you could get away with it, brother mine," she commented, then stopped where a thick growth of vines tumbled to their feet. With one hand, she swept the greenery to the side, revealing a rise of stone stairs, cleaner than most and well lit. "We're here."

With no way to see what—or who—lay at the top. After climbing the first couple of steps, Bannan stopped and turned to Jenn. "A good time for our small friend to take a look."

She nodded and looked down at the toad. "Ask for us, if you would, little cousin."

Patpat.

Though he was familiar with the yling by now, Bannan couldn't be sure if he saw it or a leaf held aloft by a breeze. Save there was no breeze and the leaf kept rising, following the stairs.

To stop, midair, then tumble back and down, now leaf, now yling.

To land in Jenn's hair, not his.

Her dear face flashed disappointment, then acceptance, and he knew what she'd say before the words left her lips. "I—we—can go no further."

Lila gave the stairs a suspicious look, shifting that look to Jenn. "What's wrong?"

"Nothing," Bannan said huskily. The yling chose to show Jenn the edge and, this time, to stay within its magic. He couldn't blame the tiny creature. The truthseer opened his arms and Jenn put down the toad to run into them, holding him as tightly as he held her. "Take care, Dearest Heart," he begged, lips to her ear. "Wait for me at the Keepers' house. We're almost done. Think of that. We'll be home, in Marrowdell, tomorrow."

"I won't leave without you," she replied, her voice no steadier. "I won't!"

It was a promise, and magic, and if he didn't come back—

He would, Bannan vowed, just as firmly. They moved apart, and he couldn't smile. "However far we are apart," he prayed.

"Keep Us Close," Jenn answered.

Words he felt, warm along his neck.

Then she went to the bottom stair, the vines a wall behind her, and stood waiting.

"If you're done, little brother?" Lila inquired with unexpected patience. When he nodded, she turned and began to climb.

"Wait." Bannan had marked the stair the yling refused to pass. "Let me go first."

"Says the man without his sword."

Bish's hung at his hip, but his sister wasn't wrong. The weapon was small and unfamiliar; he'd likely stab himself before an enemy. Not that he hoped to draw the thing. "Wait, Lila."

She shook her head, annoyed, but stopped.

Bannan eased by her and looked back at Jenn. Against the dark green, half in shadow, toad under her arm, her golden hair and the pale skin of her shoulders and face shone in the lamplight—or had their own glow—

She seemed more dream than real.

Heart's Blood. Swallowing, he turned and took not one, but several steps in haste, going past where the yling had been, making sure, before he stopped and turned once more.

Lila frowned up at him. "Before dawn, if you please?"

Not a vine or leaf had moved.

But there was no one else below.

~The edge, elder sister. The edge!~

"Hush," Jenn said soothingly, though her heart—what felt like her heart—fluttered in her chest and her stomach—for surely nothing else could churn like that—tried to climb into her throat.

The edge? She could feel it for herself, this close.

The yling had bounced back, pretending to hit a glass wall. But it wasn't a wall, it was another world, to her untouchable.

Unreal.

Bannan passed into it, looked back. Looked for her. He

couldn't see her, though she lifted a hand and waved, just a
little. Because you did, when someone tried to find you.

You waved.

Lila glanced back. "What's this about?"

Jenn made herself smile. "Saying good-bye."

"Ancestors Limp and Lovelorn. I'll get him back to you."
Shaking her head, Bannan's sister bounded up the stairs,
following her brother.

Through the edge.

In that other, unreachable, world, Lila took Bannan's
arm and pulled him with her the rest of the way. Out of
sight.

Leaving Jenn Nalynn, alone, at the bottom of the stairs.

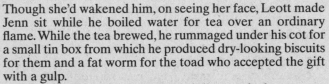

Though she'd wakened him, on seeing her face, Leott made
Jenn sit while he boiled water for tea over an ordinary
flame. While the tea brewed, he rummaged under his cot for
a small tin box from which he produced dry-looking biscuits
for them and a fat worm for the toad who accepted the gift
with a gulp.

After they'd sat and sipped and devoured what were—
somewhat to Jenn's surprise, as she'd planned to eat anything he provided without comment—delicious and
satisfying treats, she told the artisan of the night's events as
frankly as she would Wainn. Leott listened, eyes hooded
with thought, the lion on his shoulders pacing back and
forth, until she reached the staircase that led beyond the
edge.

"They've gone where I cannot," Jenn finished, tired
enough her voice quivered despite her best effort to be stalwart, that being, she'd decided, what she would be until
"they"—being everyone, from Bannan and his sister to
Herer and his clockwork—returned safely.

Though it was impossible not to think about swords and
blood and traps of magic, not to mention outright war.

Laughable now, her dire warning to Bannan of the dangers of Endshere's homely inn, had she been at all inclined
to laugh.

"The shadow lords, is it?" Leott murmured, unsurprised.

"A whisper from any of them's worth all the shouting in either House."

While not saying much for the government of Mellynne, Jenn thought, it did bode well for Emon's mission and Rhoth. "Where they meet—" she began, then hesitated.

"More tea?" As he poured, Leott gave her a keen look. "You understand why the sect meets outside the Shadow District, don't you?"

She'd thought of little else, riding back here. To evade the turn-born seemed the obvious reason, though she couldn't see the point. Mistress Sand and the rest had no interest outside the edge and absolute power within, when they agreed to use it. Whatever the shadow lords might decide in secret would fail if it went against the Keepers' smallest whim. Still, like her and Peggs sneaking to the privy for a conversation their father and aunt couldn't overhear, there was something to be said for privacy.

But privacy wasn't the most important thing about leaving the edge.

"They remember what others forget," she said quietly. "They know that makes them special. Meeting outside lets them prove it."

Leott clapped, startling the now-dozing toad. "It's a test," he agreed. "One all who would rise with the sect must pass."

Jenn stared into her cup. "Has anyone ever—" it wasn't quite cheating "—found a way not to forget?" When he didn't answer, she looked up.

He'd stood and walked away.

"I'm sorry," Jenn said at once. "I didn't mean to—" what might she have done? "—offer offense."

The lion's face looked from his shoulder at her. "You could never offend me, Dear Heart. Your presence is a gift from the Source." But Leott didn't turn around, busy, as Jenn rose to join him, his fingers traveling the worn spines of books.

At her approach, he glanced at her with a reassuring smile. "I don't know how to keep memories the Source wishes lost. However, somewhere in here," he stroked a volume, "are stories of those blessed by the Source to remember."

Like Bannan, receiving the mark from the moth. The sei, Jenn thought suddenly, had that power.

Did she? If she did, she frowned inwardly, how did she use it?

"You worry," he perceived. "Is it of being forgotten by this Lila?"

"I worry about Lila," Jenn corrected, and sighed. "Though she'd not thank me for it. Winter in Marrowdell isn't like here. Our rivers freeze; our roads are choked with snow. She won't see her sons again till spring. Ancestors Witness, it's not right, a family being so divided. If only I could take her with us."

The lion opened its jaws in a silent roar as Leott twisted to face her.

"Not that I can, or would even try," Jenn added, before the toad or kruar could add their own objections. "Bannan and I will leave tomorrow—" Ancestors Witness, it must be nigh dawn. "—today, I mean. Lila will know he's with them."

The lion hadn't relaxed. "Remember, Dear Heart. You and Bannan must be seen to leave as you came, both of you, and no one else. The sect will be watching."

Good, she thought. Let them prove to themselves Bannan Larmensu was a Keeper. Let them continue to believe only a Keeper could pass between worlds.

Both worlds would be safer for it.

So when at last Jenn Nalynn returned to the house the Shadow Sect had prepared for their magical visitors, the kruar again seeking their rooftops, she smiled at Appin as though he were an ally and friend, and thanked him for the bed.

Not that she'd sleep, until Bannan was safe and back with her.

Moonlight gilded the cobblestones, stars twinkled above, and Jenn had vanished from his sight as if erased from the world. Sick inside, Bannan stumbled more than ran behind Lila along now-deserted roadways until they reached the alley that was her goal.

Once within that cover, she stopped and he did and

where was his courage, that he couldn't ask what she remembered—

Lila punched him in the shoulder. "Smarten up, little brother. You look like your Jenn's died instead of taking our very good advice."

He hugged her then, he couldn't help it, and laughed like a fool. Though startled, Lila patted him on the back instead of objecting.

"I should have known. I should have," he gasped when she'd had enough and, not gently, shoved him away.

"Yes, to whatever and all of it," his sister agreed absently, looking down the alley. It was more a small road, wide enough for a cart, and doors broke the walls on either side. "Come."

They surprised a cat as Lila led the way to a small wooden door within a pair of larger ones meant to receive goods; proof the manor had been a warehouse once, like the other buildings along the greater canals.

Implying there hadn't always been a need for the shadow lords to meet here. Or shadow lords at all. Marrowdell's crags bore the scars of the last time the edge had been disturbed and worlds convulsed.

At that moment, what had happened elsewhere along the edge? Bannan wondered suddenly. Here, the other world met this one above the ground, not within it. Had the sky torn open?

"Ancestors Witness, you'd think they could afford better locks," Lila murmured, having made short work of the one on the door. "This leads into the servants' corridors," she reminded him. "We'll start looking for Glammis where he took you—"

"Heart's Blood!" Bannan said abruptly. "The barge!"

She swore in understanding. Abandoning the door, they ran to the iron gate at the alley's end, scrambling up and over.

The Straight loomed before them, stroked by moonlight. Barges lined the bank on which they stood, tarped and quiet, waiting for dawn. Barges as far as his eyes could see, tied by the embargo with Rhoth.

Except for a new gap, where the barge of Glammis Lurgan had moored.

"We're too late. He's gone."

Lila went to the edge. "And not planning to come back, by what he's left behind."

Bannan joined her, looking into the water. Bodies bumped restlessly against the stone, tangled in lines. "It's my fault," he said grimly. "I had us follow the moths."

"There are always consequences, little brother." Lila looked up at the building behind them. Light outlined closed curtains and slipped by shutters; windows on the lowest level were bricked closed. "If your Jenn hadn't summoned us, Emon wouldn't be in there," a tip of her head "hauling Ordo's arse from the fire. Nor," grimly, "would you have exposed Bish in time."

All well and good, but of one thing he was certain. "Glammis must be dealt with, Lila. He's a threat to Werfol—"

"No."

If Glammis had heard that denial, he'd not sleep again, nor believe there was any place in all of Rhoth where he could hide.

"Now," Lila said in a completely different tone, "what say we find a decent vantage point and wait for my dear husband?" She pointed to where a pair of crows paced the wide sill of the rightmost window, heads bobbing with each step.

Bannan raised a brow. "And how do you propose we get up there?"

Lila merely smiled.

A short while later, the truthseer rested his chin in his hands, arms supported by his elbows. "I was afraid you'd go for the roof," he admitted.

His sister grunted something uncomplimentary. They lay on their stomachs, stretched out on a pile of crates, those crates beneath a canvas Lila had considerately untied rather than slit before squirming into place. The manor was in view; they weren't.

More importantly, they were steps from both the side alley and the building front, the only way, Lila had assured him, Emon and his companions would exit.

An excellent vantage point and a fortunately uncomfortable one, given neither of them had slept.

Not that Lila would. "Back in the alley," she whispered

without preamble. "That nonsense. What should you have known?"

Bannan told her of those who remembered, and those who forgot.

"Interesting," was all she said at first.

Which it was, he gave her that.

Then, "So that's why they meet here."

He blinked. "Pardon?"

Lila nudged him with her shoulder. "Really, little brother. Isn't it obvious? If so few can remember this magic beyond the edge, the lords of the Shadow Sect have to be among them. If I were one of them, I'd take full advantage and—" slower, as if thinking aloud, "—I'd not take seriously anyone who can't prove they remember too."

"Emon."

He felt her shrug. "If he senses they've secret knowledge, my so-clever husband will be the last to reveal his own ignorance. Besides," comfortably, "he's been here before and come back full of tales for the boys. I'd not bet against him."

"I never would," Bannan said fervently.

She chuckled. "At last, wisdom. Now, little brother. To keep us from nodding while Emon does his part in things, tell me of Werfol and Semyn—as well as what you didn't put in your letters about Jenn Nalynn. How you came here from Marrowdell is also of great interest to me. And—" another low laugh, Lila being well-pleased after all, which eased Bannan's worries immeasurably, "—more concerning toads."

So he did.

"M'lord couldn't have done better," Dutton said quietly.

Herer nodded, his eyes bright. "He was brilliant. Timed each revelation to counter the next naysayer, not that any denied what you'd brought us, Bannan."

"When those shadow lords laid eyes on the tokens, it went so quiet we could hear one of m'lord's birds outside the window. Forbidden magic, that's what they called it. Foul."

And the man who'd been willing to use them had escaped—news no one had been pleased to hear.

Emon Westietas didn't have the look of a man freshly triumphant. He'd left his companions with Bannan to go to his wife, dropping his head to her shoulder.

"M'lord's exhausted," Herer explained in a low voice, his eyes on Emon.

Dutton looked to disagree, then rubbed a hand over his face. "He's not alone." After battle, came its cost. Bannan knew it. They all did.

The three had come out of the manor through the main door, unescorted, just as dawn drew its fiery promise along the horizon. The crows had swooped down to circle Emon, then flown to where Lila and Bannan waited; a sign they could trust, Lila said, climbing from their hiding place at once.

By mutual consent they'd moved down the bank until out of sight of the manor. Racks of barrels waiting to be shipped made a convenient shelter. More racks than should be. The barges swaying with the river's current were loaded and ready. They'd been that way for weeks now.

Bannan leaned against a barrel, eyeing Emon's companions. Did they remember? Should he even try to ask?

Before he could, Herer chose his own barrel, made himself comfortable, then said with a casual air, "Ancestors Witness. Seems a rare number of moths, hereabouts."

Dutton, pretending great interest in a loose button, shot a keen glance at the truthseer.

Why—they were testing him?! Bannan grinned. "It's the lady who sends them I love best."

The two men chuckled. "Good to know," Dutton said, then grew serious, nodding toward Emon and Lila. "Our lord baron brought seven of us on his last visit to this city of magic. Only we three—" a pained pause, then he went on determinedly. "—That's why m'lord chose us for this mission."

"We hope," Herer added, "to speak as freely before our lady baroness."

Not a question, but Bannan was glad to answer. "Lila remembers."

Their faces lightened at this.

Lila and Emon joined them, the baron waving to dissuade the crow intent on landing on his head. "My friends. Brother," this to Bannan, with warmth. "We've done what we came to do, thanks to you. Hearts of my Ancestors, I am truly Beholden for such—"

"Idiocy," Lila interrupted pleasantly. "Or should I use a stronger term, Dearest Heart? How does madness suit?"

Emon shook his head. "My lady wife worries how my failure will be received at court." One crow landed on his shoulder. The other chose to perch atop a barrel, bending its head to caw in disapproval.

"'Failure,' m'lord?" Dutton broached, after a quick look to Herer. "But we thought—"

"Oh, Mellynne will vote to restore normal relations with Rhoth. Given the public will, I expect a courier, perhaps a noble delegation, underway as early as this afternoon. Matters needed but gentle encouragement in that direction. No one is as relieved as I."

"After your 'failure,'" Bannan observed grimly.

"Exactly. I did nothing that was expected of me." A peaceful smile.

Lila began to pace, outrage in every step. "You'll lie to the prince. You'll expect us to do the same. And when he publicly accuses you of being a fool and coward? When he tosses you from court?"

Still the smile. "I'll miss a session at most. I've friends in the House and Commons, dear wife. Ordo's one voice—granted the loudest—but just one. He'll call me back to my seat, pleased no doubt to mention at every opportunity how miserable an envoy I was and how he alone kept the peace."

She walked up to him, eyes green with fury. "You saved it!" The crow soared up and away in a flurry of wingbeats.

"Lila. The Shadow Sect cannot be exposed as having dealt with Rhothans. Nor would any Naalish thank me for showing them the rot in one of their noble houses." Emon cupped her face in his hands. "To sink in the estimation of a fool is no lasting loss to me or Vorkoun. This was the price set by the shadow lords, Dearest Heart, for their cooperation. I gladly pay it."

"I don't like this," she said so softly Bannan barely heard.

Emon's smile grew tender. "I never thought you would." He kissed her soundly.

"—then we're off to Avyo," she stated when they stepped apart, her cheeks decidedly pink.

"As quickly and quietly as possible," the baron agreed. "We've arrangements in place. Herer?"

"About that, m'lord." Herer pulled out a leather-wrapped document. "Bish vouched for the boat and crew."

"I'd prefer," Emon said dryly, "to survive my skulking home, tail between my legs."

With a nod, the other man removed the document, tearing it once, then again.

" 'Skulking,' husband-mine?"

"The best way across the border—given none of us entered Channen legally," the baron pointed out.

"There is that."

"I've a smuggler who owes me a favor," Bannan said ruefully, "but he's in Avyo—wait." Ancestors Dear and Departed. He'd carried the brooch through everything. Could it be? "I may have a way." He caught Lila's eye. "I've the name of someone who worked the river barges, years ago. Who might be willing to help." If they could find him. A dead woman's lover, who'd—how long ago?—taken a barge to Avyo. That was likely half the adult population of Channen. Left, right. Either way were barges. Dozens. Hundreds, more likely. Moths. He could use moths, right now.

"Who?" Lila pressed.

"Baldrinn. Baldrinn Duart. We've mutual friends." He gave a helpless shrug. "But I've no idea where he is."

Emon's eyes widened, then he broke out in the most wonderful laugh. When he was done, he wiped his eyes. "Ancestors Rare and Remarkable, brother of my wife. Are you sure? Baldrinn the Bargemaster?"

"You know him?"

Dutton and Herer had cheered as well. "We know of him," the latter said with a relieved grin. "And well know where to find him."

Emon nodded. "I should have thought of Baldrinn myself—"

"Bish spoke against him, m'lord. Said he was feeble-minded."

"A recommendation if ever I heard one," Lila snapped.

Bannan looked from one to the other. "You know him?" he repeated, feeling left behind.

"Your pardon," Emon said. "Baldrinn's famous—or

infamous, depending who you ask." He chuckled. "Despite his years, he remains a force in Channen. The man's written daily—or more—to the prince about the embargo. A correspondence neither flattering nor pleasant, believe me. He's sent, among other things, a package of spoiled meat from a shipment held at the border. And demanded, loudly, nothing less than an envoy from Avyo come straighten out the mess."

Dutton's eyes gleamed. "Such a man would be glad to hear things are about to move again on his river."

"News we can't give," Herer protested.

"No matter." Bannan took out the brooch, handing it to Emon. "When you meet Baldrinn, return this before asking for passage."

The baron examined it, then glanced at Lila. "It's an endearment."

"Yes." The truthseer found himself smiling. "Tell Baldrinn Frann wore it with love until she joined her Blessed Ancestors." His smile widened. "And Lorra sends her regards."

That those formidable ladies of commerce would help the baron and baroness of Vorkoun, who'd ended the choke on trade caused by the very prince who'd exiled them?

Something to savor, Bannan decided, for a very long time.

He wished he'd dared tell Lorra Treff.

She'd neither meant nor wanted to fall asleep, but Jenn startled awake to find her bed covered in sunshine.

And Bannan Larmensu snoring, very quietly, beside her.

Though it was day and, as Aunt Sybb was fond of saying, sunlight was for working by, lamplight for finishing, and candlelight a poor substitute for either, Jenn Nalynn rearranged the covers over them both.

Then curled herself around the man she loved and went back to sleep.

"I believe you've killed him this time," the dragon observed calmly.

Scourge bent his great head to the boy's chest, nostrils flared, lips working. "He's not dead."

They spoke in breezes to include the boys. Perhaps a mistake, Wisp decided, as Semyn came running through the snow. "'Dead!?' Weed!!"

"Not dead!" the old kruar reiterated somewhat nervously, backing away.

Not fast enough, so the boy simply dove beneath his belly to reach the too-still form in the snow.

"Weed! Werfol!" After a look into his brother's face, Semyn pulled him up and over a knee, then began striking him between the shoulders.

~Shouldn't we stop him, elder brother?~ The agitated house toad, watching from the porch, actually hopped into the snow.

"Wh—?" The word garbled in a wheezing cough.

Semyn grabbed Werfol's shoulders, sitting him up. "One breath at a time, Weed. It's just like when I fell from the tree. You've the air knocked out of you, that's all. By a bloody idiot!" With a glare at the kruar. "How many times must we tell you? He's too small!"

"Am—am NOT!" Werfol struggled to stand, accepting his brother's help only after it became clear he remained wobbly. "With Uncle Bannan gone, Scourge is mine and I'm to ride him."

Semyn glared a second time at the kruar, who was doing his utmost to appear blameless. The result was more like Wainn's Old Pony, a conniving creature at the best of times, the dragon thought with amusement, not that the boy was fooled. "Weed can't get up on you without help," the baron's heir stated, making his case. "That makes this your fault. Again. This has to stop!"

"He's MINE!" Werfol punched his brother.

Semyn pushed him back into the snow. "Listen to your elders!"

Werfol launched himself at Semyn's knees and they both went down, fists flying.

"What's all this?" roared Tir, coming out of the house.

Spoiling everyone's fun, in the opinion of a dragon.

Scourge, the old coward, twitched his tail and bolted from the farmyard. He left not a dimple in the snow.

But two red-faced, angry warriors.

Who, after Tir did nothing but look down at them for a long moment, became two shivering, pale, and ever-so-contrite little boys. A trick worth learning, Wisp thought with envy, the disciplining of the truthseer's nephews having become something of a sore point.

Tir shook his head. "Dragon, you were to stop this."

He'd have pretended not to hear—or even be in the vicinity—but the truthseer looked right at him, lower lip trembling. "Wisp, it wasn't your fault."

So of course it was. "Scourge cannot resist the boy," the dragon began.

"Oh, and you're better at it?" Tir scowled where he thought the dragon to be, then turned back to the boys. "In the house. The pair of you," he ordered gruffly.

Inside was warmer. With biscuits, Tir being the better cook. But when Wisp tried to slip through the door behind them, the man stepped in his way, then closed it, leaving them outside.

Where it was colder. Wisp wrapped himself in light, Tir being annoyed by invisibility.

"There you are," the man said unnecessarily, then spat to one side. He lowered his voice conspiratorially. "Any sign of them yet?"

Efflet and ylings having taken up posts at each crossing, with the little cousins eager for their reports, the dragon would know before anyone. "No."

"I thought they'd be home by now."

He wanted reassurance. Wisp had none to offer. "They went swiftly through the Verge. They must still be in Channen, delayed by your kind, not mine."

Tir seemed pleased by the answer. "Sir's no fool," he declared. "Between him and the baroness, I can't see any Naalish stopping them."

If that were true, thought the dragon, would Bannan and Jenn not already be home?

Perhaps it was time he crossed. Looked for himself.

Tir opened the door. "C'mon, dragon. There's biscuits."

He would cross tomorrow, Wisp decided comfortably. And—

"Tir! Wisp!"

Man and dragon rushed inside, the dragon veering up and sideways to avoid a crash in the doorway sure to end his chance at more biscuits. Together, they entered the house.

Semyn knelt beside his brother, crumpled amid a pile of jackets and boots. "He just fell," the boy said tearfully. "I didn't push him, Tir. He just fell."

"Don't move him," Tir cautioned the dragon. "I'll have a look. Semyn, go stand by the fire."

The boy took two steps away before he stopped and turned, arms wrapped around his middle. Tir took a look at his face, then nodded. Wisp flew to a rafter where he could watch without being in the way.

The house toad eased closer. ~Is this a new game, elder brother?~ An understandable confusion, the little cousin having witnessed innumerable tumbles, fights, and—yes— games in which the winner was the one who remained motionless the longest while the other made faces.

This was no game. The dragon lowered his head. Werfol's face was sickly pale and covered in sweat. Beneath blue-tinged eyelids, his eyes were in constant motion. ~Something's wrong, little cousin.~ But what?

"He fell from Scourge. More than once. The last time knocked his breath out, but he was fine after," Semyn said all at once, his voice cracking with worry. "Why isn't he fine?"

"Give'm time," Tir said gently. Finished his examination, he gathered the child in his arms. "Your uncle's bed." That was a mattress in a corner of the room and Semyn ran to pull down the covers. After putting Werfol in bed with great care, Tir looked up. "Dragon. Bring the healer."

~

*A snip of thread, touched by skin and warmth . . . a drop of*
*sleep, under the tongue . . .*
*And the dream unfolds . . .*

Falling . . .
Falling . . .
No. A road, blinding white, stretching to a point of
darkness.
Darkness widens. Opens. It's a mouth!
FALLING FALLING FALLING
*The dream shatters . . .*

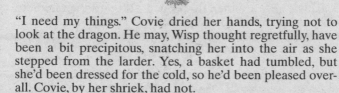

"I need my things." Covie dried her hands, trying not to
look at the dragon. He may, Wisp thought regretfully, have
been a bit precipitous, snatching her into the air as she
stepped from the larder. Yes, a basket had tumbled, but
she'd been dressed for the cold, so he'd been pleased over-
all. Covie, by her shriek, had not.

"Tell the dragon what to fetch," Tir said, by his tone
more concerned with speed than manners.

Wisp sent a polite little breeze. "A list would do."

"Ancestors—" She closed her mouth, nodding. "First, I'll
take a look. Poor lad."

Semyn looked up. "He's dreaming. He can't stop."

The healer frowned, then bent over Werfol. She ran a
fingertip between his brows, to the tip of his nose.

Then lifted her hand in haste, as though she'd touched
flame. "This is no natural sleep. You say he'd had a few falls
into the snow. Did he strike his head on anything harder?"

"Not that I saw, mistress," Semyn said very quietly.

"Nor I," volunteered Wisp.

Her eyebrows rose. "Thank you."

~He did not, elder brother!~ as if they'd asked the toad.
Being a sincere creature, the little cousin clarified, ~That I
witnessed.~

Tir hadn't taken his eyes from Werfol's face. "He'd another of his tempers."

Covie frowned. "What do you mean?"

Semyn looked miserable. "I made Weed mad. We were
fighting."

"Being angry doesn't cause—" the healer gestured at
Werfol, seeming lost for words.

"Begging your pardon, healer, but it might. I've seen the

like, once." Tir shook his head. "Sir—Bannan lost his temper. Ancestors Witness, he'd every right and reason—I'll say no more—but what happened next was worse. His gift, you see. He lost control. Couldn't see what was in front of him— or saw too much that wasn't." His voice turned grim. "Tied him to his bed, we did, and had to stuff a cloth in his mouth or our camp would have been found for sure. To this day, I don't know how he survived it."

"Weed?" Tears flowed over Semyn's cheeks.

Covie gave another, slower nod. "If that's the case here, we need Bannan. How long until he's home?"

"Dragon?"

But the air was empty.

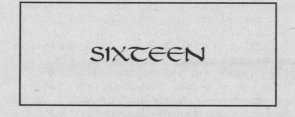

# SIXTEEN

*J*ENN STRETCHED LUXURIOUSLY, scented bubbles sliding over her skin, and still couldn't touch the far side of the bath. Her toes did find Bannan.

"Careful there!" He sank under the water, then appeared laughing beside her, covered in bubbles.

"Hold still." Jenn skimmed the offending bubbles from his broad shoulders and strong arms, then worked her way—oh, quite methodically, this being an important task—over his chest and down the line of wiry curls. With an incoherent moan, Bannan pressed his whole length against her and, not for the first time, they lost themselves in the delirious possibilities warm wet skin afforded lovers.

Really, Jenn thought a while later, she could stay in this tub the rest of her life. Especially as she was now, half-afloat with her back along Bannan's chest, his arms and legs entwined with hers.

He nibbled her ear, then her neck, and she might have mentioned they'd both eaten their fill from the refreshments provided, except she'd no wish for him to—

A crow flew in the arched window, to the wrath of the house toad. ~ELDER SISTER!~

"It's all right. A messenger," Jenn told the creature as Bannan pulled himself from the tub and padded over to the bench where the crow now perched. She floated where she was, enjoying the slip of bubbles down the pleasing landscape of his back.

Bannan bowed to the crow. "Scatterwit. What news?"

A messenger in truth. How could it talk? If so, could she understand it?

Curious, Jenn half-swam to the edge closest to them. The crow twitched, regarding her with a bright black eye. Judging her harmless, it turned back to the truthseer.

Balanced on one foot, it raised the other, unrolling four scaled toes, each ending in a sharp black claw. Three faced forward, one—the longest—behind. Toes that began to make small deliberate movements.

Signs! Making no sense to her, but there was meaning, she could tell. "What a clever bird," Jenn praised, delighted. The crow bobbed its head, uttering a series of low throaty clucks. Smug, that was.

Bannan nodded, not looking away. When Scatterwit stopped, standing again on both feet, he signed something back to it. The bird watched intently.

The truthseer finished, pressing his hands flat over his heart. After a shake to settle its feathers, Scatterwit flew back out the window.

With a reply to the message it had delivered.

It was all quite amazing and Jenn resolved, then and there, to learn some of these signs for herself. With two boys and Tir now living with Bannan, and herself with the Emms, she'd been resigned to any private conversations being outside. With this? She could imagine several charming possibilities.

First, though, they had the bath.

"Lila's on her way." Bannan wrapped himself in a towel before turning to face her.

Ending any thoughts of lingering in bubbles. "What's wrong?" Jenn asked worriedly as she climbed out. For he thought something must be, she could see it in his eyes.

"Scatterwit's message said only to meet Lila at the

canal." He came close, wrapping her in one of the sheet-sized towels, then in his arms. "How long do I have?"

Before they were to cross, he meant. "The best part of an hour," Jenn said. She might not own a clockwork, but she needed nothing to remind her of the approaching turn. It sang in her blood—or what was inside her—a song that today was stronger and more beautiful than ever.

Because they were going home.

She watched him dress in haste, choosing the clothes the yling had mended and Appin cleaned. They'd both new boots and cloaks like the sect member's, for they'd be moving in daylight. Bannan had filled his pack from the generous platters of food and drink, while Jenn had a new sack full to bursting.

Having dried herself, she reached for her clothing.

"Please wait for me here, Dearest Heart," Bannan said quickly. "Unless I misread, Lila's asked to meet me alone. Probably," he made a face, "for a lecture."

Jenn sat, clothes in her lap, so he knew she'd wait, and searched his face. "That's not what you believe," she concluded.

A face set to mild exasperation, perhaps to hide concern. "There's no guessing, with Lila." He tied back his hair. "Maybe she wants to send something for her sons."

Jenn nodded. "Anything," she urged. "We can carry it."

Warmth in those apple butter eyes. "I'll tell her you said so."

"And that when she comes for them, in spring," Jenn went on impulsively, "we'll have a Beholding to thank the Ancestors your family is back together."

More than warmth. As if uncertain of his voice, Bannan sketched a quick but dashing bow before striding from the room.

The turn was coming. Jenn dressed slowly and with care. She hadn't bothered to warn him not to be late, for what did it matter? This turn or the next. She wouldn't leave without him.

How could she?

Pat. Pat.

The yling having announced his intention to come along, Bannan took care donning the cloak and hood. He covered his head, grateful for the disguise. Being dressed once more as Rhothan felt a step closer to home. He wasn't there yet.

The wide cobbled street was busier than he remembered, or the alarm racing along his nerves since the crow's arrival made the bustle of strangers and wagons and other vehicles somehow ominous. Act as if it were all familiar, he reminded himself, and walked the pace of a man on business but in no hurry for it, managing not to flinch when a crack like pistol shot marked the end of an axle and the beginning of a traffic knot.

Once through the gate and sheltered within the walled landing, Bannan abandoned his pose, going down the steps as quickly as the slick of leaves and mud allowed. At the bottom, he eased around the column that hid the opening of the stair from the walkway beyond.

And there was Lila, standing by one of the other columns. Scatterwit perched atop it, quiet as Bannan approached but ever-so-curious. The crows could initiate a report, as well as carry a message, and no one read their clawed toes better than Emon, who'd taught his birds to so speak.

Unlike the crow, his sister appeared a statue till he was near enough to see her tremble. He closed the space between them in a rush, put his hands on her shoulders. "What's happened?"

Lila looked at him with such horror his breath caught in his throat. "Werfol. He's trapped in a dream. A nightmare!"

How she knew was plain; safe with Emon, Lila'd taken the chance to truedream. What she believed? "In Marrowdell—" Bannan stopped himself. Jenn had told him she'd wished both boys freedom from the valley's dreams. Then what Lila believed sank home. "You think his gift's out of control."

"I know it," low and hoarse.

Ancestors Torn and Terrified. The truth. It pulled free his own dreadful memories: of being unable to stop seeing beyond the now and the real. The faces of friends rotting to bone. Trees around him burning or falling to axes or turning to tall dead stumps filled with carrion birds and decay. The sky's ending . . . "Heart's Blood."

Lila seized his forearms. "Weed's a child. How can he understand what's happening? How can he free himself?" She shook him. "Brother, I must get to him and quickly. Take me with you!"

"Dear Heart." He stiffened in protest. "You can't cross with us."

"The beasts like Scourge, then. Give me one of them!"

"A kruar can't bring you with it. Only Jenn—"

"Then take me to her!"

"Even if she would, Lila, trust me, you can't." Bannan stared into his sister's desperate eyes, his heart hammering. "You 'dreamed the madness. You've seen it. That's the Verge and you wouldn't survive it."

She shook her head impatiently, as if he hadn't heard, her hair flying. "Blindfold me. Lead me through. Bannan. Carry me unconscious. I've my draught. But you must take me with you. I beg—" And her voice failed, as Lila's voice never did, and her face was full of fear, as Lila's never was.

And he knew, no matter what he said, this she would do.

"Come with me."

There had to be a way, Bannan thought furiously as he led his sister up the stairs. Appin had granted them the privacy he and Jenn had requested, and would meet them at the turn. Being witnessed was vital, Jenn had explained. Two Keepers having come?

Two must go.

Mounted, in his cloak, Lila had the height to pass for him. He could make it back to Marrowdell on his own.

By spring. With no way to know if Lila had survived the Verge or not. To know if Werfol—Bannan refused to think it.

And he'd thought waiting for news of Channen would be difficult.

They reached the landing. At the gate, Bannan warned, "Not far, but it's public."

A nod. His sister had kept her Naalish clothing and, likely Emon's doing, no longer wore her sword in plain sight but a full pack hung from a broad strap over one shoulder and hip. Ready for travel, that said. Fair enough. Doubtless word had spread that Channen's barges were leaving their moorings, perhaps why the streets were busier.

His skin crawled during the walk to the door, but he strode with confidence. If any observers from the Shadow Sect watched, let them think him one of theirs, escorting a last minute delivery.

Inside. Lila took in the empty room, with its polished floor and ornate lamps, with a sweeping glance, a brow rising in question at the three closed doors along the far wall.

Bannan pulled off his hood. "Let me talk to Jenn."

"I won't be denied."

A battle line, that, drawn as much by the set of the jaw as the tone.

"Nor will you be a fool," he said with matching strength. "You're no good to Werfol dead." Bannan circled his fingers over his heart. "Hearts of our Ancestors, I swear to you we'll find a way. But you have to trust us. For once, Lila, listen to me."

Her eyes searched his. Unexpectedly, the corner of her mouth twitched. "Listen to my little brother? I suppose the time had to come."

He didn't smile, couldn't. Not even when the leftmost door opened and Jenn Nalynn stepped out to join them, toad under one arm.

Seeing her face, hers turned sober. Quickly, she closed the door behind her, motioning to the half door of the kruar. "Appin's back," she explained as they went through and she closed that. "He came to tell me one of their lords waits to watch our crossing. Why are you here?" to Lila. Curt, that demand, and uneasy.

"She's—" started Bannan.

"To save my son," Lila answered.

Jenn put down the toad, it being easier to do than meet the other woman's eyes. "Werfol," she guessed as she straightened.

"He's lost in a dream. A nightmare." The effort to keep

those words calm and steady showed in Lila's face. "Unless I go to him, he'll stay trapped there. He'll die. I must go. Take me with you." The last spoken with all of a mother's terrible need. "Bannan's told me. Only you can do it."

~Elder sister, is this wise?~

In no way. Jenn didn't dare look at Bannan. "I will not," she said, knowing he'd see the truth of it.

Lila's face hardened. "I accept the risk—"

"Because you don't know what it is," Jenn replied, relieved to see a flicker of doubt. "Can't Bannan help Werfol?"

"Our gifts aren't the same. I can see what my son dreams. I can share that dream, once we touch, and show him how to free himself. I can save him, Jenn! You must help me."

Tears burned, spilled cold over her cheeks, as Jenn fought to say what she must. "If you entered the Verge, you would share madness and death with your son."

Lila might have been stone. "Without me, that will be his fate."

For the first time, Jenn wavered. Bannan had endured. Might his sister, despite her different gift?

The toad waited. The kruar had arrived, ready to leave this world and be themselves again.

Be themselves. "How long does he have?" Jenn asked abruptly. "Werfol."

Lila frowned. "He suffers now."

"He's a healthy lad," Bannan declared, stepping forward. "And brave. Covie will care for him." He stood near his sister, their faces like reflections. "Lila, he's yours. You know him best. How much time do we have?"

"If Werfol stays in the dream," she said after a dreadful moment, "the damage will be to his mind first. I can't— Heart's Blood." A quick breath. "A couple of days, if the Ancestors care at all. After that—" Lila pressed a fist to her mouth.

Bannan put a protective arm around his sister. "Why?" he asked Jenn angrily, as if she'd been needlessly cruel.

Instead of answering, Jenn turned to the kruar. They lifted their heads, snorting with suspicion as she walked up to them, for that was their nature. But they didn't back away.

Being brave. That too.

She let herself be glass and tears and light, light that caught in their wild, red-rimmed eyes.

And asked a question.

Two cloaked figures led their horses under the arch of a bridge to where the canal widened into a small lake. Disks of dark silver lay beneath the surface, like platters or wide steps, and the day's last light gilded the mist above but didn't break it. Beside the lake stood not one but three observers, in cloaks of the same shape and style. No others were allowed here. No others would dare.

The turn was coming.

The figures mounted, sending their horses down a step into what seemed water but stirred with movement and glinted silver and wasn't, quite. Boots were raised as the horses waded, belly-deep, then lowered as first one, then the second climbed on what lay below. Steps then.

Built by rain.

Those watching knew more was imminent, for it rained every sunset, as if the dimming of light woke the clouds. Those swimming knew as well, growing ever more hungry.

Once in place, the horses stood with unhorse-like patience, their riders silent and hooded.

As if holding a breath.

Then the rain came, and the light changed, and all became a swirl of color and possibility. Those who watched saw the horses leap upward, to disappear within the clouds.

And were content.

The turn came, and Jenn Nalynn stepped from stone to what wasn't.

~Myturn.~Don'tpush~Higher~MORE~Holdon~-Holdfast!~

Nyim scampered and clawed on top of each other, their true color revealed by the light of the Verge. Patterns and whorls. Bright flashes by eyes more red than yellow. Beautiful, in their way.

If prone to bite. She stepped with care, but quickly.

~Higher~MORE~HIGHER~ Now she could stand, for the mass of them rose beneath her as more and more shoved their way into the pile. Hundreds, perhaps thousands. Ignoring the rain in their determination.

High enough. She'd have thanked the small creatures, but she found herself inside a drop and quite unable to speak.

For it was time. The turn came. With a thought, with a wish, Jenn Nalynn crossed into the Verge.

Warm and bright and mad with color and she . . .

Blinked.

The toad squirmed from her pack. ~Where are we, elder sister?~

"I've no idea," she admitted.

. . . staring out over purple-kissed hills that rolled themselves into the sky and curled back down like sleeping dragons.

No idea at all.

The turn came.

And kruar landed, soft as feathers, on the cloud-wreathed rooftop above the small lake. Pigeons scattered.

No outcry from below. Heart's Blood. They'd done it.

"What of Jenn?" Bannan demanded.

His kruar bent her neck to regard him. The breeze in his ear was reassuringly confident. "The turn-born crossed into the Verge."

"They can talk!?" Lila asked, her eyes wide. Then mouthed, "Scourge?"

He nodded, pleased the beast included his sister, less pleased by what lay ahead. "You must stay near me," he cautioned the kruar yet again. Heart's Blood. "Beyond the edge, you won't be able to speak. You won't remember who you are. I will remember for you."

"Truthseer." Acknowledgment.

Lila's threw up his head. "Soon, we will have names to remember!" A different breeze, hot and eager.

"Names!" from his.

Ancestors Witness, they were like recruits before their first battle.

"Bannan," his sister cautioned, hearing that as well.

These were kruar and fire was in their blood, he reminded himself. Jenn had challenged them, had shown them a path to glory.

Had crossed alone into the Verge, to give Werfol this chance.

Bannan leaned forward. Seeing him, Lila did the same. "To Marrowdell!" he cried, uncaring who heard, and dug in his heels.

For the turn-born had asked the kruar one question.

Can you outrun death?

Time they proved it.

Where were they?

Goodness, this was a pickle. Jenn decided to sit and think a moment. It didn't help matters that she felt more than a little light-headed.

And alone, she sighed. Though she had her guardian, and the yling, presently in her hair. Much as she prized both, it wasn't at all the same as having Bannan with her.

Which she didn't and wouldn't. There was, as Aunt Sybb would surely say, nothing to be gained by sighing about what wasn't right with the world. She'd usually add that extra chores were the best cure, having an infallible list of those at the ready.

"We've a chore of our own," Jenn told the toad. "Finding the way home." She might have guessed a crossing contained in a drop might be blown or move or simply not be where it should; another question for Mistress Sand.

Still, she'd expected—for no good reason, it seemed now—to simply "know" the way, much like a spring duck.

She got to her feet. Feet covered by new boots. Boots she couldn't wait to show Peggs, bringing on an entire wave of longing. "Yes, home it is." But which way?

She looked down at the toad. "Which way looks best to you, little cousin?"

It shrank into a distressed and pale ball, eyes bulging.

Oh. "Sorry. Well . . ." Jenn popped a finger in her mouth, then held it out to detect any breezes.

None.

About to decide based on where she could see the most blue, it seeming a trustworthy color, she felt a patpatpat. "What is it? Do you know?"

Out flew the yling, to hover before her eyes and his six hands waved with distinct urgency. Alas, no two in the same direction.

"What's it saying?" she asked the toad, disappointed.

~To run, elder sister!~

The bloody beasts. You could love them, Bannan decided in a rare moment of clarity, but it'd be the same fondness you felt for the lightning that struck your enemy's camp and missed yours. There but for chance was my death.

These kruar must have ambled through the Verge. Scourge at his wickedest, heart-stopping best must have trotted, likely bored.

This?

They'd leapt through Channen on rooftops. Leapt across the Straight, bouncing from barge to barge too quickly for any to do more than glance up and wonder.

Beyond the city, once their hooves touched soil, it was as if the kruar moved the world.

Forget passing other riders on a road. He'd glimpse flashes of light and guess those to be towns and villages, lamps lit against the dark.

Dark mattered nothing to the kruar. That he'd already known.

Did their riders? Ancestors Witness, if the saddle hadn't held him tight, he'd have been left, on his rump, in Channen. The grip of his hands, his arms' strength had failed long since. He'd tried to gain his mount's attention, worried for Lila, afraid, frankly, for himself. As easily talk to the wind.

Manic, this race, and magic. That too.

For Werfol, he told himself, and buried his face against a hot neck.

~

*A drop of blood, bitten from a cheek . . . a chewed sleeve,*
*threads once touched by other skin and warm . . .*
*And the dream unfolds . . .*
What is this?
Soft, white. A blanket?
For it covers. Soothes.
Chills.
SMOTHERS!
CAN'T GET OUT! CAN'T GET OUT! CAN'T—
*The dream splinters . . .*

Running in the Verge was a peculiar thing. Jenn had picked up the toad and, to be sure, the yling did fly ahead, hands beckoning, so she ran as quickly as she could in its wake.

But sometimes she ran up and sometimes sideways and several times, most disconcertingly, she was upside down. It helped profoundly, she discovered, to focus on the yling.

Flying being a more straightforward business.

She didn't run out of breath, which was a comfort. Though troubling, if she thought about it, so she did her best not, other than to remember to breathe.

That being important, since she took Mistress Sand's warnings about the risky nature of flesh seriously indeed, and ran as turn-born.

While thinking, always, of what else she was and intended to be.

After a while, which might have been an afternoon or hour, Jenn began to think about something else. "Little cousin, why are we still running?"

~This is not a good part of the Verge, elder sister.~ In much the same tone as she'd warned Bannan about Palma's inn.

"So there are good parts."

She felt it swell under her arm. ~Yes, elder sister! Wonderful parts. Where our—~ It stopped mid-rapture.

Jenn slowed to a jog. "'Where our—' what? Is there a

part where little cousins live?" Bannan's toad had been pleased when she'd offered, she recalled with a twinge of guilt, to look for other toads. "Is it far?" If on the way home, surely she could accomplish at least that much.

~We are not yet worthy, elder sister.~ Sorrowfully.

Meaning there was such a place, she decided, but what could be more worthy than the stalwart toads of Marrowdell? If they needed an advocate—

A shadow scented with cinnamon crossed her path, and Jenn looked up—

—down. Below flew a dragon, larger than Wisp. She stopped in her tracks, trying to puzzle out what wasn't right about it. The emerald green was a bit gaudy, but she'd once seen dragons in great numbers, and they came in colors like the sky of the Verge.

Emerald green not being one.

Oh, but she'd seen eyes of this color, hadn't she? Glimpsed a head of that shape, before all had become a moth, then been gone. And this dragon didn't fly, for its wings didn't move, so what held it in the air was another strangeness. She grew quite dizzy, looking down and up and at it, but not afraid.

For this wasn't, Jenn realized, a dragon at all, but a sei.

"I wouldn't listen to it, Lovely Jenn," said a hatefully familiar voice.

Crumlin!

The world stopped moving. Or they had. Bannan was fuzzy on the details. What he did know was Lila'd fallen off.

Fall off a horse? His sister?

It did strain credulity, but he found himself dropping to the ground, able to stagger, if not walk, to where she lay curled in a ball.

A groan.

"Ancestors Blessed," Bannan said then, startled—awake by his own voice? Had he been sleeping?

No. Riding. As he went to check Lila for broken bones, he glanced up.

The kruar stood, heads lowered. Their sides worked like

bellows and sweat darkened their hides, where it didn't cling in streaks of white froth. Spent, they looked, as he'd never seen Scourge.

Feeling his gaze, heads lifted, lips curled. Ready when you are, that was.

Lila first. "Dear Heart," he urged. "Are you hurt?"

Her head lolled back against his arm, eyes open but upturned, staring at nothing. No, he thought in horror. She truedreamed. "Wake up!" He shook her, gently then hard enough to rattle teeth, though what he hoped to accomplish the fall from the kruar hadn't done— "Lila!!"

"Heart's Blood—Bannan. Stop!"

He snatched her to him, despite a protest involving most of their ancestors and a suggestion regarding his progeny, should he live so long, letting her go only when she boxed his ear. "Ow!"

His sister glared. "Exactly!" She stretched, rubbing the back of her head. "What happened?" Then looked around. "Where are we?"

Being the better question. Bannan stood, turning in a slow circle. The sun was up, but barely. They stood in the midst of flat land, dusted with snow. On every side, hedges marked neat fields of—"Those are grapes. We're in Lower Rhoth. I remember—" his turn to rub his head. "We crossed the Kotor in the night, I swear it."

Lila got to her feet. "Halfway." She looked at the kruar. "Ancestors Wild and Wondrous. From Channen to the heart of Rhoth in a night." Then her face changed. "Bannan. I 'dreamed Werfol. He's no better. Might be worse. We can't stop now."

"We have, so let's use it. Food and drink," he ordered bluntly. "And your promise not to 'dream in the saddle—unless you want to be tied to it."

Her lips twisted. "No more dreams. I'm not helping him," Lila admitted. She nodded to the kruar. "They are."

"Then a short break and, our brave mounts willing, we go on." He kept a straight face. "Unless you wish a rest?" he asked the kruar.

Snarls were his answer.

Bannan shook his head and smiled. Halfway.

With the Northward Road closed by snow? With who knew what storms ahead?

Halfway, he told himself.

Home.

Alone had been better.

Keeping her eyes on the yling, still fluttering ahead, Jenn did her best to ignore her unwanted company. If she didn't look, it wasn't hard to pretend the sei-dragon had left her in peace.

Crumlin was another matter. How had he found her? Possibilities abounded, none pleasant. Had he followed the crossing drop and laid in wait? Did he share her gift for finding? Set traps?

The toad had swallowed something of his magic. Had that betrayed them?

It could be all of those, or something worse.

"Why are you going this way, Lovely Jenn?"

She gritted her teeth. The bodiless voice would fall behind and grow faint, each time giving her hope she'd left it—him—behind, only to start again from ahead or the side as if he'd found a swifter path and outpaced her. All the while, Crumlin chatted as if they were friends out for a stroll. If she answered, she knew she'd never be rid of him. It was, in a way, like dealing with Roche in one of his moods.

Except that Roche was a person and, however annoying, could be fun and even reasonable.

Unlike what pestered her now.

"There's nothing nice that way, Lovely Jenn. You should go to the right."

Where gloom filled the space beneath tall stalks of something, and little red eyes blinked?

She was not going there.

But when Jenn passed it, her head high, Crumlin laughed, a soft and happy laugh, as if she'd done what he wanted after all.

Roche, she'd thrown into the sows' pond.

She walked and walked, the sei-dragon staying with her

and Crumlin keeping up, though neither of them were walking that she could tell, which was rather unfair.

As well as alarming.

Still, walking was progress, Jenn told herself. She moved away from them, or tried to, and moved toward home, or somewhere that wasn't here.

Tried to. A peculiar thought, suited to the Verge.

Yet was the yling leading her somewhere?

Or for something.

Perturbed, Jenn stopped, lifting the toad so she could look into one of its eyes. "Where are we going?" she whispered. "Is this the right way?"

A leg lengthened, clawed toes stretched, then the toad settled peacefully in her hands. ~Trust in us, elder sister, as we trust in you.~

Because she did, Jenn kissed it, then tucked it safely back under her arm. She looked for the yling, sorry for her doubt.

There it hovered, waiting.

Jenn nodded to it, and began to walk again.

"What's the hurry, Lovely Jenn?" Crumlin asked, falling behind. "Where are you going?"

To wherever those she trusted wished her to be.

Though part of her hoped that meant home and Peggs and—oh, Bannan and Lila with Werfol safe and Semyn happy—

—the rest and better part now understood.

The small ones had risked themselves in the Verge and Channen to help Bannan. To help her. They'd proven themselves not only worthy, but selfless and true friends.

Now it was her turn.

He'd crossed into the Verge. Flown to the turn-borns' cursed fountain and back. Roared at the impudent and curious who'd come to see why.

When they scattered, the dragon thought the better of it and commanded their help. Not trusting his temper, they'd flown away even faster. Younglings.

He'd have been proud, if not for the inconvenience.

Kruar were no better help, refusing to leave their hiding places for a question. As if he'd trick them.

As if, the dragon smiled to himself, he hadn't many times before.

He sought the girl, not the truthseer, knowing Bannan would be with Jenn or dead. Dead was of no use to Werfol.

After his second futile flight, Wisp realized searching was of no use either.

He considered approaching the turn-born, who knew the crossing to Channen, only to discard the notion. They'd been reluctant to see the girl cross. To suggest something had gone amiss would be like stirring up a nest of nyphrit.

Only worse and without the tasty result.

Leaving this.

The blue door stood open and waiting. The dragon ignored that invitation to stay on the path, crystal breaking in protest. He would remain here, and be found by the sei.

First? An interesting question. The dimming would soon begin and the hunt.

Wisp let his jaws hang open, dragonfire warm in his throat.

Let them come.

But what arrived first was neither sei-dragon nor hunter. It was a moth.

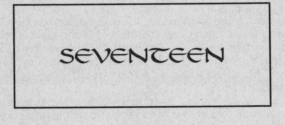

# SEVENTEEN

"WHERE ARE WE going, Lovely Jenn?"

Crumlin asked more and more often. Did he grow anxious? More likely, Jenn thought, he'd been one of those children who'd pestered adults with repetition.

She'd lost track of time long ago, having not the usual clues of sore feet or an empty stomach or even thirst. Mistress Sand had warned her not to forget herself, and what held her to flesh thinned, in some fashion, the more she walked as turn-born. Jenn felt lighter, might have become insubstantial.

But she remembered and refused and began to walk as woman. That meant feeling the weight of the toad, which she found herself shifting from arm to arm as each wearied in turn. A weight and weariness she treasured, for they reminded her of who she was, and meant to stay.

"You will lose your shape, Lovely Jenn."

Something new at last, as if Crumlin heard her thoughts, which he couldn't. Even so, she came close to protesting and had to catch herself.

"That's the price, to stay here. They take your shape! That's the price. The price! The price!" His voice, so long the same, became louder and more shrill.

Encumbered by the toad, Jenn couldn't cover her ears. Just when she thought she'd have to respond if only to stop him, Crumlin fell silent. Then, almost a whisper, close as could be. "I could show you. I could prove it. I could save you, Lovely Jenn."

She'd preferred it when he was annoying. To distract herself, she looked for the sei-dragon.

It was gone. When had it left? Having worried over its presence, Jenn felt abandoned.

"Let me save you, Lovely Jenn. One boon, the smallest of services, a nothing, and I would save you."

Everything Crumlin said was a lie, she told herself, walking faster.

"You will lose your shape."

Even what sounded all too true.

Winter met them at Weken, where smoke blew sideways from chimneys and not a soul stirred outside.

The sun crouched, distant and chill, above the road—or the expanse of unbroken white that had been the road. Once on the snow, the kruar slowed perceptibly, as if some of their strength now went to keeping aloft, but still ran faster than the fleetest horse. Bannan held on, knew Lila did the same; hope gave them strength. The Northward Road wasn't closed, not to the mighty beasts they rode.

But even kruar had limits. The body beneath him was furnace hot, saving him from frostbite, but at what cost? Bannan could feel a change in the kruar's once-effortless strides, a shortening. He shouted at his, tried to stop it.

Felt a snarl of denial through his legs.

They needed rest. Needed meat, he was certain. Bloody idiots, he told himself worriedly. They risked everything, risked leaving him and Lila to freeze. Why wouldn't they stop?

Then Bannan stared ahead, at first bemused to see their way blocked by a range of massive white mountains, like those to the south near Vorkoun.

But they were clouds, not mountains, and beneath them was night.

Heart's Blood. The kruar wouldn't stop because they saw what was coming. A storm. Between them and Marrowdell.

The road was closed after all.

They'd die together, Bannan realized. This close, and they'd fail.

Why make it easy?

"Hyah!!!" he shouted, and leaned over as far as he could to slap the beast on the shoulder. "You want a name? Claim it!"

The kruar heard.

And began to hum.

The yling clung to a long silver thread by the hands of his feet, gossamer wings limp. The fragile-looking thread was one of many over Jenn's head, extending from where she stood over a wide lake of pure mimrol, like the web of a too-daring garden spider across a garden path.

What might have been the nests of weaver birds hung from the threads, except these were far more than nests. Each teardrop shape had doors like windows, complete with balconies and delicate perches. Yling homes.

No, Jenn realized, as she tried to estimate their number. A yling city. A very quiet city.

With only one yling, hers, in sight.

The toad squirmed gently. ~We have arrived, elder sister.~

She put him down on what wasn't sand or a beach but a woven carpet that met the silver of the lake or became part of it. She knelt to take a closer look, entranced by map-like patterns in the design, though like no map she'd ever seen. There were stories in it, layers upon layers of stories, as if the carpet surrounding the lake was an ever-growing quilt.

"Are you sure you want to be here, Lovely Jenn?"

The hoarse whisper broke a lengthy silence she'd quite enjoyed, having guessed it meant Crumlin recognized where the yling would lead her and didn't care for it.

Making the ylings' extraordinary city a place she liked very much, Jenn told herself, despite there being no signs of life.

The ylings' webbing was secured, on this side of the lake, to rocks that jutted from the ground. The rocks were remarkable—for the Verge—in appearing to be simply rocks, gray and rough. The tallest was about three times Jenn's height, its girth that of a privy, though most were no larger than the toad. In fact, the toad, having turned itself gray, might have been one of them.

Not wanting to break a thread, she watched for them as she explored, but those she found were well above her head. Finally, she chose a rock the size of a chair and tapped it politely. When it remained a rock, Jenn sat gingerly.

"Leave, Lovely Jenn. Leave while you can!"

Leave to go home she'd do and happily. Once they were done here.

Done what? Jenn touched the toes of her new boots together, regarding their scuffs and marks wistfully. She moved her toes apart.

To find something stood behind them. Something no larger than her hand.

A yling?

But they didn't stand on the ground.

Or rather, half in the ground.

Curious, she leaned forward, elbows on her knees, chin in her cupped hands. What was this?

It had wings, like a yling, but withered and curled against its back. The chest was little more than ribs over a hollowed belly and, though it had a pair of arms, those were thin and ended in stubby claws. As she watched, it struggled free, revealing legs very much, she thought with a horrid growing surmise, like those of a nyphrit, but more bone than flesh.

Then it lifted its head, and it wasn't just a head, but a man's head, with a mouth and nose and ears.

Except for eyes that were yellow and round with pupils like pits of darkness.

Crumlin.

The wind howled and raged, sending drifts of snow and shards of ice, and Bannan knew only that they moved through it.

He couldn't imagine how.

The kruar fought the storm as they might an enemy of flesh, snapping and snarling. They hummed too; he heard it. The idiot beasts expected their riders to die first.

And planned to honor them, by taking his and Lila's last breath.

Well, they weren't, that was all. If the kruar could keep going, so could they. When he could see his sister, she was a mound of white crusted to her mount's back. Holding on, his Lila. She'd make it.

He'd better, or he'd not hear the end of it.

It was then Bannan felt something wet and hot strike his cheek. Then again.

He brought up a hand gloved in a sock, wiped it away. Somehow brought it close.

Saw a dark stain.

Ancestors Dire and Doomed.

Blood.

The kruar refused to fail. They ran themselves to death, for glory.

And for a child.

Bannan lowered his face to that burning hot hide, and wept.

Old, he was. That too. Wrinkles seamed a face no larger than the tip of her thumb and his body was hunched over, so he must use the claws of one arm like a cane. She'd have judged him a pitiful, miserable creature.

Except that he'd escaped her dragon. Harmed him. Jenn sat straight, resisting the urge to rub her arm where Crumlin had put his shackle, and stared into those too-familiar yellow eyes. "What do you want?"

Oh, and didn't the wee thing bow, then, and didn't the tiny mouth smile? "To save you, Lovely Jenn." The same voice, from everywhere as well as before her. A trick. "Or would you become like me?" The free hand gestured from head to toe.

"I will never be like you," Jenn countered, for she knew—didn't she?—why he was so monstrous. Everything he'd consumed had left its mark on that twisted body. "The Verge shows your true shape, Crumlin Tralee. Stealer of lives!"

"I harvest magic, Lovely Jenn, from those who need it less." A blink, *rustlerustle*. "I can show you how."

"I am magic," she told him and was.

He pretended to cower, then straightened with a triumphant laugh. "So you are. Such a waste in someone who cares so little for it."

Was this the shape he wanted? Jenn quickly became herself again. She could step on him. Squash him flat.

But this was the Verge. She couldn't trust size here. Perhaps Crumlin had made himself small to avoid notice.

Or set another trap.

It was then Jenn realized they were no longer alone.

Ylings filled the air between the rocks, some clinging to the surface, others balanced along silver threads. They were armed, these ylings, some even armored, and in such vast number that the light of the Verge shattered within their hair, making it impossible to look up.

The little cousin. Her yling. They'd planned a trap!

"Your turn!" she exclaimed with fierce joy, surging to her feet. "We've caught you!"

"Have you, now?" A chuckle, dry and dusty, made her hesitate and doubt, then Crumlin bowed once more. "How very, very, kind of you and your friends, my dear and Lovely Jenn, to be all here, together, away from their nasty lake. Just for me."

He raised his tiny arms.

Nets sprang from the ground, black and twisting as if alive. Nets that climbed faster than the ylings could fly, that their weapons couldn't cut—though they tried desperately to free themselves and those near them. When this failed, masses flew at the nets, offering themselves so those behind could escape—

But it was a dreadful mistake.

As the sparks within their hair failed, as they died, the nets grew darker and stronger. More nets loomed, filling the sky!

"No!" Jenn changed to turn-born, lunged at Crumlin.

Hearing him laugh as his nets caught her too.

"Sir."

He'd fallen. No, the kruar had. Ancestors Despondent and— Bannan tried to feel the great beast, his eyes refusing to open.

"Sir! Ancestors Witness. Give me a hand. He's not hearing me."

Of course he heard, Bannan thought, but didn't bother to respond. He'd dreamed they'd arrived over and over. Dreamed that voice, in particular. Dreamed falling.

Falling.

"Momma!!"

Heart's Blood. Hands held him and were real. Arms steadied him and finally, at last, he opened his eyes.

Marrowdell.

They were in his farmyard, by the fountain! He gripped Tir's arms, staring around. "Werfol—" That first. "Get Lila to Werfol—" he couldn't speak in more than a whisper. "She can save him."

"That's Werfol's mother!" A parade-ground bellow. "Get her inside to the lad! Hurry!"

Figures began to move on every side, making Bannan dizzy. Big Davi, with Lila in his arms. Dusom. Kydd. Peggs. Semyn, running beside his mother.

Who roused herself at the porch. "Put me down!"

Ancestors Blessed. They were home. Because of— Bannan leaned on Tir, shaking his head to clear it, looking for the kruar.

They'd gone down, the female on her side, the male with his legs under him. Blood dribbled from their nostrils and mouths, staining the snow. They breathed still.

Enough to snarl warningly at the surrounding villagers.

Bannan pulled himself toward them, Tir tucking a shoulder under his arm. "Two more?" the man muttered, but it was with respect and remorse.

Lips curled over bloody fangs as the truthseer knelt in the snow between them, but they endured his hand on their necks. He could feel their hearts laboring. "The bravest of us all," Bannan told them. "That's what you are. Please. Let these people help you."

Though he knew not what could be done. Were these horses, it would have been mercy to dispatch them.

Tir helped him stand. "Werfol," Bannan said next.

His friend nodded, helping him to the house. "The lad's hardly in better shape than yon beasts," he warned.

"Lila will save him."

Unless, despite the kruars' great sacrifice, they were too late.

The warmth indoors hurt, after the bitter ride, smarting his cheeks and bringing tears to his eyes. Blinking his eyes clear, Bannan saw Lila already beside her son. She'd paused only to strip off what covered her hands. Looked only at Werfol's too-pale face.

Semyn stood beside her, doing the same, taut with hope.

Tir pulled at his coat and the truthseer accepted that help before going to his sister. "Lila—"

Ice melted in her hair and shivers wracked her body, but the eyes that glanced at him were green and bright and fierce. "I will save him."

She kissed Semyn, then pushed him to Bannan. Without another word, Lila lay on the bed at Werfol's side.

And took his little hand in hers.

 

*And the dream unfolds . . .*
Into darkness and cold, without hope or light . . .
*See the candle . . .*
A flicker, smaller than a teardrop. Too far. Too small!
*Bring it closer . . .*
Closer?
*You can do this . . . bring it closer . . .*

Near now, the candle. In a holder shaped like a crow. On
a . . . on a . . .
*See the table . . .*
Dark and cold but there, a candle. In a holder shaped like
a crow. On a table, round, and carved, with a . . . with a cup,
steaming . . .
*Taste it . . .*
There was nothing here and nothing was ever here and he
was alone and . . .
*Taste it, Dearest Heart. I brought it for you . . .*
Because Momma did that, every night. She brought a
cup . . . a cup . . . but he had no hands . . . he had no
hands . . . he couldn't stop falling without hands . . .
*I've got you . . . taste it . . .*
For there was a candle, in a holder shaped like a crow that
his father had given him, on the table he shared with
Semyn, and on that table was the warm drink Momma
brought them every night, to have with their story . . . and
it . . . tasted like . . .
Love.
*The dream gently fades . . .*

"Momma?"

As Werfol opened his eyes, Lila sat up and gathered him
to her, tears slipping down her cheeks. Semyn jumped on
the bed to join them, landing on Werfol's foot so he kicked
at his brother who shouted. And their mother's laugh as she
straightened out matters to take both in her arms was surely
the most wonderful sound Bannan had ever heard.

So his eyes filled and Tir's did as well, though his friend
wiped his with a rough sleeve and mutter about fool boys
who scared their elders.

And the second best moment came next, when Werfol,
who didn't recall being in bed so long, realized he urgently
needed the chamber pot but insisted he would not, under
any circumstances, use it in front of his mother because he
was a big boy.

At which Lila laughed again, though she did grant him
privacy.

Privacy she used to come to Bannan and Tir, with abrupt concern. "The kruar?"

"Look!" Semyn called.

"What?" Werfol demanded. Bannan picked him up and brought him to the window with the others.

Scourge had come.

Bannan handed his nephew to Tir. "I'd best go outside." There could be only one reason, he knew. To take the final breaths of their mounts. "Wait here."

Lila shook her head. "We'll all go." She wrapped Werfol, who didn't protest about being too big after seeing her face, in a quilt, then waited while Semyn threw on his own coat.

Bannan went to the door, to find the house toad there and waiting. He nodded and let it precede them all.

The sun was low over the Bone Hills, the sky free of cloud. He could see his breath, but there was no wind. They'd left the storm on the road. Too late for the kruar.

Scourge stood near his fallen kindred, neck and tail curved. When Bannan stepped out on the porch, the old kruar turned to regard him.

Waiting.

"Brother," Lila said quietly. "Their names."

The truthseer nodded. It was the least they could do. He walked to his former mount, stopped before him, and stared into a barely open eye. "Whatever you require of your kind to earn a name, by the Hearts of my Ancestors," he said, circling fingers over his heart. "I swear to you both of these have done so."

The fallen pair roused at this, eyes widening, and Bannan felt a surge of hope. Could it be?

Scourge let out a roar!

More than a roar, a summons!

The kruar on her side flung up her head, fought to bring her legs under her, then lurched to stand, limbs shaking. The other rose to his knees, fell back, then surged up.

Scourge circled them, nostrils flared. The kruars' struggle to stay upright was pitiful and Bannan's heart went out to them.

But they had to stand, if they were to live.

Scourge came back to him, bent his head to push, gently, at the truthseer's chest. "Name them."

Bannan glanced back at Lila, who must have heard for she gave a tiny shrug. Your problem, that was.

Ancestors Witness.

He could only go with what he felt. Bannan went to the male who had carried Jenn through the Verge and Lila across Rhoth. "Spirit."

Eyes lit, at that. A neck curved.

Next the mare, who'd carried him. "Dauntless."

Lips pulled from fangs. Was that a purr?

Scourge went to each in turn, nipping them on the nap of the neck. "You have been named."

Werfol cheered, surprising everyone, but why not, Bannan thought, and let out a "Hurray!" of his own.

As if names were a tonic, Dauntless and Spirit took a step, then two, aiming for, to Lila's obvious consternation, Werfol.

And didn't that bode something for the future, that they recognized another truthseer?

Ancestors Witness, he wanted a sleep, dry clothes, and a drink—and explanations—and not in that order.

Because first and most of all, he wanted someone.

Someone who should . . . should be here. Should have been here long before and waiting.

Bannan turned to Tir, a terrible fear growing.

"Where's Jenn?"

Though everything in her screamed to struggle, and fight the net, Jenn held herself still, knowing she couldn't, not alone.

"That's a good girl," Crumlin told her. He might not have had hands to rub together gleefully, like a story villain, but he managed with his voice. "Such a good girl. Stay—"

Stay? She was in his net already.

As a woman. Even as she thought it, Jenn felt it. A draining, a loss. She stared down at herself as if it could be seen, but it couldn't, this theft. And it wasn't of the magic she possessed as turn-born or sei—

Magic, as she kept thinking, Crumlin hadn't dared take, or couldn't.

He feasted on the magic of small things. Ylings. Efflet and nyphrit. Of—of real things, like this shape she remembered for him. This flesh.

Making it Melusine's gift being taken by this sneak! Her mother's magic. Hers! That was how he could use her.

"I don't think so," Jenn Nalynn said, and wasn't a "girl" anymore.

Her hands opened.

Out flew moths. The first few stuck to the net, but those behind pushed at it, stretched it, twisted it. As more and more pushed, stretched, and twisted, parts of the net came free from the ground.

To wither, like the tops of uprooted carrots. That was it! Jenn thought. Crumlin lived in the ground, hid there. His power was there.

Her moths, untold, fluttered to where the nets began, pushing with delicate legs and wing beats against what should have been too strong, but wasn't.

Because they wouldn't stop. She wouldn't stop. And now she knew he couldn't steal magic from what of her was sei.

Crumlin took a step back, eyes blinking. "What are you doing?"

Jenn thought it obvious, but she didn't waste her breath. Not that she breathed, at the moment, but something she did used the same feeling and effort, so she wouldn't spend a bit of it on him.

She didn't notice the moment she was freed, too intent on freeing the ylings as well.

"NO!"

More nets around her, thicker, darker. Those around the ylings fell away as Crumlin turned his remaining might against her, nets adding to those sticking to her hair and clothes. Smothering, the nets, and they pulled at her, even as the ground softened so she sank. To her knees.

To her waist!

~Elder sister!!~ The toad crept toward her, as if swimming.

Even as the ground took her deeper—

And she heard Crumlin laugh—

Then.
A roar!

Wisp roared again, for the sheer joy of it. How clever of the girl to draw out their enemy! Under the ground, Crumlin laid his traps, used the earth itself. But above? Exposed?

~ELDER BROTHER!~

The dragon veered, wing joints straining, in time to save himself.

Ylings!? He roared again, this time in fury. Their threads, studded with poison darts, formed a glittering fence between him and his prey!

Between him and the girl!

Had the toad not warned him—

No matter. Wisp flew frantically this way and that, seeking a way through. The moth who'd led him had no such problem, joining what seemed a blanket of their kind around where Jenn struggled.

~Wait!~

For what? Disaster? The dragon roared again, rock shattering.

Then, to his astonishment, ylings flew to their webbing and began to cut.

Homes splashed into the mimrol, but still they cut, destroying their city.

To let death through.

# EIGHTEEN

*T*HE NETS BOUND her arms and Jenn lifted her chin to keep from sinking below the surface. She could see Wisp above, trying to reach her. Hold on, she told herself. Just hold on.

Crumlin walked up to her face, giving her much too clear a view of his distorted body. "Don't hope for the dragon, Lovely Jenn," he told her. "Or for yourself. I must go home."

It wasn't her nature to be cruel, angry as she was at the foul being, but she wouldn't—couldn't—allow anything made of these—these loathsome pieces back into Marrowdell. "You can't," she told him. "You don't belong there anymore. Not as you are."

Yellow eyes blinked. *Rustlerustle.* "I won't be, Lovely Jenn," as if she'd missed the point.

She must have. What she didn't miss was that as he talked to her, she'd stopped sinking. Keep talking, Jenn decided. "Why go back? You've power here."

"I'm old," the tiny not-a-man reminded her. "And Rhothan. I must bring my bones back into our world."

Wasted arms formed a caricature of a shrug. "How else will I live forever?"

The freed ylings flew up and away, but Crumlin hadn't noticed. Keep him talking, Jenn told herself. "You want to become a Blessed Ancestor?" Heart's Blood. She could, she supposed, understand that.

Crumlin laughed, spittle on his lips. "Silly girl. I haven't spent a lifetime here to die there. My bones are all of me I've left." He tapped a yellowed claw to the side of his head. "But I've learned what I need to restore my true self. To live forever!"

Jenn ignored him, as silver threads broke and fell.

The ylings had cut down their city!

The dragon followed.

Jenn made herself glass and pearl just in time for Wisp to seize her in his claws and pull her from the ground. She came free with a horrible sucking sound, as if leaving a mouth, even as netting snapped all around.

Wisp set her down, as gently as a rose petal.

Then *SNAPPED* up something tiny before it could dig itself away.

Crumlin.

"Wait!" Jenn cried.

The dragon hesitated, Crumlin neatly between his jaws. Wild violet eyes regarded her with understandable disbelief. ~Why?~

Because bright yellow eyes peered at her between fangs like old bone, and seemed not the least afraid.

Dragons, Jenn thought suddenly, being magic. She shuddered to think of Crumlin and his nets, growing within Wisp's body. "I don't believe he'd be good for you," she cautioned as she thought what else to do and quickly.

~Elder sister?~

The toad. It hadn't been much help, to be truthful, but then again, neither had she. "What is—" She blinked. "What are you doing?"

For it was, to her surprise, more square than round, with sharp little corners protruding behind its eyes.

"Why?" Wisp asked again, the little breeze snapping with impatience. "Is it your good heart?" With a tinge of despair.

"It's not," Jenn replied absently. "Don't let him get away, please." She crouched by the toad. "I think the little cousin is making something."

An incredulous silence.

But she was right. The toad opened its mouth, wider and wider, and she could see it, now. Some sort of— "It's a box!" Jenn exclaimed, as indeed one popped out of the toad.

Who settled back, pride in every wart.

Not any box, she realized, picking it up. This was made of an all-too-familiar metal, bound like a tiny chest with leather straps. The outline of two eyes shone dully on the top, blood red, for hadn't a traitor's blood gone into this and a brave man's tunic, as well as the shackle and chain she'd worn, cleansed by dragonsfire? Not to mention whatever else the toad might have fancied while out of sight. To make this.

A cage.

Jenn undid the straps and opened the lid. Inside was larger, which it couldn't be. Larger, and she found she didn't like to look there.

The little cousin watched her, something ruthless in its gaze. Ylings hovered, those not bent or broken by Crumlin's nets, weapons in hands.

She could imagine the eyes of efflet, cold and grim, and knew what all of them asked of her.

Justice.

"I will take you to Rhoth, Crumlin," Jenn Nalynn said and showed the open box to Wisp's prisoner. "In this. It's your choice," she added, for it should be.

The dragon snarled, offering his.

Crumlin considered the box, then stared at the toad. "You can't hold me. I am magic's master!"

The toad stared back.

Like a dare.

And Jenn wondered for the first time about Crumlin and the toads, and why he'd never harmed them, but now was not the time for questions.

"I must go back." A mutter. Claws wrapped around a fang, Crumlin peered out at her. "You must promise to take me with you, Lovely Jenn. I insist on your promise. You wouldn't lie." He made it sound a flaw.

"If you are in this box," Jenn stated with the greatest care, not trusting him at all. "I promise to take you to Marrowdell."

He looked back to the toad and frowned, his face a contortion of wrinkles, as if trying to spot the trick in it. "Toads. Useless things. She trusts you?"

Jenn waited, for she did.

Crumlin laughed. Climbing from between the dragon's fangs, he jumped neatly into the box.

Jenn shut the lid and fastened the straps. Answering to impulse, she held it up.

Two ylings flew down, to weave a thread of silver over and around every side. When they were done, the thread became bands of silver that sank into the iron and gripped. Overhead, the rest of ylings began to dance, trilling their joy.

Jenn brought down the box. It was no heavier, but she knew beyond doubt what it held.

For where the toad had made eyes from dried blood, now a pair, bright yellow and pupiled in darkness, stared out. They didn't blink or move. They might have been of paint.

Save they held horror.

Finding her sack, Jenn hastily shoved the box inside. "That should do it," she said shakily, brushing at her clothes. What should have been soil avoided her fingers, slipping away to drop on the ground. The toad glared at it, but didn't, this time, eat anything.

Being done. The small ones had triumphed and were safe from Crumlin.

Jenn didn't feel triumphant. She felt a little sick, truth be told. And tired. "Take us home, Wisp," she asked.

"Now? We can't go now. Where is Bannan, Dearest Heart?" Wisp said. His wings jerked open and closed. Worry, that was. "You said stay in Marrowdell, but the young truthseer needs his help and you were not back. You were not there." With a chill nip. Frantic, now. "Did you lose him again?" Breezes whirled and breezes fretted.

Ancestors Witness, she'd thought toads fussed.

To be fair, Wisp had every reason and right. "Bannan's home," she said quickly, though it was more hope than surety.

She'd done all she could, and must trust the kruar.

"Home?" Wisp echoed, head rising in surprise. "How? Why? When?" With dark suspicion. "Did he lose you again?"

"He went to save Werfol." Jenn picked up the toad, Marrowdell's yling settling in her hair with a patpatpat. "Let's go home, Wisp. I'll tell you the rest on the way."

Then, because her heart was full, she put her arm around his cold, scaled neck and pressed her cheek to his, close to that wild violet eye. "Thank you, for coming here to look for him and find me." An escape whose closeness and result she refused to consider until safe in Bannan's arms.

When she'd know everyone was safe.

Though first? Jenn wished the air warm and dry, only here, only now, and there was no *disagreement*. And Wisp used his breezes to pull threads and homes from the lake in case, as he told her, other dragons thought to take advantage.

The delighted ylings trilled and danced, some bold enough to caress his wings, and Jenn had to laugh at the dragon's dismay.

Then she didn't laugh, but stood still in amazement, for something moved within the lake of mimrol as if disturbed by their antics, or curious, something larger than barge or dragon, and beneath that silver surface, Jenn thought she saw red eyes, ancient and wise, and glimpsed a yellowed beak, and was that a hint of shell?

The lake stilled, reflecting the many colors of the sky and the glittering sparks of ylings, and surely she was mistaken.

Jenn curtsied, nonetheless.

The table was set with plates from Weken and cups from Marrowdell. Tea from Vorkoun filled those cups and eggs from toads would be on those plates, once Tir finished whatever he did at the stove.

The stove being from Weken and Tir being from some village in Upper Rhoth whose name he didn't recall but should. Why didn't he? Hadn't he ridden across the bloody whole of Rhoth! Bannan scrubbed at his eyes. Ancestors Lost and Abandoned.

Jenn had sent them. Known what she was doing.

But how could she? The Verge—it wasn't her home, this was.

She'd known what she was doing, Bannan repeated to himself. Known if they took the kruar, she'd have no guide, no means to travel quickly or safely. Jenn had saved Werfol.

Could she save herself?

"It's ready," Tir called. The boys rushed to the table, Lila coming from her seat by the fire to join them.

Bannan made himself smile, fooling no one. Nodded thanks to Tir, who scowled back, just as worried, no doubt, but kind enough not to say what they all were thinking.

Where was Jenn?

Scourge had crossed in search, Dauntless and Spirit as yet unable. He'd hope yet.

"The Beholding, brother. Unless you want Tir to say it?" Lila didn't smile, though it was a private joke the former guard shouldn't be given that particular task before a meal they planned to enjoy while hot, and she looked at Bannan with sorrow in her eyes, though her heart was whole again.

As his was not.

When he hesitated, Semyn looked at him, then said, very earnestly. "Wisp isn't back either, Uncle."

Tir nodded. "Aie. Missing a good meal too." A hint that was, not to let the eggs cool on their plates.

So Bannan roused himself to really smile this time, for Semyn was right and Tir. Though in his heart he knew the dragon stayed in the Verge for only one reason. Wisp hadn't found Jenn.

Yet. Heart's Blood, they'd been through worse. He circled his fingers over his heart and began, "Hearts of our Ancestors, we are Beholden for the food on this table, and that Tir didn't burn the eggs—" to make Semyn hide a smile and Weed giggle, "—for it will give us the strength to improve ourselves in your eyes. We are Beholden for—" so much, his voice stuck in his throat.

"We are Beholden," Lila said then, "for the strength and courage of our new friends, Spirit and Dauntless, and for the bravery of our old one," a nod to Tir, who blushed bright red, "for bringing us together to share this meal. We are Beholden my dear husband vowed to clean house before we get home," this with a grim finality that sparked golden fire in Werfol's eyes. "We are Beholden for the gifts that both saved us and healed us," her voice grew husky now. "Hearts of our Ancestors, above all we are Beholden for this time we've spent together, as family. However far we are apart, Keep Us Close."

"'Keep Us Close,'" echoed the boys and Tir.

About to say the words, Bannan felt a burning on his neck!

He surged to his feet, his stool clattering to the floor. As the others looked to him, Tir with pity, he shook his head, starting to smile. "'Keep Us Close!'" He kissed Lila, rubbed the boys' hair, and slapped Tir on the shoulder. "'Keep Us Close!'"

"Sir?"

"Can't you feel it?" Bannan cried. "'Keep Us Close!'"

"Gone mad, have you?" But Tir was on his feet now, and the boys and Lila, their faces filled with the same hope.

"What is it, Uncle?" Semyn asked, because he needed to be sure.

Bannan, already at the door, looked back at his family. "It's the turn."

Scourge ran across the snow, Wisp flew above it, her sack—and toad—in his claws. Being neither kruar nor dragon, Jenn pulled up her skirt to run through the new drifts, Night's Edge having more snow than she remembered, and laughed.

She was glad to have such fine new boots.

Glad of so much.

The turn went ahead of her, catching the eyes of efflet, sparkling the hair of ylings, burnishing the mail of toads, for little cousins squatted in the snow as though to show her the way.

Her heart knew it.

There was the gap in the hedge, which wasn't a gap in a hedge but the door to everything she held dearest and wanted most.

And there, as if he'd known, was Bannan. He began

wading through the snow toward her, struggling and as desperate to reach her as she was him, both laughing for the joy of it.

Though Jenn was ever so impatient.

All at once, what had been snow and a struggle pending flew into the air and out of their way, becoming a cloud of tiny moths, then a twinkle, then gone.

"'Keep Us Close,'" Bannan said as they came together at last.

Jenn Nalynn couldn't agree more.

"Turtles." Peggs shook her head, smiling. "That's what you remember most?"

Turnip in hand, Jenn used her wrist to push hair from her forehead. Her sister reached across to tuck the stray lock behind her ear and she smiled her thanks. "If I could, I'd have brought my clothes to show you. Especially the simples," she added, managing not to blush. "But they're in Channen." Not to mention coated in slime and mimrol from her time in the canal, being carried by those turtles.

Peggs had heard the entire tale while they prepared supper together, their father listening to the part about riding kruar through the Verge while he'd tea, and Kydd, though presumably busy painting, eavesdropping shamelessly through everything concerning the Shadow District and artisans, though Bannan had spoken to him in private.

The Uhthoffs' having been most helpful and needing to know.

Peggs waved steam aside as she inspected her stew. "I wonder if Mistress Sand could bring some," she mused aloud, "to trade, of course."

She'd not thought of that. "I could ask," Jenn offered.

A glance from knowing dark eyes. "So you'll be going back. To the Verge."

Jenn twirled the turnip idly, then aimed her knife at it. "Not right away," she said comfortably, though in truth she hadn't left.

For she was whole, now, and knew herself. She was more than the memory of flesh, held within glass, filled with tears.

She was woman, and turn-born, and sei. Marrowdell. The Verge. Magic itself.

One and the same.

"Good," Peggs declared, and Jenn didn't for an instant think her perceptive sister had missed a thing. "Now—tell me more about these artisans."

So she did.

Leaving out the rabbits.

"We'll be fine." Lila refolded a shirt Werfol had left on the bed, tucking that into a bag. Her youngest was off playing with Cheffy and Alyssa. "Will you?"

Semyn, in the bedroom to help his mother pack, looked up. "Wisp says he'll be here."

As now-permanent guest, it would seem. Must be in the rafters, there hardly seemed space amid the bundles. "I'm not the one returning to Vorkoun." Bannan leaned against the window frame and frowned. "Is it so bad here?" She'd seemed content, in Marrowdell, teaching her sons when not helping the villagers. The breadth of Lila's skills never ceased to amaze, but even he'd been surprised to learn she knew how to make cheese.

And Werfol could reliably sit the now-healed kruar.

His sister gave him a look he knew very well. She'd sat still long enough, his Lila. No longer.

He'd expected it. She'd waited for the kruar to heal, that was all. "Stay till after the celebration," he urged. "That at least."

"Please, Momma?" Semyn asked. "I promised to play."

Her lips quirked. "Well, then. We mustn't break a promise."

Meaning nothing so benign as the boy's pipes and the dance. They'd talked it through—he, Lila, and Tir. How Glammis might have learned of their gifts, be it a slip from someone trusted or malice left from the marches. What he wanted with them.

How to prevent it.

In Lila's hands, that, as was her pendant. She'd heard how Werfol had used it more than once, something new in her experience with truedreaming, and intended to learn more. Though Kydd, knowing something of such magic, had cautioned it might not have been the endearment alone, but Marrowdell. Oh, the gleam in her eye then. Bannan thought it more than likely his sister would be back. With her family, of course.

A joy in itself to believe.

Last and not least, Lila had put the box, with its weight of letters and seals and dire guilt, in his care, to keep in Marrowdell and safe. She'd not said what to do with it, should the need arise.

Making him her threat, his sister, which was no joy at all.

"The celebration and no longer," Lila said then, reaching for another small shirt like any mother packing for her children. "I've 'dreamed. Your father's ready for us." She eyed her son. "We've a new cook."

Semyn went still, then nodded. Heart's Blood, he'd wish she spare the boy—but that wasn't the life they led, his family. Not and be safe. "I'll write," Bannan promised gruffly.

Lila raised an eyebrow. "Is that an invitation, little brother?"

He pretended to grimace, then smiled. "If you must."

To his surprise, her face softened. "Thank you." More briskly, with that familiar glint to her eye. "Now, what's left to pack? Semyn, be sure to check every bag."

"For what, Momma?"

Lila glanced at Bannan, a dimple in one cheek.

"For toads."

The Midwinter Beholding was held in Marrowdell, as it was throughout Rhoth and her neighbor, Mellynne, on the longest night of the year. Boughs of fragrant cedar were tied throughout the mill, and lanterns carefully lit. A feast was prepared, as feasts should be, using the best from larders and shelves.

Plus an immense platter of ompah, to the particular joy of Master Jupp.

Baking there was, all the favorites plus puddings and sweet sausage pie, being traditional at this time. As, in

Marrowdell, was the wearing of one's very best winter coats, it not being possible to heat the mill.

Dancers would warm themselves, once the meal sat comfortably in stomachs, though most would return to nibble, there being sweet trays to come later and savory and surprise treats tied in little bags.

Bags used the last year and years before that, and those not frayed saved for next year, it being one of the Ancestors Blessings to add the old to the new.

Added to this year were the Westietas, mother and sons, as well as Tir Half-face, being himself of Marrowdell as much as any place or more. Semyn played on his old pipes, his new flute packed to be taken and repaired, with Weed helping Cheffy keep the beat on a drum.

When they weren't playing tag with Alyssa.

Lila and Lorra, having discovered they'd much in common, sat together. Plotting to take over the world, Bannan would say, only half in jest, but he was as pleased as any there, to see color in Lorra's cheeks and hear her argue to her heart's content.

While she could. Zehr and Davi had crafted a sled from the wood of Lila's wagon, for as she'd put it, Emon would need the tools of his office soon.

Though a little anarchy, she'd grinned, was good for him.

A bagful of letters would return with them as well, the opportunity to send word midwinter not to be missed. Aunt Sybb wouldn't be the only one surprised and pleased.

The sled and all its contents would be pulled, much to the astonishment of those who knew kruar, by Spirit and Dauntless. Jenn had gladly wished away the saddles grown onto their backs, expecting the pair to seek their freedom. But once healed, they'd accepted the traces without demur, being, it turned out, enamored of Werfol and Lila.

Semyn, ever prudent, kept his distance.

According to Wisp, the kruar vied to be fools like Scourge. Scourge seemed content, having proclaimed he was, in fact, too big for Werfol. Anything but admit to being glad to have his own truthseer back and safe.

And so worlds tugged each other this way, then that, Jenn Nalynn thought, gazing down at all this from the attic, her chin on the rail around the stair, her legs and feet—bare—dangling over. She could feel it, how the light of the Verge would begin to retreat before the light of the sun, days longer here, but not necessarily shorter there.

The Verge hardly so predictable.

"May I join you?"

She smiled and patted the floor. A moth flew up and away as Bannan slipped his legs through and sat. "Our first Midwinter Beholding."

Jenn looked askance at him. "What do you think?"

He put his arm around her. "I like it."

"The dancing will—" She paused, it being hard to speak and pay proper attention to a kiss at the same time, and the kiss being the more interesting process, then continued, breathlessly, "—start soon."

"I like dancing. I like the food. I like almost everything."

She looked askance at him for the second time. "'Almost.'"

Bannan could look remarkably innocent. He did now, widening his apple butter eyes and smiling. "I'll have my house back, in a couple of days. You know what it will need then?"

Her heart began to pound. "Why don't you tell me?"

He put his face close hers, lowered his voice to a delicious rumble, and said, "Another toad."

She sat back and pushed at him. "You have your own."

Bannan laughed, undeterred. "A map, then. I need a map for my wall."

Why . . . catching on to the game, Jenn took a breath, feeling giddier than a couple of ciders and happiness could explain. "I suppose you need another pair of boots too."

"How did you know? And clothes. Drawers full of clothes." He ran a finger through her hair. "And a hair brush," this tender and soft and now she saw the hope in his eyes and realized he was more than a little giddy too.

Before the sun had set, they'd all stood in the ossuary, snow to their knees, to silently tell their Ancestors Dear and Departed, including Frann, of every fault and every triumph of the past year, then every hope for the next.

She'd not looked at Bannan then, nor wished. She'd simply told her Ancestors of her new and special hope, for this very year.

So, it seemed, had he.

"A toad." She pretended not to understand. "A map. Boots, clothes, and a brush?" Then Jenn Nalynn smiled, from her heart. "I believe all that could be arranged."

They kissed, then and again, and whether she had a heart or simply the memory of one didn't matter, for Jenn felt hers about to burst with joy, and they might have kept kissing, but the music started below and tables were moved and someone—likely Hettie—shouted up at them to come down, then everyone did.

With Lila's voice the loudest.

Bannan helped her to her feet. He blew a kiss down to his sister, then glanced at Jenn. He started to frown, muttering, "Ancestors Bothered and Brash," as if struck by sudden concern. "I'd best tell you now, Dearest Heart. You may—" oh, and this so grim and serious she knew it was nothing of the sort and managed not to smile, "—change your mind."

She wouldn't, of course, any more than he. Playing along, Jenn arched a brow, as Aunt Sybb would when suspicious. "Tell me what?"

"We won't be alone." The truthseer's grin was full of boyish mischief. "There's a dragon."

The dragon coiled in the rafters above the dancers. It wasn't warm enough.

But it would do.

The younger truthseer saw and pointed him out to his brother, who didn't see but seemed pleased. Having been seen—again—Wisp flew to a different rafter and waited. Hide and seek being a dragonish sort of game.

The girl was happier than he'd ever known her to be. Happier and different. He'd seen it first in the Verge. She was more sei now, yet more herself.

Beyond a dragon to ponder.

A little cousin squatted in the shadows. Not the only one, there being food dropped from tables and the possibility, however scant, a nyphrit might dare the lights. But this toad was hers.

This toad had crossed into the Verge and back.

Of this toad, even a dragon would be wary.

It had taken the box, with its straps and bands. The girl had been glad, being too good-hearted to savor revenge. Unlike a dragon.

It had taken the box, but why? A dragon could be, Wisp decided, curious.

Marrowdell's little cousins did other incomprehensible things. They built a throne for their absent queen from pebbles they earned by their service. Sent one of their own into the Verge, to swallow a bit of sei and burp out a mask.

This box, though.

A dragon could be, Wisp decided, concerned.

"I see you!"

When not playing a game.

"Where?" said Semyn, squinting up.

Because there was a box, with Crumlin safe inside, and the girl was happy, and he felt particularly generous, there being more children soon to arrive . . .

Wisp shaped himself from light, then swooped down to skim over the dancers' heads, to oohs and ahhhs and at least one very satisfying shriek.

Before slipping out, another shadow in the night.

# Concerning the Denizens of Marrowdell

**Alyssa Ropp**, daughter of Mimm and Anten, sister of Hettie and Cheffy, stepdaughter to Cynd, stepsister to Roche and Devins. Born in Marrowdell. Helps in dairy.

**Anten Ropp**, brother of Cynd, father (with Mimm) of Hettie, Cheffy, and Alyssa. Widowed then married Covie. Stepfather of Roche and Devins. Tends the dairy.

**Aunt Sybb** (the Lady Sybb Mahavar, nee Nalynn), sister of Radd, aunt to Peggs and Jenn. Spends summers in Marrowdell. Wife of Hane Mahavar. In Avyo, they own several of the better riverside inns.

**Bannan Marerrym Larmensu**, brother of Lila, rider of Scourge. Former Vorkoun border guard who went by the name of "Captain Ash." Truthseer and, in Marrowdell, farmer.

**Battle and Brawl**, Davi Treff's team of draft horses.

**Cheffy Ropp**, son of Mimm and Anten, brother of Hettie

and Alyssa, stepson of Covie, stepbrother of Roche and Devins. Born in Marrowdell. Helps in dairy.

**Covie Ropp**, mother (with Riedd) of Roche and Devins, stepmother to Hettie, Cheffy, and Alyssa. Widowed then married Anten. A baroness in Avyo. Tends the dairy. Village healer.

**Crumlin Tralee (Lost One)**, once resident of Marrowdell. Disappeared under magical circumstances.

**Cynd Treff**, nee Ropp, sister of Anten, wife of Davi. Aunt to Hettie, Cheffy, and Alyssa. Gardener and seamstress.

**Davi Treff**, son of Lorra, brother of Wen. Husband of Cynd, Anten's sister. Uncle to Hettie, Cheffy, and Alyssa. Village smith.

**Devins Morrill**, son of Covie and Riedd, brother of Roche. Stepbrother of Hettie, Cheffy, and Alyssa. Stepson of Anten. Came to Marrowdell as a boy. Tends the dairy.

**Dusom Uhthoff** (Master Dusom), father of Wainn and Ponicce, husband of Larell (widowed), brother of Kydd. Formerly professor at Avyo's University of Sols. Village teacher and helps tend the orchard.

**Frann Nall**, former business rival and now friend of Lorra Treff. In Avyo, holdings included riverfront warehouses. Village weaver, quilter, and trader.

**Gallie Emms**, mother of twins, Tadd and Allin, and baby Loee, wife of Zehr. Author and sausage maker.

**Good'n'Nuf**, Ropps' bull.

**Hettie Emms,** nee Ropp, daughter of Mimm and Anten, sister of Cheffy and Alyssa, stepdaughter of Covie, stepsister of Roche and Devins, wife to Tadd. Came to Marrowdell as a child. Village cheese maker.

**Himself**, boar.

**Jenn Nalynn**, daughter of Melusine and Radd, sister of Peggs. Born in Marrowdell under magical circumstances. Turn-born.

**Kydd Uhthoff**, brother of Dusom, uncle of Wainn and Ponicce, husband of Peggs. Came to Marrowdell as a young man. Formerly a student at Avyo's University of Sols. Tends apple orchard. Village beekeeper and artist.

**Larell Uhthoff**, mother of Wainn and Ponicce, wife of Dusom. Died by misadventure on the Northward Road.

**Loee Emms**, daughter of Gallie and Zehr, sister of Tadd and Allin. Born in Marrowdell.

**Lorra Treff**, mother of Davi and Wen. Great-aunt to Hettie, Cheffy, and Alyssa. Formerly head of Avyo's influential Potter's Guild. Village potter.

**Melusine (Melly) Nalynn**, nee Semanaryas, mother of Peggs and Jenn, wife of Radd. Died by misadventure in Marrowdell.

**Mimm Ropp**, mother of Hettie, Cheffy, and Alyssa, first wife of Anten. Died by misadventure in Marrowdell.

**Old Jupp** (Wagler Jupp), great-uncle of Riedd and Riss. Former Secretary of the House of Keys in Avyo. Currently writing his memoirs.

**Peggs Uhthoff**, nee Nalynn, daughter of Melusine and Radd, elder sister of Jenn, wife of Kydd. Came to Marrowdell as a babe. Village's best baker and cook.

**Ponicce Uhthoff**, daughter of Dusom and Larell, sister of Wainn, niece of Kydd. Died by misadventure on the Northward Road.

**Radd Nalynn**, father of Peggs and Jenn, husband of Melusine, brother of Sybb. In Avyo, owned mills and a tannery. Village miller.

**Riedd Morrill**, father of Roche and Devins, husband of Covie, cousin of Riss, great-nephew of Old Jupp. In Avyo, was a baron and served in the House of Keys. Died by misadventure in Marrowdell.

**Riss Nahamm**, cousin of Riedd, great-niece of Old Jupp, wife of Sennic. Came to Marrowdell as a young woman. Creates tapestries and cares for her great-uncle.

**Roche Morrill**, son of Covie and Riedd, brother of Devins. Came to Marrowdell as a young boy. Left for Ansnor with the Demas.

**Satin and Filigree**, sows.

**Scourge**, the Larmensu warhorse. In Marrowdell, his true nature is revealed.

**Semyn Westietas**, elder son of Lila and Emon, brother of Werfol, nephew of Bannan.

**Sennic Nahamm**, formerly known as Horst, former soldier, husband of Riss. Took the name of Horst from baby Jenn, who continues to call him Uncle Horst. Hunter and village protector.

**Tadd Emms**, son of Zehr and Gallie, brother of Loee, twin of Allin, husband of Hettie. Came to Marrowdell as a babe. Tends livestock.

**Tir Half-face** (Tirsan Dimelecor), former Vorkoun border guard. Bannan's friend and companion. Has taken service with the Lady Mahavar in Avyo.

**Wainn Uhthoff**, son of Dusom and Larell, brother of Ponicce, nephew of Kydd. Came to Marrowdell as a young boy. Injured by misadventure on the Northward Road.

**Wainn's Old Pony**

**Wen Treff**, daughter of Lorra, sister of Davi. Came to Marrowdell as a young woman. Prefers to talks to toads, but recently has been known to talk to people.

**Werfol (Weed) Westietas**, younger son of Lila and Emon, brother of Semyn, nephew of Bannan.

**Wisp the dragon**, once Wyll the man, Jenn Nalynn's dearest friend and protector.

**Zehr Emms**, father of the twins, Tadd and Allin, and baby Loee, husband of Gallie. A fine furniture maker in Avyo. Village carpenter.

# Concerning the Denizens
## of Endshere

**Allin Anan**, formerly Emms, son of Gallie and Zehr, brother of Loee, twin brother of Tadd, husband to Palma Anan. Came to Marrowdell as a babe. Now lives in Endshere as barkeep in Palma's inn.

**Bliss**, not nice person.

**Cammi**, postmistress.

**Dinorwic**, thief and smuggler.

**Great Gran** (Caryn Anan), great-grandmother of the family. Former resident of Marrowdell.

**Hager Comber**, son of Harty, village smith.

**Harty Comber**, father of Hager, village smith.

**Larah Anan**, Palma's brother. Clears tables in the inn.

**Palma Anan**, sister of Larah, wife of Allin. Born and raised in Endshere. Owns and operates *The Good Night's Sleep* inn. Author.

**Shedden**, village healer.

**Upsala**, one-eyed trader who sold Bannan his ox.

# Encountered in Channen

**Abeek Harrow**, baroness.

**Appin Arkona**, sect member.

**Baldrinn Duart**, bargemaster, former acquaintance of Frann and Lorra.

**Birr**, artisan.

**Bish Fingal**, one of Emon's companions.

**Cheek**, one of Emon's crows.

**Dawnn Blysse**, artisan.

**Dokis**, another not nice person.

**Dutton Omemee**, one of Emon's companions.

**Emon Westietas**, father of Semyn and Werfol, husband of Lila. Baron, holding the seat for Vorkoun in the House of Keys.

**Glammis Lurgan**, collector.

**Herer**, one of Emon's companions.

**Leott**, artisan.

**Lila Westietas**, nee Larmensu, mother of Semyn and Werfol, wife of Emon, sister of Bannan. Baroness.

**Plevna**, artisan.
**Rhonnda Taff**, artisan.
**Scatterwit**, one of Emon's crows.
**Thomm**, artisan.

# The Making of the Shadow District

Before I sat down to start *A Turn of Light*, I'd found my inspiration for the next fantastical setting to be encountered by Jenn Nalynn—and you. I needed somewhere very different, yet as grounded in reality as Marrowdell's village. What did I have in mind? Everything a writer experiences is grist for the creative mill. After my guest stint at Armadillocon 2006 (a simply wonderful convention in Austin, Texas), Roger and I took a couple of days to explore the famed River Walk of San Antonio, Texas.

It was late August and the air at street level was closer to a sauna than anything I'd encountered outdoors. The skin of my legs actually hurt. Being determined tourists, we followed a small sign to a staircase by an arched bridge. The stairs seemed to take us inside a tree. (Interesting of itself.)

But they led down to another world. The air turned to silk, cool and moist. Music was playing, softly. A canal of dark, gleaming water—with turtles—curled into the distance. On either side, walkways followed along, here lined with planters of flowers and little cafes with bright awnings, there between old stone walls and writhing roots. While around every bend, bridges arched overhead and vegetation cloaked the world above.

What better mix of inspiration (for us both, as my other half is a photographer) and romance (need I say more?)? We'd leave to walk to our hotel (mistakenly up in the concrete jungle and blocks away), only to turn back to the canals for relief. Trust me, sometimes we'd stand there and laugh at the amazing change. At others, we'd be silent and in awe.

Roger Czerneda Photography

*"Timeless Romance" along the River Walk, San Antonio, Texas*

Roger had his photos, I had my memories, and all I needed was the go-ahead from my beloved Editor to write the book in your hands, in order to bring Channen's Shadow District to life.

Of course, then I had the pleasure of adding details. Much of what you've read in the story is straight from real life. So is the cover. I sent several of Roger's photos to Matt Stawicki for his reference. You'll recognize both fountain and bridge, as well as the stonework.

*Fountains and ornate stonework were everywhere along the River Walk, San Antonio, Texas*

The turtles, you ask?

We'd met already, at Armadillocon. The concom took us for a fabulous Texas BBQ and behind the restaurant happened to be one of the, to-me, strangely dark, warm rivers. To our surprise, our hosts had us toss rib bones into the water. Instantly ripples formed everywhere as hundreds of turtles swam up and close to seize the offering. The nyim were born, then and there.

Having decided there would be turtles, I knew I'd want them to be like Marrowdell's house toads and somehow different when seen at the turn. Though I could have made something up—that's my job, after all—there was no need. I came across the research of Dr. Abigail (Abby) Dominy with terrapins.

Terrapins live in brackish water and, to most of us, look a great deal like a larger version of the common red-eared slider turtles found in rivers and lakes across North America (including Texas). Terrapins are, however, quite different and remarkable in their own right. How different?

Dr. Dominy discovered, as I read in *Science News,* that terrapins have markings only visible in UV light, and that they can see that portion of the spectrum. She's hypothesized this may play a role in their social interactions.

Imagine the vastness of my joy! Remember, I'm a biologist by training and inclination. Here was a chance to slip something real and astonishing about the natural world into my fantasy one.

I contacted Dr. Dominy at once. She graciously sent me information on her research, adding reference images I could pass along to Matt for the cover, for all of which I am most grateful. (I love my job, btw.) The passage within the book where Jenn Nalynn recites what she's read about turtles, terrapins, etc, is part of my promise to inform the public about these fascinating creatures. There's also a page on my website, with links, for those of you who wish to know even more.

I'd turtles. I'd firsthand experience with a truly unique environment. All I had left to do was create the magic of the Shadow District, and that came to me while I wrapped a birthday present. The edge, as I see it, is like a ribbon twisted through the world. Not simply along the surface, as in Marrowdell, but at times plunging below.

Or above.

It was raining outside, when I took a length of ribbon in my hand, lifted it up, and gave it a thoughtful twist.

That, dear readers, is why magic rains in Channen, to collect in dark canals. That's why nyim rise to catch mimrol drops—and whatever else falls in. And that's why, as I wrote about the Shadow District, I smiled to myself.

Remembering two days of inspiration.

And a certain timeless romance.

# Put Me in the Story!

A veritable host of dear and familiar folk have wound up in Marrowdell, Endshere, and even Channen. Some generously bid on a character name in support of charity, for which I thank you. Others are here as part of a tribute to my now-ended and beloved sff.net newsgroup (which lives on as the Grey Stone Tower on Facebook, if you've missed the company). The rest of the namings were special gifts, from me to you. To all, I'm privileged to be trusted with your names, or variations thereof, and appreciate any character details (or challenges!) you provided. I hope you enjoy the result. (The usual proviso applies, in that I make stuff up to serve the story first and foremost, so it's entirely possible you won't recognize yourselves. Hence the following list. However, any resemblance you do spot? Please take it as the compliment I intend.)

Here's the full list. Some are characters who are mentioned, but don't appear in the story. Others walked in and took over the place. A few wound up on a map. Again, thank you to all, and I hope you enjoy!

## Marrowdell:

Alyssa Ropp — Alyssa Donovan
Hettie Emms nee Ropp — Henri Reed
(Treffs' friend) Frann Nall — Fran Quesnel
Treff, Cynd — Cindy Hodge
Treff, Davi — David Trefor James
Treff, Lorra — Lorraine Vivian James
Treff, Wen — Gwen Veronica James

## Endshere, Channen, and Other Mentions:

Bish Fingal (Emon's companion) — Anne Bishop
Caryn Anan (Great Gran) — Caryn Cameron
Clairr River — Claire Eamer
Dawnn Blysse (artisan) — Dawn Bliss
Herer (Emon's companion) — Robert Herrera
Jym Garnden (astronomer in Avyo) — James A. Gardner
Kimm Larmensu (Bannan's great-uncle) — Kimberly Marie Antell
Koevoets and Moniq (fair goers) — Monique Koevoets
Kotor and Mila Rivers — Janet, Willem, Leora, and Mila Chase
Larah Anan (Palma's little brother) — Lara Herrera
Lehman (that infamous author) — Susan Lehman
Leott (artisan) — Elliot James Godfrey
Lianna (wife of Stevynn) — Liana K
Loiss (Bannan's former friend) — Lois Gresh
Lornn Heatt (Lila's assumed identity) — Lorne and Heather Kates
Palma Anan — Shannan Palma
Renee (Bannan's former friend) — Renee E. Babcock
Rhonnda Taff (artisan) — Rhonda Donley
Rowe Jonn (Lila's guardsman) — Jonathan Crowe
Ruthh (that infamous seamstress) — Ruth Stuart
Sarra River — Sarah Jane Elliott
Seel Aucoin (Lila's guardsman) — Jennifer Seely

Stevynn (artisan)—Steven Kerzner
Thomm (artisan)—Thomas Czurgai

*Elliot, your Auntie Jen and I look forward to hearing how your dear parents explain to you, years from now, how you came to be a character dealing wisdom and joy from a tent in a fantasy world. Perhaps, though, it will be easy. After all, you've begun your life doing both for us in the real one. Happy Birthday!*

# We'd like to Invite You...

And an array of wonderful events ensued! If I've missed thanking anyone involved, please blame my hasty note-taking. It's been something of a blur.

Marrowdell, the scale model, made its world debut in the model room of Polaris 24 to my great delight. Thank you for taking such great care of it—and me! As for the model, I'm very proud to say it was accepted by the World Fantasy Art Show jury and exhibited at World Fantasy Toronto, 2012. I was able to show Betsy Wollheim! (If it hadn't been for a dastardly hurricane, Sheila would have seen it then, too.) My thanks to Christopher Roden and Kim Kofmel who saw me through my "I'm an artist?" jitters.

I happily attended SFContario, Ad Astra, and Polaris. These are my "home" conventions and a treat. Congratulations to the concoms for their always-excellent work. I was privileged to be a guest of Laurention University, Sudbury, as part of its "Social Science on the Final Frontier: a Conference on Science Fiction and Society" (special thanks to

Dr. David Robinson, Alain Boulay, and our other charming hosts) as well as to be part of the Toronto SpecFic Colloquium.

Thank you, Fred Addis and the Leacock Museum, for hosting not one, but two events: my workshop at Literary Lapses and the splendid gallery show of Roger's photographs ("Look. Magic!") with its finale night of readings and feast ("Here Be Dragons") featuring Anne Bishop, Mark Leslie, Adrienne Kress, and myself. You not only support the arts, my friend, you elevate us all. (While providing a Very Fun Time. People came from afar. There were gambols.)

My thanks to Anime North and Fingers Delarus for having us as guests and workshop presenters. Thanks also for giving me the honor of hosting the opening ceremonies (complete with hat). An amazing event and I look forward to coming back.

Pi-Con and Albacon were great events. Pi-Con was a new convention for me and quite wonderful. My thanks (and hugs) to Kris Snyder, Persis Thorndike, and Tom Traina. Albacon followed, where we met new friends and familiar ones. Kudos and hugs! to Chuck Rothman, Christopher J. Ford, Debi Chowdhury (who always smiles!), Bryan Connell, and Elizabeth McLaren. A special shoutout to my newsgroup friends who came out to find us, including G'leep (Pi-Con), Morgan (Albacon) and Kay (in Baltimore). Lovely to see you all.

Launches for *Turn* were held at Bakka Phoenix Books in Toronto, and in Buffalo with my dear friend, Anne Bishop. I must make special mention of Minicon 48 (where the con suite was renamed "The Claw and Jaws!"). Thank you, Joel Phillips and Steve Hubbard, as well as liaison extraordinaire Anton Petersen, along with all those at this terrific and warm convention.

The most unusual—and meaningful—event for *A Turn of Light* was hosted and planned by Cam Trueman, master miller. Yes, we did *Star Wars* Day at Watson's Mill, Manotick, outside under a tent, complete with a band and folks in period costume.

That fall, I attended my first Baltimore Book Festival, thanks to Catharine Asaro and SFWA, as well as Danielle

Ackley-McPhail. It turned into something of a book tour, including a wonderful event at Flights of Fantasy. Thank you, Maria Perry, for your hospitality both within your home and your fabulous store, and to the ever-gracious Joe Berlant. I should mention this trip included not only a terrific stint with my beloved DAW kin in New York, but Julie's Video Day at Penguin! Thank you all for making me look and feel like a star.

Thank you, Reversed Polarity, for letting us help celebrate 50 years of the Doctor with you!

It wasn't all fun and games. Okay, most of it, but I was privileged to make other authors sweat—I mean to conduct workshops—for the following groups: Writers Community of Simcoe County (thanks, Deepam Wadds), Toronto ChiSeries (and a reading! with thanks to Sandra Kasturi and Michael Matheson, and hosts Bakka-Phoenix), and Ottawa Comiccon (thanks, Cliff Caporale).

There were special online events this past year, starting with the immense Blog Tour for *A Turn of Light* organized by Jessica Clooney of Penguin Canada, assisted by Kelsey Marshall, and Katie Hoffman of DAW Books. I can't thank the bloggers who hosted me and helped promote my very new book enough. There's a list, and links to archived posts, on my site for readers who may have missed it. I'd also like to thank Bryan Thomas Schmidt for inviting me to my first ever twitterchat on Sffwrtcht. Such fun! (For me. I know Bryan worked very hard behind the scenes.) My sincere thanks to Jim C. Hines for hosting the cover reveal for *Species Imperative*. You're a good friend and kind. Last, but not least, my thanks also to Kristen Bell of Fantasy Café for hosting the cover reveal for *A Play of Shadow* with such enthusiasm and class.

As I write this, I'm looking ahead to what's to come. Signings for this book, absolutely. Favorite cons to revisit and enjoy; new ones—and friends—to meet! For what I love most about writing—what still blows me away every time—is how it's introduced me to so many fine people I'd otherwise never have met. Hugs to those I have! Hello (and hugs) in advance to those I will!

# The More Usual Acknowledgments

Though perhaps . . . not!

You see, during *A Play of Shadow*, I would dash over to Marrowdell—the village on Facebook, that is—to ask questions, seek thoughts, and generally hang out with readers familiar with, and fond of, house toads. One such dash led me to a contest called "Aunt Sybb Said . . ." because I was, well, stuck that day. The responses were many and I let the others on the page vote for their favorite. Heather Dryer won, and I admit her saying posed, at first, something of a challenge. "Aunt Sybb had said a whistling woman and a crowing hen never come to a good end . . ." Where to put that? As you may have read by now, I found the perfect spot and am delighted. Thank you, Heather!

I also needed help visualizing Lila Larmensu. Oh, I had my notions. Clear ones. So clear, in fact, that it suddenly dawned on me this was someone I knew! Yup. I'd been inspired by a dear friend of our daughter. Nothing for it but to ask permission, which Lauren Burger (being our friend too), graciously granted. While I'd never call Lauren lethal, she's lovely, inside and out, brilliant, and oh-so-easy to underestimate at first glance. Lila, in truth.

Then there was the inn at Endshere. In *A Turn of Light*, I'd established that Palma Anan (based upon our friend Shannan Palma) owned and ran it. Little did Shannan suspect that I'd be dashing back to her (there was a great deal of dashing during *Play*) for more. A name, for one thing. It became "The Good Night's Sleep" aka the "G'Night." I ran the depiction of the interior past her as well. Just when Shannan probably thought her involvement done, I learned that she made her own ginger beer.

Joy!

Yes, the beer Allin serves Bannan in the G'Night is Shannan's, in truth. I hope to taste it myself soon. (Authors. So demanding!) Thank you, Shannan, for your help and patience.

Now we come to Nathan Fillion. (Yes, that Nathan.) We've never met, but like many, I'm a huge fan. Have been since *Firefly*.

As it happens, I wrote a huge book.

You can guess where this is going, can't you? Thank you, very much, to my friends Bobbie and Sandra (no last names, to protect the innocent), for getting that gleam in your eyes of "we can do anything and would, for you!" at the Watson's Mill signing. I won't say it's your fault, but you certainly facilitated. In short, upon my envious sigh hearing they were to meet him, these fine ladies left with said huge book. They carried it to the Ottawa Comiccon where Nathan was appearing, had their picture taken with the poor man (and huge book), then calmly informed him the huge book? Was his.

To take home on the plane.

Okay, as plans went, there may have been a flaw or two. But this wee story deserves to be here because I still smile to think of it, no matter what happened to the book. This is a perfect example of the kindness, enthusiasm, and derring-do! of my friends and readers. A power I should, admittedly, use more wisely in future.

On to the more usual acknowledgments? Not yet.

We've arrived at the mirror. If you've read the book, you know whereof I speak. If not, suffice to say that in the interests of accuracy and detail, I had to know what happens when a mirror melts. Not something easy to find, it turns out. I'm grateful to Tim McManus of BlownAway Glass Studio for his kind assistance, as well as Jenn Wanless-Craig of Artech Studios. Always go to those who know, folks. Trust me.

After the mirror came the coinage of Rhoth. I needed names for coins, which led to the discovery that such names come with history and meaning to the society! Luckily, I met the talented author Krista (K.V.) Johansen at Ad Astra. Not only was she expert in such research, but her husband knew coins! Thank you, Paul Marlowe, for your helpful replies to my questions, and for "drogues and sprats."

Now, for the more usual acknowledgments. Thank you, Sheila Gilbert, for not only being a superb editor and colleague, but for being the best of friends, for being here, when I needed you most. Words cannot express. To all at DAW Books—Joshua the Mighty, Katie the Brilliant, Briar the Vigilant, Peter the Charming, Betsy the Wonderful, George the Unstoppable, and Paula the Wise—my heartfelt gratitude. The quality and care you pour into everything you do is outstanding and always appreciated. (Of course, toads ARE watching ...)

Matt Stawicki? Working with you was pure delight! Thank you not only for this gorgeous cover, but for all you did to help me blend our visions of it. You see, dear readers, Matt used the references I provided to create his masterpiece. I then wrote the actual scene based on what he'd created. The final step? Matt read and critiqued my descriptions from that scene, to be sure I'd got it right. Brilliance!

Ed Greenwood? I owe the speed with which I wrote to you and your wisdom. Thank you!

Jennifer, my indispensable alpha reader, thank you for your keen eye and true heart. In every sense, I owe the quality of this book to you.

Erin Stirling, thank you for letting me impose on your enthusiasm for *Turn* by reading *Play* in ragged draft, and for going over the maps with Jennifer. Roger? Thank you for looking after everything (truly), so I could get it done. Scott, you've been an inspiration.

There were those who held me in their hearts as I wrote *A Play of Shadow*. To you, I won't say thanks. How could I? To you, I say:

However far we are apart,
Keep Us Close.

# Author's Note

Dear Reader,

Are you like me? When I'm near the end of a special story, one that's won my heart and mind, I do my best to make it last. It never works, of course. Instead, I'll linger after closing the book, happily caught in the fullness of feeling. Wipe a tear. Smile and sigh. Laugh, curl my toes, then, ever-so-reluctantly, rejoin the real world. After all, I know the story isn't really over, only resting awhile.

Waiting for me to pick it up again.

If that's how you felt after finishing *A Play of Shadow*, I've some good news. Like you, I love Marrowdell and all its denizens, be they dragon or aunt or toad, and there will be more, I promise, once I finish my current project. The next in the Night's Edge series is called *A Change of Place,* and will see Jenn Nalynn caught between the sei and the toads' indomitable queen. Meanwhile, a letter (remember the winter mail bag) arrives where it shouldn't and Bannan finds himself on a train. Intrigued? I hope so, because all this is merely the start. You'll meet another dragon and—oh my!

So you see, the story of Night's Edge isn't really over, only resting a while.

Waiting for me to pick it up, again, and give it to you.

However far we are apart,
Keep Us Close.

Julie Czerneda

# Julie E. Czerneda
## *Species Imperative*

"This novel bears the hallmarks of Czerneda's earlier books: strong, complex, and appealing characters and a thoughtful, intricate plot. Czerneda creates an original and terrific alien species...and the plot is packed with vivid images and events. Czerneda is a masterful storyteller and one of the best of the recent voices in science fiction."  —*Voya*

## SURVIVAL
## MIGRATION
## REGENERATION

The entire trilogy, now available in a single volume for the first time!

ISBN: 978-0-7564-1014-8

*"A creative voice and a distinctive vision."*
—*C. J. Cherryh*

To Order Call: 1-800-788-6262
www.dawbooks.com

# Joshua Palmatier
## *Shattering the Ley*

"Palmatier brilliantly shatters genre conventions. . . . An innovative fantasy novel with a very modern feel. . . . For readers who are willing to tackle a more challenging fantasy, without clear heroes and obvious conflicts, *Shattering the Ley* is an excellent read."　　　—SFRevu

"*Shattering the Ley*, the terrific new fantasy from Joshua Palmatier, is built of equal parts innocence, politics, and treachery. It features a highly original magic system, and may well be the only fantasy ever written where some of the most exciting scenes take place in a power plant. I couldn't put it down."　　　—S. C. Butler, author of *Reiffen's Choice*

ISBN: 978-0-7564-0991-3

**And don't miss the *Throne of Amenkor* trilogy!**

THE SKEWED THRONE　　　978-0-7564-0382-9
THE CRACKED THRONE　　　978-0-7564-0447-5
THE VACANT THRONE　　　978-0-7564-0531-1

To Order Call: 1-800-788-6262
www.dawbooks.com

# Michelle Sagara
## *The Queen of the Dead*

**SILENCE**
978-0-7564-0799-5

**TOUCH**
978-0-7564-0844-2

And watch for the third book in the series, *Grave*, coming soon from DAW!

To Order Call: 1-800-788-6262
www.dawbooks.com

DAW 192